The
MX Book
of
New
Sherlock
Holmes
Stories

Part XXXI – 2022 Annual
(1875-1887)

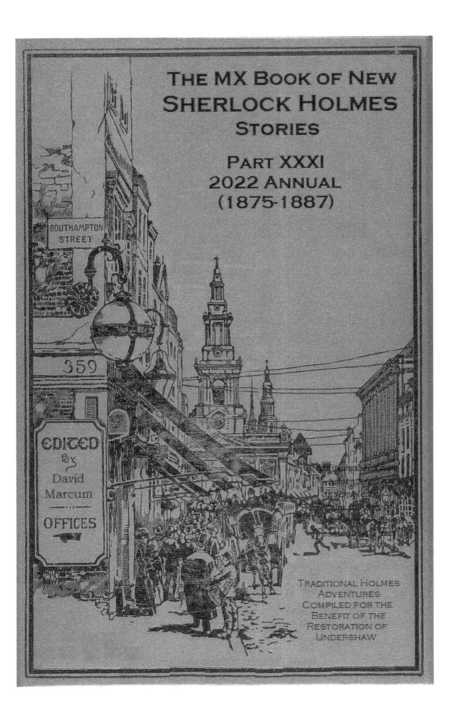

THE MX BOOK OF NEW
SHERLOCK HOLMES
STORIES

PART XXXI
2022 ANNUAL
(1875-1887)

SOUTHAMPTON
STREET

359

EDITED
By
David
Marcum

OFFICES

TRADITIONAL HOLMES
ADVENTURES
COMPILED FOR THE
BENEFIT OF THE
RESTORATION OF
UNDERSHAW

ISBN Hardback 978-1-80424-005-2
ISBN Paperback 978-1-80424-006-9
AUK ePub ISBN 978-1-80424-007-6
AUK PDF ISBN 978-1-80424-008-3

Published in the UK by
MX Publishing
335 Princess Park Manor, Royal Drive,
London, N11 3GX
www.mxpublishing.co.uk

David Marcum can be reached at:
thepapersofsherlockholmes@gmail.com

Cover design by Brian Belanger
www.belangerbooks.com and *www.redbubble.com/people/zhahadun*

Internal Illustrations by Sidney Paget

CONTENTS

Forewords

Adventures

(Continued on the next page . . . .)

(Continued on the next page . . . .)

These additional Sherlock Holmes adventures
can be found in the previous volumes of
The MX Book of New Sherlock Holmes Stories

(Continued on the next page . . . .)

(Continued on the next page . . . .)

PART V – Christmas Adventures

(Continued on the next page . . . .)

PART VI – 2017 Annual

(Continued on the next page . . . .)

(Continued on the next page . . . .)

Part IX – 2018 Annual (1879-1895)

(Continued on the next page . . . .)

(Continued on the next page . . . .)

The Adventure of the Silver Skull – Hugh Ashton
The Pimlico Poisoner – Matthew Simmonds
The Grosvenor Square Furniture Van – David Ruffle
The Adventure of the Paradol Chamber – Paul W. Nash
The Bishopgate Jewel Case – Mike Hogan
The Singular Tragedy of the Atkinson Brothers of Trincomalee – Craig Stephen Copland
Colonel Warburton's Madness – Gayle Lange Puhl
The Adventure at Bellingbeck Park – Deanna Baran
The Giant Rat of Sumatra – Leslie Charteris and Denis Green
    Introduction by Ian Dickerson
The Vatican Cameos – Kevin P. Thornton
The Case of the Gila Monster – Stephen Herczeg
The Bogus Laundry Affair – Robert Perret
Inspector Lestrade and the Molesey Mystery – M.A. Wilson and Richard Dean Starr

Part XII: Some Untold Cases (1894-1902)
Foreword – Lyndsay Faye
Foreword – Roger Johnson
Foreword – Melissa Grigsby
Foreword – Steve Emecz
Foreword – David Marcum
It's Always Time (*A Poem*) – "Anon."
The Shanghaied Surgeon – C.H. Dye
The Trusted Advisor – David Marcum
A Shame Harder Than Death – Thomas Fortenberry
The Adventure of the Smith-Mortimer Succession – Daniel D. Victor
A Repulsive Story and a Terrible Death – Nik Morton
The Adventure of the Dishonourable Discharge – Craig Janacek
The Adventure of the Admirable Patriot – S. Subramanian
The Abernetty Transactions – Jim French
Dr. Agar and the Dinosaur – Robert Stapleton
The Giant Rat of Sumatra – Nick Cardillo
The Adventure of the Black Plague – Paul D. Gilbert
Vigor, the Hammersmith Wonder – Mike Hogan
A Correspondence Concerning Mr. James Phillimore – Derrick Belanger
The Curious Case of the Two Coptic Patriarchs – John Linwood Grant
The Conk-Singleton Forgery Case – Mark Mower
Another Case of Identity – Jane Rubino
The Adventure of the Exalted Victim – Arthur Hall

PART XIII: 2019 Annual (1881-1890)
Foreword – Will Thomas
Foreword – Roger Johnson
Foreword – Melissa Grigsby
Foreword – Steve Emecz
Foreword – David Marcum
Inscrutable (*A Poem*) – Jacquelynn Morris

(Continued on the next page . . . .)

PART XIV: 2019 Annual (1891 -1897)

(Continued on the next page . . . .)

(Continued on the next page . . . .)

Part XVII – Whatever Remains . . . Must Be the Truth (1891-1898)

Part XVIII – Whatever Remains . . . Must Be the Truth (1899-1925)

(Continued on the next page . . . .)

Part XIX: 2020 Annual (1882-1890)

(Continued on the next page . . . .)

(Continued on the next page . . . .)

Part XXII: Some More Untold Cases (1877-1887)

(Continued on the next page . . . .)

(Continued on the next page . . . .)

Part XXV: 2021 Annual (1881-1888)

(Continued on the next page . . . .)

(Continued on the next page . . . .)

Part XXVIII: More Christmas Adventures (1869-1888)

(Continued on the next page . . . .)

Part XXIX: More Christmas Adventures (1889-1896)

Part XXX: More Christmas Adventures (1897-1928)

(Continued on the next page . . . .)

The following contributions appear in the companion volumes:
Part XXXII – 2022 Annual (1888-1895)
Part XXXIII – 2022 Annual (1896-1919)

*Dedicated to
these friends of the
MX Anthologies who
recently crossed over
the Reichenbach:*

Carole Nelson Douglas
Greg Hatcher
Carl Heifetz
William "Bill" Lawler
Mark Levy

R.I.P.

Editor's Foreword:
"We can but try."
by David Marcum

Some approach the Sherlockian Canon, that small batch of just five-dozen original Holmes adventures, as if that number – *Only sixty stories!* – is unalterable. They're quite firm: *Verily, verily, the Canon shall be sixty stories – No more, no less!* But then the exceptions creep in . . . .

Sixty may be absolute – *No more, no less!* – but then there's *The Apocrypha*, that extra-Canonical material that maybe ought to be included too. "How Watson Learned the Trick" and "The Field Bazaar", though not full-length adventures, are important slices-of-life from the famed Baker Street sitting room. And if one accepts those, then there are the Canonical plays – all by way of the First Literary Agent: *The Crown Diamond* and *The Speckled Band*. Then onward to the lesser-known (and most confusing) play *Angels of Darkness*. And don't forget the two stories which clearly feature Holmes in an off-stage setting, "The Man with the Watches" and "The Lost Special". So already the pure Sixty-story Barrier has been breached.

And then there are those absolute purists who make other exceptions. "*Sixty adventures – No more, no less!*" they cry, prepared to defend that idea to the death. But then, a moment later, they follow with, "Well, except for these two or three pastiches written by a friend of mine, or by the person whose attention I'm seeking or whose celebrity favor I want to curry with my praise." Thus, their conviction of The Immaculacy of The Canonical Sixty is already cracked and compromised.

Along the same lines, some insist that The Canon be insulated from the bigger picture, keeping Holmes's world a cozy little place solely defined by only what is found recorded in the "official" sixty tales. If it isn't recorded there, they insist, then it didn't happen. But there's a loophole for that: The Canon mentions over one-hundred-forty "Untold Cases" in addition to the Told Sixty, and the details of these are often so vague that they are very much open to infinite interpretation. It's a bold concept, and too much for some to assimilate: Holmes and Watson are doing things off-stage that we don't get to witness in the Canonical Sixty.

I haven't done the math, but it would be a good project for someone to make a solid estimate of just how much time accrues in just the events of The Canon that we actually see recorded and presented. For instance, the bulk of "The Five Orange Pips" – around 82% – consists of just an hour or so in the Baker Street sitting room on a late September 1887 night, either hearing the client's story, or discussing it after he leaves to go be murdered. The rest occurs in a short breakfast scene the next day, followed by another concluding conversation that evening.

It would be interesting if someone were to calculate the amount of time that is actually recorded in The Canon – either passing from the beginning of a case to the end, or simply what's shown "on screen", against how much total time that passes within the forty years between Holmes's first *recorded* Canonical case, "The Gloria Scott" (in Summer 1874) and the last, "His Last Bow" (in August 1914). I'm certain that it would be stunning for some just how much unrecorded time there is, wherein Holmes and Watson live all those other parts of their lives beyond the lens of the pure Canon that so many defend.

And in that recorded time, there are historical events occurring all around them. Many don't want to acknowledge those either. They like the idea that Holmes and Watson interact with anonymous folk like Jabez Wilson or Hall Pycroft, or others that no one has never heard of before or since. They don't want to hear about Holmes actually functioning in *The World*. But he does. In some of those Canonical Untold Cases, there are references to Holmes's interactions with historical figures, so it isn't a total impossibility, even for the Defenders of the Sixty, that he had contact with others. Holmes assisted the Pope (Leo XIII, whose Papacy ran from 1878 to 1903) in two Untold Cases, that of the Vatican Cameos, and also the death of Cardinal Tosca. He assisted the Royal Family of Scandinavia (as mentioned in "The Noble Bachelor" and "The Final Problem"). He was hired by the King of Bohemia (although such title was rather flimsily moribund by the late 1880's), and he assisted the British Prime Minister (whose name was changed for security's sake.)

So when Canonical purists dislike those post-Canonical stories wherein Holmes is involved with recognizable historical figures, they really don't have a Canonical leg to stand upon. The door for this was thrown open with the publication of Nicholas Meyer's Game-changing 1974 work, *The Seven-Per-Cent Solution*, wherein Holmes and Watson meet Sigmund Freud. Before that, in Canonical adventures which had been prepared for publication in *The Strand*, Watson and the First Literary Agent had pointedly changed names to protect identities. But not so in the document that Meyer uncovered. And when it was understood that Watsonian manuscripts could be published without the need to cross the First Literary Agent's desk, such editorial protections were no longer honored – or necessary.

The list of historical figures that Holmes and Watson have encountered who appear under their own names in latter-day post-

2

Canonical adventures is staggering, and many show up multiple times: The Queen of England and the Prince of Wales (and later the King). Gladstone and Disraeli and Lord Salisbury (and other Prime Ministers). Actors like Ellen Terry, Henry Irving, Lillie Langtry, and Basil Rathbone. Writers such as Bram Stoker, Henry James, Charles Dickens, H.P. Lovecraft, H.G. Wells, and F. Scott Fitzgerald. Inspector Abberline and Montague Druitt. The Dalai Lama and Henry Ward Beecher. Dr. Joseph Bell and Dr. Cream and Dr. Joseph Lister and Dr. Crippen. Both of my grandfathers, William Marcum and Ray Rathbone. Bismarck and Kaiser Wilhelm and Winston Churchill. Theodore Roosevelt and Franklin Roosevelt. J. Edgar Hoover and Adolf Hitler.

The list is overwhelming – although the *School and Holmes* website has made a good start at cataloging various figures encountered by our heroes in post-Canonical adventures. Here's the link for the letter "*A*" – Dive in, and like Jabez Wilson in "The Red-Headed League", you can progress through that letter, and "*with diligence [you] might get on to the B's before very long. . . .*"

https://www.schoolandholmes.com/charactersa.html

Many who try to limit Holmes to the Canonical Sixty are unwittingly limiting what makes him the greatest detective. If we only accept what's presented in The Canon, then we find that a good many of Holmes's cases are small affairs indeed, giving the impression that Holmes is a very skilled *but very small-time* problem solver. Of course, he loved the problem for the problem's sake, no matter its size or seriousness, and to him it didn't matter if a client was a pawn-broker or a king, a stockbroker or a banker or baronet. Yet many of the recorded Canonical cases are rather insignificant in the great scheme of things. If not for being memorialized in The Canon, for example, no one would have ever known or cared about the existence of Jabez Wilson or Hall Pycroft.

Holmes was involved with so many people over the course of his career, and his reputation grew and grew through the decades. Therefore, it's certain that even though a sizeable percentage of his clients were those who lived *small* lives, there were also just as many who lived *big* lives. And if Holmes was interacting with these historical *figures*, then he was interacting with *history* as well.

Many Canonical limiters don't want that. They *want* Holmes to be a shabby small-timer who mopes around the sitting room in brown studies, getting in the dumps at times and not opening his mouth for days on end, until he's consulted by an otherwise unimportant figure who has a curious vexation – five orange pips, for instance, or a blue jewel in a bonny goose

3

container. Granted, there are the occasional cases of greater importance – stolen naval treaties and that irksome Napoleon of Crime – but many stories presented in The Canon are much smaller in scale. Yet just because that's what's on the "accepted" Canonical stage doesn't mean that it's the whole story.

In 1989, one of my few heroes, Billy Joel, released "We Didn't Start the Fire", a nearly-five-minute long song detailing the events from 1949 (the year of his birth) to 1989. He wrote it after speaking to a twenty-one-year old who told him that things were much rougher in 1989 than it had been when Joel was in his twenties. Joel responded by pointing out all of the historical events – some quite grim, like the Korean War – which occurred in those bygone days, all just as rough as what the young man was facing in the present. The chorus states, *"We didn't start the fire – It was always burning since the world's been turning. We didn't start the fire, No, we didn't light it, but we tried to fight it."* The implication of this is that these historical challenges have always been with us, but that one can meet them as they appear and do one's best to succeed.

And this, believe it or not, is rather like Sherlock Holmes's own creed.

In both "The Problem of Thor Bridge" and "The Creeping Man", Holmes makes a statement that's easy to slide over too quickly, but which, in fact, is something well-worth remembering:

> *"We can but try."*

In context, Holmes first makes the statement in "Thor Bridge" when explaining that he has a theory, but it might be wrong:

> *[Y]ou have seen me miss my mark before, Watson. I have an instinct for such things, and yet it has sometimes played me false. It seemed a certainty when first it flashed across my mind in the cell at Winchester, but one drawback of an active mind is that one can always conceive alternative explanations which would make our scent a false one. And yet – and yet – Well, Watson, we can but try.*

"Thor Bridge" was first published in February and March 1927. The next Canonical tale to be published was "The Creeping Man", a full year later (in March 1928, just a little over a year before Watson's passing). In that, Holmes is suggesting that he and Watson bluff their way into seeing an antagonist, to which Watson replies:

4

"We can but try."
"Excellent, Watson! Compound of the Busy Bee and
Excelsior. We can but try – the motto of the firm."

The motto of the firm indeed! Even though this statement only
appeared in the fifty-fifth and fifty-sixty published Canonical adventures,
it was certainly Holmes's philosophy long before that. It served him well
as he carried out his investigations, and also as he lived his life – for
besides encountering many historical figures, Holmes encountered a great
deal of challenging history as well.

Holmes was born in 1854. Watson's birth was two years earlier. We
can look at the world around us now and bemoan all that is legitimately
wrong – and it truly is wrong in so many ways! – but the challenges people
faced in those days, while different, were also quite grim indeed. Disease
and genocide – different forms then and now, but still the same human
suffering under different guises. Wars and starvation on all levels – they
had it, and we have it. Societal unfairness, foul corruption, and evil
injustice and from top to bottom, with the haves always greedily clutching
at theirs while the have-nots scramble – some surviving and others not.

Google, that amazing tool undoubtedly brought back from the future
to this time by some as-yet unborn time-traveling Prometheus, provides an
instantaneous way to find out this or that fact. It is truly an amazing thing.
A quick check shows that between 1854 and 1900, there were nearly *three-
hundred wars* around the world! Eight of those were in the year of
Holmes's birth. And while that seems like a long time ago, and they might
have been small compared to the World Wars and possible Nuclear Wars
and Cold Wars that we've been conditioned to in our lifetimes, they were
very real and devastating and disruptive and deadly for those who were
involved. Lives were ruined or lost.

During that same period, there were several dozen pandemics and
endemics and plagues – fevers and cholera, influenza and bubonic plague,
malaria and smallpox.

The world was a dangerous place. It *is* a dangerous place. It always
has been. It isn't just bad now. This – the history we're living in right now
– is just a different kind of bad.

*We didn't start the fire. It was always burning since the world's been
turning.*

But we can be strong and face it.
Like Sherlock Holmes . . . .
We can but try.

5

I had the idea for *The MX Book of New Sherlock Holmes Stories* in early 2015 as a way to have more stories about the *True Canonical Holmes* – a hero, and not a modernized broken sociopathic murderer who had stolen Holmes's name, a version that was insidiously creeping into the world's perceptions of him. The idea for volumes of stories about the True Holmes was more popular than I could have ever imagined, as so many people still need *Heroic Holmes*. My 2015 hope for possibly a dozen or so new stories grew and grew over that year to become the first MX three-volume set with over sixty new adventures – the largest Holmes anthology collection of its kind ever produced. (We've since regularly surpassed that.)

It quickly became obvious that both authors and readers wanted more, so the series was established as an ongoing venture. From nearly the beginning, it was decided to direct the royalties from the books to a school for special needs children that was located at Undershaw, one of Sir Arthur Conan Doyle's former homes in Hindhead, England. The school was originally called *Stepping Stones*, but it has since been renamed to match the building where it resides, *Undershaw*. As of this writing, this series, by way of the incredible contributions from over 200 authors and the amazing support of countless fans around the world, has produced nearly 700 new traditional Holmes adventures and has raised nearly *$100,000* for the school. That's nearly *One-Hundred-Thousand Dollars!* That number will almost certainly be exceeded by mid-2022. (And I'm told that even more important than the money has been the spread awareness of the school around the world and its valuable work.)

When COVID-19 came upon us in early 2020, I was worried about this series, and how everyone's suddenly upside-down lives might be affected in terms of contributing new Sherlock Holmes stories. While some people found it more difficult to write when conditions became unfavorable, most rose to the challenge, and the books continued as before, with multiple volumes of high-quality traditional Holmes adventures. There were six volumes in 2020, and six more in 2021. Now as I write this, the world watches as a vile Beast has invaded Ukraine, and still the contributors have done an amazing job, and I continue to receive stories for the next set of books, *However Improbable* . . . . planned for Fall 2022.

I cannot express my admiration and gratefulness enough for those who have provided stories under ongoing challenging conditions.

Each and every contributor who has added to this series with stories, poems, forewords, and artwork are the finest kind of people, and they are heroes of the first order, and should all be incredibly proud of what we've accomplished. And as conditions still prove to be challenging . . . .

We can but try.

"Of course, I could only stammer out my thanks."
– *The unhappy John Hector McFarlane, "The Norwood Builder"*

As always when one of these sets is finished, I want to first thank with all my heart my incredible, patient, brilliant, kind, and beautiful wife of nearly thirty-four years, Rebecca – every day I'm luckier than the day before! – and our amazing, funny, brilliant, creative, and wonderful son, and my friend, Dan. I love you both, and you are everything to me!

In late 2020, I was fortunate to obtain my dream job, working as a municipal civil engineer for the city whose specific infrastructure had inspired me to go back to school in my thirties to be an engineer. It's the best job I've ever had with an amazing group of people – and the learning curve has been amazing in its own way as well. I knew the engineering, but learning things from the municipal side is a new challenge. On top of that was family time – most important – and also the various Sherlockian efforts that I've pursued.

In 2021, through the new job, I found time to write a number of new Holmes pastiches and essays, and also to edit and get published twenty-two different books. (These included six of my own books, six MX anthologies, five Holmes anthology volumes for Belanger Books, the remaining four volumes in *The Complete Dr. Thorndyke* collection, and a book of Holmes stories by Nick Dunn-Meynell.) Then, in late 2021, the boss I was hired to replace retired, so my work responsibilities increased exponentially.

Thus, the editing of the *2022 Annual* took on new challenges as it fit in around my real life. Thankfully, the various contributors were wonderful as usual, and I can't thank them enough for their patience, and for the stories that they sent, even as they worked around their own ever-more-complicated lives.

For the *2022 Annual*, some contributors simply couldn't join the party this time, due to all sorts of reasons – too busy or too stressed. Perhaps there were health- or job-related issues, or burnout. Several experienced tragic deaths of their loved ones over the past few months. I completely understand, and cannot express my gratitude enough for their past participation, and I hope that they'll be back in the future.

Other authors found that Watson was whispering to them much more urgently than before, and they ended up with more than one story to submit. Some had two or three, and in a couple of cases, a full half-dozen tales. In these trying times, I was incredibly grateful to receive them, and they are invaluable additions to the latest set.

Back in 2015, when the MX anthologies began, I limited each contribution to one item per author, in order to spread the space around more fairly. But some authors are more prolific than that, and rather than be forced to choose between two excellent stories, I began to allow multiple contributions. (This also helped the authors, as their stories, if separated enough from each other chronologically, could appear in different simultaneously published volumes, thereby increasing their own bibliographies.)

Hal Glatzer and David MacGregor each contributed two stories this time. Dan Rowley, Tim Symonds, Arthur Hall, and me (your editor) provided three, and the indomitable Tracy Revels wrote an amazing six of them.

Also of note are the six stories contributed by the late Terry Golledge. In early 2022, I received an email from Niel Golledge, Terry's son, with a sample story, "The Addleton Tragedy". Terry had written it, along with nine others, in the 1980's, but they were never published. Niel had recently approached another editor about them, but that chap felt that it would be too much work to prepare the original typewritten manuscripts for modern publication. That was his big mistake, for it was absolutely worth the extra editorial work, as Terry Golledge's stories are wonderful and Watsonian. Niel graciously agreed to let me edit and include six of them for this collection, and later in 2022 they, along with the remaining four stories, will be published in their own separate volume, to the delight of Sherlockians like me who can *never* have enough tales about the *True Sherlock Holmes*. (An interesting side-note: Terry Golledge's mother worked as a governess for Sir Arthur Conan Doyle for several years in the early Nineteenth Century, so these tales have a bit of extra associational history.)

I can never express enough gratitude for all of the contributors who have donated their time and royalties to this ongoing project. I'm constantly amazed at the incredible stories that you send, and I'm so glad to have gotten to know so many of you through this process. It's an undeniable fact that Sherlock Holmes authors are the *best* people!

There is a fine group of people that exchanges emails with me when we have the time – and time is far too rare for all of us these days! I don't get to write back and forth with these fine people as often as I'd like, but I really enjoy catching up when we do get the chance: Derrick Belanger, Brian Belanger, Mark Mower, Roger Riccard, Denis Smith, Tom Turley, Dan Victor, and Marcia Wilson.

There is a group of special people who have stepped up and supported this and a number of other projects over and over again with a lot of contributions. They are the best and I can't express how valued they are: Ian Ableson, Hugh Ashton, Derrick Belanger, Deanna Baran, Andrew Bryant, Thomas Burns, Nick Cardillo, Chris Chan, Craig Stephen Copland, Matthew Elliott, Tim Gambrell, Jayantika Ganguly, Paul Gilbert, Dick Gillman, Arthur Hall, Steve Herczeg, Paul Hiscock, Mike Hogan, Craig Janacek, Susan Knight, Mark Mower, Will Murray, Tracy Revels, Roger Riccard, Jane Rubino, Geri Schear, Brenda Seabrooke, Shane Simmons, Robert Stapleton, Tim Symonds, Kevin Thornton, Tom Turley, DJ Tyrer, Dan Victor, I.A. Watson, and Marcia Wilson.

Next, I wish to send several huge *Thank You's* to the following:

- *Jeffrey Hatcher* – I missed my chance to meet Jeff in person at *From Gillette to Brett V* in October 2018, although I very much enjoyed his presentation. I was already aware of him for the incredible work that he had done in bringing a rather grim Holmes novel with a remarkable lack of hope, Mitch Cullin's *A Slight Trick of the Mind* (2005) to the screen in the form of *Mr. Holmes* (2015). My deerstalker and I were at the theatre on the film's opening day, having just re-read the book in preparation, and I wasn't sure what to expect. An elderly Holmes's life in the book is very bad, and it only get gets worse, with more bad piling high with each new chapter. Still, I normally defer to the printed version of things as the "true" version – especially when changes are made for a film. In this case, I happily made an exception to my rule.
    My own father had passed away in 2011 after struggling for several years with both Parkinson's and Alzheimer's, and to see Holmes's decline on screen was almost too vivid to bear – but Jeff's deft handling of the script, and the wise changes he made to the original plot in order to give Holmes a happier better future than shown in the book, were exactly what was needed.
    When Steve Emecz interviewed Jeff for the MX Publishing Audio Collection and then put me in touch with him, I was very pleased, and this was exceeded when Jeff agreed to write a foreword for this collection.
    Jeff, thanks very much for all your work, and the contribution of your time to these books. It's very much appreciated!

9

- *Steve Emecz* – As I've explained elsewhere, Steve works a way-more-than-full-time job related to his career in e-finance. MX Publishing isn't his full-time job – it's a labor of love. He, along with his wife, Sharon Emecz, and cousin, Timi Emecz, *are* MX Publishing. In addition to their very busy real every-day lives, these three sole employees take care of the management, marketing, editing, production, and shipping, and they absolutely cannot receive enough credit for what they accomplish.

Some people have a picture in their minds of a publishing company with several floors on some skyscraper, hundreds of employees running around like ants, with vast departments devoted to management, marketing, editing, production, shipping, etc. That is not always the case. Those old giant dinosaur publishers are still around, and they might squeeze out a Sherlockian title or two every year for those readers who foolishly think that there are only one or two Sherlockian titles every year (thus cheating themselves of some really incredible stories), but those publishers don't represent the modern way of doing things. MX has become the premiere Sherlockian publisher by following a new paradigm: Avoid the sucking whirlpool of traditional publishing and get books to readers as soon as possible. And they manage to get all of this done with a truly skeleton staff.

From my first association with MX in 2013, I saw that MX (under Steve's leadership) was *the* fast-rising superstar of the Sherlockian publishing world. Connecting with MX and Steve Emecz was personally an amazing life-changing event for me, as it has been for countless other Sherlockian authors. It has led me to write many more stories, and then to edit books, along with unexpected additional Holmes Pilgrimages to England – none of which might have happened otherwise. By way of my first email with Steve I've had the chance to make some incredible Sherlockian friends and play in the Holmesian Sandbox in ways that I would have never dreamed possible.

Through it all, Steve has been one of the most positive and supportive people that I've ever known.

With his and Sharon's and Timi's incredible hard work, they have made MX into a world-wide Sherlockian publishing phenomenon, providing opportunities for authors who would never have had them otherwise. There are some like me who return more than once to Watson's Tin Dispatch Box, and there are others who only find one or two stories there – but they also get the chance to publish their books, and then they can point with pride at this accomplishment, and how they too have added to The Great Holmes Tapestry.

From the beginning, Steve has let me explore various Sherlockian projects and open up my own personal possibilities in ways that otherwise would have never happened. Thank you, Steve, for every opportunity!

- *Brian Belanger* – Over the last few years, my amazement at Brian Belanger's ever-increasing talent has only grown. I initially became acquainted with him when he took over the duties of creating the covers for MX Books following the untimely death of their previous graphic artist. I found Brian to be a great collaborator, very easy-going and stress-free in his approach and willingness to work with authors, and wonderfully creative too.

    Brian and his brother, Derrick Belanger, are two great friends, and several years ago they founded *Belanger Books* which, along with MX Publishing, has absolutely locked up the Sherlockian publishing field with a vast amount of amazing material. The dinosaurs must be trembling to see every new Sherlockian project, one after another after another. Luckily MX and Belanger Books work closely with one another, and I'm thrilled to be associated with both of them. Many thanks to Brian for all he does for both publishers, and for all he's done for me personally.

- *Roger Johnson* – I'm more grateful than I can say that I know Roger. I was aware of him for years before I timidly sent him a copy of my first book for review, and then on my first Holmes Pilgrimage to England and Scotland in 2013, I was able to meet both him and his wonderful wife, Jean Upton, in person. When I returned on Holmes Pilgrimage No. 2 in 2015, I was so fortunate that they graciously invited me to stay with them for several days in their home, where we had many wonderful discussions, while occasionally venturing forth so that they could show me parts of England that I wouldn't have seen otherwise. It was an experience I wouldn't trade for anything.

Roger's Sherlockian knowledge is exceptional, as is the work that he does to further the cause of The Master. But even more than that, both Roger and Jean are simply the finest and best of people, and I'm very lucky to know both of them – even though I don't get to see them nearly as often as I'd like, and especially in these crazy days! (The last time was in 2016, at the Grand Opening party for the Stepping Stones School (now called Undershaw) at Undershaw in Hindhead.

In so many ways, Roger, I can't thank you enough, and I can't imagine these books without you.

And finally, last but certainly *not* least, thanks to **Sir Arthur Conan Doyle**: Author, doctor, adventurer, and the Founder of the Sherlockian Feast. Honored, and present in spirit.

As I always note when putting together an anthology of Holmes stories, the effort has been a labor of love. These adventures are just more tiny threads woven into the ongoing Great Holmes Tapestry, continuing to grow and grow, for there can *never* be enough stories about the man whom Watson described as *"the best and wisest . . . whom I have ever known."*

David Marcum
April 5th, 2022
128th Anniversary of
"The Empty House"

Questions, comments, or story submissions
may be addressed to David Marcum at

thepapersofsherlockholmes@gmail.com

Foreword
by Jeffrey Hatcher

I've never written a Sherlock Holmes pastiche. At least not in prose. I've written the plays *Sherlock Holmes and the Adventure of the Suicide Club*, *Sherlock Holmes and the Ice Palace Murders*, and *Holmes and Watson*. I also wrote the screenplay for the film *Mr. Holmes*, based on Mitch Cullin's novel *A Slight Trick of the Mind*. But I've never attempted a classic short story or novel of the sort Arthur Conan Doyle excelled at. The reasons are two-fold:

I've never had the stamina to write prose fiction, be it the short story or a long form narrative. There's something about the density of the words and the requirement to depict a complete world with both exterior action and interior thought that defeats me. When I was in junior high, I started writing a shorty story – maybe it was going to be a novel, I can't remember – and around that time I'd read Dashiell Hammett's *The Maltese Falcon*. Its opening is devoted entirely to a description of what Hammett's private eye hero Sam Spade looks like:

> *Samuel Spade's jaw was long and bony, his chin a jutting v under the more flexible V of his mouth. His nostrils curved back to make another, smaller, V. His yellow-grey eyes were horizontal. The V motif was picked up again by thickish brows rising outward from twin creases above a hooked nose, and his pale brown hair grew down – from high flat temples--in a point on his forehead. He looked rather pleasantly like a blonde Satan."*

So, I figured that's what a writer's supposed to do. Start with your main character and describe him in laborious, infinitesimal detail. So that's what I did. I can't remember who my main character was or if he even had a name, but I was onto my third page and hadn't gotten below his upper lip. And he wasn't going to be the only character in the story. I was going to have to do this with all the characters. Then I'd have to describe the rooms they inhabited, their homes and offices, their cars. Not to mention the outdoors. It came down to this: I don't like having to describe what the tree looks like. I never finished that story or novel or whatever it was supposed to be. It was properly abandoned. Instead, I turned my interest to dramatic story telling: Plays and screenplays, the first fully executed one being a one-hundred-forty page film adaptation of Ian Fleming's *Moonraker*, five years before the Roger Moore movie. (Mine was better.)

The second reason I've never attempted a Sherlock Holmes story is that although the form seems simple enough, schematic even, the content, tone, and style that Conan Doyle mastered with such apparent ease is actually very hard to impersonate. The joy in a familiar form such as the Holmes stories lies in the reader experiencing the changes the writer rings within the form.

I wrote a few *Columbo's* in the 1990's and each classic *Columbo* episode had the following structure:

Act One: *Meet the polished, sophisticated murderer and watch him or her commit the ostensibly perfect crime.*
Act Two: *Columbo investigates, discovers a clue that tells him the perfect crime isn't so perfect.*
Act Three: *Columbo and the murderer play cat and mouse as more mistakes are uncovered and more chess moves take place.*
Act Four: *The murderer finds the means to save himself.*
Act Five: *Columbo tricks the murderer into incriminating himself or reveals the final damning clue that closes the case.*

The fun was in watching the form reenacted in different settings with different characters, clues, twists, and surprises.

Similarly with Holmes, we start a story expecting a scene in Baker Street, the arrival of a client, a mystery posed. "Will you help me, Mr. Holmes?" Then Holmes and Watson set forth into the streets of London or the Great Grimpen Mire to investigate the case. They meet increasingly desperate and malevolent characters. Another crime is committed or foiled. Finally, the culprit is captured. Throughout the story Holmes will reveal his deductive powers, his psychological perceptions, his wit, his courage, his humanity – along with those of Dr. Watson's. Yes, there are occasional departures from the form, but, with rare exceptions, the departures are not what we crack the spine for.

Enjoy the stories you're about to read. Think of them as an old and dear friend who's come to visit you – and he's got something terribly new and exciting to tell you.

Jeffrey Hatcher
March 2021

"These little narratives"
by Roger Johnson

Younger readers – and writers, for that matter – may not be aware that it's not so very long since the choice of new Sherlock Holmes stories was very limited indeed. If you were lucky, you might find a copy of *The Misadventures of Sherlock Holmes*, edited by Ellery Queen and published in 1944. There were two printings before the Conan Doyle family's lawyers spotted a copyright infringement in another Ellery Queen anthology and used it as a reason to have *The Misadventures* withdrawn. Sir Arthur's sons could never be persuaded that the non-canonical stories might encourage readers to seek out and read the great originals.

The occasional new story did get published. In 1945 J.C. Masterman, a distinguished Oxford University academic and wartime intelligence chief, contributed "The Case of the Gifted Amateur" to *McKill's Mystery Magazine*, and S.C. Roberts, the no less distinguished Cambridge University academic who became the first President of the Sherlock Holmes Society of London, included a short story, "The Adventure of the Megatherium Thefts", in his classic 1953 book *Holmes and Watson: A Miscellany*. The specialist Holmesian journals occasionally published good new stories, but until 1974 the only book of consequence was *The Exploits of Sherlock Holmes*, comprising twelve tales written by Adrian Conan Doyle and John Dickson Carr, and published in 1954. (Adrian had made himself so intensely disliked among American Sherlockians that Edgar W Smith, head of the Baker Street Irregulars, dismissed the book as "Sherlock Holmes Exploited". In fact, the stories are never less than good, and several are excellent.)

1974 was the year of wonders, beginning with the Royal Shakespeare Company's hugely successful new production of William Gillette's play *Sherlock Holmes*. Adrian Conan Doyle had died in 1970, predeceased by his brother Denis, and, despite some subsequently dubious handling of Sir Arthur's estate, the attitude towards sincere fictional tributes to his most celebrated creations was now more relaxed. The first novel-length pastiches had only recently appeared, derived from the scripts of successful movies: *A Study in Terror* and *The Private Life of Sherlock Holmes*. More would come, but the real breakthrough was Nicholas Meyer's *The Seven-per-Cent Solution*, which would itself become a notable film.

The floodgates were not yet breached. That would come with the expiry of Sir Arthur's British copyright in 1980 – and would be followed by problems when copyright in all countries of the European Union was extended to seventy years after the author's death. Freedom was finally declared in 2000 – except in the U.S.A., whose copyright laws are unlike any other nation's. Nevertheless, it was now legal to write and publish new Holmes stories almost everywhere, and, as long as publication was a matter for the professionals, we could be pretty confident that the result would be of at least reasonable quality. But fashions in the book world change, and even Sherlock Holmes doesn't always appeal to the professional publishers.

What actually destroyed the floodgates was the rapid development of the home computer and the world-wide web. Self-publishing became much easier and cheaper, and in time the authors didn't even have to produce a printed version of their works, as the internet made it possible to post them online for anyone to read. One result is easy access to stories created with admiration and affection. Another, alas, is that the good stuff is vastly outnumbered by the less good – often poorly constructed and badly written, sometimes actually offensive.

Fortunately, it isn't hard to find new Sherlock Holmes stories of genuine quality. The book you're reading now is evidence of that. This series began in 2015, with the publication of three volumes, whose editor, authors, and publisher generously donated all their royalties to the restoration and maintenance of Undershaw, the house that Arthur Conan Doyle had built in the Surrey Hills for himself and his family. The fact that *The MX Book of New Sherlock Holmes Stories* continues, six years on, is heartening. That it now exceeds *thirty* volumes is amazing!

The apparently indefatigable David Marcum ensures that the standard remains high, and the proceeds still go to the upkeep of Undershaw, which since 2016 has been home to the Undershaw School, providing care and education for children aged 8 to 19 with Autistic Spectrum Disorder and associated learning needs.

Could there be a better recommendation?

Roger Johnson, BSI, ASH
Commissioning Editor: *The Sherlock Holmes Journal*
December 2021

An Ongoing Legacy
for Sherlock Holmes
by Steve Emecz

Undershaw
Circa 1900

*T*he *MX Book of New Sherlock Holmes Stories* has grown beyond any expectations we could have imagined. We're very close to having raised $100,000 for Undershaw, a school for children with learning disabilities. The collection has become not only the largest Sherlock Holmes collection in the world, but one of the most respected.

We have received over twenty very positive reviews from *Publishers Weekly*, and in a recent review for someone else's book, *Publishers Weekly* referred to the MX Book in that review which demonstrates how far the collection's influence has grown.

In 2022, we launched *The MX Audio Collection*, an app which includes some of these stories, alongside exclusive interviews with leading writers and Sherlockians including Lee Child, Jeffrey Hatcher, Nicholas

Meyer, Nancy Springer, Bonnie MacBird, and Otto Penzler. A share of the proceeds also goes to Undershaw. You can find out all about the app here:

https://mxpublishing.com/pages/mx-app

In addition to Undershaw, we also support Happy Life Mission (a baby rescue project in Kenya), The World Food Programme (which won the Nobel Peace Prize in 2020), and iHeart (who support mental health in young people).

Our support for our projects is possible through the publishing of Sherlock Holmes books, which we have now been doing for over a decade.

You can find links to all our projects on our website:

https://mxpublishing.com/pages/about-us

I'm sure you will enjoy the fantastic stories in the latest volumes and look forward to many more in the future.

Steve Emecz
March 2022
Twitter: *@mxpublishing*

The Doyle Room at Undershaw
Partially funded through royalties from
The MX Book of New Sherlock Holmes Stories

19

A Word from Undershaw
by Emma West

Undershaw
September 9, 2016
Grand Opening of the Stepping Stones School
(Now *Undershaw*)
(Photograph courtesy of Roger Johnson)

I am delighted to bring you news of Undershaw . . . from Undershaw. Since September 2021, under our new name, vision, and values, our wonderful school has been focussing on Undershaw community pride. To that end, we have focussed on recruiting, retaining, and upskilling a talented staff cadre, each one a specialist in their field, experienced with SEND education, and each one an innovator of new teaching and learning practices.

We have fortified our school life with robust qualifications and have strengthened our relationships with exam boards to ensure our students leave us with the qualifications they deserve, and of which they are eminently capable. Our school is awash with academic, artistic, and musical talent, and we feel privileged in our role of unleashing that potential in a way that works for our learners.

Our traditional classroom learning is complemented by a variety of other techniques. For example: Our outdoor learning area, for which we are currently fundraising. A Fire Pit shelter will double as an outdoor classroom, and will enable us to continue our learning in nature all year round and in all weathers. We know that learning outdoors amidst nature does wonders for well-being and contentment. We have such a beautiful and inspirational campus and, as much as it is our *raison d'etre* to equip our provision for all our learners, it is also our role as caretakers of Undershaw to nurture and improve the campus for the generations to come.

It is only through our relationships with benefactors such as MX Publishing, and the wonderful authors who support its charitable giving, that we are able to thrive through 2022 and beyond. The culture at Undershaw is an extremely positive one, and we're delighted that you are joining us on our journey. For up-to-date news about our school and our work within the Special Educational Needs sector, please see our website at www.undershaw.education. Our newsletters carry a vast array of student activities and daily goings on, while our news articles take a deep dive into some of the ways Undershaw is redefining opportunities for our young people.

As ever, my heartfelt thanks to you all for your unrelenting support. Our students, staff, and families are full of pride at belonging to #teamundershaw, and I look forward to writing to you again soon with more tales from the Surrey Hills.

Emma West
Acting Headteacher
March 2022

"Undershaw" Hindhead Conan Doyle's House.

Editor's *Caveats*

When these anthologies first began back in 2015, I noted that the authors were from all over the world – and thus, there would be British spelling and American spelling. As I explained then, I didn't want to take the responsibility of changing American spelling to British and vice-versa. I would undoubtedly miss something, leading to inconsinstencies, or I'd change something incorrectly.

Some readers are bothered by this, made nervous and irate when encountering American spelling as written by Watson, and in stories set in England. However, here in America, the versions of The Canon that we read have long-ago has their spelling Americanized, so it isn't quite as shocking for us.

Additionally, I offer my apologies up front for any typographical errors that have slipped through. As a print-on-demand publisher, MX does not have squadrons of editors as some readers believe. The business consists of three part-time people who also have busy lives elsewhere – Steve Emecz, Sharon Emecz, and Timi Emecz – so the editing effort largely falls on the contributors. Some readers and consumers out there in the world are unhappy with this – apparently forgetting about all of those self-produced Holmes stories and volumes from decades ago (typed and Xeroxed) with awkward self-published formatting and loads of errors that are now prized as very expensive collector's items.

I'm personally mortified when errors slip through – ironically, there will probably be errors in these *caveats* – and I apologize now, but without a regiment of professional full-time editors looking over my shoulder, this is as good as it gets. Real life is more important than writing and editing – even in such a good cause as promoting the True and Traditional Canonical Holmes – and only so much time can be spent preparing these books before they're released into the wild. I hope that you can look past any errors, small or huge, and simply enjoy these stories, and appreciate the efforts of everyone involved, and the sincere desire to add to The Great Holmes Tapestry.

And in spite of any errors here, there are more Sherlock Holmes stories in the world than there were before, and that's a good thing.

David Marcum
Editor

Sherlock Holmes (1854-1957) was born in Yorkshire, England, on 6 January, 1854. In the mid-1870's, he moved to 24 Montague Street, London, where he established himself as the world's first Consulting Detective. After meeting Dr. John H. Watson in early 1881, he and Watson moved to rooms at 221b Baker Street, where his reputation as the world's greatest detective grew for several decades. He was presumed to have died battling noted criminal Professor James Moriarty on 4 May, 1891, but he returned to London on 5 April, 1894, resuming his consulting practice in Baker Street. Retiring to the Sussex coast near Beachy Head in October 1903, he continued to be associated in various private and government investigations while giving the impression of being a reclusive apiarist. He was very involved in the events encompassing World War I, and to a lesser degree those of World War II. He passed away peacefully upon the cliffs above his Sussex home on his 103rd birthday, 6 January, 1957.

Dr. John Hamish Watson (1852-1929) was born in Stranraer, Scotland on 7 August, 1852. In 1878, he took his Doctor of Medicine Degree from the University of London, and later joined the army as a surgeon. Wounded at the Battle of Maiwand in Afghanistan (27 July, 1880), he returned to London late that same year. On New Year's Day, 1881, he was introduced to Sherlock Holmes in the chemical laboratory at Barts. Agreeing to share rooms with Holmes in Baker Street, Watson became invaluable to Holmes's consulting detective practice. Watson was married and widowed three times, and from the late 1880's onward, in addition to his participation in Holmes's investigations and his medical practice, he chronicled Holmes's adventures, with the assistance of his literary agent, Sir Arthur Conan Doyle, in a series of popular narratives, most of which were first published in *The Strand* magazine. Watson's later years were spent preparing a vast number of his notes of Holmes's cases for future publication. Following a final important investigation with Holmes, Watson contracted pneumonia and passed away on 24 July, 1929.

Photos of Sherlock Holmes and Dr. John H. Watson courtesy of Roger Johnson

The MX Book
of
New Sherlock Holmes Stories
Part XXXI – 2022 Annual
(1875-1887)

The Nemesis
of Sherlock Holmes
by Kelvin I. Jones

By a window in a fog wrapped street,
At the end of a darkening day,
A figure locked in reverie
Watches the cabman's dray.

He wears no slippers,
Dishevelled stands,
His gaunt face lined and dark.
There are scars upon his weathered hands
That marked his ordeal on that path.

The nemesis
Of the King of crime,
A creature of decadence,
That aged body
Stained with sweat and grime,
Locked with him in a deathly dance.

That demon's visage, etched with blood,
That thin voice choked with ire.
That dreadful, oscillating head,
Those eyes like balls of fire.

That visage,
With its hell-hound's bark,
Still watching from the dark.

Much will never be the same,
Despite his illustrious rise to fame,
And his dreams are fuelled with brimstone now
And have left their branding mark.

On nights like this,
His pipe alight,

Holmes scans the silent street,
Remembering that deadly fight,
Hearing his faint heart's beat.

As the fog swirls down on Baker Street,
And shadows loom from alleyways,
He hears the church bell's dull and melancholy beat
Mark the ending of the day.

He recalls now it was ever thus,
And ever shall it be,
And he draws the slim syringe along his sleeve,
Haunted by shades that will not leave,
A man bereaved,
In search of Morpheus.

The Unsettling Incident
of the History Professor's Wife
by Sean M. Wright

A Word to the Reader: The present account of a case in which Mr. Mycroft Holmes assisted his brother Sherlock took place in 1875, predating by only two weeks "The Affair of the Queen's Necklace" – published as Enter the Lion: A Posthumous Memoir of Mycroft Holmes *(Michael P. Hodel and Sean M. Wright, Hawthorn, 1979). At the time of this story, Mycroft was twenty-eight years of age, and Sherlock was twenty-one. In the foreword to that earlier adventure, I referred to the discovery of a folder containing the manuscript of the novel and notes to more of Mr. Holmes's reminiscences, including this unfinished manuscript.*

The present narrative appears to be a first attempt at novelization, given up and left unfinished by Mr. Mycroft Holmes when it became evident that the events did not warrant a lengthy presentation. Fortunately, the solution to this case was discovered among his memoranda, so I have taken it upon myself to complete the tale. I hope the seam will not be too noticeable.

The Foreign Office was abuzz with the news. Diplomatic cablegrams had arrived announcing an excited – nay, a *tumultuous* welcome given the Prince of Wales upon his arrival at the port city of Bombay. Lord Northbrook, the Viceroy, was mightily gratified.

Before continuing, the reader will want to stoke the fire and settle more firmly into his armchair as I endeavor to explain events beginning on the 6th of November in the Year of Grace 1875. Having a tumbler of Scotch whisky to hand, perhaps fortified by a touch of soda, would not be amiss. My narrative will encompass both a political situation coming to fore at the time, and what transpired after I received the following telegram, the first of several I would receive over the years when my brother found himself in a quandary:

Mycroft –

Will you be in tonight? I should like your opinion regarding a police matter. It is sufficiently outré *to appeal to your sense of the grotesque.*

Sherlock

Despite a minor note of apprehension struck by one or two Cabinet ministers, Her Majesty's Government had dispatched His Royal Highness the Prince of Wales on what became an eight-month-long Royal Progress to India. Leaving behind a distraught Princess Alexandra, [1] the Prince selected fifty male companions, many titled, all members of his socially prominent – and latterly scandalous – Marlborough House set. [2] These lords and gentlemen accompanied the Prince as a hunting and shooting party set on enjoying the astonishing beauty of the land of the *Parsee*, the *Hindoo*, and the *Musselman*, [3] intent on bagging enough game to keep a dozen taxidermists busy for the rest of the next year.

Two months had passed since the Prince and his party had boarded *HMS Serapis* on an excursion ostensibly seen as a manifestation of good will extended the Crown Colony by Queen Victoria. The following week, Lord Northbrook would escort the Prince and his friends to Government House, the Viceroy's palatial residence in Calcutta. [4] The next several days would be filled with grand banquets to which were invited princes and pashas undecided about pledging loyalty to the British Raj, accompanied by concerts, levees, [5] drawing rooms, and even an elephant ride.

Within European embassies it was an open secret that, as the Great Powers had divided China into spheres of influence, Russia, Japan, and even Siam were queueing up to use the Balkan hostilities as a pretext to subdivide the subcontinent. Some of these same Indian potentates and satraps had earlier besieged the Viceroy with anxious expressions of alarm when insurrection against Turkish rule erupted in the Balkans. Later dispatches would show the Prince of Wales at his most charming, exchanging gifts and information with along with promises of protection as Mr. Disraeli had planned.

The true reasons for this expedition are not so well known, even as I recollect events a third-of-a-century after Her Majesty's demise. [6] The Royal Progress tested the water for yet another aspect of Mr. Disraeli's statecraft, one directly involving the wishes of Queen Victoria: For some years, she had desired Parliament to grant her the title *"Empress of the British Isles"*.

Clearly, the great respect accorded the Prince of Wales by assorted regional rajahs, maharajahs, and sultans demonstrated their acceptance of Victoria as sovereign successor to the imperial tradition of the Padishahs, as the now dispossessed Mogul Emperors had been styled. [7] By their acquiescence to the Queen's succession, Indian rulers would help ease yet another, more delicate, political difficulty in England.

The reason for wanting this title as her own lay in the fact that Her Majesty became discomfited when the German Empire was newly recreated in 1871. Prussia's King Wilhelm IV was chosen to lead a Second Reich in succession to the Empire founded by Charlemagne in 800, and ended in 1806 by the Little Corporal. [8] In maintaining a connection with the Roman Empire, Wilhelm acceded to his new throne, styling himself *Kaiser*. [9]

The coronation dismayed Queen Victoria. Her Majesty realized that Wilhelm's son, Frederick, husband of her daughter, Victoria the Princess Royal, would succeed to an Imperial throne. The Queen found it unseemly that her son-in-law and daughter, as *Kaiser* and *Kaiserin*, would both possess titles of greater dignity than her own. From that time, Her Majesty resolved to have the title Empress as her own. [10]

My superior, the Right Honorable Mr. Jerrold Moriarty, the military liaison, advised restraint. The idea was sound. Yet it seemed odd that the military liaison would voice worry about trade. A few weeks later would I learn why. That, however, is another tale to be told. [11] There was much agreement with the change of government in 1874 from Mr. Gladstone to Mr. Disraeli. Taken into the royal confidence, Mr. Disraeli well understood that Her Majesty's subjects would never stand for her assuming an imperial style over England which would imply subordination of the parliamentary system of government, Albion's bulwark against autocratic rule. It was, therefore, with great delicacy that Mr. Disraeli was expending considerable effort within the Commons in order to fulfill Her Majesty's desire.

A Royal Titles Bill was being prepared for consideration after the Prince's return. Mr. Disraeli's plan was to have the title "Empress" modified as representing, not the British Isles, but as an expression of British hegemony over lands across the seas. The title would thus inspire pride in the hearts of Her Majesty's subjects while, at the same time, thwart any charges of absolutism from Mr. Gladstone and the Liberals.

My brother's telegram arrived at the Foreign Office as I neared the end of my workday.

I sent a reply that I should expect him after dinner at my home in St. Chad's Street.

Amid his desultory university studies, Sherlock was taking full advantage of a letter of introduction I had procured from Mr. Richard Cross, the Home Secretary. He was fascinated by the notion of a young gentleman wishing to study criminal conduct in order to combat it. The letter from Mr. Cross to Sir Edmund Henderson, the Commissioner of Police, allowing my brother access to the study of police methods was met with rather less enthusiasm in some quarters within the purlieus of Scotland Yard.

For more than half the year, Sherlock had accompanied police on such occasions as were permitted. Some Scotland Yarders were leery of a young man armed only with a cascade of deductions. Others welcomed his observations and theories.

Sherlock was in a querulous mood as he strode into my tiny foyer, laid down his walking stick and yanked off his gloves.

"How can I make a living as a consulting detective if my efforts to learn more precisely the habits and practices of the criminal mind are treated in so careless a manner by the professionals? Ofttimes when accompanying one of them, I feel as if I were a Borneo bushman hunting game, and finding himself suddenly transported to the throne room in Balmoral."

Hanging his hat, ulster, and comforter on clothes pegs, he paused to observe, "Have you told your landlady about the woodworm in the corner?"

"I have," I replied dryly. "And I see you've been working with poisons again."

He stared at me for a moment.

"The sticking plaster on your left hand. It almost came off with your glove. Now take a chair by the fire and have some brandy so you can warm yourself and stop shivering."

"It isn't the cold which caused my shiver just now," said Sherlock, wheeling 'round on his heel and gazing at me sharply. "It is the memory of the sight I beheld earlier today." So saying, he picked up his walking stick and stalked into my sitting room. Slumping into the overstuffed barrel chair set across the hearth from my own Morris chair, Sherlock leaned forward, resting his chin on his hands grasping the brass knob of his stick.

A scrimmage of dead leaves blew past my window to rustle down St. Chad's Street as a chill wind whistled ominously round the corner of my snug sitting room. In silence Sherlock sat, staring at the crackling flames of the fireplace. The state of his shoes bespoke how my brother had prowled the streets to clear the cobwebs from his mind.

"Share the details, Sherlock. Let's see if I can help you find a solution."

A few more moments passed before he stirred. "I believe I will take you up on that brandy now."

I made as if to rise, but my brother stood and pushed me back. "Stay there, Mycroft. I know how much you hate to stir once you have made yourself comfortable." At my sideboard, he poured himself a brandy, swiftly downed it, poured himself another, then poured some in another snifter for me.

"What, then?" I asked, stoking the logs, grateful for the fire's cheery warmth for, even wrapped in a heavy dressing gown, the cold vice of autumn was dispiriting. My brother's reply made the room all the more chill.

"This morning I accompanied an acquaintance to the scene of a grisly death." Bringing the decanter with him, my brother handed me a snifter and sat down again.

I shrugged. "You will have to inure yourself to such sights if you wish a career in police work." He set down the glass with a sharp thump on the side table next to his chair. Once more resting his hands on the knob of his walking stick, he again stared at the flames.

"Do you know Shimon Alexandros Egenburg, a tall, vigorous, older man with a luxurious black beard lightly streaked with grey – the Jew broker in the Tottenham Court Road?" [12]

"No."

"Among a clutter of sundry other items in his shop are a number of second-hand musical instruments. He does a brisk trade in sheet music as well. I found the shop over a year ago when I had difficulty finding copies of the score for Offenbach's *Orpheus in the Underworld*, which was then being revived in Paris."

My brother's attitude lightened a little. "You may recall, Mycroft, several members of the critical press originally resented the operetta, attacking it as a satiric depiction of the court of Napoleon III. Their attitude notwithstanding, the operetta was a resounding success. With its revival, Mr. Egenburg told me, the same critics were now dismissing Offenbach's work as having become *passé*. 'Why should I stop selling good music simply because of a few self-important critics in France? Besides,' he said with a wink and a laugh, 'Louis Napoleon, himself, is now *passé*.' [13]

"Admiring the man's pluck, I continued my patronage, and we've shared several conversations since. Making his home in the rooms above the shop, he makes his own hours.

"In need of some rosin for my bow, I stopped by Mr. Egenburg's shop this morning and found him standing in front, in company with a constable and a police van. In great distress, Mr. Egenburg told me the policeman had come to fetch him to his daughter's home.

"'My Susie, Mr. Holmes!' the shopkeeper exclaimed, 'The constable here tells me her husband has died, and the police want to ask me some questions.'

"He seemed to have aged twenty years, becoming stooped as he wrung his hands. Knowing him to be a widower and quite devoted to his daughter, I asked if I might be of service. He looked back at me with doleful eyes and shrugged. I asked the constable the name of the inspector

37

in charge. He gave me a quizzical look but told me that Inspector Tobias Gregson was conducting the investigation. Nodding, I told him that I was known to the inspector, and so I accompanied Mr. Egenburg in the van.

"We rode in silence. I had no wish to interrupt his thoughts as the old man prayed under his breath, his hands anxiously clasping and unclasping. Aware of how gently she had been raised, I was astonished to learn that his daughter and her husband made their home in Mornington Crescent, Camden. She was living in one of those large houses which have been made into a honeycomb of flats for paupers.

"I made out the tall figure and florid face of Inspector Gregson. He was standing on the front step of a residence, writing in a notebook. An expression of surprise crossed his features upon seeing me alight from the van, but he directed his remarks to Mr. Egenburg, who was eager to see his daughter. The inspector expressed his regrets for having to detain him to ask a few questions, but promised that he would be able to see his daughter forthwith. I took the time to inspect the porch and exterior of the flat. There was nothing of interest save a single window on the south side of the house, below which is a window-box containing a hardy strain of begonias.

"'While you speak to Mr. Egenburg,' I asked, 'would you mind if I look inside, Inspector?'

"'This is a straightforward matter, young Mister Holmes,' he said – not unkindly. 'I dare say your theories will shed no light on the subject.'

"'Then, perhaps,' I replied smoothly, 'I will learn something from you as a professional, experienced with this kind of misfortune.'

"Gregson hesitated, then said, 'Very well, young man, I believe I will let you in. Be warned, however, the dead man doesn't make a pretty sight. This gentleman's daughter is within, accompanied by a constable. I don't want you bothering her.'"

Sherlock reached for the decanter. After gesturing I wanted naught more, he poured another half-glass for himself.

"I thanked Gregson, assuring him that I'd follow his direction. The inspector turned to the policeman who had accompanied us, gesturing to him to open the door to the sitting room."

Sherlock paused, his brow knotted. "I wasn't prepared for the *tableau* within, Mycroft. A man's body lay on the floor. "The wall behind it was spattered with gore." Again, he shivered. "It took but a moment to see why: Half the man's head had been blown away."

He took a deep breath. "I have imagined encountering such a scene and thought my nerves fairly proof against what I might come across in such an investigation. Beholding the wreckage of a man's body, so recently alive, roused in me mixed emotions of sadness, anger, and eventual pity."

"I see. Well, your telegram promised me something grotesque."

"Ah!" said Sherlock. "That isn't the only incongruity. The man's wife – Mr. Egenburg's daughter, Susan – was sitting on a rickety wooden chair appearing to be perfectly composed. She was doing needlework, in fact – much to the consternation of the constable assigned to watch over her. He seemed frustrated in that she wasn't collapsed in tears."

"You haven't as yet mentioned the name of the man who died, Sherlock."

"His name was Jack Bridgeford," said Sherlock, taking another drink. "He and the young woman were married six years ago "I turned back to view the scene once more. Incredibly, nothing had been moved. The police hadn't stamped about obliterating evidence, praise be. I credit Gregson for that. He's among the more thorough of the Scotland Yarders.

"Taking it all in, I was able to confirm for myself that the death followed a self-inflicted gunshot. Bridgeford, in his shirtsleeves, had been sitting in another wooden chair in the sparsely furnished room. Falling from it, he rolled onto his back, his left arm flung out. A torrent of blood had rushed from the wound, flowing across the floor and eddying into the curve of his right elbow. His right hand still clutched the revolver. A few rills of blood running under his right hand were clotting.

"Certain that my promise to Gregson didn't include the constable. I waved him over and explained my presence as an investigator known to the inspector. In lowered voices, we chatted for a few minutes.

"After the shooting, Mrs. Bridgeford had rushed out into the street till she found a constable. She was all disheveled, he informed me. Upon finding two others, himself one of them, she brought them back to her flat. Upon their return, she left them to gaze at her husband's body while she tidied herself, rinsed off her face, and brushed her hair. Thereafter she had shown not the slightest bit of emotion.

"The other constable left to bring word to the Yard. Briggs, the one I spoke to, assured me that no one had approached the body. 'We were concerned about the lady since the gentleman was beyond medical care,' he told me. Since that time, he further informed me, Mrs. Bridgeford showed no emotion. He thought it strange that, without so much as a by-your-leave, she took up her sewing basket and began her mending. I thanked him and left the room.

"Inspector Gregson suggested that Mr. Egenberg might help his daughter put some clothes together and take her to his home. I agreed, adding that he might want to avoid glancing at the left-hand portion of the room.

"'Is my Susie all right?'

"'She's quite self-possessed, under the circumstances.'

"'Thanks be to the Lord our God!' said Mr. Egenburg. As he walked by me, he placed his left hand upon my shoulder, nodding his thanks, his eyes welling up before entering the room.

"'So, young sir,' Gregson smiled, 'will you be favoring me with any deductions, or do you agree with me in citing the cause of death as a single gunshot to the head – the manner of death being suicide?'

"'I saw all that you saw, Inspector, and was glad to find nothing disturbed. With a certainty, all signs point to the dead man having shot himself. No other conclusion is possible.'"

"'Aye, now, young Mister Holmes,'" said Inspector Gregson with an expansive smile, 'it seems as if you might yet have the makings of a detective in you.'

"I fail to understand, Sherlock," I interposed, "If you and the inspector are so much in accord, what use is my opinion?"

"An excellent question, Mycroft. I've come because, having found ourselves in such close agreement, Gregson allowed a small, self-satisfied smirk to cross his features, as he continued in a low, conspiratorial voice, 'D'ya know the lady claims to have murdered her husband?'"

"Ha!" I exclaimed. "There's the rub, right enough! And yet you both saw traces of a powder burn on the man's right hand – correct?"

"Yes, Mycroft. That, along with intense powder burns on the man's neck and on what was left of his face, indicated the pistol was held close to the head."

"It was, of course, a large-bore weapon?"

"Ah," my brother responded. "That was a feature Gregson noted as well. In Mr. Bridgeford's hand was a .45 calibre, nickel-plated American Colt revolver."

"That is of some interest, no doubt. Was this Jack Bridgeford from America?"

"Gregson noted that Mrs. Bridgeford told him that her husband was born in Lichfield of a good family. He attended Cambridge, spent nearly a year in Canada, staying with an uncle and aunt, where he learned how to fish. He then served for a time as an officer in the Militia Artillery. [14]

"What other traces did you note?"

"The walls were bare save for a food cupboard and a few, small, unframed, original still-life landscapes. A terribly old, swayback divan sits along the east wall. Meals are made on an old stove, which is also the only source of heat. A cheap, varnished kitchen table was covered by a chintz cloth. Dishes were clean, stacked on a wash-hand stand opposite the stove.

40

"The floor is uncarpeted but clean – the floorboards show signs of frequent scrubbing, although there were some heel marks from a man's shoes in front of the food cupboard and a man's jacket lay flung in the corner. I noticed that Mrs. Bridgeford had swept the floor earlier in the day. There wasn't a bit of house dust or a cobweb anywhere, not even in the corners. She was interrupted in her work, however."

"No doubt by whatever led to her husband's death," I said. "Explaining why you saw her cleaning implements: The broom and dustpan were still out and the pail filled with dirt and old newspapers hadn't been emptied. Even in reduced circumstances so meticulous a woman would scarce lose her sense of sell-respect."

"My thoughts, as well."

"Could it be," I mused, "that Mrs. Bridgeford cleaned her floors to hide traces of a third person?"

"I could find no indication of a third person leaving the room."

"Not even by a window?"

"There is but one window," Sherlock replied, shaking his head. "Come, Mycroft, I am not so benighted as to overlook the obvious. Blood spatters on sill and drapery were without smudges, and there were no recent marks to show the window had been raised. Beyond that," my brother concluded with a sardonic smile, "when I saw it, the earth and begonias in the window-box were undisturbed."

Removing a notebook from his coat pocket he asked, "Would you care to know the contents of Mr. Bridgeford's pockets?"

"It may be instructive."

"While old Egenberg and his daughter were in her bedroom packing some clothing, Gregson and the constable went through the dead man's trouser pockets. They found sixpence, a cigar-end, some vestas, a clasp-knife, and a pack of playing cards, within which was placed a ticket coming from a nearby pawnbroker's shop bearing today's date."

"The cigar-end," I asked. "Was it from a decent smoke?"

"A Jamaican cheroot."

"It's curious that Bridgeford placed the cigar-end in his pocket instead of throwing it away," I mused. "Was it cut or bitten off?"

"It was cut," said Sherlock. "Undoubtedly by the same clasp-knife he carried."

"So," I said, enjoying the comfort of my Morris chair, my fingertips placed together, "we know Jack Bridgeford had a decent start in life with a sound education. He married a caring wife and had good prospects, but has come down in his fortunes. He has been making a living, of sorts, as a gambler. And although he knew a fine cigar, he had lost his taste for tobacco. You said he was in the military?"

41

"A former member of the Military Artillery. A folded handkerchief was found in his left shirt cuff."

"Another indication of his being right-handed," I nodded. "An officer of course."

"Non-commissioned. A sergeant-major."

"I'm impressed with your exactitude, Sherlock. How could you tell his rank?"

"His widow told me when I asked her," Sherlock said as he lit his pipe.

"*Touché*," I chuckled. "Asking questions is always a good thing. Any other discoveries?"

His smile departed on the instant. "Five bullet pocks adorn the west wall of the bedroom, all located above the bed."

"Truly," I remarked. "An intriguing sign. What did you learn about their existence?"

After a few moments' silence, Sherlock asked, "Have you discerned anything of the character of Susan Bridgeford?"

"You have told me precious little about her, save that she was gently raised, confident, self-possessed, with a streak of the romantic tempered by a good deal of self-respect. She is given to painting, has an inclination to independence which she keeps submerged, is a thorough housekeeper, and a loving wife, intent on keeping her marriage intact. I am surprised," I concluded, "that you didn't remark on there being a bookcase filled with the poetry of Byron, Keats, Shelley, and Wordsworth."

"There are no books at all in the flat."

"That's odd, considering how both were so well-educated. Might Susan Bridgeford have been cleaning up after being visited by a caller," I wondered aloud, "a man, perhaps, toward whom Jack Bridgeford was ill-disposed, and was interrupted by her husband's unexpected return. It isn't an unreasonable assumption."

"Certainly not unreasonable, but equally as unlikely," Sherlock replied intensely. "See here, Mycroft, you have noted that she was a loving wife – "

"You misunderstand me, Sherlock," I quickly interposed. "I didn't mean to imply any kind of romantic connection. I wondered only if she had a visitor to whom her husband was ill-disposed."

"I see," my brother replied. "Yes, that is a possibility. Anything less an implication is greatly at odds with every other indication of the woman's character. Here is a woman putting on an heroic front in the face of her husband's adversity, making her home as endearing as possible. She has hung draperies of a dreadful, catchpenny sort, but brave with color.

She maintained a window-box, and had even hung her own paintings attempting to mask the drabness of the couple's surroundings."

"Your conclusions are perfectly sound," I interjected.

"As her father protectively hovered over her – and by Gregson's leave – I questioned Susan Bridgeford. She unburdened herself of her personal history quite willingly, but dispassionately, her voice listless.

"Susan Egenburg met Jack Bridgeford seven years ago at a dance put on for the Military Artillery. Attending with another young lady, Susan didn't consider herself as beautiful as many of the other belles present. Nonetheless, Jack Bridgeford stood before her, bowed, and asked her to dance. In conversation, she learned Jack was a sergeant-major in the Militia, but was more impressed by his scholarly bent – impressed that Jack's keen knowledge of classical Roman life and personalities matched her own.

"Writing each other and meeting on occasion over the next several months, they discovered they shared a number of other interests, including a love of poetry. Even when disagreeing with him about one thing or another, he loved her all the more, he told her, because she didn't simper, but could hold her own. When Jack asked her to marry him, Susan decided to 'take a stab at it', as she put it with an American colloquialism, and they were wed.

"A few months before, Jack had secured a position in a small finishing school. At the end of the term, he was offered a post as a history instructor at a small college near Kensington, very close to their home at the time, and the future seemed assured. Yet this was the beginning of their calamities.

"The dean of the history department was an envious old don whose chief asset in teaching was a ready birch rod, which he applied vigorously to his students. He made life unbearable for the instructors as well, brow-beating the more talented into obsequiousness or departure.

"The old reprobate made life particularly difficult for Jack Bridgeford, whom he rightly recognized as a serious challenger to his imperious sway. With his military training, Jack wasn't about to, 'take any guff from anyone', as his widow so strikingly said. He regularly stood up to this dean, even defending other instructors he bullied.

"The situation continued for some time. Jack Bridgeford made a mistake, however, allowing it to become known that he was writing a new history of the first five Roman Emperors, the Julio-Claudian Caesars. The dean was soon piling extra duties on Jack during the next two terms, his widow believes, to prevent him from spending much time in researching his book.

"In other respects, all went well until the end of that second term. Mrs. Bridgeford went out one day to shop. Upon her return she found their home in a jumble. It seemed at first that only few oddments had been taken and some loose change. However, she soon realized her husband's unfinished manuscript and the pile of notes it had taken him four years to compile were also missing. The police were alerted but, when they found little of actual value and just two-and-six missing, they lost interest, suggesting that the manuscript's theft was merely a student lark and would soon be returned.

"Jack was willing to believe this at first. Yet, as the days passed and no one admitted to the prank, he became more distraught. It came to a head when he heard the dean describe a student party as being marked by 'Caligulean' enormities – hardly a word in common parlance – but one which Jack knew to be in his manuscript.

"Convinced that his dean was now in possession of his manuscript and notes, on the evening before commencement ceremonies, Jack imprudently brought his service revolver with him to school, denounced the dean, and waved the gun under the old man's nose, threatening him if his manuscript and notes weren't returned upon the morrow. Instead, the dean denounced Jack Bridgeford before the headmaster and demanded his arrest. The head, however, called Jack in and simply dismissed him, explaining that he would do that rather than cause a scandal for the school by having the young man charged by the police for committing a felony."

"Heavens, Sherlock!" I said as I refreshed my drink then settled my bulk more comfortably. "This tale is beginning to show all the elements of one of Mr. Dickens' more sordid novels. Can the death of Little Nell be long in coming?"

"I grant you the melodrama," my brother said rubbing his eyes, "and, yes. it becomes worse. Attempting to find employment at other institutions, Bridgeford discovered that he was thoroughly blackballed. Due to letters sent out by his nemesis, the dean, he was unable to find employment even at lesser senior and public schools.

"As his savings dwindled, Jack became embittered, took to drink, and began associating with an unsavory lot. Before long he was enticed to gamble, ignoring the loving pleas of his wife to find some other kind of employment. If he couldn't follow his chosen profession, he told her, he would have no other.

"September, a year ago," Sherlock continued, "his savings close to being exhausted, and having sold most of the family's furniture, wedding China, and silver to settle affairs, he and his wife were forced to give up their cheery home in Kensington for the bleakness of Mornington Crescent. Mrs. Bridgeford offered to sell paintings, but Jack would have

44

none of it, having convinced himself that he could make a living by gambling.

Pausing his narrative to take a drink, I was allowed a few moments to consider the unvarying pattern of ruin, self-inflicted by minds suffering mental trauma, unable to cope with reverses, and set upon a path of self-destructions.

"I have been reflecting on the ruinous road Jack Bridgeford was on, while his wife, I take it, found some way to eke out a living."

"Yes. She attempted to hire herself out as an art tutor. Mrs. Bridgeford had cards printed up which she left on the counters of grocers', greengrocers' and butchers' shops, but to no avail. Yet in my estimation, having viewed her still-life paintings on the walls of the flat, she displays a fine sense of composition and design, worthy of display at any decent gallery. Without her husband's knowledge, she brought in a pittance by washing clothes for neighbors.

"You mentioned the absence of books," I interjected. "It is singular that there are no books in a household of two educated persons."

"Very true," Sherlock replied. "Jack had forbidden the presence of books in their home. He cursed them as the tools of scoundrels, the source of all his troubles. His wife, however, couldn't do without books. Susan Egenberg's parents had a great devotion to music and learning in Russia, but the threat of a pogrom caused them to flee, forcing them to leave most of their possessions behind. Susan was born in Kent three years after, her mother dying when she was five. Mr. Egenburg devoted himself to imparting an appreciation of literature, music, and art to his daughter.

"During Jack's frequent absences, and with an all too frequent leisure, Mrs. Bridgeford occasionally visited the British Museum and Carlyle's London Library in order to expand the limits of her knowledge. [15]

"Late last year, while entertaining what she admitted to be a rather naïve hope to form a literary connection for her husband at the library or museum, she came in contact with Andrew Colley, one of his former students. From him she learned that his younger brother, Peter, would be attending a new Methodist public school, the Leys, in Cambridge. The school began its courses in February last." [16]

"Andrew was enthusiastic in his belief that Jack could be the school's teacher of history. Not many boys had been signed on as yet. The position, therefore, couldn't promise much in the way of money, which explained why the position had yet to be filled. With Andrew promising to set up a meeting for Jack with the headmaster, Mrs. Bridgeford profusely thanked the young man, positive that striving to gain the position, and it being so near to the university whence he had been graduated, would appeal to the better angels of Jack's nature.

"He was pleased to hear that a position might be open to him, and he gave up his drinking bouts and became much like the Jack Bridgeford of old. The appointment was made, but Jack Bridgeford never appeared before the headmaster at the Leys School. He made the mistake of visiting one of his old haunts on the day of the interview, and what was supposed to be a visit to ask luck from his tavern friends turned into an afternoon of darts and drinking, his interview completely forgotten until he came home."

"That should bring us to the night of the tragedy," I remarked.

"I haven't as yet explained the presence of bullet pocks in the wall of their home."

"Of course. Pray continue."

"Basing himself on the fact that, when removed from Bridgeford's hand, the Colt revolver had but one cartridge in the chamber, Gregson is of the opinion that the five bullets were shot there last night, on the order of a drunken, if dangerous, prank. Having seen how it upset his wife, he emptied the spent cartridges into the dust pail, saving the last for himself: A self-inflicted punishment which came to him in his drunken state."

"I congratulated Gregson on concocting a neat, if somewhat implausible, theory. I then held up a hand lens to the bullet pocks so he might see a fine accumulation of dust settled on the edges of the holes, verifying them to be a week or more old, thus proving my belief that, in detection, one should never guess in advance of the facts."

"What did happen?"

"Susan Bridgeford explained that her husband, home from a day of winning at gambling, was soon deep in his cups. As she made dinner, Jack, in the bedroom, saw a fly buzzing about. He decided to kill it with his Bull Dog service revolver, laughing throughout, his wife told us, until he believed it was dead."

"Did she say anything further?"

"Actually not," my brother replied, "save that, once again, she told us she had murdered her husband."

"Yet all the facts tell against her admission?"

"Without question."

"What was Inspector Gregson's attitude?"

"He confessed that his first inclination was to arrest Susan Bridgeford upon her admission of guilt," answered Sherlock. "When I protested, he raised the possibility of her being whisked out of the city by the Jewish cabal before a coroner reported on the death. [17] I snorted at that, pointing out that his own investigation contradicted the woman's confession. All the evidence led to the inescapable conclusion that Jack Bridgeford killed himself. Gregson finally concluded that seeing her husband die in such a horrendous manner caused Susan Bridgeford to undergo grievous shock and distress of mind."

I swirled the brandy in my snifter for a short time.

"Gregson's decision notwithstanding, you realize Susan Bridgeford has given a jury an excellent motive for finding her guilty, should an enterprising prosecutor elect to take her at her word and place her in the dock for being the impelling catalyst behind her husband's death?"

Sherlock nodded. "Yes, I do," he replied with an edge to his voice. "Her statement might yet be used in evidence and place her under suspicion of murder, wishing to rid herself of the man who had brought her to so low an estate. Considering her reaction to her husband's death, Susan Bridgeford might just confess to whatever charge might be laid against her.

"And yet, Mycroft, had you listened to her describe her early life with her husband, you would be quite convinced of her deep love for him. She was capable of living with him throughout the worst of it." He grimaced, removing his pipe from his mouth and staring at it. "I'm so tired I can't even keep my pipe lit." He tamped down the tobacco with his finger. I continued to regard my brandy.

"Yes, in the face of his obstinance and dereliction," he continued, "she stood by him, cheerful and optimistic, ready to believe that their travail was transitory. I am convinced that she believed she could, in time, defeat his stubbornness, help him redeem his self-respect, and overcome all their misfortune." His hooded eyes gleamed in the flare of the match he struck. "Such women are rare."

"So you can exonerate her of possibly being a shrewish nag, now feeling pangs of guilt because she drove her husband to an early grave?"

"Yes."

"On the other hand, she may be trying to spare her dead husband's reputation. 'Suicide' has an ugly ring when used as an epithet."

"That may come closer to the truth," Sherlock conceded. "It is Gregson's thesis as well, and I gave him his due for the nobility of the suggestion. My own conjectures want me to place the truth somewhere between that and Jack Bridgeford being in a drunken rage and shooting himself quite by accident with Susan Bridgeford in despair, taking the blame for not having earlier disposed of the revolver."

"But that is exactly what she had done, my dear Sherlock," I said quietly.

On the instant my brother's eyes opened wider.

"Indeed," he said, the smoke of his pipe curling overhead. "Now how can you know this, having not observed the scene for yourself, relying only on what I've told you?"

"From the bullet pocks in the bedroom wall."

I sipped my brandy, allowing him a moment to reflect.

"You were so anxious to prove to the inspector that the bullet pocks weren't coeval to this morning's shooting, you inadvertently talked him out of searching the dust pail for the spent cartridges. Talked yourself out of the same action as well, I fear. I would be interested to know what was pledged. I daresay it would be some keepsake of more value to Jack Bridgeford than to the pawnbroker. A pocket-watch for instance, which brought him only a few pounds – five or six at most."

"Gregson retains the ticket, but I copied the number." said Sherlock. "*Jack Bridgeford received £6/2'*."

"Very enterprising, brother."

"The broker, a man named Kerrigan, was at first disinclined to reveal the details. He grew more co-operative when I suggested he might be called in as a material witness to the death of one of his clients. The watch – " I smiled, nodding graciously. " – was a testimonial to Sergeant-major John Bridgeford from his commander, presented at the time of his separation from the Military Artillery."

"Capital!" I cried. "Now, why would Jack Bridgeford pawn his presentation watch, an item he certainly valued highly? Despite living in Mornington Crescent for nigh over a year in reduced circumstances he was getting by with his gambling. So why the sudden need for cash in the early evening, and why last evening? Think, Sherlock!"

A hint of animation brightened his tired aspect. "The revolver! He wanted the money to purchase a revolver. I assumed the Colt was a souvenir from his stay in Canada."

"Right. Now, why was he holding an American revolver at the time of his death and not his own service revolver? You said he owned a Bull Dog, I believe."

"Yes, as his widow told us," said Sherlock with a grimace, puffing violently at his pipe all the while. "A reasonable young man to start out, Jack Bridgeford was pushed out of a promising career as a history professor. When another chance came his way, he muffed his opportunity. My brain is rattled by what became a wasted life. The man's death was so unnecessary." His frown deepened. "And I have been slow to fit together the pieces of the puzzle."

"We may take comfort in the knowledge that Gregson is slower," I said with a small smile. "However, as I see it, there are three threads to this business. First, that the broom and dust pail were left in view. Second, that the pawn ticket bears this morning's date. Third, that there are bullet pocks in the bedroom wall. You observed each of these threads, but failed to follow each one to its proper end.

"So then, the threads in this skein are woven on this wise: First, in a drunken state, Jack Bridgeford severely frightened his wife, shooting five bullets into the bedroom wall. Next, scared to death, Susan Bridgeford, fearing her safety, took her husband's revolver and bullets – "

"And hid them in the only place possible," Sherlock erupted suddenly, "in her dust pail, taking care to cover the top with a crumpled newspaper."

I nodded. "And lastly, there are the foot marks in front of the cupboard. In my experience, drunken men have little appetite, but Jack Bridgeford stamped back and forth in front of the cupboard, as his heel marks show. If not for food, for what was he searching? Surely that is where he kept his revolver."

"And so," added Sherlock excitedly, "at a loss to explain its disappearance, he probably accused his wife of taking it. Perhaps she feigned ignorance. In any case, he began to ill-use her, doubtless hoping to force the secret from her. Since there were no bruises to be seen, I suggest that he shook her violently."

"Explaining her unkempt appearance, as noted by the constable she found," I said. "Since she had refused to reveal where she had hidden the gun, in a drunken fury Jack stormed out of the house in search of another."

"A scant three streets away, Jack came upon Kerrigan's establishment, pledged his watch, and returned to one of the pubs he frequented where he purchased the American revolver from one of his cronies, late of the army of the United States, who, it would seem, had but the single load in it."

"Explaining why a former military officer shot himself, not with his own sidearm, but with an American revolver uncommonly found in England," I concluded. "As regarding what took place afterward, we can suppose that it is for this reason that Susan Bridgeford thinks herself the cause of her husband's death."

"While I distrust forming theories in advance of the facts," my brother responded in a pensive voice, "I agree with your deduction. [18] I further suggest that there is evidence enough for Inspector Gregson to support a coroner's finding of death by misadventure, rather than listing it as death by suicide. [19]

"When Jack Bridgeford, possibly fortified by another drink or two, returned home, he triumphantly brandished his newly-acquired gun, just to spite her."

"And his death?" I asked.

"Only Susan Bridgeford can answer that question positively," my brother replied, his eyes narrowing. "Perhaps Jack aimed with sodden delight at various items in their home, the crockery or her paintings. Upon seeing her fright and alarm, Jack came to himself a little, and attempted to assure his wife that there was nothing to fear.

"Perchance he then attempted to prove that no harm would come of it by bringing the hammer of the revolver down on empty chambers. Seeing no change in his wife's demeanor he then pointed the gun to his own head, proving there was no need for worry. His mistake would prove fatal."

It was my turn to frown.

"You find a flaw in my reconstruction of the situation?" my brother asked.

"Yes, indeed. A telling one in my estimation," said I. "It is difficult for me to believe that, even in an inebriated state, a highly-trained soldier – a sergeant-major at that – would fail to examine and unload a weapon he didn't plan to use. Such care with arms would become a second nature."

Sherlock's state of exaltation remained undiminished.

"The problem is that you haven't yet set the final piece of the puzzle in place. Jack Bridgeford died, not because of his own carelessness. He died a victim of his own recklessness."

"Well, of course, anyone who would drunkenly wave a loaded – "

"No, no, no, Sherlock!" I interrupted. "It is the man's own innate recklessness, aggravated in no small part by ignorance, that was his undoing, not the influence of drink."

"But Mycroft, Jack Bridgeford had no idea of the presence of that single bullet in the Colt revolver."

"Oh, he knew that bullet was in the chamber," I countered. "He was, however, convinced that the hammer wouldn't strike it."

Sherlock's brow arched. "How so?"

"Without that broker's ticket," I began, "I might have supposed those five bullet pocks in the bedroom wall of the Bridgeford home were fired by the same Colt revolver. It has six chambers and five were empty."

"I dare say Gregson holds the same opinion at present, despite Susan Bridgeford having told us both that her husband owned a Bull Dog revolver."

"And the Bull Dog is the answer to the mystery, Sherlock."

Sherlock looked at me guardedly. "To be sure, the five bullets shot in the bedroom wall emptied the service revolver. A Webley Bull Dog has only five chambers. How does that fact provide the answer to Jack Bridgeford's death?"

"Sherlock, it comes down to the respect of a military man for his firearms. The former Sergeant-major Bridgeford, despite his intoxication, took care not to shoot off the one bullet in his American pistol. '*Abuent studia in mores*,' as Mr. Burke would have it." [20]

"You and your politicians," was Sherlock's disdainful reply.

"Tut, tut, Sherlock. Jack Bridgeford was bound to follow no other course. He would have been sure to take care to know the location of the chamber with the bullet in it. The instant before his death, Jack Bridgeford saw the rim of the cartridge in the chamber on the left side of the barrel. He pulled the trigger and died."

"Which shows me that he was too intoxicated to realize where the bullet was," shrugged Sherlock. "The cylinder of a Colt revolver turns clockwise."

"The cylinder of a Webley Bull Dog service revolver turns anticlockwise."

Sherlock paused, pipe in hand. A blank expression eroded his countenance. "That feature never occurred to me," he confessed.

"It might have escaped me as well," I conceded, "had I not supervised the compiling of a report a month ago regarding the effectiveness of small arms and long guns issued troops during our last expedition against the Ashanti Empire. [21] That is how the British Bull Dog five-chambered revolver manufactured by Webley and Scott came to my attention." [22]

I rolled a long, white ash from off the tip of my cigar into the ashtray. "An investigator needs must be aware of such variations in so ordinary an item as even a handgun."

Sherlock nodded and rose. "It will give me great pleasure to accompany Inspector Gregson to Mornington Crescent tomorrow morning. When he unlocks the door of the Bridgeford residence, I will stride across the room, reach into the dust pail, and remove a service revolver and box of cartridges. That should convince him of her good intentions and exonerate Susan Bridgeford."

Thanking for me for my aid, Sherlock gathered his habiliments. I saw him out, lingering at the door of the foyer to watch my brother enter the roiling, white billows of mist rapidly undulating from over the Embankment and filling St. Chad's Street.

Postscript

Returning home from the Foreign Office next evening, my landlady, Mrs. Crosse, informed me of a visitor awaiting me in my sitting room. Entering, I was momentarily surprised finding a lovely young lady sitting on the settee. She rose, stately and graceful, despite the twice-turned dress under a heavy, black cloak and her careworn features beneath a black bonnet which had seen better days.

"Good evening, Mrs. Bridgeford. Welcome to my home."

A light blush appeared beneath her red-rimmed eyes. A slow smiled defied her air of mourning.

She rose. "Good evening, Mr. Holmes," she replied. "Your brother told me not to be startled if you appeared to know me and greeted me by name." She lowered her eyes. "I understand from him that I have you to thank for my freedom."

"Sherlock makes too much of it," I said, 'I simply led his thoughts to the correct solution, May I take your cloak and hat?"

"I won't stay long," said Susan Bridgeford, "Nevertheless I wanted you to know how grateful I am."

"In that case," I said, "you're very welcome." Hanging up my own hat and coat, I continued, "But allow me to offer you some sherry. And do please feel at home." She thanked me and resumed her seat.

"Your brother came to my father's home this morning to tell us that he had invited Inspector Gregson to meet him at my home in Mornington Crescent and that, despite my confession, he knew how to destroy any thoughts the inspector might be entertaining about making a case against me that would satisfy any police court."

Handing her a glass of sherry, I told her, "I'm sure that is so."

She took a sip and a small smile appeared.

"It is a good thing your brother stopped at my father's shop before visiting Scotland Yard. There was one thing wrong with the details you worked out."

"Indeed. What was that?"

"I would never treat a revolver so poorly by placing it in the dirt of a dust pail. It's true I put the box of bullets there. I placed the revolver in my sewing basket."

I returned her smile. "I take it you gave the gun to Sherlock so that he might still mystify the inspector?"

She nodded. Her eyes welled with tears as she said, "I tried to press a sovereign into your brother's hand in payment for his services, but he would have none of it." She quickly removed a lace-trimmed handkerchief from her beaded hand-bag and pressed it to her eyes. "You have both been so kind. I really should like to repay you in some fashion."

"I pray you not concern yourself about it," I answered in a kindly manner. "You may be sure that my brother is glad to set you and your father's minds at ease. He will be repaid by proving to the inspector how foolish it is to hold you responsible for your husband's demise."

"Oh, but Mr. Holmes, I am responsible for my dear Jack's fate. How you and your brother came to know with such accuracy the events surrounding his death I shall never understand. Nonetheless, I am responsible. I didn't tell your brother because he was in such a jubilant state. It weighed on my soul not telling him, and that is why I asked him for your address. I had to tell you what neither of you could possibly have realized."

"I understand, in your state of mind . . . ."

Mrs. Bridgeford stopped dabbing at her eyes. Quite frankly she said, "No, Mr. Holmes. I *knew* Jack would kill himself and I did nothing to stop him."

Returning her gaze I asked, "You knew the cylinders of an American Colt and a British Bull Dog turn in opposite directions?"

"Yes, Mr. Holmes." Her mouth set as she continued, "My father is a cultured gentleman. He instilled in me a love for good literature, good food, fine art, and encouraged me to develop a sense of curiosity. How often my father would tell me, 'The Lord God gave us curiosity to discover the secrets with which He blessed the world so mankind wouldn't tire of it.'

"In his brokers' shop over the years, my father has had pledged a number of extraordinary items, as well as veritable armory of firearms and other weapons. Papa showed me how they were operated. Indeed, Papa took pleasure acquainting me with such varied artifacts as guns, dark lanterns, paintings, photographs, razors, microscopes, artificial kneecaps, surgeon's instruments, stuffed armadillos, potted palms, illuminated manuscripts, and jewelry of all kinds."

Her hand went to her necklace. A small, irregular triangle of iridescent glass hung from a thin, gold chain. Yellow, streaked with hues of green, purple, and blue, it shimmered in the firelight.

"This was Jack's present to me on the occasion of our engagement. Mr. Holmes. He found it amid the ruins of Pompeii. It might have been part of a cup, or a bowl, perhaps a piece broken from an amulet." She regarded the artifact for a moment, her eyes shining. "He treasured it – as now do I.

"Oh, I wish you had known Jack as he was then," she continued ardently. "We shared a love for art and a passion for the ageless grandeur

53

that was Rome: The Republic and the early Empire. His book on the first five Caesars was to have reflected not only history, but also the satires of Juvenal and the precepts of Horace. He so loved the wisdom of the ancients." She paused, gazing at the small table on which her sherry glass sat, seeming to study the lace edge of the table cloth."

"Quite so," I said letting a moment pass, "*The pen is the tongue of the mind.*"

Of a sudden she looked up smiling. Recognition danced in her eyes.

"*A poem is a picture without words.*' Oh, Mr. Holmes, you know Horace! Many's the time my Jack and I spent an evening capping Horace to each other."

"You're fortunate to have those memories, Mrs. Bridgeford."

"And I thank you and your brother for acquainting me with the coroner being able to declare a person's manner of death as by 'misadventure'."

"It seemed much more likely, Mrs. Bridgeford, than – pardon my saying – *suicide.*"

"If you had known Jack when first I met him, you would know that suicide was never in his mind. He was tall, strong, young, brave. His brown hair turned lighter the more sun he got, and his very smile warmed you. His students enjoyed the way he made Roman history come alive. Indeed, I heard Mr. Wetherby, the Latin instructor, compliment Jack for making the boys attend his own class all the more interested in learning the language of Antony and Augustus after being treated to one of Jack's spirited descriptions of Cincinnatus at the plow, Horatius at the bridge, Caesar chasing pirates, or Cicero denouncing Catiline before the Senate."

"Then why . . . ?"

She lowered her eyes again. "For over a year, most nights he'd go to a pub on a carouse. The first night Jack brought me along for company. The pub was The Crown and Scepter, where he soon fell into conversation with some other retired military men. They began regaling each other with tales of this battle and that, one commander after another.

"Someone suggested a game of darts. I was forgotten. Jack is – was – particularly good at playing darts. Gambling ensued, and we came home with a quid or two more than we had at the beginning of the evening."

"And this happened regularly?"

Susan Bridgeford sighed. "It became a nightly ritual, Mr. Holmes. When the pubs closed, he and his new cronies went off to other premises and played cards. Jack began to carry a deck with him. Sometime before dawn he managed his way home to sleep throughout the morning.

"Jack became indifferent to me. I kept the house, made the meals and cleaned his clothes. Depending on his luck the night before he'd leave a few shillings, perhaps a pound or two – as if I were little more than a charwoman."

"I can see how you would suffer with so drastic a change," I offered sympathetically.

Susan Bridgeford fell silent for a time. Her expression became more pained.

"I hadn't meant to tell anyone, but I shall trust you with something else, Mr. Holmes, since you perceived the truth. I told your brother and the inspector about how my husband emptied his service revolver in pursuit of a fly. That wasn't the only thing he did with his gun.

"A few weeks ago, Jack began playing a dangerous game. He'd remove all but one bullet and spin the cylinder of his revolver. He'd then aim at a spot on the ceiling, or a picture on the wall. He never aimed the gun at me, but often he'd point the barrel at his own head and let the hammer fall. It never failed to terrify me. As much as I begged him to stop, the more he delighted in my fear, laughing at my panic.

"Jack did this, Mr. Holmes, only when drinking at home. After several days of this game, I noticed that, before his pretense at shooting, he would engage my attention elsewhere, to distract me from seeing him move the cylinder ahead one space if needs be, so that the chamber with the bullet wouldn't be in position to fire and so eliminate any danger.

"Jack knew I respected safety in regards to firearms. Several times in our early life together, he had shown me how he took apart his service revolver for cleaning and reassembled it after. Even later it was obvious he hadn't totally forgotten his military training. Nevertheless, I despised this game and determined to remove this menace from our lives."

I saw at once to where Susan Bridgeford's narrative was leading. "And so, after your husband stepped out for a time, you removed his service revolver and box of cartridges from the food cupboard," I said, "hiding them only moments before he returned."

"Exactly, Mr. Holmes," she nodded. "He soon went to the cupboard. I picked up a handkerchief I had been mending and began sewing. He didn't at first comprehend that the gun was gone. Befuddled by drink, he searched for some time before it came to him that it was gone and that I was the only one who could have taken it."

"'Where's my Bull Dog?' he demanded. I said nothing, but continued my sewing.

"He stamped about the room, then stumbled into the bedroom and privy before returning in a cold rage. I was frightened, but tried acting unconcerned as I plied needle and thread.

"Standing before me, he again ordered me to produce the gun. When I made no reply, he brushed aside the sewing, yanked me off the chair, shaking me violently, all the while insisting I tell him where his revolver was hidden.

"He threw me back onto the chair at last. I was horrorstruck. He had never laid rough hands on me before.

"'Very well, my sweet, never mind,' he said thickly while making a mocking, unsteady bow and sweep of his hat. 'I shall simply thwart your plans.' With that he clomped out the door.

"I sat, stricken, my mind awhirl. Within fifteen minutes Jack returned, triumphantly brandishing another gun, the Colt revolver. He danced around the room, laughing, pointing the gun at various objects and each time saying, 'Boom!'

"I took heart at this, hoping that it meant he'd found no ammunition, but he grabbed the other chair and set it opposite my one. Shoving the revolver into his belt, he removed his jacket. He tried to hang it up, but each time he did, he attempted to reach into a pocket and it slid off the peg.

"Finally, in frustration, he picked up the jacket, removed something from its pocket, then flung it across the room. He sidled back to the chair, pulled the revolver from his belt, and sat down.

"Smiling vacuously, he held up a bullet. 'Look what I found.'

"I was appalled, Mr. Holmes. As he clumsily attempted to load the bullet into the chamber. I pleaded with him to put the gun down and have some breakfast.

"'I'm not hungry as yet, my girl,' he said, his efforts to get the bullet in the chamber resembling his trying to thread a needle. I fled to the bedroom.

"From the time my father showed me how firearms worked, I was aware that the cylinder of a Colt turns clockwise. When Jack cleaned his service revolver, I had noted in passing how its cylinder turned anticlockwise.

"I heard the hammer fall and Jack laughed boisterously. I began praying most fervently to God that, in his stupor, Jack would weary of the game and go to bed.

"'You missed it, my sweet,' he called out. 'I'll do it again. Come see, my darling.'

"I was rooted to the floor. I heard Jack laugh. Then I heard the revolver's report. Jack's laughter stopped." Quietly she began to weep, her handkerchief at the ready.

"I begged him put down the gun, Mr. Holmes. I swear it." Tears glistened on her cheeks.

"Months ago, he cursed me. He cursed the day we met, cursed the military, cursed the abominable dean who stole his manuscript. He cursed the headmaster and every school in the land. I knew it was the drink talking. Still, when he raised his hand to his head, *I* shot him. I should have told him the cylinder turned in a different direction."

"Is it possible," I suggested, "that upon his return with the American revolver, you thought of how he had humbled you, his mocking laughter a reproach, as if none of your earlier happiness mattered?"

She considered my words. After some moments she replied, looking down at the handkerchief in her lap. "There may be some truth in what you say, Mr. Holmes, but not much."

"Exactly. You loved him still," I continued. "So much so, you were willing to be incarcerated, perhaps lose your own life for his sake, with no other purpose in mind but to protect his good name, to keep him from being dismissed as a suicide."

Susan Bridgeford threw back her head, her eyes on a level with my own. "When we were married, we vowed to love each other for better or for worse, Mr. Holmes. Jack Bridgeford was the bravest soldier who ever served your Queen," she replied firmly. "He was a beloved schoolmaster, admired by his students and respected by his fellow masters. It isn't right that his last act of folly should color the good he accomplished in life.

"My Jack died months ago. His mind stopped functioning rightly when his manuscript was stolen, his job lost, and finding himself blackballed from teaching throughout the area. The man I revered and loved had vanished, unable to comprehend how men of learning could be so evil. The mean-spirited drunk and gambler who died yesterday wasn't the man I loved.

"I have one joy in his death," she said, her lip trembling. "The last words he spoke, 'My darling', was his favorite term of endearment for me. I'll always know I was his darling to the end."

I rose as she took her leave. Opening the door for her, Susan Bridgeford took my hand and squeezed it affectionately.

"God bless you," she said with great emotion. "God bless both you and your brother."

It struck me how Queen Victoria's desire to maintain a title commanding more dignity than that of her daughter really came to nothing. In 1875 Prince Albert, whom I had literally run into and came to admire greatly, had been dead for fourteen years. [23] It is well known how much our Queen Victoria loved the Prince Consort

I prefer to remember my Queen as a woman who so carefully guarded intimate recollections of her Albert as lovingly as Susan Bridgeford regarded the memory of her Jack.

In setting down this account, the story told by Plato, in *The Republic*, about Gyges and his ring came to mind. Gyges faced the dilemma of choosing between the act of committing an injustice or suffering an injustice. Old Socrates, the philosophical moralist, argued that Gyges should have chosen the former in order to avoid the latter. Socrates explained that, in choosing to suffer injustice, Gyges made the wrong choice, not only morally, but also in terms of self-interest.

Susan Bridgeford turned that conclusion on its head. She was willing to endure the injustice of being considered a murderess in order to prevent the injustice of her husband being considered a suicide – a moral coward. Her conclusion is more in line with a Jewish philosopher, the Master Philosopher, He who stated that greater love hath no man but that he lay down his life for a friend.

A week passed. Mrs. Crosse, my pert Irish landlady, caught a glimpse of my brother on one of her market days. Arriving home from Whitehall, I met her in the foyer. She spoke of Sherlock, lamenting, "Mr. Holmes, your brother is nothing but skin and bones. Does he eat regularly?" Without waiting for a reply, she demanded, in her charming way, "You get him over here for dinner tomorrow evening. It will be Saturday so won't interfere with his classes. Now, mind!"

There was nothing left for me to do but say, "Yes, ma'am," turn around, and make for the corner telegraph office.

Next evening, Sherlock came round to my home in St. Chad's Street. From his wallet, he removed a clipping taken from *The Gazette*.

The newspaper's reporter relayed details of a minor theft from the office of the dean of the history department of a small college in Kensington: Some Red Indian artifacts, papers, and notes. The dean averred that, while nothing of great value was missing, it was unconscionable that his sanctum had been invaded. When the artifacts were located in the college's kitchen in a pot of stew, the constabulary put it down as a student prank.

"And they are confident the missing papers would soon be returned," Sherlock dryly quoted the newspaper's final statement. "When the police have no answers, they feed the press hackneyed phrases."

I arched my brow.

"Why, Sherlock, do I feel there is some jobbery afoot?"

Just then, Mrs. Crosse called us to dine.

Over the five-course meal provided by my inestimable landlady, we spoke of the events I have related in this account. Starting with a thick ham-and-lentil soup, we continued with a *ceviche* of filet of haddock steeped in lime juice, seasoned with shallots, diced tomatoes, coriander leaves, and a sprinkle of nutmeg.

It was easy to become a discerning gourmand at one of Mrs. Crosse's boards.

"On Wednesday, I stopped by Mr. Egenburg's establishment in the Tottenham Court Road," said Sherlock spreading some venison *pâté* on a water cracker.

"I hope that gentleman is well. And his daughter?"

"Mr. Egenburg is well indeed," my brother replied. "His daughter, Susan, remains somewhat withdrawn. She is in better spirits than she was, however. She told me that her husband's manuscript and notes arrived anonymously by afternoon post the day before. She was profuse with her thanks but, while expressing my happiness at their return, I professed to know nothing about the matter. Mr. Egenburg gave me a sly wink.

"The reason for my visit, I explained, was to tell them that I had spoken to one of the art instructors at college, who suggested I give her the addresses of two art schools – either of which, he is confident, would be interested in hiring her as an instructress."

Following the salad course, Mrs. Crosse carved several slices from a fine joint of roast beef chosen for each of us for our *entrée*, accompanied by Yorkshire pudding, carrots and honey-glazed parsnips, scalloped oysters, and creamed onions. The gravy-boat contained a delectable garlic-mushroom beef gravy. The spread was topped off by a tolerable Burgundy provided by my brother. We both were hungry and our conversation dropped off.

"I'm proud of you, Sherlock," I declared over the trifle provided by Mrs. Crosse for our dessert course. "Helping the young lady secure a position as an art instructor was an inspired and truly noble gesture."

"Nonsense," said he, brushing away the compliment. "Mr. Egenburg supplied the truly noble gesture."

I looked up. "And that was?"

"Oh," he replied offhandedly, "he presented me with a violin."

"That was very kind."

"I dare say," replied Sherlock.

"On Thursday," he continued, "I received a letter from Mr. Egenburg at first post requesting I come by his brokers' shop. I replied that I would come after my one o'clock class. Upon my arrival he greeted me effusively. As he had no customers, he took me to a door in the rear of his shop which he unlocked.

"Entering, he shut the door behind us. 'Few people are aware of this room,' he told me. 'I keep my most valuable pieces here.' He led me to a large safe and unlocked the door. On the shelves within were a number of violins. Mr. Egenburg reached in, taking hold of one which he then held out to me. 'Look,' he instructed, pointing under the bridge to a maker's label. It read, '*Antonius Stradivarius Cremonensis Faciebat Anno 1709*'.

I was stunned.

"Did I hear correctly? A Stradivarius?"

"Indeed."

"My word! What a grand gift."

"Mr. Egenburg explained that, as I had saved the one thing in the world which he most loved and cherished, it would be churlish to offer me anything less than the best thing he owned."

"Back in his shop, two customers had arrived and were searching through the hodge-podge of objects for sale. In a box behind his counter, Mr. Egenburg located an appropriate violin case.

"Placing the violin with its bow in it he said, 'That will cost fifty-five shillings,'"

"I looked at him. 'You're serious?' I asked in bewilderment.

"'What? You think violin cases grow on trees?' he said affecting a wheedling voice. 'Mr. Holmes, the fiddle is yours with my blessing, but you have to keep it in something to protect it. My daughter, whom I love more than my life, is back in my home. I have to protect her. Besides,' he concluded with a smile, 'I must needs start saving for another dowry.'"

And that is how my brother became the owner of a Stradivarius for fifty-five shillings.

NOTES

For some years Mr. Alexander Egenburg, with myself and the late Dennis Ashby of happy memory, has been one of Three Musketeers in an online Wireclub chatroom. Alex was kind enough to email copies of records from his family archives which helped fill in a few details regarding events alluded to in this narrative.

There is reason to believe that Christopher John Bridgeford's unfinished history of the first five Caesars was sold to Alfred Perceval Graves (1846-1931), an Irish poet, songwriter, and folklorist. If so, it would then form part of the research used by British poet and critic Robert Graves (24 July, 1895-7 December, 1985) for his well-known volumes, The Twelve Caesars, The Golden Ass, I, Claudius, *and* Claudius the God.

For his assistance and enthusiasm for this project I am happy to tender Alex my most sincere thanks and appreciation. I remain in hopes of raising a pint or two of McSorley's Best with him when next I visit New York City. – S.M.W.

1. Daughter of Christian IX, King of Denmark, sister to George I, King of Greece, Alexandra Caroline Marie Charlotte Louise Julia of the House of Schleswig-Holstein-Sonderburg-Glücksburg married Prince Albert Edward in 1863. Princess of Wales longer than anyone before or since (1863 to 1901), Alexandra became Queen Consort when her husband acceded to the throne as King Edward VII.
2. The Marlborough House set – *aka* The Smart Set – was made up of young, titled couples with whom the Prince and Princess felt at ease. Several commoners were in the set, including wealthy Americans and even Anglo-Jewish subjects previously ignored by British Society. Members of this clutch of glitterati were good company and often sexually permissive. While personal immorality was winked at, breaching their Eleventh Commandment, "*Thou shalt not tell*," could be disastrous, as was discovered by a few individuals while pursuing divorces. Making public certain scandalous communications and details led to their social ostracization for a number of years.
3. *Parsees* are Zoroastrians living in India, descended from those who fled Persia during the Moslem persecutions of the seventh and eighth centuries. *Hindoo* is a now archaic variation of *Hindu*, one who follows Hinduism. *Musselman* is a word found within late-sixteenth-century Persian manuscripts, originally used as an adjectival referencing of Moslem (or Muslim).
4. Calcutta was the capital of India during the British Raj (*Rule*) from 1858 to 1911, after which the capital city was changed to Delhi, then to New Delhi, which has served as the capital of India since 1947, when independence was proclaimed. India remains, however, within the British Commonwealth of Nations.
5. A "Levee" was a festive gathering wherein socially prominent gentlemen were presented to the Sovereign. A "Drawing Room" was a formal function

at which debutantes were "presented at Court". During the reign of Queen Victoria, Levees occurred in the morning, Drawing Rooms took place in the afternoon.

6.   This aside indicates that Mr. Holmes wrote the present account close to the same time as when he penned the manuscript regarding "The Affair of the Queen's Necklace".

7.   The Mogul (Moghul or Mughal) Emperors of India were a minor dynasty founded by Prince Babur, a direct descendant of Timur (known in the West as Tamerlane). By 1700, most of the Indian subcontinent was under their control but, due to extensive corruption, Mogul power declined significantly by the 1850's. The last Mogul emperor, Bahadur Shah II, was deposed in 1857 when the British Raj was established. After the Indian Mutiny of 1858, Britain imposed direct control over much of India. Various Governors-General – later Viceroys – were named to preside over federal and provincial legislatures.

8.   During a battle in the first Italian campaign (1792-1797), General Napoleon Bonaparte, the artillery commander, dismissed incompetent artillery officers then took charge of a unit of cannoneers as a "gun commander", a position usually filled by a corporal. The battle ended with Bonaparte grimy and reeking of gunpowder, but the ordinary soldiers, seeing his willingness to fight alongside them, hailed him as *Le Petit Caporal*, "The Little Corporal." British admirers appropriated the title, in grudging respect for a charismatic adversary. Sir Arthur Conan Doyle wrote an enjoyable series of tales centered on Brigadier Gerard, a member of *La Grande Armée*, and one of Bonaparte's most ardent – and braggadocious – devotees.

9.   *Kaiser* – the obviously German rendering of *Cæsar* – understood as equivalent to the title *"Emperor"*.

10. As Empress Consort in Germany. Victoria reigned ninety-nine days with her husband, Kaiser Frederick III. He died of laryngeal cancer in 1888. As the Empress Dowager, "Vicky" was styled *Kaiserin Friedrich*, dying in 1901, soon after her august mother's demise.

11. Mr. Jerrold Moriarty's scheming came to fore two weeks later and forms much of the tale Mycroft set down, published as the aforementioned *Enter the Lion*.

12. Sherlock's use of the term "Jew broker" may jar readers' sensibilities today. *The Oxford English Dictionary*, however, shows that use of the term "Jew" as an adjective was identified as being merely colloquial and was, for some time, commonly descriptive without intending offense. Writes Mr. Andrew Solberg, BSI, ("Professor Coram"): *"'Brokers were, of course, money lenders, just as pawnbrokers are today. It isn't surprising that there were Jewish brokers. As for the use of the word "Jew" as an adjective . . . it was an acceptably neutral figure of speech that wasn't meant as an opprobrious phrase."* ("Sherlock Holmes: Anti-Semite?" *Baker Street Journal*, Vol. 51, No. 1, Spring 2001, pp. 35-41)

13. The ironic jest is understandable when one realizes that Charles Louis Napoleon, having become the Emperor Napoleon III, was defeated in the

Franco-Prussian War of 1870. Losing his throne, he and his wife, Eugenie, exiled themselves to Chislehurst, Kent, where he died in 1873.

14. Militia Artillery: Fearing invasion by France in 1852, Her Majesty's government re-established the Volunteer Force, including the Militia Infantry reserves. Units were eventually designated to include artillery and engineering branches. Volunteers didn't sign on for a term of service. Except in times of actual warfare, members were allowed to quit after giving a notice of fourteen days.

15. Forbidden to borrow books from the British Museum Library, Thomas Carlyle, the Scottish academic who developed "the great man" theory of history, was forced to do research on the premises, sometimes while seated on a ladder instead of in a chair. He convinced influential friends to begin a private subscription lending library in 1841. Initially renting premises in 45 Pall Mall (above what had been a gambling den), the library was moved in 1845 to Beauchamp House in St. James Square where, greatly expanded, it remains. Dickens, Thackeray, Darwin, Gladstone, and even Prince Albert are found among many other illustrious names on the list of the library's patrons and subscribers.

16. In February 1875, the Wesleyan Methodist Church Conference opened this senior school on the former Leys family estate along the River Cam in Cambridge. Sixteen boys formed its first student body. Novelist James Hilton, an alumnus, was inspired to base events in his novel, *Goodbye Mister Chips*, on a schoolmaster and several of his own experiences at the Leys School, which still exists.

17. Slanderous gossip like this haunted Jews throughout Europe, often spread by well-meaning yet misinformed people. It was otherwise fostered by paranoids, opportunists, and bullies displaying what the Germans call *schadenfreude*: The enjoyment of the misfortune of others.

18. *"While I distrust forming theories . . . ."* Obviously a lesson learned at an early age, this is one of Sherlock Holmes's most important *dicta*. Dr. Watson quotes his friend stating this axiom in various ways:
    - *"It is a capital mistake to theorize before you have all the evidence. It biases the judgment."* (*A Study in Scarlet*)
    - *"I never guess. It is a capital mistake to theorize before one has data. Insensibly one begins to twist facts to suit theories, instead of theories to suit facts."* (*The Sign of Four*)
    - *"It is a capital mistake to theorize before one has data. Insensibly one begins to twist facts to suit theories, instead of theories to suit facts."* ("A Scandal in Bohemia")
    - *"It is a capital mistake to theorize in advance of the facts."* ("The Second Stain")
    - *"I never guess. It is a shocking habit – destructive to the logical faculty."* (*The Sign of Four*)

19. Coroners within the United Kingdom record death as "by misadventure" on death certificates and associated documents when describing persons expiring due to a fatal accident. It applies when death is primarily

63

attributable to an action or actions having occurred due to a risk voluntarily taken by the deceased individual.

20. *"Practices pursued become habits"* aphoristically translates this advice, first given by Edmund Burke (1729-1797), a distinguished and highly quotable Member of Parliament, in his Speech on Conciliating with America, delivered before that body in 1775.

21. Mycroft speaks of the third war (1873-1874) pitting the British Empire against the Ashanti Empire (now Ghana, Togo, Ivory Coast). The Treaty of Fomena demanded Ashanti withdrawal from coastal areas of sub-Saharan Africa and banned human sacrifice while compensating the United Kingdom for its trouble with 3,125 lbs. of gold.

22. It would now be called a snub-nosed gun. *"The British Bull Dog was a popular type of solid-frame pocket revolver introduced by Philip Webley & Scott of Birmingham, England, in 1872, and subsequently copied by gunmakers in continental Europe and the United States. It featured a 2.5-inch barrel and was chambered for .442 Webley or .450 Adams cartridges, with a five-round cylinder."* Vide: *The Military Factory* website, ABAA VBF: California Edition, Infantry Small Arms / The Warfighter, Webley Bull Dog Five-Shot Pocket Revolver [1872]. Electronically retrieved 8 February, 2022: *https://www.militaryfactory.com/smallarms/detail.php?smallarms_id=305.*

    Some commentators have believed this to be Dr. Watson's oft-mentioned "service revolver" since, in *A Study in Scarlet*, he says, *"I keep a bull pup,"* but no such animal ever appears in company with Watson at 221b Baker Street. Some readers may find it of interest to know that Charles Guiteau assassinated U.S. president James A. Garfield with such a weapon on 2 July, 1881.

23. The episode of Mycroft's blundering into Prince Albert in his youth is recounted in "When the Prince First Dined at the Diogenes Club" in *The MX Book of New Sherlock Holmes Stories, Part XIX, 2020 Annual (1882-1890).*

The *Princess Alice* Tragedy
by John Lawrence

"I sometimes think it remarkable that the government hasn't more often called upon your talents," I remarked to Sherlock Holmes in late October of 1888 as we breakfasted in our rooms in Baker Street. "You obviously made a decision quite early in your life not to affiliate with the Metropolitan Police or Scotland Yard. Instead, you invented this curious role as a 'private' consulting detective, a profession that didn't even exist outside of Mr. Poe's imagination."

We had recently concluded a number of harrowing adventures, including the terrifying case involving the Baskerville hound and the matter of the Greek interpreter. It was during the latter case that I had been introduced to Holmes's enigmatic older brother. Mycroft Holmes, frequently but secretly, provided assistance to Her Majesty's government. (Some even suggested he *was* the government!)

"Official England is the provenance of my brother," Holmes replied, not even bothering to look up from his morning paper. "My interactions with the elected and the titled have been among the less fulfilling experiences of my career. I prefer the gratitude of the terrified clerk who has misplaced the monthly payroll to the aristocrat who views the need for my services as distasteful."

"Surely it is their loss," I replied, recalling silently that in those cases involving the upper crust of society, such as that of the noble bachelor, Lord St. Simon, and the Bohemian Prince, there had been little empathy from Holmes towards his elite clientele. "Yes, I understand. The aristocracy can be so presumptuous."

"Pomposity if far from the worst of it," Holmes sharply responded. "A most unfortunate case in which I was engaged quite early in my career considerably shaped my prejudice in the matter. Indeed, I'm not sure I have ever shared the tale with you."

"You know very well which of your cases you have related to me and which you have kept buried in those boxes and files," I corrected, pointing to his bookcase that overflowed with the records of dozens of adventures. "Of course, if you have a hitherto undisclosed narrative to share – well, it is a slow morning, the fire is comfortable, and I would be delighted to hear the story."

A gray look passed over Holmes's face as he removed one of his well-broken-in briars from his pipe rack and filled it with the morning's first

65

bowl of shag. Settling into one of the comfortable chairs before the fire, he motioned for me to join him. I brought my coffee over and sat across from him. He grew pensive for a moment, taking a deep mouthful of smoke, the lids on his eyes half-closed as he conjured up the memory of the long-ago case

"Several years after I left university, in September of 1878. I had opened my practice as the world's very first consulting detective. I admit the world wasn't exactly beating a path to my door. The case of the *Gloria Scott* a few years earlier had been very helpful in establishing my credentials, and had persuaded my brother that my unique talents in the field of deduction might yield me a comfortable living. It was undoubtedly he who directed Sir Fitzhugh Wombley to my very modest flat.

Here Holmes paused and looked over to me. "Do you recall the *Princess Alice*?" he inquired.

"The Queen's daughter?" I responded. "The Grand Duchess of Hesse. I recall that she died of diphtheria, I believe – and yes, it was in 1878, the year I completed my medical degree."

Holmes slowly shook his head. "No, Watson, not *that* Princess Alice," he corrected me. "I'm referring to the saloon steamer that met its untimely and tragic end in September of that same year while rounding Woolwich Point on the Thames. I presumed it might have slipped your attention, as you undoubtedly were out of Britain serving with the Fusiliers or some such thing."

"Of course," I recalled. "I recall the replacement troops mentioning the accident. I had no idea of your involvement in the inquiry."

Holmes again sat quietly for a moment. It was unusual for anything to affect him emotionally, as evidently did his recollections of the *Princess Alice*.

"September 3rd, a decade ago," he resumed, "a black day for London. And yet it had begun as a cheerful one for those aboard the ship – an old side-paddle wheeler." He took a pull on his pipe and shook his head before blowing out a thin stream of blue smoke. "Six-hundred passengers at least, mostly from the lower classes, twice the permitted number, but the captain ignored the warning." His voiced drifted off for a moment before he picked up his tale.

"She had gone down to the Nore, where the Thames meets the sea, stopped at Gravesend to let off some fortunate passengers. Then she picked up less lucky replacements before beginning the voyage back up to London, leaving behind several hundred more who wanted a place on the ship.

"The remainder of the voyage was uneventful until they approached the North Woolwich Pier near Tripcock Point." He paused again, closing

66

his eyes to conjure the image in his mind. "There's a bit of a blind spot there as you round the point. And coming down river was a great iron ship, far larger than the *Princess Alice*: The *Bywell Castle*, a collier, just starting its journey up to Tyne to pick up a load of coal."

Holmes stood up and walked over to his bookshelf. He reached up to the thick file marked with a "*P*" and pulled it into his hands. Leafing through it, he found a sheaf of pages that had been tied together with twine and handed it to me. On the top was a yellowing illustration from one of the newspapers. "*The Terrible Accident on the Thames*" read the bold heading. Several additional clippings and crumbling papers were tied up with a thin ribbon into one package.

THE TERRIBLE ACCIDENT ON THE THAMES
MANY HUNDREDS OF LIVES LOST

SINKING OF THE PRINCESS ALICE ON HER RETURN FROM SHEERNESS SEP 3 1878

"Here are the clippings from the days following the sinking," he said, handing me the packet of papers. As Holmes puffed on his pipe and stared lazily out the window, I removed the frail newspaper and read the first person account of the unspeakable tragedy:

> *The steamboat was on her way from Sheerness to London, in completion of her day's excursion at about 7:20 p.m. as the sun was setting,* [read the account in the *Greenock Telegraph and Clyde Shipping Gazette* the day after the calamity.] *As the heavily-loaded paddle wheeler turned around Tripcock Point, where the river is about a half-mile wide, it encountered the massive three-masted steam ship weighing nearly four times its tonnage bearing*

down on it. Captain Grinstead had cried out an order, and the ship had "spun round like a top," a witness claimed, in an effort to slip past the much larger collier. It was no use. As the Princess Alice continued its turn to port, the larger ship crashed into it at full speed, almost directly on the paddle wheel.

"The blow was fatal," the account continued, with the side of the passenger steamer crushed below the water line. Cleaved nearly in half by the force of the collision, the *Princess Alice* quickly began sinking as hundreds of people were thrown into the river. Many hundreds remained below in the rapidly inundated lower levels of the ship from which there was no chance of escape. Within five minutes of the collision, the account noted, the tragedy was complete. What had been a vessel filled with hundreds of laughing day-trippers, children, courting lovers, and more – many of them dancing as the orchestra played a lively tune, was sunk in nearly twenty feet of water.

"The loud laughter was succeeded by the wildest and most pitiful shrieks that could render the steel air," one surviving passenger from the *Princess Alice* declared. There had been "a fruitful struggle on the deck as men, women, and children rolled over and clutched and tore at each other." The overcrowded ship was ill-equipped to provide aid. There were only two lifeboats and a few flotation vests." Many of the women were dressed in heavy clothing, including layers of petticoats, that absorbed water rapidly. Unable to swim, most clutched their children and sank like stones into the rancid Thames.

I sat shocked by the description of the catastrophe and the illustrations in the newspaper. Holmes sensed my horror and turned to me.

"Yes, those gay vacationers were crushed and drowned, nearly within sight of their own homes," he said quietly. "The public response was overwhelming, leading the city government to promise a swift and thorough investigation."

"Several days later, Sir Fitzhugh appeared at my door, soliciting my participation in the official inquest. He was a large man, arrogant in his bearing, contemptuous of my admittedly modest rooms, and his offer seemed more a command than a solicitation."

"'Mr. Holmes, I have heard of your somewhat peculiar line of work,' he began after the briefest of introductions. He didn't bother to sit down, although the inferior quality of my furnishings might well have provided him justifiable cause. 'You may offer us some valuable assistance in the conduct of this review.'

"'I'm honoured,' I replied, but the distinguished gentleman entirely missed my youthful sarcasm.

"'Doubtless you have heard of the tragedy that befell the *Princess Alice* the other evening on the Thames,' he began.

"'Yes, and the unfortunate passengers as well,' I added.

"His face bespoke a look of reproach, but he continued.

"'There is to be an official inquiry into the causes of the crash – obligatory you understand,' he said. 'Of course, the press demands an accounting for the mistakes, if mistakes were in fact made.'

"'You will forgive me, Sir Fitzhugh,' I responded, 'but it seems incontrovertible that 'mistakes were made'. This is, after all, hardly the first time that two ships have passed Tripcock Point simultaneously, and yet a collision of such magnitude is, I believe, unprecedented.'

"'Undoubtedly,' he replied, shrugging his shoulders.

"'The light was good, visibility clear, the river seemingly calm,' I continued, 'So it seems obvious that a grave error of judgment was made.'

"'And yet – ' the distinguished visitor interrupted.

"'And yet,' I interjected, 'I make it a matter of principle never to speculate without facts. The newspaper accounts are rarely to be believed. Even the testimony of eyewitnesses can be faulty at such times. An independent review is certainly warranted, in my opinion.'

"'And that is precisely what we are intending to initiate,' Sir Fitzhugh replied. 'I am here to request your assistance. We believe your unique skills could be of invaluable service to our official investigators, and your reputation for integrity and accuracy would build confidence in the inquiry.'

Holmes paused in his narrative and stared into the fire, evidently lost in his recollections of the discussion with Sir Fitzhugh.

"Well," I said, hoping to draw him back into his recitation, "I presume you agreed to assist in the inquiry . . . ."

Holmes's Account

I had an uncomfortable feeling about what I was being asked to do by Sir Fitzhugh, [he continued]. It almost appeared that he wished my involvement to give credibility to the investigation. It struck me as shamelessly opportunistic on his part. So I turned him down. I thought it probable that I would hear no more of the *Princess Alice* until the issuance of the formal report.

Two days later, I was looking out my window when I noticed a man pacing in the street before my flat. Occasionally he stopped and look towards the building before resuming his aimless walking. I thought that if he sought to speak with me, he would do so in his good time and returned to my chemistry experiment.

Shortly, the expected knock came on my door. When I opened it, to no great surprise, the wretched man was standing before me, suffused with a degree of heartbreak such as I had never before observed. He was around thirty-five years of age, I should say, but the stoop of his back, the grief in his eyes, and the dark circles underneath them made him appear twice that age."

"Mr. Holmes is it then?" he asked in a plaintive voice.

"I am Sherlock Holmes," I confirmed.

He nervously clutched and unclutched the cheap cotton hat he held before him. "I wanted to speak with you."

"And so you are," I replied, hoping to ease his discomfort. "How may I be of service?"

He looked to the table on which the remnants of my breakfast remained and then back at me.

"Would you care for some coffee?" I inquired. "Perhaps some toast? I seem to have some extra portions here."

The man slowly made his way to my table and poured himself a cup of lukewarm coffee. "I don't mind if I do," he said, reaching tentatively for one of the pieces of toast and then slathering it with butter and jam. "I haven't eaten since . . . ." His voice drifted off as he sat, holding the bread halfway elevated to his mouth, but frozen in the air.

I sat across from him, resolved to allow him to begin the conversation.

"My name is Edmund Wool, Mr. Holmes. I know it is presumptuous of me to come see you like this," he began, "but I have friends who says you're a clever fellow what can figure out things others can't, if you know what I mean."

"I try to do my best, Mr. Wool," I replied. "You are here to see me about the *Princess Alice* tragedy, I would expect."

He turned his mournful eye towards me, tears forming in his eyes. "And how would you come to know that, sir?"

I hesitated before informing him. "I am a prodigious reader of newspapers. One could hardly read of the tragedy without noting what has befallen the Wool family."

"A 'tragedy'?" he cried. "That is hardly adequate! My wife Ann, and my daughters – my *five daughters!* All lost on that cursed, infernal ship!" he cried before becoming overcome with grief.

It took several minutes for the over-wrought man to regain control over his emotions. I pushed aside the morning's newspaper where I had read the story containing the names of his wife, Ann Bird Wool, and their five daughters, Annie, Lydia, Minnie, Mable, and Kate. All of them pulled had been pulled from the Thames. Only the youngest, Kate, was still alive when the rescuers found them, and she had perished in agony before even reaching the shore. I had resolved to be of help to him before he had wiped the tears from his face.

"Yes," he began. "I will tell you straight off, everything you said is true as true can be. But I'll also tell you I haven't a penny to pay you."

"Whatever you're asking, Mr. Wool, will be provided without charge, if it is in my power to provide it."

"Find out what happened, Mr. Holmes. I've lost everything. Everything!" And he again collapsed into inconsolable sobbing.

"The authorities have assured me those responsible will be held to account," I explained.

His sobbing stopped abruptly and he looked coldly into my eyes.

"D'you really believe that, Mr. Holmes? Do you think they'll find fault with the coal shippers or the captains?" He shook his head violently from side to side. "They will shut down the inquiry before they've even found all the bodies, mark my words! Look how fast they're burying them out in Woolwich. Some people can't even find who they're lookin' for before the burying's done."

His sorrowful account persuaded me that I had no choice but to reconsider my decision to reject Sir Fitzhugh' entreaty, and no sooner had Wool departed my rooms than I sent a note to the statesman informing him I would agree to serve as a consultant to the investigatory commission.

Late the following morning, I stood on the bank of the great river where the crumpled remnants of the *Princess Alice* had been taken. The extreme damage to the ship's midsection illustrated the force with which the collision had occurred, and ascertained why the human losses were so high. I have never been to war like you, Watson, and I pray I shall never see anything comparable to the dreadful sights I witnessed as they removed the victims, some of whom had remained submerged for several days. The bodies of entire families tumbled out of ship as the doors to various cabins were pried open and attendants picked up the cadavers to move them to a temporary mortuary on the riverside. They treated the dead gently and with dignity, but several bodies simply tore apart at the shoulders or the hips as they were raised up from the deck. And the odor, Watson! The stench couldn't have been more revolting if the vent of Hell had been pried open and the putrid gases of Hades were forced into my nostrils!

From Limehouse to Erith, bodies had been washing up on the banks of the Thames, dozens every day. At the Beckton Gas Works, the Woolwich Dockyard, the office of the London Steamboat Company, and even the Woolwich Town Hall, temporary mortuaries were created where bodies were scrutinized, but efforts at identification often proved fruitless.

Given the advanced decomposition, many victims remained anonymous when consigned to a mass grave hurriedly dug at the Woolwich Cemetery.

"After four days in the water, it isn't surprising the cadavers would have begun to bloat and decay," I replied, repulsed by Holmes's gruesome account. "But I am surprised by the foulness of the odor you describe. I saw more than my share of decaying corpses during my military service in Afghanistan and know what several days of exposure can do to a body. Having been submerged in the chilly waters of the Thames shouldn't have produced such advanced putrefaction."

"Something else quite peculiar occurred as we were examining the remains of the ship," Holmes added. "We heard a loud ship's horn and looked up instinctively as the Bywell Castle, *the very ship that had collided with the* Princess Alice, *made its way down river past the crumpled wreck . . . ."*

I rushed to the director of the recovery team, Percy Blowell. "Surely that ship ought not be departing before the inquiry has been completed!" I protested.

Blowell regarded the departing ship and waved his hand dismissively. "Oh, it has been looked over," he said.

"But *I* have hadn't opportunity to examine it," I protested, "nor to speak with the captain or crew! Such examinations are crucial to my assessment of what occurred."

"I believe they interviewed Captain Dix yesterday," he blithely replied. "We have gathered what we need, Mr. Holmes."

"Yes, perhaps *you* think they have," I admonished, "but that isn't the same as what *I* need in order to investigate this tragedy completely." To my exasperation, no effort was made to recall the ship, which continued down the Thames and out towards the sea, carrying its captain and potentially valuable evidence about the recent catastrophe.

I insisted that the evidence provided by the crushed remnants of the *Princess Alice* couldn't indisputably establish the cause of the collision or which ship bore the major responsibility. There were reports of alarms sounded by both captains as the collier bore down on the much smaller ship. But events moved so swiftly, it was impossible to record with certainty the precise order in which they had transpired.

"It indisputable that the major fault lay with the captain of the *Bywell Castle*," I insisted, noting the larger collier had been headed down river and turned into the *Princess Alice*, which was closer to the shore and had already rounded Woolwich Point.

There was no doubt that insufficient attention was paid to the physical evidence, intentionally so. Only a desultory effort had been made to interview the surviving officers from either ship, let alone the fortunate surviving passengers who had managed to make it to shore or had been picked up by another ship in the area.

My conclusion, therefore, was that the collier had turned too abruptly to starboard, crashing into the smaller ship and causing it to sink. Yet the commissioners indicated little interest in my opinions, citing their own inquiries and the pressing deadline for issuing their report.

"We are all knowledgeable and honourable men, Mr. Holmes," one of the commissioners assured me. "We are grateful for your speculations, but we are perfectly capable of examining the facts we have gathered and coming to an impartial conclusion."

"Just two days later, those results were released to the public," Holmes continued, a grim look passing across his face. *"The tragedy was dismissed as 'misadventure'."* He handed me a paper from the bundle he had been perusing. *"*Report of the Inquiry into the Sinking of the *Princess Alice,"* the sheaf of papers was entitled. I quickly scanned several pages of findings, interviews, and questions before arriving at the report's conclusion: The Bywell Castle should have anticipated the collision and reversed its engines before crashing into the much smaller ship. However, the captain of the* Princess Alice *also had erred by failing to turn his ship astern to avoid presenting a broadside target for the larger ship. The large number of casualties, it insisted, were attributable to the severe overcrowding failure of* Princess Alice *and the insufficiency of lifesaving equipment.*

The report appeared to ignore every observation Holmes had offered. "Did they solicit your thoughts before issuing this report?" I inquired.

"Not at all!" he replied. "The superficiality of the entire investigation was appalling, and my time had been entirely wasted – or so I believed." He paused as his voice rose with indignation. He looked at me with a hard glint in his eye. "I am not used to my insights being flouted, as you know!"

Holmes picked up a piece of coal and added it to the blaze. "But something else was deeply troubling," he added. "The members of the panel insisted that I had been a part of the investigatory team."

"What!" I cried. "Without engaging you properly or heeding your cautions?"

"Very much so," he confirmed. "Look here at this story in The Times," he said, pointing to a short paragraph halfway through the story.

"'The inquiry was aided by the insights and recommendations of the celebrated young private detective, Mr. Sherlock Holmes, it was reported','" the story read.

I was astonished. "But this is untrue, Holmes! You have said they all but ignored you!"

"A painful lesson to be learned," he replied. "The use of my name was valuable, but my insights were unwelcome. I had no choice but to tell poor Mr. Wool that I had been prevented from gaining access to the evidence and testimonies that would have helped him to understand the tragedy that befell his family. However, the appearance of that single line in this newspaper story turned out to be the key to the next phase of the whole case."

"So there is more to the story?" I asked.

"Oh, quite a bit more. We have only scratched the surface of the horror of the event and the perfidy of the response . . . ."

Mr. Henry Hollingsworth

The ink of that blasphemous newspaper story had barely time to dry before another caller appeared at my flat wishing to speak to me on the matter.

"Are you Mr. Sherlock Holmes?' the young man inquired when I answered his knock. He was about my own age, of medium size, in an inexpensive jacket and tie, his long brown hair somewhat disheveled by the wind. "I would like to discuss your role in the *Princess Alice* inquiry."

"I presume I am addressing Henry Hollingsworth of *The Times*," I ventured as he strode into the room.

The young man was stunned by my statement and looked about him as if to try to discover how I might have discerned his identity in advance of his introducing himself.

"Yes, I am Hollingsworth, but how the deuce did you know?" he asked incredulously.

This was, of course, a bit of shameless showmanship on my part, Watson, I admit. You have seen me perform such analysis on many occasions.

"Really quite elementary," I responded. "You have an early edition of *The Times* in your hand, an hour before it would arrive at the kiosks. You are too well-dressed to be a printer and not quite at the sartorial level of an editor. (You should excuse the observation, but your frayed cuffs suggest so.) I perceive smudges of ink on the paper, indicating you had handled it before the printing had time to dry, almost assuredly within moments of its removal from the press. Obviously, you have special access to the newspaper's production facilities. Therefore, someone working at the newspaper office. A clerk? Perhaps. But I perceive a number of pencils stuffed into your breast pocket and a reporter's notebook in the side pocket of your jacket, all suggestive of someone expecting to take notes – hence a reporter. And if you are a *Times* reporter anxious to see me about the *Princess Alice* inquiry, I presume you to be Henry Hollingsworth, the reporter whose name graced the byline of today's story about the inquiry report."

"You saw all that in the few seconds that I've been standing before you in this room?" a perplexed Hollingsworth asked.

"Actually, I *observed* all these facts the moment I opened the door," I replied, "just as I noted that your father was a minister, that you are a swordsman, and that your write with your left hand but perform most other functions with your right. But enough with this banter. What are the points in the inquiry report that disturb you?"

He paused to collect his thoughts.

"Mr. Holmes, I believe there is devilry afoot. Ah, I see from your expression you aren't surprised by that opinion."

"I agree wholeheartedly that the investigation was hurried," I replied. "I remain perplexed as to my actual purpose in being asked to assist in the inquiry."

"You were there solely to lend credibility to what I believe to have been a manipulated and distorted proceeding,' Hollingsworth responded.

"Did you share these suspicions with your editor and employers at *The Times*?" I inquired.

"My *former* editors and employers," he said glumly. "When I expressed my concerns, they dismissed my suspicions. When I insisted earlier this morning on greater latitude to probe the matter thoroughly, I was summarily sacked!"

"Well, I am certainly sorry to hear that so reputable a newspaper has taken such precipitous action against a reporter who was merely doing his job."

"Not in their mind," he replied. "I was accused of insinuating myself into complex matters that were well beyond my level of expertise. I offered what I consider to be indisputable evidence that the findings of the inquiry had been manipulated, but that disclosure only seemed to aggravate my supervisor even more."

"What direct evidence?" I asked.

"The Board of Inquiry wasn't truly of the opinion that 'misadventure' was the cause of the collision," Hollingsworth declared. "I've discovered that eleven members of the board voted to bring a charge of manslaughter against the captain of the *Bywell Castle*, but twelve votes were needed. As a result, Captain Fox, his ship, and the company that owned the collier utterly escaped responsibility for hundreds of deaths for which they clearly bear culpability."

"And now, the *Bywell Castle* is long-departed and Fox is beyond apprehension," I added to his narrative.

"Not only that, but the Board of Trade has prepared an inquiry of its own, without bothering to take even the limited testimony of the official inquest. It should come as no surprise, Mr. Holmes, that the business leaders point the finger of culpability directly at – "

"The *Princess Alice*'s captain," I interrupted.

"Exactly!" the young man cried. 'The Board of Trade chose to defend its commercial fleets – fully exonerated the *Bywell Castle*!" he added disgustedly. "They blamed the *Princess Alice* for violating 'waterway regulations'. Looking out after their own, they are, and d--n the women and children rotting on the banks of the Thames!"

The young man had become distraught, and I urged him to sit down while I went into the corridor to call down and request that my landlady bring us some tea.

"What are you planning now?" I inquired, upon returning to my room.

The reporter stood up abruptly. "I'll not be silenced!" he insisted. "I've found people who survived the crash willing to share their accounts with me. But having been sacked by *The Times*, I wonder if I will be able to find someone willing to publish my story."

"I should like to carry on with you, Mr. Hollingsworth, if you don't mind," I offered. "I have little doubt that my unique skills can help expose the true reason behind the calamity, I would like to redeem my own reputation, which has been sullied by association with this disgraceful charade!"

Hollingsworth mentioned three people he planned to interview about the disaster and invited me to accompany him the next morning: Alfred Thomas Merryman (the chef on the *Princess Alice*), Robert Haines (a ship-board musician), and Julian Carttar, the London City Coroner. We agreed to meet near the waterfront and, after expressing his appreciation for my willingness to join him, the young man departed.

The following morning, I awaited my colleague, but Hollingsworth never made an appearance. After an hour's wait, I returned to my flat and found a small envelope affixed to my door. Quickly, I tore it open.

Mr. Holmes:

I should not have involved you in this matter. There is great risk to anyone who pursues this inquiry outside the formal channels. I apologize for placing you in jeopardy and request that you abandon the interviews which I had arranged, as shall I.

Yours faithfully,
Henry Hollingsworth

The note had been written by a man under great duress. The roughly-formed letters indicated the shaking of the author's hands as he wrote swiftly, as evidenced by his lack of caution in allowing his cuff to sweep across the writing while the ink was still wet. He had neglected to place a dot above several *I*'s, indicating haste rather than normal penmanship. It seemed likely that someone had warned Hollingsworth that persisting in his inquiries into the *Princess Alice* inquest could result in consequences far more serious than discharge from *The Times*.

I brushed off the warning and, after making inquiries amongst several journalists I had formerly befriended, located the young reporter's lodgings in a small building near King's Cross. Later that day, Hollingsworth was undoubtedly startled to find an ancient peddler selling second-hand clothing from a rickety cart on his doorstep.

"No, please," he protested. "I cannot consider such things now."

"Ah, but please, sir, surely there is somethin' in my inventory to enhance your wardrobe," the peddler loudly protested. "Here, let me in to demonstrate some of my wares."

Hollingsworth had objected vigorously, but the old man had more strength than it would have appeared, and in a moment, I was standing with the reporter in the vestibule of his building.

"Goodness, Hollingworth, I wasn't sure I would ever get you to invite me inside," I laughed, revealing who I was, to the young man's astonishment.

"But why the disguise, Mr. Holmes?' he had asked in puzzlement.

"If you are truly in danger, you might be under observation," I explained. "It's one thing to allow an old beggar-man admission to your rooms, but I suspect whomever might be watching the street would recognize my undisguised arrival. So I thought it best to choose another identity to preclude any possible effort to thwart our enterprise."

"You're willing to take such a chance?" he asked in amazement.

And this is where the story became truly interesting . . . .

"I'm not one to abandon a fight or a courageous young man because of some threats," I assured him. "'The game is afoot!' as one of my old professors used to say, and we are on the hunt together."

The young reporter was apparently delighted by my refusal to be intimidated. My "beggar-man" soon departed, rendezvousing shortly thereafter several streets away with the journalist, who had heeded my instructions to ensure he wasn't followed. In a half-hour's time, we were in Hitchen Square and knocking on the front door of Alfred Thomas Merryman, the chef on the doomed ship. We identified ourselves and explained our purpose in visiting him, and after furtively casting his eyes up and down the Zealand Road, we all went indoors.

"You can't be too careful these days," he advised as he escorted us into a sitting room. Merryman was a young man, about thirty, with a small moustache and several rowdy children noisily running through the house. Closing the pocket doors behind him, he motioned for us to be seated. His face was a mask of exhaustion and fear.

"No one saw you coming here, did they?" he anxiously asked, looking back and forth at us. "I'm not a man what frightens easily, but these last few weeks, they have been a terror. I don't mind saying and I'd prefer no one knows I'm talking with you, since I still have hopes of finding work on a ship."

I raised my hand in assurance. "You have nothing to fear, Merryman,'" I promised. "Nothing you say to us will be attributed or traced to you, I give you my word." Merryman seemed comforted, but his face still bore the look of a man living in fear.

"Can you tell us what you remember," I asked, "about the accident?"

"Accident?" Merryman snorted. "That collier must have seen us. How could it not? Full light, calm river. Turned right into the *Princess Alice*. Once it hit, the panic on board was terrible. The boat shook something frightful and seemed to be cut in two. The women and children were screamin' and tryin' to rush up to the deck as the water poured down the stairwell.

"I made it up to the bridge and found the captain, but he seemed paralyzed in disbelief. 'What should we do?' I cried.

"'We are sinking fast!' he intoned. 'Do your best.'" Merryman paused again and took a drink of water before continuing. "Those were the last words he said," the chef recalled. "At that very moment, down she went."

Once in the water, a piece of wreckage had helped him stay afloat, but within moments, twenty more people swam to grab onto it as well and it quickly plunged under the surface, taking several unlucky people with it, many of them clad in saturated clothing. Merryman was among the lucky ones who knew how to swim, and he made his way toward the hulking *Bywell Castle* that had stopped its engines and was throwing down ropes, pieces of wood, and even chicken coops for use as flotation.

"They pulled me up," he said in a dazed voice. "Me and maybe four or five others." He stood and walked over to a table and picked up a newspaper. "I was awfully lucky, compared to these poor devils." He handed me the copy of *The Illustrated Police News* with a horrifying cover illustration.

"They took us to the South Woolwich Pie, where we had been headed only a few minutes earlier, and I saw some other people who had been brought ashore. I was holding one little boy who had swallowed a lot of water. A few minutes later," he said flatly, "he died, right there on my lap."

The cries of his own children elsewhere in the house rang out, and the miserable man looked off towards them. "And I've heard that many of those dying since the crash were so sick, they couldn't even attend the inquest or give testimony as to what had occurred."

"You gave this account to the inquiry board?" I asked.

"'Just as I have told it to you,' he responded.

"And how did they respond?"

"Most seemed awful sympathetic, but this one fellow seemed quite skeptical and kept asking whether the *Princess Alice* didn't bear responsibility for the crash."'

"Do you know who that was?" I asked.

"I was told it was one of the city people," he said. "Someone responsible for discarding the river, I was told."

"'*Discarding* the river'?" I asked, somewhat confused.

"I dunno what it meant," the chef said. "But he kept insisting both ships shared responsibility and then, once everyone tired of his line of questioning, I was dismissed."

"Hmm. 'Discarding the river'?" I wondered as Hollingsworth and I set off for our second interview of the day with Robert Haines, the musician whose small home wasn't far from Merryman's. Once again we were greeted warily, with many looks up and down the street before settling into chairs near a crackling fire.

"I was but three feet from the bow railing when I saw the collier bearing down on us,'" he recalled. "I was certain they saw us, but then it hit right at midsection. Good Lord, it made a terrible noise!" Involuntarily, he gave a shudder as he relived the terrible moments after the collision. "There I was with my big bass and the ship's nearly cleaved in half, water pourin' in, people running about, jumpin' into the river, screaming. The smell was terrible. I looked for my mates in the band, but I saw them all go down, every one, except me.

"I figured I was cooked as well, when suddenly this lifebuoy floats by me, and it's a good thing it did because I am no swimmer, so I grabbed onto it," the musician said. "It was all I could do to hang on while I waited for a rescue by one of the little boats from the steamer. I don't mind telling you, I was sick as could be from fear, and dizzy as well. They threw me into the bottom of the boat and continued rowing about looking for others to rescue, but most of them they picked up was either already dead or died before we made it to the shore."

"These people who died before reaching Woolwich," I asked, "they had been swimming in the water?"

"Oh, yes, they was kickin' about," Haines recalled, "at least most of 'em. But somethin' got to them – the cold, the current, the fear – and a lot of them just stopped swimming, gave up, just started floating or sinking into the river." His voice drifted off again. "By the time I got to shore, my knees were shakin' awful bad and I was retchin' up – you'll pardon my description, but you asked. I guess I was convinced I wouldn't survive, just like my mates."

"And the day after?" I pressed.

"Well, I stopped shaking from fear, I'm glad to say," Haines continued. "But I certainly felt poorly and stayed that way for days. My insides were all aching and 'misbehaving', if you know what I mean. I must've been sick for a week or more. And then I heard that verdict saying both ships were to blame." He shook his head. "That's a travesty, that is," he declared. "That collier ran us down as clear as day, and it looks like nobody at the company is the worse for it."

He had talked himself into a severe state and fetched a bottle of whisky from an ancient sideboard nestled into a corner of the darkened room. "To steady me nerves," he explained. "Hard on my stomach these days, but I need something to calm me." He drank a glass of the brown liquid and smacked his lips. "Ah, that helps a bit, and every bit helps," he declared, holding the bottle out to Hollingsworth and myself. "You gents care for a taste?" he inquired, but we declined, and he poured himself one more glass.

"And when you spoke to the inquiry board, did you mention all this information?" I asked.

"Oh, yes, just like I told you. But they just hustled me off with a quick 'Thank you very much.'"

"A valuable conversation," I remarked after we had left the musician's home.

"'His account was vivid, to be sure," Hollingsworth inquired, "but it seemed to me rather redundant to what we already knew. Did you discern anything new?"'

"Possibly, yes, possibly," I replied. "His statement certainly contained some unique pieces of evidence, particularly when combined with the report from Merryman."

"It seems very odd," said Hollingsworth. "The testimony of both leaves little doubt the *Bywell Castle* bore the major responsibility, as does other evidence. Yet the inquiry board, despite eleven votes for charging the captain with manslaughter, found no blame at all, and within days, the *Bywell Castle* has taken its leave of British jurisprudence. How do you make sense of that, Mr. Holmes?'

"Well, one conclusion might be that the shipping officials closed ranks around their fellow captain and shipowner," I said. "Between an old tourist boat and a great coal and shipping fleet, it isn't hard to guess where the inquiry board might come down – especially if, as I suspect, the inquiry board's ranks were tilted towards the shipping industry. I'm hoping our next interview will provide some additional insights."

The last visit was to the office of Julian Carttar, the local coroner who had supervised the identification of the bodies and conducted the main inquest into the tragedy. Carttar's review had taken two weeks, during which he had met Hollingsworth, whom he greeted cautiously.

"Hollingworth, is it?" Carttar said as we were shown into his office. "What more will you be needing now?" he inquired, while cautiously regarding my companion. "And who's this, come nosing about with you?"

"My name is Sherlock Holmes, and if it isn't as yet familiar to you, it might become so in the years to come."

"Will it now?" Carttar replied skeptically. "And what might your role be here?"

"I am a consulting detective, working with Mr. Hollingsworth on the *Princess Alice* tragedy."

"Detective? I don't seem to recall your name as being on the London force."

"A *private* consulting detective."

"I wasn't aware of such an occupation," Carttar replied.

"I wouldn't expect that you would be," I answered, "as I am the only member of my profession. But I have little doubt we shall get to know each other quite well in the years to come."

Carttar seemed unimpressed. "Well, you are likely wasting your time around here. You know we completed our report several days ago. Your friend, Mr. Hollingsworth, covered the inquiry for *The Times*, though I seem to have heard you have been sacked by the paper for your troubles."

"How did you hear that news?" questioned Hollingsworth.

Carttar ignored the young man and turned his attention to me. "What did you say you were looking for, Mr. Holmes?"

"The *post mortem* reports," I replied. "I presume you must have catalogued each of the deceased before dispatching them to the family or the common grave. I wonder if I might look over that list?"

"What would you be looking for?" Carttar asked, suddenly more suspicious of my intentions.

"I am not altogether certain at this moment, but I think a review of your reports might be illuminating."

"There was hardly time or necessity to complete *post mortems* on each of the victims," he said, "but what I found, I provided to the commissioners and it was included in their inquest report." He reached up to a shelf above his desk and took down a thin sheaf of papers, motioning towards them so as to clarify that they constituted the aforementioned report. He thumbed through several pages, then handed it to me. "Most apparently drowned within eight minutes of the collision," he said grimly. "We estimated six-hundred-and-forty lost, and a majority of them . . . women and children."

"Yes, I know that drowning was the *reported* cause of death, but only in the aggregate. I am interested in the individual cases. Who died, and from what cause? That sort of thing. A curiosity of mine."

"There you go," he said, ignoring my question. He pointed to a paragraph declaring that nearly each victim had perished by *"drowning in the waters of the River Thames."*

"Drowning, pure and simple. Many were trapped in the ship and never had a chance of escaping. Those that made it into the water didn't do much better."

"There were reports that the crew of the collier were drunk," I noted.

The coroner nodded his head, putting down the report. "Yes, I heard that accusation," he replied. "But we investigated and found that was certainly not the case."

"Which is why you allowed the ship and crew to depart within a few days?"

"There seemed little more to learn from them."

"You seemed to be in quite a rush to conclude the inquiry, if I may say. I myself had been recruited to offer expert advice to the investigation, and yet the proceedings moved so swiftly I was able to offer almost no insight whatsoever."

"Undoubtedly our loss," Carttar observed derisively. "Look, Mr. Holmes, it was a nasty business and we found there was no one to blame. Yes, we moved fast, but the scene was tragic. Did you know there were pickpockets on both sides of the river, stealing from the dead as they washed up on the shore? Disgraceful! People rowing up to the wreck to break off pieces of wood for keepsakes. Watermen were paid five shillings for every body that they recovered, and they were fighting with each other over the corpses. It was beginning to look more like a *Fez souk* than the scene of a dreadful tragedy. And people were making all sorts of accusations – this crewman was drunk, this crewman ignored drowning people to save himself." He waved his hand dismissively. "So, yes, Mr. Holmes, we wanted to bring the inquest to a close as quickly as possible and file our report."

"I understand," I replied, but continued to press him. "The individual *post mortem* reports: Am I going to be able to see them?"

"I am afraid they aren't available," Carttar replied brusquely. "I only did a few, after establishing that most had drowned. There was no information of importance in them."

Such a comment quite sparked my interest, as you might imagine, since destroying the individual reports, if that is what happened, would have been a highly irresponsible and doubtless illegal act. There might be valuable medical information, of course. There also might be evidence of criminal activity pertinent to legal action against either captain or shipping company.

"There seems a concerted effort here to conclude the inquiry and remove evidence of whatever actually occurred," I told Hollingsworth after we departed the coroners' office. "Both suggest to me there is more to this matter than meets the eye."

"What comes next?"

"My next step is to go to Woolwich," I said. "There I might find sources willing to answer questions that are unwelcome in official offices."

"Am I not to accompany you?" asked Hollingsworth. "I have rather begun to enjoy seeing a detective ply his craft. Perhaps I will write up a story about how you do so!"

"Narratives about my methods are bound to be a waste of time that no sensible person would care to read," I had replied. "What I do next is best done alone," I explained. "I am going to interview some of the Woolwich watermen who were engaged in removing the corpses from the river. I don't think two gentlemen from London would be trusted or welcome, so I intend to employ another of my rather theatrical disguises to appear more of a local."

The next morning, I boarded the early ferry and an hour later disembarked at Woolwich dressed in the rough clothing of a waterman. A judicious application of stage make-up had transformed my face into a somewhat rougher and less-kempt version of its normal appearance. On my head was a cheap woolen cap, and I wore torn gloves and heavily scuffed boots.

I stepped off at Woolwich docks and ambled around, looking for a cluster of men who might serve as sources of information and within only a short time, I located several watermen gathered by their small boats, waiting for jobs to come their way. Causally entering the group, I waited for several minutes before speaking up. It wasn't difficult to steer the conversation to the recent tragedy.

"It must have been a dreadful sight, especially all those children," I offered. "I thank my stars I was off visiting the missus' family in Birmingham when that happened."

"Lucky enough to make four pounds from hauling them in," said one grizzled chap who the cast a suspicious eye in my direction. "Say, who are you anyways? I don't recognize you being from around here."

"Oh, I am not here all that often," I countered. "I work in London mainly, but I thought I'd come down here and see if there was any more money to be made."

The men suddenly became quiet, as if alerted by their friend's comment that they ought not be speaking so frankly before a stranger.

"Can you tell me more about what happened," I pressed. "We didn't get much of an account up in Birmingham, as you can imagine."

"It was a collision, the ship sank, a lot of people died," another waterman offered brusquely. "What more did you want to know?"

"Well, I am something of an amateur anatomist – birds, dogs, that sort of thing – so I'm interested in the victims' appearance. You know – how they looked when you fished them out. Were any of them still living when you pulled them from the river?" There was only more silence from the gathering.

"Well, ah, I seem to recall some details I'd be happy to share with a fellow waterman, but not here around all these roughnecks!" one young man said jocularly. The other men shook their heads knowingly. "Why don't we go find a pub and I will give you more information than you probably need, though I'll tell you right now, it's goin' to cost you a pint or maybe even two."

"That will be no problem," I replied, "and I promise you the best brew in the house."

Together, we took our leave of the gathering of watermen who watched us walk off together. Beyond the quay, we turned up Mortgramit Square, a small side street where this man, named Aikers, assured me that the Mermaid's Braid had a good selection of ales and spirits. Then, once away from the bustle of the port, Aikers roughly shoved me up against the wall, pinning me with one burly forearm and withdrawing a knife from his jacket pocket.

"All right, now, Mr. 'Birmingham', why not tell me what you're really up to?" the man growled. "Come 'round here, askin' questions about the *Princess Alice*. What makes you think we want to be talkin' about what we saw and did to get a few quid? Who are you, and what do you really want, 'cause you ain't no waterman, that's for sure!"

I was taken by surprise, and despite my mastery of *baritsu*, was barely able to move, given the man's heavy pressure on my neck and the knife blade resting disturbingly close to my throat.

"You're mistaken," I replied. "I'm curious about the accident. That's the whole of it."

"No, *you're* the one who's mistaken." Suddenly, I felt the man's arm relax against my throat as he teetered for a moment and then slumped to the grimy street. Standing triumphantly behind him, wielding a heavy walking stick, was none other than Henry Hollingsworth.

"You didn't think I was going to allow you to have the adventure all to yourself, did you?" he asked with a broad grin. "I know how to get a story, too! I was careful to hide myself aboard the ferry from London this morning, and it was a simple matter to follow you and observe your conversation with that gang down by the docks. I figured there was at least an even chance this fellow was up to no good, so I kept behind him as he steered you up this alley."

"And I am grateful you did!" I responded, rubbing my throat when the man's arm had been pressed and managing a weak smile of appreciation. "But now, let's take our leave of this spot before our friend here regains consciousness and takes another swing at me – and likely you, too!"

We walked down several streets hurriedly, with occasional gazes over my shoulder to ensure we weren't being followed, and finally ducked into a small café where we ordered a late breakfast of tea and scones with clotted cream and raspberry jam. No sooner were we alone at our table than a man – coarsely dressed and unshaven – slid into one of the other seats. Hollingsworth started, but I immediately recognized him as one of those at the riverfront only a half-hour earlier.

Sam Phillips' Story

The man sat quietly for a few moments, glancing out the window and looking hard at our faces, measuring us, before finally beginning to speak.

"I was there," he said. "I can help you." He waited for a reaction. "Name's Sam Phillips." He paused again to gather his thoughts. "I was on one of the boats fishing them out of the river." He again seemed to expect a response. "But I need to know what you want the information for. You ain't a copper, are you, comin' after my mates? You tell me why the information is important, and I'll tell you everything you want to know." He looked around furtively. "*Everything*," he added for emphasis.

"Since you have played straight with me, I will do the same," I answered. "My name is Sherlock Holmes. I am a private detective." The young man was startled. "I said, a *private* detective. I have no connection with the official police." I pointed to Hollingsworth, who was studying the conversation intently. "This is Hollingsworth, a newspaperman who's been writing about the crash. We aren't interested in what you or your friends might have done, although it seems you deserve much credit, even if you earned some reward for your rescue exertions. We are interested only in what you saw, and I would happily compensate you for useful information."

"How much?" the man asked eagerly.

"For good information, one pound."

"Not likely!" the man snorted. "More like three!"

"Well, why don't we start with one, and if your information is valuable, I shall be happy to give you three." The young man contemplated the offer and shook his head affirmatively.

"Describe for us the scene on the river after the crash," I said.

A gray look crossed the waterman's face as he conjured up the scene in his memory.

"Oh, it was hell, I tell you, Mr. Holmes, it was hell. The screamin' and wailin' – you could hear it from shore, and when we went out amongst them, it was just pitiful. And the stench – ah, that was beyond belief.'

"The stench of what, Mr. Phillips?" I asked. "The bodies hadn't been in the water long enough to decompose."

"Oh, it was over-powerin'," he protested, "the most god-awful smell you've ever imagined. Offal and sewage and oil and who knows what else. Even them that was lucky enough to know how to swim couldn't help gulpin' in mouthfuls of it whilst they was thrashin' about, waiting to be rescued.

"The others, the ones who couldn't swim, you could see 'em just disappearing under the surface like they was being sucked under by a giant vacuum. We'd row round to the ones who stayed on the surface and grabbed 'em and tried to pull 'em into the boat before they went under, too. No sooner were they aboard than they commenced retchin' and swoonin', cryin' out for help. But there was nothin' to do. I had to keep paddlin' around to try to get more on board before they slipped under for good.

"By the time I got to shore, more than half of them were dead, or as good as gone. We dragged them onto the shore, dozens of 'em. You could see them struggling, but they were goners as soon as they dropped into the river.

"'The bodies kept washing up on the shore for days, piles of 'em, and we'd bring them to one of the morgues the coroner set up." He shuddered involuntarily.

"The coroner?" I asked. "Carttar?"

"Yeah, that's the man," he replied. "Carttar. But most of them were hardly even recognizable, what with their faces eaten away."

"Wait!" I cried. "What do you mean – their 'faces eaten away'?"

"Just that – there wasn't much left of them after a few days in the water."

"Could the damage have been caused by fish?" I asked.

Phillips grunted. "Not many fish livin' in the Thames up there!" he declared. "Not with all the discharging into the river."

I sat bolt upright. "*Discharging* into the river," I muttered, leaning forward – Not "*discarding*" as the chef Merryman had said. "What discharges do you mean?" I demanded.

The man regarded Hollingsworth and me suspiciously and said nothing. Finally, I broke the awkward silence, reaching into my pocket and fishing out three pounds, which I put it on the table in front of him. "What discharges?" I slowly demanded.

The man's eyes widened at the sight of the money. "Why, the sewer discharges," he said. "There's two big outfalls that ain't far from Tripcock Point. There was a rumor they'd dumped a lot of muck into the river only a day before. And a lot of chemicals, too, from them factories just upstream. Ordinarily it don't smell too good, of course, but if you stay in your boat and sail through it quickly, it won't kill you. Although," he added, "breathin' it in can make you light-headed – 'specially when the discharges are heavy."

"And what if you are swimming in it?" Hollingsworth interjected. "Swallowing the filthy water?"

The man leveled his eyes at us and stared for a long moment. "If you're in that water, sir, you're going to die," he said, shaking his head slowly. "If you swallow it," he shook his head, "you die faster. No two ways about it. Those people were dead the minute they went into the river that evening, but they didn't know it. The ones that drowned straight off, well, they might have been the lucky ones. The rest rotted fast from the inside. The sawbones knew it, too, and shipped them off quick to the big grave out at Woolwich Cemetery."

He grew quiet and then silently slid his hands across the table for the three pounds, but I pulled it back quickly.

"What about the inquiry?" I asked. "Did they know about the discharges? I don't remember seeing any references to all this in the inquiry report."

"Ha, that report wasn't about sayin' what happened, everybody knows that," he said with a hollow laugh. "They just wanted to get it over with fast. Nobody responsible. Not the captains, not the sanitation commission, nobody. They wanted the dead in the grave, the *Bywell Castle* back on its way to Tyre, and no questions asked by busybodies like you."

"'And why didn't you come forward with this valuable information?" Hollingsworth pressed.

Phillips regarded the reporter dismissively. "Who, me?" he asked. "A nobody waterman challenging the coppers and coroners and the whole group of high-and-mighty officials? You think I was gonna risk the permit for my boat? Ha! 'Nope, no thanks,' my mates and me said," his voice defiant as his face grew grave.

"But I kept seein' those faces and I knew I couldn't keep it bottled up forever. I decided I'd take a chance on you, sir." He shook his finger in my face for emphasis. "If you double-cross me, I might as well have been cast into the river from the *Princess Alice*."

"Who is threatening you?" I asked. "Why is everyone so frightened to tell the truth?"

"'The men who run the waterfront – they've got powerful friends," Phillips replied. "Some of them are powerful enough themselves. Your boat gets sunk, your crew frightened off. Maybe you can't rent out your boat, or maybe you take out the wrong people in your boat and it comes back without you. They make it pretty clear they don't want no big scandal when somethin' goes wrong. But this one," he shook his head again, "this one, I just have to talk about it, and I trust you'll be protectin' me."

With that, he grabbed the three pounds on the table and rushed off into the street. I never saw him again.

"I don't mind telling you that I was outraged by the young waterman's report," Holmes confided all these years later as the fire continued crackling. "If what he was telling us was true, there was a grave conspiracy amongst the city officials."

"But why would anyone behave so monstrously?" I asked. "Permitting the discharges and then covering up the consequences?

Wouldn't honest public officials want to expose such inhumane behavior?"

"'Honest' officials, yes, but the waterfront is the Devil's playground. Smuggling, polluting, illegal trafficking in people – it's a sorry portion of London, where criminality has been elevated to commonplace and the public officials are greasing the wheels of corruption – for a price, of course.

"I suspect the cost of building new sewers was regarded as exorbitant. The government has dragged its heels, indifferent about spending tens of thousands of pounds to benefit mainly the lower rungs of our society who live near and work on the river.

"I wouldn't be shocked to learn that the city barrister counseled against a public discussion of these events, since disclosure would almost certainly prompt legal action and political retribution. There may even have been bribes paid to cover it up." His mouth tightened into a hard line of distaste. "Crowding, crime, and contamination – they are the dastardly byproducts of what makes our industrial and urban age so grand: Great cities, enormous wealth, an expanding Empire, and the unglamorous costs no one wants to discuss or take responsibility for addressing."

Holmes re-lit one of his old briars and gazed out the window. "Of course, I was a good deal younger in those days, and perhaps more impetuous in my behaviour than the man you have grown to know over these recent years," he said. "But I nevertheless was determined to expose the scandal and do what I could to hold accountable all those who had concealed the real reason so many of these victims had died such horrible deaths."

"That is perfectly understandable!" I assured him.

Holmes continued his account, which began with his appearance at the office of a municipal official who, for legal reasons (my publisher informs me), must remain unnamed, even at this late date. The detective's arrival was, not surprisingly, decidedly unwelcome . . . .

"I am here to see the commissioner," I announced upon entering the official's office.

"Have you an appointment?" the clerk responded.

I brushed aside the young man with a brisk forearm and strode through the door leading to the private room of the government official. Several men considering a number of official-looking documents laid out on an elaborate oval wooden table were startled by the abrupt interruption. The clerk quickly entered, offering his profound apologies.

"I regret this intrusion, Commissioner," he began in an exasperated voice. "This man pushed his way past me. I will summon the constable and have him removed immediately."

"Yes, by all means, do call the police," I replied. "And I shall summon my friends amongst the press. They are always such a rapt audience when I regale them with the stories of the many criminal enterprises I have succeeded in exposing."

The men in the room stared at me, astonished by my utter indifference to the clerk's threat or the prospect of imminent arrest. "Well, hurry up, let's get those officers in here," I admonished. "I have no doubt they will include several with whom I have collaborated. We can have a good chat about the growing incidence of criminality in London, at all levels of society." I took the cheeky step of sitting down in one of the available chairs, holding my hat in my lap and with an expectant expression on my face.

The man in whose office this extraordinary confrontation was occurring looked gravely at me and raised his hand in a cautionary gesture. "That will do, Davis," he said to the clerk and he turned to face to me. "Your name, sir? I am at a loss, since your entrance wasn't properly announced."

"My name is Sherlock Holmes, Commissioner, and I have business with you. I can explain the nature of that business here and now, with these gentlemen present, or they may retire to their own pressing interests while you and I conduct our conversation. I assure you it makes no difference to me whatsoever."

"And the subject of that conversation?" the commissioner inquired.

I cast my eyes down at the papers covering the oval desk and considered them briefly before one of other men hastily gathered them into an untidy bundle and shoved them into a large folder.

"Really, sir," I asked, "will we be compelled to prevaricate about so tragic and consequential a misfortune as the sinking of the *Princess Alice*?"

The commissioner gestured for the others to leave the room. He pulled out the chair from behind the desk and sat down. He leaned forward on the desk and stared hard at me.

"'Holmes', you say?" he repeated.

"Have I not sufficiently indicated the seriousness of my purpose here? You know exactly who I am, just as I know of your membership in the Diogenes Club and your familiarity with my brother, Mycroft." The commissioner appeared startled by my mentioning the secretive fraternity. "I have seen you there upon occasion. Let me assure you: The manner in which you respond to the matter at hand will surely determine whether you are ever welcome in that august building again."

"Is that some sort of threat, Holmes?" the commissioner seethed.

"Do not test me," I replied. "I assure you I have confronted far higher and mightier men in the dock and sent them on their way to Newgate Prison."

The commissioner's eyes widened and his demeanor underwent a sudden change. He slumped slightly into his chair and sat quietly for a few moments.

"What is it you want?' he asked in a fatigued voice. "This office has nothing whatsoever to do with the safety of navigation on the river, and I assure you, the appropriate offices have conducted a very proper inquiry."

"I assisted the committee investigating the collision of the *Princess Alice* and the *Bywell Castle*," I responded.

"I am aware of your participation in the committee's work," he said, "just as you are aware that the matter is considered closed."

"Not by me," I corrected. "You see, my role was circumscribed by those in charge of the inquiry. Since I found their conclusions quite superficial and at variance with my own observations, I have decided to continue the inquiry employing my rather unique investigative skills."

"Hardly necessary," the commissioner commented.

"I also took the liberty of familiarizing myself with the most recent rules governing navigation on the Thames, and it is indisputable that the report of the investigatory commission was preposterously incorrect."

The commissioner's eyes narrowed. "How so?"

"It is beyond question that culpability for the tragedy rested squarely with the *Bywell Castle*, as the inquiry voted with but one dissenting vote. And yet that consensus was ignored in favour of a finding of shared blame, which allowed the *Bywell Castle* and its captain to escape any responsibility for the tragedy. Please do not deny that there was tampering with the inquiry board to influence its finding! You and I both know the heavy hand of the Board of Trade weighed in on behalf of the coal shipper over the welfare of a few hundred afternoon pleasure seekers."

The commissioner said nothing, but stared at me with a cold attitude.

"But as you say," I continued, "navigation safety isn't the provenance of your office, and so I will not focus my attention today on the whitewash about the causes of the collision. I'll take up that matter with the proper authorities. Instead, I've come here to address the deplorable culpability of your own bureau in the deaths of more than six-hundred victims."

"But the victims drowned as a result of the sinking," he protested. "'My office bears no responsibility for their deaths!"

I stood and walked closer to the commissioner, who seemed to shrink into his leather chair as I approached.

"That would be true if, as you say, they had drowned. But like you, I am well aware that most of them didn't drown. They were *poisoned*, which left them incapacitated in the water. Dozens more perished once aboard rescue boats or, in some cases, after they had managed to swim to the shore. You bear a very great responsibility for those deaths."

The commissioner's face had drained of color, and his chin quivered involuntarily. He licked his lips several times and removed a large yellow handkerchief from his coat that he used to dab the perspiration on his large forehead.

"You see, I am not a physician, but I do have considerable knowledge of the effects of poisons," I continued. "And when I saw the corpses of many of those victims and heard the descriptions of how they had drawn their last breaths, they didn't seem to me like people who had drowned. And they appeared to have endured grievous pain and distress. They looked, sir, as though they had swallowed poison, with the most calamitous of responses."

Here, Watson, I admit to some duplicity. I hadn't had sufficient time to conduct the experiments I was about to describe, but I was absolutely convinced the commissioner would recognize the inevitability of the finding had I sufficient time in the laboratory. It was a risk, I admit, but a risk worth taking.

"My suspicions were confirmed by my experiments in the chemical laboratory at Barts," I declared. "Several physicians who were treating the victims of the sinking provided me with biological samples from the dead and dying, which I subjected to rather intense analysis. It was, I might add, not amongst the more challenging research in my career, but the findings were absolutely dispositive."

The official, now grave and deflated, sat with both elbows on the desk and his hands supporting his head.

"Go ahead, Mr. Holmes," he said, staring stonily at me.

"They found that many of the victims hadn't drowned at all! There was little if any water in their lungs, an indisputable indication of drowning. But there *was* water in their stomachs, water contaminated with raw sewage and industrial chemicals." I paused momentarily for effect. "They were poisoned by vile contaminants that had been dumped into the Thames not a quarter-mile from the site of the sinking: Toxins far in excess of the levels permitted by the woefully low health standards that exist."

The commissioner shifted in his chair, but remained silent.

"And the decision to permit such illegal discharges, in violation of the safety practices set by this very department, was made by whom?"

The commissioner sighed deeply and raised his face. "By me," he said gravely. "It was my decision, it is true, to open the watergates. But it wasn't the first time such large quantities had been discharged into the river. We had the bad luck of doing so immediately before the collision, just before hundreds of people were cast into the river." He paused to collect himself. "There was nothing to be done. I realized immediately that even if they were able to swim to safety or were rescued, most would likely have consumed enough of the bacteria and poison to be fatal.

"We tried, Mr. Holmes. You cannot believe I didn't attempt to provide as much emergency aid as possible, but there were so many of them, and their condition deteriorated so rapidly . . . ." His voice petered out to a near whisper.

"So you conspired with the navigation board to exonerate the *Bywell Castle* and expedite its movement out of this region in order to curtail a thorough inquiry," I charged. "And you secured the approval for mass graves to be filled with victims before proper *post mortems* could be ordered to conceal your culpability. And knowing the medical implications of ingesting sewage-tainted water or chemical wastes, you have allowed weeks to go by after the incident without providing the survivors proper notice about the nature of their illnesses, let alone aiding them in securing necessary medical treatment?"

"Yes," the commissioner declared, asserting an officious demeanor. "I stand by that decision to protect the city and its leaders from condemnation. The calamity and the deaths were, after all, not the result of the discharges, but of a collision for which the city bore no responsibility. Had that accident not occurred, the discharge would have impacted no one, just as past ones have gone unnoticed."

I shook my head sharply.

"No, that will not do. Your office and others in positions of responsibility in this city owe a great deal to the victims of this tragedy and their survivors, and it is my intention to ensure that debt is paid. Wives have been lost. Children killed by the score. Lives have been ruined."

"'And I ask you, Mr. Holmes: What good it is to ruin still more? I assure you we are changing our operations – all of the improvements people expect of their government. What more can be gained by exposing whatever shortcomings you believe might have occurred, setting Londoner against Londoner, exciting agitation against the government for what cannot in any fair way be termed anything but a terrible oversight, and an error that can never occur again?"

Holmes sat back in his chair and we looked at each other for several long minutes.

"What did you do?" I finally questioned.

"What I probably shouldn't have done," he replied. "I went to the Diogenes Club and arranged to meet Mycroft in the one room in the establishment where one can converse aloud. I told him of my discoveries, of my conversation with the unnamed commissioner – of course, he immediately deduced the man's identity – and asked his advice."

"You really have no choice, Sherlock," he insisted. "As a member of the inquiry board, you were sworn to secrecy. You cannot violate that pledge now by disclosing such sensitive information. It just isn't done! And, I might add, if you are perceived to have violated that oath, whether for personal gain or other reason, I would be concerned about your future working with the police in your own curiously concocted occupation."

"So if I'm not part of the inquiry and have no data, I can make no charges because I lack the necessary knowledge," I responded. "And if I possess that information because of being a part of the inquiry, I am prohibited from a public discussion because of my oath!"

"As is typical of your deductive skills," Mycroft replied, "precisely so."

I wasn't surprised at Mycroft's response. He is very much a man of the state and honours the oath of secrecy to Queen and country. But I admit I was deeply disappointed in his rationalization of such misbehaviour. I certainly didn't view matters in a similar light and had little faith in those responsible for releasing the poisons, issuing inaccurate death notices and digging mass graves."

"You were a young man," I counseled. "One can understand not choosing to endanger your career with a public spectacle – especially if you were confident the practices were to be reformed."

"But I had no such confidence," he responded. "Nor did I have, in my opinion, an obligation of confidentiality since I had uncovered these dastardly facts on my own and not as part of any official inquiry."

"What did you do?" I asked.

"I returned to the commissioner's office, and this time was immediately ushered into his room."

"Well, Mr. Holmes," he archly declared, "I trust you have come to your senses and recognize that it is best to trust the authorities."

"What *I* trust, Commissioner, is that you will comply with several demands I will make, in return for which I shall continue to treat this matter in confidentiality."

94

"Why – !" the commissioner gasped. "I have never been spoken to in such a manner, let alone by someone well below me!"

"Need I remind you that should I not agree to hold my tongue, you may well find yourself regarding those 'below you' from a perch upon the gallows!"

The commissioner blanched and sat, motioning for me to do the same.

"First, you will use your influence to have Hollingsworth, the reporter, restored to his position at *The Times*," I began. "This young man showed great courage in pursuing this story and was sacked for his troubles."

"I think I can accomplish that goal. The publisher is a longtime – "

"And at a salary increase of twenty-five-percent above his past rate – still a penurious amount, but one from which he will swiftly rise," I interrupted.

The commissioner slowly nodded in agreement.

"Second, the city must provide financial compensation to every family that lost members due to the collision, beginning with the Wool family that lost six of its members! Enlist the owners of the *Bywell Castle*, use municipal funds, or take them out of your own well-lined purse, but every family must have some measure of financial assistance. Five pounds for any woman or child lost, and ten for any wage earner."

The commissioner's mouth opened in silent response, but then closed it before he uttered a word.

"In addition, you must erect a suitable monument over the common grave at the Woolwich Old Cemetery. These are my absolute conditions – in addition, of course, to your promises of restricting the future discharge of toxic waste and improvements to navigation safety."

The commissioner lit his pipe and thought for a few moments. "All right, Mr. Holmes, I can see you intend to hold us accountable – no matter how unjustly, in my view. I will intervene with those in higher positions of authority to ensure they are fully met."

He stood behind his desk. "I believe that concludes our business, and perhaps our paths will cross again in less contentious circumstances.' He extended his hand, but I naturally ignored the offer.

"I sincerely doubt that will be the case, sir," I replied. "I shall hold you to your pledge, however, and if you meet your promises, I shall do the same."

"With that, I turned and walked out of the room," Holmes said gravely.

"And did they comply?"

"Yes, each of my conditions was met. Hollingsworth was given a senior position and salary and assignments, although he never learned of my role in his re-securing his position with The Times. *The survivors also received the compensation I had demanded. And within a short period of time, the sanitation officials of London had instituted improvements to the city's discharges into the river. Equally important, new safety rules for signaling and separating large ships from smaller craft went into effect."*

"What a testament to your skills, I congratulate you," I responded, *truly impressed with the outcome of his dogged investigation. But my friend stood and walked to the window overlooking Baker Street, an expression of great sadness on his visage.*

"Thank you. I do mean that, my friend. But I fear the outcome of this case has caused me more grief in the intervening years than any other to which I have applied my powers. Perhaps I was too young and too wary of crossing swords with the London authorities. Perhaps I was too cowed by Mycroft's remonstrances. The fact is, I was persuaded to accept a settlement that allowed those guilty of gross negligence – or worse – to escape accountability for their actions, and of that, I am not proud."

"I completely understand. But you may draw great satisfaction that the health and safety of millions of Londoners and likely others around the world are attributable to your actions and yours alone. But for your steadfastness, years might have passed before some further tragedy spurred the authorities into action."

Despite my assurances, however, I could see that Holmes drew no comfort from my rationalizations, all of which he doubtless had long ruminated upon himself. At last, I understood his distrust of government and his discomfort at being engaged by those in positions of authority.

At the moment, however, there was little more to do but to entice my friend to join me for a late lunch at The Boar and Beagle, where our conversation was considerably lighter than the morning's discussion of the Princess Alice *tragedy. Never again did I mention the distressing case, not even when I learned that five years after the tragedy on the Thames, the* Bywell Castle *had disappeared somewhere off the coast of Portugal with the loss of all hands.*

The Memorial to the victims of the
Princess Alice *at Woolwich Cemetery*

The Adventure of the Amorous Balloonist
by I.A. Watson

Archivist's Note: Inside the lid pocket of the document dispatch box which was formerly secured by Dr. John Watson at his bank, Cox and Company of 14-16 Charing Cross, is a laced leather wallet containing several crumpled loose-leaf accounts not found elsewhere in his casebooks. These neglected items were evidently returned to Watson with notes scribbled across them by his literary agent, Conan Doyle. The manuscripts were each variously rejected for publication in Watson's lifetime, principally due to content which might in that era have been considered salacious or in poor taste. The ribald amusements of William IV's reign and of the first days of Victoria's sovereignty had long since been stifled by austere late-Victorian values.

Publishers were careful not to risk public opprobrium or official censure, and Doyle knew better than Watson where readers' sensibilities might lie. The present account, recovered from that file of "damned" material and representing one of Watson's earliest efforts at chronicling his friend's investigations, was set aside by Doyle with the simple phrase, "The editors wouldn't stand it, old fellow. Too Continental, eh?" Presentation of this lost episode here must therefore come with a caveat lector *as including mention of a topic which rendered it unpublishable in 1890 - that of sex. Readers of a robust constitution, mature nature, and steady moral character may now review the matter for themselves.*

– I.A.W.

"You need a distraction," Holmes told me.

I looked up from my newspaper's sporting pages and realised that my fists were crumpling the broadsheet.

My new flatmate regarded me with concern. "Will you instead consider a puzzle that you might perhaps be able to solve? For your health's sake?"

"I am not unwell," I denied.

"You are reading the latest on the cricketer's strike at Trent Bridge, and the Nottinghamshire Cricket Club's attempts to thwart their players demands of a twenty-pound minimum fee for playing. It always causes your choler to rise."

I had lived with Holmes at our digs in Baker Street for close to six months by this time, and knew that my flatmate had little interest in or knowledge of sport. "The bowler Alfred Shore and six other of the best players on the Nottinghamshire team have refused to attend any further dispute negotiations if County Secretary Captain Holden is present. How can the issue be properly resolved if the two sides will not even meet?" [1]

"I have no idea," Holmes replied indifferently. "I doubt that your spleen knows either. Might I divert your attention elsewhere, to a professional matter?"

"It's all very well saying gentlemen should play for the love of the sport, but with clubs profiting from the matches and fielding many players of limited financial means, why shouldn't – " I went on, before I parsed what my friend had said. "A professional matter? Yours or mine?"

Sherlock Holmes was a detective, or rather a *consulting detective*, the specialist to whom other investigators referred when their resources were exhausted. I had been privileged to accompany him on his investigations before, and had found these mysteries almost as remarkable as his capacity to solve them.

In the lazy summer of '81, I was slowly recovering from a serious injury that had ended my military service as an army medic, eking out my pension until the pain and bad dreams passed. I was a doctor, but a doctor without practice or patients.

"Both your trade and mine," Holmes told me, his eyes twinkling. "I am going to your *alma mater*, Barts, to visit a young lady who is recovering there from some injuries she sustained earlier today. You might come along as a native guide. She may prefer having a medical man present when she makes her statement."

"I shall be pleased to oblige, of course," I agreed, folding away the accursed newspaper with its accounts of unsporting behaviour. "Might I ask the nature of the lady's injuries?"

"I believe she has a broken leg, a fractured arm, and some damaged ribs," Holmes told me. "She was involved in a balloon crash."

"A gas balloon, you mean? It landed on her?"

"She was in it when it foundered. Her gentleman companion is dead."

"Killed in the crash landing?"

"Murdered in the gondola, at five-hundred feet," Holmes told me with satisfaction.

"By whom?"

"The police are somewhat fixated on the fact that the young lady was the only other person aboard."

"Then . . . surely . . . ?" I ventured.

"Her sister has retained my services to consider other possibilities."

"And you wish me to be present at your interview with this unfortunate lady."

"It would be preferable, certainly. You see, the young woman has a rather temperamental husband – and it wasn't he with whom she decided to go ballooning."

Mrs. William Sangfirth wasn't the adventurous aviatrix, but rather the elder sister who had appealed to Holmes. She rose from her seat in Barts visitor's tearoom and proffered her hand in greeting as Holmes identified and closed in on her. We made no mention of her reddened eyes and unhappy expression, instead observing the usual courtesies of introduction and the ordering of a fresh pot of tea.

"I may have called upon your services in vain," the lady warned us. "My sister's husband continues to be truculent. He will not allow visitors to be admitted to see Lucy. Even I have been . . . excluded from her room."

That was Sir Trinian Fledger's right as a husband, of course, but it was a right he was using rather heavily-handedly.

"I have brought along a medical man," Holmes mentioned to Mrs. Sangfirth. "It may be that he can gain access to your sister where others cannot. In the meantime, if you wish to be of utility to Lady Lucy, you might brief us on the detail of the matter you described in your note of hand."

I poured the distraught visitor a cup while she gathered herself to speak.

"You must excuse my distress. It has been a horrible day. First news of Lucy's accident, then of the circumstances around it, then seeing her here swathed in those bandages and plaster – and then policemen and that awful scene with Fledger. I have never been spoken to so, never! Mister Sangfirth shall hear of it!"

"You are right to bring the matter to Holmes, Mrs. Sangfirth," I assured her. "The best you can do now is to render him a full, clear account. How did your sister ever come to be ballooning?"

"She has always been the wayward, adventurous one. Mother hoped that marriage would settle her but . . ." The tearful lady caught herself, took a sip of her undistinguished hospital canteen tea, and started anew.

"Lucy married Sir Trinian Fledger almost four years ago. It was a good match. He has extensive lands in Essex and she brought over two-hundred acres and some properties in Chelmsford and Colchester, as well as woods near Thurrock. And she retained our late father's house at Ingatestone, near Brentwood, which is where she was staying these past few months. She was nineteen when she wed. Fledger was a retired naval officer of forty-six, a widower who sought a suitable new wife since he intended to run for Parliament."

"She was content with the alliance?" I surmised. Such matches aren't uncommon when a man wishes to enter the political arena and requires the support of his county.

"We convinced her, mother and I and Mr. Sangfirth. Lucy needed a steady hand. Sir Trinian, knighted for his military service, newly retired from the Royal Navy, experienced and ambitious – he seemed like a decent prospect."

"But the marriage isn't a happy one?" Holmes suggested.

"Not then, less now." Mrs. Sangfirth paused and found a handkerchief to dab her eyes. "I shall spare you the domestic gossip. Suffice that Lucy spends most of her time at Ingatestone and Fledger uses the London house or his Club. He is deeply involved in opposition to Irish Home Rule and is active in the campaign around the implementation of the Coercion Bill."[2] Lucy . . . Lucy has much time on her hands."

"For ballooning?" I suggested.

"For entertaining. One frequent visitor was Lieutenant Ward Wakelyn."

"The pilot of the vehicle," Holmes recognised, "who died in the air."

"Indeed. I am given to understand that Lt. Wakelyn is an – *was* an avid balloonist. It was perhaps this aspect of his life that most interested Lucy. He visited her to discuss it on several occasions."

"Without Sir Trinian being present?" I checked. I began to see why Lady Lucy's husband might be somewhat sensitive to her having male visitors at her bedside.

"Yes," Mrs. Sangfirth admitted, almost inaudibly. She resorted to her teacup again for a moment's recovery.

"What do you know of today's events?" Holmes demanded.

"It is my understanding that Fledger, having learned of the visits to Ingatestone from a junior Naval officer, issued instructions to staff that Lt. Wakelyn wasn't to be permitted in house or grounds again – that the dogs should be set upon him if he attempted entry. There are a number of former military staff in Fledger's employ at the estate that would be more than happy to carry out such orders. However, though the gates might be locked, that is no bar to a gas balloon."

"Lt. Wakelyn arrived by air," I understood. "He wasn't seen?"

"It is coming up to harvest time," Mrs. Sangfirth pointed out. "Most of the ground staff are engaged in the fields, supervising the tenants. Lt. Wakelyn knew to approach over the long lake and ornamental gardens. Indeed, he landed his vessel close to the boathouse and tethered it there."

"Was Lady Lucy expecting him?" Holmes asked.

"Evidently. She slipped out of the house and met him beside the lake. They had apparently arranged that she might at last fulfil her desire to fly in his balloon."

"Wakelyn came alone?"

"I think he may have brought a servant with him. The intention was evidently to fix cables to the ground to hold the balloon in place, so that Lucy might ascend vertically and see over the grounds and the county beyond while not risking being blown away. Her absence would certainly then be noted."

"That's a common method at fairs and displays," I knew. "The chap on the ground pays out the cables that hold the gas bag, the gondola goes up, and the whole thing floats there up in the sky, but anchored. It is the safest kind of ascent." Indeed, I had seen similar things on occasion during my military service, where such tethered baskets were sent up to spy the terrain and to observe enemy movements.

"Times," Holmes demanded. "Facts."

"I had only a little while to speak with Lucy in her hospital bed before Fledger arrived, but my understanding is that she left the house to meet the Lieutenant at a quarter-past-ten. The accident was a little before eleven."

"You mean the murder of Wakelyn," Holmes clarified. "A gunshot wound to the head is hardly an accident."

"What happened after was the accident," Mrs. Sangfirth rallied. "Horrified at the sudden demise of her pilot, his tumbling over the side of the box in which they flew, and afraid of more gunfire at her, Lucy tried her best to bring the vehicle to ground. Instead, she managed to loosen the balloon from its tether and set it flying free, carrying her away."

"Those things are hard enough to control for experts," I knew. "A young woman on her first flight could hardly be expected to handle such a machine."

"The balloon was out of control. It moved with the wind and changed direction several times before veering too low and brushing the roof of a factory in Basildon. From what I could gather, that spilled the gas more and sent the vehicle crashing to the ground, causing poor Lucy's injuries."

Holmes demanded details, locations, times, and collected what he could, but Mrs. Sangfirth wasn't an ideal testatrix and had no first-hand knowledge of events.

Her main focus of concern was on what had happened since. "Lucy was brought to St. Bartholomew's, of course, so that a specialist might be sure that her injuries had been properly treated and set. She gave my name as the person who should be summoned, but naturally they sent for Fledger also. When I arrived she was already in casts, woozy with the morphine

102

she had been given, but she confessed to the nature of her . . . adventure as I have just recounted it. But then a horrid policeman arrived."

"He didn't interview your sister while she was drugged and in pain?" I checked.

"He wanted to, but her doctor was firm."

We determined that the inspector's name was Brecknell, from the Essex Police headquarters in Chelmsford. Unable to interview Lucy Fledger, he had instead contented himself with terrorising her sister.

"He asked some quite awful questions, imputing disgusting things. Eventually it became clear that he believed that Lucy had murdered Lieutenant Wakelyn in some sordid lover's quarrel."

"Because of the close-quarters nature of the fatal bullet wound," Holmes recalled from Mrs. Sangfirth's original letter.

"Yes. Something about powder burns and so on. He seemed convinced that only Lucy might have taken the shot that spilled the young lieutenant over the side. He wanted to know where she had cast the weapon overboard during her flight. He asked all kinds of ridiculous things."

"This is how you came to hear of the close-quarters nature of the fatal wound."

"The supposed close-quarters, yes, although I am convinced that must be false, some ploy by the police or some silly medical error. Lucy would never . . . She has always been the silly, romantic one. I have to look after her. But now she is hurt . . . ."

We waited while Mrs. Sangfirth overcame her upset again. Relatives of the injured often suffer shock and remorse even when the events have nothing to do with them.

At last the lady continued her recitation of woes. "And then Fledger arrived, furious at what he had heard, and tossed the policeman out. He threatened to wire the Home Secretary. [3] And then he ejected *me* from Lucy's private room as well. The audacity! The rudeness of that man!"

"Do you know this Brecknell, Holmes?" I enquired.

Holmes shook his head ruefully. "I am afraid that my comprehensive knowledge of the police detectives of London doesn't yet extend into the Home Counties. An omission. All that I can say is that I haven't heard of him, which may mean he is new, or undistinguished, or just that he has never handled a case worthy of my attention. I shall learn about him now."

"They are trying to say that Lucy killed Lieutenant Wakelyn," Mrs. Sangfirth told us. "They are trying to make a case for murder! She is too drugged for pain to understand it yet, but soon she must recognise her danger. Fledger is furious. Scandal like this will end his political hopes of selection. He is . . . he has a temper on him. A vengeful man. I am afraid for Lucy."

"You fear his behaviour?" I asked.

"It wouldn't be the first time he has taken the crop to her. And I have never seen him so furious as this."

A husband has a right to chastise his wife, but that can be quite unpleasant. [4]

When Holmes had finished his interview he was ready to depart, but I lingered to make polite and proper farewells with his client. "My advice is to go home for now, Mrs. Sangfirth, if you cannot be with your sister. Holmes and I shall do what we can to untangle this mess. He will send a telegram if anything happens that you should know about – or I will."

Sir Trinian Fledger had evidently been the kind of military officer who believed that shouting was the way to have his orders carried out. Now pensioned out after injuries during the hunt for the stolen Peruvian monitor *Huáscar* in '77, [5] he had evidently channelled his thwarted ambition into political wrangling and harassing medical staff who had better things to do.

Nor was he amenable to allowing a former army surgeon who was no longer attached to Barts into his wife's recovery room to enquire about her airborne adventures,

"You can go to the devil, sir," he told me, "and take your long-nosed friend with you!"

Holmes regarded the ruddy-faced sailor with a detached calm. "You have been interviewed by the Essex Constabulary, then. Is the ink upon your knuckles from dispatching a telegram of complaint in haste to their Chief Constable?"

"None of your d----d business! Get out of this ward before I call the porters to eject you."

"You will not allow us to do what we can to see if the charges against Lady Lucy can be disproved?" I attempted.

"My wife is a sick woman, physically and mentally. When she is sufficiently recovered from her present injuries, I shall see to her incarceration in an institution that can treat her behavioural condition." [6]

"Her sister may have concerns about that," I warned.

"Her sister may go to the devil with you!"

"I don't have time for the visit you suggest, Sir Trinian," Holmes answered him. "I have too much to do resolving the murder of Lieutenant Wakelyn. You knew the man?"

"Get out! Out, I say, before I take my stick to you!"

That was as far as we got with the unhappy husband.

The trains are good to Brentwood, and thence to the pleasant little station of Ingatestone. It took us less than half-an-hour from Liverpool Street, but it gave me some time to pick Holmes's brain on the case at hand.

"Do you often encounter obstructions like Sir Trinian?" I wondered.

"On occasion. The art of detection lies in learning their stories from their belligerence. For example, when I suggested the telegram to the Chief Constable, I saw the expression upon Fledger's face. It was an idea that hadn't yet occurred to him, though he didn't say it, and one that he seized upon with intent to perform. That tells me that the note he wrote in haste, splashing ink carelessly, was unlikely to be the Home Secretary, whose good opinion he must court. Likewise, the tightening of his fingers, the instinctive desire to form a fist, when I enquired of his acquaintance with Wakelyn, betrays his prior knowledge of the fellow."

"And likely that he knew much of the lieutenant's friendship with Lady Lucy," I supposed.

"Most probably. It is a strand to pursue. So although Sir Trinian Fledger denied us access to the primary witness for now, he had been quite helpful in our investigation."

I began to understand how Holmes approached hostile witnesses. Even their belligerence might offer him valuable data. "What of those telegrams that awaited your collection at Liverpool Street Station Post Office?" I ventured.

"Ah, these contain useful background information for which I wired at the start of my researches. Here are replies from the Essex and East Anglia Balloon Club, from an Admiralty clerk of my acquaintance, from a Probate Office secretary, and from our regular visitor Inspector Lestrade. Can you surmise what each of them has to tell us about our investigation?"

"Well," I considered, "I suppose that the Balloonists can tell us somewhat of Lt. Wakelyn and his machine. He was presumably a member of that club, or at least known to them. The Admiralty will have details of the Naval service of the dead man and Sir Trinian. Lestrade may know something of the Essex police detective Brecknell. As for the Probate Office . . . ?"

"It can inform us of the terms of Lucy Fledger's father's last will and testament," Holmes supplied. "That tells us the inheritance and dowry settled upon the lady, and the terms under which Sir Trinian controls the income and properties after marriage."

"In other words," I recognized, "would he lose her assets if there was a divorce?" [7]

"Yes. And I read now that such is the condition of the late Sir Henry Drustan's will. Interestingly, if Lucy predeceases her husband without living issue, then the bulk of her inheritance reverts to his other daughter, Mrs. Sangfirth, if she lives, and otherwise descends to any issue of hers, or else to a cadet branch of the Drustan family."

"You think this relevant?"

"I think that Lady Lucy's estates bring Sir Trinian sixteen-thousand a year, forming a significant part of his income. A man with political ambitions might require such money. But likewise, his loss of that income is another's gain. It is all useful data."

I recognised that a detective's work required assembly of many facts that must be sorted into the proper pattern. "What other information have you received?"

Holmes flicked through the yellow telegram sheets. The one from Lestrade was the briefest, within the minimum twenty word basic rate. [8] It informed us that, in the Scotland Yard man's opinion, "*B – Complete bumbler, No experience, No common sense. Expect Essex refer case Yard soon. Wife responsible. Don't waste time. Lestrade.*"

Holmes regarded the message with amusement. "If the police investigator is such that Lestrade regards him so poorly, then he must be dull indeed."

"You have said that Lestrade is the best of the Scotland Yarders," I reminded my companion.

"It was faint praise."

"How then shall you deal with this Inspector Brecknell?"

"I sent him a telegram also, but he has failed so far to respond."

The Balloonists Club response contained some useful material. Lt. Wakelyn had been an avid member, staging his machine from an airfield the club retained at Great Baddow, a couple of miles west of Chelmsford and only seven miles as the balloon flies from Ingatestone. He had departed from the field that morning at 8:45, trailed on the ground by his man Avewick. The club secretary from whom our reply came suggested that we might learn more from Lt. Corcoran, another member and Wakelyn's closest friend.

"Shall you interview this Avewick and Corcoran?" I asked Holmes.

"Both will have useful things to tell," my friend agreed. "However, unless Brecknell fulfils Lestrade's estimate, he will have spoken with them first."

The Admiralty communication offered us the insight that Sir Trinian, then Captain Fledger, and Lt. Wakelyn, then Ensign, had served together on the *Signal* for four months in 1876, before Fledger's transfer to Rear Admiral Algernon de Horsey's staff aboard HMS *Shah* and his subsequent injury during the Battle of Pacocha.

106

"So they did know each other in military service," I recognised. Of course, there was no way to know what relations there might have been between a senior and very junior officer.

The Admiralty note also mentioned that Lt. Ward Wakelyn was presently on half-pay without posting, which explained why he was at liberty to be ballooning around the countryside descending upon married women.

"It has nothing to say about why he hasn't been given a berth?" I asked.

"I doubt that the Admiralty would disclose that information to a casual enquirer," Holmes pointed out. "Perhaps his friend Corcoran might tell us."

The process of Holmes's professional investigation fascinated me, but our conversation was truncated by our arrival at our destination.

Holmes gained access to Sir Trinian's Ingatestone estate by the simple expedient of announcing that he was investigating the unfortunate incident that morning. He failed to mention that he wasn't one of the several members of the constabulary that had visited throughout the day.

He was quick to ask decisive questions of the various staff we encountered. From the gate porter we confirmed that Lt. Wakelyn was well known at the house, being a frequent visitor, first as a dinner guest and then later in attendance of her Ladyship only. Sir Trinian had recently instructed that the young man not be admitted to the property.

From the butler, we gleaned that Sir Trinian had first extended Wakelyn an invitation to dine in hopes of recruiting Wakelyn's support for the would-be politician's planned candidacy. Such endorsement had evidently not been forthcoming, Wakelyn's Irish family connections setting him at odds with Fledger's strong views on Irish nationalism. Sir Trinian had spoken opprobriously about the young lieutenant thereafter, using salty Naval language I shall not here record.

From the head gardener, we learned that Sir Trinian has recently issued a fiat that if Wakelyn attempted to enter the grounds, "the dogs should be set upon him", or that if he was discovered "he should be given a thorough thrashing and thrown out". From this, the staff had surmised that their master had learned of the dashing lieutenant's visit to their mistress. The orders had come via "Sir Trinian's man" Turpin, now appointed gamekeeper to the estate.

However, the country house at Ingatestone had formerly been the property of Sir Henry Drustan, father of Viola and Lucy – Viola being the given name of Mrs. William Sangfirth. It was the estate at which the girls had spent their childhood summers. Many of the staff remembered her

Ladyship from her tender years there and were more inclined to her part than that of her dour, domineering husband. I sensed a divide between the longer-term staff of the property and the few ex-Naval appointees imposed upon the household by the new master.

Given such sentiment, I wasn't surprised that Lieutenant Wakelyn had been able to pay visits to the lady of the manor despite any prohibitions by its Lord, or indeed that it took some time before Sir Trinian Fledger had become aware of them.

From Lady Lucy's personal maid we heard of the regular attendance of the young aviator after his initial dinner visits, of walks in the grounds with her mistress – "All proper, with me walking after as chaperone, mind" – of long correspondence that wasn't passed through Sir Trinian's inspection, [9] and of their meetings at a tea shop in Brentford. Nor was the girl surprised that Lucy Fledger had been willing to dare a balloon ride. "Mistress was always that daring – properly game for aught," she told us. "She were mad keen on trying that flying lark ever since she 'eard about what Lieutenant Wakelyn did. Try getting me up in one o' them contraptions, though. Brr!"

It seemed as though the balloonist's arrival that morning had been by appointment. Lady Lucy had ordered her warmer outdoor clothes to be made ready three days running, presumably warned that aerial ascents might get chilly. Holmes observed that today was the first day this week that wind and weather were favourable for a flight southwest from Great Baddow Field.

Uncertain of how long our licence to poke about might last before we were challenged, Holmes passed down into the grounds to find the place by the lake boathouse at which the balloon had been tethered.

We were just in time to see the grounds staff hauling out the three-foot long pitons that had been used to pin the craft to the ground. There had been twelve such spikes, eight of them hammered down equidistantly in a square some five yards across, with four more to the north, presumably to shore the craft against the prevailing southerly wind.

One mystery was solved when we discovered that the reparations were being undertaken at the direct command of Sir Trinian himself, who had dispatched one of his attendants with a hastily-scribbled note of hand that all should be set in order. I remarked to Holmes that it was curious that, discovering of his wife's injuries and of murder at his home, the man's first instinct had been to send a furious and urgent message to erase all traces on his property.

Between them, the gardeners and the police before them had done much to obscure the scene of Lady Lucy's rendezvous. The only other signs of the balloon's visit were a crushed patch of rough grass some four-feet-nine-inches square where the basket had rested, six ballast bags of sand that Inspector Brecknell had already removed, and a discarded bottle of Perrier-Jouët *brut* champagne. [10] Of the heavy mallet that must have driven the pitons in, of the ropes that had bound the craft in place, and of whatever other equipment had been required to hold Wakelyn's anchor or to launch it, there was no sign.

"There was a carriage, though," Holmes observed to me, indicating one set of tracks below the muddy mess caused by several other carriages and innumerable footprints of the subsequent investigation. "These prints here, bisected by all the others, crusted somewhat before being churned up in flakes by all these later marks. A four-wheeler gig with an axle-span of five-feet-eight, coupled to a pair of cobs, one of which kicks out with its left foreleg. I shall recognise that vehicle again if I see it."

"We heard that the intrepid lieutenant had a man following him on the ground," I recalled. "Avewick? Yes, Avewick."

"Indeed. It is customary to have some crew trailing the balloon, to assist with its landing and recovery. The pilot has limited choice as to direction or touchdown site and must rely upon others to retrieve him and his equipment. Discovering the presence of Avewick's carriage is most helpful."

"You will be able to trace it?"

Holmes snorted. "I am not a scent-hound, Doctor. No, it tells us that the servant and his vehicle were allowed access to the grounds via the gatehouse. The gate staff interpreted Sir Trinian's prohibitions very literally and obtusely. They didn't bar Wakelyn's man from entering, nor from driving in his rig."

There was one area behind the boathouse that had already been raked over and covered with sand. Even now, a gardener's boy was tipping a load of fine gravel over what had formerly been a small viewing circle with a fine vista over the tranquil ornamental lake. A stone bench that had served as a sitting point had been removed except for the bottom layer of pillar foundation.

"Where the dead man landed," I presumed.

"The evidence has been thoroughly wiped away," Holmes answered sourly. We attempted to discover what the workmen present might have seen when they were first called to the lakeside, perhaps when the death of Lt. Wakelyn had been initially discovered, but they had all been cautioned to silence on threat of losing their places.

Holmes made another check of the area, beating through the box bushes and long grasses that lined the lakeshore, and returned to me looking more satisfied. "There are two places obscured in the high shrubbery that all earlier search had omitted," he reported to me. "It is too early yet for me to determine which, if either, is relevant to the murder, but either are sites where a man might conceal himself, and indeed did. I see no need to call the ground-staff's attention to them."

"Certainly not to this fellow," I suggested. I indicated the path to the main house and the fellow striding down it. We were noticed at last.

A burly gamekeeper in rough tweeds stalked over to ask us who we were and what our business might be. Here, by his tattoos, was one of Captain Fledger's retired seamen, a fierce brute carrying a broken-open shotgun under one arm.

"Who are you and what are you up to?" he asked us abruptly.

"We are here to investigate the demise of Lieutenant Wakelyn, and the injuries to Lady Lucy Fledger," Holmes told him loftily. "You?"

The fellow bristled. "I'm Turpin, game warden. You are not policemen."

"You weren't on duty at the time of the incident?" Holmes surmised, reading some sign on the fellow's person invisible to me. "It wasn't your shift. Your work necessarily keeps you out late into the night, stalking the grounds – yesterday in the woodland to the east where there are ground-burrs and sedge grass. Your weapon is .45 calibre? You have others?"

"What's that to do with aught? You are trespassers!"

"Trespassers who came via the gatehouse and have talked to many of the staff? We are investigators, Mr. Turpin. At the moment our area of enquiry is the presence of firearms on the estate. I shall need a listing of them, and preferably a chance to inspect them to determine when last they were fired."

"You'll be on your way!"

"The quickest way to be rid of me is to show me what I wish to see."

"A murder has been committed, Mr. Turpin," I interjected. "That is an affront to all decent people. You were a Navy man? Surely you uphold the Queen's justice?"

"I am under instructions to keep out all busybodies and unauthorised persons."

Holmes noted that. "Then show me your firearms, answer my questions fully and clearly, and we shall be on our way."

Turpin was confounded, faced with a confident gentleman whose assumed authority daunted the usually-forceful warden. In the end he relented, taking the quickest evident path to shepherd Holmes and me to the gate.

It was indeed Turpin who had received and promulgated Sir Trinian's orders regarding Ward Wakelyn. Fledger had portrayed the young officer as a cad, a serial seducer of dubious moral character. A similar prohibition of access had been issued regarding Lt. Corcoran. Turpin was furious that

110

"toothless older staff" had turned a blind eye to Wakelyn's visit this morning. This is what happened when discipline in a household was lax. Changes would be made, see if they weren't.

"And now you must go," he told us, closing up his shotgun warningly. Perhaps he felt he had said too much. His employer might have preferred him to say nothing.

Holmes pressed his hands into his pockets and turned away. "Come, Watson. We have seen all we may in this sorry unpreserved crime site." To Turpin he said, "You have been of more help than we shall let your employer know. Good day."

With a tip of his hat, Holmes left the confounded warden and we departed Ingatestone.

The radial nature of the public transport system made it impossible for us to take a cross-country train to nearby Basildon, less than six miles away. Instead we engaged a local fellow to trot us there in his trap, and less than half-an-hour later we discovered the site of Lady Lucy's crash landing at Sumpter's Digestive Biscuit Works.

My impression of Basildon was of a pleasant rural landscape laid in old patchwork fields sewn with rye and peas, root vegetables and strawberries, sprawling out from a church and manor house. New rows of small terraces were beginning to spring up along the thoroughfares, signs that the London, Tilbury, and Southend Railway was making it possible for workmen to live cheaply outside the capital and commute to their labours, but the country was unspoiled and pleasant on a summer's early evening.

The so-called factory was hardly what a Londoner would recognise as such, being a mere three-storey brick shed beside the River Crouch, but it was a busy site compared to the languid and lazy farm acres that we had recently traversed. The factory foreman had evidently had enough interruptions to his production schedule that day, referring us off to a junior who didn't even bother to check our credentials. There had evidently been a number of sightseers wishing to view the crash site and the wrecked balloon.

I tipped the fellow and took the tour. We saw the damaged roof where the descending gondola had displaced some tiles and, below the wall, the downed remains of the basket and silk gas-bag. The tank of hydrogen that had fuelled the flight had evidently been exhausted, but had been taken away by the police just to be safe.

Holmes examined the remains. The wicker gondola hadn't survived its final landing intact, having cracked along one corner seam, but was still largely held together by the hemp ropes that bounded it. Of special interest to my friend were the long trailing lines that had now been neatly coiled beside the wreckage but which showed signs of mud, suggesting that they had trailed loose before that.

Holmes waved his magnifying lens over them and then at me. "This is telling, Watson. Come and bear witness. You see the ends of these cables. You will observe that they haven't been cut, nor frayed and snapped. That means that they have been loosed. The hitch-knots that held them to those pitons at Ingatestone were deliberately freed."

"Lady Lucy's attempts to control the craft couldn't have detached these from the ground."

"Indeed not. Some other actor released these ties, and in the correct manner."

"The murderer wanted the balloon to fly away?" I wondered. "But why? Some attempt to also kill Lucy Fledger?"

"Or to remove her from the scene, more likely. A marksman who can shoot a fellow who is at the full length of these ropes, five-hundred feet in the air, could presumably also place a second shot into another victim."

Another thought occurred to me. "Where was Avewick when all that happened? Was it not his duty to attend to matters on the ground? Would he not have seen the murder, Wakelyn's fall, and Lady Lucy swept away on a loosed balloon?"

"Those are good questions," Holmes approved.

He turned back to the wreckage. The basket had been decorated with purple and green sashes. A nameplate pronounced the vessel the *Letitia Sage*. A Fortnum and Mason's luncheon basket that was strapped to the interior of the wicker frame had been emptied out, but I saw that it had fitted compartments for well-wrapped delicacies to accompany the abandoned champagne bottle we had previously located.

From the junior official who had been made available to keep the curious from interfering with daily business, we learned that the downed balloon had also been packed with several comfortable cushions, blankets, a sunscreen, a telescope, a map case, and a hand-anchor to assist with emergency landings. Some of these items had been confiscated by Inspector Brecknell. Others had been taken as souvenirs by sightseers.

Holmes examined the wrecked machine with some interest. He traced his lens over some wrinkles on the cloth cladding at one side of the basket's rim, indicating to me a few traces of blood flecked on the purple swathing below. He indicated a few other barely-discernable splashes on the wicker weave on the opposite interior.

Holmes particularly showed me four places close together where the fabric covering the lip of the box had been crumpled. "Note the location where Lieutenant Wakelyn's hands convulsed on the rail, creasing the

112

fabric as he gripped hard. Observe the lack of major bloodstains on the interior of the vehicle. The victim perished looking over the side of the gondola here, leaning down as if to see something below."

"Leaning out to speak with someone?"

"Perhaps." Holmes sounded uncertain, though I could imagine such a conference turning sour and leading to a gunshot.

"Wasn't he shot in the forehead?" I remembered from our enquiries so far. "If he was facing outwards from the basket, then it could hardly have been a bullet fired by Lady Lucy."

"Geometry suggests not," my friend agreed. "And yet geometry sets other problems. A shot from the ground must have had a trajectory that avoided the large gas-bag above. Assuming Wakelyn was a man of average height such as yourself, Watson – we shall ascertain his dimensions when we inspect his body – and assuming he was standing upright at the side of the basket, then the bullet must have come from a significant distance away to achieve an angle that avoided the balloon itself. Yet such a lateral impact would have, should have, left significantly more splatter on both the interior of the vehicle and upon his passenger."

"Mrs. Sangfirth said nothing of that as part of her sister's ordeal. Nor was the state of Lucy Fledger's clothing remarked upon."

"Furthermore, if that was the aviator's position at the time of death, when the bullet impacted into his skull, I fail to see how he might have been propelled past the other occupant in a smallish box, to tumble over the opposite side."

"He must have fallen forward, then." It was the only other option. "But . . . wouldn't the bullet jerk him backwards?" Had Lady Lucy helped him over the side after all?

"There is also the question of the two patches of broken shrubbery beside the lake, well apart from each other. Given the site of Wakelyn's impact below, his position in the basket would determine from which location a shot might have been fired."

I regarded the sad broken remnant of the *Letitia Sage*. "Then what are we to make of this?"

"I see possibilities . . . but it would be an error to make anything of it at all yet, ahead of having all the evidence before us to compile adequately. That is the mistake of the amateur, to theorise ahead of the facts. We shall simply set what we have observed amongst our store of data and carry on until informed solutions suggest themselves, and then test those possibilities with further research."

The role of the consultant detective was more complex than I had first apprehended. I was pleased to trail along with Holmes to understand more of what it entailed.

We couldn't access Wakelyn's rooms at the Standard Hotel in Chelmsford. Evidently much of their contents had been cleared by the industrious Inspector Brecknell, and the chambers sealed at his command. Holmes was displeased at this block to his investigation and sent off a second telegram to the policeman urging a conference.

The day was lengthening. No point now in heading to the airfield to seek the man Avewick, or Wakelyn's friend Lt. Corcoran. Sir Trinian Fledger had forbidden access to his wife. The last witness we might find was a silent one, the mortal remains of the fallen aviator.

I know now from experience that had Ward Wakelyn's body been taken up to any of the hospital mortuaries in London, Holmes might have been welcomed by whatever pathologist had been appointed by the local police division. He would have greeted each doctor or orderly by name, aware of their skill and competence, and they would know him and respect his insights. However, the dead balloonist's body had been conveyed to Brentwood Cottage Hospital, [11] to be held until Inspector Brecknell cleared it to be passed on to Wakelyn's distant relatives for reverent disposal.

Hence Holmes and I found ourselves facing a truculent local porter with little understanding of medicine and an insistence on holding to the letter of his tasks. He refused us access to the tiny local hospital's mortuary basement until Holmes demonstrated his acuity.

"You have two choices," the severe, unremitting detective told the sour steward. "You may take this half-crown and allow us access to the mortal remains of Lt. Wakelyn now, and go forth to purchase more of the cheap whisky to which you are irredeemably addicted, or you may withhold access and tomorrow I shall draw your drinking habits and the slovenly service you therefore give to the Board of Trustees of this institution."

The man blanched and stammered denial, but Holmes was inexorable. "Even if the proof weren't written in your eyes and nose, in the fumbled buttons of your waistcoat and scratched pocket-watch fob, there are a dozen details of your workplace that betray your addiction. You have the choice before you: The half-oxford [12] or dismissal."

Faced with that implacable diagnostic stare and the silver coin, the stubborn night-porter quailed and granted us access. He melted away, presumably to fortify his nerves after encountering so disquieting a fellow as Sherlock Holmes.

The cottage hospital's cluttered basement room was little more than a cold-store. Wakelyn's was the only cadaver present. I drew back the sheet and we examined the stripped corpse.

"The clothing has been removed and the bloodstains and powder residue washed off," Holmes objected. "Inspector Brecknell may as well have danced over the cadaver and rolled it down a hill too! Still, we shall see what may be recovered."

The deceased wasn't a pleasant sight. The frontal skull was shattered at the forehead, with an exit wound through the parietal just above the lamboid suture, a little to the right side of the back of the head. The spray of blood and brain matter had been diligently cleaned off, leaving the entry and exit wounds rawly exposed. Death must have been instant.

Holmes frowned as he tested the wound, first with his magnifying glass and then with one of the probes lying to hand. "Interesting," he muttered.

I tried to find what fascinated him about the dead man's injuries, and then I saw it. "The shot penetrated above his eyes and exited through the back of his head. The gunman, or woman, must have been level with him. We might have expected some shot from the ground to pass instead through the crown."

Holmes nodded absently. He indicated the reddened flesh around the forehead. "You see these powder burns?"

Though any granular discharge had been sponged away, the stippled sear-marks were still evident. "Sure proof of a very close shot," I admitted. "The weapon must have been virtually pressed to his head. Then it *was* Lady Lucy who fired the gun."

"Much can still be read from the entry wound and tunnel of passage. A ball of .355 calibre, jacketed, rifled, did this damage."

I examined the remainder of the corpse. The broken limbs from a high fall had been straightened. It was evident from the split flesh that the lieutenant had landed left leg and hip first, for those were shattered. The lower abdomen and part of the chest cavity had burst, leaving a gory mess.

"From the lack of bruising around the trauma points on the body, the heart had already ceased pumping before he hit the ground," Holmes mentioned in passing, still taking measurements of the trauma insult to the skull. "Else there would have been a significantly greater sanguine effusion. I have no doubt that a gunshot was the cause of death, sustained while he was airborne, and that he was deceased before reaching the earth."

He requested that I venture upstairs into the hospital to enquire who had stripped and cleaned the body and to arrange an interview if possible. I should also ask where Wakelyn's aviation gear and other clothing had gone.

I diligently pursued his request, but by now it was seven in the evening. The day shift had gone home. Only a single night nurse maintained a watch upon the hospital's dozen beds, with a junior doctor on call at need in the adjoining apartment. Any further enquiry must await the day roster.

Holmes completed his investigations of the body and we retired to Baker Street. "There is naught else we can do until the morrow, Watson," he advised me. "You may go back to gnawing away at the Nottinghamshire Cricket Club."

The doings of the NCC and their strike had lost their capacity to arouse my ire. I found myself instead drawn into Holmes's investigation, to the plight of the yet-unseen Lady Lucy Fledger, coupled to the fierce and unpleasant Sir Trinian, and to what had really happened in the *Letitia Sage* that summer morning. Had there been some quarrel between the married woman and her illicit visitor? Had she used a weapon in self-defence and was now ashamed to say it? Might there be some stranger possibility, such as a denied lover's perverse aerial suicide?

I went to sleep with my thoughts buzzing with the case, and dreamed not of Afghanistan, but of balloons.

Holmes and I rose early the next morning. Fortified by one of Mrs. Hudson's excellent breakfasts, we set forth to the Great Baddow airfield of the Essex and East Anglia Balloon Club. There we hoped that Holmes's telegrams of yesterday might secure us access to Wakelyn's man Duncan Avewick, and to Lt. Corcoran.

Corcoran wasn't yet arrived when we made enquiries for him. The club secretary with whom Holmes had corresponded attested that the aviator wasn't known for his early starts and might be expected presently.

Avewick awaited us nervously in one of the sheds. He had evidently "bunked down" at the field overnight, since Wakelyn's rooms at the Standard had been denied him.

"I already told that inspector all that I saw," he protested. "I'm only 'ere 'cause I don't know what else to do."

Indeed, the fellow was now unemployed. He had done what he could to communicate with his former master's family, an uncle and aunt who still lived in Belfast, but had so far received no instructions regarding the dispositions they might wish to make for their nephew's body and estate.

"You are a naval man yourself," Holmes observed, evidently from the servant's posture, dress, and hands. "Did you ship with Lt. Wakelyn?"

"Yessir. We served together. So when my service was up and the Lieutenant was put on shore leave, 'e called me up to steward for 'im as 'is man."

"Did you also share a ship with Sir Trinian?"

116

"Captain Fledger? Oh yes, sir. A right sour martinet, and that was before 'e took a bit of scrap to the gut in that encounter with the Peruvians. We knew 'im on the old *Signal*, me and the Lieutenant and Lieutenant Corcoran."

It turned out that Corcoran and Wakelyn had both been "snot-faced ensigns" aboard *HMS Signal* at the time of Fledger's captaincy, advancing in rank only after his redeployment. The young junior officers found much in common. They were both of Irish descent, both adventurous spirits, and both enjoyed private if limited incomes that allowed them to indulge their sporting inclinations. Their friendship and their friendly rivalry had seemed only natural.

Avewick asserted that their "shoring" was a consequence of the general cutback in Royal Navy expenses, which had seen the number of sea berths reduced in line with government policy and spending, although I knew that such cutbacks had also allowed a certain weeding of less reliable and capable officers. Pressed further, Wakelyn's man admitted that several "japes" that the two adventurous young junior officers had committed might have had something to do with their lack of preferment. Evidently Lt. Corcoran had suspected a bad report from Fledger to have been added to their records.

"You were a witness to the events yesterday?" Holmes enquired of Avewick.

"No sir. I already told that Brecknell fellow, a dozen times. A score. But 'e just kept asking, again and again."

"How were you not there?" I wondered. "You had brought a carriage to follow the balloon, had you not?"

"Every time, sir, and a right merry chase that can be, I'll tell you. Balloons can go where roads don't, and keeping the *Letty* in sight can require some pretty sharp driving – aye, and navigation."

Holmes was pleased to confirm with the manservant the details he had read about Wakelyn's carriage. The actual vehicle was present in a stable on site, although the splenetic Inspector Brecknell had mauled it too.

"'E even tore up the upholstery, a-looking for a gun," Avewick complained. "'Did Lady Lucy toss me down the murder weapon and 'ave you set 'er flying off?' Indeed! Pah!"

Holmes indicated the still-muddy patches on the knees of the manservant's tweed overalls. "It was you who drove in the pitons to hold the *Letitia Sage* in place?"

"Yessir. And 'itched the guy-ropes with good knots, sir. But as for yesterday, I was under strict orders once the Lieutenant was up in the air with 'er Ladyship to make myself scarce for an 'our or so."

"What time would this be?" Holmes always likes times.

"We got the *Letty* up again, with the Lieutenant and the lady aboard, by about ten-forty, maybe just after," Avewick recounted. "The gondola was tethered – well tethered, sirs, whatever that inspector says, so it weren't going anywhere. Wind was no more than a light breeze from the nor'-nor'west, no threat of breaking the anchors, nor pulling the pins. So once the basket was up to full stretch, I did as I was told and took the cart off to water the 'orses."

"You were granted admittance to the estate."

"Well, they pretended not to see me, even while they was opening the gates."

"This was a planned visit."

"Aye, sir. In fact, the Lieutenant was just waiting for a clear day for it. Right frustrated 'e was about the weather not co-operating."

"What was his relationship with Lady Lucy?"

Avewick stiffened. "I don't think it proper for you to ask or me to answer. It's none of my business. I didn't see aught amiss."

Holmes moved on. "At what point did you return?"

"When I saw *Letty* was loose. 'Ard to miss, really, and the lady screaming over the side, and no sign of the Lieutenant. So I raced back to the mooring site and . . . well, there was the Lieutenant."

It was Avewick who had summoned other assistance, who had commanded the staff at Ingatestone to call the police. By then the balloon had passed out of view, so it was impossible for him to follow it. "I'm to go clear it up from where it crashed later today," he told us. "I doubt there'll be much to salvage, except maybe the silk."

Holmes sought further details. In what position was the corpse? Sprawled on his back, twisted with one leg bent backwards all wrong. Was there blood? Yes, but most of it had soaked into the ground. The head wound was quite obvious despite the falling injuries. Did he hear a gunshot? No, but he had been some distance away and might not have heard it anyway because of the altitude. Did he observe anyone else about? Not at the time, although there were grounds staff nearby when he called for aid.

"What shall you do, once your duties to your late employer are completed?" I asked him sympathetically.

"I'm not sure," the ex-sailor admitted. He looked uncomfortable. "Lt. Corcoran 'inted that 'e might take me on, but I don't know 'ow serious 'e was. If not, I'll just 'ave to look around."

"Your former master's friend may find you a place?" Holmes asked. "But you are unsure. Of the likelihood of the offer or whether you should accept it?"

118

"Bit of both," Avewick admitted. "Lt. Corcoran can be a bit . . . sharp – 'specially when 'e loses at a game or a bet."

It came out that Corcoran and Wakelyn were more rivals than friends, perhaps. They were certainly competitive with each other. Wakelyn had believed that Corcoran only took up ballooning because he had, seeking to overmatch his habitual sparring partner. The wagers between the two young men had sometimes been for large sums, other times for mere dares.

"I don't know 'ow comfortable I would be as 'is man," confessed Avewick. "I shall 'ave to think on it." His lips tightened, as of a fellow with a difficult problem ahead of him.

When Holmes was satisfied with his interview, he allowed Avewick to go about his duties.

"Do you think this Lieutenant Corcoran might have had reason to kill his friend?" I wondered to Holmes. "If there were gambling debts between them . . . ?"

"It is certain that any shot that killed Wakelyn from the ground must have come from a skilled marksman," Holmes allowed. "Possibly with military training."

"But the shot couldn't come from the ground," I reminded him. "The powder marks."

Holmes made no reply to that, but instead led us to see if the sporting Corcoran had yet roused himself and arrived at Great Baddow.

Corcoran was an amiable-looking young man with fashionable moustaches and a regrettable straw boater. He lifted his lid to us in salute as we found him by the shed where his own balloon was being prepared. "You must be the sleuth-hounds set on by the redoubtable Mrs. Sangfirth."

"So we must," Holmes agreed, taking in the fellow's flight jacket, riding breeches, thick boots, and padded gloves, and doubtless learning far more than I could of Corcoran's habits, character, and behaviour. "Thank you for consenting to speak with us."

"Well, you asked a lot more politely than that blustering policeman," he admitted. "Or those burly bullies that Sir Trinian sent round yesterday to find out what I might know."

"Sir Trinian was asking questions?" I interjected.

"Of a kind. His bruisers aren't really that well-suited for doing much more than frightening his tenants. I sent them off with a flea in their ears. Today I'm heading upwards, where I can't be disturbed by annoying henchmen." He gestured at the ballooning apparatus that was being assembled outside his hut. His vehicle was the *Lord Derby*.

"How much did you know about Lt. Wakelyn's plans to visit Lady Lucy Fledger?" Holmes began.

119

Corcoran gave us a sour grin. "Too much, old chaps. I had regular and detailed progress reports from Ward regarding the sweet Lucy. Very annoying."

"Progress reports?" I echoed.

"Yes. Regarding his progress, you know?" The rival aviator sighed and leaned in closer. "You are gentlemen of the world, unlike that clod-footed policeman with his ridiculous barrage of pompous enquiries. You understand how two young fellows might enjoy the frisson of a wager or two to pass the time and to spice up their days."

"And what has that to do with 'progress reports'?"

Corcoran sighed. "You haven't heard the name of Ward's balloon?"

"It was the *Letitia Sage*," I recalled.

"And that name means nothing to you?"

Holmes had probably not known it until yesterday, but he certainly knew it now. "Letitia Anne Sage was an actress in the 1770's who became known for being the first female to go aloft in a balloon, at the dawn of the age of flight. There was a certain scandal attached to it."

"Women were expected then to be rather meeker than they are today," I suggested.

Corcoran snorted. "That wasn't the scandal," he told me. "Mrs. Sage was to go aloft with the pioneer Italian aviator Vincenso Lunardi and his sponsor, one George Biggin. Great crowds appeared to watch the event, and on the second attempt the balloon went aloft, although Lunardi himself had to stay behind because of weight problems. Allegedly. As the gondola rose, the wind blew aside the curtains that shielded it, revealing the actress in a compromising position. She claimed that she had been thus to try and secure a loose part of the awning. The crowd drew lewder imputations." [13]

"And Lt. Wakelyn named his vessel after her," Holmes observed.

"Of course." The lieutenant leered unpleasantly. "Haven't you heard of the famous wager recorded in 1785 in the Brook's Club betting book? Five-hundred guineas between Lord Cholmondeley and Lord Derby that the latter couldn't have a woman at an altitude of one-thousand yards? There was much speculation in eighteenth-century society about the amorous possibilities of ballooning." [14]

I frowned. "Are you suggesting that a similar wager took place between you and Wakelyn regarding Lady Lucy Fledger, sir?"

"No need to be offended, old chap. You'd be surprised how excited the ladies get flying in the sky."

"I shall take offence as I wish, sir," I told him.

"As you please." The bounder sneered again.

"The wager was mutual, I deem," Holmes interrupted before I could thrash the fellow. "And Lt. Wakelyn's suit prospered the more."

"Perhaps. Or he bribed her staff for better access."

"Seduction as sport?" I snorted.

"And perhaps revenge," the arrant knave suggested. "Neither Ward or I had much reason to be fond of Captain Fledger – 'Sir Trinity' as he is now. He's a brute and a bully. Lucy would have been happier with either of us."

"Until your wager was won."

"And perhaps after. She is a beautiful and personable woman."

"You were unhappy that she preferred Wakelyn to yourself," Holmes observed. "You need not deny it. The digging of your nails into your palms as you speak tells all. Your bravado in attempting a decadent *savoir-faire* is somewhat shallow, Lt. Corcoran. What may have begun as an ill-favoured lark between you and your friend turned serious when you contracted genuine affection for the lady."

Corcoran breathed deeply. "Perhaps. I wasn't pleased that Ward so lightly regarded his liaison. I had come to . . . reconsider our wager."

"As you should," I hissed at him.

Holmes restrained me and addressed Corcoran. "You knew of Wakelyn's intent to take his balloon to Ingatestone yesterday. You must have done, for it had been his objective for two days running before that, thwarted by the weather. Did you expect that such a visit might be the occasion when he would win his wager?"

The scoundrel wouldn't meet our eyes. Perhaps he was regretting his earlier swaggering candour. "Possibly."

"Did you tell anyone of Wakelyn's intended visit? Perhaps to thwart him winning your inappropriate gamble?"

"Of course not. Why do you ask?"

"Because someone knew to be at Sir Trinian's estate with a firearm. A weapon that shot a .355 cartridge, unlike the heavier and shorter-range weapons a groundskeeper might have to hand to deal with vermin. Indeed, I have examined and eliminated the firearms available at Ingatestone."

"Lucy shot Ward! That loud policeman Brecknell confirmed it."

"I have yet to have a conversation with Inspector Brecknell," Holmes responded. "You are certain you didn't tip off some third party to Lt. Wakelyn's intent? Her sister or her husband?"

"I have said not!" He turned away.

Holmes called after him. "You weren't at Ingatestone yourself yesterday?" The fellow had betrayed motive and was a trained shot.

"I was aloft. I should be aloft now. I have to get my balloon in the air. I am too busy to answer any more of your questions. Or to suffer your ignorant judgements."

"I fear our judgements aren't so ignorant at that, Corcoran," Holmes told him sharply. "A man who has climbed the fence into a country estate and progressed through woodland filled with burrs is wont to leave traces – even threads of his clothing. When he conceals himself in cover to observe a moored balloon, he leaves bootmarks, the imprint where he laid his field glasses – just such binoculars as are stowed on your basket there, Lieutenant. And when he does all of that during a busy harvest-time when there are many people in the fields – "

The airman blanched. "If . . . if I was seen, then they can witness that I bore no rifle."

"So you were there!" I seized upon the admission. I was fairly certain that Holmes had found no such traces or witnesses. Nor had he actually claimed any.

"I went to prevent . . . to save Lucy from Ward Wakelyn. But I couldn't get past the gatehouse. I had to find a way over the woodland fence, and it took too long. By the time I arrived, they had already gone aloft."

Holmes gave no indication that he had tricked a confession from the cad. "Describe the location from which you tried to keep watch upon the balloon."

Corcoran frowned in doubt. "I thought you said you knew – ?"

"There were two positions where men hid in the bushes by the lake. At least one intruder intended murder. Which site did you occupy?"

Corcoran haltingly described the further of the two positions that Holmes had marked yesterday. My friend nodded as if that confirmed something. "What did you see through your field glasses?"

"Very little," Wakelyn's rival answered sourly. "Lucy and Wade were looking out at the view over the lake, the other side of the gondola. I could scarcely glimpse then because of the angle. I took my eyes off them for a moment to see if there was a better vantage point when I heard a shot fired. I recognised the sound at once. Looking back, I saw Wakelyn topple to the ground after Lucy killed him." He shuddered in reaction at the memory.

"You saw her fire?" I asked urgently.

"No. I told you, they were masked from my view by the basket, but I know from Inspector Brecknell's questions that – "

"Stick to what you witnessed," Holmes told him sharply. "What did you do then? Could you see where Wakelyn was landed?"

"No. I did see the *Letty* begin to shift position though. She had been loosed. That was when I acted – tried to act. I wanted to seize a rope and somehow tether the basket. But by the time I reached the site, the *Letty* had risen too high for me to reach and was being blown across the lake."

"Then you saw Wakelyn's remains."

Another shudder. "What was left of the poor b-----d. Then I realised that I had better get away sharpish, before I was found standing beside him. I had to get away."

"You had hitched your own balloon somewhere off the premises. Determining its location will be no difficulty. Such craft are hardly able to be concealed," Holmes considered. "Before you departed though, what else did you do?"

"What could I do? I simply left, as fast as I might without being seen."

"You are a material witness, sir," I informed the feckless airman. "You told nothing of what you saw to the officer of the law who questioned you. You have admitted your presence at the location of the crime."

"You can prove nothing!"

Holmes snorted. "I advise you to immediately contact the constabulary and make a full statement. If you seek to avoid liability for a larger transgression, you must make confession of the lesser. If you don't inform Brecknell of your involvement, then I must."

Corcoran swayed like a drunkard. "I will . . . I will consider it."

"You and your friend were both cads," I told him firmly. "I don't say he deserved murder, but the both of you require sound drubbings."

Thus that interview ended.

"Do you recall the forgery case I closed last February?" [15] Holmes asked me as we returned to Baker Street.

"I remember the mass of visitors that kept me out of our sitting room," I allowed. "I didn't know then that you were a detective."

"You will at least recall the effusive thanks of the banker Chesterlaine, whose career and fortune were saved by the exposure of the fakery?"

"The fellow who wouldn't stop shaking your hand?"

"The same. I have drawn upon that debt of gratitude to discover some confidential financial information about some of our present principals. I expect a letter to await us on our mantelpiece."

"In regard to the case before us?"

"Very much so."

"And then you might solve the murder?"

"My dear fellow, I solved it all some time ago. I am now merely verifying my conclusions."

Holmes had now interviewed, or at least encountered, all the principals in his investigation except the most significant one, the accused Lady Lucy herself. He therefore marshalled the support of Mrs. William

Sangfirth and her husband and leveraged his relationship with the senior staff of Barts to override Sir Trinian's prohibition of access.

By the time we had rendezvoused with the unfortunate invalid's sister and gained the appropriate administrative overrides, Inspector Brecknell had arrived at Lucy Fledger's sick room with a warrant of arrest for the murder of Lieutenant Wakelyn.

We therefore arrived at a scene of loud confrontation, with the red-faced former Naval captain rowing with the red-faced Essex police officer. Two uniformed constables drawn from the local station and a pair of Sir Trinian's burly enforcers watched in consternation as the law and the knight clashed.

Lt. Corcoran had also visited before us, evidently with some intention of throwing himself upon Lady Lucy's mercy and perhaps confessing his supposed affection. He too had encountered her husband, and from the split lip he now nursed had equally made acquaintance of the ex-Navy men in Sir Trinian's employ. His bloody countenance wasn't preventing him from adding his voice to the clamour.

Nor were matters assisted by a severe ward superintendent loudly demanding quiet since there were patients convalescing nearby.

Sir Trinian indicated that he gave not a d--- for them all, but that he wouldn't have his wife disturbed by any hayseed buffoon of a jumped-up policeman. Lady Lucy was sick, and when her physical wounds had sufficiently recovered, she would be removed to a place of long-term treatment for her mental defects.

Inspector Brecknell, a burly, portly officer with a country accent, indicated just as forcefully that he had a judge's warrant that he must serve, and that he expected unimpeded access to the murderess to achieve a statement of confession. Sir Trinian was thwarting the law and risked arrest and confinement if he didn't now step aside and allow police business to proceed.

Corcoran roared that he would save Lucy from the lot of them, no matter how many thugs were set on him. He loved her, he said, and there was nothing that could be done about it.

The superintendent indicated that the Board of Trustees would bring suit against all of them if they didn't immediately depart from disturbing the peace of the private recovery ward. He had summoned porters to effect such ejection, who would be here shortly.

Mr. Sangfirth, arriving with us in support of his spouse, decided that now was the time to express his affront at his brother-in-law's previous rudeness to her, and stepped in to add to the ruckus.

Into this chaos strode Holmes, tall, gaunt, controlled, and somehow without ever raising his voice, caught the attention of all present. "Good

124

afternoon, gentlemen. I am Sherlock Holmes, retained to solve this puzzle and uncover the truth of the murder. This I have now accomplished. I am ready to present my solutions."

Everyone was caught by surprise. Inspector Brecknell recovered first and blustered, "The murderess is known. It could only be Lucy Fledger. Her husband is delaying the law from its duty!"

"You are mistaken about Lady Lucy," Holmes told him. "A proper review of the evidence still available is unassailable."

"Who are you? Are you the fellow who keeps sending me those deuced telegrams?"

"If you had evinced the courtesy to reply to them," Holmes told him coolly, "you would already know."

"You again!" Sir Trinian recognised. "I already told you – "

Holmes held up his hand for silence, restraining Sir Trinian's expostulation. "A man has died. This matter mustn't descend into farce. If you would all be so good as to step aside with me, I believe that a few moments of discourse will resolve this problem. Given the stakes, I cannot call it trivial, but as an intellectual exercise, it lacks challenge. If all parties can refrain from shouting for a moment, I shall be glad to unfold the facts of the matter."

"What facts?" Brecknell rumbled, unhappy at being shorted.

Holmes penned in his audience. "The matter becomes plain when one considers the physical evidence on Ward Wakelyn's corpse and the traces on the grounds beside the lake."

"If Lucy killed Wade," Corcoran insisted, "then he must have deserved it."

The airman should have remained silent, for now he gained Holmes's attention. "Lt. Corcoran, you are caught in a lie. If you believe from Inspector Brecknell that Lucy Fledger shot Lt. Wakelyn, then it must have been with a handgun. Why then were you at pains to insist to Watson and myself earlier that any witness to your trespass could confirm that you didn't carry a rifle?"

"I – " The bounder was caught short.

This exchange puzzled the rest of the people gathered, and necessarily required a brief recap of Holmes's discovery of not one but two places of concealment near the balloon's moorings.

"You must have known that the shot came from the ground," I accused Corcoran. "Perhaps you could tell from the report of the bullet? Perhaps you even saw the murderer – if it wasn't you who did the deed."

"I tell you, I had no rifle!"

"I believe you," Holmes assured Corcoran. "There were no traces in the further of the two hides where a long-gun might have been stood, no butt-imprint on the soft soil."

"But you were there?" Mrs. Sangfirth demanded of the half-pay officer. "Why?"

"As I warned you when Lucy began to see Ward, he had bad intentions for her," Corcoran insisted.

"You told us earlier that you had sent no message about the liaison," I chided the bounder.

"Not that day. Weeks ago. How do you think Mrs. Sangfirth became aware of her sister's delusion?"

Mrs. Sangfirth conceded that she had received anonymous information of that kind which had first set her on to seek information from Lady Lucy about her infatuation.

"You said nothing to me, Corcoran," Sir Trinian growled.

"Nor ever would I," the junior officer snarled back. "Why give you more excuse to whip your wife?"

Inspector Brecknell stirred. "So you were there at the scene, at the time, and you lied to me about it," he said to Corcoran. I could see him mentally considering whether he might transfer the blame to the immoral aviator.

"I had no rifle. I couldn't have killed Ward!"

Holmes intervened. "Of course, you might have carried a revolver."

"What? Why . . . why would I?"

"You claim belated affection for Lady Lucy. Either you crept to spy upon her tryst to verify the outcome of your sordid wager, or else in hopes of preventing Wakelyn from taking advantage of her. If it was the latter, then you might well have brought your service weapon to support your endeavour."

"I didn't kill Ward. I swear it!"

"Did you not?" rumbled Brecknell.

Holmes again: "I fear he is innocent – of that. The facial injuries tell all." To the police inspector he said, "You have observed the cadaver? Probed the gunshot wounds in the skull?"

"Wounds?" I caught the plural.

"The killing shot that hit at range, and the second impact that left burn evidence at close quarters," Holmes prompted. "The passages of the two missiles were slightly different. Close and expert examination of the exit wounds will easily confirm it."

"But Holmes . . . when Wakelyn fell from the basket he was dead on impact with the ground." It came to me then. "A second head-shot must have been *post mortem*, point blank, only to disguise the killing shot that had come from range."

"Then it was *not* Lucy," Mrs. Sangfirth insisted. "The murderer wanted to make it seem as though only she might have done the deed! The second shot proves it!"

"Not precisely, Mrs. Sangfirth. The second shot was fired by *someone* who wished Lucy Fledger to be blamed for the killing."

Sir Trinian wasn't keeping up. "Make sense, man!"

Holmes sighed, trapped in a room full of people whose intellects couldn't keep up with his own, in a world of people similarly handicapped. "Corcoran claims great affection for Lady Lucy. He has even apparently come here to declare it – albeit only after he knew that Watson and I had uncovered his part in this plot. Suppose, however, that this affection was somewhat soured when she responded instead to the approaches of Lt. Wakelyn. Suppose Corcoran came yesterday to prevent the young couple from their balloon adventure."

"Corcoran was delayed," I recalled. "He said he 'arrived too late'."

"Too late to threaten or kill Wakelyn, if that was his intent. But not to fire a second shot in revenge into the dead man's skull, with the intent of disguising the first wound by the application of powder burns. Was that revenge on Lucy too, Lieutenant? Or had you hopes of saving her from accusation and still obtaining her affection?"

Had there not been a crowd of witnesses, I swear that Corcoran would have gone for Holmes then and there. Instead he was restrained by the strong hand of Inspector Brecknell on his collar. He decided to take his right to remain silent seriously and sealed his lips.

"What you claim about this second shot must be checked – verified, Mr. Holmes," Brecknell allowed. "It will all be gone into."

"There have been several deficiencies in your handling of the case so far," Holmes ticked him off imperiously. "You will find that a trawl of the lake near the boathouse shore will likely render you two firearms discarded under the water – the long rifle used for the murder and Corcoran's service revolver used to disguise the distance of the killing shot. Corcoran's balloon landing can be verified. The physical traces of concealment are still there in the bushes, undisturbed by your former search or by Sir Trinian's attempts to obfuscate matters."

"But if not Corcoran or the lady, then who killed the balloonist?" Brecknell demanded.

"Ah, for that we must return to the positional evidence. The nature of the first injury is telling. For Lieutenant Wakelyn to have been shot at that angle from the other hidden spot on the ground, and to have taken that insult, he had to be leaning forward quite significantly over the lip of the basket, bending at forty-five degrees or more. This is why the dead man toppled forward not backwards and why the shot missed the balloon sack."

"Leaning forward?" Brecknell tried to follow the reasoning.

Holmes went on. "You will likewise have noticed that Lady Lucy wasn't bespattered when the shot caught Wakelyn. Yet both she and Wakelyn were gripping the edge of the gondola tightly enough to crumple its covering material."

"There were four sets of marks," I recognised.

"Yes. Lady Lucy was below the level of the wicker basket, crouched out of sight with the Lieutenant behind her and leaning over her."

Sir Trinian's fists doubled. I feared for his blood pressure.

"That was why Corcoran couldn't see them in his field glasses," I surmised. "Wakelyn was leaning far out on the other side of the balloon and his passenger was . . . below the lip of the basket."

Everyone looked uncomfortable or wrathful, except Holmes who carried on calmly and dispassionately.

"The amorous balloonist was betrayed. His presence was expected. Arrangements had been made. A marksman with a long-rifle was in place. The shot came upwards from a prepared position, a hide set up in a known locale."

Another thought came to me. "For the position to be prepared, the assassin must have known not only that Lt. Wakelyn was going to be there that day, but exactly where his balloon would alight."

Holmes shot me a tight smile, as if I was a puppy who had finally learned a new trick.

"But the killer failed to get Lady Lucy too," I went on.

Holmes's pleased look faded to a mild despair. "The killer never intended to murder her. Yes, she was in cover below the lip of the basket, but wicker is hardly proof against .355 rounds. He might have peppered the whole gondola – or detonated the hydrogen sack above her, for that matter. No, he instead loosed the bonds that held the *Letitia Sage* in place, to remove a witness who might otherwise see him leave."

"Or she did it herself, seeking her getaway," Brecknell muttered, dissatisfied that he must divest himself of his original theory.

"She certainly couldn't cast herself loose," I argued. "Only an expert knotsman as well as a marksman might untie ropes hitched by a sailor. And the knots were on the ground, which she was not."

"Setting her flying away could still have killed her!" Mrs. Sangfirth objected bitterly.

"I don't think that the murderer considered how dangerous a gas balloon can be without a competent pilot," Holmes considered. "Else he would never have risked his fee by setting her adrift in that manner."

"His fee?" Sir Trinian repeated.

"The killer was paid?" Mrs. Sangfirth cried. She stared accusingly at her brother-in-law.

"An examination of Sir Trinian's correspondence and accounts may be interesting," Holmes owned. "In particular, letters and telegrams between Sir Trinian's London house and Club and Ingatestone yesterday, and perhaps with his man of business and attorney-at-law."

"My correspondence is a private matter!" Fledger thundered.

"But murder is a public affair," Holmes rejoined.

"You accuse me, sir? Before witnesses?"

"I accuse you of seeking profit from the murder, Sir Trinian," Holmes answered implacably. His calm surety was chilling. "The majority of your fortunes derive from your wife, and much of her holdings revert to her family on her death."

Mrs. Sangfirth nodded in acknowledgement of it. "He daren't divorce Lucy. It would ruin him financially as well as politically."

I began to understand. "However, if his wife were arraigned for homicide – discovered mentally incompetent to avoid the hangman, but confined for life in some asylum – "

"He retains her fortune and preserves some public sympathy," Brecknell reasoned with me.

"This is outrageous speculation!" the would-be MP insisted.

"There are arrangements already made for just such an incarceration," the ward superintendent interjected.

"And you sneered at me for fortune-hunting," Corcoran broke his silence, evidently raking up some ancient quarrel from their Naval service days.

"Committal to an institution is far preferable than an ongoing scandal," Holmes suggested. "Or a series of scandals. And Fledger doesn't like Irishmen."

"Keep talking. I shall see you in court for slander!" Sir Trinian threatened.

Holmes was uncowed. "I think you might regret that case, sir."

"This can all be examined," Brecknell insisted. "Examination of the runners and smallfolk at the airfield will determine whether Corcoran sent any of them racing to the post office to dispatch a telegram to warn Sir Trinian of Wakelyn's coming. For that matter, Sir Trinian's household staff and the post office nearest to his London address can confirm delivery of such an epistle."

Mrs. Sangfirth's brows rose at this new line of enquiry.

"Holmes," I reminded my friend, "you haven't yet said who the man that shot Wakelyn is."

"You know?" Corcoran gasped.

"Then who?" Brecknell demanded.

Holmes explained. "Once I ascertained the location from whence Corcoran had sought to spy, I knew that the other hide must be that of the killer. Given the ground traces left at the ambush site, the nature and identity of the assassin easily follows."

"What do you mean, sirrah?" demanded Lucy's choleric husband.

"I refer to the footprints and knee-prints of the rifle-wielder who crouched in cover, creeping to his prepared position in the bushes. Brecknell's hob-nailed constables fortunately failed to discover and trample upon any relevant evidence there. A match with the traces by the lakeside hide can be found on the boots and tweeds of the man Avewick."

Indeed, Holmes had seen both boots and clothing only yesterday. So had I.

"Avewick?" growled Brecknell, champing his bulldog jaws on a different bone. "Wakelyn's man?"

"The same, and a trained shot like his employer and his employer's friend. Apart from the evidence of the hide, prepared by one who knew the grounds from prior visitation, and with intelligence not only of the intended balloon jaunt but where it would alight, there is also the sequence of events. Avewick claimed to have heard no gunshot, supporting the idea that it must have taken place aloft in his absence. But Corcoran heard the first report, and himself caused the second to simulate a close-quarters murder, close to where Avewick claimed to be running to see how the *Letitia Sage* had come free of anchor."

I understood. "He couldn't but have heard that report if it had been fired by any other, and would only deny it if he held the weapon."

Mr. William Sangfirth spoke up for the first time. "So the batman Avewick committed the murder, and this man Corcoran tried to pin the thing upon my sister-in-law?"

"For pay," Inspector Brecknell seized upon the point. "He was set on."

Holmes passed across the letter from his former client banker. "I have confidential information that three days ago, Duncan Avewick deposited into his bank a substantial payment of five-hundred pounds."

That was a lot of money for a discharged non-commissioned Navy veteran to have at hand, representing perhaps ten years income at a manservant's pay rates.

"He was paid in advance?" I checked.

"Perhaps in part. You will note, Watson, that Avewick hasn't fled. Perhaps he is confident that he will not be identified, but I suspect he is also awaiting a second installment of his fee."

"You may also wish," Mrs. Sangfirth advised the Essex policeman, "to seek a judge's warrant to inspect the bank accounts of Sir Trinian Fledger for a withdrawal of five-hundred pounds."

"What?" Fledger exploded. "How dare you – !"

"I can hear you all out there, you know," Lady Lucy called from within her recovery room. "I am convalescent but not deaf. Nor am I so drugged as to be unable to follow what is being roared outside my door. Come in, all, and I shall tell you everything I know."

"I fell in love with Ward Wakelyn," the battered lady told us when we were all assembled round her bed. Sir Trinian's attempts to thwart us had been stifled by the constables and Barts porters who outnumbered and overawed his bravos. Nothing could now prevent her confession.

"He was a vile seducer!" Corcoran warned her.

"He came to seduce me. He had taken a juvenile and cruel bet with you, part mischief, part revenge. He confessed it, before we became lovers, because his feelings for me had changed. He told me the story of Letitia Ann Sage too, and I consented to facilitate him winning his wager with his rival."

"You faithless hussy!" Sir Trinian gargled, but was silenced by Brecknell.

"You left me lonely and ignored, Trinian!" the lady accused. "A man so cold and loveless, so calculating and ill-tempered! Why should I not go to a better? It isn't your junior officers only who can plan their revenges! So Ward became my lover after I knew all, and we were happy together. All those who wished us well knew it. And evidently one who didn't, who told Trinian here, from what Mr. Holmes says."

"Remain with your first-hand testimony," my friend advised her.

"Yesterday was the culmination of our adventure. You have already discerned the details of it. I was . . . preoccupied when Ward jerked, toppled forwards, and fell from the basket. I knew at once there had been a shot fired. I believed that I must stay low so as not to be likewise targeted."

"That was very sensible," I assured the lady.

"Then I felt the balloon shift," she went on. "It was unmoored and rose swiftly, crossing the lake and thence away. I had little idea how to control it. And Ward was dead."

She wiped away a tear and told us something of her frenzied flight and of the painful crash that ended it. Yet I adjudged that she had been lucky to escape with her life.

"And you," she gestured to Corcoran, "who had protested so sweetly of your affection, defaced poor Ward's corpse, to put the blame on me."

131

"I . . . I wasn't thinking right," the living Lieutenant stammered. "I was jealous, heart-sick, and stupid. Forgive me!"

"Never," the bereaved adventuress told him.

"The law has him now, your Ladyship," Brecknell promised, still clutching his prisoner.

The convalescent lady hadn't finished, She pointed to her husband, accusingly. "And then *he* . . . he – the bully, the brute, laid out his own revenges, his long-planned goal of seeing me shut away forever, leaving him with my fortune." She shivered. "And so he shall, for the law has given me to him, unless you can prove him the murderer behind the assassin."

"Not so," her sister cut in fiercely. "Even if no proof is found in his account books, if the manservant *cannot* name his patron and the inspector *cannot* bring a charge, there is enough in this matter to bring petition of divorce. You shall be unentangled of him, Lucy. I shall see to it."

"Just so," Mr. Sangfirth agreed, careful not to contradict so fierce a wife.

"You may all go to blazes!" Sir Trinian told us. He swivelled on his heel and marched out.

"Never fear," Inspector Brecknell announced. "The law shall pursue him. We have Corcoran. We shall take up Avewick. Be sure we shall get Sir Trinian in the end."

Holmes and I finished the case where we had started it, in Barts tearoom with Mrs. Sangfirth. Her husband wrote a cheque of hand to cover the detective's fees.

"You asked me to prove your sister's innocence," Holmes told his client. "I have done so. The murderer Avewick will certainly be convicted. He shall hang. The police will never prosecute Sir Trinian Fledger."

Mrs. Sangfirth accepted this. "So that the law can separate him from Lucy, I am content."

"Might we not investigate further, Holmes?" I appealed to my friend. "What the constabulary might not be able to prove, your acuity could penetrate."

"That is beyond my remit, my dear Doctor," he replied. "No amount of investigation could prove that the unpleasant Fledger was warned by Corcoran, or that he fee'd Avewick to kill Wakelyn. Because he did not."

Mrs. Sangfirth stopped stirring her tea. "Then who did?" she enquired quietly.

"Someone clever enough, I am sure, to not withdraw equivalent sums from a bank account to pay for a killing. Someone more sceptical of Wakelyn's reform than Lucy Fledger. Someone who cared enough about

132

the lady to see her delivered of cruel husband and unsuitable swain both. Or else who knew the benefits of Lucy's inheritance reverting if she perished. Which was it?"

The Sangfirths had both gone quiet.

"I would never wish Lucy harmed," Mrs. Sangfirth said at last. "I am sure that whosoever instructed the man Avewick wrote nothing of loosing the balloon's tethers. That at least he may be convinced to confirm."

"Certainly the remainder of his fee hasn't been paid," Holmes remarked. "Perhaps his sponsor is unsatisfied that Lucy Fledger was hurt by his actions?"

"I suppose that is possible."

"He cannot be blamed for the charges laid against your sister, though. That was her other suitor, the one who first alerted you to the threat that Wakelyn posed."

"I am grateful that you exposed the truth about that. Lt. Corcoran is an unhappy man."

"What might have happened had I not pointed to the evidence of the second wound?" Holmes wondered. "Or not discovered the traces of the assassin's hide? Would some other clue have appeared to point to Avewick? Perhaps some correspondence from him to his unknown hirer? Something to cast suspicion on Sir Trinian and see your sister exonerated, for certain."

"I would never wish Lucy harmed," Mrs. Sangfirth repeated. "I have always saved her, even from herself."

Mr. Sangfirth rose from his seat. "My wife has had a difficult two days," he declared. "If . . . if there is any additional expense for which you think I should be billed, Mr. Holmes – "

"I am satisfied that Lady Lucy is to be separated from her unpleasant spouse," my friend declared. "Whatever other secrets remain are matters of the conscience, incapable of proof in law. I require no other fee. I recommend future restraint." He rose from his seat. "I shall be keeping an eye on the wellbeing of Lucy Fledger."

Holmes folded away his payment inside his jacket. We bade the couple good day.

Once out in the sunshine, passing under King Henry VIII's gate onto Smithfield, [16] I turned to Holmes and asked, "Did I understand that right? About Wakelyn's murderers?"

"Without proof there is no case, Watson. My methods are effective, but require evidence. We cannot convict on faith alone."

"Sir Trinian is a regrettable fellow, and Wakelyn and Corcoran no better than they should be. Still . . . ."

"An imperfect world suffers imperfect justice. '*Though justice be thy plea consider this, that in the course of justice none of us should see salvation.*'" [17]

"Lucy Fledger has a future," I conceded. "There is that."

"There is that," Holmes agreed. We breathed in the summer and passed by St. Bartholomew the Great. "So come," he said at last. "You have indulged me, Watson. Instruct me on the bowler Alfred Shore."

NOTES

1. Eminent Victorian cricketer and rugby footballer Alfred Shaw (1842–1907) bowled the first ball in Test cricket and was the first to take five wickets in a Test innings. In 1881, he led a controversial and lengthy strike of Nottinghamshire Cricket Club professionals for formal contracts of employment that guaranteed benefits at the end of an agreed playing period. The national debate caused by the strike and its leadership by so prominent a cricketer highlighted the different ways that "gentlemen" players of private means and "other" players were treated by cricket clubs, including different accommodation and travel arrangements, whilst poorer players had no guarantee of any income, disability pay, or pension. It was one of the first "professional sportsman"' arguments.

2. For the majority of the Nineteenth Century, the "Irish Question" regarding home rule, or independence of Ireland from the United Kingdom, was a hot political topic, as well as the cause of violence and suppression. In February of 1881, the controversial Coercion Bill temporarily suspended *habeas corpus* so that those suspected of committing an offence in Ireland could be detained without trial.

3. That is, the senior politician appointed the charge of "home" (domestic) affairs, including oversight of the police forces of the United Kingdom. In 1881 this was the Right Honourable Sir William Harcourt K.C., M.P. for Derby, known as "The Great Gladiator", and notorious for his temper and bullying.

4. Codification of a husband's right (and responsibility) to discipline his wife, including the use of force, dates back at least to Romulus, founder of Rome, who reportedly asserted that women must "*conform themselves entirely to the temper of their husbands and the husbands to rule their wives as necessary and inseparable possessions.*" Friar Cherubino of Siena's fifteenth-century *Rules of Marriage* recommends, "*When you see your wife commit an offence, don't rush at her with insults and violent blows . . . Scold her sharply, bully and terrify her. And if this still doesn't work . . . take up a stick and beat her soundly, for it is better to punish the body and correct the soul than to damage the soul and spare the body . . . then readily beat her, not in rage but out of charity and concern for her soul, so that the beating will redound to your merit and her good.*" The Napoleonic Code regarded women as minors without legal and social privileges, and authorised husbands to beat their wives for acts of disobedience.

    Victorian British law, as summarised in Sir William Blackstone's seminal *Commentaries on the Laws of England* (1865), was that "*for as [the husband] is to answer for her misbehaviour, the law thought it reasonable to intrust him with this power of chastisement, in the same moderation that a man is allowed to correct his apprentices or children . . . this power of correction was contained within reasonable bounds . . .*". Blackstone then notes some examples of "*reasonable bounds*"' in civil law, "*allowing him for some misdemeanours, to beat his wife severely with scourges and cudgels . . . for others only moderate chastisement.*" He suggests that, as a measure of what might be reasonable, husbands could beat their wives with sticks which were no thicker than the husband's thumb – the infamous *"rule of thumb"* test that was applied thereafter in many British and American courts.

Established tort immunity made it almost impossible for a wife or her family to bring a legal case against a violent husband until well into the twentieth century. *In extremis* a wife might petition a court for a writ of *supplicavi*, which required her husband to post a bond in guarantee of not exceeding his legal right of chastisement. Marital rape didn't become a comprehensive criminal offence in the U.K. until the passing of the *Criminal Justice and Public Order Act* 1994, and is still legal in many places across the globe.

5.   As part of an attempted coup in Peru, rebels boarded and seized the Peruvian vessel *Huáscar* and began to harass merchant shipping. When British merchant ships were boarded, a Royal Navy detachment under Rear Admiral Algernon de Horsey was dispatched to address the outrage. There was an indecisive engagement at Pacocha on 29th May, 1877, notable only for the first use of torpedoes in Naval combat, but the rebels escaped under cover of darkness to surrender shortly after to Peruvian authorities.

6.   This was a standard Victorian response to *"moral degradation"* such as female infidelity or unmarried maternity. As late as the 1980's, there were still elderly women in Britain's mental health system who had been committed to asylums as young women or girls for "moral lapses" in the early years of the twentieth century and had become perm

For example of the Victorian practice, letters from Mr. Dutton Cook to journalist friend William Moy Thomas record testimony from Charles Dickens' widowed wife that after the Dickens's 1858 separation because of Charles's affair with the actress Ellen Ternan, *"he [Dickens] sought to have shut her [Mrs. Dickens] up in a lunatic asylum, poor thing! . . . But bad as the law is in regard to proof of insanity he couldn't quite wrest it to his purpose."*

Writing on the subject in *The Times Literary Supplement*, 22nd February, 2019, Professor John Bowen comments that, *"assertions about his wife's 'languor' and 'excitability' [were] sufficient basis to draw up a certificate of 'moral insanity'."*

7.   Since the 1857 *Matrimonial Clauses Act,* divorce no longer required an Act of Parliament (after a debate in the House of Commons), but still involved a lengthy and expensive public trial. The press were always ready to publish salacious details of the usually-private affairs from those relatively rare cases that were brought before the Bench. Until the *Matrimonial Causes Act* 1923, proven adultery alone was sufficient for a husband to divorce his wife, but a wife needed to bring additional charges such as cruelty, desertion, or incurable insanity to be awarded a dissolution.

8.   Telegram costs varied by company, but by the 1880's had largely standardised with the United Kingdom Telegraph Company's rates, with

which its rivals fiercely competed (to the extent of petitioning Parliament to have any UKTC cables that crossed railway lines removed, and sometimes even illegally cutting down UKTC telegraph wires). A twenty-word message cost one shilling within a hundred miles and two shillings beyond that, with costs multiplying in twenty-word blocks. In comparison, a second-class letter (usually for next-day delivery) was 1d, one-twelfth of the cost of a basic telegram. A shilling was the day rate for the poorest paid labourers, so sending telegrams was a luxury – or a necessary business expense.

9. Until the *Married Womens Property Acts* 1870, 1882, 1884, and 1893 weakened and finally dissolved the medieval common law of *coverture* – the principal that a married woman has no legal or financial existence outside her husband's authority – a husband enjoyed full disposal of his wife's property and control of and responsibility for her behaviour.

    Blackstone's *Commentaries on the Laws of England* summarised this thus: "*By marriage, the husband and wife are one person in law; that is, the very being or legal existence of the woman is suspended during the marriage, or at least is incorporated and consolidated into that of the husband; under whose wing, protection, and cover, she performs everything.*"

    In particular, custom and law both allowed and expected that a husband had access to his wife's ingoing and outgoing correspondence and might forbid either.

10. Tastes in champagne developed even during the years of Holmes's casework. The formerly popular sweet champagnes of the first half of Queen Victoria's reign were gradually replaced with *demi-sec* or half-dry brands. Russia, Scandinavia, and France were slow to adopt the sharper flavour, but the British palette preferred it. In 1843, Perrier-Jouët in the Épernay region of Champagne produced the first wine with no added sugar at all. Criticised at first for being "*severe and brute-like*", *brut* champagne gradually became the fashionable norm and most modern champagne is made this way. Had Watson discovered a bottle of champagne later in his life, he wouldn't have felt it necessary to record that it was *brut*.

    1881 was early for champagne to have become the default good-time drink of young romance, suggesting that the futurist Lt. Wakelyn was ahead of his society in more than the matter of aviation.

11. A Cottage Hospital was a humble rural medical establishment, often literally housed in some cottage or townhouse, with perhaps a dozen or twenty beds, mostly used for treatment of poorer locals. By the end of the nineteenth century, there were over three-hundred such institutions in Great Britain, mostly supported by charitable donation.

12. The colloquial term "half-oxford" for the silver half-crown coin worth two shillings and sixpence (half the value of the five shilling crown in a currency with twenty shillings to the pound) derives from its earlier nickname, the half-dollar, five shillings sterling then being the general exchange rate for a U.S. dollar. The application of rhyming slang changed "dollar" to "Oxford scholar", and may refer to some part of a student's annual fees at that

137

institution. The term is first recorded in literature in 1885, so Holmes is probably using the student slang from his own days as an actual Oxford scholar.

In any case, a two-and-six tip is a reasonable and substantial bribe in an era where sixpence was usually a suitable reward for service.

13. The historic flight took place on 29th June, 1875 from St. George's Field in London.

Mrs. Sage published her ballooning experiences the very next day (without confirmation of her founding the Mile High Club) in the pamphlet *A Letter, Addressed to a Female Friend, By Mrs. Sage, the First English Female Aerial Traveller*, priced at one shilling. From this account we learn that the balloon, lacking any pilot who had previously flown, was blown north-west for an hour-and-a-half before crashing near Harrow, causing damage to a farmer's field. Rescue came from the headmaster and boys of the famous public school of the town, who compensated the irate farmer and bore the slightly injured actress back to their quarters and tended to her whilst other help arrived.

14. The actual bet, made shortly before Mrs. Sage's memorable pioneering flight and preserved in the records of the gentleman's club, reads: *"Lord Cholmondeley has given two guineas to L[or]d Derby, to receive 500 G[uinea]s whenever his Lordship ------ a woman in a Balloon one-thousand yards from the Earth."*

"Cholmondeley" is, of course, pronounced "Chumley". Five-hundred guineas in 1785, meaning five-hundred pounds and five-hundred shillings (from a time when tax was a shilling to the pound, or five percent) would be in excess of £3-million pounds today. There is no account of whether the bet was won.

15. This case was mentioned in passing in *A Study in Scarlet* (1887).

16. This ornate main entrance to St. Bartholomew's Hospital was erected in 1702 to commemorate patron Henry VIII who had supported the foundation after his dissolution of the monasteries in 1536-1541. It is the only outdoor statue in London of the controversial monarch.

17. *The Merchant of Venice* Act 4, Scene 1.

The Pilkington Case
by Kevin Patrick McCann

We were pinned down. The position was hopeless, and I knew at that moment I was going to die. I could hear the screams of the wounded, the bullets buzzing past my ears like so many enraged wasps, and even though she was long dead, I called for my mother – screamed for her to come and save me. Somebody was calling back to me. I could hear my name, but the other words were muffled as if heard from the other side of a wall. They got louder though and finally I heard clearly –

"Watson! Watson! Wake up!"

I forced my eyes open – they felt glued shut – and saw Sherlock Holmes standing by my bedside, his face a mask of concern. "Wake up man. You're having a nightmare."

I sat up in bed and began, "I'm so sorry – " but the words seemed to clog my throat and I realised I was weeping. It was as if the gates of some castle keep finally gave before a battering ram and all the memories I'd tried so hard to hold at bay for almost a year now – it was coming up to the first anniversary of Maiwand – finally burst through. They overwhelmed me.

I was aware of a strong pair of hands holding my shoulders, of a woman's voice saying, "What's wrong with him, Mr. Holmes?" and a younger man I thought was Murray my old Orderly saying, "Here's the brandy!" My head was tilted back, and liquid poured in. I coughed, but some of it went down my throat. I heard the woman again saying, "Give him another dram, Mr. Holmes," and more liquid that this time I managed to swallow.

I felt my body going limp, felt my limbs grow heavy as I sank into darkness and merciful silence.

I woke up to the sight of Holmes sat in a chair by my bedside. "Ah, Watson," he said. "Back with us?"

I sat up, mouth so dry my lips were stuck to my teeth, and croaked, "Holmes, I'm so sorry . . . ."

He waved his hand in a vague gesture that said, *Think nothing of it*, and poured me a glass of water from the carafe on my bedside table. As I drank, he leaned forward and patted my arm. "I think . . . ." he began before lapsing into silence and then proceeding to fill his pipe. That done, he produced an envelope from his dressing gown pocket and handed it to me with, "What do you make of this?"

I examined the envelope. "Good quality paper, and addressed in an educated hand." I then took out a single sheet and read the following.

Dear Mr. Holmes,

> *I am reliably informed that you have a talent for explaining the seemingly inexplicable. Now the thing is this: I pride myself on being a rational man, not given to either superstition or imaginative flights of fancy, yet I appear to be the victim of a haunting. However, as I do not believe in ghosts or goblins, I feel sure there must be a rational explanation, just as I feel sure that you are the very man to discover it.*

> *I am not without means and can offer you a fee of five guineas a day as recompense for your services. If you are agreeable to my terms, please indicate by sending a telegram to Hoglin Grange, Wighton, Herefordshire.*

Yours sincerely,
Alexander Pilkington

"Your thoughts?"

"He sounds rather pompous, but five guineas a day . . . ." I didn't finish the sentence. I didn't have to.

Holmes rubbed his hands together happily. "There's money in this case if nothing else."

As he stood up to leave, I said, "There's just one thing. I know for a fact that you've turned down at least three cases that seemingly involved the supernatural, so why are you accepting this one?" I saw him hesitate and added, "I also note that this letter was posted three days ago. The postmark is for the seventh. It is now the tenth."

"It's the eleventh actually, but no matter. I'll go and see about breakfast."

So it was that later that morning I found myself sitting opposite to Holmes in a first-class compartment bound for the Midlands. We – or rather *I* – had enjoyed a good lunch in the buffet car, and it was during this time that Holmes explained why he'd taken the case. "As you know, I've no time for table turners, and I feel certain that this case will turn out to be a waste of time. However, it has two merits: It will give a much-needed boost to our flagging finances, and it will give you what I suspect is a much-needed holiday."

140

Our carriage was warm, the train was moving at a steady pace, and I began to feel that weightless detachment that always precedes sleep. Holmes was lost in a book, so we were observing what I'd come to call The Grand Silence. I remember just as I was nodding off having this fancy that each fence post we passed peered briefly in through our carriage window before snapping back to attention . . . and then of course I couldn't find Holmes anywhere . . . .

It was pitch dark and I was feeling my way along a rough stone wall. I was aware that I was not alone, but whatever was in there with me wasn't friendly. I could hear its rasping breath and a faint click-click as its claws came in contact with the floor. I was in a room with neither door nor windows and this thing was blindly groping for me, searching for me in the utter darkness. I knew if I stayed still, it would find me later and if I moved it would find me sooner. Get it over with! *I thought,* Get it over with! *And I tried to yell, but the words were too big and had jammed in my gullet, so I coughed like a cat with a furball and –*

"Watson! Wake up!" I unglued my eyes. Holmes was looming above me. "Wake up," he said gently. "Wake up."

I could feel the train slowing down and was aware of the conductor passing our carriage shouting, "Wighton. Next stop Wighton."

Holmes had telegraphed our client to expect us that afternoon, and we were met outside the station by a young man alone and palely loitering who introduced himself as Newman. He took our bags and led us to a small dog-cart with, "It's only a short drive, gentleman."

Holmes bared his top teeth in what he imagined was a friendly smile but said nothing until our journey was underway. For some reason he wanted details as to the domestic arrangements, and questioned Newman about the number of servants who lived in, what kind of a master Mr. Pilkington was, and so forth. I was far too busy enjoying the fresh country air to pay much attention, but what little I did listen to informed me that Newman and his sister Angela (who was the cook) were the only servants that lived in, though there was a gardener, one Turner by name, who came in daily, that Mr. Pilkington was as good a master as could be expected – an odd choice of words I thought – and that he and his sister had neither seen or heard anything unusual.

"So far as I know," he said, "there's never been any stories about the Grange. None that I've heard of anyway."

Hoglin Hall wasn't quite the ancient ivy-covered manor house I was expecting. It was comparatively small (only eight bedrooms), whitewashed, cruciform in shape, and reached by a short gravel-covered driveway that curved from a front gate, through a virtually treeless meadow edging a well-kept garden, and up to a nail-studded front door. As we climbed down from the dog-cart, the door opened and a short stout man stepped onto the porch. He was clean-shaven and completely bald with a bottom lip that protruded out from under his top one, so I was irresistibly reminded of a fractious baby. I also noted flakes of dry skin on his lapels and a small but noticeable patch at one corner of his mouth.

He made no further move towards us and instead barked, "Which one of you is Holmes?"

My friend and I exchanged a glance, and then he smiled broadly and said, "I am, and this is my colleague, Dr. Watson."

He responded with, "If you'd like to follow me, gentlemen, Newman will bring in your bags." Then, turning on his heel, he went back inside.

Holmes and I followed. We went through a short hallway and into a rather pleasant sitting room. There were three comfortable looking armchairs, a long sofa, and an oak table with a vase of flowers as its centrepiece. Holmes and I sat down and a few moments later a rather handsome young woman bustled in with a tea trolley. I saw that as well as tea, there was also what looked like ginger cake.

I saw at once the close resemblance between her and Newman, and so surmised that this was his sister. As she handed me a cup of tea I thanked her with the words, "This is very welcome!" and gave her a warm smile. She responded with the briefest of nods and, having served all three of us, left the room.

Holmes took a sip of his tea and then turned to our client. "Now Mr. Pilkington, perhaps you could give us a full account of your alleged haunting. Omit nothing, no matter how trivial."

Pilkington drained his teacup in two huge swigs and then began. "I've been living in this house since I was a child. My late father bought the place back in the forties with proceeds of his investments in the West Indies. I was an only child. My mother died in childbirth, along with a sister who didn't survive. My father died in sixty-nine, and I took over running the family business."

"Which is?"

Pilkington looked put out and said gruffly, "I was just coming to that. I own an iron foundry, and also have properties. I've lived here contentedly all my life, and nothing has ever happened to disturb that equilibrium until about six months ago. I began to feel a growing sense of unease. Nothing had happened, and yet I felt something had changed.

"I have an aversion to cats, so won't allow one in the house. I know they keep the rats down, but so does poison. I've forbidden the servants to feed any strays that wander onto the grounds. Just over a month ago, I went

142

up to bed a little later than usual. I'd been reading and was enjoying a rather excellent port. It was a still night and rather close. When I got upstairs, I saw my bedroom curtains were still open. I went to draw them and looked out onto the grounds and saw a huge cat. It was crouched by the undergrowth at the far end of the lawn. Its eyes looked huge, and even though it was some distance away, I could swear I could see an expression of utter hatred on its oddly human face."

"You mean," asked Holmes, "that it had a human face?"

"No, I mean that its face seemed fluid, and shifted between cat and human. And you may laugh, but the face seemed familiar. It reminded me of someone, I just can't remember who. Since then, things have got worse. I hear cats in the house. I see them out of the corner of my eye. I've been awakened twice now by the sound of one outside my bedroom door, scratching and yowling, yet when I've rung for Newman, he's found nothing."

I glanced across at Holmes and could see he was fighting a losing battle between his desire to laugh and the prospect of five much-needed guineas-a-day, so it was with some relief I heard him say, "What do you believe is happening?"

"I really don't know, which is why I sent for you. I don't believe in ghosts and goblins and things that go bump in the night, and yet . . . I want you to find out if I'm haunted, or simply going mad."

"My colleague is a medical man, and I have had some experience with the so-called supernatural already. Have no fear, Mr. Pilkington. Between us we'll solve your little mystery." Then Holmes stood up. "If you have no objection, I should like to examine the grounds. Watson, perhaps you might stay here and keep our client company"

By the time Holmes had been gone for well over an hour, I was beginning to tire of Mr. Pilkington. I'd observed him closely for any tell-tale signs of drug use – living with Holmes had already given me some expertise in that area – but saw none. What I saw instead was a man who insisted on going over all the events he'd already described in even more tedious detail. But I knew that it might help Holmes if I managed to find out more about his life. There was nothing to tell. The foundry was run by a manager, and the rents on what I had no doubt were slum properties were collected by an agent.

I observed his barely hidden nervousness, the scratching at his neck, and when he stretched his arm to reach for a third slice of cake, his sleeve rode up, I saw red lesions on his wrist.

At one point I got up and looked out of the window. I could see Holmes talking to a young man whom I took to be the gardener. To my

143

amazement, they seemed to be sharing a joke, and Holmes was actually laughing.

That evening as I was changing for dinner, there was a light knock on my bedroom door. It was Holmes, who came in and sat down on the edge of my bed.

"Well, what do you make of our Mr. Pilkington?"

I finished tying my tie. "I think the man is mildly delusional. He lives in this house alone, has no family or close friends, and from what I can gather from our conversation earlier, never visits the foundry he owns. He also used to sit on the Bench as a Magistrate, but no longer does even that. His life is dull and solitary. I think this is a case of an overactive imagination, combined with a desire for attention. The flaking patches of skin are most likely the product of nervous tension and a lack of exercise."

Holmes smiled broadly. "I think you could very well be right. I examined the undergrowth carefully and found no trace of cats. No paw prints, no feathered remains, and the gardener, Turner, tells me if ever one ventures near the house, he sees it off."

"So can I assume our stay will be a brief one?"

Holmes smiled again. "Perhaps, perhaps not. We are after all being paid handsomely for our time. Perhaps we should see it as a much-needed holiday."

That evening as we sat down to dinner, Newman came in wheeling a trolley on which were set three bowls of delicious-smelling soup. "I'm very sorry, sir, but I accidentally dropped the tureen and smashed it. I will of course replace it out of my own resources."

Pilkington scowled. "That was damn clumsy of you."

"Indeed, it was, sir. Vegetable broth?"

Pilkington nodded and Newman set a bowl down in front of him. Holmes declined, but I accepted mine gladly. It was quite delicious. We ate in silence. Pilkington was a noisy eater, and I found his slurping quite off-putting. I glanced across at Holmes, who raised an eyebrow in what was clearly a shared distaste. Our main course was roast beef with a Beaune to accompany, and finished off with apple pie and cream.

During the course of the meal, Pilkington's behaviour was odd to say the least. He seemed fascinated by the graining pattern of the table. I also saw (more than once) that he was muttering to himself, and at one point began giggling. I looked across the table to Holmes for guidance. He briefly shook his head and mouthed the word "*Observe.*"

I observed that Pilkington barely touched his wine and, when we adjourned for an after-dinner cigar, he drank down one glass of port but

144

didn't take a second. His conversation became increasingly difficult to follow. He would pause in mid-sentence, seem suddenly to be concentrating his gaze on something way off in the distance, and then when he did resume talking, it would be on an entirely different subject.

I sat as quietly and patiently as I could until the clock struck eleven, at which point, I claimed fatigue and said I was off to bed. Holmes indicated that he was going to sit up a while yet, no doubt to continue to observe our client. Personally, I felt there was little need. The man was clearly suffering from some form of psychosis which could only get worse if left untreated.

I was awakened from one of the best night's sleep I'd had in months by the sound of screaming. I sat up, lit my bedside candle, and consulted my watch. Two-seventeen. I got up immediately, pulled on my dressing gown, and was out on the landing in time to bump into Holmes. We were joined a few moments later by a night-attired and dishevelled Newman, who was carrying a lamp. We followed him down the landing and stopped outside the master's door. Pilkington's screams were still shrill and clear, so after one token knock with Holmes leading the way, we went in.

We found him crouched in a corner of the room, pointing at his crumpled bedsheets and screaming uncontrollably. Holmes gripped his forearms and shouted, "What is it man? What is it?"

At first Pilkington didn't respond, but as Holmes persisted, he gradually became quiet. He was shaking violently, with a long strand of drool hanging from one corner of his mouth. Holmes looked up at Newman. "Towel, face cloth, and water. Now please."

Newman nodded and left. As soon as he was gone Holmes said quietly, "Help me get him up on his feet and into that chair." It was easier said than done, but eventually we got Pilkington up and into a high-backed chair by the window. Newman returned carrying a bowl and ewer, accompanied by his sister who was carrying a fresh towel and facecloth. I couldn't fail to note that with her hair down she was an exceedingly handsome woman.

I became suddenly aware of Holmes's voice. "Watson, could you assist please?"

I took the proffered facecloth and wiped away what I now saw was a copious amount of sweat on Pilkington's face. That done, I checked his racing pulse. Holmes then repeated his question. At first Pilkington didn't appear to hear him, but then suddenly leaned back into his chair and said, "Faces. Dead faces." Then collapsed into uncontrolled weeping. We tried getting him to his feet, but it proved impossible, so eventually it was decided to fetch another chair and take turns in watching over him for the remainder of the night.

Newman offered to take the first watch, but Holmes declined his offer with, "That's quite all right. Doctor Watson and I will take it from here." As soon as Newman and his sister Angela had left us, Holmes turned to me. "Go and get some rest and I'll wake you in three hours."

Pilkington was still clearly agitated (though less so), and I felt uneasy about leaving Holmes alone. "Don't worry, Doctor," he said obviously reading my thoughts. "I feel sure the worst has passed, but I'll call you if needed."

Holmes didn't wake me three hours later. I woke myself and when I consulted my watch found it to be past nine. I got up and went straight to Pilkington's room. He was now in bed, was sleeping peacefully, and Holmes was still sat in the same chair, a window open behind him, puffing at his pipe.

"Ah," he said quietly as I came in. "Good morning."

"Holmes," I hissed, "you were to wake me hours ago!"

He smiled, stood up, stretched his long frame, and said, "Shall we adjourn to my room? If we leave both this and my door open, we should be able to hear Mr. Pilkington if he wakes."

"Well, what do you make of it all?" Holmes asked.

"It's clear to me," I began, "that our client is suffering from some form of dementia. I would recommend placing him in an institution where he would be well cared for." Holmes said nothing. Instead, he gave me one of his irritating half-smiles. "It's obvious," I went on. "Obvious, and it explains everything." Holmes continued looking at me in silence. "What other explanation could there be?"

He reached into his dressing gown pocket and produced a small screw-top jar which he tossed over to me. I unscrewed the lid and saw a white cream containing flecks of green, as well as red and yellow fragments of rose petals.

"I found it on Pilkington's bedside table. What we have here is a cold cream to which herbs have been added to make an ointment for his patches of dry skin. When applied, it soaks into the skin." He paused and smiled at me. "Not much of a holiday is it? Why don't you take the air while I ponder all this?"

I smiled back. "Breakfast first I think."

After doing full justice to my meal, I went outside to take the air. It was a hot morning and I ventured under the shade of the trees at the far end of the garden. My eye was caught by some shrubs I immediately recognised as belladonna, also known as deadly nightshade. The flowers were bell-shaped and a deep blue, but what really drew my eye were the berries. They were black and shone like burnished metal.

"Can I help you?" I spun round to see the gardener, Turner. "I wouldn't advise you to go eating them though. They's deadly nightshade, and well named too."

I frowned. "I know what they are. Why have you got them growing here? Wouldn't it be safer to get rid of them?"

"Master told me to leave 'em. They kill cats as well as us, but birds is immune."

He took a small clay pipe and a tobacco pouch out of his pocket. "Do you mind, sir?"

I shook my head. "Certainly not." I took out my own pipe and tobacco. "I'll join you if I may."

He nodded back and we both filled our respective pipes, lit them, and then shared a gradually easing and companionable silence.

"Your Master isn't overly fond of cats, is he?"

He looked around as if afraid of being overheard and then said, "Scared stiff of 'em."

I noted that his face was now flushed with obvious anger, so I asked, "You don't care for your employer?" He looked down and I realised that he saw me as a "toff" and not to be trusted, so I added – rather feebly – "Because I most certainly don't!"

"Likes and dislikes don't come into it, sir. I'm paid to take care of Mr. Pilkington's garden, not comment on his character."

I'd noticed his hands were shaking with barely suppressed emotion, so decided to try a different tactic. I'd seen Holmes on more than one occasion deliberately goad someone to the point where they let slip something in anger – something about which they would normally keep silent.

"Do you believe your Master is being haunted?"

"No," he replied, "Not unless it's by a guilty conscience!" He immediately reddened. "I'm sorry, sir. I spoke out of turn."

I lowered my voice, "What has he got to be guilty about?" Turner's face remained impassive so I added, "I'm a doctor trying to arrive at a correct diagnosis. I believe your master needs help – special help – and it would hasten proceedings if you tell me now everything you know."

The ghost of a smile flickered across his lips at this last, and I could see he was torn between his mistrust of me and his quiet delight at the thought of his master being declared insane.

"Well," he began, "there was the cat for one thing. That nightshade poisoned a little stray that my Angela – Miss Newman that is – was feeding

147

on the sly. I went to the Master and told him what had happened and asked permission to dig 'em up, but he wouldn't have it. Said it was only a d--- cat and it didn't matter."

"He showed no sign of regret?"

"No sir, but my old Dad, God Rest, always said you can lie to everyone but not to yourself. So maybe it's preyed on his mind."

Not on his, I thought, but certainly on yours. The fog was beginning to clear, so I pressed on, "You and Angela – "

"We have an understanding. I'm saving every penny I can, and we plan to marry soon."

"Will she stay on here as cook?"

"No sir, not if I have any say in the matter."

"Because of the cat, you mean."

I sensed an inner conflict in the man, so I stood silent and unmoving as he considered his response. Finally he hissed, "Not just that. Something much worse."

It was time to be silent and so waited. The silence grew, and I was about to say something to prompt him when he began.

"It's on account of her dad. He was a union man and he got sacked from the foundry when the manager found out. After that he was blacklisted – he couldn't pay his rent – so him and his wife and Angela and her brother John was evicted. Well, her dad couldn't get no work, so eventually his wife had to go on the Parish. John and Angela too, while their dad went on the tramp looking for work. Their dad was arrested for vagrancy and given twelve months hard labour. While he was inside his wife died, and John and Angela, only being nippers, was put in an orphanage. When their dad got out, the parish wouldn't let him see them on account of him being an ex-convict. In the end he went mad – drowned himself in the canal. And a few years later, along comes Mr. Pilkington, looking for a slavey and trainee footman who he can work for just their keep. That were just on a year ago."

I didn't know what to say, so eventually spluttered something along the lines of, "At least he took them out of the orphanage – "

"You don't understand, sir. See, the man who owned the foundry, the landlord, and the magistrate were all the same man: Mr. Pilkington, I mean, and you know – he didn't even recognise the name Newman when he picked John and Angela out the orphanage. He destroyed that man's family and it meant nothing to him." He paused, "Didn't even remember their dad enough to see the resemblance, even though Angela tells me her brother's the image of her dad."

I went back into the house and was joined in the sitting room by Holmes. I told him everything that Turner had said, ending with, ". . . so either our Mr. Pilkington is going mad as the result of a guilty conscience or – " And here I paused, but Holmes gave me an encouraging nod, so I went on. " – or he is being drugged in some way, and I begin to suspect that the drug in question is belladonna."

I glanced across at Holmes, who I was expecting to dismiss my theory, but all he said was, "Go on."

"Well," I continued, "it was the ointment that you found in Pilkington's bedroom gave me the notion. We both noticed it had plant matter mixed in with it. When I was a medical student, we had a number of lectures on toxicology and herbal medicine. As I recall, women in the Middle Ages who believed themselves to be witches smeared themselves with goose fat that had been mixed with belladonna. The mix was then absorbed through the pores and induced temporary madness – visions of demons and so forth. Now our client has a minor skin disorder and presumably rubs the ointment you found onto his skin on a daily basis, most likely last thing at night."

Holmes nodded and said, "And whom do you suspect?"

"Turner for one, and Newman for another. Turner could provide the belladonna, and Newman could mix it with the ointment."

Holmes smiled, "And dear sweet little Angela knows nothing about it?"

I reddened and said, reluctantly I admit, "She probably bought the face cream."

"And the motive?"

"Revenge for what he'd done. I believe it was their intention to drive Pilkington mad. Once they told Turner what had happened to their father, I've no doubt he agreed to help them. The fact that he and Angela have an 'understanding' will have encouraged them to confide in him. The hallucinogenic properties of belladonna aren't generally known – most people think it's simply a straightforward poison, Turner is a countryman, and it's likely he would know. Imagine it though: Every day, slaving for the man who destroyed your family, and him not even remembering."

Holmes nodded. "Not consciously perhaps, but it is possible that Newman's resemblance to his father might have been just enough to trigger some unconscious recollection. Hence the growing sense of unease. And what did you make of the broken soup tureen? You will have seen that when Newman wheeled in the trolley last evening, the two bowls intended for us were close together and Pilkington's stood slightly apart. During my walk yesterday, I observed some small mushrooms growing by the woodpile. I recognised them as psilocybin, a species of fungi that when ingested causes hallucinations. Turner does probably know about belladonna's hallucinogenic properties, as well as those of the mushrooms. I suspect some were added to our client's broth in order to push him right over the edge in front of witnesses, and convince us that he is insane.

"You do realise that if we go to the police with this, all three of them will receive hefty jail sentences, and if Pilkington dies of fright and the truth comes out, it will be the rope." He paused. Then: "We need to find a way of putting a stop to this before it's too late."

"Pilkington is still sleeping?"

"Yes, but I think it would be wise for one of us to stay by his bedside."

I stood up. "Very well. I'll take first watch and give the matter some thought."

It was (as Holmes would say) a three-pipe problem and, as I sat by the open window in Pilkington's room, a solution began to take shape in my mind. We had to find a way of letting all three of them realise we were on to them and put a stop to this before it was too late.

And by the time Holmes came up to relieve me, I knew what to do. I put my proposal to him, and he smiled broadly, saying, "Excellent – truly excellent!"

It was just at that point that Pilkington began to wake up. Holmes nodded to me and said quietly, "Go. I'll take care of things here."

I found Turner sitting on a garden roller. "I was just remembering," I began, "a case I heard about some years back. It seems a servant who hated his Master decided to frighten the man for a joke. He knew that belladonna in the right quantities can induce terrifying nightmares, so he mixed some juice from the berries in with the man's food. It had the desired effect, and so he continued. Unfortunately, on one occasion he overdid the amount, the Master died, and the servant was hung. Tragic really, as the whole thing began as a prank that got seriously out of hand."

Turner gave me a hard stare and said, "Why you tellin' me this . . . sir?"

"No reason in particular. Just your belladonna plants put me in mind of it."

I then turned on my heel and went back into the house.

Later that day, Holmes told Pilkington that he could find no evidence that his house was haunted. Then I gave him a thorough examination and told him he was clearly suffering from nervous tension, and this had been exacerbated by an allergic reaction to the ointment he was using. I gave him a bottle of pills which I told him were a far more effective treatment for his condition. In fact, they were nothing more than sugar tablets which I, like all doctors, know will work because the patient believes they will work.

Holmes and I stayed another three days ("just to be sure"), during which time our client experienced no further night terrors. Newman, his sister, and Turner (much to Pilkington's chagrin) all gave a week's notice. Turner explained that, "Me and Angela's getting married and John's coming to live with us."

Holmes and I enjoyed what had finally turned into a holiday. As we were taking our leave, Pilkington presented Holmes with twenty-five guineas in cash – less five that he held back to pay for our expenses there – and he presented twenty to Turner and Angela as a wedding present.

As I've observed elsewhere, Holmes's knowledge of toxicology and poisons was vast, and I found it hard to believe that he hadn't begun knowing what was going on as soon as he saw the belladonna. I realised that he had let me solve the case. On the train back to London, I asked him why.

He responded with, "Are you still troubled by nightmares?"

I shook my head. "No."

He smiled again. "That's why," he said.

The Adventure of the Disappointed Lover
by Arthur Hall

From the early days of our association, it had been apparent to me that my friend, Mr. Sherlock Holmes, held a great mistrust for the female sex. The initial cause of this was never revealed to me, but it is certain that a case that was put before him not long after we took up our rooms in Baker Street served to convince him of the correctness of his conclusion.

The affair began, at least for my friend and myself, at the instant we heard the startled cries of our landlady. There had hardly been an exchange of words between her and whomever had summoned her to answer the door before Holmes and I heard her surprised exclamation, followed by heavy footfalls upon the stairs. A moment later the door of our sitting room burst open to admit a dishevelled young man in a highly nervous state. He came to an instant halt at the sight of us, his hat crooked upon his head and his tie askew.

I lowered my newspaper and turned in my armchair, as did my friend.

"What is the meaning of this, sir?" I asked angrily.

He seemed to be quite breathless as our landlady appeared behind him in the doorway.

"Mr. Holmes, I am sorry. I couldn't prevent this gentleman from entering."

Holmes got to his feet, completely unruffled. "Don't concern yourself, Mrs. Hudson. I'll attend to this."

Before our visitor could speak, Holmes told the fellow that he hadn't requested tea or coffee before our landlady withdrew because it was obvious that something stronger was required. He then introduced us.

"Do take the basket chair, opposite Doctor Watson. Allow me to pour you a brandy, for I perceive that your nerves are agitated."

"Thank you, sir. I'm having great difficulty keeping down my anger. I fear that I might do some harm that will bring the law down on me."

Holmes handed him the glass. "Pray drink this, and when you've calmed yourself, take a moment to collect your thoughts. Then, when you're ready, you can tell us your name and something of the problem that has brought you to us today. There is no need to hurry."

Our visitor sat and accepted the glass gratefully. He gulped the harsh liquid down and made a visible effort to get to grips with the fury that possessed him.

"Thank you, gentlemen," he began when he had attained a more settled state. "I cannot apologise sufficiently for my entrance. I am emotional by nature – excessively so, I'm told – and I'm given to such unfortunate displays."

"An apology to us is unnecessary, but may be better directed to our landlady. I fear that she was rather upset."

"I will indeed express my regrets for my inexcusable conduct as I leave, be assured."

"Very well, then. Kindly state your case. Pray pay special attention to detail."

Holmes lowered his thin form into his armchair and regarded our visitor critically. The man, I would have said, appeared to be of twenty-six or twenty-seven years – about the same age as Holmes and myself – with unruly dark hair and eyes which, to my mind, held a surprising look of innocence. His morning suit, although visibly worn and creased, seemed to be of good quality.

"My name is Ebenezer Barlow," he informed us. "I'm a junior clerk at the establishment of Berryman's, the well-known manufacturers of artificial hearing appliances. I'm here because the woman I love is being cruelly treated, and I'm helpless to intervene."

"Who is this lady?" Holmes enquired. "Presumably she is suffering at the hands of her parents, or a sibling?"

Mr. Barlow let his ashamed glance fall to the carpet. "No, sir. Her name is Mrs. Martha Roper, and she is being mercilessly beaten by her own husband."

"Martha Roper?" I repeated. "Are you referring to the former actress?"

Our client nodded. "She left the stage five years ago. There was no further need for her to work, since her husband's sugar importing company has prospered a great deal."

"You must understand," Holmes said then, "that, as a consulting detective, I cannot interfere with what passes between a man and his wife. Depending on the circumstances, the law may even be on his side. Tell me, Mr. Barlow, does the lady know of your feelings for her? Have you actually met her face to face, or are your liaisons confined to your imagination only?"

Our visitor's mouth dropped open, and I saw that he was fighting against the rising of renewed anger.

"I am not mad, Mr. Holmes! Nor am I an impressionable schoolboy given to romantic daydreams. Mrs. Roper and I met at the reception that followed a wedding of a mutual friend, about two months ago. Even then I could see that her husband has little interest in her, since they hardly conversed and he seized the earliest opportunity to leave her to join a circle of local businessmen who were drinking excessively as they discussed their various occupations."

"Did she approach you, or did you seek her out when you perceived that she was neglected?"

Mr. Barlow hesitated. "I . . . I cannot remember. I just recall that I stood alone with a glass of wine in my hand, and the next moment I was in the company of an intelligent and beautiful woman."

"And she proceeded to tell you of her plight?"

"No, not at all. It was weeks later, during one of our subsequent meetings, that I enquired as to the extensive bruising which had swollen the side of her face. At first she explained that she had fallen while descending the stairs at their Mayfair home, but when I pressed her, she told me all."

Holmes rested his chin on his interlaced fingers. "Has she reported further injuries since?"

"Indeed she has. On one occasion she was limping noticeably as we met, and on another one of her eyes was bruised and half-closed, and her hearing was temporarily impaired from a heavy blow."

"This is monstrous!" I interjected. "If this is true, the man should be dragged into court."

Holmes gave me a disapproving glance, but I chose not to see it.

"Has she not consulted the official force about these assaults," he asked after a moment, "with a view to getting her husband cautioned, or even leading to the end of the marriage?"

Our visitor shook his head. "When I asked her that question she replied, as you did Mr. Holmes, that they wouldn't interfere with goings-on in the marital home. Also, her husband has friends among the higher ranks of the police who would inform him of her complaint, leading to further punishment."

"You have presented me with something of a dilemma," Holmes took a cigar from the coal scuttle, then apparently changed his mind and set it down on a side-table. "I cannot approve of the friendship you describe with a married lady, for it can lead only to trouble and heartbreak. On the other hand, it would lie heavily on my conscience if this lady were to suffer further punishment after you have brought the situation to my notice." He regarded our client with a cool stare. "What then, would you have me do?"

154

Mr. Barlow shifted uncomfortably in his chair, seemingly racked by an agony of indecision.

"Truly, I don't know what I was thinking of, by relating this to you. I must apologise again for occupying your time with such matters. What could I have expected? I really cannot conceive of any other way to assist Mrs. Roper, yet to think of her subjected so is unbearable to me."

For a few moments there was silence, except for faintly heard shouting in Baker Street as someone impatiently attempted to procure a hansom.

"We understand and appreciate your feelings," I said to our visitor, "but to intervene here would be to – "

"Perhaps," Holmes interrupted, "Watson and myself could call at the Mayfair house a little later. I can promise nothing, you understand, but I will attempt to convey to the husband that his actions are known and make him aware of the possible consequences."

For the first time, a strained smile spread across Mr. Barlow's face. His relief was evident.

"I cannot thank you enough. To know that I have at least caused something to be done in her defence is of comfort to me."

"In return," Holmes continued a little sternly, "I must ask for your word that you will make no attempt to see this lady until after I have spoken to both her and her husband."

"You have it! My word on it!"

My friend nodded. "Thank you, Mr. Barlow. If you will allow Doctor Watson to make a note of the lady's address and your own, and any other details that you may think relevant, I think we need not detain you beyond that."

We rose all three together, and I took up my notepad and pencil as Holmes crossed the room to stare from the window. I didn't hear him answer our client's farewell, and the front door had closed before he spoke.

"I don't expect this to be the most interesting of cases, Watson. On reflection, I would say that it is much nearer to your department than mine." He sighed heavily. "But I have undertaken to look into this, and so I must. Be so kind as to hand me my hat and coat and accompany me, if you have nothing better to do."

A surprise awaited us as the hansom delivered us to a quiet side-street in Mayfair. A police coach waited near the gate at the end of the long garden, while the driver conversed with a burly constable. Holmes introduced himself and the constable saluted uncertainly while the driver, no doubt in disapproval of unofficial agents, stared into the distance.

"What is happening here, Officer?" my friend enquired.

"I don't know if I should discuss police business, sir. Inspector Lestrade doesn't like too much to be known too quickly."

"Inspector Lestrade? He and I are acquainted. I have been of some small assistance to him from time to time."

The constable was suddenly more forthcoming. "Oh, in that case, sir, I can tell you. It's murder, for sure. There's blood all over the place. You'll find the inspector in the dining room, straight through the garden."

Holmes thanked the man and we took the path, edged by roses and clusters of dahlias, to the front door. The constable on duty there asked us our business, but Inspector Lestrade appeared in the doorway before any reply could be made.

"Mr. Sherlock Holmes, is it?" he enquired unnecessarily. "I don't think we need your skills here, sir. It's all straight forward enough as I see it. Someone was burgling the house when Mr. Roper disturbed them during the night. He's wearing his night-clothes, you see, so I saw that immediately. Anyway, the burglar stuck a knife in the poor man's heart and made off with a few things. I've got men all over the district looking out already, since there's been a number of robberies in the area lately."

"Very efficient and commendable, Inspector. Would you object to my examining the scene? If you have finished, of course."

Lestrade considered briefly. "I don't see that it would do any harm, Mr. Holmes. Mind you, I don't think you'll find anything either, but you've been a bit of help to Scotland Yard before now, so I suppose that's all right. I'll tell you what – I'll come with you."

Only I saw Holmes's irritated expression at this last remark as we entered the house. Lestrade led us down a short passage hung with portraits to a large airy room containing a sideboard and a long table and chairs. Near its centre lay a grey-haired man of average height in a nightshirt, with a kitchen knife protruding from his chest. Blood had spread down almost to his waist, indicating to me that death wasn't instantaneous.

Holmes immediately whipped out his lens to examine the body and the surrounding area. He then extended his search to the perimeter of the room. Many of the panes of the full-length window at the far end of the room had been broken, probably by the bronze statuette lying on the carpet nearby, to the extent that a man could have passed through. Two of the sideboard drawers were half-open, and their contents disturbed.

Holmes ceased his inspection suddenly, replacing his lens in his pocket and standing in a pose of contemplation. No more than a few moments passed, before he turned to the inspector.

"Call off your men, Lestrade. The murderer of Mr. Roper hasn't left this house."

"Did I miss something, Mr. Holmes?" The official detective was aghast. "Surely, the entrance and exit of the intruder is obvious."

Holmes declined to comment on the question, but explained his findings. "The hole in the window is certainly of a width to admit a man, but the glass fragments lie on the loose soil *outside*. This indicates, as does the fact that there are no footprints out there, embedding shards of glass in the earth or otherwise, that the window was smashed from within. Also," he wore a condescending smile for an instant, "it has surely occurred to you that the noise resulting from this would have woken the household well before entry could be gained."

Lestrade looked over his shoulder, I thought to ensure that no one else, particularly a constable, was in earshot. "Quite right, Mr. Holmes, I had of course taken that into consideration. In fact, I was about to confer with you about it. Would it be right then, do you think, to say that Mr. Roper was killed as a result of a burst of anger, or something like that?"

"Undoubtedly, for if it had been planned in advance, the scene would likely have been better prepared. There is no question in my mind that the decision to kill was taken on the spur of the moment."

"That was my conclusion, exactly."

"The household then, comprises of how many?" Holmes asked with a straight face.

"Three," said the little detective. "Apart from the murdered man, that is. Mrs. Roper of course. Then there is the butler, Danvers, and the maid, Carlotta. As you'd expect with a name like that, she's Spanish, and speaks no more than a few words of English. I'm told she understands it, though."

"Naturally, you will want to interview these immediately, Inspector. Perhaps you would allow Doctor Watson and myself to be present, in order to learn from your expertise and possibly to add a different point of view. In addition, Watson may be able to assist if Mrs. Roper or the maid are excessively distraught."

This time, Lestrade needed little time to consider. "Very well, gentlemen. I have asked them to remain in the parlour together for the time being, under the watchful eye of one of my constables." He covered the body with a sheet that someone, presumably an officer, had obtained and left for the purpose and strode over to the door to call out. "Newton, ask Mrs. Roper to step in here, if you please."

We heard a distant door open and close before she entered. I had once been enthralled by her in a performance at the Theatre Royal in Drury Lane, and the magnetism she had exuded then hadn't diminished. Even in these sad circumstances, and in distress, her personality seemed projected before she had uttered a word. She appeared more mature, it is true, but her hair had retained its gloss and her face much of its beauty. She was dressed in a simple dark-coloured frock, and her features were swollen by the tears of her grief.

"Please be seated, Mrs. Roper," Lestrade said in a kindly voice, which was unusual for him. "Let me first express our condolences at your loss. You will appreciate, I'm sure, that these gentlemen and I will need to ask you certain questions in order to discover who has done this terrible thing."

As she sat, tears welled up in her eyes, but she spoke bravely. "Don't spare my feelings, Inspector. This man must pay for his crime. Ask me whatever you wish."

"When did you first become aware that someone had entered your house?" Lestrade enquired after allowing a short while for her to compose herself.

"I awoke early and realised at once that my husband had gone downstairs. I heard movement, which I thought must be him since it was too early for the butler or maid to have risen. After a while, as he hadn't returned, I went to look for him. I found him as you see him now."

"You saw no one fleeing from the house, or attempting to hide within?"

Her expression was one of extreme melancholy as she shook her head. "There was only my poor dead husband. I cried out to raise the alarm, and Danvers came out of his room half-dressed. When he saw what had happened, he went to the local police station."

"Who promptly called us." Lestrade's bulldog-like face looked as confused as ever.

"If I may ask." Holmes looked at Mrs. Roper, and spoke in his most soothing voice, "about something that puzzles me. We have seen how the murderer apparently entered your premises, searched through your sideboard drawers, and disturbed your husband. This must have entailed considerable noise, which doubtlessly woke him. Did you, yourself, hear nothing, or either of your staff?"

She looked at him silently for what seemed to me a long time. Lestrade had made no introductions, so she probably assumed that we were his colleagues from Scotland Yard.

"As I indicated, I heard nothing," she said at length. "As for the butler and the maid, they will answer for themselves."

"Indeed they will," confirmed Lestrade. "I think that we have troubled you quite enough, Mrs. Roper. I will see the butler now."

She rose and left slowly, visibly distraught. Some minutes passed, during which Holmes remained impassive while Lestrade became increasingly impatient. I believe that he was about to utter some remark about having to wait while a servant condescended to join us when the door, which had been left ajar, opened fully. The man who entered, wearing butler's attire, was more elderly than I had imagined, tall but bent and darkly saturnine. His harsh demeanour was belied by his calm and gentle voice.

"Gentlemen, I cannot apologise enough. Earlier, I was sharpening the cutlery and, unfortunately, I was careless. I was obliged to bandage my hand," he indicated a dressing stained with a spreading spot of blood, "before I could present myself."

"If you wish," I said at once, "I could assist if the bleeding is profuse. I am a doctor."

"My thanks to you, sir, but it is nothing. It will heal in a day or two."

"Listen, my man," Lestrade interrupted then, "Danvers, is it?"

"It is, sir."

"Very well. I want you to tell me all that you know about this business. Don't try to lie or mislead me – we take a very dim view of that kind of thing at Scotland Yard."

"Yes, sir. I was alerted by Mrs. Roper's screams, and got to her as soon as I could. She was very upset of course, and instructed me to go to the local police station to report her husband's death."

"How did you get there so quickly? We were called in soon after."

"I have a bicycle, sir."

"I see. What happened then?"

"Sergeant Hollis came out here in a borrowed cart, but he didn't stay for long. He looked at Mr. Roper, said that this was a matter for his superiors to deal with, and left."

Lestrade scratched his head. "Did you return on your bicycle?"

"I did, sir."

"Then how did you occupy yourself from the time you got back to the house until my constable ordered you to remain in a room with the maid and under guard."

"I spent most of the time doing what I could for Mrs. Roper, which was very little, I'm afraid. I found a clean sheet which I gave to your man, since I knew it would be needed. I also acquainted the maid with the situation as best I could, which was difficult because the girl is foreign. I think she knows now, though."

"All right," Lestrade viewed the man suspiciously. "You can go, but I'll want to talk to you again, I don't doubt." He looked at my friend. "Do you have any questions for this man, Mr. Holmes?"

"Only two." He looked directly at Danvers. "Did you, at any time, approach the body?"

"No, sir."

"And how long have you been in Mr. Roper's employ?"

159

"Fifteen years, sir. I served with Mrs. Roper's family for many years previously, since she was a small child."

"You came with her, as it were, when she married?"

"That is correct, sir."

"Thank you, Danvers. That is all I need to ask."

"Be good enough to send in the maid," Lestrade said to the butler's retreating back.

Shortly after, the maid entered. She was far from the exotic beauty I had imagined, being short and rather narrow-faced. I saw at once that her most noticeable features were her shining black hair which she had tied with a ribbon, and her dark eyes which seemed to hold a resentful glitter.

Lestrade didn't invite her to sit, but launched immediately into his questioning.

"What can you tell us about this dreadful business, girl?"

It took her a moment to answer, perhaps to understand the question in a tongue that wasn't her own.

"I know nothing of killing, sir."

Now it was the inspector's turn for slowness, the girl's English was so heavily-accented.

"Oh, yes. Have you seen your master quarrel with anyone, or did you happen to see whoever broke in here?"

She shook her head vigorously. "I see nothing."

"You heard no raised voices, or noise of someone smashing their way through that window back there?"

"Nothing," she repeated. "Mr. Roper was a good man."

Lestrade was finding communication difficult and he fell silent, I thought, while he decided whether to continue.

"Senorita Carlotta, did you see anyone watching the house beforehand?" Holmes asked suddenly.

Again, the girl took some little time to reply. "I saw the man who is my mistress' friend."

"Yesterday?"

She shook her head again. "It was days ago. I saw no one after."

"Did this man enter the house?"

"No. I saw him walking past, two or three times. He was always looking at the windows." She hesitated, as if uncertain whether to elaborate. "I saw mistress wave to him once, when my master wasn't there."

"Thank you," Holmes said.

"You can return to your duties for now," Lestrade told her, evidently with some relief at not having to struggle to understand her further.

160

"Well, I don't know, Mr. Holmes," he confessed when the door had closed behind her. "It seems as if we have someone else to consider here. I shall have to speak again to Mrs. Roper of course, but the lady is too distressed at the moment. I will return to Scotland Yard, where I'll consider your observations also."

Holmes nodded. "Quite so, Inspector. It is always best, I find, to think at some length about the facts and their implications before reaching any conclusions. Doubtless our paths will cross again before long, but for now we will bid you good-day."

"Well, Watson, what do you make of this?" Our hansom was on its way back to Baker Street, and my friend had spent some time in contemplation.

"I have solved it," I answered triumphantly.

"Indeed?" His suppressed smile didn't deter me, for I knew that my theory was sound. "Pray explain."

"The butler, Danvers, explained his injured hand as the result of his carelessness while sharpening knives. I'm inclined to think that the damage was incurred by broken glass as he smashed the window to create the apparent means of escape."

Holmes raised his eyebrows. "Excellent! You go from strength to strength. All that you have said is correct, but I don't think that the butler is responsible for Mr. Roper's death. I watched his response to Lestrade's questions carefully, and they convinced me that there is no malice in the man, and certainly no reason for him to take the life of his master."

"Then I confess to being in the dark as to who actually killed Roper. The maid seems an unlikely prospect."

"Perhaps, but do remember that we know little about her. However, it has crossed my mind that our client may be more deeply connected to this affair than he would have us believe, whether or not he is aware of it."

"What then, is your intention now?"

Holmes adopted a thoughtful look and, as our cab turned into Baker Street, he replied briefly, "I suppose I shall have to keep an eye on Mr. Barlow for a day or two. However, that is for later. First, we'll partake of the fresh salmon which I know that Mrs. Hudson has procured for our luncheon."

We did indeed enjoy an excellent lunch. As soon as it was over, Holmes vanished into his room, to emerge a short while later in the guise of a rather well-dressed man-about-town.

"I think this will suffice," he remarked as he studied himself in the full-length mirror. "Kindly inform Mrs. Hudson that I'm likely to be a little late for dinner."

There my friend was mistaken, for he reappeared at the moment our landlady served the chicken pie. He quickly shed his disguise and in moments we were eating a steaming meal together.

"Were you successful in finding Mr. Barlow?" I enquired when the coffee pot was empty.

"There was no difficulty there. I simply waited near Berryman's until he left, and then followed him to his home in Highgate. It appears that he has kept his word to us in not attempting to approach Mrs. Roper – at least since this morning. He sent no telegram on his way home, and posted no letter – although, as this evening's newspapers are full of the incident, he must know of Mr. Roper's murder by now. I must return to Highgate this evening, tomorrow, and possibly the next day for, if our client is involved he will certainly wish to ensure that everything in Mayfair has turned out as he intended. I don't think he'll visit her otherwise, despite her apparent need for comfort, because this will not only bring their friendship into the open and cause a scandal for them both, but will, in the eyes of some, implicate him in the crime. Now a change of appearance again, I think, and I must spend the next few hours in a rather uninteresting fashion."

I saw little of him during the following day or two, except for some meals and his brief appearances in a variety of different guises. A plumber, a window-cleaner, a tramp, and a tinker all came and went until finally, once more at breakfast, he sat at the table restored to himself.

"Have you been successful in discovering our client's connection to Mr. Roper's death?" I asked when our meal was over.

"I have been successful in establishing that he had nothing to do with it. He has made no attempt to see Mrs. Roper, or to be anywhere near Mayfair, as far as I can tell. It was a false trail, but I am glad to discount it from our list of possibilities."

I nodded. "How then, will you proceed?"

We heard the doorbell ring, and were immediately still to listen. The caller spoke briefly to Mrs. Hudson, before we heard the door close and she returned to the kitchen. For once, this didn't concern us.

"I have an appointment," Holmes continued, "with Mr. Artemis Blunt. From him I'm expecting to learn the reason behind this crime, and possibly how to obtain a confession."

"But who is this Mr. Blunt, and who are you expecting to confess?"

"He is Mr. Roper's solicitor, who controls the estate. As for the murderer, I must admit that I was in no doubt from the beginning. The difficulty was in obtaining some sort of proof that would convince Lestrade, before his blundering obscured or ignored every indication."

"Who, then, is responsible?"

He consulted his pocket-watch. "You will find out very shortly. For now I must depart to avoid keeping Mr. Blunt waiting. I will however, leave you with one thought: What evidence did you see of our client's claim that Mr. Roper was a violent man?"

With that he was gone, and from the window I saw him board a passing cab. After a while I settled myself at the table to perform the long overdue task of bringing some of my medical notes up to date. Less than an hour had passed when the doorbell rang once more.

I strained my ears to listen, as I had seen Holmes do in order to prepare himself for a visitor, and heard a woman speak briefly to our landlady. The door closed and I heard footsteps on the stairs before Mrs. Hudson knocked and entered our sitting room.

"Doctor Watson," she began, "A lady downstairs is here to see Mr. Holmes. I have explained that he is out, but she insists on leaving a message. Will you see her?"

I put aside my pen. "Of course. Please show her in."

A moment later the lady entered. She was dressed completely in black, her bonnet and veil hiding much of her features, and she said at once that her message was brief. I introduced myself and offered her a chair.

"No, thank you, sir. I have little time. As you see, I am here to attend a funeral. I must return to Norwich on the afternoon train."

"Very well. What is it that you would like me to tell Mr. Holmes?"

"Simply this. I am Miss Jane Roper. My brother, Mr. Andrew Roper, was a good man. Whatever you are told to the contrary, I beg you to disbelieve. Please don't proceed with your investigation deceived by anyone who would tell you otherwise. That is all I have to say, sir."

"Yes, but – " I said no more, for I was speaking to an empty room. She had fled abruptly, and I heard her descend the stairs and close the door.

For some time after, I wondered how that distressed and tearful lady could know that Holmes was concerned with the affair of her brother's death, and concluded that she had probably visited Scotland Yard and learned it from Lestrade. I wondered also whether she was acquainted with Mr. Ebenezer Barlow, our client, or if Mrs. Roper had remarked about her late husband's ill-treatment.

It was almost time for luncheon when Holmes reappeared, and he listened intently as I described Miss Roper's visit.

"You may take the lady at her word, Watson," he said as I concluded my account. "As I suspected, and Mr. Blunt confirmed, Mr. Roper wasn't known to be violent."

"Then what of our client's fears?"

"Unfounded, all of them. I hope to demonstrate this later."

"The visit to Mr. Blunt was satisfactory then?"

"Very." He hung up his coat and we repaired to our armchairs to await Mrs. Hudson. "He confirmed much that I had surmised. Mr. Barlow will be distressed to learn that Mrs. Roper has no affection for him, nor any use either, save to rid her of her husband."

"Our client is the killer, after all?"

Holmes shook his head, smiling at my lack of comprehension. "Not so, but that was Mrs. Roper's reason for allowing a friendship between them to develop. I believe that she was making him progressively anxious for her by means of her accounts of ill-treatment, intending to do so until he felt bound to act in her defence. His feelings for her would have dulled the enormity of taking her husband's life, had it come to that."

"Did he refuse then, necessitating her use of another?"

"There was no need. According to Mr. Blunt, Mr. and Mrs. Roper's marriage had been faltering for some time, despite the image they projected in public. Mrs. Roper made several attempts to induce her husband to sign a large part of his fortune over to her, but to no avail. When she met Mr. Barlow, she apparently saw her opportunity to take it all, since it would revert to her on her husband's death, but she needed time to convince our client gradually. Then an event occurred which compelled her to act immediately. You see, Watson, Mr. Roper had a previous marriage. He was in fact a widower when he met his current wife. From that first marriage came a son, Anthony, from whom his father has been estranged for years, until a chance meeting in a London club saw them restored to an amicable state."

The situation was now clear to me. "Whereupon Mr. Roper intended to change his will in favour of the son, leaving his present wife with much less?"

"Precisely. He had intended to do this the day after Mrs. Roper put a knife in his heart, which is why she acted so quickly. He made a fatal error by informing her. She would still, on his natural death, have inherited a substantial sum but, as in many situations that I've encountered, that wasn't enough – she wanted it all. The timing of the murder made Mr. Blunt suspicious, and so it was easy to persuade him to assist in obtaining a confession, which he and I will do this afternoon. As I've indicated, it was obvious from the first: You will recall our client's description of Mrs. Roper's facial injuries, of which there was no sign when we met her."

"Her skill with theatrical face-paint, from her previous profession."

"Exactly."

"But Danvers, the butler – was he a party to this?"

"Yes, but I doubt if he will suffer for it. The man has loved her since her childhood – you will recall that I questioned him about the length of

164

his association with the family – and it may well be that she somehow presented him with another explanation of what had occurred."

"But for such a great actress, admired by many, to have done such a thing – I would never have believed it."

"That, if I may say so, has also been obvious to me from the outset. As I have stated before now, there is no place for sentiment or preconceived impressions in the methods of the ideal reasoner. Now, the only missing piece for the case to be complete is the lady's confession." He inclined his head, listening. "Ah! But I believe our luncheon is on its way. Let us take our seats and see what our good landlady has prepared for us."

He could hardly contain his impatience to begin upon his plans for the afternoon, although it was with some surprise that I watched him consume his meal, since I had become used to him eating only a small amount or leaving his food entirely untouched.

No sooner had he replaced his teacup in its saucer than he sprang to his feet.

"I regret that I cannot ask you to accompany me on this occasion. However, you have my solemn word that I will relate the occurrences of this afternoon in their entirety to you, upon my return."

With that he withdrew to his room, emerging in a remarkably short time as a rather prim young man in the subdued dress of the legal profession.

"Mr. Blunt requires a clerk to be present to witness his dealings with Mrs. Roper," he explained. "He and I have come to an agreement as to what she should be told."

With that, he picked up a battered briefcase and left without another word. I confess to feeling disconcerted at my exclusion, but I couldn't see how I could have been of service in Holmes's plan. I resumed my study of my medical notes but found concentration difficult, so that I took up my book after a while to lose myself in the exploits of the great explorers in the days of sail. After a chapter or two I became drowsy but shook myself awake, as I had heard the door close loudly before quick footsteps sounded upon the stairs.

"Ah, there you are!" Holmes said as he entered. "Did I not say that I would be away for no more than a short time?"

"It all went well, then?"

"Exactly as I anticipated. Pray contain your impatience until I have resumed my normal appearance, and I will tell you all."

He vanished into his room abruptly, and I heard water splashing as I retrieved my notebook. Shortly after he reappeared, and I poured us each a glass of brandy as we seated ourselves.

Holmes consulted his pocket-watch. "I see that there remains almost an hour before dinner. Ample time, I should think, for me to acquaint you with all that has transpired." He took a sip from his glass, before replacing it on a side-table.

"Mr. Blunt and I discussed our intentions further during our journey to Mayfair," he began. "By the time we arrived he was quite clear as to the part he should play, and I must say that he did so faultlessly. We were admitted by the Spanish maid, Carlotta, and shown into the room where Mr. Roper died. I observed that the window had been repaired. Mrs. Roper appeared in high spirits, apparently having convinced herself that her role as a grieving widow could be dispensed with. I believe that she had deluded herself that her crime was undiscovered, possibly encouraged by Lestrade's erroneous conclusions."

"The inspector has made further investigations then?"

"Apparently he could make nothing of my recommendation that he search for the intruder within the house and decided to concentrate his efforts externally. At Mr. Blunt's suggestion, and after he had introduced me as his clerk, we sat around the table and he produced documents relevant to the estate. I watched as the expression of expectation grew on Mrs. Roper's face. Seldom have I seen more pitiless greed than that which filled her eyes. When the solicitor reached the false clause that I had convinced him to mention, stating that her husband had already altered the beneficiary of his entire wealth, her face froze as if encased in ice. All animation drained from it and she exhibited symptoms of profound shock.

"'Anthony?' she whispered. 'No, not him! Why did I not act sooner?' She jumped to her feet and hammered on the table with her fists, terrifying Mr. Blunt and making it apparent that she had lost all reason. Eventually she became calmer, and I asked her when she had decided to kill her husband and she replied that it hadn't been her original intention. She had, as I suspected, begun to prepare Mr. Barlow for that role. 'What would I want with a penniless clerk otherwise?' she enquired of herself. I saw then that she was probably unaware that she was confessing, but she surprised me by fixing me with a hateful stare and saying that she knew that she had met me before."

"She must be a most perceptive woman. I would not have recognised you."

"I can only suppose that it was a similarity in the voice I had adopted. Playing so many parts on the stage, she would be sensitive to such things."

I nodded. "Doubtless. Did you then send Danvers to the local police station?"

"It was unnecessary. I had telegraphed Lestrade earlier, and he arrived at precisely the right time accompanied by two constables. Mrs.

Roper, I fear, will spend some time in the cells at Scotland Yard before the trial. I have no doubts that her performance then will equal any of those enacted upon the stage, but let us hope that the jury is composed of level-headed men." He sat back in his chair and inhaled deeply. "But Watson, today is one of those rare times when my appetite has become considerable. Let us finish our brandy, before doing justice to the chicken that I smell as the aroma increases with Mrs. Hudson's approach."

The Case of the
Impressionist Painting
by Tim Symonds

Chapter I: A Prospective Client Arrives

I was by myself at 221b Baker Street. Sherlock Holmes had yet to return from a clandestine visit to the Royal Albert Dock, this time disguised as a tramp. Those were early days in his career when he was still building his reputation, before the cases arrived which were to make him the most famous private consulting detective in Europe. I wondered whether to remind our landlady, Mrs. Hudson, of her recent generous offer to pull a bottle of Hochheim's *Königin Victoriaberg* from her "wine cellar" (the coal room), gifted to her twenty years earlier. She would, she had said, uncork the bottle in a few days' time when Holmes and I celebrated our first year as co-lodgers.

Mrs. Hudson came up the stairs. "There's a gentleman at the front door," she said, handing me a calling card. "He insists on seeing Mr. Holmes." The card read *"William Henry Perrin, Fellow Royal Chemistry Society, Proprietor Perrin Dyeworks"*. I asked her to see him up. A man of a pleasant but troubled demeanour entered the sitting room. Before I could introduce myself, he grasped my hand and exclaimed, "Mr. Holmes, it's extremely good of you to – "

I interrupted, smiling. "I'm Dr. John Watson, Mr. Holmes's flatmate. He'll be returning shortly. Meantime," I added, "do sit down and tell me the purpose of your visit."

He looked reticent. I said, "You may be absolutely frank with me, Mr. Perrin." I took his valise and invited him to hang his tailored velvet opera cape on the coat rack. The lavender silk lining matched the colour of his bow tie.

We settled into the comfortable chairs by the fireside. My visitor offered a heartfelt, "Dr. Watson, you invite me to be frank. I have no need to tell you my presence here indicates my situation is bleak. I presume we can agree that being blackmailed is a desperate situation! Blackmailed by a fiend!"

He then related how some twenty-five years earlier, he'd been a student of chemistry at the Royal College where he made a chance discovery: From a derivative of coal-tar, he produced the most wonderful

168

light-purple dye now universally known as "*mauveine*", or Florentine Mallow. The colour became the height of fashion among the *beau monde* of Paris and London – so much so that the frenzy became known as "mauveine measles". Queen Victoria appeared at the 1862 International Exhibition wearing a silk dress coloured by his dye. In France, Empress Eugenie, wife of Napoleon III, and her ladies-in-waiting wore mauveine-dyed dresses to state functions.

Restless, he stood up and crossed to the windows and peered down at the street. "That opera cape, Dr. Watson," he clarified over his shoulder. "I'm a man of considerable wealth, but not a patron of the Arts. I had it specially made for my visit here today, aiming to throw anyone off the scent. I booked a seat for the matinee at the Opera House and walked straight through the building to the stage entrance at the far side, to be certain no one was following me."

He bent down to withdraw a thin sheaf of documents from the valise.

"Being able to speak freely after three weeks during which I have trusted no one will be a considerable relief. You are a doctor of – ?"

"Medicine," I replied. "Until last year, I was a surgeon attached to the 66th Berkshire Regiment of Foot in Afghanistan."

He nodded and began to describe the parlous situation which had brought him to our Baker Street sitting room.

"It started when I received this telegraph . . . ." In capital letters it read:

IN MEMORIAM R.M. OBIIT MDCCCLXXXI

"*R.M.?*" I enquired.

"Robert Miller. I was surprised to receive this," he continued, "because I wasn't aware that Robert had died."

He explained Miller had been the owner of a large dye works in Mill Street, Perth, a remarkable chemist in his own right.

"I first reached out to him years ago, when I was a student at the Royal College, studying under Dr. August von Hofmann, a pioneer in the chemistry of carbon-based molecules, and specifically chemicals being isolated from coal-tar. Dr. von Hofmann encouraged me to seek a natural alkaloid substitute for quinine, for the treatment of some forms of malaria. Doubtless you know from your time in the Far East that the world is critically short of medication for malaria parasites. I decided to start by oxidising allyl toluidine."

Quinine was derived from the bark of the cinchona tree, grown mainly in South America. Its cost was exorbitant, and the supply far short of the amount needed for the vast number of malaria cases. I said I could

169

only imagine the formidable task ahead of a chemist who ventured into quinine synthesis. "The development of synthetic quinine would be a milestone in organic chemistry," I stated, "but I don't recall reading about any such discovery."

"For good reason," my guest replied wryly. "Oxidising allyl toluidine was a route doomed to failure from the start. I tried formulation after formulation. No quinine was formed – only a dirty reddish-brown precipitate."

"What made you communicate with the proprietor of a dye-works?" I queried. "It's quite a leap from looking for an artificial remedy for plasmodium parasites to entering the field of dye-making."

"As you say," Perrin agreed, "but I sought Robert's advice for a quite separate reason. As I explained earlier, during my coal-tar experiments, I chanced upon a rare form of purple dye. I wanted to know if the dye might have any commercial possibilities. If so, should I apply for a patent?"

"Ah," I said, smiling, "Kismet! What are the chances of experimenting with coal-tar derivatives for a quinine substitute and by chance discovering . . . ."

For the first time a glimmer of a smile crossed my visitor's face.

"Am I to understand you believe in Fate, Dr. Watson?" He added impishly, "A result of too long spent in the mystic East, perhaps?"

"No and yes," I replied. "No I do not, because it's irrational. Yes I do, because otherwise I cannot properly divine how I came to meet Sherlock Holmes a few days short of one year ago."

I recalled how I'd planned to live out my professional life as an Army surgeon, until Fate decided otherwise. A Jezail bullet shattered my shoulder at the Battle of Maiwand. Overnight, I became a discarded pawn, a forgotten element in "The Great Game" played out between St. Petersburg and London for supremacy in Central Asia. Had the damage not been so serious, I would never have returned to England so precipitously. Then once more Fate stepped in, this time at Piccadilly Circus.

I was standing at the Criterion Bar when someone tapped me on the shoulder. Turning round I recognised young Stamford, my former orderly at Barts. Later that fateful day Stamford introduced me to Sherlock Holmes, who was in need of someone to help share the expenses of these bachelor's quarters.

"Then Destiny must have two faces," my visitor replied, "like the Roman deity, Janus. One looking forward, one looking backward. I've done well in the world of chemistry," he added, "yet now I sit here awaiting the arrival of a private consulting detective, to beg him to save me from a blackmailer intent on murdering my very soul!"

At this he broke down. Pitifully he cried out, "What have I done to bring this about?"

The sound of the front door opening and banging shut was followed by Holmes's familiar footsteps taking the stairs two at a time. Perrin and I got to our feet and turned to greet him.

Holmes shook hands with our visitor in a business-like manner and waved him back to the chair by the grate. I handed over the telegraph concerning the passing of Robert Miller and gave a synopsis from my notes of my conversation with Perrin.

"Mr. Perrin," my comrade continued, "first may I say that to those of us with a particular interest in chemistry, your fame goes before you."

Holmes motioned towards his chemical table in the corner of the sitting room.

"Dr. Watson will tell you that I myself experiment with coal-tar derivatives. But please go on."

Perrin's worried expression returned.

"Soon afterwards, I received a second communication, a cutting from *The Perthshire Constitutional and Journal.* I'll read it to you."

> *It has been revealed that during the very early hours of the morning a* cluinntinn mèirleach *(phantom thief) entered the premises of the North British Dyeworks, formerly J. Miller and Sons Ltd., on North Street, Perth. The office filing cabinets were jemmied open and some files removed. A nearby safe known to contain a large amount of money for the weekly wages was not broken into. Consequently, it seems the thieves may have lost their nerve and left with nothing of value.*

Perrin looked up.

"The break-in must have taken place just an hour or two after poor Robert's death."

Holmes asked, "Did you have any idea why this was sent?"

Perrin replied, "At the time, no."

Again he reached into the valise.

"A week passed and I received this letter. It bears no signature and as you can see, it was produced on a typewriter."

> *Dear Mr. Perrin,*
>
> The Perthshire Constitutional and Journal *was misguided in saying nothing of value was taken. Files dated to 1856*

171

concerning the discovery of an interesting new purple dye
were removed. The drawer contained a wonderful mauve
bow-tie and extensive correspondence between you and the
lamentably deceased Robert Miller, also taken.

"This can't be the last communication," I said, puzzled. "While they've been odd, so far I see no sign of blackmail."

"It wasn't the last," Perrin confirmed, passing over an envelope. "This came only a day or two later. It contains a letter in Robert Miller's own hand, meant to seem as if it were written many years ago in reply to my very first letter to him, but never sent."

I asked, "The earlier reference to *'the lamentably deceased Robert Miller'* – why did the writer use the word *'lamentably'*?"

"The fact Robert died is lamentable enough, but the circumstances of his death were doubly lamentable. He always worked late at the factory, but one night he worked even later. The weather was inclement. He beckoned a cab waiting for custom on the other side of the road. He was crossing to get into it when the horses bolted straight at him. Before Robert could save himself, he was under the horses' hooves and died within the hour. The cabbie was never traced."

"There was no one else in the street?" asked Holmes.

"Just a passer-by walking a dog. He had noticed the cab, a heavy coach pulled by four horses. He hadn't seen one plying for trade that late before. He said the horses took off as if they'd been raced – as though trained to bolt out of a starting gate."

"Did this witness give any details of the carriage?" Holmes asked.

"It was too dark for him to make out the driver or a cab plate, but the passer-by must have had some knowledge of the equine world. He said the four-in-hand were American Quarter Horses, an unusual breed for a hackney carriage," Perrin replied.

I opened the envelope and took out a vellum sheet. The heading was that of the dye works in Perth. It was signed *"Robert Miller"* and dated more than two decades earlier:

Dear Mr. Perrin,

Thank you for the letter of the 5th instant regarding your chemical experiments with coal-tar derivatives. You say your initial experimentation to discover an artificial alternative to quinine failed, but you believe there could be a particular colourful dye inherent in the derivatives. As the owner of dye works, I can be of considerable help regarding aniline dyes. I

172

have been experimenting in such matters for some time for commercial purposes, especially in the light-purple range. My works have recently received a Royal Warrant from Her Majesty, and we refer to ourselves as silk dye makers to the Queen.

You report that your efforts resulted only in a reddish powder and an oily pitch-black substance, rather than the glistening white crystals of quinine. I had similar results in my search for a new dye, but by persevering I have recently made a break-through by introducing alcohol into my experimentation. I have discovered an entirely new way to produce a colour very similar to the flower of the Mallow plant. For some two-thousand years, a major colourant in this spectrum has been Tyrian Purple, obtained at immense cost from Murex brandaris *and* Murex trunculus. *It took thousands of the molluscs to dye one toga – such a rarity that Julius Caesar decreed the colour could only be worn by Roman emperors and their families.*

The new dye has proved fast on silk. Regarding its commercial possibilities, it is vital that it also be fast on cotton, an immensely larger and more challenging market. If it is, it will be worth my company's while to apply for a patent.

I admire your enthusiasm. These are wonderful times for the advancement of chemistry. Being eighteen, you are at the right age to take advantage to the full. May I suggest you come to Perth to discuss whether you should take leave of the Royal College and assist me in my work on the cotton challenge and in my preparation of a patent application? I shall be delighted to cover all your expenses.

Yours very sincerely,
Robert Miller, Proprietor

I remarked, "A very pleasant letter."

Our visitor looked at me with a strange expression.

"Very pleasant indeed, Dr. Watson," he acknowledged, "but I don't think one syllable of it was composed by Robert. I had never had sight of it until it was delivered to my home in the early hours a fortnight ago. Despite the date on it, the content convinces me it could only have been counterfeited following the theft of those files."

I started to ask, "Then why would anyone compose such a remarkably welcoming – ?"

173

"Gentlemen, Gentlemen!" Perrin broke in impatiently, "if you read it as I read it, it makes out with devilish cunning and in no uncertain terms that Robert, not I, discovered mauveine, that I stole the credit, and worse, that I knavishly patented the dye in my name. That artful letter prepared me for the worst – and then this came."

He brought out a further piece of paper.

"This arrived yesterday – typed, as you see. Especially note the post-script."

I read out: "*I suggest we meet soonest,* en-plein-air, *and forestall any difficulties which may arise between us. Place an advertisement in* The Evening Standard. *State a precise place, date, time.*"

The post-script added, "*It strikes me that the Royal Chemistry Society might find the Miller letter of great historical value for their annals, don't you agree?*"

"It came with these two cuttings from *The Illustrated London News,*" Perrin continued, "enclosures so idiosyncratic, so odd, I assume they were included by mistake. What bearing they have on any matter of concern to me is unfathomable."

I took them from him. The first indicated that Christie's was holding an auction: "*A great sale of pictures, sculpture, Sevres, Dresden, Chinese, and Japanese porcelain, decorative furniture, bronzes, and works of ornamental art and fine materials, brought from a Duke's Palace.*"

The first excerpt was followed by a second: "*A painting of especial interest is the portrait, by Valasquez, of Philip IV of Spain, which was taken from the Palace at Madrid during the Peninsular War by the French General Dessolle, from whose family it found its way to the Estate of the Duke. It is one of the finest portraits by Valasquez.*'

It concluded with: "*An anonymous bid of six-thousand guineas has already been submitted.*"

I remarked that the final sentence was doubly underlined in red ink.

"Good Lord!" I continued. "Six-thousand guineas! It's astonishing to think any painting could be worth as much as a fine house in Grosvenor Square or Belgravia!"

I pointed at the newly framed portrait of General "China" Gordon on the wall of the sitting room. "I paid only twenty guineas for that, including the cost of the frame."

"When did the auction take place?" Holmes asked.

"It hasn't yet," I replied, looking at the cuttings. "It's in a few days' time."

"Mr. Perrin," Holmes asked, lighting his pipe, "was it you who underlined that last sentence?"

"I did not," came the response.

174

"Then we must presume the blackmailer is the anonymous bidder," Holmes continued. "He will be calling on you to provide him with the six-thousand guineas to secure the Velasquez portrait."

In a voice breaking with despair, Perrin wailed, "Money I have, but payment would be an admission of guilt – what would stop this vampire leeching and leeching, and then deciding through some malevolence of mind to send that forgery of a letter to the Royal Chemistry Society anyway! With Robert's death and the evidence stolen from the factory cabinet, I have nothing to disprove the calumnies implied in it. My career and reputation will be at an end."

I asked, "The patent in question: Did Mr. Miller ever take one out?"

"Not on mauveine," came the reply. "He was perfectly aware I alone had made the discovery. I even sent him the prototype of the once-white bow-tie I'm wearing today which I had plunged into the dye. As you can see, it turns the white silk into a wonderful pale violet."

"How close is the writing to Robert Miller's own?" Holmes asked. "The shape and slope of the letters, regularity of the spacing?"

"I cannot find one jot of difference," came the unhappy response.

"Blackmailers can be seen off, Mr. Perrin," I remarked. "A book printer threatened to publish a salacious memoir by a former mistress of the great Duke of Wellington. It was made clear only money – in copious amounts – could keep his name out of those red-hot pages. Wellington sent the letter back with a message scrawled across it: '*Publish and be damned!*' Why not emulate the Duke?"

"Doctor," Perrin returned morosely, "were I the Iron Duke, I would reply in exactly those terms. His hard-won reputation as the conqueror of Napoleon was hardly at stake. Besides, half the aristocracy of Great Britain and even the eldest son of our Great Queen indulge in such affairs."

At this he clambered out of his chair and strode to the door leading to the landing. He thrust it open, checking for listeners, before closing it and returning to us. He withdrew a sheaf of telegrams from a pocket.

"Look at these, gentlemen. They will impress upon you the seriousness of my predicament. La Société Chimique de Paris is considering offering me their most prestigious medal. It will mean thousands of pounds – possibly millions – in further revenue for my factories. The Technische Hochschule of Munich is offering me an Honorary Doctorate. So too is the University of Leiden, and also my alma mater Würzburg. As to America, I am invited to make a tour – New York, Chicago, San Francisco! If that letter goes to The Royal Chemistry Society, all and sundry will consider me a plagiariser, a counterfeiter, a forger, a copier, a cheat, an impostor, and a cribber.

"I shall no longer hear a word from any of them. Every such offer already made will be withdrawn, every likely offer of awards nipped in the bud. Such is the suspicion this wretched letter will instill in their minds. Seven years ago, the Royal Society awarded me the Copley Medal for my numerous contributions to the science of chemistry. It will be taken from me, together with the Royal Medal. They may even strip me of my Fellowship. I shall no longer be welcomed by Her Majesty and the Prince Consort at the Palace.

"I tell you, Mr. Holmes and Dr. Watson: Before you is a desperate man. This is no ordinary blackmailer. He has the heart of a cobra, a king cobra. All my wealth is as nothing when I consider how bleak my life will become if this criminal is allowed to proceed at will. You must fend him off. Trounce him. Otherwise, no one in all England with means and reputation will be safe."

"Then, sir, we must start right away," Holmes ordered. "Place the advertisement in *The Evening Standard* exactly as he asks. He is hoist with the petard of passion to possess the Velasquez. There could be opportunity in that for us. He'll want to impress upon you precisely how well his plan has been prepared to your extreme disadvantage, as indeed it has. I don't doubt the scheme was long in gestation. If his case appears strong, you must tell him you will pay, but you'll need several days. By then we may have a chance to discover his identity. Mr. Perrin, I must warn you: Dr. Watson and I can offer no guarantee. This is no ordinary criminal. He displays immense cunning, the like of which I've never encountered."

Soon after, I saw our new client down to the street. As he entered a cab he looked back.

"Dr. Watson," he asserted bravely. "You have given me courage. I shall try to muster enough to stand up to this snake of a human being."

"Good man!" I called back.

Holmes was still in his position by the window when I returned. I gave a questioning look.

"What do you make of it all?" I asked. "I take it you've had quite some experience of blackmailers?"

He shook his head.

"None."

He crossed the room to knock out his pipe in the grate.

"Blackmail is a curious crime, a common object of criminal prohibition, the ugliest of transgressions. It's rightly said that when a portion of wealth passes out of the hands of him who has acquired it, without his consent, to him who hasn't created it, whether by force or by artifice, property is violated, plunder perpetrated – yet it can be paradoxical. Take the Miller letter. On one reading it threatens Perrin –

176

pay up or your reputation in the world of chemistry will be put in extreme danger. Yet on another reading it could be taken as a demand for justice for the unfortunate Robert Miller, deceased."

With an unexpected change of subject, Holmes asked, "You had horses out in India, didn't?"

"I did," I replied, "though never American Quarter Horses. Two Walers. Wonderful breed."

"Then I shall be questioning you further on the characteristics of our equine friends," Holmes replied.

That evening we dined at Simpson's, a ritual we practiced whenever we had the chance. Holmes chose the steamed steak-and-kidney pie. I preferred the hand-dived Scottish scallops. Both of us decided on a dessert of vanilla, cinnamon, cream, and bitter and sweet almonds.

Two days later I left our lodgings and went to the one-legged news-vendor at the Baker Street Station to purchase *The Evening Standard*. I turned to the personal ads. The first one read: *"CAD: Utterly miserable and broken-hearted. I must see you my darling. Please write and fix time and place, at all risks. Can pass house if necessary unseen, in close carriage."*

Starkly, the next read: *"Tomorrow Highgate Cemetery one p.m. Grave of Alfred Swaine Taylor."*

I took the newspaper home. Holmes was at his chemical table. The sitting room was filled with acrid fumes. I told him, "The meeting is set for tomorrow at Alfred Swaine Taylor's grave. It has to be Perrin's advertisement. Taylor was a chemist, wasn't he?"

"He was," Holmes replied. "Author of *On Poisoning by Strychnia*. I attended his funeral. His grave lies near a very grand mausoleum, that of Julius Beer."

Chapter II: A Fraught Encounter in Highgate Cemetery

At around a quarter-past-two the following day, Holmes and I were in a cab being pulled up the steep hill to Highgate Cemetery. We paid off the driver and took a side-path to the Circle of Lebanon, the most circumspect way to reach Alfred Swaine Taylor's grave. The Cemetery was a fashionable place to bequeath one's corpse to the soil. Lower down, a combination of coal-fired stoves and poor sanitation made the air heavy and foul-smelling. By contrast, the air of Highgate was fresh. Flowers and trees grew well. The labyrinth of Egyptian sepulchres, Gothic tombs, and a litany of silent stone angels were safe from extremes of pitting and weathering.

At the heart of the Circle was a Biblical "First of Trees'", a massive cedar which towered over the landscape like a huge bonsai, the base surrounded by a circle of tombs. We paused under its graceful branches to survey the route ahead. Holmes pointed across a patchwork of toppled gravestones and grandiose mausolea to where a man was standing at an easel.

"Where the artist's at work," he said, "that's the Julius Beer Mausoleum. Taylor's grave is close by. In fact," he added, "look over there. There's our client."

Perrin was slumped down. He had been scribbling notes. He looked utterly woebegone. On seeing us he cried out, "It's no use, Holmes. Unless I pay whatever he demands and for as long as he demands, I am lost. The man's the Devil – the Devil incarnate!"

"So the blackmailer arrived?" I prompted solicitously.

Perrin paled at the memory.

"He did," came the reply.

"And?" I prompted.

"He congratulated me on my cranium. He told me I have a marked 'patch of wonder' – hence my inventive ability."

I said, "I presume he then – ?"

"He did. He told me he was here solely to impress on me why I should hand over six-thousand guineas in not more than three days."

"Conveniently in time for the auction of the Velasquez," I said.

"His age?" Holmes asked.

"About the same as mine," Perrin estimate. "I'd hazard over forty. Perhaps forty-five."

"Height?" I prompted

"That was notable," Perrin replied. "Very tall, accentuated by being thin."

"The face?" I asked.

"Even more notable – the forehead especially. It domed out in a white curve. Eyes deeply sunken for a man of his relative youth. The shoulders rounded, as though from much study."

He paused, reflecting. With a shudder he burst out, "Then he began to speak. Every sneer was a hammer-blow. I was writing notes when you arrived, but I hardly need them. His words will remain etched into my brain for the rest of my life. He addressed me as 'My dear Perrin.' Then he went on, saying, 'You and I are here for the sole purpose of deciding whether you should hand over a considerable amount of money – six-thousand guineas, in fact. I am here to convince you that you should. I suggest our business together will be done faster if I go first, to convince you a refusal will have the most deleterious effect on your well-being.

178

"'On the one hand, we can agree a time for you to return here within three days with such a sum. On the other, you can refuse, and the Miller letter will be delivered to the Royal Chemistry Society. If by chance you discover my identity and report matters to Scotland Yard, and were I consequently to be placed in the dock, I would convince judge and jury that I'm a humble citizen who chanced across a letter proving it was the late Robert Miller, not you, who came across Florentine Mallow in doing his own scientific experiments with coal-tar derivatives. By contrast, I would point out your experiments under Dr. von Hofmann were seeking a substitute for quinine, but quinine is achromatic. It has no colourant properties whatsoever. It wouldn't turn silk or cotton purple.

"'The letter proves it was Miller who determined a purple dye could be derived from coal-tar. He had the factory and the financial capacity to conduct every experiment imaginable. Your laboratory was a hut in your back garden. Further, I would put it to the Court the letter shows it wasn't you but Miller who planned to apply for a patent, but you cheated him out of it through your deplorable opportunism.'"

Perrin produced a handkerchief and wiped his brow. I offered him a gulp of restorative liquor.

"Mr. Holmes, he is a man of implacable evil who has done his research formidably well. I was a mere eighteen years of age. A jury wouldn't believe I alone carried out the experiments leading to the discovery and patenting of Florentine Mallow, although that's the truth of it. Plainly they would take the blackmailer's side – that I stole the formula and patented it in my name."

"On what terms did you part?" I asked.

"He said I should return here on Saturday at the same hour, bringing the money," Perrin cried out. "I can see no way out but to comply with his demand."

"We have three days," Holmes murmured. "We must allow our client to wend his way home."

Perrin shook our hands. Despite the cold his face glistened with sweat. He started towards the path leading to the great cedar of Lebanon and the exit beyond. After a yard or two he halted.

"Mr. Holmes," he called back in a voice which shook as though his oppressor was still present, "there was something . . . something about him, like a predatory reptile of the order *Crocodilia*. When he turned his back on me, I expected to see a row of spines sprouting from the nape of his neck to the tip of a tail."

We stood watching his departure.

"We can be sure of one thing," Holmes muttered. "If we fail, it won't be Perrin's reputation alone the press and public will shred like Savoy cabbage."

We passed close to the Julius Beer Mausoleum. The artist was still there, dabbing at a convincing watercolour. My comrade left my side and stepped across to him and asked, "Did you get it?" The artist pulled out a charcoal sketch from under the canvas. A face leered out, the forehead white and domed, the eyes deeply sunken, the shoulders hunched, exactly as Perrin had described his tormentor.

"Take it to Scotland Yard immediately," Holmes ordered, handing over several guineas. "Ask for Inspector Lestrade. Tell him Sherlock Holmes should be glad of any information which could help identify this man. Inform Lestrade we need to discover who he is before Saturday. Make it clear this isn't a missing person or an unidentified corpse. His likeness must not appear in any newspaper."

The following morning, Holmes joined me at the fireside as I caught up with the Court and Social page of *The Times*. We began to sort through the first post of the morning when a banging came at the street door. This was followed by the sound of a visitor greeting Mrs. Hudson in familiar terms before hurrying up the stairs to our sitting room, chortling loudly. It was Inspector Lestrade.

"Gentlemen!" he cried out, waving the depiction of the man who had so terrified our client at Highgate Cemetery. "I circulated this around the Yard. There was nothing remotely like him in our files." He shed his coat. "However, by chance we have discovered his identity – except we can't possibly have the right man. He can't be your blackmailer, Mr. Holmes!"

The inspector's eyes sparkled as he spoke. He was evidently in a state of barely-suppressed exultation. He slapped the drawing with the back of his hand.

"This man was recognised by a constable who joined us after deciding not to pursue the priesthood at Hackney College – the Divinity school. He's certain it's the man who taught him philosophy and astronomy, a Professor O'Clery. If you're seeking a ruthless, cunning, and decisively malicious person, it can't be O'Clery. His career has been spent among seminarians preparing for life in the Church."

He looked from one to the other of us to gauge our reaction. I was about to say this wasn't the most welcome piece of news we had ever received when Holmes asked, "How long ago was this constable at the College?"

Lestrade looked at the paper in his hand.

"He left four years ago, but the Professor's still there. My constable was on a return visit to his old academic haunt the other day and spotted him crossing a courtyard."

"He's quite certain the sketch identifies O'Clery?" I asked.

"Adamant! The seminars were held in the Professor's study. Our constable remembers them well. If a seminar got boring, he'd spend the time gazing at an oil-painting above the mantelpiece – copy of a beach scene in France, he said."

Holmes asked, "Did your constable learn the name of the artist who painted the original?"

"A Frog – " Lestrade checked back with his notes. " – by the name of Claude Monet."

"The title?" Holmes asked.

"Holmes, for heaven's sake!" I cried out in exasperation. "This Professor O'Clery can't be our man! The inspector has work to do, yet you keep him here discussing a painting! What does it matter what it was called – or who painted the original? What can it have to do with blackmailing Perrin?"

"The title of the painting, Lestrade?" Holmes repeated. "Did the constable recollect the title?"

"As a matter of fact he did, Mr. Holmes," Lestrade replied, addressing his notes again. "On one occasion, waiting until all the students had turned up, Professor O'Clery talked about the picture. The original was titled '*La Plage de Trouville*'. Two ladies with parasols on a sandy beach and so on. Painted ten or twelve years ago, on the artist's honeymoon."

With nothing else to report, Lestrade turned to go. I stood up and helped him back into his coat. I thanked him and saw him down the stairs to the front door. Disconsolate, I returned to the sitting room.

"Clearly we haven't found our blackmailer," I reminded Holmes. "I'm astonished you kept Lestrade here as long as you did, going on about a copy of a Monet. It's ludicrous to suppose a professor at a seminary of all places could be the – "

Holmes interrupted my flow. "Nevertheless, tomorrow we shall pay the Theological College a visit." Then he added, "We could find the Monet very interesting." He reached for his coat. "In the meantime, I'm off to Lumber Court."

I stared after him as he headed for the door. The narrow thoroughfare at St. Giles was known only for tradesmen dealing in old clothes of a most varied and dilapidated description.

Chapter III: We Take a Cab to Hackney College

The next day, a cab dropped us off at the College entrance. Holmes had been in the best of spirits on our journey, prattling away about Cremona fiddles, and the difference between a Stradivarius and an Amati. We were in priestly garb. Rummaging around Lumber Court the previous evening, he had come across two sets from a royal peculiar which had found their discernibly weary way to St. Giles from St. Katharine's by the Tower. A young seminarian standing at the College entrance offered to show us to Professor O'Clery's study. He was one of his students, he informed us.

Conversationally Holmes asked, "I've heard he has an interest in the French Impressionists?"

Our escort smiled.

"He has," he replied. "All of us seminarians have become very familiar with the copy of a Monet over his study mantel. Not just Impressionists, though. He could lecture on the whole of European Art, right down to the Flemish and Dutch Bamboccianti if he were so inclined – but he sticks to astronomy and philosophy."

He left us at the study entrance with a polite bow.

I knocked on the door. A voice called out "Come in."

Professor O'Clery was precisely as portrayed in the sketch. He came towards us, hand outstretched. As soon as we'd shaken his hand, Holmes pointed at the painting in pride of place over the mantelpiece. Conversationally he remarked, "Professor, I hear you are attracted to the French Impressionists."

"I am," came the professor's reply. "Renoir, Sisley, Bazille, but – " He gestured at the painting. " – this Monet in particular. How perfectly it captures a moment by the sea. The windswept beach. The unmediated colours. Alas, this isn't the original. As a humble professor, I must make do with a copy, naturally."

"Naturally," Holmes murmured. "I believe the original was stolen and has yet to be recovered."

"So I've heard," the professor replied.

With a polite, "If I may," my comrade crossed to the painting. He lent forward, peering closely at it.

"This figure of a woman lost in thought," he remarked. "Is she Camille-Léonie Doncieux, Monet's wife? And the second woman – would that be the wife of Eugène Boudin?"

"So we are told," came the reply. He added, "You seem surprisingly well-acquainted with it."

La Plage de Trouville – Claude Monet (1870)

"My parents went to Trouville once," Holmes explained. "The summer Monet made this sketch."

A small movement of Holmes's hand caught my attention. Visible to me though concealed by his back from our host, Holmes had pressed his thumb against the canvas and was pulling it across the paint.

A moment later he took a seat.

"A most exceptional copy," he concluded.

Our host smiled.

"As you say," he responded.

To my consternation, Holmes continued. "I have a question for my friend here. He's been taking instruction at the National Gallery, reproducing copies of the great Masters."

He turned to me with an encouraging smile. "I recall your effort at a Raphael – Saint Catherine of Alexandria, wasn't it?"

On my occasional visits to the famous gallery I would pass huddles of copyists spending painstaking hours before the Raphaels, but not once had I been among their number.

Holmes gestured towards the Monet.

"Now if you were commissioned to copy an Impressionist, one painted *plein-air*, like this Monet, where would you undertake the work, if not at a gallery? Most probably an *atelier*?"

"Most probably an *atelier*, yes," I parroted, responding to his nod.

Holmes asked, smiling encouragingly. "To avoid the elements – wind, rain?"

"Precisely," I replied, bewildered by the topic.

Holmes pointed again at the Monet.

"Though surely in this case you'd want to stand at the exact spot on the beach in Normandy, surrounded by wet panel carrier, palette cups, French easel, paints, brushes, brush cleaning water, and all the rest of the artist's paraphernalia?"

"Only if I've been hit with a stick as heavy as a Penang-lawyer," I replied jocularly, entering with brio into a game I failed to grasp. "Outdoors would be absurd! I would in any case have to take along the original or a copy as exact as Professor O'Clery's."

To be sure I had made the point my comrade clearly wanted, I added, "Even then, how could I be sure the light would be the same?"

A short uncomfortable silence ensued. I was convinced Holmes had made a hideously embarrassing mistake. Engaging me in a discussion so far removed from our reason for being there was undoubtedly a desperate resort. Regardless of the facial similarity to the drawing, in no way did O'Clery live up to William Perrin's alarming description of the malevolence the blackmailer radiated at the cemetery. He was the very epitome of hospitality and courtesy. Fortunately there would be a limited time for small-talk before the seminarians arrived for a tutorial.

Chapter IV: The Denouement

"Now, gentlemen," Professor O'Clery commenced, "you still have the advantage of me. I don't recall you giving me your names, nor the reason you chose to visit. I see from your dress you are from a Royal Peculiar. St George's Chapel at Windsor, perhaps? You can hardly have made your way here just to discuss the French Impressionists."

He looked over at the mantel clock.

"I have a mere five minutes left, so perhaps you can tell me how I can be of – "

In a preternaturally calm voice, Holmes broke in with, "Certainly, Professor O'Clery. Allow me to introduce my colleague. Despite his clerical apparel, this is Dr. John H. Watson. And I am Sherlock Holmes – a consulting detective."

"But your clothing – " said O'Clery. "Well, you really don't look much like priests after all. I don't suppose that you're here to help propagate the Gospel, or to alleviate Swaziland's dire need for evangelists. But I must ask why the two of you are disguised as clerics to gain entry to a theology college. To what do I owe the honour?"

Holmes's tone sharpened as he replied. "Professor, we came to discuss your attempt at blackmail of the notable chemist, William Perrin. Your preparations have been at the level of genius, from the murder of a dye-factory proprietor Robert Miller to the subsequent break-in at his factory in Perth, to the sequence of notes and clippings. Above all the forged Miller letter. You must stop as of now, you really must. Otherwise the consequences will be as injurious to your reputation, even to your freedom, as any you might inflict upon Perrin himself."

Even as I glanced at Holmes upon his use of the word "murder", the professor slowly rose from his chair to his exceptional height.

"Sir, you astonish me. You astonish me!" he repeated, coming closer. "You enter my study unannounced. You call me a blackmailer – a murderer even! It's a case of mistaken identity as ever there was! My life is here, among priests and seminarians. My occupation is studying the Cosmos. I am a student of Euclidian planes and solid figures on the basis of axioms and theorems. Nevertheless," he said, now pausing quite close to Holmes, "for amusement before you go through that door, never to darken it again, let's say I *am* this blackmailer, and now you are here in turn to blackmail *me*, threatening the ruination of my reputation, and even snatching away my liberty. How will you do that?"

Without directly replying, Holmes repeated, "Cease and desist immediately, or the consequences for you will be dramatic."

Then he turned to me. "Come, Watson. I'm afraid that in the pleasure of this conversation, we are neglecting business of importance. The Moravian virtuoso, Norman-Neruda, is playing a trio of Schumann pieces rearranged for violins and cello at the Hallé."

As I retrieved our shovel hats, I was puzzled by the abrupt turn in the conversation. Why had Holmes so brusquely revealed we had come under false pretences – why we had even come in the first place? What had he learned from our brush with the professor, other than the latter was an aficionado of French Impressionists, something we already knew from the Scotland Yard constable's recollection of the Monet over the mantel?

Holmes reached for the hat in my hand, and then halted as though struck by an afterthought.

"Professor," he said, pointing at the painting. "One other thing. I believe I mentioned my mother and father spent that one summer in Trouville."

185

"I believe you did, Mr. Holmes," the professor answered, his voice tense with anger. "I take it they enjoyed their stay?"

"They did – except for one minor inconvenience," Holmes replied. "When the temperature rose each day, the wind would pick up. Sand would blow everywhere. They had to forsake the beach and take their picnics *sur l'herbe*."

"How very interesting," our host replied, observing my friend carefully.

Holmes glanced my way. "Imagine Monet at his easel on the beach – painting with all that sand blowing about."

He glanced back at O'Clery. "We mustn't leave without once more congratulating the professor on the rigour and detail of his copy of '*La Plage*'. It even replicates the hundreds of particles of sand that the sea-breeze spattered over Monet's canvas while the paint was wet . . . I wonder if the accuracy of each particle's placement could be confirmed by the Deuxième Bureau in Paris?"

The professor's cheeks flushed. In an alarming *volte-face*, the brows had come down, almost touching each other, and the look had turned malevolent.

"For my amusement, Mr. Holmes," he snarled, "tell me of this Robert Miller's death. You say it wasn't an accident. What sparked your suspicion? Did this malefactor – whose preparations you say were at the level of genius – make a – "

" – Serious blunder? Only the one," Holmes confirmed.

"Go on," O'Clery demanded.

"His choice of the four-in-hand – the American Quarter Horses. For power and speed from a standing start they are nonpareil, entirely suited to his devilish purpose, but I could find no other instance in the whole of the Queendom where they would be used to pull a cab."

Holmes turned and walked toward the door. I followed. "A last word," O'Clery called out as we opened it and passed into the hallway. "You praised the blackmailer regarding his preparations, and the forged Miller letter – 'above all', you said. Wouldn't such a skilled practitioner of coercivism have a second, even third and fourth exact copy to hand? Food for thought, Mr. Holmes . . . ."

The door shut behind us and we walked back outside, neither daring to look around. The young seminarian who led us to the Professor's study caught sight of us from the quadrangle. He hurried over to escort us out. Conversationally, Holmes asked him, "How do you get on with the professor?"

"He's all right – as long as you stay on the good side of him," he replied, glancing towards O'Clery's rooms. With a wry smile he added,

"But heaven help you if you rile him, as I did once. In an instant he turned into a chthonic Fury."

Back on the road, Holmes selected a lone barouche from a line of hansom cabs.

"That's the first I've heard about a Schumann concert this afternoon," I said. "A bit feeble as an excuse to get us out of there, wasn't it?"

"Not at all. You and I *are* going to the Hallé straight after we change our clothes. I ordered the tickets last night."

"That terrifying eruption and the threats have convinced me O'Clery's our blackmailer. The explosion was triggered when you mentioned grains of sand. Can you explain? And why are we now going to a concert?"

Holmes chuckled. "I assume you noticed I drew my thumb across the painting the moment I had my back to O'Clery?"

"Yes, I did," I replied, "though I haven't the faintest idea why you should want to leave a thumb print on it."

"About ten years ago," Holmes began, "a Parisian art gallery dealer by the name of Durand-Ruel became interested in the new exponents of Impressionism – Monet and Pissarro, for example. He was intrigued by their preoccupation with surface texture. He grew into a connoisseur, buying up their paintings by the dozen, adding works by Sisley and Degas and Manet. He organised a series of exhibitions which transformed the art world's former hostility into acceptance and admiration. It was evident to art dealer and crook alike that in time the paintings would shoot up in value, Renoirs and Monets not least. Six years ago, a criminal mastermind organised a break-in at the Durand-Ruel Gallery on the Rue Laffitte. Hundreds of thousands of francs-worth of paintings were cut from their stretchers and spirited away, including '*La Plage de Trouville*'. All were returned for a ransom except the Trouville painting. Clearly it was a favourite of the mastermind behind the theft."

I gestured back towards the College. "But that was a copy. It can't be worth ten guineas. If it were the stolen Monet, the professor would hardly hang it in full sight over the mantelpiece in his study!"

Holmes replied, "You've heard the adage, if you want to hide something, do so in full sight. O'Clery knows that."

"You have yet to explain why you ran your thumb along the paint. If it wasn't to leave a print on it, why?"

"Some time ago, an acquaintance with the Deuxième Bureau's Paris headquarters notified me. They knew my grand-uncle was the French artist, Horace Vernet. They asked me to keep an eye open for the stolen Monet. Remember, it was never ransomed. The Bureau felt it might well have been hidden within France's borders for a year or two until the search went cold. Then it could have been smuggled abroad. They told me of a clue hidden in the paint, a clue which – if you can get close enough – would show it really was '*La Plage de Trouville*' rather than an excellent copy. Like other Impressionists, Monet layered dabs of pure colour on the canvas, sometimes wet on wet – you apply a new layer of oil paint on top of a still-wet layer, rather than waiting for one layer to dry before applying the next.

"A major feature of a coastal resort like Trouville is of course the beach. From the artist's point of view, a less desirable feature is the in-shore wind which sent my parents packing into the interior for their picnics. Monet was working on '*La Plage de Trouville*' when that wind came up and peppered the still-wet paint with grains of sand, hundreds of which became set in the paint as it dried.

"It's almost impossible to see the individual grains unless you're within two feet of the painting and know what you are looking for and where to look. Even then you may have to be near a window letting in bright clear sunlight, which the professor's jabot curtains certainly did not allow. When I ran my thumb across the painting I could *feel* the grit. Think how unlikely it is for someone making a copy to have a spoonful of Normandy sand to hand, to scatter on the canvas before the paint dried, placing every fleck at the exact locus as the grains on the original, yet managing to do so before the final layer of paint dried.

"Nevertheless, O'Clery apparently felt perfectly safe keeping the painting on the wall. Monet skilfully captured the exact colour of the beach. When I remarked how accurately the copyist had included particles of sand spattered by the sea-breeze over Monet's canvas, and referred to the Deuxième Bureau, O'Clery realised the game was up. The painting is the genuine Monet and worth far more than he could ever legitimately have afforded. His ferocious reaction merely confirmed we had the proof we needed."

I sat back in my seat, staring out. The streets grew more familiar as we followed the signs towards Paddington.

"All right" I cried. "I give up! Do you want O'Clery to get away? We're stuck in heavy traffic! In heaven's name, why did you choose a stately barouche and not an agile hansom? Even now he could be packing up to make good his escape. Why tell the driver to take us to our lodgings? Why are we to go on to the Hallé instead of driving furiously to the Yard to inform Lestrade?"

"My dear chap," Holmes replied calmly, "we are on our way to our lodgings and the concert for good reason. When I said the blackmailer possesses one of the finest brains of Europe, with all the powers of darkness at his back, I meant it. From the moment we took Perrin on, there was never a likelihood we would inform the Yard or the Deuxième Bureau of the blackmailer's identity, even that we have discovered the Monet."

"And never a likelihood we would take the matter to the authorities is due to – ?" I asked.

"We couldn't leave O'Clery's study and rush off to Scotland Yard – quite the reverse. We had to make it clear that was exactly what we were *not* going to do. Hence my purchase last night of tickets for the Norman-Neruda matinee. The letter purporting to be from Robert Miller was a fake, but utterly brilliant in preparation, down to Miller's own vellum stationery, script, and execution. If it were to arrive at the Royal Chemistry Society, Perrin would have no answer to the danger it presents to him, even now. The professor made it plain he has an entire barrage of equally convincing fake letters at the ready. He could as readily send one from a cell at Pentonville Prison as from Hackney College. Our only option was to force a *quid pro quo* on him – he would forego the Velasquez but keep the Monet, and never again hold the forged letter over Perrin's head. We in turn – "

"We in turn – " I interrupted with disbelief. "We in turn," I repeated, "would let him keep his freedom, even though you believe Robert Miller was murdered, presumably on O'Clery's orders?"

"The timing of Miller's death and choice of horses convinced me it was murder, yes, but a forensic impossibility to lay at the professor's door."

He leaned to one side to catch our driver's attention.

"Cabbie," he called out, "be a good chap, zig-zag a little now and then, and let us know if we're being followed. There's an extra guinea in it."

He turned back to me. "I wouldn't be surprised to find the professor or an acolyte following us in a hansom right now, to be sure we're keeping to our side of the bargain."

That evening we reminisced over a fine meal prepared by Mrs. Hudson where a bird was the chief feature, washed down by the promised bottle of Hochheim's Königin Victoriaberg. The dessert of wine-marrow pudding followed, straight from Godey's *Lady's Book*. At the end of our meal, Holmes folded his napkin and sat back, staring into the fire.

"Watson, I do not say this lightly: A shiver went through me at the look in O'Clery's eye when I revealed our identity. I have never before felt so deeply we were in the presence of some vast potency, a power of evil . . . ."

189

The time limit imposed by the blackmailer came and went. Four days later, Mrs. Hudson's stately tread was heard on the stairs. She brought a sealed package for Holmes which he asked me to open. It contained a letter from William Perrin expressing the warmest gratitude for our services. Our client had received no further communication. The anonymous bid of six-thousand guineas for the Velasquez had been withdrawn and the painting put into Christie's next auction of Old Masters. Perrin's letter was accompanied by an extremely generous cheque.

The Adventure of the
Old Explorer
by Tracy J. Revels

It was a lovely spring day in 1882 when I came down to the breakfast table and found a note from Sherlock Holmes, chiding me for being a slugabed. He stated that he had gone out on an investigation with Inspector Gregson to the London home of Sir Lionel Stedwell, and that he hoped to return by luncheon. I confess a bit of a wounded pride, for I would have greatly enjoyed an outing that introduced me to one of Her Majesty's most famous adventurers, a man who had paddled down the Amazon, scaled the Andes, battled fearsome jungle tribesmen with nothing more than an army pistol and a machete, and lived to tell the tale. Instead, I was left to the coffee pot and, much to my surprise, a short time later, a visit from Inspector Lestrade.

"Gone out, is he?" the ferret-faced man asked. "Not Gregson's case, I hope."

"I believe it is."

Lestrade rolled his eyes and helped himself to a biscuit. "Bit of nonsense, that one. Sir Lionel is returning from a Continental speaking tour, and his niece believes that someone broke into the home last night. Yet according to her young husband, nothing at all was taken. Not much of a case there. I hardly understand why Gregson thinks it's enough of a fuss to involve Mr. Holmes."

"You must have a more serious one."

"That I do and – here, now, Doctor. None of that deducing on your part! One Sherlock Holmes in the world is enough."

I couldn't resist a chuckle. "Can you tell me about it?" I asked as Lestrade lit a cigarette.

"No harm, I suppose, but I cannot stay for long. I was called over to the old burial ground in the parish of St. Phillip's, near the docks. Seems that about three weeks ago, a young fellow named Hood died in a charity hospital after being trampled to death by a runaway cab. He was clearly a decent sort of chap, though known only at his lodging house as a temporary visitor to the city. There was no paperwork about him, no way to contact any family. The vicar of St. Phillip's – who was serving as a chaplain in the hospital where the fellow died – took it upon himself to give the man a funeral, with services provided by the Grady and Garrison

Undertaking Establishment. Well, several days ago the grieving widow arrived at St. Phillip's. Seems Mr. Hood had taken a dislike to being married and was attempting to give his lady the slip. If you saw her, Doctor, you'd understand why! But she was a determined old girl and she'd been tracking him down. Hood was a Catholic, and his widow couldn't abide the thought of him resting in Protestant soil. She demanded that he be dug up so she could cart him away to replant him in whatever miserable little village she calls home. There was a bit of a fuss, as you might imagine, but yesterday permission to exhume was granted and a bunch of lads applied shovels to the soil. Said widow demanded that the coffin be opened so she could say a last goodbye – or maybe it was so she could give her late husband a final dressing down for having tried to wiggle out of their sacred bonds. Not a pleasant business, but the undertakers obliged her, and what should they find – ?"

"The body was missing?"

It was Lestrade's turn to grin. "Only the head."

"Good heavens!"

"It really is a puzzle. The days of the resurrection men may be past, but there are still plenty of anatomical lecturers who need fresh bodies and prefer the formerly young and strong ones. Mr. Hood was a prime specimen. Most of the lecturers and schools pay decently for the unclaimed dead from the poorhouse, but this chap was put into the coffin whole – or so it is that the undertakers and the vicar who buried him claim. But . . . I shouldn't laugh. It is rather undignified. And yet . . . ."

"Spit it out, Inspector."

He had begun to shake all over with amusement. "You see, there *was* a head in the coffin – it just wasn't his! It was a plaster bust, painted with remarkable skill. I suppose if you didn't look closely, or if a linen shroud was draped over the face, you'd hardly notice that it was a fake head. But the question I have is – who'd go to such trouble?"

"The poor widow," I sighed.

"She fainted, of course, but once she revived, she threatened to bring all manner of lawsuits against the hospital, the undertaker, and even the half-blind vicar."

I leaned back in my chair. "This sounds like a medical student prank."

"My thoughts exactly, Doctor. I'm sure Mr. Holmes would agree. Tell him if he's interested, it might be one of his stranger cases." With that, Lestrade snuffed out his cigarette, reclaimed his hat, pilfered another biscuit, and made his way downstairs. I was left to ruminate on the disreputable behavior of many of the young men in my field until I heard Holmes's tread upon the stairs.

192

"You missed nothing of interest," Holmes assured me. "Other than a tour through one of the most bizarre mansions in the metropolis, and a conversation with a strong-willed young woman. She may even have been beautiful, but I tend not to notice such things."

I groaned in disappointment. "Tell me about it anyway."

Holmes sorted out his pipe and tobacco. "Gregson called upon me at six this morning – heirs of national heroes have a great deal of persuasive power at Scotland Yard, and the young lady and her husband had arrived there at five, just as Gregson was beginning his day. Her name is Mrs. Silvia Russell, and her husband is Wilbert Russell. They have been married just a little more than a year, I gathered, and in that time, they have resided at Sir Lionel's. He is the girl's paternal uncle and protector – it is clear that the couple depends on him for their livelihood, a situation that no young man of pride would gleefully stomach. Mr. Russell informed me that his current occupation is cataloging all of Sir Lionel's trophies and artifacts, in preparation for a book upon the vast collection.

"According to the pair – the lady, mainly, as the young man was embarrassed and preferred not to speak unless directly questioned – the house was burgled in the night. Five servants – two maids, a page, and the butler and housekeeper, who are a married pair – sleep in the house, in rooms on the fourth floor. The ground-floor French doors, which give access to the large garden, had been left open, and the thief clearly traipsed through the trophy room and the library. He tracked a good bit of red clay soil in on his boots, which were rather thin with pointed toes. You know my methods, Watson. It was child's play to trace him from where he climbed the fence to where he forced the door, a task of no difficulty, to where he stomped around amid the old explorer's things."

"There was no dog?" I asked. Holmes smiled.

"There was quite a large dog, a mastiff, but when we arrived it was still snoring loudly upon the front step. The lady believes, and I concur, that whoever climbed the stone fence first tossed drugged meat to the dog, which it gulped down readily. No one heard any clamor. Yet at around four a.m. something woke the lady, who says she is a light sleeper. Finding herself alone, she lit a lamp and went downstairs to spend an hour reading in the library. She saw at once that it had been disturbed and immediately raised the alarm."

I held up a hand. "The lady was alone?"

Holmes smiled. "You are wondering whether there is already trouble in such a young marriage. The gentleman assured me that he has been suffering from a rather nasty cold for several days and didn't wish to inflict his misery upon his wife. He had therefore taken up temporary residence in a secondary bedchamber. Of course, it would have been valuable to have a doctor's opinion as to the severity of the illness or the veracity of his claim."

"Next time," I grumbled, "wake me up. I would have enjoyed seeing Sir Lionel's lair."

Holmes shrugged. "You and every schoolboy in the Empire, I imagine. It is a quite spectacular Mayfair mansion, with multiple rooms filled with mounted animal heads, curios from savage tribes around the globe, artifacts and weaponry from every age of man, and a library of several thousand volumes. It is, without doubt, the finest collection outside of the British Museum, and from Mrs. Russell's testimony, there are always offers being made to buy parts of it, but Sir Lionel says it shall never be broken up until he dies. It seems that the old explorer has a bit of a superstition about his collection and believes that if any part of it should be discarded or disturbed, ill fortune will follow."

"So what was taken?"

"That is the curious thing, Watson. *Nothing* was taken. Judging by the tracks, the thief wandered through two rooms, looked around a bit, lit a candle, and blew it out within five minutes, then returned the way he had come. His only crime, besides accessing the interior of the house, was soiling the fine Oriental carpets of the rooms with his clay-covered boots."

"No articles or relics were taken? How could they be so sure?"

"As its cataloger, Mr. Russell is exceeding familiar with the collection, and he assured me that nothing had gone astray, and that he was embarrassed by his wife's immediate summoning of both official and unofficial forces. His belief is that the thief was sent by some higher criminal agency to burgle the house of their nearest neighbor, Lord Elsworth, who possesses a much more traditional pile of loot, including a good bit of gold and silver plate, as well as a rather famous tiara said to have once graced the head of Queen Anne. Upon realizing his critical error, the thief panicked and fled the scene."

"And what do you make of his theory?"

"Utter rubbish, of course. A thief bold enough to break into a mansion in that neighborhood would hardly confuse the house numbers. Drugging watchdogs is not an unknown ploy, but it would have been safer to have poisoned the canine instead, and criminals are rarely sentimental. No, Watson, I am not a child, nor am I as gullible as Lestrade – who, I note, was here earlier. Don't look so surprised – you never eat that much for breakfast, despite our good landlady's efforts to fatten you, and Lestrade's cigarettes leave a very distinctive aroma in the air. As I was saying, I am left with only one mystery: Why did Mr. Russell burgle his own residence and then take nothing?"

"Russell! You are certain?"

194

"Of course. If his strange behavior and his convenient absence had not been enough to convict him, there was the evidence of his narrow, pointed-toe boots. The butler's feet are too large, the page's too small. One might admit that his wife could have procured his footwear, but this hardly seems the kind of prank to have been staged by a lady, especially one who is so obviously devoted to her uncle. So what was the purpose in Russell's little nocturnal adventure?"

I certainly couldn't think of an answer. Holmes rose from his chair and went over to the window. I told him of Lestrade's visit, receiving only grunts in reply, until I reached the end of my story and my personal theory as to it being a lark of some medical students.

"For what purpose?"

"They wanted the head, of course."

"Yes, but why go to such trouble to replace it? What could it have mattered to medical students if a corpse went to the graveyard headless? Whoever was so careful as to replace a head with a decent facsimile was concerned that the funeral and burial take place without incident – a concern that would hardly have occurred to a party of possibly intoxicated medical school lads."

Having my pet theory shot down so cavalierly, I decided to say no more about it. I picked up my paper, noting the headline on the second page which announced Sir Lionel would be returning that very evening from his Continental speaking tour. I wondered if the incident at his home had any relationship to the old explorer's return.

"According to *The Times*," I said, "Sir Lionel's health has suffered of late."

Holmes, who had resumed his seat, nodded grimly. "His immediate homecoming following a medical crisis was part of the niece's concern. Once we assured her that we saw no evidence of a crime or any danger, she decided she wouldn't tell the gentleman about the incident. He suffered a mild stroke while lecturing in Prague, and she is very determined that he should now rest and recuperate. By the way, did I mention the unique family heritage of her husband?"

"No – what do you mean?"

Holmes leaned forward. "Perhaps you recall, since you clearly idolize the old fellow, that he wasn't alone in his explorations of the Amazon back in '67? There was a *second* explorer, Neville Russell."

"I do recall! He was an academic from Oxford."

"And that rarity among academics, a man of action, as comfortable in the wilds of Africa or South America as he was in a classroom. I saw a picture of Sir Lionel and Neville Russell today, one that was made just

195

before their final voyage together. They looked ready to conquer the world."

"But there was a tragedy."

"Yes. Russell went off with a scouting party while Sir Lionel was suffering from nasty bout of malaria. The native guides returned in terror, saying the men had been attacked by savages. Sir Lionel, despite his weakness, led the rescue party, but Russell and his helpers were never found, though some bloody clothing and discarded weapons indicated that their end was not a pleasant one." Holmes gestured with his pipe. "Wilbert Russell was Neville's nephew. Sir Lionel took him in and educated him, and young Russell fell in love with Miss Silvia. I gathered, from a few indiscreet comments made by the lady, that her uncle never completely approved of the match, despite his goodwill toward his late partner."

I folded my paper. "Is it fruitless to speculate further?"

"I have no data," Holmes said. "Therefore, let us avail ourselves to lunch, and perhaps swing round by Scotland Yard and see what Lestrade has made of his case."

The inspector, it appeared, had made nothing of the case, despite having endured a rather painful interview with Hood's distraught and infuriated widow. He tossed a photograph at Holmes.

"Here, do take a souvenir for Baker Street. The lady brought me twenty of these. She seems to think that such pictures will be useful in tracking down her husband's remains – as if his head is somehow wandering blithely about London."

I studied the image. Mr. Hood had been a handsome, robust chap, with perhaps the largest walrus moustache I had ever laid eyes upon. Holmes tucked the picture into his pocket, and later that evening I found him staring into it, frowning.

"Is something wrong?"

"The face, Watson. It reminds me of . . . no, that is a foolish thought. It is time for me to retire. Let us hope something more intriguing arises in the next few days or . . . ."

He cast a greedy look towards the old morocco case. I gave a loud harrumph. Holmes smiled, patted me on the shoulder, and took himself off to bed.

It was two days later, and I was just returning from an early afternoon walk around Regent's Park, when I heard the first shouts of "Sir Lionel Stedwell dead! Read all about it!" from a one-legged newsman. I tossed him a coin and seized the paper. Details were scarce, but it seemed that the old man had suffered some type of fit in his home in the middle of the night and had been found dead on the rug in his trophy room. By the time

I climbed up to our Baker Street suite, Inspector Gregson was perched on the sofa and Holmes was throwing on his coat.

"Ah, see the perils of exercise for exercise's sake, my boy? You almost missed the second opportunity to visit your hero's home."

"Sir Lionel is dead."

"Aye, and that's what brings me here," Gregson said. "There's something just – I can't quite put my finger on it – but something feels *wrong* about the business. Not that a man his age shouldn't fall dead on the rug, but my God, surely no stroke could do that to a man's face. I saw his body very early this morning, when we were first called to the home, and that's a visage that will follow me into my dreams."

"How do you mean?" I asked, as we came down the stairs, Holmes leading us like a hound catching the scent.

"His face was twisted and distorted, his eyes were wide, his lips pulled were back over his teeth, as if he died in a moment of supreme terror."

"Was there any indication of intruders in his house?"

"None," Gregson continued, as we climbed into a four-wheeler. "But there were some queer doings that I'd appreciate Mr. Holmes's assistance in getting to the bottom of."

My friend gave the slightest of nods. I noted that he had something in his hand and was studying it intently. To my great surprise, it was the picture of Hood, from Lestrade's case. Holmes slipped the image back into his coat, shaking his head.

"Tell Watson what the maid said," Holmes instructed the inspector.

"She claims that in the nights since Sir Lionel's return, she has been awakened by drumming sounds, very soft and distant. She wasn't bold enough to investigate, and no one else in the house heard them. The butler, who found his master this morning, noted that there was a strange odor lingering in the trophy room, a smell that he describes as being almost like incense. But he also said that Sir Lionel was fond of experimenting with various native powders and potions, many of which gave off strange aromas."

"Perhaps this was what killed him."

"Surely a man as well-versed in native lore wouldn't accidently poison himself with an ordeal drug," Holmes said. "Nor is the idea of suicide to be entertained. Sir Lionel was, according to everyone Gregson interviewed, very happy to be home and rejoicing in a certain bit of domestic news. On the night he returned, Mrs. Russell revealed that she is in the family way."

"I'm glad you're along, Doctor," Gregson said, "I'm not much for dealing with hysterical women."

A short time later, we were ushered into what was clearly a home in the first stages of mourning. A massive wreath already hung from the door, and every mirror was draped in linen or silk. The deferential servants moved about with their heads down, and the female staff was red-eyed from weeping. The dignified old butler, who told us he had been with Sir Lionel for almost forty years, ushered us into the trophy room, the very space where the great man had died. His niece was seated on the sofa, her young husband beside her. She was already clad in a full mourning gown, he with an armband on his sleeve.

"Must you really come again, at such a time?" Russell asked, the fierce, angry gleam in his eyes belying his chilly composure. "As you may imagine, this business is very difficult for my wife to endure."

"Oh, do hush, Bertie," Mrs. Russell said, firmly. She was a beautiful woman, blonde and stately, with a determined expression on her face. Her husband slunk back at her rebuke, while she leaned forward. It was clear to me that she was the much stronger and more practical of the pair. "Think how ashamed Uncle Lionel would be of me, if I couldn't keep calm and carry on with his great work. Thank you for coming again, Inspector, and you too, Mr. Holmes." She smiled gently as I was introduced. "I am grateful for all your help. I cannot stop thinking that the strange occurrence on Monday night, and now dear Uncle's death, might be connected, but I cannot understand how."

"There was no sign of a burglary last night," Gregson said. "We've already had men around at all the houses in the neighborhood. Nothing amiss. No alarm raised anywhere."

Holmes had begun walking leisurely around the room, studying the many native curiosities inside their glass cases.

"You didn't hear the drumming that the maid described?" he asked.

"Why, no," Mrs. Russell answered. "I am sure Alice was dreaming. There was so much excitement to have Uncle home again, and we were all working hard to please him. Surely she was just overtired and imagining things."

Holmes gestured towards one case. "Ah, but a drummer would have much to choose from, would he not? You are certain there were no doors left unlocked, for someone to slip within and cause a bit of mischief?"

"Ridiculous!" Russell snapped. His wife reached backward and gently patted his hand.

"I have already thought of that, sir. I even asked Bobby, our page, if he had been getting up to naughtiness, but he of course denied it. He is a sweet lad, and he has never given us trouble. I cannot imagine that he would have done such a thing, which would have disturbed Uncle's much-needed rest."

Holmes lifted his head, squinting at the high walls lined with animal heads. "Please tell me about your uncle, Mrs. Russell. How was he when he returned?"

"Exhausted, Mr. Holmes. He wasn't well when he left for his Continental tour a month ago. I begged him not to make it, but he had given his word to old friends at the various universities that he would come and reminisce for their students. About three weeks ago, he suffered a small stroke while in Prague. Alice and I went to Prague to care for him. He claimed we made too much of a fuss, and promptly sent us home again, determined to finish out his tour."

Holmes turned, leisurely crossing the room behind the couple. "You didn't go, Mr. Russell?"

The young man bristled.

"I had pressing business here. And I knew that Sir Lionel would be angry with me if I didn't finish all the jobs that he had set for me to complete."

"Your patron was a harsh taskmaster."

It was not a question. Russell twisted, the muscles in his face jumping nervously.

"He held high expectations, Mr. Holmes. He was a famous man and – forgive me for saying so, darling Silvia – but he could be demanding. We lived here because he wished it. I worked for him because he wished it. We were never in a position to tell him no."

"Bertie!" the lady scolded. "Uncle was generous to us. Neither of us would have a farthing to our name if not for him. Oh, I only wish he had lived long enough to see the child we will name for him!"

Holmes knocked against an ornate brass cabinet, a strange piece of furniture that looked like a small barrel upon legs. "What is in here?"

"Horrors, Mr. Holmes," Russell answered. "That is where Sir Lionel kept some shrunken heads, collected from South America."

"Indeed? I have heard of such things but never seen one."

"They are grotesque. No, sir, the cabinet will not pull open. It requires a key."

"I would like to see them. I am certain Dr. Watson would as well."

Russell shook his head. I noticed that a sheen of perspiration had erupted upon his brow. "Please, sir, they are distasteful. My wife, in her condition – "

The lady's laughter rang out. "Really, Bertie! How many times have I seen those horrible talismans in the past? They are called *tsantsas*, Mr. Holmes, and are collected by tribesmen of the Amazon as an offering to their gods. I don't understand why my husband is so – Oh, very well, if you insist, Bertie, I will leave the room. Is there is nothing more that our guests require?"

Holmes gave her a short bow. "I believe your spouse may assist us with further inquiries."

"Very well, I shall retire." She swept from the room, and a moment later we heard her soft tread upon the stairs, and the anxious voice of her maid. Holmes folded his arms.

"The key, Mr. Russell?"

The man made a show of patting down his pockets. "Strange," he murmured, "I was certain I had the set of trophy room keys. I will need to go into the library to look for them."

Gregson, who had been studying my friend intently, stepped between Russell and the library door. The man whirled around, but I had quickly taken a stance between him and the French windows. Holmes pulled something from his vest.

"No need to exert yourself, Mr. Russell – this tool, favored of criminals, will make short work of the lock. I trust the inspector will not arrest me for using it?"

"Go on, Mr. Holmes."

Russell whimpered like a whipped spaniel. Holmes quickly sprung the lock and opened the rounded sides of the cabinet.

Within, displayed on several hooks, was a collection of severed, shrunken heads, a truly vile and disgusting display of native ingenuity. Each head was no larger than a china doll's, its skin leathery and its eyes and lips sewn shut with heavy leather thongs. All but one was dark, with long black hair. But the relic which dangled foremost in the cabinet was the most shocking of all, for it was the head of a white man, and possessed of an enormous flaxen moustache which dropped over its lips and dangled almost to the bottom of the cabinet.

Russell moaned and wavered on his feet. Holmes produced Lestrade's photograph.

"I believe we have solved two mysteries with one skull. Here is the missing element of the mortal remains of Mr. Hood, a most unexpected addition to Sir Lionel's collection, which he no doubt found shocking. Ah, there Russell drops – I thought there was very little blood in him. And now, Inspector, you see the value of having a medical man as an assistant! Watson, I trust you have your flask?"

A short time later, we retired to the old explorer's private study, a room that was three chambers removed from the hallway, where privacy could be assured. Russell sat on a chair before a majestic mahogany desk, upon which Gregson commandeered to take his notes. The pale and nervous gentleman had decided that his best hope laid in a full confession.

"You cannot know what it was like! You cannot imagine the suffering I have been through. But I promise you, upon the angels and saints, that I never laid a finger on Sir Lionel. God struck him down – God and his own guilty conscience. As for the other fellow, Hood, I had nothing to do with his death, nor did I turn him into a relic. I only sought justice, for myself, my uncle, and even for Edwardo."

Holmes leisurely lit a cigarette. "If you wish to elicit any sympathy from us, you must begin at the beginning."

The man nodded mournfully. "Perhaps you know my antecedents. My parents died when I was just three, and my uncle, Neville Russell, took me into his household. He was a good and kind man, though I saw very little of him, for he was often away on his adventures with Sir Lionel, and I was raised mostly by servants and tutors. But what I recall of him was endearing, and he promised me that when I was grown and properly educated, he would take me along, to India or Egypt or Africa. There was nothing more likely to incite a lad's imagination, and so I made myself a diligent student, awaiting the day when I might join him.

"But then, in 1867, when I was just fifteen, came the terrible news that Uncle Neville had been killed in the Amazon. By the terms of his will, I was given into the care of Sir Lionel, who immediately brought me to London, where I met Silvia. It was in those months, as I mourned my uncle, that I was drawn to her, and soon I had no greater ambition in life than to grow into manhood and make her my bride.

"But something was wrong. I felt it from the time Sir Lionel came to collect me. He didn't care for me – it would be too strong to say he hated me, but his dislike was made clear in his eyes, in the slight sneer he gave whenever I asked a question or told him of some youthful accomplishment. He never abused me, but he kept me at arm's length, even as he spoiled and coddled Silvia. He sent me away to college as quickly as possible, and more than once found some excuse to prevent me from returning to his home for the holidays. I searched myself for what offense I had given and could find none. It was as if the mere sight of me disgusted him. I promise you, sirs, that if my heart hadn't been given to Silvia – who returned my love – I would have bid Sir Lionel farewell upon my majority and never darkened his door again! But I couldn't have her without him, and he loved her too much to utterly forbid the match, though he didn't approve of it. He took me in and gave me menial tasks, nothing more than busy-work that was hardly worthy of my Oxford education. He held the purse-strings, and while Silvia might have any foolish thing she craved, any hat or dress or necklace, I was limited to my meager salary, and treated with no more respect than the page boy or the carriage driver.

"It might have gone on this way for eternity, hadn't a strange event set my mind in motion. An old retainer of Sir Lionel's, long retired, died several months ago. I was sent to Garrison and Grady's Undertaking Establishment, to see that the man was put away properly. I was standing in the store, talking with Grady, when a strange-looking man – small, dark-skinned, with black eyes and his hair cut in a bowl shape, like a child's – emerged from an inner room to ask some question. He threw up his hands and gave a cry when he saw me.

"'Russell has come back from the dead!'"

"It took us some time to calm him, to assure him I wasn't a ghost. I insisted, as my business was complete, that I be allowed to take him next door, to the public house, and buy him some whisky to calm his nerves.

"There, I learned the truth. He was a native of the dark jungles where my uncle had gone on his fatal voyage. Missionaries gave him a new name – Edwardo – and taught him the English language, though they had never succeeded in weaning him from his pagan religious practices. Because he could speak our tongue with some proficiency, he was hired by Sir Lionel as the chief of the native bearers who hauled the tents and scientific equipment into the tangled forests.

"Everything Sir Lionel claimed about that expedition had been a lie. Sir Lionel had never suffered from malaria. Indeed, he was the driving force of the party, and diverted it even deeper into uncharted regions when he heard a rumor of gold being found along the river. My uncle warned against this, but Sir Lionel prevailed, and the men plunged into the land claimed by the most dangerous of the local tribesmen. It was while in this land that the two halves of the expedition became separated. Sir Lionel and Edwardo, as well as a few others, were making their way back toward a rendezvous point when they heard the sounds of battle, the screams of the warriors and, above the din, my uncle crying for help. Edwardo and his men were ready to fight, but Sir Lionel's nerve failed him, and he ordered his party to retreat.

"'We could have perhaps saved them,' Edwardo told me, 'but Sir Lionel had us flee instead. Never will I forget their shouts and cries. Those were the most savage of the tribes, I have no doubt that their victims were tortured until they died.'

"I asked how he had come to be in London. He told me that Sir Lionel sent the rest of the bearers back into the jungle, retaining Edwardo only because of his language skills and his strong back. Edwardo knew he would be treated as an outcast, should he try to return to his own tribe. Sir Lionel grudgingly agreed to take him to England as a servant, but upon disembarking in London, he threw the man over. Edwardo had already heard Sir Lionel's account of the death of Russell, and he knew it for a falsehood, but Sir Lionel told him that should he ever speak out, he would never be believed. Indeed, who would take the word of a 'dirty savage' over the account of a white man who had received a knighthood for his services to the Crown? It was only by good fortune that he was able to find the most menial of employment, and eventually came into the service of the undertakers, for he was very skilled with his hands and a master of woodworking.

"I gave him what little money I could spare, for I felt some responsibility, as he was the only person in the world who had protested my dear uncle's fate. To test his tale's veracity, I began to grow out my moustache, so that I more truly resembled my relative. This action clearly distressed Sir Lionel. Every day, my very presence reminded him of the man he had betrayed. Few people knew it, but Sir Lionel was deeply superstitious, and believed in some of the strange omens and augers that he had encountered in his travels. That was why he would never sell any aspect of his collection, for he felt bad luck would follow. I suppose it was also why he allowed me to marry Silvia, and held us close, despite my heritage. Lying in bed at night, brooding over this knowledge, I devised a plan to use his past against him. But I swear to you that, at the time, it was only a vengeful fantasy.

"Then Sir Lionel departed on his European travels, much against the wishes of his physician, who had warned us privately that his nerves were very bad, that any sudden shock might kill him. The very next day, Silvia told me she believed she was expecting our first child. I knew I must act, for I was certain she would name my son after my tormentor, and that we would be required to raise the lad in this house. I felt I must win our freedom before our child came into the world. And so, I determined to deliver a fatal jolt to Sir Lionel's unsteady heart.

"I paid a visit to the rooms where Edwardo lived, a sordid set of chambers above Garrison and Grady's Mortuary. I described to him what I wanted. He never turned a hair, for as I have mentioned, our Christian faith had made little impression on him. Our plan all depended on locating the proper head, of the right sex and age, with the same bold moustaches that had distinguished my uncle. Edwardo soon sent me a note that just such a trophy had been found, borne upon the body of a man who had been run down in the street and had no relatives. The nearest church had offered to arrange the burial, and as Edwardo lived at the undertaking establishment, it was easy enough for him to slip down in the night and do the deed. He even went to the trouble of replacing the human head with a painted plaster one, covering it with enough shrouding that any mourner giving it just a moment's glance would be readily deceived.

"Edwardo transformed the head into the grisly trophy you now hold in that box. I will spare you the details of how such gruesome work is done, only to say that it takes time and must be handled with care. When the news arrived from Prague that Sir Lionel had suffered an attack, I had hopes there would be no need for our work to be revealed, but a telegram from Silvia, saying Sir Lionel had improved, made me stiffen my resolve. I had hopes of placing the head in the cabinet while Silvia was away, but the work wasn't complete, and the thing couldn't be rushed."

"Ah – that explains the need to secretly enter your home at night," Holmes said.

"Yes, for there was no way I could get it into the house otherwise. Silvia is most dear and clings to me, even when I work in these rooms. I saw no other way to deceive her. I feigned illness, and then sent a note around to Edwardo, who brought the thing to me in a bag. We met in the wee hours of the morning, several streets away. I had drugged our dog and left the French doors open so that I could most easily get into the trophy room. I climbed the wall, crossed the yard, and put the shrunken head where Sir Lionel shouldn't fail to see it once the cabinet was opened. I had no intention of staging a robbery, only of slipping the horrible relic into place. What I didn't anticipate was that my wife would awaken and the alarm go up so quickly. I was fortunate that I was able to run away, scale the fence, and then come back up the path, use my key, and race up the servants' stairs while my wife was still shrieking in the trophy room. Thus, I evaded detection. Of course, I claimed nothing was amiss, that the 'robbery' had been foiled, but you saw Silvia's insistence upon an investigation."

"What of the drums, and the strange smell?" I asked.

"When Sir Lionel returned, he was pale and unsteady. I thought perhaps I could hasten his demise by creating an atmosphere that played upon his guilt. The first evening, at supper, Silvia told him our happy news, and I used it to speak of perhaps giving the future child his old friend's name as well as his own. I even urged him to tell the story of their last adventure. I saw at once that this gave him discomfort. I later made sure to place some sleeping powders in the drinks of all the household, including my wife's, with the exception of Sir Lionel's. I knew him to be a light and restless sleeper, so in the deep hours I slipped downstairs and hid myself, beating softly on some drums from his collection. Twice he came down, looking about wildly. These nocturnal adventures taxed his strength and nerves. Silvia and the staff had sworn they wouldn't tell Sir Lionel of the break-in, but I did, in private, enhancing the story. I even claimed I had discovered naked footprints on the rug, and that I sensed some strange curse had descended upon our home.

"Then last night, I not only beat the drums, but I tossed a ball of incense into the fireplace. It was one which involved the lush smells of the tropical jungles. I also scrawled a note and placed it on his chair, bidding him to look in the cabinet. He came down at just after one a.m., sweating and staggering. When he read the note, he grabbed the key and opened the cabinet.

"There, hanging on the closest hook, was what he took to be the head of his friend, Neville Russell. I saw him step back, his face contorting in horror. Then he made a soft sound – barely a moan – and dropped to the floor. I hurried from my post, moved him closer to the fireplace, burned the note, and locked the cabinet. My plan had worked – the old murderer was dead, and my uncle's soul could finally rest."

Russell slumped forward, his head in his hands, and began to softly sob. I looked around the room. Gregson had gone pale, and his pencil was still. Holmes considered the weeping man with a solemn, appraising gaze, then motioned for us to retire into the next chamber. He closed the door behind him.

"There is no exit from that study besides this one, so we need not worry about Russell slipping away."

"What in blazes do I charge him with?" Gregson muttered. "He killed Sir Lionel as surely as if he put a bullet through his head, but what jury would condemn him on such evidence?"

"Rest assured, Gregson, that even if English justice doesn't prevail, he will answer to a higher judgement. It would be wise of you to immediately arrest the accomplice Edwardo, for the act of desecrating a corpse if no other, though – "

Holmes clipped his words, holding up his hands for us to remain silent. I thought I heard the faintest of sounds, like someone gently tiptoeing in the distance, in the hallway, but I could easily have been mistaken. Holmes sniffed, coughed, and then returned to his thoughts.

" – I expect you will find the bird flown back to his tropical paradise," Holmes continued. "My sympathies lie with the ladies in this case. One has been forced to endure losing her husband to tragedy and then learning that his body was disrespected. The other will know, in time, of her husband's perfidy. No matter how he may try to explain it, the lady's love for the man who raised her may be stronger than her love for the man who married her."

Readers of the history of the Empire, as well as those patrons of the sensational press, will surely recall the great honors that were heaped upon the late Sir Lionel Stedwell, along with the large and public funeral that drew mourners from across the nation and floral salutes from individuals scattered throughout the colonies. While the respectable *Times* attributed the old hero's demise to a chronic heart condition, the more lurid papers claimed he was the victim of a native curse, a fate brought on by his habit of stealing idols and offending pagan gods. This ridiculous story gained even more adherents and sold many more papers when, not a month later, the son-in-law of Sir Lionel, Wilbert Russell, perished while cataloging the explorer's massive collection of artifacts. He was found dead at his desk, having accidentally pricked himself with a poisoned dart, which he had mistaken for a harmless one while working late at night.

It was perhaps a year afterward that we encountered the widowed Mrs. Russell in Hyde Park with her baby and a nursemaid. She remained as lovely as ever. Indeed, the black mourning attire flattered her blonde hair and splendid complexion. Holmes rarely expressed interest in clients once their problems had been resolved, but in this instance, he drew me along to make a pointed effort to speak with the lady and inquire into her health and that of her little daughter. No mention of the case was made, and after a few polite exchanges we tipped our hats and sauntered along the pathway. I asked Holmes why he had stopped.

"Verification," Holmes said. "Her perfume was very distinctive, and I remember it well from that afternoon, outside of Sir Lionel's study. It lingered in the air as we discussed the case. Clearly, she eavesdropped and heard her husband's confession. I only wonder: Did she exchange the darts, making a poisoned one appear harmless? Or did she stand before Russell with a pistol pointed at his head, and he had no choice but to prick his own finger? The former, I suppose. Women are usually more cunning than men."

Dr. Watson's Dilemma
by Susan Knight

The following troubling narrative should, I think, make clear why I, a doctor bound by the Hippocratic Oath, have delayed decades in recording it, the events here described relating to the earliest years of my association with Sherlock Holmes, when we were first residing together in Baker Street. It was early January, a miserable damp and foggy month. Christmas, a season I love but which my associate abhors, had passed, hardly remarked at Baker Street, despite Mrs. Hudson's best efforts at festivity.

"Goodwill to all men, indeed," Holmes would blast. "Look around you, Watson. Truthfully, how much real goodwill do you see? Sentimental twaddle. I blame Mr. Charles Dickens for this mess."

He was hardly less enthusiastic about celebrating his birthday which followed hard on the heels of Yuletide, on 6 January. The first couple of years I spent with Holmes, I made the mistake of purchasing a gift for him, only to have it dismissed out of hand.

"You keep this scarf, Watson," he would say, "for I shall never wear it. I cannot abide a checkered pattern."

Or, "Do you not consider, Watson, that if I had need of a leather bound notebook embossed with my name, I could have purchased it myself?"

Needless to say, he never reciprocated with a gift for me on my birthday which falls in the altogether pleasanter month of August, and thus it was that I had decided not to buy him anything on this occasion. It was to my considerable surprise, therefore, that over the New Year, as we were finishing our supper, he gave a great stretch and said, "I have been thinking, Watson, of what gift you might buy for me this year. Rather than the dreary little surprises that it is your wont to offer, how much better if I tell you exactly what I should like to have."

"Well now – " I started to reply, but he held up his hand.

"Please do not tell me I am too late, that the wretched thing has already been purchased," he said, a smile tempering his harsh words.

I shook my head.

"Then I should like very much for you to go to Charing Court, one of those paved alleyways between the Charing Cross Road and St. Martin's Lane, where you can find all manner of fascinating book and print shops."

"Yes," I replied, "I know the place."

"Good. Well about halfway along you will find a dingy-enough establishment with, in the window, some ancient maps. I am particularly interested in the one featuring Asia Minor with its illustrations of the preposterously exotic humans imagined to inhabit those wild places."

An inscrutable expression on his face, he then reached for his pipe and stuffed it from the Persian slipper with the abominable weed it pleased him to smoke.

As it happened, I had business in the West End district on the following morning, and, that accomplished, made my way on foot to Charing Court. The day was cold, dank, and dismal, with a chill that penetrated to the very bones, a stink of smoke infecting the air and turning it yellow. My spirits thus being already low, worse was to come. The shop in question turned out to be a dark hole of a place hardly warmer inside than out, with a door bell that clanged like a veritable knell of doom. Nor did my mood lift, when, on requesting the Asia Minor map displayed in the cobwebbed window, I was informed that the price was six guineas, much more than I had intended to spend, especially for something so stained and torn at the edges. The grey-bearded elderly owner, as cobwebby as his establishment, saw that I hesitated.

"It is a beautiful map, your honour. An antique. Eight-hundred years old, it is. One of a kind. You won't get anything like it anywhere else."

As it happened, my business in town had resulted in an unexpected bonus payment, so that I had coins a-plenty rattling in my pocket.

"Will you take five guineas?" I heard myself say, having judged from the man's face that he would be ready to bargain."

"Oh sir, your honour," he replied. "You want to rob a poor bookseller of his profits . . . ." He paused. "Well, let's say, five-and-a-half guineas."

He held out a hand for me to shake.

Holmes is, after all, a very good friend, I thought, relenting, and I grasped the man's horny claw.

"Since I know what it is you have bought me," Holmes said, on my return to Baker Street, observing what I was holding, "you might as well give it to me at once."

This being three days before the anniversary in question, I was somewhat bemused. However, I duly handed the thing over and wished him many happy returns, receiving only a perfunctory nod and no thanks as he eagerly pulled the map from its tube. He spread it out on the table and pored over it.

"So how was old Balthazar?" he asked me.

"Who?"

"The bookseller. How did you find him?"

"Easily enough," I said, deliberately pretending to misunderstand, for I was annoyed with him. "Given your most precise directions."

He looked up at me. "No, what were your impressions of the man? How did he look?"

"Not very prepossessing," I replied. I hadn't realised I should be required to make a report and had not paid the man any particular attention.

"No more than that? You disappoint me, Watson."

"Old. A grey-beard."

"Yes . . . and?"

I closed my eyes to think. "A foreigner, though he speaks good English. Wearing a long robe and a kind of turban. An Arab, perhaps. A Jew."

"An Arab," Holmes said. "I should say so."

"You have met him yourself then?" I asked. So why then did you need to hear it from me, I wondered? It was all most provoking.

"No, I have never met the gentleman," Holmes replied. "Though I have heard of him, and, moreover, in more precise detail than you have been able to give me."

"I didn't take to him," was all I replied to that remark.

"Let us hope, anyway, he didn't charge you overmuch," he said after a while, studying the map. "A guinea or two would be a reasonable price, I think."

I wasn't about to reveal what I had paid – it was a gift, after all – but my dismay must have shown on my face, for Holmes exclaimed, "More! Much more! Oh, Watson, Watson. He saw you coming."

After a few moments, he continued. "And what of his esteemed companions, Mr. Kaspar and Mr. Melchior. Were they in attendance too?"

"I saw no one else, "I replied. "Only Balthazar." Whereupon Holmes raised quizzical eyes to mine, and I grinned. "Of course, the three wise men. Apologies, Holmes. I am very slow today."

"Not at all, dear friend. I have been teasing you. But come. There isn't a moment to be lost." He rolled up the map again, and replaced it in its tube.

"Where are we going?" I asked.

"Back to Balthazar, Watson. I'm afraid he has sold you a fake."

As we approached the alley, dark as a tunnel in the fading afternoon light before the gas lamps were lit, Holmes seized my arm.

"Now I'm going to surprise you, Watson, but whatever I say, keep a straight face and back me up if necessary."

My suspicions were growing by the moment that I had been used, and not for the first time, in one of Holmes's investigations. Why the man felt he couldn't fully confide in me was beyond my comprehension. However, I was becoming intrigued enough with the present case not to turn on my heel and abandon him, despite a little voice telling me I should do just that, to serve him as a lesson.

We entered the dusty shop to the clang of the doomful bell, Holmes stumbling somewhat and having to cling to my arm. At first it seemed as if the place were empty. Then, from the shadows, the old man emerged – again, to my mind, looking as if the cobwebs everywhere in evidence were clinging to him too.

Holmes raised his head and sniffed appreciatively. "Ah, the musty scent of old books."

"Good day again, honoured sir," Balthazar said to me. "Have you come to buy another of my fine maps?"

"Not at all," Holmes cried out angrily. "We have come to demand my friend's money back. You have sold him a modern forgery."

The old man shook his head vigorously.

"Certainly not, honoured sir! The map is genuine. One-thousand years old."

"You told me eight-hundred," I said.

Holmes removed it from its roll.

"I doubt it is one-thousand hours old," he said. "Where do you make them, old man? In the back of the shop? Is it coffee you use to stain it to look so ancient?"

"No, sir. I assure you. My reputation as an honest man is well known. Ask anyone. If it is a fake, as you say, then I too have been fooled, although . . . ."

To my horror, at that moment, Holmes clutched at his breast and staggered, falling against the counter.

"Sacker!" he gasped. "My elixir . . . ."

It took me a moment to realise that he was addressing me. Had he gone mad? Was he having a stroke? A man not yet thirty!

"My elixir, if you please." His voice was barely above a murmur. "In my breast pocket."

I reached in under his jacket and drew out a little vial of I knew not what. Uncorking it, I put it to his lips and he drank of it, seeming to find therein some assuagement.

"Thank you, dear friend," he muttered. "Thank you. Then he turned to Balthazar, who had been hovering anxiously.

"Is there somewhere I could sit down," he asked, "until the worst has passed?"

"Come back here, honoured sir," the old man replied, drawing aside a ragged curtain. "Rest for as long as you need."

Given the sharp way in which Holmes had previously addressed him, Balthazar's behaviour now showed, I judged, an unexpectedly worthy degree of compassion.

The room we were in was small and windowless, furnished with a table and three spindly chairs into one of which Holmes fell as with great relief. Bookshelves, filled with dusty tomes surmounted by rolls of ancient looking manuscripts, lined the walls of this gloomy space. A map lay spread out on the table, apparently of an age with the one I had so foolishly purchased. An antique or another fake?

The old man's eyes lit up as he smoothed his hand over the map.

"The North Atlantic, honoured sirs, as imagined by the old cartographers. See what monsters they thought to be lurking there."

It was hard to make them out but gradually I discerned grotesque forms emerging from the waves, threatening tiny ships with certain destruction.

"What fancies they had!" Balthazar remarked. "No sirs, it would be beyond my powers to make copies the likes of these."

He poured a cup of water from a jug and offered it to Holmes.

"I am sorry if we offended you," the latter said, accepting the drink. "Only I was sure, you know, the map was forged. It is this damned condition of mine. It gives me brain fever."

"You are badly afflicted then, honoured sir?" Balthazar asked.

"Sacker could tell you," Holmes replied looking at me. I was about to speak, not quite sure what to say, when Holmes went on. "It will prove fatal in the end, an end I confess that I crave, for the pain and suffering are sometimes beyond belief."

"Yes indeed," I said at last. "My friend's suffering is indescribable." True enough, I thought, for I had no idea what he was talking about.

"We are quick to put common beasts out of their misery," Holmes continued, "but when it comes to human beings whose awareness of pain is so much more acute, those of us suffering unutterable torments must endure until nature takes its course. It isn't right. And yet – and yet I fear the final coup. I tell you frankly, my friend, I would end myself this minute, if I had the courage to do it."

After this astonishing speech, Balthazar sat looking at Holmes for a while, then said, "Honoured sir, fate has led you to me."

"Indeed. And how is that?"

"For the moment, I should prefer not to say." He glanced at me. "However, if you would care to return tomorrow, alone, at this same hour, I shall be happy to enlighten you."

Holmes leaned across the table and grasped the man's hand.

"Can you help me then? Do you have some elixir stronger than the one I have to take away the pain?"

"I can most certainly assist you – but tomorrow, honoured sir, if you can wait that long."

"Every instant will drag for me until that moment," Holmes said rising, staggering again so that I was obliged to support him.

"In the meantime," Balthazar remarked, "I shall be glad to return the five guineas your friend here spent on the map."

"Five-and-a-half," burst out of me.

The old man regarded me with lidded eyes. "Five-and-a-half. Just so."

"Not at all," Holmes replied. "I was mistaken. I shall treasure the map for as long as – " His voice broke a little. " – for as long as I live."

"Till tomorrow then, honoured sir," the old man said. "By what name shall I know you?"

"You can call me Sherrinford," said Holmes. "Henry Sherrinford."

We left the shop to the accompaniment of the clanging knell of doom.

It wasn't until we were well away from Charing Court that Holmes no longer leaned on me but regained his normal sprightly step.

"That went rather well," he said cheerfully.

"I hope you will explain to me now what it was all about."

"My apologies, dear fellow. Yes, indeed. I shall be glad to tell all as soon as we get back to Baker Street."

"I am surprised you decided to keep the fake map," I said, chafing at the thought of my wasted five-and-a-half guineas.

"Good heavens, Watson. It's no forgery. Do you doubt I could recognise the genuine article? The map is exceedingly old and worth as much if not more than what you paid for it."

"But . . . but . . . ." It was all quite beyond me.

"A ploy, don't you know, to get me an introduction to the old gentleman. By the way, Watson. Remind me what it was that the original Balthazar brought as a gift to the child in the manger."

I paused for thought. "Hmm . . . Gold, frankincense and myrrh . . . But which . . . ."

"Myrrh, that's the thing. Myrrh, a reminder of mortality, used to anoint the bodies of the dead." He nodded as if it was all now quite clear to him. As for me, the foggy miasma rising about us was hardly thicker than the fog of incomprehension in my head.

Holmes could really be the most aggravating of men. It wasn't until we were warm and comfortable in front of a good fire, with glasses of Mrs. Hudson's fine Smoking Bishop in our hands, that he started to explain.

212

"You recall no doubt the circumstances relating to the death of Mr. Alfred Parkinson."

I nodded. The sorry accident that had caused the demise of that well-known merchant had filled the newspapers for a brief time some weeks before. It seemed that Mr. Parkinson had been heading on foot to his club when he had become disoriented in the fog and had stumbled into a ditch, drowning in just a few inches of water. As well as a glowing obituary of the merchant, I recalled that *The Times* had taken the opportunity to print a cautionary tale regarding elderly gentlemen who might (reading between the carefully worded lines), have over-indulged in spirituous liquors, thus rendering them incapable of clear thought and subject to unfortunate accidents.

"I have been approached," Holmes explained, "by Mr. Parkinson's nephew, a Mr. William Darnley, who suspects dark doings with regard to his uncle's death. Acting as one of the executors, Darnley recently received a bill from something called The Proxy Club, of which Mr. Parkinson was apparently a member. It seems the Club was looking to be paid what seemed an excessively high membership fee, the strange element being that payment was only to be made after the member's death."

"*After* the death! How very extraordinary."

"Yes, indeed. In fact, it was quite by chance that the nephew uncovered this detail. In the normal course, had Mr. Parkinson not retained the original contract – which I understand was hidden away in a secret compartment of his desk – the sum would have shown as a simple fee owing, which the executors would have paid among all other such pending debts." Holmes made a steeple of his hands and tapped the forefingers against his lips before continuing. "The other factor, of which Darnley informed me, was that in latter years his uncle was suffering from a painful wasting disease."

Holmes leaned back and looked at me.

"I see," I said.

"Do you? Do you, Watson? Tell me exactly what you see."

"Well . . . ." Of course, he had thrown me off kilter again. I had not a notion in my head.

"I have, as you may surmise, been looking into this same Proxy Club," Holmes went on, ignoring my confusion. "With some difficulty, I might add. It isn't listed among the regular clubs of the country. A lucky chance meeting with Inspector Lestrade recently – you recall of course, the Barlow case, in which I was instrumental in returning a fine Stradivarius to its owners – revealed to me that Lestrade wasn't unaware of the existence of this club, having noted it, without realising its

213

significance, as having among its members such dignitaries as Maria Angelotti, the opera singer, Herr Gartner, the German cultural attaché, and Benjamin Mortlake, the portrait painter."

"All dead!" I exclaimed.

"Precisely. And all suffering from incurable diseases."

"Good heavens, Holmes. What evil lurks here?"

He sipped his Smoking Bishop, smacking his lips. "There is after all one good thing to be said for the present season: It encourages Mrs. Hudson to brew up this most delectable and cheering beverage."

I refused to be distracted. "This Proxy Club is somehow linked to Balthazar, is it?"

"At last, Watson, light dawns in your benighted brain." He smiled, again to mitigate the stab of his words. "A complex trail, which I won't bother you with, has indeed led me to those unlikely premises at Charing Court. Today I essayed an experiment, and must thank you for playing your own part in it most admirably . . . ."

Had I? All unbeknownst, anyway. However, I nodded acceptance of this unwonted compliment.

"You think the bookseller is behind these deaths, then?"

"From my investigations, it seems most likely."

"And yet he seems so kindly! Good Lord, Holmes, what a cunning villain to be able to dissemble so well."

"Indeed, as you say: A cunning villain . . . ." Holmes nodded. "However, to be sure, I shall return tomorrow, as he requested, and beard the old greybeard in his lair."

"Is that safe?"

"Until this poor suffering individual signs a contract with him, yes, I am sure it is."

On the following day, I was most unwilling for Holmes to venture forth alone. However, he reminded me of Balthazar's stipulation.

"I don't think he will reveal himself fully if you accompany me."

"Can I not at least bring you to the shop? Ill as you are." I sniffed. "After all, you can hardly reach it safely alone. What if you were to collapse in the street?"

He regarded me quizzically. "My word, Watson, you are becoming as devious as I. An ungainsayable argument. Yes, by all means, bring me, limping and staggering, to the shop and then, if required, make yourself scarce until the time comes to remove me again."

I noticed that his skin was turned grey and that his eyes seemed shot with blood. Was he truly ailing?

"You are looking askance at me, Watson. I haven't over-done the cosmetics, I hope."

Understand that in those days I was still unused to the degree to which Holmes could change his appearance in the twinkling of an eye.

Once again at the appointed hour, what light there was already fading, we made our way to the dingy little shop in Charing Court, Holmes becoming ever more reliant on my support the nearer we approached.

"Who knows who might be keeping a look-out," he whispered to me.

The old man frowned as we entered.

"Alone, I said, Mr. Sherrinford."

"I cannot manage by myself for any distance," Holmes replied. "And Sacker here is entirely in my confidence."

"Not possible, honoured sir," Balthazar replied firmly. "There must only be the two of us."

"So be it," Holmes replied with a sigh. "I suppose you can occupy yourself elsewhere, my friend, for – " He looked at the other. " – a half-hour?"

Balthazar nodded.

I was loth to leave, but Holmes nodded reassuringly. However, just as I was on my way out, a little girl entered. She was thin, with tangled dark curls and a grubby face, wearing a ragged dress and shawl, hardly sufficient for the chill of the day. At least she wasn't barefoot as were so many of her ilk, even if the boots she was wearing were several sizes too big for her.

"Ah, Sal," said Balthazar kindly. "Have you come for your basket?"

"Yes, if you please, Uncle," the girl replied, watching us warily.

"Wait just a moment," the old man said, disappearing into the room at the back of the shop.

"Are you sure?" I started to say softly to Holmes. "I'd much rather stay."

Sal's bright eyes passed from one of us to the other.

Holmes just shook his head as Balthazar returned, carrying a large basket, its contents covered with a cloth.

"How is little Tommy?" he asked the girl.

"Not so good, Uncle. A bit better, mebbe."

"I hope so. I've put in some linctus. It should help him. Now will you be able to manage by yourself?"

Sal lifted the basket. It was evidently almost too much for the little mite, but she nodded.

"Why don't I carry it for you?" I said. "I have time on my hands, after all."

The girl looked reluctant to yield her treasure until the old man said, "Thank the kind gentleman, Sal." While to me, he added, "It isn't too far. The Devil's Acre."

I shuddered. Despite efforts to clear that particular district in recent times, it was notorious as a dangerous slum. Still, I had offered and couldn't now very well demur, so lifted the heavy basket and accompanied Sal from the shop.

The girl kept a close watch on me as if suspecting that at any moment I might make off with whatever was in the basket. Together we dodged the traffic to reach Trafalgar Square, Sal more adept than I at circumventing the rushing hansom cabs and carriages, even with the handicap of the too big boots. She waited for me by one of the great bronze lions, a mocking expression on her face.

"That's a scary beast," I said, attempting to engage her in chat.

"It isn't real," she replied dismissively, tossing her curls.

This wasn't at all promising and I resigned myself to a silent trek, down Whitehall with its imposing buildings and palaces, past the gothic glory that is Westminster Abbey, such a contrast to the place whither we were bound. Indeed, all too soon we found ourselves in the warren of slum streets known as the Devil's Acre. I had visited here several times before in the course of my medical duties, on each occasion ever more horrified at the conditions these poor people had to endure. Tumbling down tenements with broken or no windows, tiles fallen from roofs, leaving interiors open to rain, hail, and snow, the wretched inhabitants crammed to overflowing in mildewed rooms, unspeakable filth running in the streets between, fat rats glimpsed in all corners. Still today it makes me angry that the authorities have failed so dismally to improve the lot of this portion of the population, some self-righteous individuals even justifying their inactivity by claiming, erroneously, that it is their own immorality that has reduced the poor to this level.

Meanwhile, Sal had stopped at a door patched up with odd planks of wood. She stretched out her hand for the basket.

"This is us," she said. "Upstairs."

"Let me bring it for you," I replied. For it was indeed very heavy.

She shrugged and led the way up a gloomy stairwell, the treads treacherous from rot.

The room occupied by her family was in no way luxurious, but at least it was clean. Clearly some effort had been made to render it homely with pictures from almanacs pinned to the walls and a bunch of those flowering weeds that grow so freely on waste ground set in a jam jar, but it was very cold, a miserable fire struggling in the grate. Two little mites

216

played on a thin rug on the wooden floor. A thin and harassed looking woman stared at us in astonishment as we entered.

"Who's this then, Sal?" she asked

"Don't know, mammy," came the reply. "He *would* carry the basket for me."

The woman's eyes lit up at the sight of that receptacle.

"Oh, you got it. God bless the old man," she said. "And you too, sir," she addressed me, "if you have anything to do with it."

I quickly disabused her of any association with Balthazar.

"He may not be a Christian by religion," the woman went on, examining the contents of the basket which seemed to me comprised of meats and cheeses and other comestibles, combined with items of woollen clothing, even a woven blanket, "but he's more of a Christian than many who call themselves that."

She picked out a bottle that was lying on top, "What's this?"

"Something for Tommy, Uncle said," Sal replied.

I became aware of a bed in the corner covered, as I had thought at first, with a heap of rags. But they shifted from time to time, and now a small wan face emerged from under the sheets. A paroxysm of coughing ensued.

"Here Tommy, love," his mother said. "Here's something to make you better."

I stepped forward.

"May I see it, Madam?" I asked. "I happen to be a doctor."

Perhaps she was astonished to be addressed so politely, but she handed me the bottle readily enough. I opened it and sniffed at the linctus provided by Balthazar. If the man was indeed a murderer, I was disinclined to let the boy partake of anything he provided. However, it smelt sweetly of elecampane and I judged it harmless enough, and indeed, even perhaps efficacious.

"Would you like me to examine the little fellow?" I asked, giving the woman back the bottle.

She stared at me for a moment.

"I can't pay you, sir," she said finally.

"No. I wouldn't look to be paid," I replied. "Just to see if there is anything I can do for him."

"Well, God bless you too, then, sir."

Poor Tommy had a racking cough and a fever that caused his body to go into frequent convulsions. Recovery from what was clearly a bad chest infection wouldn't be helped by the fact that he was clearly undernourished. In my opinion, which I expressed to his mother, Tommy should be in hospital. She looked horrified.

217

"Oh no, sir. Not the hospital. When people go in them places they never come out again."

I was taken aback at the force of her words.

"Not at all, my dear woman. They help the sick get better."

"Not my mother nor my father neither. Never seen them again after, except they be cold and dead."

She wasn't to be convinced and Tommy clung to her in terror at the very suggestion. I therefore relinquished the idea, and instead gave instructions as to his further care, writing out what medicines he should be given, and handing her a couple of sovereigns to cover the cost and more.

"Plenty of beef tea, too," I said, "for all of you."

Mrs. Mullins, for that had proved to be the poor woman's name, was overcome, tears streaming down her worn face as she grasped at my hand. I think she would have kissed it, had I not gently withdrawn it.

"What of your husband?" I asked, since I had discerned signs of a man's presence in the shape of a cocked hat and a waterproof coat. "Is he a working man?" A seafarer I was thinking.

Mrs. Mullins lowered her eyes, silent.

"Working, is it!" exclaimed Sal, with a cynicism way beyond her years. "Oh yes, Mister. Working hard lifting mugs of ale in the Pig'n'Whistle."

"Sal!" said her mother, blushing with shame.

"Well, it's true and you know it, Mammy."

I was careful not to express a judgement and just remarked, "Be sure, then, to keep those sovereigns for the purposes I told you of. In fact, Sal, why don't you come with me now to buy that medicine for Tommy?"

Thus it was that I was tardy enough returning to Charing Court where I found Balthazar and Holmes sitting together in that same poky back room. There was a tension in the air. Balthazar looked to be almost pleading with Holmes, who, I noticed, was no longer acting the invalid.

"It must stop right now," Holmes was saying, "or I shall be forced to take further action."

"But honoured sir – consider the unnecessary suffering."

"Mr. Alfred Parkinson – " Holmes began.

Balthazar interrupted him. "I have already tried to explain that the case of Mr. Alfred Parkinson was a terrible mistake. No one expected the old gentleman to attempt to walk out to his club on such a terrible foggy evening. When I left him, he was as comfortable as he could be, with his glass of brandy to hand – "

"His poisoned glass," Holmes said.

218

Balthazar lifted his shoulders, making that open-palmed gesture of submission with his hands that I recalled as characteristic of persons encountered on my travels in Asia.

What was going on here? Had Parkinson been poisoned? In error?

"Ah, Watson," Holmes exclaimed. (So I was no longer to be – what was it? – *Sacker* any more then.) "Mr. Balthazar here has been explaining to me the mysterious workings of the Proxy Club."

"You tricked me, honoured sir," Balthazar said reproachfully, shaking his hoary locks. "I took you on in good faith."

"A necessary deceit, I'm afraid."

"Can anyone tell me what you are talking about?" I said.

There was a pause. Then Balthazar spoke in low tones.

"It began with my wife," he said. "Mariam. A wonderful woman. The light of my life." The depth of his emotion could be read on the man's face. "But she fell sick – so very sick that nothing could be done to ease the pain. I saw this strong woman turn to a skeleton. And yet she didn't die." He wiped a tear from his face.

"Go on," I said gently. I had seen many cases like it in the course of my work, a cruel fate indeed.

"Mariam begged me to help her pass," he said. "At first I was shocked – *horrified* at her request. She confessed that she had wished to end it many times but couldn't bring herself to take that final step. I tried to convince her that it was a terrible sin, but as you said yourself, honoured sir, on that first visit, she asked me in reply how is it that we don't hesitate to put beasts out of their misery, but refuse that mercy to our fellow humans. Allah would understand, she said, hanging on to my hand." He shook his old head. "That night Mariam's suffering was unspeakable. For hours on end she screamed out in agony. I couldn't bear it." He wrung his hands. "Honoured sirs, I have some knowledge of herbal remedies, and so, like the Ancient Greeks, prepared a concoction of opium and hemlock that would cause her to die quickly and without pain. Her last words to me were a blessing and a promise to meet me one day again in Paradise."

He fell silent. We too were lost for words.

"I then swore to myself, honoured sirs," he said, "to assist similarly any poor suffering soul who wished it, and the Proxy Club was born."

"Death by proxy," I muttered grimly.

"Precisely," he replied. "An acquaintance of mine is a medical man – like yourself honoured sir," he said, bowing to me. When I looked surprised that he knew of me, he added, "Oh, I have heard many times of the esteemed Dr. Watson, associate of Mr. Sherlock Holmes here."

I inclined my head, though rather suspecting that he flattered me more than I deserved.

219

He continued to explain. "This acquaintance, whose name I shall never reveal, will indicate to me from time to time anyone he thinks might benefit from membership of the club, any suffering soul who dares not take that final step or who has scruples regarding suicide."

"A doctor sends you people to kill!" I exclaimed, deeply shocked. "But that is against all our principles. Our calling, as medical men, is to preserve life, not to take it. Good Lord, man, has your friend not sworn to the Hippocratic Oath?"

"Have you never administered a medicine to a dying patient that eases the pain but speeds the end?" Balthazar asked me. "It is a question of humanity, honoured sir."

We gazed at each other. Truly, the man had answers for everything.

"Putting ethical questions aside for a moment." Holmes interrupted the silence, "how exactly does it work, Balthazar – this club of yours? You told me earlier that the subject of your dubious ministrations knows not the day nor the hour when their end will come."

"Not exactly true, honoured sir. Some wish to know it and that obviously makes it easier for me. Others prefer not, for whatever reason. In addition, as I indicated, I like to wait a while after they have signed the contract in case they change their minds. Few do, I might add. In that case, since payment to the club only occurs after the . . . er . . . *passing*, no funds are sought and the contract is torn up."

"Yet many of your clients are rich and pay well for your services. At least, I assume so," Holmes remarked with disdain, "given what you suggested I should pay,"

"I charge what I think each person can afford, which sometimes is nothing at all," the other replied with some dignity. "Look at me, honoured sir. Am I a rich man? No, I live off what I earn from this little shop, which isn't very much. All the money from the Club goes to help the living – people like little Sal who was here earlier. You will have seen how that poor family lives, Doctor," he said, bowing again to me. "But there are so many, so many in the same predicament. What I can provide is a mere drop in a great ocean."

Again we fell silent. For me, while I couldn't in any way condone the source of the man's philanthropy, yet I was beginning to understand why he acted as he did, misguided though he was. As for Holmes, he stood up abruptly.

"Give me your word, Mr. Balthazar," he said, "that the Proxy Club will cease its operations as of today, and no more will be said on the subject."

"But Holmes," I interjected, "surely the police must be informed."

"Mr. Balthazar?" he said again, ignoring me.

220

"I cannot make such a promise," the old man said. "So many depend on me. Do what you must, honoured sir, as will I."

"Come, then, Watson." Holmes swept from the room, I following out of the shop, that awful bell clanging behind us.

"Straight to Scotland Yard, I suppose," I said.

He didn't answer me, and I was most surprised when he turned, not to Whitehall, but homeward, to Baker Street.

All the way through the foul fog of the streets, he kept silent, his head down as if deep in thought. Finally, he muttered, "If there are any more 'mistakes', like in the case of old Parkinson, I shall surely inform Lestrade. Otherwise – "

"Otherwise?" I stopped short. "Holmes, I cannot believe it of you. Are you really intending to let Balthazar continue with his murderous ways?"

He turned towards me then. I was shocked at the agonised expression on his face.

"I have never told you this, Watson, but someone very close to me suffered the way the old man described the sufferings of his wife. That person had no means of liberation, and lived on in agony until at long last succumbing to the disease. It was terrible to witness. Terrible."

"I understand," I started to say. "But as a doctor – "

Holmes laid a hand on my arm.

"Hush," he said. "Hush."

My friend didn't bid me stay quiet about what we had discovered: He left it to me to decide, which in some ways was worse. How I struggled with my conscience. It wasn't right. It couldn't be right. And yet, and yet . . . Many a night turned to dawn before my exhausted brain succumbed to a disturbed sleep. In the end, Holmes not reporting any crime and even letting Mr. Parkinson's nephew understand that there was nothing untoward about his uncle's demise, I kept silent too, though whenever I heard of a sudden and unexpected death I couldn't but wonder if we had made a morally justifiable choice.

It is only now when both Holmes and I are old and approaching that same portal with its ominously clanging bell, that I have felt able to reveal all. Balthazar is long gone, his shop sold, the Proxy Club, as far as I know, no longer in existence.

As far as I know.

The Colonial Exhibition
by Hal Glatzer

Prologue

Sherlock Holmes had no use for games. He admired the athleticism of cricket, football, and rugby, but joined no teams. In his youth, he'd computed how roulette wheels favored the casino, and eschewed gambling thereafter. I never saw him take a flutter with a bookmaker. He refused to trust in luck.

The conviviality of men around a table at whist, poker, or bezique might have been a healthy distraction from his darker moods. With his enormous intelligence, Holmes could have made a fortune at cards. But they held no fascination for him. Even on dismal winter nights when I suggested cribbage, Holmes always declined. "I get no thrill from the turn of a card," he said. "And the only 'knaves' that pique my interest are the perpetrators of crime who remain at liberty."

So it was surprising to discover he kept a board-game in our sitting room.

In 1898, toward the end of August, I was reorganizing volumes in the tall bookcase I shared with Holmes and spotted an old edition of *Bartlett's* on the topmost shelf, where I must have left it years ago. I stood on tiptoes to retrieve it, but as I snagged the binding with one finger, down it came, along with a colorful game board and deck of cards. The book struck my shoulder, the board glanced off my temple, and the cards scattered across the carpet.

Holmes laughed. "Does *Bartlett* have a quote about parlor games?"

"What is this?"

"A souvenir."

I picked up a few of the cards. On one side the words *"Tentoonstellings Spel"* were printed.

"What's this? It isn't English."

"Dutch, old chap. I brought it back from Amsterdam in '83."

"Has it been up on that shelf these past fifteen years?"

"I suppose so. I never told you about that case, did I?"

I always hoped to learn of cases that he'd worked on without me. "Perhaps you could do so now. How did you come to possess this . . . souvenir? I don't recall seeing it before."

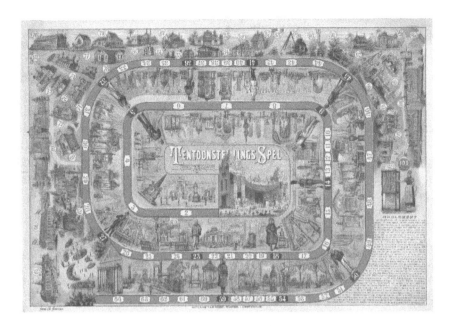

A *Tentoonstellings Spel* Game

"We were not so well acquainted, then," said he, "and I was still very much a 'lone wolf', distrustful of other people. You know, it was only to share the rent that I was willing to live with a stranger. And you have chronicled how difficult a flat-mate I was – then."

He waited for me to make the obvious retort, but I merely smiled.

"The fact is, Watson, it took me well over a year to grow accustomed to your constant presence, and almost three to include you in my work. Don't take offense. You befriended me before I reciprocated. You are the first real friend I have ever had, and I have known you longer than any other."

"You trusted me from the start, Holmes. You brought me along on cases."

"Some, but not all. In those early years together, you will recall, there were times I would absent myself for days."

"A 'lone wolf' on the scent, were you?"

"In this particular instance, and at that particular time, this particular case had to be concealed from the public – even from you, Watson."

"So . . ." I could not keep from smiling, "is there is no longer any reason to keep it from me? Or from the public? Has something happened to – ?"

223

"Just this year, yes. Cast your mind back a decade-and-a-half to 1883, and I shall put you in the picture."

While I gathered up the board and the cards, he took soda water from the gasogene in his whisky and leaned back on the sofa. I did likewise to my own whisky, settled into the basket chair, and put my feet up on the ottoman.

"In those days, and in my mind's eye, Watson, I was still as much a chemist as a detective. The success of my test for haemoglobin had made me keen to do something even greater in the laboratory. I was still conducting experiments over there at my table, some of which released such noxious odours that you would throw open the windows and go away for a few hours to escape the fumes."

"I remember!"

"It was on one such day in June. You'd gone off to your club or somewhere, because an especially unpleasant aroma was lingering. I hoped no one but I would notice, but there was a knock at the door. I opened it, and there stood Bradstreet, who had recently been promoted – the youngest Inspector in the Metropolitan Police."

"What did he want?"

"Ah! Let me reconstruct the case for you. Would you care to take notes? If you should publish, I insist you attain the highest degree of accuracy in your report, for this turned out to have enormous significance for an entire nation."

"As I was not there with you, would you consider letting me write in your voice? To have you narrate your own case?"

He drew twice on his cigarette. "No romantic excess! Will you promise? Just facts and deductions."

"Now, Holmes, you must give me some leeway there, for the smooth flow of storytelling. Please relate the process by which the facts you observed led to the deductions you made. And it would greatly help if you would take me through the case from start to finish in chronological order."

"All right. But I must have final approval of the manuscript before you send it off someday to your editor at *The Strand*."

"Of course . . . ."

Chapter I

"Can you come and view a body, Mr. Holmes?" asked Inspector Bradstreet as soon as I opened the door. "If you're free, that is."

I had been, stoically, trying to ignore the malodour with which my latest chemical experiment had filled the room. So I leapt at the opportunity to leave for a while.

The cab let us out in a narrow Soho street lined with two-story houses. A constable who'd been on watch in front of one of them opened the outer door and took up a post on the steps.

A vain, Napoleonic bureaucrat came through from the parlor to meet us in the vestibule. Short, with a pugnacious sneer, he was nearly a caricature of the small man attempting to project strength. Over a round and shiny bald pate he'd brushed the few remaining threads of his hair, to appear younger. Hunched shoulders implied much desk-work. Bradstreet introduced us.

Edward Stanley, Earl of Derby, said, "Thank you for coming so swiftly. I was to meet a fellow here, found the front door unlocked, and came inside to wait. I saw . . . him . . . there, ran out and fetched the constable who was walking in the next street.

Bradstreet said, "I was on duty when Lord Derby and the constable came in to report what they'd found. My superior was out on an important case, so I came back here with them. But there's something queer about this business, Mr. Holmes."

"I told Inspector Bradstreet that Her Majesty's government will need to have . . . an ongoing presence in this investigation," added the Earl. "And that it must be conducted with great delicacy."

"I suggested to Lord Derby, with all due respect, my Lord, that he might want to consult a certain enquiry agent in Baker Street."

"When the inspector said your name, Mr. Holmes, I knew I could trust him. I've heard of you through . . . official channels. And the fact is, it would be in the interest of the government to keep this incident out of the public eye for as long as possible."

Words like "official channels" and "in the interest of Her Majesty's government" always bring Mycroft to mind. Likely, at some point, I would hear from my brother.

I smiled. "Thank you for the recommendation, Inspector. Now, if you please . . . ." I parted them and opened the inner door from the vestibule.

There had been a meeting in the parlor not long before, to hear an informal lecture. Seventeen chairs had been set in two imperfect but concentric rings. A small table alongside one chair held a glass tumbler and a ewer of water for the speaker.

But six of the chairs were scattered, and where they'd stood, a man's body lay face-down on the wooden floor. Struck from behind, the impact had propelled the victim forward, to land flat on his face. Blood had seeped out of his head and coagulated beside his neck. I examined the wound

225

through my lens. The parietal had been crushed. The shape of the depression suggested a dowel or broomstick, but heavier.

Bradstreet pointed to one of the overturned chairs. "Could that have been the murder weapon?"

There was a bloodstain on one of the legs, with hairs and bits of flesh adhering. "Good eyes, Inspector! This was not premeditated. It was an impulsive act. The killer picked up the chair, swung it into the fatal blow, let it fall, and made no effort to hide it. Notice that there's plenty of blood around his head, and on the floorboards, but no streaks. What does that tell you?"

"I think . . . he was killed right where he fell. If he'd been attacked elsewhere and dragged here to where he lies, there would be blood evidence."

"Correct. Please roll him over."

By his face, the victim was young – the early twenties, I should say – but with a prematurely retreating hairline. He was fully dressed, his black cravat still snugged at the neck. The fall had broken his nose and shattered his eyeglasses. His suit-jacket and trousers were of fine Harris tweed, but *prêt-a-porter* – not bespoke. I rolled up his sleeves and trouser legs but found no additional injuries.

Lord Derby, keeping his distance from the body, called out, "Could a burglar have come in intending to steal something, and . . . found the place wasn't empty?"

"He was not killed by a burglar. In light of your call for discretion, do you know this man? He was left-handed, and earned a respectable living as a librarian."

Bradstreet laughed. "What did I tell you, my Lord? I've seen Mr. Holmes name a man's occupation from the callosities on his hands!"

I nodded. "Hands, yes, but more than that, this time. His clothes are dear, though not an extravagance, and his eyeglasses are rimmed in eighteen-karet gold which, likewise, means he had a sufficient income to afford quality accoutrements. The remains of the eyeglass lenses show they were ground to correct for hyperopia. Thus, the man was farsighted, and needed spectacles to read or do close work. Do I need to say more? Lord Derby: The fellow you came here to meet – is he the dead man?"

"No."

"Excuse me, Mr. Holmes. Could it not have been a burglar? There was no billfold or money in his pockets – that suggests he was robbed. Perhaps the burglar intended only to knock the man out, to facilitate his burglary, and didn't realize he'd killed him."

Lord Derby nodded. "Would you let the record say so, Inspector? To forestall any further enquiries."

"Oh, my Lord, I don't know if I can – "

"He was killed by someone he trusted."

Lord Derby demanded, "How do you know that, Mr. Holmes?"

"He was upright and wearing his spectacles when he was struck. Most likely, he had been reading or examining something close-up while he stood or walked. And was likely also talking with his attacker, for he had no hint of danger. There are no defensive wounds on his arms. Whatever he had been carrying, his attacker took the thing away with him."

Bradstreet looked perplexed. "You said a moment ago that he was a librarian – and left-handed."

"Do you see?" I pointed to the body. "His palms are not calloused, so he did not do manual labor. His cuffs and sleeves are worn shiny on the outer side. That comes from resting his arms on a desk. But he did not write a great deal, nor did he use a mechanical adding machine very often. There is only a slight indentation from holding a pen between the forefinger and second finger of his left hand. As to his right, there is only a very thin callus on the fingertips from striking keys. But there is a small blue stain on the outside edge of the little finger of his right hand, which I recognize as ink from a stamp-pad. So . . . what kind of work is done, sitting at a desk, that involves reading but not much writing, the occasional use of an adding machine, but the far more frequent use of a gutta-percha stamp? That of a librarian, of course. Oh, and he also had some recent experience with chemistry."

Lord Derby stepped closer to me. "The chemistry of explosives?"

That was unexpected! But it opened a fresh line of enquiry. "Possibly. I should know for certain, later in the day."

Bradstreet smiled. "You say he knew chemistry, Mr. Holmes. Was that by the discolorations on his fingers?" He pointed to my own hands. "You have similar stains."

"Excellent, Bradstreet! Most likely, the library where he worked specializes in the natural sciences, where he would have easy access to chemistry texts. My Lord, I suggest you delegate someone from your bureau to visit the London libraries that have scientific collections. One of their assistants is absent from work today."

I took a small envelope from my pocket, broke a splinter off a safety matchstick, slid it under the victim's fingernails, and saved the scrapings in the envelope. "I will examine this in Baker Street, under a microscope, and let you know what I see. Bradstreet, you found no billfold in the man's clothes. What did he carry in his pockets?"

He reached in, and withdrew a handkerchief and a latch key. "This was all, so I put it back."

"Nothing in his jacket?"

"No, sir."

"Check it again. The lining, too."

Bradstreet had to turn him over again to reach the back of the jacket. There was a flap in the silk, closed by a button. That was not how a tailor would repair a torn lining. He undid the button and extracted something thin and hard that had been concealed within. "Here's a postal card."

I took hold of it. "This is not a postal card. There is printed matter on both sides, but no space for an address or a stamp."

The card stock was white cardboard, measuring a little over three by four inches. On one side were the words "*Tentoonstellings Spel*" in ornate black letters in a fancy frame. On the reverse, the words "*Verenigd Koninkrijk*" in serif capitals ran along one of the short sides, forcing the card to be regarded vertically with that word at the bottom. Above it was a collage of images that had been printed first in black ink and then hand-colored: Tiny brush-strokes were visible where watercolors had been applied. Among the illustrations were the interior of a cotton textile mill, a locomotive beside a canal-lock within an industrial landscape of factories topped by smokestacks, and two ships at sea on a common course – one a merchantman, the other a Royal Navy gunboat. The collage was surmounted by a silhouette of Victoria in profile.

Lord Derby took it from my hands and said, "I know what this is and what it represents. I must return immediately to my offices and discuss what I have learned here. But let the three of us meet in your flat, Mr. Holmes, in two hours' time. There, I will tell both of you what I know, and you will understand why we need to keep this out of the public eye."

Chapter II

Open windows had largely cleared the air in the sitting room, and tobacco fumes soon overwhelmed lingering traces.

Lord Derby set down his cigar. "I realize, Mr. Holmes, that you did not recognize my name this morning. I am rarely seen or quoted in the newspapers."

"I deduced that are a senior government official, but I take little interest in politics. What position do you hold? And why are you taking such a keen interest in this little murder?"

"I am Prime Minister Gladstone's Secretary of State for the Colonies. There is, right now, an international fair in Amsterdam – the Colonial and Export Trade Exhibition – and in my official capacity, I'm responsible for how Great Britain and our colonies are represented at this Exhibition. We and the Netherlands are the largest exhibitors. The other colonial powers exhibiting are Spain, France, Germany, Portugal, Belgium, Russia,

228

Austria-Hungary, Ottoman Turkey, the United States, our South African Republic, and the Transvaal, which is allied with the Netherlands. Since the Exhibition opened last month, thousands of visitors have already come. The fair's administrators expect hundreds of thousands will have toured the exhibits by the time it all closes in October."

Bradstreet was growing impatient. (That is perhaps his only flaw as a detective.) His eyes wandered about the room. But a moment of silence had just opened, and he blurted, "Please, my Lord. Mr. Holmes needs to know why he has been consulted. And I need to know why you want me to attribute this murder to a burglar."

"I am coming to that!" he retorted. "All across Europe there are socialists, communists, and anarchists who are opposed to colonialization. At least two such cells – that we know of – are plotting to detonate explosive devices within the exhibition grounds, and that little parlor in Soho is where the English cell was planning its campaign. Mind you, these are not Russian revolutionaries. These are English socialists – members of a subversive organization here in London that was formed up at the beginning of this year, and is rather philosophically named 'The Fellowship of the New Life'."

That rang a bell. I drew on my pipe and recalled seeing the group. They were pamphleteers. I'd passed one of their gatherings in Hyde Park a few weeks previous, and stopped to listen to an oration. A young man called Havelock Ellis was advocating the abolition of marriage in favor of something he called "free love". But as I have never loved, and have no interest in marriage, I did not take their pamphlets.

Lord Derby, however, had brought along some of their tracts and spread them out on the side-table. Only one dealt with unconventional nuptials. The others were a reckoning of the evils of capital, a screed against leading financiers, praises for the nobility of the laboring classes, and a call to action for a socialistic future in Europe. There was also a fresh edition of Marx's *Communist Manifesto*.

"This card that the dead man carried in a secret pocket," said Lord Derby, holding it up, "is one of a set from a parlor game that's sold in Amsterdam as a souvenir of the colonial exhibition. '*Tentoonstellings Spel*' means '*Exhibition Game*'. Each of the colonial powers is represented by a card, similar to this one. '*Verenigd Koninkrijk*', is Dutch for '*United Kingdom*'. And the illustrations depict of some of the U.K.'s characteristic industries. Each of the other countries is represented by a card, with pictures of what that country is best known for. The various colonies around the world are represented on cards as well, with what they export to their mother country. The colonies and industries also appear on the

229

game board, as stations along a spiral track – a labyrinth in reverse – that starts at the center and ends along one edge.

"Each player takes a great power for himself, and progresses along the track around the board in increments, set by the throw of dice. The object of the game is to collect the greatest number of cards for colonies and industries."

"In effect, to acquire the largest empire."

With that pugnacious sneer, he said, "Yes, Mr. Holmes. The anti-colonial forces at work in the world are keen to point to a few bad apples among the empires, and to claim, therefore, that the whole ton of apples is rotten. Their latest target is Leopold, King of the Belgians, who – we must admit – has been treating the blacks in his Congo shamefully. But I'm sure you will agree that Britain's administration of India is exemplary. Under English law, everyone in the subcontinent benefits from being subjects of the British Empire. We have given them modern medicine, government, and schools – 'Civilization', if you will. As a principle of governance, one should exercise enlightened benevolence toward one's inferiors."

"There is opposition to colonialization. It has been growing ever since the American Revolution a century ago. But fortunately, colonials do not break free of their masters easily. Even when they do – "

"I'm sorry, Lord Derby. International affairs stand far outside my bailiwick."

"The important thing, Mr. Holmes, is that colonial rebellions must be suppressed. Ideally, they must be prevented. And the best way to do that is to ensure that our subjects are happy, or at least satisfied, under the *status quo*. No one wants them incited to rise up against their masters. Which is why if a bomb should be detonated at the trade fair in Amsterdam, especially if it were directed against the United Kingdom's exhibit, or the Netherlands' own, that could spark conflagrations at home and abroad. A raft of bombings in Europe, or in the principal cities of the colonies, might well follow."

Explosives, at last!

"Excuse me, Lord Derby," interrupted Bradstreet. "The Metropolitan Police has had a bit of surveillance going on with regard to this Fellowship of the New Life. We always want to keep sharp, don't we, in case a rally turns into a riot. I've talked with some of the coppers who've been keeping watch in Hyde Park, but none of them's ever heard talk of any bomb business."

"The socialists in this Fellowship, I admit, are a harmless lot. They talk of resisting authority, they make angry speeches, they paint slogans on walls, but they don't break icons or tear down statues. And they don't hurt people. But we have reason to believe that anarchists have lately

230

infiltrated the Fellowship. They are the ones we must watch out for. They advocate the overthrow of governments, and they're prepared to kill and be killed for their cause. We believe that the dead man was one of these anarchists, and that he was making a bomb."

I opened my hands, by way of asking: *How?*

"I have an agent posing as a member of the Fellowship."

"I thought as much. And you ought to have told me at the start. You were foolish not to."

He scowled. Men in high positions bristle at criticism. But he knew I was right. "Last week," said he, "my agent reported that an anarchist in the Amsterdam Fellowship cell contacted one of the anarchists in the London cell, asking him to send over an explosives expert – someone unknown to the Dutch authorities – to make a bomb that they will set off to disrupt the Exhibition. Such an action would, obviously, discredit the colonial empires which extend farthest around the world – particularly the empires of Great Britain and the Netherlands."

"I would question your agent's effectiveness."

"Why, Mr. Holmes?"

"In a group like this, with at least seventeen members – the chairs," I explained. "There could well be a pacifist, humanitarian faction, opposed to violence and bombs – opposed to the anarchists, that is. Has your agent never reported on such opposition? And if there truly is no pacifist faction, couldn't your agent form one up, and lead others to break free of the bomb-throwers, without exposing his role as an informer?"

Lord Derby looked away for a moment, then faced me. "No one in my office has heard from our agent since yesterday morning. He has not responded to our entreaties, which we continue to send in cipher to his lodgings. We are concerned that he has been discovered. So now we fear for his life."

"The dead man, then, was not your agent?"

"No. Could he have been the bomb-maker?"

"We shall know in a few minutes."

I set up the microscope in my laboratory, angled the mirror to catch the daylight, and peered through the eyepiece at a slide that I smeared with what I'd scraped from the victim's fingernails. Immediately, I saw that it was a conventional gunpowder mixture, but with pale gray particles added.

While Bradstreet and the Earl conferred quietly across the room, I edged the detritus into five test-tubes and dripped a different chemical into each. When one of them reacted as I expected, I held up the test-tube.

"Sometime during the day on which he met his death, the murdered man had been making a bomb."

"I feared as much," said Lord Derby. "But why do you guess he was doing it on that day, and not, oh, the day before or the day before that?"

"I never guess. Despite his anarchism, or perhaps to disguise it, he was a fastidious man who dressed well in good clothes. He would not go out in public with so much dirt under his fingernails."

Bradstreet peered at the test-tube. "Do you think his killer has the bomb now?"

"I would take that for a working hypothesis."

Lord Derby strode to the door and donned his hat. "I will have to report this development to – Umm, to report it."

"I need to return to my regular duties," said Bradstreet.

"And I have an idea I wish to pursue. Let us return here at, say, seven o'clock, and talk further." I put on my hat, took my stick, and accompanied them down the stairs and out into Baker Street.

As we looked up and down for cabs to hail, a short fellow in a dark suit, holding a bowler hat against his chest, strode up to us.

Lord Derby hailed him. "Oh! Whitmore. I'm glad you've come. I've tried to reach you all day. Mr. Holmes, this is our agent in the Fellowship. He – "

The man yelled "Slave-driver!" into his face and took away the hat. A heavy black object dropped to the pavement. It was the size and shape of a small cannonball, with flame sputtering down a short fuse.

I grabbed Lord Derby by the sleeve and yanked him into the road. Bradstreet leapt away from the bomb, yelling, "Look out! Look out!" and waving his arms, to scatter the passersby. I left Lord Derby on the far side of Baker Street and dashed after the man who'd dropped the bomb at our feet.

He was just rounding the corner when I hurled my stick at his legs. It caught him between strides and tripped him up, knocking him prone to the pavement. I flung myself on top of him, and caught his neck in the crook of my left elbow to put him in a choke-hold. After a few seconds, he ceased to resist.

In all this time, and to my great surprise, there'd been no report. No bang. No noise at all except shouts of warning and confusion. No one was crying or screaming. I dragged the man up, yanking the lapels of his jacket backwards over his shoulders for a makeshift restraint, and pushed him ahead of me, back into Baker Street.

Smoke was seeping out of the bomb from the hole where the fuse had been, but it had not exploded. No one, however, was moving in for a closer look. Indeed, everyone in the street had backed far away, including three of my young "Irregular" agents, though they continued to stare at the thing, waiting – hoping, I suppose – to see it go off.

Bradstreet joined me and immediately snapped irons on the fellow's wrists. "Nice work, Mr. Holmes. There's a police box in the next street. If you hold him here, I'll put in a call for the men who deal with bombs to come 'round."

"Where is his Lordship?"

"Over there – " he pointed. "Sitting in the doorway of the stationer's shop."

I hauled my prisoner over. The Secretary of State for the Colonies blinked, then stared hard at the fellow and shouted, "Traitor!"

Chapter III

Some twenty minutes later, the bomb had still not exploded. A crew from the Metropolitan arrived in a special wagon with an iron box on the back. Bradstreet told the men that he would bring in the prisoner later. They lifted the bomb with a canvas sling, lowered it into the box, locked the top down, and drove off with it.

Leaving a constable and a regular police wagon at the doorstep of 221b, Bradstreet, Lord Derby, and I pushed the miscreant ahead of us, up the stairs, and put him into a straight-back chair with his wrists cuffed behind his back.

"This is Paul Whitmore, Mr. Holmes," explained Lord Derby. "He was our informer in the Fellowship." To him, he said, "Joined the anarchists now, have you?"

"Are there more bombs?" Bradstreet asked.

"Wouldn't you like to know!"

I leaned close to him. "Last night, after the speaker had left and the meeting was concluded, all the others in your Fellowship departed – all except you and the amateur chemist. You had a spirited conversation about the bomb. Likely he even let you handle it, and told you how to use it. But then he took it back and prepared to leave with it. That's when you picked up a chair and knocked him down – killed him, by the way. Then you stole the bomb. You also filched his billfold and coins, so anyone who found him would think he'd been robbed."

"How could you know that?"

"It is my business to know things that others conceal."

"Why did you turn against your country?" Lord Derby demanded. "Aren't you proud to be British?"

"It was the opium," he said.

"What? I never heard of anyone becoming an anarchist after a pipe-dream."

"Not from taking it, you idiot! From trading in it – something that has made Great Britain very rich. Myself, too, I'm sorry to say. Opium is my family's business. We have had an import license for opium since the 'Forties. That's how we got acquainted, my Lord – remember? Your office staff handles the working papers from your end, and I handle them on ours. Anyhow, a year-and-a-half ago, we had just imported a hundredweight from India, but our laboratory said the potency wasn't up to par. I got tagged to go out there, to where the poppies grow, and find out what the trouble was. Ever seen poppies in the field? Lovely flowers, they are."

"Come to the point."

"I am! Once I got to talking with the peasant farmers, I learned that we're forcing them to cultivate more poppies than anybody actually needs for making medicine. We're sending most of that Indian opium to China, turning the people there into addicts. But what made me truly angry was that we weren't paying the farmers a decent price. There are too many middle-men in our colonial administration, and they all take their cuts before the farmer gets his share. He's lucky if he sees a shilling for a week's work. It isn't fair.

"I returned to London in January, went back to my family's firm, and in March I was in your offices again, Lord Derby, bringing the usual paperwork, when you came through and asked me: Did I want to have an adventure? Well, I'd just had a glimpse of the world east of Suez, and I was game, all right. You took me inside, into your private office, and made me a deal. You said if I were to join this socialist tribe and report back to you, you'd grant my family a more comprehensive license – one that would enable us to import opium by the tonne, instead of just the hundredweight. That sounded like a good arrangement."

He had been sniffing our fumes, so I offered him a cigarette – put one in his mouth and held the match. "Go on."

"Well, once I started palling around in the Fellowship, I realized that the misrule I'd seen in India wasn't unique. We misrule the whole empire! We're so proud to have outlawed slavery. We sing how '*Britons never, never, never shall be slaves.*' But we work our colonials to death, with no say in how much they're paid! Are we not, in that way, slave-drivers? To own countries is to own slaves!

"Well, then, we heard about this Colonial and Export Trade Exhibition that was opening in Amsterdam. As I've told you several times, a few of the fellows aren't socialists. They're anarchists who want to abolish all governments – every kind of government. One of them said he knew how to make the bomb. Said the cell in Amsterdam wanted somebody to go over there and build them one.

234

"Well, he wanted to go and do that. He said making a bomb wasn't hard, because anybody could mix up the basic ingredients and make gunpowder. But he'd been reading chemistry books, and he said he'd found a way to make gunpowder almost as powerful as Nobel's Dynamite. He used the empty flat upstairs for his laboratory, and last night he brought his bomb down to show us."

"The men who came today," said Bradstreet, "I'll send them to investigate that upstairs flat. Go on, Mr. Whitmore."

"Before he could go to Amsterdam, he needed to know how big a blast his bomb would make. So he proposed holding a demonstration. Set it off in a park at night, when no one's around. Make a big noise. Then we could threaten to use it if the government didn't stop treating our colonials like dirt."

"You had a different idea, didn't you? Assassinating me would draw more attention. You'd be famous!"

Whitmore spat in his face.

Lord Derby inelegantly wiped off the spittle with his sleeve. "There is competition among anarchists," he explained. "Each one wants to be the leader of his cell, but people opposed to the very idea of governance do not yearn for leaders. Instead, he seeks notoriety. Likewise, every cell of anarchists desires to be the top dog in the pack, by being seen to perpetrate an outrage. And that encourages other cells to do something even more outrageous. Thus, if one cell should detonate a bomb, other cells, anxious to make a name for themselves, will detonate more or bigger bombs. And that is the greatest threat facing Europe today."

He turned to Bradstreet. "We've delayed enough. Take Whitmore downstairs, and have the constable take him in the wagon to Whitehall Place. Get him into a gaol cell. See that he is held incommunicado. At all costs, keep him from talking with members of the Fellowship, for a week, at least – two, if you possibly can. We don't want anyone to learn that the bomb-maker is dead."

When they'd gone, Lord Derby said, "I still want to know if he made more bombs."

"If he did, they will be duds like this one. Under the microscope, I could see that he added a mineral catalyst to the gunpowder which, when it's fresh, is extremely dangerous. Fortunately for us, he was untrained, and working solely from books. He must have read about this catalyst, for it does, indeed, vigorously enhance the gunpowder's explosive energy. But the mineral is mined in one of the driest parts of the world, and the latest research shows that, in a humid climate such as ours, the catalyst is prone to oxidize. Likely, he failed to keep it an air-tight container. Exposed to London's humidity, it slowly but steadily lost its effectiveness. After a few hours, it no longer acted as a catalyst. Instead, it became a deterrent, inhibiting the black power from exploding. Without a test, he couldn't know how potent his bomb would be, which is why he urged them to set it off in an empty park. But Whitmore kept the bomb overnight, and didn't try to detonate it until this afternoon. By then, the catalyst had deteriorated even further, and turned into a suppressant."

Taking the "*Tentoonstellings Spel*" card from his Lordship, I said, "I can picture a cell of anarchists sitting around, playing this Exhibition Game for their amusement. But when a man carries one of these cards in a concealed pocket, it isn't for fun. Most likely it's a *shibboleth* – a way to identify himself, to establish his membership in the anarchist fraternity, and his concurrence with the strategy of inciting violence and terror."

"Then surely you see what we must do next."

"Infiltrate."

"Yes, Mr. Holmes. We need to recruit another agent and send him to Amsterdam, posing as the English bomb-maker they're expecting, but stopping them from detonating one."

I had, of course, foreseen this. "Do you propose that I become this infiltrator?"

He nodded.

I leaned back and took my time before speaking. "For a spy to discover the greatest amount of information, he should have first-rate language skills. I speak French. But I have no skill in the Dutch tongue beyond the social pleasantries."

He shook his head. "Englishmen are disliked around the world for refusing to speak any language but our own. But anarchism is an international phenomenon. Most likely the majority of those you may meet will, to some extent, speak English. You should not have any difficulty in that regard. Besides, you are ideal for our purpose. You are a genius at uncovering facts. You have enough knowledge of chemistry to pose as a manufacturer of explosives. And in all these activities you are neither a policeman nor a government agent – so you can act independently, and by your own rules of conduct, if – "

"If I should have to kill someone?"

He shrugged.

I stared at him. "If I were revealed to be a spy, would you acknowledge me? Would you intervene to protect me from the group's retaliation? If I should cause someone's death while in another country, would the British ambassador take me in his charge? Extradite me, so I could not be prosecuted?"

"So . . . you refuse?"

"Actually, I accept. But first I need to send a wire."

Chapter IV

I had just enough time to pull together a kit of theatrical makeup and costume for disguise and pack them in a carpet-bag. In response to my wire, I had a brief meeting at the Diogenes Club with Mycroft. He arranged for me to carry a British passport in the name of Milton St. Cloud, along with a *carte-de-visite* as an instructor of chemistry in a small college. I was whisked to the station to catch the next train to Folkstone, and from there I boarded the overnight ferry to Holland.

Mycroft was concerned that the Dutch government would not take kindly to the British sending an agent-provocateur into their country. It would be better, he felt, to cast my presence there as a police matter, so he cabled ahead to a senior officer in the Amsterdam police, whom he knew to be incorruptible. And what he and Lord Derby communicated to the Dutch government was that I was going to Amsterdam to work with the police, to help evaluate the extent of the socialist and anarchist threats. This way, I could be vouched for and presented at court in my own person, and in my ordinary capacity as a consulting detective.

I was met at the station in Amsterdam by Politie Onderzoeker Martijn Schotten, a police investigator whose rank was comparable to that of an Inspector in the London Police. He alone had been briefed on the real nature of my mission. Schotten was a decade or so older than I – tall and clean-shaven, not only of chin but nearly of scalp as well. The *Politie*, as the Dutch force is called, requires men to crop their hair very short, like soldiers.

"*Welkom*, Mijnheer Holmes!" he said right away. "Now we will give these anarchists a thrashing!"

In a one-horse cabriolet he drove us to Dam Square, at the center of the city, and pulled up before the Royal Palace, which rose above the western side of the plaza. We were escorted to a reception room on the second level and greeted at the door by a tall, muscular man in a morning-suit. He smiled broadly as he shook Schotten's hand and mine.

An attorney, obviously (he carried a leather case of the right size for legal briefs), he was thirty or a little more, with brown eyes, a fair complexion, and a huge black moustache twisted up and waxed at the tips. From his left temple back past his ear, thinning black hair could not cover a narrow, white front-to-back scar.

"I am Johannes Van Limburg," said he, with a nod and an almost imperceptible click of heels. "Chief Counselor to His Royal Highness Alexander, Prince of Orange, to whom I shall now introduce you." He waved us into the room.

The prince was standing in the center of the room, dressed like a prosperous businessman in a fine bespoke suit. Age about thirty, he had a high forehead and a full but closely trimmed brown beard. Bags under his eyes suggested he had a nervous disposition, and was not sleeping well.

Despite having stood stiffly erect while awaiting us, the prince proved to be the modern kind of royalty. He eschewed Van Limburg's ceremonial protocol and stepped forward to greet us as we entered the room, smiling as he shook our hands. That he had progressive tendencies was reinforced by the square-and-compass ornament depending from a chain at his waistcoat: He was a Freemason, and a Grand Master of his Lodge. We exchanged hearty greetings. The Prince took my arm and led us to an anteroom where a buffet luncheon was set out.

As I am not well-up on international affairs, Mycroft had given me several pages of notes, which I had read during the crossing. Now I reviewed them in my mind while I ate smoked salmon and liver sausage and drank the local beer.

Prince Alexander was heir to the throne of the Netherlands. He was the third and youngest son of King Willem III, but the eldest son had died young, and the middle son died in 1879.

Their mother, Queen Sophie, had died in 1877, leaving Willem a widower at the age of sixty. His agents thereupon opened negotiations with various Royal families on the Continent, in search of a suitable new wife. But none of the eligible women proved eager to wed him. Willem was a starchy, old-fashioned monarch who always resented parliamentary and constitutional limitations. A big man with a loud voice, he was also hot-headed, though quick to forgive and forget.

During the two years' search for a new queen, Willem carried on a scandalous morganatic flirtation with a French opera singer. (I was reminded of this, years later, in the case of the King of Bohemia and Irene Adler!) But propriety was restored in 1879 when Willem married young Emma of Waldeck and Pyrmont, a German principality. The Queen Consort is young indeed – a full forty years younger than her husband, and five years younger than his surviving heir apparent, Prince Alexander. Emma and Willem have a child together – a three-year-old princess called Wilhelmina.

After luncheon, over coffee and tobacco, the prince rose and said, "It is good that you have arrived, Mr. Holmes. We hope you and Onderzoeker Schotten will be able to gauge the threat from socialists and anarchists and make a report to us."

"Indeed, Your Highness, I will need to do that quickly."

"Is a threat imminent?"

238

"I have been informed," Schotten explained, "that anarchists have taken control of a socialist cell here in Amsterdam. Mijnheer Holmes is well spoken-of by the Metropolitan Police. That is why they asked him to work with us in the *Politie*, to help us discover what threats this cell may pose."

"The Amsterdam cell," said Van Limburg, "is one of many within the larger, international organization known as the Fellowship of the New Life. It has always included anarchists among the socialists. We have some knowledge of them. Please memorize this." He passed me a paper on which were four names. "See if you can find these people. They are the anarchists who are known to us. They must be somewhere in the city."

I shared the list with Schotten, lit a cigarette, and burnt the paper in the ashtray before stubbing out the match. "I must ask you gentlemen what I asked my own countrymen: Is there no pacifist faction in this cell? No opposition to a campaign of terror? Can no one persuade some of these people to give up all thought of bombs?"

"That was our hope," said the prince. "Counselor Van Limburg had an agent in the cell. But he . . . disappeared. We have had no word from him since January."

"He was instructed to try that approach," said the counselor. "But he was quickly rebuffed by the anarchists, who want 'action'. So we instructed him to keep a low profile and not be prominent. Better that he stay among the followers than try to lead. That way he would still be trusted, and able to keep us informed of any movement in the direction of bomb-throwing. But he has sent no message in six months. I worry that he was killed."

"We do not need to convert the cell to pacifism," said the Prince. "We need to prevent them from setting off a bomb."

Schotten turned to me. "Since construction of the Exhibition began in January, the *Politie* keeps a squad of constables there always. They have a small accommodation, so they are ready day and night if trouble-makers come."

Van Limburg laughed. "One of them took me to see it. He said it is a finer billet than his regular barracks! But His Highness is right. A bomb set off at the Exhibition could well encourage rebellion among our colonies."

"And bring the kingdom into disrepute for failing to prevent the atrocity."

Schotten slapped the table. "We will act quickly!"

"Mijnheer Holmes," said Van Limburg, "You shall stay in a room here in the palace while you conduct your investigation. The resources of the kingdom are at your disposal."

"With respect, sir," said Schotten, "it would be better for him to stay in the pension which the *Politie* keeps for visiting policemen."

"Yes," said I. "A small hotel is better. To pursue my enquiries, I will need to meet frequently with Onderzoeker Schotten. From his headquarters, I can wire my contact in London at all hours."

"I understand," said the prince. "Onderzoeker Schotten, we are counting on you and Mijnheer Holmes to expose the anarchists, so we may bring them to justice." He rose, beckoned Van Limburg to accompany him, and left the room.

Schotten's cabriolet was at the gate. We drove to the pension, but not for my accommodation.

In a small room, I totally changed my appearance. I built up my nose with putty to look swollen, adding an ugly red boil near the tip to discourage people from staring too long at me. I applied a narrow moustache, in black, to match the color of a wig in need of a haircut, to which I added a bit of gray paste at the temples to make me look older.

As my own frame is lean, I donned padded underclothes to appear heavier. My costume was that of a man not poor but down on his luck: A gray wool suit that had once been costly, but now worn thin at the seat. I added a striped cotton shirt, collars and cuffs that were starting to fray, a cravat with a small tear along one seam, scuffed brogues, and a felt hat with an age-softened brim.

Schotten yelled something fierce at me, in Dutch, as I stepped into his cabriolet. Then he caught himself, peered at my face, and smiled. "Truly, Mijnheer Holmes, I did not recognize you."

"When I left London," I said, as we drove away, "I was given information about the Royal Family, but Van Limburg was not mentioned."

"He fills a special role. Not so much *avocat* as – "

"Bodyguard? Yes, I thought he was more than a mere attorney. He still has the posture and carriage of a soldier. At some time he went into battle, for he has a scar – " I touched my head. " – where a bullet grazed him."

Schotten smiled. "*Avocat* Van Limburg is native to Württemburg, in Germany. In 1870, he was a soldier in a Prussian regiment, wounded in the invasion of France. In 1872, he moved to the Netherlands and studied in the University at Leiden, where Alexander was also student. Their ages are nearly the same. They become friends. In 1876 Van Limburg was made *avocat*, and joined the retinue of Alexander in the palace.

"But in 1881, the Tsar of the Russians was assassinated by a bomb in St. Petersburg. Now there was panic all over Europe. Every king was

240

afraid he would be the next to be murdered. The *Politie* always keeps eyes and ears on every man and women at work in the Royal household. Two disloyal people were let go. And Willem had, now, near to him a squad of trusted guardsmen, day and night.

"But Alexander wasn't comfortable with guardsmen. He wished to go about as ordinary men do. Yet he must be protected also. Van Limburg is a strong man with soldiering skill. Quickly, he was promoted to Chief Counselor, which means, in truth, that he kept watch over the Prince by day. Palace guards keep watch through the night."

He drove me near to a house which he knew was occupied by the Fellowship cell, and I walked the rest of the way, so as not to be seen with a policeman.

Chapter V

The house was in a workingman's neighborhood called Jordaan, in a narrow street that ran between two canals. Like most of the others in its row, the outside wall in front was not perpendicular to the road – it leaned over the street, a few degrees off the vertical. Though it must have been that way for a hundred years or more, my first impression was of imminent collapse.

My knock was answered by a woman of forty years or so – a short-sighted cook who had formerly worked in a textile mill. (There was her apron, of course, but she squinted at me, and the bridge of her nose had red marks on either side, from *pince-nez* on a ribbon around her neck. She wore a snug white cotton bonnet, typical of those that mill-girls tie on to keep their hair from catching in the machinery. She wore it now to keep her graying hair out of pots and pans.)

She had opened only the top half of the door. "*Ja?*"

"I am looking to join the Fellowship of the New Life," said I. "Have I come to the right place?"

"*Misschien*," she replied. Seeing I had not understood, she said, "Maybe."

"I am a utopian socialist, anxious to meet others with a like mind. My life's purpose, I believe, is to improve the lives of the workers of the world, and their children. Tell me Miss, please – Is this, in fact, where I may find brothers and sisters who share my beliefs?"

"Should you not be at work?" She had a German accent.

"Ah, well . . . that is . . . I'd rather not discuss that, out here on the doorstep. May I come in?"

She eyed me head to toe, gave a nod, and opened the bottom half of the door.

To the two men who were sitting in the front room, she said, "Interview this fellow, please. He wishes our cause to join." Then she went into the narrow hallway and continued down to the kitchen.

The men stood and introduced themselves as Oswald and Sidney – first names only. I replied, "Milton."

They were Englishmen, and had been relaxing without collars or cuffs, their sleeves rolled up past the elbows. Oswald, whose accent was that of south London, was in his forties, and stood about as tall as me, but weighed far more. He was a pugilist – obvious by the punched-down nose and thickness of speech from taking blows to the head. Sidney, by his accent, was from the north of England. Short and thin, age about forty, he had quit the sea at least a dozen years ago, and was working now in some janitorial capacity. (The anchor with an inscription, tattooed on his left forearm, had faded considerably. And I caught a whiff of spirits of ammonia from his shirt and trousers when we shook hands.)

"What brings you here?" asked Oswald.

"Aye," said Sidney. "You look like a man accustomed to work. Why aren't you working?"

"I had a . . . disagreement with my superior."

They bade me sit and waited for me to elaborate. From the sagging cushions of a tattered sofa, I began to spin the tale that Mycroft and I had concocted . . . .

"It's this way: I read chemistry at university, and for the past ten years I've been teaching chemistry in Hertfordshire, in a boy's school. During recess weeks I always go on a walking tour. Last year, I was near to Bath when I happened to pass a stone quarry. I was curious to see the operation, but the workers were on strike. I'd never thought much about men like them, but they're the fellows who do the real work. It's dangerous work. And they weren't being paid enough to compensate for the risk. They might as well have been slaves.

"D'you know – I'd never seen men go on strike. It got me thinking how there were poor chaps all over Britain, digging out tin in Cornwall, or coal in Wales. Then I realized there are even more men out in our colonies who go down into the earth so they can feed their children, and they get even less money! There's boys scratching out diamonds down in South Africa. And what about all the field hands picking cotton in Egypt, or tea-leaves in Ceylon? Grand-mams in Burma, stooped over, water up to their knees, plucking rice out of paddies? There's just so many people who do the real work, all over the world, while Britons – and we three are Britons, aren't we? – we take what they make and don't pay them a living wage for it. I ask you: Is that right and just? I say it is not!"

They nodded and started to smile.

242

"Well . . . so . . . I was out for a stroll in Hyde Park of a Sunday, a month or so ago, and I stopped to hear this fellow that was talking about how socialism would make things better for the people who do the real work around the world. How there ought to be a union in every factory, to fight the bosses for higher wages. He gave me this tract – " I pulled one of the London Fellowship's pamphlets from the inside pocket of my jacket. Along with it, the "*Verenigd Knonkrijk*" game card came tumbling out. I hurriedly snatched it up and returned it to my pocket.

I had deliberately let them see it, of course. But I proffered the tract and went right on with my story. "Once I'd read this, I went back the following Sunday, heard more speeches, read quite a bit more about the Fellowship . . . and I guess you can figure out what happened next. I took a bunch of these pamphlets back to school with me the next day, and tried giving them out to my fellow teachers. The dean obtained a copy, saw what it said, and gave me the sack.

"I've been living off my savings since then. But I learned that a big fair was opening here in Amsterdam, with exhibits from all the colonial powers and their colonies. And I thought: Where there are colonialists, there will be anti-colonialists, socialists, and communists. And if they are mounting some kind of opposition, I want to be there too and join with them. Your Fellowship in London gave me this address, so I sold all my books and my best clothes to raise the fare, and . . . . well, I just got off the boat today. Here I am. Can you use me?"

"Aye, maybe," said Sidney.

Oswald nodded. "Where're you beddin' down?"

"Well, that's . . . another reason why I came here. I didn't realize that, with a big fair in town, all the hotels and rooming houses are charging double their rates. That's capitalism for you!"

I joined in their laughter, then said, "Do you suppose I could spend a few nights here, while I look for something more permanent?" Oswald's eyes narrowed, and Sidney paid somewhat more attention to my clothes than he had before. Hastily, I added, "I can contribute toward the rent. I brought a few quid. What's the rate of exchange?"

"D'you think we're runnin' a bank?" Oswald got up and took a tin box down from a shelf and said, "You can stay for a week. Give us five bob." I passed the shillings to him.

"Back in a minute," said Sidney. He strode out into the hall, and disappeared up the narrow stairs.

243

Chapter VI

There were seven in the cell besides myself, and we ate as if in a family home, around a single large table, passing the serving dishes around. Afterward, we each washed our own dishes and silverware (pewter, actually) in the scullery.

The woman who'd originally let me in was called Grete. She was, as I'd deduced, the cell's cook, but she was more than that. As soon as the meal and the washing-up were concluded, we returned to the great table, where she took the head chair and rapped with her knuckles to open the meeting.

"If you have not yet his acquaintance made," said she, pointing, "this is Milton, from . . . London." Most of the members called out their names and gave me a little welcoming wave of the hand. But two, in addition to Sidney, spoke their names softly and nodded. I took that to mean they understood, from the way Grete said "London", that they were the anarchists, and that I was the man they were expecting.

Frijof was a painter – of signs or houses, not works of art. (Long, thick, blond hair fell to his shoulders, but splotches of gray and black paint had dripped from above and clung to the top.) He was about my age, tall, fair, and broad-shouldered – not as massive as Oswald, but two stone, at least, heavier than me. When he joined the conversation around the table, his accent was that of a Dutchman.

Victor was nearer fifty than forty, and for many of his years had been an equestrian. (He walked bowlegged to and from the table.) His skin was sunburnt and leathery, his hands were thickly calloused, and his face bore the scars of smallpox in childhood. His accent was Russian, and a Russian who spends years on horseback is either an aristocrat or – far more likely in this case – a Cossack.

A discussion commenced around the table that was evidently a continuation of one begun before my arrival. Everyone wanted to visit the Exhibition, but some members did not want everyone to go.

The proponents felt we would benefit by becoming more knowledgeable about the colonies. An Italian fellow called Romulo said, "More than likely, and especially if we are subtle in asking around, we will discover that some people working at the fair, or within the exhibit halls, are sympathetic to our cause."

Oswald spoke in opposition. "If we do that, we might be seen and remembered by the police. The risk is too great."

"Once we are known to the authorities," added Frijof, "we can easily be rounded up and arrested."

I raised my hand and was pleased to be acknowledged by Grete. "Perhaps," said I, "we should not all go at once. I, myself, would like to visit the Exhibition. Perhaps, over the course of a day, we could go individually, or in twos. May I suggest, however, that we do not, as – Romulo is it?"

"*Si.*"

" – that we do not, as Romulo said, make conversation with the workers. The temptation to do so will be great, and it could well add to our numbers. But as Oswald said, it would be unwise to call attention to ourselves. Let us keep our eyes and ears open, and our mouths closed – except, perhaps, to partake of food and drink."

This drew a big laugh. Grete said, "Milton a good compromise proposes." And by show of hands, everyone agreed that the following day, we would, singly and two at a time, walk to the Exhibition, use the money in the tin box to pay our admission fees, and spend a little more inside for refreshments.

Afterward, Sidney beckoned me outside. Victor and Frihof joined us for a private meeting. We walked down the street and stopped at the verge of a canal, where we shared a single cigarette.

"Let's see that card again, Milton," said Sidney.

I took it from my jacket and passed it around.

"Good!" Sidney shook my hand. "We asked the London cell to send us an explosives man. That story you told us: Strikers in the quarry, fired by your dean. Was that true?"

I smiled. "True enough, if you were not who I expected to meet."

"What caused the delay?" asked Frijof. "We are waiting two days for you."

(Thankfully, word of the murder had not reached them.) "I needed a key ingredient, and had to wait for the chemist to stock it. I'm not too late, am I?"

"There is no problem," said Frijof as he opened a shirt-button and extracted a card which he held up for me to see. The legend was "*Nederland*" and the illustrations were of a tropical spice-tree plantation, a dairy with great wheels of cheese piled high, and a windmill, all topped by the burly Willem III, standing full-figure in an oval frame,

Victor waited a few seconds, then produced a card but did not show us its face. "In this game there is a card for Russia. The comrade who would have carried it is dead – arrested and tortured by the police after killing the Tsar. So it is thought best, in tribute to his brave action, never to use the Russia card."

The others murmured assent, so I did too.

"The card I hold now," Victor continued, "was first to a Belgian given. But he, too, is dead. Caught by Leopold's men before he can join us here. One of those men was secretly on our side, and smuggled the card out of Belgium. This I show you now."

The word "*Belgie*" was prominent, but above it was a singular illustration. Around the perimeter were trees tapped for rubber, and in the center an outline map of Africa, with the Congo – a huge area in the middle – delineated. And inside that, a finely detailed color portrait of Leopold, seated upon a throne whose back and arms were fashioned of elephant tusks.

I saw a shadow move nearby. Grete was approaching. I slipped my card into my pocket, but the others continued to hold theirs. She reached into the pocket of her apron and withdrew a game-card. Its images depicted the harbor at Trieste, a wedding celebration in a Balkan village, and the Schönbrunn Palace in Vienna, surmounted by a cartouche with a drawing of Emperor Franz Joseph. "*Oosenrijk*" (That is: *Austria*) was printed along the bottom edge.

I had now confirmed Van Limburg's suspicion. The names he'd written on the paper I'd burned were Grete, Victor, Frijof, and Sidney.

"You have a very nice house. Have you all been living here a long time?" I asked.

"This house is by my family owned," said Grete. "I made it open to the cell in '81. Victor, you here came in '82, Romulo also. Sidney at Christmastime, *ja*?"

"Aye. And Olaf right after me." He glanced at me and added, "He went away in January. Joined another cell, we figure."

"Frijof, you came in February. Oswald showed up in March. And now, Milton, you come to us in June."

"Thank you, Grete. I hope, with what we do, that we will draw more and more to the cause."

We wrapped our arms around each other's shoulders and clasped ourselves in a tight circle.

After a moment, Frijof broke away. "We must to business now go. I have to the fair been one time before." He pulled a colorful paper from his jacket and unfolded it, then pointed as he spoke. "This is the official plan of the Exhibition, which they sell where you enter. Here is the main gate and the Main Building. It has various exhibits. Here is the City of Amsterdam pavilion, the Machinery Gallery, the Music Pavilion, and a Japanese Bazaar. This blue line is a canal, spanned by a bamboo bridge. A Chinese junk floats there, also. All around there are restaurants for German, English, and Dutch food. An English tea shop, too, open to the air, with a roof overhead. But here – " He pointed to a separate building. "

246

– this is the Netherlands' Colonial Pavilion. That is where we should go tomorrow. to make examination, to find best places to . . . leave our *package*."

Victor said, "I have already an empty iron ball. It lacks only to be filled and fuse inserted."

"Am I to fill it?" They answered me by looking at me. "All right. Where shall I do the work?"

Grete said, "Attic."

"And how long do I have, before the package is to be . . . delivered?"

They glanced at one another. Sidney motioned for us all to come closer. "On the King's agenda, there's a ceremony at half-past-eleven on Thursday. He's to open a special exhibit of diamonds from the Transvaal in South Africa."

Victor squinted. "Point to where on the map is this exhibit."

He did so. "Inside the Dutch Colonial Pavilion."

"How do you know this?" Grete asked.

"There is a guard at the palace," he replied, "who's in sympathy with our cause. When I walk through Dam Square, if he's at his post, and has information for me, he'll set the butt of his rifle down beside his right boot. If he needs to warn me against approaching him, he shifts the rifle to the left."

"What if he should be re-assigned one day," I asked, "and lose his post on the Square?"

"What if he should be discovered?" asked Grete.

"And tortured?" Victor put in.

"That's possible. But I'll go to Dam Square tomorrow and confirm the agenda. If the king will be at the Exhibition on Thursday, we'll need to act."

Grete, fortunately, spoke what I had wished to say: "Is it our intention – speak truly, now, all of you! Do we mean for this bomb to assassinate the King?"

There was silence. I spoke first. "That would not be my preference. I should like to see my bomb set off out of doors, ahead of time, in an open field. We would prepare a feuilleton – a handbill, a manifesto – taking credit for the explosion, warning the colonial powers to beware our wrath, and further promising further action if they do not start to divest themselves of – "

"Ha!" That was Victor. "They will never read your little paper, and they will never do as we ask. They will hunt us down and kill us for making a 'manifesto' just the same – just as fierce – as if we killed the king. So we might as well kill him."

Grete asked, "Frijof – where do you stand?"

247

"I stand with Victor. Half a measure is not enough."

She nodded, said, "I also," and put her hand forward. "We are pledged to do this deed. Milton, will you do this with us?"

I laid my hand on hers, and the others put theirs on top.

"Let us visit the pavilion tomorrow," said I, "and see where the most effective location may be to produce the desired effect."

Chapter VII

I rose early Tuesday morning, and saw Frijof leave at sunrise for his house-painting job. Over coffee, I told Grete, "I need to purchase the . . . ingredients. They must not all come from a single shop. Can you or someone here give me addresses for two or three chemists?" She squinted, not understanding the English word. "*Farmacia*? *Apotheek*?" I suggested.

"Thank you." She jotted various locations on a scrap of paper.

In truth, I did not need to buy anything. I had brought the bomb-making components with me. What I really intended to do that morning was follow Sidney.

In the night, I'd had to correct my impression that he worked as a janitor. The odor of ammonia on his clothes had come from within the house, for I saw him swabbing the hallway and kitchen floors, and cleaning the privy. Likely he exchanged these chores for room and board.

Romulo greeted me at the table, asked if I had ever been to the Continent before, and urged me to visit Rome someday.

Victor shattered this bonhomie. "When anarchy is triumphant," said he, "there will be no need for capital cities. Or capital!"

Sidney stood up, took a hat from the hall-tree, and left by the front door. The previous night, he'd said he would visit his informer at the palace. If I did nothing else in Amsterdam, I would at least uncover a subversive element among the guardsmen. I excused myself, waved Grete's note at her to show I was off to the chemists, and departed.

It was not easy to follow him – and I say this as someone adept in the art of surreptitious pursuit. It was as if he were accustomed to being followed, for the route he took was irregular, with some doubling-back and sudden reversals of direction. I must admit it was a challenge, but at last he came to Dam Square, where there were crowds milling about, and I could slip among knots of passersby while keeping watch on him.

He strode past the main gate of the palace, with no glance toward the uniformed guard who stood there holding his rifle across his chest. As Sidney passed, however, the guard released his rifle and rested the butt beside his right boot.

Sidney pretended to take no notice. He walked about thirty paces into the Square before he turned around and walked back along the wrought-iron fence at a leisurely pace. Close to the guardhouse he stopped to pull a cigarette from his shirt pocket. He offered one to the guard, who shook his head to decline. But the offer brought them into close proximity. I saw the guard whisper something, while Sidney was striking a match against the fence, shielding the flame from the wind, and lighting his cigarette. Then he walked away from the guardhouse, rounded the far corner of the palace, and stepped into the busy street behind, where he dodged a couple of carriages and swung himself onto a passing omnibus.

Chapter VIII

The weather in Amsterdam is much like the weather in London – they are very nearly on the same parallel of latitude. Although the summer solstice was approaching, the sun over the Dutch capital was never bright and hot while I was there.

On Wednesday morning, rain drizzled out of overcast skies, as each of us in the Fellowship set off, at five-minute intervals, to walk to the Exhibition. It was in a swampy, as-yet unpopulated part of the city, south of the old hub of government and commerce, and beyond the concentric canals where the city's wealthiest lived.

To approach the Exhibition, one walked under and through the long archway of a new museum that was under construction. Emerging into the light from that dark tunnel gave a dramatic impact to the broad vista of the fairground beyond. Floral gardens and fountains surrounded the main entrance – an enormous ceremonial gateway, bracketed by highly ornamented turrets festooned with fluttering ribbons in a rainbow of colors.

Most of the colonial powers' exhibits were housed in an enormous edifice, roofed with glass like an orangerie, where they displayed the fruits – literal and figurative – of their colonies. What the Netherlands extracted from its colonies was housed in a separate building, which was a smaller version of the main hall, with a similar glass roof, and an entryway in a similar gate-and-turret motif.

I went there straightaway. The glass overhead brought in daylight, and made the interior hot and humid. Palms, flowers and foliage rose high out of cachepots everywhere, enhancing the sense of traveling through colonies in the tropic zone.

Sidney and Grete had left the Jordaan together. In the hall, now, I saw them strolling arm-in-arm. Whether this was a pantomime to obscure their mission, or evidence of romantic attraction, I was not prepared to discover.

Victor, like me, had gone to the fairground on his own. Frijof did not go, since he had previously been there. But before he left for his painting job, he said he would tell his foreman that a family matter would keep him from working on Thursday.

We'd all agreed not to acknowledge one another at the fair. We would discuss what we'd seen when we met again after supper, to make final plans for carrying out Thursday's action.

So as not to be seen lingering in any one spot, I strolled up and down the hall's central corridor, measuring its length by my strides. Almost halfway along stood the Transvaal's stalls, decorated with South African flowers and taxidermy heads of wild animals. Workmen there were installing glass shelves in an empty display-case that was surmounted by a sign reading "*Diamanten*" in bold red capitals. This was where the new collection of diamonds would be presented on the following day. Occasionally, a worker would consult with a fellow holding a notebook and pen. I put myself in the mind of that supervisor, crediting him with intelligence and logic. After a few minutes I had worked out the most likely arrangement for accommodating the Royal visitors and their entourage at the opening ceremony.

I returned to the Jordaan house, took my carpet bag up to the attic where Grete had said I should work, and made the bomb.

Before leaving Baker Street, I had combined crystals of the mineral catalyst with gunpowder, and brought the mixture to Amsterdam in a small jar. After three days' exposure to the air – tomorrow would add yet another day – the gunpowder would be inhibited from exploding. Like the dud in London, it would produce only smoke. The little iron ball that Victor supplied had a hole already drilled. I poured my mixture in through a funnel, and closed the opening with the cord for the fuse.

After supper, Frijof, Grete, Sidney, Victor, and I met where we'd met the previous night, beside the canal.

Sidney reported, "The palace guard confirmed that the Royal party will arrive at half-eleven. Oh, and by the way, the Prince, the Queen Consort, and the little Princess will accompany him. The mayor of Amsterdam as well. The more, the merrier, eh?"

I had brought my carpetbag. I motioned for the others to circle tightly around me, and pulled the bag open to show them the bomb.

"Why leave you such a long tail on the fuse?" Victor demanded.

"This type of cord – " I touched it. " – burns one inch, or two-and-a-half centimeters, every second. When we decide how long we want it to burn down, I will cut it to the appropriate length."

"How big a blast will this make?"

250

"Well now, Frijof," said I, "that is a good question! The charge is extraordinarily powerful. But without conducting a test, I have no way of knowing how the ball will respond to the blast. If you're asking: What will be the radius of destruction caused by the percussion and the scattering of iron fragments? That I cannot tell until I see it go off. If it's too powerful, I may be, as Shakespeare put it, '*the engineer hoist with his own petard.*'"

Victor drew a deep breath. "That is a gamble. Every anarchist who does this thing must confront this fact: A bomb can bring upon him his own death."

Sidney chuckled. "Perhaps we ought not to stand too close."

"We do not know who in the Royal party will be standing closest to it," said Grete.

"Nor, yet, who will ignite and throw the bomb," I added.

"That is the big question," said Frijof. "Who shall carry the bomb? Who shall bring it out from under his coat, light the fuse, and send it sliding across the floor to the feet of the King?"

"I will not do it," declared Grete. "It is possible that all of us may die. And if only some of us die, the others will be arrested. Someone must live to return to the house, which is my house, and tell the Fellowship what happened. Everyone trusts me. They know I say truth. Do you all agree that I must survive? That I must not throw the bomb?"

We nodded agreement.

Victor lofted his shoulders and chin. "I will do this in honor of my comrades of 1881 in St. Petersburg. Revolution will come one day. Maybe I live to see it. Maybe I do not. But I am prepared to be martyr for the revolution."

"It may not be wise for you to be the bomber," said Sidney. "Your connections to anarchists in Russia will become known, and publicized, and we will have lost the chance to promote *our* cause: Opposition to the colonial powers. So . . . the perpetrator must be me." (A little gasp escaped Grete's mouth, but Sidney pretended not to notice.) "I have some skill at nine-pins. I know how to send a ball skidding along the floor in a straight course."

"That will not be necessary," said I. "I have devised a method by which we will accomplish our purpose with the least possible risk to ourselves." The others leaned in, as closely as they had when I showed them the bomb. "Let four of us do what we did today: Be ordinary visitors inside the hall. The fifth will carry the bomb. He will be stationed out of doors, beside the – "

"Out of doors?" Frijof exclaimed. "How can he – ?"

"Hear me out, please. Surely the palace has prepared plans in case of emergencies or attacks. Can we not expect armed guards to accompany the Royal party? If I were in charge of securing their safety, I would position the guards to face outward, during the ceremony, to spot trouble-makers, or anyone that even looks suspicious."

"Then we will have no chance to – "

"Please, Victor, let me finish. Our man will, indeed, wear an overcoat to conceal the bomb. But he will be stationed out of doors, by the entry to the hall. When the Royal party enters, he will note the time from his watch, and then walk along the outside wall, to a spot corresponding to the location of the diamond display inside. Exactly ten minutes from the time the Royal party enters, he will ignite the fuse, and then he will toss the bomb up in the air, making it arc high enough so that it will fall through the glass roof and land in the middle of the display. Then he will shed the overcoat, run away, mingle with the crowd, and leave the fairgrounds. The rest of us will be inside, far enough from the Royal party to avoid the worst of the blast. This way, we will all live to report back to the Fellowship."

No one spoke. But each one nodded, or grinned, or shrugged. Finally, Frijof declared, "That is brilliant!"

Grete said, "You have got it, Milton. No one will expect a bomb to fall from the sky."

Sidney added, "And they will not have time to react. They will hear the glass break and look up – not down."

Victor held up a hand. "I have considered what Sidney said. But I must insist to carry the bomb myself."

There was silence for a moment, but eventually we all nodded, and clapped Victor on the back.

"How will I know where to stand with the bomb?"

"I measured the building, inside and out, yesterday. I will show you the exact spot, ahead of time."

Victor picked up some rocks, hurled each of them high up over the canal, and we all timed the duration of their flight from release to splash. Between four and five seconds was the consensus.

I reached into the bag and cut the end of the fuse five inches from the bomb. "The rest of you must stay as far away as you can. I will stay close, inside. After all, I am as curious as you are to see how big a bang I can make!"

Chapter IX

Thursday morning, Frijof volunteered to go to the Exhibition first, to enter as soon as the gate opened at ten and scout around to see if additional guardsmen, or if any members of the *Politie*, might have joined the regular

252

contingent. He would thereby discover if the palace had taken extra precautions.

Sidney said that the day before, he had noticed a clutch of guards stationed at the far end of the Netherlands Colonial Hall, so he and Grete would stay close to them. When the bomb went off, she would pretend to faint, and thereby impede their response to the blast.

Victor, Grete, Sidney, and I arrived at the fairground just after ten-thirty, and immediately walked near to the open-air English tea shop, where Frijof sat with a cup of tea and a biscuit. The signal we had agreed upon was that, if security had been tightened, and we needed to postpone the operation, he would turn his teacup over and lay his spoon on top of it. If he left it right-side up and set his spoon down beside it on the saucer, our operation would commence.

Just as Frijof lifted his spoon, a stiff breeze suddenly whipped up, lofting flags and ribbon streamers almost to the horizontal, and making his long blond hair flap up and down all around his head. With the spoon still between his fingers, he reached both hands up and patted down his locks. A moment later the wind was calm again. Frijof looked about, saw we were waiting for his signal, gave a little nod, and laid the spoon down on the saucer beside his upright teacup.

We all headed to our agreed-upon stations at the Netherlands Colonial Hall: Frijof on the outside, to watch for extra guards, Grete and Sidney on the inside, to linger at the far end of the hall. Victor followed me and watched from a distance as I paced along the outer wall, then stopped to light a cigarette. Crushing it out with my shoe marked the spot.

I made my way into the hall and strolled up the central corridor, stopping every few feet to admire something. Then, as I took up a position just beyond but quite close to the Transvaal stall, I heard a hubbub of shouting and cheering from the direction of the entryway. Guards suddenly formed themselves up in lines along both sides of the corridor, opening their arms or holding up their hands, to keep visitors at bay.

The Royal party had come. I checked my watch. It was 11:35.

First to enter was a thick-set man in a morning-suit – prosperous-looking, like a businessman, but by the silk ribbon sash he wore from one shoulder down to the opposite hip, I deduced he was the Mayor of Amsterdam.

He made a brief announcement in Dutch, then stepped aside as the Royal Family entered: First King Willem III, with young Queen Consort Emma on his arm. Behind them came Prince Alexander. At his side walked Chief Counselor Van Limburg. Joyous shouts greeted each of the Royals as they arrived, but the loudest, heartiest cheer erupted when three-year-old Princess Wilhelmina trotted in.

It sickened me to know that the anarchists with whom I had plotted with were willing to kill her too.

Though crowds had followed the family all through the fairground, guards now stopped additional visitors from entering the hall. The Royal party proceeded up the corridor, nodding acknowledgments left and right, until the guards gathered them into a semicircle at the Transvaal diamond display.

It was 11:40.

The Mayor spoke for a minute or so, introducing two men in formal attire. Though I knew little of the language, it was clear that they were the diamond merchants who had brought the precious stones from South Africa.

11:42.

At first the King paid attention, but soon he was glancing around, nodding to his subjects and giving them tiny waves of his hand. Alexander and Emma were more dutiful – standing still and listening to descriptions of the various gems. Wilhelmina was more interested in the giant flowers that decorated the stall, and tugged her mother's hand, trying to get close enough to smell them.

11:44.

One of the merchants held up a ring, and then placed it in William's palm. It could never fit onto his thick fingers. He gave it back, and the merchant presented it to Emma. She held it out and showed it around, so everyone could see the remarkably brilliant stone glitter. Only Van Limburg was not watching. His eyes darted all about, ever alert. He touched his enormous moustache. He consulted his watch.

I did, too. It was 11:45.

Van Limburg lifted his chin and looked up at the roof. Just as the bomb crashed through the glass, he grabbed Alexander's sleeve, pulled him out of the semicircle into the corridor, and down onto the floor, covering him with his own body.

Everyone else, startled by the noise of shattering glass, looked up. Shards struck the diamond merchants, the mayor, and the King. Tiny fragments sprinkled down on Emma and her daughter. The bomb landed on the floor and rolled, fuse sputtering with yellow flame and white sparks. It stopped at Wilhelmina's tiny feet. Emma swept up her daughter with one arm, and used the other to open a path through the crowd.

Someone shouted "*Bom!*" A dozen others shouted "*Bom!*", and then more and more. Willem leapt backward, knocking over one of the display cases, and barged into the corridor.

As if giant hands were pushing them, everyone in the crowd backed away, then turned to flee. Van Limburg hauled the Prince up from the floor and lugged him, stumbling, down the corridor toward the exit.

The bomb lay still, with smoke pouring out of the fuse hole. Because the guards had limited the size of the crowd in the hall – and because I had ensured that there would be no explosion – the rush to the exit was surprisingly safe. I heard only a few cries of pain, but I did not see anyone crushed or trampled. As Sidney passed me, he sneered and whispered, "No hoist with that petard, eh?" Grete tugged his sleeve, and they hurried out. I remained where I'd been all along until everyone else had fled. I was the last to leave the hall.

A cordon of fairground guards and Amsterdam *Politie* stood in a circle, facing outward, rifles at the ready, protecting the important guests in the center. There, a policeman was applying iodine and bandages to the mayor and the merchants, who'd sustained glass-cuts to their heads. The king had a bandage on the back of his right hand. Wilhelmina was still wrapped up in her mother's arms, but she wasn't crying. A lady-in-waiting was combing bits of glass out of their hair. Alexander sat on the lawn. Van Limburg stood watch over him.

I saw Police Investigator Schotten walking around the perimeter of the cordon, thanking each of the constables. As he neared me, I stepped forward, caught his eye, and beckoned to him. He said something to another officer who then continued the patrol, and joined me a dozen yards away.

With a clap on the back, he said, "Good work! Mijnheer Holmes. Of course we would have no bomb preferred. But no blast is also good. We will now to the Jordaan go and make arrests. Come with us."

"No. Send your men immediately. But you must make an arrest here."

He looked around. "Do they stay here, the conspirators?"

"No. I'm sure they have fled. But a dangerous man remains, and we will need to question him before he has a chance to make up a story."

"Certainly. Show him to me, please."

"Take me into the cordon."

Two constables came to attention at Schotten's approach. He said something and pointed to me. They opened a gap through which I followed him into the protected circle. Then I took the lead and brought him over to Alexander.

The prince looked up from where he sat, squinted, then said, "Who are you? How did you get in here?"

"His job was very well done!" boomed Schotten. "Reveal yourself, Mijnheer Holmes."

With my fingernails, I scraped the putty and boil off my nose. I pinched the moustache, pulled it away, and then yanked off the wig.

Van Limburg's brown eyes widened. He grinned, grasped my hand, gave it a hearty shake, and embraced me, exclaiming, "What a spy you are!"

I broke away. "Investigator Schotten, you must place this man under arrest."

The prince stood up. "What are you saying? He got me away just in time!"

"He got you away before time. I had my eye on him. He looked at his watch because he knew that, exactly ten minutes after you entered the hall, a bomb would fall through the roof. He took hold of your arm and pulled you away just before the bomb came down. Notice, Your Highness, everyone but you was hit, or cut, by falling glass."

Alexander thought for a moment. "It all happened so quickly, but . . . now that I think of it – "

Van Limburg seized my jacket and pulled me close, seething. "This is an outrage, Mijnheer Holmes! Obviously you have joined with the anarchists you were supposed to spy on. You are lucky that the bomb failed to explode, or you would not be standing here to charge me with treason!"

"If it had been a real bomb – if I had made a real bomb, and not a dud – you and the prince would be the only members of the palace household standing here, alive. You got him out of the way, so that the king, the queen consort – even the little princess – would all have perished. Then your friend Alexander would ascend to the throne. And you would serve as his chief counselor throughout his reign. Likely one day *you* would be the power behind the throne."

"Johannes? Is this true?"

"Of course not!" Van Limburg shouted. "This is a madman's tale!" He glared at me, then leaned in close, his mouth just an inch from my ear, and whispered, "I will kill you."

By now, Willem and Emma had joined us. I gave a little nod of respect to them, and to Wilhelmina as well. "My name is Sherlock Holmes. I am a consulting detective and a British subject. I was sent here by Her Majesty's government, as a detective, to help the *Polite* discover the extent of anarchist activity in Amsterdam. At Onderzoeker Schotten's suggestion, I infiltrated a cell of anarchists here. It is thanks to the leadership of Onderzoeker Schotten that the cell was prevented from exploding a bomb."

"My constables are making the arrests right now."

"What was unexpected in the cell," I said, "was the discovery of an agent-provocateur in disguise."

I reached over and snatched the great waxed moustache off Van Limburg's face. He jerked back and stood – stunned – breathing heavily.

"This is the anarchist Frijof," I declared, "who joined the cell shortly after a man called Olaf departed from it."

"Olaf was our agent!" said the prince.

"There is a policemen's barracks in the fairground. Somewhere inside, he has hidden the long blond wig and workingman's suit of clothes that he wore while among the anarchists. Some of his own hair will be in the band that secures the wig."

Turning to Van Limburg, I said, "Splotches of paint on the wig – that was a touch! I was already suspicious after learning about Olaf, but the wig betrayed you this morning at the tea shop. When the wind freshened, the blond hair blew up and all around your head, exposing your scar."

Then, to the Royal Family, I said, "As the anarchist Frijof, he was prepared to kill you all – King, Queen, and Princess."

Willem strode over and confronted the counselor, his authority profound, his bulk intimidating, and his voice stentorian. "Speak, Johannes? Did you have knowledge of this plot?"

After a silent moment, he said, "I did, Your Highness."

"And what this Englishman says: That you participated. Is that also true?"

Van Limburg nodded. "It is true, Your Highness. I disguised myself as one of the anarchists. I encouraged them to make a bomb. And I conspired to set it off. But I have killed no one!"

I leaned in. "What do you know about Olaf?"

"I dismissed him. He would have recognized me as Frijof. So I sent him to Berlin, to spy for me there."

The King turned to Schotten and said something in Dutch. Schotten waved over two constables. They put Van Limburg's wrists in irons and, with Schotten, led him away.

Emma touched my arm. "You have saved our lives, Mijnheer Holmes. I would like to shake your – oh!" She had extended her hand, but suddenly realized that her fingers were still nervously clutched in a fist around the diamond ring. "Here," she said, placing it in my hand. "Let this serve as a reward. And if there is anything else that my country can do while you are our guest, you have only to say. I thank you."

Wilhelmina beckoned to me. I dropped down on my haunches to face her. She planted a tiny peck on my cheek, and said, "I thank you, too." If it would not have been a breach of protocol, I would have returned the ring and called that little kiss sufficient thanks.

"There ends my tale, Watson." Holmes drew on his pipe. "Have I given you enough material with which to work?"

"It would be good to conclude with what transpired after that charming moment with the princess."

"Well, it is something of what you writers call an anticlimax. The socialists in England's Fellowship of the New Life kicked out the anarchists and re-grouped, changing the name of their organization. They are now known as the Fabian Society, which is a famously pacifist organization to which, as you know, many statesmen and intellectuals belong. Investigator Schotten remains one of the most important men in the Amsterdam *Politie*. And I remain in touch with him when something on the Continent piques my interest. Van Limburg was tried, convicted, and incarcerated. His behavior in prison, I am told, is exemplary. He has been made a 'trusty' – one who informs on other prisoners, and enjoys extra privileges in return.

"Watson, you follow international affairs more assiduously than I, so perhaps you know this already, but Alexander, the heir apparent, contracted typhus and died in June of 1884. Emma had no more children. With no sons to inherit the throne, Willem proclaimed that his daughter Wilhelmina should succeed him. But as she was only ten years old when he died in 1890, her mother Emma has been serving as regent. Emma is widely admired. She is warmer, more congenial, and more popular than her stern, blustery husband was."

"What is the reason that you are now willing to let this tale be told to the world?"

"Why, because now, in 1898, Wilhelmina has reached her majority. She has just turned eighteen. Look at this!" He tossed to me a stiff white card with a coat of arms and Dutch words in fancy gravure. "I am invited to The Hague next month to see Wilhelmina sworn in and crowned Queen of The Netherlands."

The Adventure of the
Drunken Teetotaller
by Thomas A. Burns, Jr.

*I*t was a snowy winter's night, in 1895, I think, when Holmes and I were ensconced in Baker Street. A cheery fire burned in the grate, and Holmes had grown bored with updating his indices – a never-ending occupation. In order to distract him from the task, which I knew could continue all night, I lowered the copy of Lloyd's Weekly that I had been perusing and addressed him. "I have just finished an interesting article about the contradiction that our era embodies," I said. "The writer specifically refers to the spectacular increase of wealth and power that the Empire has enjoyed during these last few decades, and contrasts it with the disreputable state of the poor and the working classes."

"That is no contradiction," replied Holmes. "Everything has a rational explanation. The cognoscente who penned that piece has doubtless advanced a specious argument for his position, which would inevitably lead to his labelling his conclusion as a contradiction. He obviously doesn't consider the premise that the state of the individual and the state of the Empire may be mutually exclusive. A spiritualist employs a similar strategy. When attempting to explicate so-called paranormal phenomena, the spiritualist constructs his argument so that a contradiction inevitably occurs. To resolve it, he must resort to a supernatural explanation."

"Surely you oversimplify. This world is not only stranger than we know. It is stranger than we can know."

"If I believed that, I should immediately close my consulting detective business and retire to Sussex to keep bees," asserted Holmes. "I reiterate – contradictions do not exist. If you encounter one, always return to the premises you began with. Invariably, you will find that one or more of them are in error." He paused to apply a vespa to his pipe, puffing until it was drawing to his satisfaction. "I applied this principle to solve one of the more interesting cases I encountered. You were not involved. It occurred while you weren't residing at 221b – in 1883, I think. It was an apparent contradiction that induced me to accept it."

"And that contradiction was?"

"In my case notes, I refer to it as the tragedy of the drunken teetotaller. Would you care to hear about it?"

I felt sure that Holmes had discerned what I was doing when I initiated our conversation, and simply couldn't resist outmanoeuvring me, but here was a chance I simply couldn't ignore. "Of course," I said.

"Then pour us a couple of brandies and I'll tell you the tale."

I did as he asked and settled back in my chair.

"It was a Monday as I recall, in late July of 1883. I was in Stratford, attending the appearance of Virginia Matsford in the West Ham Police Court, who was accused of poisoning her children for the insurance money . . . ."

Matsford was bound over to the Crown Court, and afterwards, removed from the court for transfer to Newgate Prison to await trial in the Old Bailey.

The unseasonably cold and rainy weather didn't discourage a crowd of about one-thousand from gathering outside. They had apparently heard of the heinous nature of Matson's crime. Holmes had joined them, his collar turned up and his hat pulled down to remain anonymous, and careful to remain on the periphery in case the mob became ugly. Sure enough, unruliness erupted when the prisoner was brought out, flanked by four burly officers who conducted her to an awaiting police van in front of the building. The mob surged forward, trying to remove her from the carriage to exact rough justice. Holmes took particular notice of an individual at the forefront of the throng who shouted loudly, "Let's have her out of there, then!" He was half-staggering and slurring his words as if consummately inebriated. The horde likely would followed his instructions, except for a dozen constables who suddenly stormed out of the building, plying their truncheons with abandon, driving back the mob, and arresting several of the rascals, the vociferous fellow among them. The rest had to give way or be trampled as the van clattered off, then they dispersed as the object of their wrath was no longer in propinquity.

Two days later, London was still atypically cold and rainy. Holmes barely noticed the weather unless it impacted his work, but he did have the sitting room windows closed and a fire smouldering in the grate. He was at breakfast when the bell rang downstairs, followed by footsteps on the stairs. A gentle knock came on the door.

"Come in, Mrs. Hudson."

The door opened and the good lady entered, carrying a silver salver. "It's a lady, sir," she said. "I informed her that you'd still be eatin' your breakfast, but she insists she must see you right away." She offered the tray to Holmes.

He picked up the calling card on its surface. *Mrs. Thomas Berry*, it read.

"Show her up," Holmes said. "If she's out so early, perhaps she's had no breakfast either."

The landlady sniffed. "Very good, sir," she answered and left the room.

Holmes rose as Mrs. Hudson returned in a moment with Mrs. Berry. The visitor was a large woman, just an inch or two shorter than Holmes, with strawberry blond hair in a bun and ringlets dangling round her ears. She affected a grey tight morning dress of the type she would wear to receive a visitor in her own home, with wide black stripes and a black ruffled collar and cuffs. Doubtless, Watson would have found her fetching. However, her face was drawn and her eyes tinged with red.

Holmes greeted her. "Good morning, Madam. Your husband must have gotten himself into serious trouble for you to come all the way from Stratford to see me in such beastly weather. Pray sit down and tell me about it. Will you have some breakfast?"

"No thank you, sir. I couldn't eat a bite." Suddenly, she started. "How did you know I travelled here from Stratford?"

"A cup of this most excellent coffee then," Holmes entreated, pouring her one. "I was in Stratford myself only the other day. You likely picked up the petals of the dahlias and cornflowers that I see adhering to your boots when you walked past the flower seller outside Stratford Station. Was your husband involved in the fracas in front of the West Ham Police Court on Monday?

Mrs. Berry had a look on her face akin to wonderment and apprehension all at once. "How did you know it was my husband in trouble?"

"For whom else would you come, Madam? Pray tell me what difficulties he has gotten himself into. And be sure to omit no detail, however inconsequential it may seem to you."

She picked up the cup and sipped the strong black brew, and some colour came back into her cheeks. "My husband Thomas is a solicitor who sometimes works in the West Ham Police Court. He often assists his clients in the courtroom of the magistrate, Mr. Ian Harris. He had a case there Monday morning." A glistening tear swelled at the corner of an eye, then she took another sip of the coffee to fortify herself before she could continue. "On Monday afternoon, Thomas was arrested for drunk and disorderly. They . . . they told me he allegedly tried to remove a woman in custody from a police van!"

"It was no mere allegation, ma'am. I was there and I observed it myself. Your husband appeared to be thoroughly intoxicated."

Her face fell, but she continued on, gamely. "Yesterday, Thomas appeared before the magistrate, Ian Harris. He was convicted of being

261

drunk and disorderly, and Harris sentenced him to three weeks' hard labour. But the drunken man you saw couldn't have been Thomas, Mr. Holmes. He's a teetotaller. He's been active in the temperance movement for most of his adulthood."

"I take it that witnesses who testified in court identified him as the man who tried to remove the prisoner from the van?"

She nodded.

"You'll pardon my saying so, Mrs. Berry, but it wouldn't be the first time a husband has lied to his wife about his vices."

"No! Not my Thomas, Mr. Holmes." She paused, the tears welling up in earnest now.

Holmes reached forward and took her hand. "There, there, Madam. Surely this is no great tragedy. The worst of it is that Mr. Berry will have three weeks' discomfort as a present from a petty tyrant."

"No, Mr. Holmes, I fear not. My Thomas has a bad heart. I fear that being put to hard labour for that time could actually kill him."

"I am truly sympathetic to your plight, but I must tell you again: I was at the West Ham Police Court during the incident in question. I saw your husband try to free the prisoner, exhorting others to assist him. He certainly appeared to be grossly inebriated."

"If it were my Thomas you saw, Mr. Holmes, then he must have been out of his mind for some other reason. He would never touch alcohol, I tell you." She paused to wipe her eyes, then went on. "You should know that I am not Thomas Berry's first wife. His Lily was killed two decades ago when a drunken drayman ran her down with his cart in a busy street. After that, Thomas vowed he would never drink again, joined a teetotaller's society, and has worked tirelessly ever since to have beverage alcohol banned throughout the kingdom."

Holmes rose to retrieve his morning pipe from the mantel, giving Mrs. Berry a questioning rise of his eyebrows. "May I smoke?"

She nodded.

He plucked a coal from the fire with the tongs and got his briar going. When it was drawing to his satisfaction, he sat and asked, "I take it there was bad blood between your husband and this magistrate? Three weeks hard labour is a severe sentence."

"Possibly. Thomas has told me that Magistrate Harris has a reputation for austerity around the court."

Holmes considered. He had often said to Watson that it is a capital mistake to theorize before all the data have been gathered. Had he been doing that? After observing the donnybrook in the square Monday afternoon, he thought that it was a certainty that the man who had tried to get to Virginia Matson was very drunk. If it was Thomas Berry, the probability that he had broken his vow was high. But there was no firm evidence that this truly was the case.

"All right, Mrs. Berry, I'll see what I can do." Holmes said. "But you must realize that the overturning of a Magistrate's sentence is no small order. I shall have to find new and compelling evidence to present to Mr. Harris, and even then, he may elect to have your husband remain where he is."

"You must tell him that even if Thomas did as it appeared, drunkenness should not be punishable with a death sentence."

"I certainly shall do that, Madam. Perhaps you would know where your husband was taken to serve his sentence?" Holmes knew that most prisoners sentenced in the West Ham Court served their sentences at the nearby Pentonville Prison, but there were exceptions.

"They told me that he was taken to Pentonville, Mr. Holmes. They won't let me in to visit him, though."

After Mrs. Berry had departed, Holmes found his telegraph pad amongst the clutter in the sitting room, scribbled for a few moments, then rang for the page. Inspector Lestrade owed him several favours for giving the Scotland Yard detective sole credit for the solutions of a few important cases. Now it was time to call a marker due. After handing his missive off to the lad, Holmes retired to his bedroom to dress. A response was waiting for him when he returned to the sitting room.

He caught a cab to Scotland Yard and asked the cabbie to wait while he went inside. He soon returned and directed the cabbie to Pentonville Prison.

Her Majesty's Prison at Pentonville occupied an area of about six acres in the north London district of Islington. It was constructed as a so-called "Model Prison", intended to remedy the deficiencies of older institutions such as Newgate, by enforcing a silent system of incarceration akin to that found in a monastery. Each prisoner occupied his own sparsely furnished cell, whose heavy stone walls muffled sound and added to the cloistered atmosphere inside. Such construction was supposed to promote penitence and introspection in the inmates, which was considered a key component of rehabilitation. The inmates were expected to remain silent except in a case of dire emergency. Penalties for noncompliance were severe.

Holmes's cab drew up before a wide square gatehouse with portcullises on all four sides, rearing high above a curtain wall that encircled the entire prison. The detective asked his cabbie to remain, alighted, and presented a letter to a guard, who conducted him through the gatehouse to a horizontal corridor that ran between two-storey administrative buildings on either side. Holmes turned neither right nor left, exiting the corridor through a door in its centre into a walled courtyard in front of the main building.

Holmes's escort led him across the courtyard and passed him off to another lackey, who brought the detective to the Governor's office, which occupied a nexus of four wings containing four floors each. The wings radiated from the rear of the central building like the struts of an open fan, and comprised the prison's living quarters. Holmes found the Governor waiting in the internal gallery outside his office, a convenient vantage point from which he could survey the entire prison from a central location.

The Governor perused the letter that Holmes gave him, then handed it back, saying, "You may visit the prisoner Berry. He is currently at his labour in the basement. You must realize that the time he spends talking to you will count against him in terms of the completion of his required tasks to earn his meals."

"Were you not informed that Mr. Berry has a heart condition that would preclude hard labour?" Holmes asked.

"Indeed I was. That is why I had Mr. Berry examined by the doctor upon admission. It was determined that he was unsuited to the treadmill, so he has been assigned to the crank instead."

"Hardly an adequate substitute," said Holmes.

"That is your opinion sir," said the Governor with a tone of finality. He addressed Holmes's consort. "Otis, take this gentleman to see prisoner Berry."

Otis, the guard, led Holmes downstairs into the basement, a dank and cheerless place that stank of mould and stale water. Cells opened on either side of a corridor. The guard conducted Holmes halfway down before stopping at an iron door. He plied a key and opened the door onto a clammy little room. Filtered daylight entering from a window near the ceiling, illuminating a man struggling to turn a crank protruding from a black metal box on a pedestal near the wall. A small meter mounted on the side of the box contained numbered wheels that advanced with each rotation of the crank. Holmes knew that turning the crank forced a series of paddles through sand inside the box, performing no useful work. Moreover, the tension of the handle could be adjusted, making it more difficult to operate the crank.

The only other furniture in the room was a three-legged stool which was too short to sit on while working, and a chamber-pot with no cover. The fellow's breathing rasped like a crosscut saw across a log as he struggled to raise the handle upright, then push it downwards again.

"Mr. Thomas Berry?" said Holmes.

The man stopped working and turned to face the detective. His countenance radiated death. His mouth hung open as he struggled for air, streams of drool ran down his chin, and his skin was an unhealthy shade of cyan. "Who are you who comes to see my misery?" he asked.

"I am Sherlock Holmes. I'm here at your wife's behest."

Berry broke into tears. "Oh, dear little Sheila! Shall I ever see her again?"

"Perhaps you shall, sir. We must talk." Holmes turned to the guard. "A little time alone with my client, if you please, Otis."

Otis clearly didn't want to honour the request, but Sherlock Holmes was a man difficult to say no to. Otis stepped outside and pushed the door to. Seconds later, the key clattered in the lock.

Holmes indicated the stool. "Sit down and rest, Mr. Berry, while we talk."

"I dare not, sir. I must turn this terrible handle three-thousand times before supper if I wish to be fed."

Holmes took Berry by the shoulder and pulled him away from the infernal machine. "Sit, sir, and let me work for you for a while." He removed his coat and jacket and handed them to Berry, then began to spin the crank much faster than the prisoner could ever hope to. However, even Holmes, a strong young man, found the task challenging.

"I must understand your actions on Monday last, which led you to this place," Holmes said.

"There isn't much to tell," Berry replied. "I had a case that morning in Mr. Harris's court."

"Did you win?" asked Holmes.

"No, but I should have done. I informed Magistrate Harris that I would be appealing his decision to the Crown Court."

"You've done that before." It wasn't a question.

"Yes, three times. Harris was overturned in each case."

"So, you went to lunch and had a pint or two to celebrate?"

As knackered as he was, Berry still managed to look insulted. "I did no such thing! I had lunch at The King of Prussia public house to be sure, but I touched no alcohol. I have taken a vow of abstinence."

"With whom did you lunch?"

"My fellow solicitors, Roger Starling and Howard Livingstone."

"Did they consume any alcohol?"

"No. They know my feelings, and choose not to indulge in my presence."

"What was your lunch?"

"I had a delightful steak-and-mushroom pie." He hesitated, then, "It was the last I have eaten before being brought here."

"What about your companions?"

"Let me see . . . I think Livingstone had the pie as well, and Starling a ploughman's lunch."

"Tell me about what happened later in the square."

Berry assumed a frantic expression. "That's just it, Mr. Holmes! I don't know! They tell me I had done outrageous things, called witnesses in court who confirmed it. But I don't remember anything!"

"Do you remember leaving The King of Prussia?"

"Yes. I had another appearance before Harris that afternoon, and I remember thinking that it wasn't going to go well because of our difficulties that morning."

"Did you feel ill after lunch?"

"A little, sir, as if what I had didn't quite agree with my stomach. But I don't remember feeling really in distress. The three of us arrived back at the Police Court and I bade goodbye to my comrades. That's the last thing I remember before waking up in jail Tuesday morning." His face fell. "I was absolutely flummoxed when they recited the list of things they claimed I had done in court."

By this time, Holmes's arms and shoulders were aching from turning the crank. He stopped and looked at the counter – barely a hundred turns since he'd begun, and poor Berry needed thousands to receive his dinner.

Holmes retrieved his garments and donned them. "Mr. Berry, I promise I will exert my best efforts to have you out of here as quickly as I can. I suggest you defy your jailers and turn that crank as slowly as you can. It will take you much longer to die of starvation than of heart failure." He banged on the door with a clenched fist. "Guard! I am ready!"

Otis apparently thought it amusing to make Holmes wait a further ten minutes before releasing him. The detective said nothing about the delay, knowing it was a battle he couldn't win. "Please take me back to the Governor," Holmes asked the guard.

Once in the presence of the great man again, Holmes expostulated, "I really must protest your treatment of my client in the strongest terms. The man is clearly not sufficiently healthy for the crank. Surely it is within your power to find an alternative. He could be assigned to pick oakum, make nets, or engage in some other trade for the benefit of all."

"Are you a physician, sir?" the Governor asked.

"No."

"A surgeon, then, or a nurse?"

"No, I am not."

"No formal medical training at all," the Governor observed, shaking his head. "Yet you presume to instruct me about the treatment of my convicts."

266

Holmes surely missed Watson now. It took every bit of willpower he possessed not to smash the fellow's nose with his fist, flat against his face. But his joining Berry here in prison would benefit no one.

Outside, the sky was painted dark grey with clouds and a cold rain fell in sheets – weather appropriate to the events of the day, Holmes thought. However, lunchtime was approaching. He mounted his cab. "The King of Prussia public house, Stratford," he said to the driver.

Twenty minutes after leaving Pentonville Prison, Holmes's cab rattled into Stratford over the River Lea on the ancient Bow Bridge. Stratford was a town in East London, a ward of the parish of West Ham that was eventually subsumed into the metropolis. Its marshy plains, inundated by the Lea, proved an ideal site for the many manufacturing enterprises that sprang up after the railroad came about forty years ago, after dangerous and noxious industries were banned from metropolitan London. Currently, Stratford served as a manufacturing hub for medicines, chemicals, and processed foods, among other goods. Holmes's cab juddered past the elaborate Italianate town hall at the junction of Broadway and High Street, whose cupola and weathervane towered one-hundred feet above the pavement. The King of Prussia occupied the lower floor of a grey-fronted building from the previous century just up the road, across the street from the West Ham Police Court. Holmes alighted and paid off his driver, as he intended to take the train back to London when he was finished here this evening.

As Holmes approached the pub, a sign on the pedimented door between two bay windows informed him that the proprietor was one *G. Demeris*. A Greek name, Holmes thought. He knew that the Greeks had a long and distinguished history in London, dating back to the Tudor Era. Many of London's Greek citizens were of humble origin – sailors from the myriad ships who docked at the port. In 1820, reprisals by the hated Turks against Greeks living in the Ottoman Empire forced many middle- and upper-class citizens to flee their oppressors. Many ended up in London where they were able to take up their lives again. It wasn't odd to see a Greek as a business owner now – some of the more prominent London Greeks had even assimilated into the upper-middle-class.

A warm, beery aroma wafted over Holmes as he opened the door to the public room and pushed inside. The warmth from the kitchen immediately seeped into his bones, driving out the chill imbued in them by the cold rain. He was in a large room that occupied most of the ground floor, full of tables and chairs. A bar to his right ran from front to back. Behind it was a pass-through to an open kitchen on which plates of food rested, awaiting conveyance to the diners who ordered them. At the rear of the room, a staircase running from right to left gave access to an upper floor – doubtless the domain of the proprietor.

The place was still three-quarters full with the lunch crowd, but a table near the bar adjacent to a bay window was clearing, so Holmes took it. A serving wench noticed him immediately and approached.

"What'll it be, ducks?"

"A pint of your best, please. What are you serving for luncheon?"

"Steak-and-mushroom pie is our specialty."

"That will be fine."

The girl brought the beer immediately. Holmes took a long draught and found it hoppy, bitter, but well-bodied. It was doubtless brewed on the premises. The tingle that suffused his muscles alerted him that it was also quite strong, but it would take much more than a pint of beer to get him into the condition that he observed in Berry during the affray outside the police court. The steak-and-mushroom pie arrived in its own ramekin in due course, steam rising from the top and a rich brown gravy bubbling round the circumference of the crust.

Holmes ate slowly, not only because the food was very hot, but also to allow the crowd to diminish, as he hoped to have a word with the landlord. He found the pie delicious and filling, and it extirpated the remains of the chill from his body.

Finally, he finished and waved at the waitress to come and remove his dishes. When she arrived, he inquired, "Can you ask the landlord to step over here for a bit?"

A look of suspicion appeared on her face. "Why? Did I do something wrong? Was the food not to yer likin'?

"On the contrary. Your service has been exemplary and the food more than satisfactory. I just wish to pay my respects."

Her apprehensive aspect transformed into a smile. "Oh! I'll let him know." A pause, and a coy look. "My name's Annie, by the way."

"Thank you, Annie." She scurried off.

A few minutes later, the landlord approached. He was a tall, grey-haired man in his sixties with a handlebar moustache and a definite Hellenic cast to his features. "You wish to see me, sir?"

"Yes, Mr. Demeris. Sit down, if you please. Firstly, I wanted to compliment you on a most excellently prepared steak-and-mushroom pie."

"Thank you so much, sir. It is an old family recipe for *kreatopita*, adapted to suit my new home here in England."

"I wonder if I could speak to you about one of your patrons? Are you acquainted with Mr. Thomas Berry?"

"*Nai fysika*! Yes, of course! He comes in for lunch, two, t'ree times a week."

"Do you remember if he came in this week?"

"*Nai*. He was here on Monday, with two friends."

"Do you remember what he had for lunch?"

Demeris gazed through the bay window into the street. "Let me t'ink . . . Ah! I have it! He had a dish of *moussaka,* I t'ink."

"Did he drink any alcohol?"

"Oh yes. Mr. Berry, he likes my beer very much! He had a pint or two. And a little glass of whisky, I t'ink, to drive off the cold."

"Hmm. Very interesting."

"If that will be all, sir, I must return to my kitchen now."

"Yes, of course. Thank you."

Holmes watched Demeris as he rose and retreated to safety behind the bar. He was nearly certain that the innkeeper had lied, and moreover, that the man was terrified. But Holmes only had the word of Berry to support his conclusion. He decided to visit the police court to gather more evidence.

The rain had abated when Holmes exited the pub, but patches of dark clouds still peppered the blue sky, promising more precipitation. Holmes was happy to be able to walk to the old court house across the square without a further soaking.

The London Police Courts were an institution unique in the European criminal justice system. Established at the end of the eighteenth century to preserve the public order after the Gordon Riots, the courts were available to all. Both the police and common citizens could seek a summons from a magistrate against someone. The magistrates themselves were paid a handsome annual stipend for their service in order to allow them to preserve their independence and remain unbiased. Even though a magistrate could convict and set punishment only for misdemeanours and certain minor felonies, his judicial power was nevertheless sweeping. He was largely unsupervised and difficult to question or reverse. A solicitor could appeal a magistrate's decision to the Crown Court, but the process was lengthy so, as in Thomas Berry's situation, it often provided inadequate requital.

However, many magistrates did much more for the public than simply render judgments. The best of them intervened pro-actively in disputes of all sorts – with family, with neighbours, with tradesmen, and even with the police. Sometimes they even interceded in the lives of their predominantly working-class clients, originating summonses, dispensing advice, and even charity from court slush funds established for that very purpose, all in the name of encouraging the common man to look to the law for redress and protection instead of fearing it as an oppressor.

After inquiring of some of the people in the halls, Holmes found Roger Starling in the solicitor's lounge, organizing his notes from today's cases.

"You've only just caught me here, you know," said Starling. "I'm off for London and won't return until next week."

"Then I am fortunate indeed," said Holmes. "I have agreed to assist Thomas Berry with his current difficulty, and I was wondering if you could provide any insight about his behaviour on Monday last."

"I'm whacked," said Starling. "I had lunch with Berry and Howard Livingstone that day, and I saw nothing to suggest he'd get himself into such a kettle of fish."

"He wasn't drinking at lunch?"

"Tommy Berry? Drinking? Good Lord, man, who told you that? Berry was the most obdurate teetotaller I ever laid eyes on. He'd sooner sip a cup of boiling lead as drink a beer with his luncheon."

"Did he seem all right when you left him?"

"Now that you mention it, he was a little green around the gills, as if his repast didn't agree with him."

"Was there anything wrong with his meal?"

"He didn't say there was. Livingstone had the same thing, the steak-and-mushroom pie, as I remember, and he was fine. I had the ploughman's lunch myself – can't stomach bloody mushrooms, you know."

"Is Mr. Livingstone here today?"

"Yes. He's arguing a case before Magistrate Harris, poor devil. Involves a young maidservant who is suing her master for her wages after she was dismissed. She claims the old man behaved inappropriately towards her, let her go without paying her when she protested. Livingstone should be here before long."

"How does an unpaid maidservant afford the services of a solicitor?"

"Some of the fellows have formed an association to provide *pro bono* services to the poor who end up in court." He hesitated. "They shouldn't have to. It's the magistrate's job to look out for them after all, but Harris doesn't always do that."

"I assume Thomas Berry is a part of that."

"He started it, sir, and roped the rest into it."

"Including you?"

"No sir. I know better than to antagonize a magistrate."

"Is Harris's behaviour why Livingstone is a 'poor devil'?"

Starling looked right and left as if to assure he wouldn't be overheard. "Harris runs his court with an iron fist. He's usually made his mind up very early in the game, according to his own view of things, and it's right difficult to change. But mind you, most of the time, he takes the correct decision."

"Did Mr. Berry have trouble with Harris?"

Starling gave a barky laugh through his nose. "You might say so," he averred. "Went after the magistrate tooth and nail, he did, even when it was clear that his cause was lost. Even took Harris to the Crown Prosecutor a few times for failure to follow proper legal procedures."

"I assume Harris took exception to that."

"Let's just say there's no love lost between the two of 'em. And Harris took Tommy's establishment of his little legal aid society as a direct affront to his authority. Couldn't do a thing about it, though."

Holmes thanked Starling for his time and went over to Harris's courtroom, where Livingstone was arguing. He pushed the double doors open, and the smell of ancient books and unwashed humanity rolled over him. The public gallery was nearly empty. Apparently only a few had chosen to spend their Wednesday afternoon viewing the police court proceedings. A plainly dressed young woman stood in the witness box, being interrogated by Harris himself, a stocky, black-robed fellow with a boxer's nose who sat behind a bar on a raised platform at the rear of the courtroom. Two solicitors occupied adjacent tables facing the magistrate and his witness. A well-dressed older gentleman, apparently the defendant, sat next to one of them while the other was by himself. The defendant was extremely tall and thin, with the protruding forehead characteristic of the scholar. He was clean-shaven, pale, and appeared older than he actually was, Holmes thought, chiefly due to his eyes, which were deeply recessed in his head. He was stooped over the table when Holmes entered, studying a paper, but he looked up, staring at the detective with his sunken eyes in a curiously reptilian fashion. Holmes felt a cold frission run from his feet to his face, as if someone had stepped on his grave.

Harris questioned the witness. "You say that the defendant's behaviour towards you was inappropriate. How so?"

"'Ee follered me into the bedroom, Your Worship – "

Harris cut her off short. "And whose bedroom was it that he followed you into, Miss Darcy?"

"Why, it was 'is bedroom, sorr, but then 'ee – "

Again, an interruption. "So you're telling me that it was inappropriate for the defendant to be in his own bedroom in his own house?"

"Why no, sorr! But 'ee pushed me against the bed, and 'ee put 'is 'ands on me – "

"Perhaps he was only attempting to get you to leave his bedroom so he could attend to private matters."

271

The lone solicitor rose and addressed the court. "Sir, if you would please to allow Miss Darcy to give her evidence in her own way . . . ." Holmes assumed that this worthy was Howard Livingstone.

Harris spitted the solicitor with a glare. "It seems that cheeky behaviour is going round today," he said. "Your client presumes to tell a man what to do in his own home, and now you tell me how to conduct myself in my own courtroom." He turned back to the woman who was now shivering in the witness box. "It seems that your employer did exactly right when he sacked you, Miss Darcy. Moreover, I find that you have wasted this court's time with your frivolous suit. Therefore, I'm sending you the Women's House of Correction in Brixton Hill for a week, so you may ruminate upon the error of your ways. Perhaps you'll act differently towards your master in your next position, assuming that you are so fortunate as to secure one." He slammed his gavel down on the block. "Constable! Take this witness into custody and see that she is duly processed."

"Your Worship, I must protest!" Livingstone shouted, but Harris paid him no mind as he rose.

Miss Darcy screamed, "No, please don't take me!" as the burly constable seized her wrists and led her struggling from the witness box.

The defendant turned to survey the courtroom, a broad smile on his face. Holmes felt that frigid spasm again as the man's eyes met his, and he smiled even more widely.

Harris moved toward a door behind his bench, and the usher intoned "All rise!" The magistrate turned and exited the courtroom.

Holmes waited until the defendant and his solicitor left the courtroom, then wended his way through the outgoing crowd to approach Livingstone at the solicitor's table. The lawyer stood there with both hands flat upon its surface, staring at the portal through which his erstwhile client had disappeared, as if he quite didn't know what had happened.

Holmes introduced himself. Upon questioning, the solicitor confirmed the information that Starling gave Holmes in every particular.

"You think that Harris sentenced Berry to such a harsh penalty because of Berry's disrespect for him?" asked Holmes.

"I'm sure of it," said Livingstone. "And the timing of it was awful."

"How so?"

"Tommy told me a few days ago that, after talking to the young woman who was just removed from here, he'd recently found out something about Harris that would really take him down a peg or two. Wouldn't say what it was, though. He said he was going to confront Harris about it soon."

At that piece of information, Holmes pursed his lips. "Tell me, was Starling present when Berry told you that?"

Livingstone looked at the ceiling for a moment then said, "Why yes, now that you mention it."

"How is Starling's relationship with the magistrate?"

"Better than mine and Tommy's," Livingstone answered. "Roger's always saying that we're hurting ourselves by antagonizing Harris. But how can we not, when he does things like he just did?"

"Did you speak to the maid about what she may have told Mr. Berry?"

"Yes, but she was terrified. Told me she just wanted her wages so she could leave London and go home."

He went silent for a moment, then continued. "Unlike Miss Darcy, Thomas Berry actually committed the crime for which he was sentenced. I think there's little chance of having him released before his time is up."

"Harris could do it," Holmes said.

"Certainly! A magistrate can do almost anything. But I think there's very little chance that he will do it."

"We shall have to see about that," Holmes said. "Thank you for your time, Mr. Livingstone."

"Good luck," Livingstone said, as Holmes walked away.

Holmes went back into the corridor and inquired about the location of Harris's chambers. Soon he was knocking at the magistrate's door.

"Come in."

Holmes opened the door upon an office filled with bookshelves, and tables that held as fine a collection of Chinese memorabilia as he'd ever seen. Harris sat at a massive desk in front of a window looking out over West Ham Lane, his black robe hanging on the back of his chair. He wore a fine tweed suit that looked as if it had come from Savile Row, and a gold ring with a large ruby glinted on his right hand. He was engaged in paging through a pile of legal documents.

"Mr. Harris, my name is Sherlock Holmes. I am a consulting detective."

"What do you want?" the magistrate answered brusquely, not even bothering to look up for the papers he was reading.

"I've come to talk with you about Thomas Berry. In particular, about the effect that the hard labour you sentenced him to is having on his health."

Now Harris looked up, a half-sneer upon his face. "And why, pray tell, should that be a concern of mine?"

"Because it's becoming increasingly likely that Mr. Berry will not survive his sentence. You didn't intend that he should suffer capital punishment for drunkenness, did you?"

273

"I didn't intend anything, sir. I merely sentenced him to what I thought was an appropriate term for the infraction he committed. Actually, I may have done him a favour. I could have easily remanded him to the Crown Prosecutor to face charges of obstructing the police, for which I'm sure he would have received much harsher punishment."

By now it was apparent to Holmes that he was flogging a dead horse. Still, he felt the need to press on.

"If Your Worship cannot see his way clear to releasing Mr. Berry, perhaps you could rescind the hard labour, or ask that the prison put Mr. Berry to some task that won't have such an adverse impact on him."

"The purpose of punishment is to have an adverse impact upon an individual, so they'll think twice before committing a subsequent crime."

Holmes hesitated, then he took the plunge. "Mr. Harris, I have evidence that Mr. Berry wasn't drunk when he interfered with the police. I believe he was suffering from food poisoning. If that were true, then he wouldn't be responsible for his actions."

Holmes thought he saw Harris's jaw drop and his eyes briefly widen, but then his expression became a sneer once more. "Balderdash! What evidence have you?"

Holmes explained that Berry was a lifelong teetotaller, and had become ill after his lunch of steak-and-mushroom pie. "If Thomas Berry drank no alcohol, as he averred, then he must have been poisoned. And some poisons can mimic the effects of drunkenness. Mushrooms, for example."

"If that were the case, we'd have had a major outbreak," said Harris. "Steak-and-mushroom pie is a speciality of The King of Pru. Nearly everyone in the place would have been sick." His eyes narrowed. "Or are you saying that Berry was deliberately poisoned?"

"I believe that is a possibility, Mr. Harris."

Harris gave Holmes a look of pure venom, and the detective wondered if he had gone too far. The magistrate could issue a summons to Holmes here and now, and he'd be in prison with Berry this evening. That would do neither of them any good. Then Harris smiled, and Holmes shivered inwardly.

"I'll tell you what, Mr. Consulting Detective. You bring me evidence that what you say is true, and I'll release Mr. Berry. I'll give you until Monday, at which time I will issue a summons for you for attempting to interfere with the legal activities of the Police Court. Now get out of here." He returned to perusing his documents.

As he walked through the courthouse, Holmes found himself quivering, not from fear but from anger. Harris was exactly the sort of person who had inspired him to take up the mantle of a consulting detective in the first place – someone who thought he could run roughshod over anybody he chose to. He silently vowed that he would see Thomas Berry safely out of Pentonville Prison, even if he had to strong arm Magistrate Harris to do it.

Holmes returned to The King of Prussia. It was suppertime. The food aroma made Holmes salivate, but he wasn't here for dinner. The detective took a seat at the bar and ordered a pint. He spotted Demeris coming out of the kitchen, inspecting the plates of food lined up on the pass-through before they went out to the customers. Holmes just sat there, watching the publican's every move. Demeris would notice him soon enough. His goal: Make the Greek nervous.

At first, Demeris didn't notice the detective, but it was as if Holmes was shooting rays of heat from his eyes. Finally, the Greek glanced in Holmes's direction, meeting that hawk-like stare. He turned away, going about his business once more. But he couldn't help himself – he looked back again and Holmes still had him on the spit. He averted his gaze once more, then straightened up as if he'd made a decision. He approached Holmes. "Can I help you, sir?"

"Tell me why you poisoned Thomas Berry."

The look in the Greek's eyes was all the evidence Holmes needed: *Fear!*

"I – I did no such thing," Demeris stammered. Unsuccessfully, he tried to mask his apprehension with indignation. "I'm afraid I'll have to ask you to leave the premises, sir."

"Or what?" Holmes said, his voice dripping with contempt. "You'll call a constable? I think that's the last thing you want to do, Mr. Demeris." An innocent man *would* call a constable, Holmes knew.

"Enjoy your beer then. It's the last one you'll be served." The publican retreated to the far end of the bar.

Holmes was now certain that Demeris was involved. He was also certain that the Greek would never admit his guilt. He was petrified, and Holmes didn't think it was himself that the landlord feared. It was whomever was behind the poisoning of Thomas Berry.

A few minutes before midnight, in the alley behind The King of Pru, a cloaked figure bent over a door, manipulating a pair of lock picks with freezing fingers. The rain had returned with a vengeance, and all was blackness. Holmes had brought a dark lantern with him, but he dared not risk a light while still outside, so he had to work solely by feel. He inserted his right-angled pick, feeling for the lever inside. Ah, he had it! Switching the pick to his left hand, he exerted slight pressure upward, taking care not to allow the pick to slide off the lever. Now he inserted a second probe beneath the first one, feeling for the deadbolt. Once he had it, he turned the second pick slowly to the right, all the while maintaining the upward pressure with the first one. A satisfying click seemed as loud as a gunshot, but the lock was open. Holmes swiftly removed the probes and stowed them in a pocket of his Inverness.

He pushed the door open and slid inside, closing it behind him, but taking care that it remained unlocked in case he had to affect a quick exit. Black silhouettes of hanging pots and pans informed him that he was in the kitchen. He was sure that this wouldn't be where he would find that which he sought, if it was present at all.

He moved silently into the public room. The gate that separated the area behind the bar from the dining area was open – was someone here? Holmes froze and listened carefully. All he heard was the rain softly pattering on the bay windows and the haunting creaks of an old building in the gusty wind. He reached inside his cloak and came out with a vespa and the small dark lantern. He struck the match on a table top and lit the lantern. A bolt of yellow light burst forth. Careful to keep it away from the windows, he played the light about until he located the staircase to the first floor. He zigzagged his way between the tables to its base, where he stopped and listened intently again. He heard nothing, but an innate sense told him that someone was there. He briefly considered aborting the mission, but he knew that if he was to free Berry, he must find evidence. He crept slowly up the stairs, keeping his light low and stepping only on the edges of the treads.

The first floor comprised one large room that had been outfitted as an office. A large dormer containing a window ten shades blacker than the dark room loomed over the square. The bullseye picked out bookcases, filing cabinets – a desk with a man in a chair behind it, slumped over, unmoving! Holmes swallowed to remove his heart from his throat, then stepped over to the body. It was George Demeris, of course.

The publican's left cheek lay on the desk, his eyes bulging, his tongue protruding, a leather belt wrapped tightly round his throat. The yellow light illuminated his battered nose, and dried blood clung to his cheeks. A closer examination revealed strawberry *petechiae* on his face, leaving no doubt to the manner of death – strangulation.

Small, irregular brownish objects were scattered around on the desktop. Holmes noticed an open strongbox to one side, the key still in the lock. He picked up one of the leathery brown objects and smelt it – a mushroom! Inside the strongbox were two leather pouches, both apparently empty. He picked each one up and shook it to make sure. One was indeed empty, but a few more mushroom fragments fell out of the other. Holmes swept up a small handful and put them back in the pouch, stowing it in a pocket.

No one locks an empty pouch in a strongbox – what had the other bag contained? It must have been gold, Holmes realized. The bag likely held the pub-keeper's nest egg.

Holmes quickly went through Demeris's pockets but found nothing: No wallet, no watch, no keychain. Apparently, the killer had picked him clean. Was this a robbery gone bad, or something more sinister? Though Holmes had no direct evidence, he suspected the latter. He suddenly realized that the absence of a keychain explained why the downstairs door was locked when he arrived – the murderer must have taken Demeris's keys and locked it behind him when he left. Did he arrive with Demeris? That would mean the killer was someone the Greek knew. Unlikely, Holmes thought. One doesn't bring company when he raids his hidden strong box. Did the murderer arrive after Demeris, who went downstairs to let him in? No again. Surely Demeris would have closed up and rehidden the strongbox before doing so. Did the fellow get in the same way as Holmes had done? He must have, and locked the door behind him. A professional, then.

And what was Demeris doing with the strongbox in the middle of the night? Getting ready to bolt, Holmes realized. It was clear then that Demeris had poisoned Berry, in all probability by slipping some of the mushrooms now in Holmes's possession into Berry's lunch. Likely, the detective's incursion into the pub at dinnertime had convinced the Greek that Holmes suspected him, and sufficiently unnerved him so that he thought flight was in order.

But why poison the solicitor at all? Demeris couldn't have foreseen the events of that afternoon, which led to Berry's incarceration. Did he intend to kill Berry, or to just make him sick? Pieces of the puzzle were still missing.

Holmes dropped to his knees, shining the bullseye on the carpet, minutely examining the fibres. He rose and went round the desk toward the dormer and inspected the floor there. Then, directing the light away from the window, he stepped up and scrutinized the glass. Fortuitously, the waning moon peeped out as a crack split the clouds, and Holmes extended a finger toward a minute crack in a windowpane. He returned to the body, shining the beam on the floor again. He reached down and plucked something from the rug, and held it in the light. A small hank of brown hair. The blood on the bottom indicated that it had been pulled out by the roots. The detective stood, stepped back a bit, placed his hands on the belt gripping Demeris's neck. Finally, he examined the Greek's hands, then smiled, as if a hypothesis had been confirmed.

277

Abruptly, a thump from downstairs, then a man's voice. "Mr. Demeris! It's Constable Pritchard! Are you here?"

Holmes's hands leapt away from the belt as if it was white-hot. The constable had probably noticed the unlocked door while on patrol and was checking to see that the premises were secure. Holmes saw his career as a consulting detective vanishing in a puff of smoke if he was found here with burglar's tools and the landlord's corpse!

The constable's voice again, louder this time. "Mr. Demeris! Are you up there?" The fellow was at the base of the stairs!

A tread creaked as the constable put his weight on it, coming up. Holmes glanced frantically about. Nowhere to hide!

He extinguished the bullseye lantern and sat it on the desk. It was much too hot to put back in his cloak. No matter – Scotland Yard would never trace it to him. He stepped round the desk, bent his head, and charged the dormer, smashing though the multi-paned window and onto the roof above the square. He rolled to the edge, clutching it with fingers made strong by years of violin playing. He pushed off the edge, hanging so the fifteen-foot drop to the street became seven feet, and let go. The shock ran from his ankles to his teeth as he hit the rain-drenched pavement and fell to his knees.

The shriek of the constable's whistle resounded through the square as Holmes scampered to his feet and dashed into the night. "Oi! Stop! Murder! Bloody murder!"

Once he'd disappeared into the darkness, all of Scotland Yard's finest would never catch Sherlock Holmes.

The next morning, the weather had finally broken. White clouds scudded across an achingly blue sky driven by a fresh wind from the Thames. The warmth of the sun promised an excellent day.

Sherlock Holmes sat in Harris's courtroom as the night charges commenced – the first order of business each morning. They comprised the relatively minor offences that occurred the previous night: Loitering, drunken brawls, petty thefts, *etcetera* . . . .

Holmes wore a Van Dyke with a *pince-nez* perched on the end of his nose. He was clad in a long-sleeved white shirt with a collar and no necktie, under an ochre tattersall vest. He held a notebook in his left hand in which he scrawled periodically as the proceedings continued. When Harris entered the courtroom to the usher's cry of, "Oyez, oyez!" and surveyed the spectators, he didn't give Holmes a second glance. The detective was present because he thought it a good bet that last night's perpetrator might end up here this morning if he spent some of that ill-gotten gold on a night's revelry. If he did not, the detective could always

278

browse the police sheets for viable candidates, which contained the results of past cases that came before the magistrate.

The parade of wrongdoers seemed to be uniformly impoverished, and most were well-known to Harris. Many were of the fair sex, most of them arrested for loitering, some for abusive language aimed at passers-by and two for pickpocketing. Harris dealt with them expeditiously. The loiters were fined and paid surprisingly swiftly, the harridans were consigned to Brixton Hill for a week, and the thieves referred to the Crown Court for more severe punishment.

Holmes perked up as the usher brought a man before the magistrate. He was about six-foot-two – the right height, Holmes thought: Slender and wiry, and dressed roughly in a canvas jacket over an open-collared work shirt. Holmes noted in passing he used a knotted rope to hold up his trousers. His brown hair was a dirty, unkempt mop atop his head, and dried blood mottled his hairline and his cheeks. Somewhat astonishingly, he seemed quite chipper, given his surroundings.

Harris knew him. "Good morning, Cyril," he said. "What brings you to my courtroom this fine day?"

"Mr. Edwards is charged with disturbin' the peace, yer worship," the usher said. "He engaged in a brawl wit' another gent in the street outside The Barkin' Dog this mornin'."

"And where is this other gent," Harris asked.

"'Ee's in hospital, sorr," said Edwards. "I'm rightly sorry about that, but I was just defendin' mesel' from a scurrilous attack."

"I am sure you were, Cyril," said Harris. "But you know that I cannot have you turning up here like this every morning. So here is my final warning – if I see you again, it's hard labour at Pentonville for you. Do you understand?"

Edward now stood with bowed head in the classic pose of the penitent. "Yes, yer worship, I surely do. And thankee for another chance."

Edwards was led out, and after a moment, Holmes followed.

The usher left Edwards in the corridor and returned to the courtroom. Edwards lost no time in heading for the front door and out on the square with Holmes on his heels. He turned south on High Street and walked briskly, crossing the river on the bridge and turning into the neighbourhood by the gas works. He entered a tenement, and Holmes waited a moment before following him inside. He heard Edwards on the stairs as he entered the darkened lobby and crept up behind the man, arriving at the top of the stairs in time to see him entering a flat. Holmes drew his revolver from his pocket and followed him inside, knocking Edwards to the floor as he pushed the door inwards.

Edwards, on his back, extended his hands upward, fingers splayed to ward off his attacker. "Oi, mate! Go easy! I got nuthin' fer yer!"

"Oh yes, you do, Cyril," said Holmes. "You murdered George Demeris last night, and I am here to see that you hang for it! Shall I tell you how you did it?"

"I never – "

"You scooped up some pebbles from the square and threw them against the dormer window. Then you went to the front door where Demeris let you in. You followed him up to his office, taking your belt from your pocket as you went, where you'd already placed it for easy access. When you arrived upstairs, you looped the belt over his head, but he managed to turn himself round and grab your hair, yanking out a thatch by the roots, so you let go of the belt and smashed in his nose with your fist. He fell against his desk, and you got hold of the belt again, turning him round so he faced the desk while you choked the life out of him. Why you left the belt behind when you were finished I cannot tell. Perhaps it was because the glint of gold from the desktop so excited you that you couldn't wait to scoop it into your pockets."

Cyril stared unbelievingly at Holmes. "Where wuz yer hidin' to see all that?"

Holmes levelled his revolver so it pointed between the man's eye's, which were as big as saucers. "Never mind. Show me the gold, Cyril. Show it to me!"

As if an unseen force governed his movements, Edwards slowly reached into his pocket and came out with a handful of sovereigns. "'Ere, yer worship. Ye can 'av it all, if ye'll only let me be – "

Holmes dashed the coins out of the killer's hand. They went spinning and ringing across the floor. "There's only one way out for you, man! Tell me who ordered you to kill Demeris!"

The level of fear on Edwards's face intensified tenfold. "I can't! It isn't just me I have to worry about. Me Mum and me Da are still with us. He'd go after them too!"

Holmes continued to cajole Edwards, promising to protect his family, all to no avail. Finally, he spat, "Pah! I'm done with you! We both know it was Magistrate Harris – that's why he went so lightly on you this morning in court." Holmes produced a pair of handcuffs from a pocket and shackled Edwards to a gas pipe. "There will be a constable up here shortly to collect you, Mr. Edwards."

Holmes left the villain pleading and struggling and sent an anonymous note about where to find him to Scotland Yard by post, being sure to mention the thatch of hair on the carpet in Demeris's office. He then repaired back to Baker Street to change clothes.

Magistrate Ian Harris heard his last case of the day at 3:50 p.m. He had sentenced a second-hand clothes dealer to six weeks hard labour in Pentonville for stealing a purse containing 11s., 6d. in coins from a woman shopkeeper. He shook his head. If he had it his way, he'd have had the man hanged. He knew that the prison sentence would have no real effect and he'd likely see the vagabond here again in a few months for a similar offence. This would go on and on until the fellow either seriously injured or killed someone, at which time he could be dealt with properly.

A knock came on the door.

"Come in!" intoned Harris.

It was the page, with the four o'clock post. He had one envelope for the magistrate. It was of fine, cream-coloured vellum, carried no stamp, and was sealed with wax. Harris rose from his chair to accept the letter from the page. He noted the elaborate coat-of-arms embossed in the upper left-hand corner, which matched the one pressed into the seal. A tremor ran through him as he retrieved a letter-opener, slit the envelope, and extracted a single sheet of heavy paper, folded in thirds. He unfolded and read the elaborate copperplate script. His hand opened involuntarily, and the letter fluttered to the floor. White as a fish's belly, he collapsed into his chair.

At six o'clock, Sherlock Holmes and Sheila Berry stood on the pavement outside the gatehouse at Pentonville Prison, next to the four-wheeler that had conveyed them there. Holmes was greatly uncomfortable, as Mrs. Berry was clinging to him as she would to a life-preserver in a stormy sea, staring into the impenetrable black depths of the structure. She gave a little start as she noticed motion within, then released Holmes and ran forward as her husband emerged into the moonlight, supported by a guard. Sobbing, she threw her arms round his neck as the guard released him, and Holmes stepped up to help conduct him to the waiting brougham.

With Holmes supporting him on one side and his wife on the other, Thomas Berry took a couple of halting steps. He stopped, and Holmes felt the solicitor's entire body go rigid as he exhaled a rattling breath. He became nothing but dead weight and Holmes had no choice but to allow him to slide to the ground.

"The poor fellow was as dead as a doornail, Watson, but at least he saw the light of freedom before he succumbed."

I held my empty snifter up to the firelight and contemplated a refill. Prudence won out, as I knew I'd regret it in the morning. I set the glass down on the side table and looked at Holmes. *"You went to Mycroft, of course."*

"Yes," said Holmes. *"Once it became clear to me that Edwards would actually rather risk hanging for murder than betray Harris, I had to take a step back and reconsider my original objective – to free Thomas Berry from his captivity. Besides, it was dubious whether testimony from the likes of Cyril Edwards would convince a Crown Court Justice to indict a colleague anyway. So I went to my brother and told him the entire sorry tale."*

"I don't suppose you're going to tell me whom it was that wrote that letter to Harris?"

"It's enough to say that it was someone very high in the British government who owed Mycroft a favour. And it meant that I now owed my brother one in turn." Holmes looked glum. *"He has yet to collect."*

There was something else I just had to know. *"Was that the first time you had laid eyes on Professor Moriarty?"*

Holmes smiled ruefully. *"Yes, it was. It was interesting – I think both of us somehow realized that our lives were to be inextricably entwined from that moment on. Of course, I didn't know at the time that the professor was the one behind all of it."*

"I assume that George Demeris poisoned Berry on Harris's orders. But why would he want to make Berry seem drunk?"

"The mushroom that Demeris employed, the fly agaric Aminita muscaria, *often causes confusion, hallucinations, and erratic behaviour. The onset of symptoms is typically half-an-hour to an hour-and-a-half after ingestion, and they reach their most severe in about three hours. In other words, just at the time that Thomas Berry would be in court. If that had happened, Harris not only could have jailed Berry, he could have applied to have his right to practice removed, permanently eliminating a thorn from his side. And I'm sure that the magistrate would have also enjoyed inflicting the professional humiliation. However, mycotoxins are known for their notoriously varied effects on individuals. The poison hit Berry hard and early so he was no doubt hallucinating before he even returned to court, while the demonstration against Virginia Matsford was in full swing."*

"And what of Harris? Did he ever receive his comeuppance?"

"A-ha! That, Watson, is another tale . . . ."

The Curse of
Hollyhock House
by Geri Schear

In hindsight, 1884 was a year of small cases, hardly worth the telling. Sherlock Holmes was nonetheless kept busy as his reputation continued to grow, both in esteem and in numbers. He was much engaged that year, doing something or other for his brother, though I did not discover this until much later. He was asked to investigate the Fenian affairs, as a number of bombs had disrupted London. His participation was minor, as he himself said, and no mention of his involvement appeared in the press.

It wasn't until late September that he was brought a case that seemed of particular interest to him.

The fog had been relentless for weeks. There were moments here and there when we thought it had lifted, but soon it descended again. That Wednesday afternoon, a knock on the door below was swiftly followed by Mrs. Hudson announcing that a young lady had come to speak to Mr. Holmes.

"She seems anxious about something," the good woman said, "though quite composed for all that."

"Send her up, Mrs. Hudson," Holmes said. "We are quite at our leisure and a visitor would be welcome." After the she shut the door, he added to me softly, "Provided she is indeed composed."

Less than a minute later, Mrs. Hudson returned with Miss Sarah Allis. She was a tall, slender young woman of about twenty years. Her soft golden hair escaped in curls from beneath her black boater hat. Despite that and the black coat and gown she wore, her air of sweetness, and the lack of guile in her cornflower blue eyes, made for a most welcome sight on that dull day.

I immediately hurried to clear a seat for her – Holmes had again decorated the sofa with newspapers – and to ask Mrs. Hudson for some coffee. As we waited, Holmes made the introductions and then leaned forward and took Miss Allis's hand in his.

"Excuse me," he said, "but as Doctor Watson will tell you, it is my business. May I first offer my condolences on your recent bereavement?"

"Thank you. I was told you were a very clever man. My friend, Helen Stoner, gave me your name."

"Ah, the speckled band," I said, recalling the case from the previous year.

"You have been in an accident," Holmes said. "If accident we may call it. There are abrasions and bruises on your hands. And I perceive evidence of recent trauma to your throat."

Despite her obvious distress, our visitor remained composed. "You are correct, Mr. Holmes. It is about those incidents that I have come seeking your guidance."

"That you may certainly have, and our protection, too, though you do not ask for it."

"Thank you. It is a relief to have two such fine gentlemen assure my safety."

"You recently moved to a new location," Holmes continued. "Somewhere north of the city – perhaps Highgate?"

"Yes. After my dear father's recent death, my mother and I moved from Knightsbridge to Highgate."

"There is a unique kind of clay in the Highgate area which I observe on your shoes. Your move is suggested by the cuffs of your gown. Packing boxes are notorious for causing damage of that sort. But your hands suggest physical labour of a more manual kind. From the blisters and scratches, I surmise that you have been gardening."

"Exactly so. Oh, Helen will be delighted I came to you, Mr. Holmes. I am sure you're the only man in London who can help me."

"Pray, make yourself comfortable and tell me everything in as precise detail as you can. You may speak freely before Dr. Watson. There is no more discreet or reliable man in London."

"I am very grateful to you both.

"In July of last year, my dear father announced that he had been diagnosed with a serious heart condition. He might live for a year, but certainly no more than that.

"For the next several months, we were utterly preoccupied with his health. Though he never complained, it became apparent that he was losing ground every day. Finally, in June, he died.

"During his lifetime, we lived comfortably enough, but we knew that things would become more difficult after his death. My father always took care of us, and so he had taken a lease on a small house in Swain's Lane in Highgate. We let most of our Knightsbridge servants go and retained only our cook and two of the maids.

"Hollyhock House is more a cottage than a house, but it is perfectly charming. It was built in the seventeenth century, and has a small, if neglected, garden."

"Hence your gardening efforts," I said.

284

"Indeed." Miss Allis smiled. "Contrary to the name, no hollyhocks have grown there for many years. Mostly, the garden is full of brambles and weeds, though I was able to rescue an apple tree, two pear trees, and several wonderful rose bushes. I'm hoping to grow some, of course – hollyhocks, I mean.

"At first, my mother and the maids were uneasy because the house backs onto Highgate Cemetery, but the house itself is very comfortable and after the first few days we all settled down. Or seemed to, I should say."

"Something happened to cause you unease?" Holmes said.

"The maids and cook began to hear noises. Their rooms are on the top floor, under the attic. I thought the house probably had mice – it had been vacant for three years before my father took it – and I set some traps. To be sure, we did catch some mice, and I thought that would be the end of it, but within a matter of days the noises returned, though no more mice were to be found."

"What sort of noises?" I asked.

"It varied. Sometimes it was a scurrying sound, as one would expect with rodents. At other times it seemed like a heavy footfall. Strangest of all was the sound of whistling."

"Whistling?"

"A tuneless sort of sound, or at least, so it seemed to me at first. After some time, I realised it was Beethoven's 'Funeral March'. That realisation was chilling."

"And no wonder," I said.

Holmes held up a hand and asked our client to continue. This she did, and I saw the concern deepen on my friend's face.

"Then things began to disappear," she said. "Just small things. The change from the milkman that cook had left on the kitchen table. Then, one of the maids mislaid her change purse. I lost a pair of earrings and a pretty brooch that had been a gift from my late father, but by far the worst was that my poor mother lost her wedding ring."

"That's dreadful," I said.

"The cat vanished for two days. I know you will say that it is in the nature of cats to disappear from time to time, but Mr. Snow has never done it before."

"Did you recover any of these items?" Holmes asked.

"Sally found her change purse on the kitchen floor, though it was now empty. None of the other things have shown up."

"Pray continue."

285

"The servants were frightened and convinced we had a ghost. I managed to reassure them that we were all safe together, and I promised that I shouldn't let anything happen to any of them."

"You know and trust these maids, I take it?" I asked.

"Most certainly. They have all worked for my family for many years. They are beyond reproach.

"For the first few days we were busy unpacking and making up the rooms in a way we liked. Then, towards the end of the week, we were running out of supplies. As the maids were busy, I decided to walk up to the shop at the top of the lane. I was feeling a bit restless from being indoors so long, and I thought the exercise would do me good. I also wanted to talk to the various tradespeople and make sure we could expect deliveries of bread, milk, coal, and so forth. It was an awful day. The rain was beating down, and it was cold, but I decided to see my outing as an adventure.

"If you are familiar with Swain's Lane, Mr. Holmes, you will know it is an extremely steep hill."

"Yes, I remember working out the gradient some time ago, merely as a mathematical exercise. The lane is a mere half-mile long, with a gradient of eight to twenty percent at various points. A strenuous climb, even for a fit man. But please continue."

"I had been walking for about ten minutes when I felt that someone was behind me. I decided to ignore it. I told myself that perhaps I had been affected by the maids' superstitious nonsense. To be clear, I didn't hear footsteps. Indeed, I couldn't, due to the noise of the rain. When I looked back, I couldn't see anything but the downpour.

"I reached to the shops, completed my errands, and then went home. I saw no one either on my way up the lane, nor coming back. But a few days later, it happened again. It was another wet and unpleasant day, but I wanted to get some seeds to plant in the garden and I decided to go right then and there. I confess, I don't like being indoors too much. Even in inclement weather, I prefer to be outside.

"About ten minutes from home, I again felt that sensation of being followed. I stopped and looked back, but I couldn't see anyone. I called out, 'Who is it? Who's there?' but there was no reply. I continued my walk, and again came that feeling of being followed. I completed my business at the shops and began my journey home. I couldn't shake the feeling of being followed."

"It sounds very distressing," I said.

"I assume the situation escalated," Holmes said, his face grave.

"I tried to convince myself that the sensation of being followed was merely my imagination, possibly due to the proximity of the cemetery, not to mention the odd events in the house. The next time I had to go out, nothing happened, and that seemed to support my theory. Then, three weeks ago, as I made my way through the fog to Highgate Village, I heard a voice whisper, *'Prepare to die!'* in a strange, sing-song voice."

"I take it this wasn't the only such occurrence," Holmes said.

"No, indeed. Since then, it has happened several more times. Always in the fog. Always when I am alone. He – it is unquestionably a man – sometimes says, *'The curse is upon you!'* or, most frequently, *'Prepare to die!'*"

"Very frightening," I said, "but perhaps someone's idea of a joke."

Holmes shook his head. His look was troubled. Before he could speak, however, Mrs. Hudson returned with a tray of scones and coffee. She placed them on the table and quietly left.

"What do you take this talk of a curse to mean?" Holmes asked as I filled the cups.

"I assume it refers to Hollyhock House," our guest replied. "When we first moved in, the man from whom my father had bought the house, Mr. Jessup, told us that the house had a long history, as one might imagine from a place so old. Over the years, a number of inhabitants died under strange or violent circumstances."

"Hardly surprising in a house of such age," I said.

"No, indeed. But with those tales, combined with the house's proximity to the cemetery – indeed, the house backs directly onto the graveyard, with only a wall between us – it doesn't take much imagination for the superstitious to create stories."

"What do you know of these mysterious deaths?" Holmes asked.

"Oh dear, I'm afraid I didn't pay too much attention. I do recall hearing that the daughter of the builder had committed suicide by hanging herself from a tree outside – at least, it was believed to be suicide, but who knows? A few years later, the builder himself cut his throat in the garden. Then, some years after that, another woman was found murdered in the attic."

"Ancient history," I said.

"Indeed," Holmes agreed. "As one might expect from any old home. Such tales are part of the legend – one might even say the mystique – that surrounds these buildings."

"Well, the mysterious deaths don't all go back so far. As recently as three years ago, the daughter of the last tenant – the house was rented for some time before my father bought it – disappeared without a trace."

"Do you know if this business of things going missing has just been since your family moved in, Miss Allis, or had it happened before?"

287

She smiled very prettily. "Oh, I believe that Mr. Jessup Junior – he's the son of the man who sold us the house – lost a very valuable fountain pen, and I don't think he ever recovered it. And the family who lived there before ours, the Bullens, lost things too. I know these things are all silly, but they are upsetting to the residents."

"And perpetuate the myth that the house is cursed," Holmes said. "But it isn't the alleged curse or the missing objects that trouble you. You haven't yet explained your injuries, Miss Allis," Holmes said.

"A week ago, I had arranged to see an old friend in Hyde Park. I was walking by the Serpentine, waiting for her to arrive. Again, came that strange sensation of being watched, then that voice came out of the fog saying, '*Prepare to die, Sarah!*' I was about to turn around and tell whoever it was to leave me alone, but at that moment, a pair of strong hands grabbed me by the throat. Only the timely arrival of a policeman saved my life, I'm sure."

"Good heavens," I cried. "The bounder!"

"I take it he wasn't apprehended?"

"No. He seemed to vanish into the fog. I was badly shaken, as you can imagine, but not seriously hurt."

"How brazen of him to make his attack in public," I said.

"He felt protected by the fog," Holmes said as he examined our visitor's throat. "The bruising around your neck tells me you had a very lucky escape. This happened a week ago?"

"Yes, Mr. Holmes. Last Sunday."

He shook his head. "Why did you wait so long to come and see me?"

"My mother became ill, and I have been kept occupied looking after her."

"What ails her, if I may ask?"

"You may of course, Doctor. She suffers badly with her nerves, and this has been very much exacerbated of late, first by my father's death, and then by the strange events that have been occurring in the house. It reached a crisis level after my attack in Hyde Park. Though I tried to keep it from her, the policeman who escorted me home was less than discreet. Since then, she has taken to her bed and has all but stopped eating. I'm very worried about her."

"Of course you are," I replied.

Holmes shook his head. His thoughts had already moved on. "Something happened that spurred you to seek help. Pray, what was it?"

She took a sip of coffee and then said, "My mother has a medicine that helps soothe her nerves, but she ran out of it. This was yesterday morning. The fog lay so thick that visibility was well-nigh impossible. I felt compelled to go out to the chemist to get it for her. I would have asked

288

one of the maids to come with me, but I didn't want to leave my mother without any assistance, especially as she was so fearful. I assured her that I would hurry up the road – the chemist isn't far away – and I should be back in no time.

"I set off up the hill. The cemetery was to my right, though I could hardly see a thing because of the fog. I hadn't gone very far when I felt that frisson of fear, that certainty that someone was watching me. I hurried my steps, but the sensation of being watched and followed didn't abate. I had worn a thick scarf around my neck, in part because my throat still hurt from my earlier experience, and in part to protect myself from any villain who might try again to harm me.

"In the distance, I once again heard that voice singing, '*Prepare to die, Sarah!*' I could tell that the person wasn't very far from me. As I hurried up the hill, a man followed me, and continued to taunt me. Then, the fog suddenly lifted slightly, and I was about to turn and see how it was when, at the same moment, I heard the rumble of a carriage coming down the hill. Before I could react or even think, I was pushed forcibly into the road.

"I'm not entirely certain what happened next. I think I fainted. When I awoke, it could only have been a few moments later, I found myself gazing into the eyes of a young man. He was deeply concerned for my well-being and insisted on taking me to his home and tending to my injuries. He was a young doctor, on his way back from visiting a patient. He was ever so kind.

"'I was alarmed when you fell out of the fog into the path of my horse,' he said. 'Indeed, I'm still unsure how I managed to miss trampling you.'

"He gave me brandy to drink and then insisted on taking me home in his carriage. Oh, he also insisted on seeing my mother, too.

"As we returned to Hollyhock House, I told him about the strange man in the fog and his previous attempt on my life. My rescuer, Dr. Forsyth, was very alarmed and insisted that I not travel anywhere without an escort.

"At home, I told my mother a rather, ah, *modified* story of my adventures. William – that is to say, Dr. Forsyth – was happy to help me. We said I had stumbled in the fog and scraped my hands and face. My mother took to him instantly and insisted he stay to tea. His mere presence cheered her up. He examined her, said her spirits were low, and gave her some medicine. He then invited both of us to dinner at his house on this coming Saturday. He will send his carriage to collect us."

"You are fortunate to have made such a friend," Holmes said. "I suppose the good Doctor didn't see the man who pushed you?"

"I'm afraid not. Although there were some patches in the fog – thank goodness, or he shouldn't have seen me when I fell – where it did accumulate it was dense."

Holmes sat back in his chair, his eyes hooded, and his expression grave.

"How did you come here today?" he said.

"I brought my maid with me. She is downstairs with the lady who let us in. We took a cab the whole way here and shall return the same way."

"Does anyone have a grudge against you?" Holmes continued.

"No, I cannot think so. I try always to treat others with respect and kindness."

"I do not doubt it," I said fervently.

"What of the servants you had to dismiss when you moved into Hollyhock House?"

"My mother and I took pains to ensure that they were all placed in suitable positions. They were sorry to leave us, to be sure, especially my mother who was a great favourite among them, but no, they understood, and there were no ill feelings."

"Do you have a former suitor who might be aggrieved?"

She flushed. "No, Mr. Holmes. I have had suitors, certainly, but the relationships all ended quite amicably. I remain on good terms with all of them."

"What do you know of the man who sold the house to your father?"

"Mr. Jessup? He lives immediately across the street from us, and he has been very kind. He brought us a pot of tea and a cake the day we moved in, and helped us with some of the heavy boxes. We are very obliged to him."

"Did he ever live in Hollyhock House himself?"

"Yes, several years ago. I believe it has been in his family for many generations. His son, Lawrence, was born there. Mr. Jessup built a new house across the street and moved in there after his wife died. That was about ten years ago, I believe."

After Miss Allis left with an assurance that we would be in touch, Holmes sat in silence for a long time. Then he said, "Watson, I would like to know more about our friend's medical rescuer. Do you think you could find out if he is a man of honour?"

"I will ask Lawson. He knows everyone and is always happy to talk about them. I take it you have some misgivings about the young Dr. Forsyth?"

"His appearance on the scene may certainly be no more than good fortune. Then again – "

"Then again, he may be in league with the person who is trying to terrorise Miss Allis. I agree. I'll go see Lawson at once."

"Tread carefully out there. It isn't only young ladies who may come foul of this filthy weather."

When I returned later that evening – Lawson insisted that I stay for dinner, then drinks, and then was kind enough to give me a lift home to Baker Street – Holmes himself was out. He returned a couple of hours later. I was relaxing by the fire reading the newspaper when he came in.

"What luck?" he said as he removed his coat.

"According to Lawson, Dr. William Forsyth is a well-respected gentleman who graduated from Charing Cross Hospital in 1879. He is the only child of Herbert Forsyth, the well-known financier. Young Forsyth set up his practice in Highgate three years ago. He is well-liked by his patients and has a spotless record. Oh, and he's unmarried. What about you?"

"I have been to Highgate. I am not a man who believes in spirits, nor, I think, am I particularly imaginative, but I vow, Watson, there is something eerie about walking down Swain's Lane in the fog, skirting the cemetery all the way. An imaginative woman would be excused for thinking she was being followed or hearing voices."

"It wasn't imagination that left those marks on her throat and hands."

"No, indeed." He flopped down on the sofa. "I didn't think Miss Allis was being untruthful, but it is wise to take nothing on face value."

"I hope you didn't spend the entire evening walking up and down Swain's Lane in this filthy weather," I said. "What else did you get up to?"

"What indeed," he said with a chuckle. "I stopped by the local inn to partake of a pint of their finest."

"I'm sure they were glad of your business. They can't be very busy in this weather."

"One would think not. However, the place was bustling. Men still work, and still develop a thirst. Many of these men, regulars all, stop by The White Horse most evenings. It was easy to get into conversation about Mr. Jessup and his son."

"Mr. Jessup – ah, he was the previous owner of the house, wasn't he? What did you find out?"

"He is known in the area, has lived there all his life, and his family before him. He is a highly successful merchant – or rather, he was until six years ago when one of his ships went down. His son, Lawrence, attended Eton, then Cambridge. He recently graduated with a degree in architecture, but seems in no hurry to find employment. 'Lacklustre Larry', the locals call him."

I chuckled.

"Yes, he seems a wastrel of the first order. Not only that, but he seemed close to Miss Bullen before she vanished."

"Indeed? And what do the neighbours say about our client?"

"That she and her mother are respectable women, very kind, and highly regarded."

"So no one seems to hold a grudge, then." I puffed on my cigarette and pondered the mystery. Why would anyone wish harm against such a lovely and innocent young woman? It was beyond me. Holmes, however, had his own ideas.

"While I was there," he added, "I brought up the curse."

"I thought you didn't believe in curses."

"Nor do I. However, I am interested in the way this alleged curse has taken root among the populace. As one might expect, there are any number of tales and legends that have cropped up over the years. Everything from murdered ladies of the manor who haunt the place to mischievous spirits are spoken of in tones of awe. The facts, however, seem much as Miss Allis told us. At least one woman died a violent death, and another disappeared without any trace. Items have gone missing, although even the most ardent believers admit that may occur anywhere."

"So what are we to make of it? I must admit that I cannot see how the house's reputation can have anything to do with the attempts on Miss Allis's life."

"Perhaps you're right." He lit his pipe and sat back in his armchair.

"You don't suppose it could be a former suitor, angry at being rejected resorted to such tactics? Miss Allis may not realise someone is aggrieved against her."

"I am the last man to speak to the behaviour of a spurned lover," he replied with a smile whose meaning I could only imagine, "Of course, resentment and jealousy are certainly motives that I have encountered any number of times. However, Miss Allis herself did state she was on good terms with her previous beaux."

"She may not realise the degree of animus harboured against her."

He shook his head but made no reply.

The following morning, the fog had been replaced by rain. Holmes was, to my surprise, already at the breakfast table when I came into our sitting room.

"You have plans today?" I asked.

"I thought I would call upon Miss Allis."

"Would you like me to accompany you?"

"Certainly, if you can spare the time."

292

And so, less than an hour later, we were in a cab headed north to Highgate. The journey made me long for sun, or even snow – something that offered visibility and light, rather than this grey and perpetual gloom. It felt as if we were trapped in some twilight world where spirits walk and stalk the living. This otherworldly sense became even more pronounced when the hansom turned onto Swain's Lane and proceeded up the hill. The cemetery to our right formed a dripping, dispiriting land of shadows. Trees seemed to moan in the wind, adding to the hiss of the rain and the distant rumble of thunder. To our left, silent husks of houses sat squat and dark, relieved only by the occasional glimmer of gaslight in a window. Shades of Edgar Allan Poe abound, I thought, and I wondered at the hardiness of any young woman who would venture into such an unsettling landscape alone.

About half-way up the hill, the cab stopped. Through the downpour, I could see the hulk of a small house set amid a tangled garden, a charming winding path leading from the gate to the door.

"I shall be glad to get out of this downpour," I said as we reached the house. Whatever Holmes was about to reply was lost when the door was opened by a young girl in a maid's garment.

"Good morning," I said. "This is Mr. Sherlock Holmes, and I am Dr. Watson. We are here to see Miss Allis."

"That's all right, Aggie," our client said, coming into the hallway. "Come in, do, please, gentlemen. I fear the weather isn't fit for man or beast."

The hallway was warm enough, and the small study at the back of the house a treat to my cold hands and cheeks. We were glad to sit in the big leather armchairs near the fire and accept our hostess's offer of coffee.

"My mother is in the sitting room," Miss Allis said, after she had instructed the maid. "She is feeling much better since William – Dr. Forsyth – came to see her. I told her I had asked you to investigate the house and examine it for any problems or difficulties. That, too, has lifted her spirits."

"She still doesn't know of your most recent misadventure?" I said.

"Goodness, no. I'm afraid my father rather coddled her and kept from her anything that she might have found unpleasant. I suppose I have inherited his trait, but she is really not able to deal with unpleasantness. Telling her would serve no good purpose. But forgive me, I am talking of matters that cannot possibly interest you. Do you have more questions, Mr. Holmes? Or, perhaps, some news?"

This last question was delivered in a hopeful tone.

"No news as yet, Miss Allis, but I wanted to examine the house, and I do have questions." As he spoke, Holmes walked to the window and looked out. "The garden would be quite charming, were it not so overgrown."

"Yes, indeed. It hasn't been touched in several years. I have been clearing it out a little at a time. I hope to plant some hollyhocks around the perimeter. After all, how can one live in Hollyhock House and not have samples of that flower in abundance?"

"Indeed," Holmes said, his voice distant. I wondered what had caught his interest. "When you spoke of the house backing onto the cemetery, I didn't realise you meant it literally."

"Yes, we are separated by nothing more than a wall."

"And the garden – all of it is to the front and the side?"

"Yes."

He fell silent, staring out the window at who knows what.

"Tell me, Miss Allis," I asked, "what else do you plan for the rest of the garden?"

"Oh, foxgloves and roses, of course, and a pretty selection of spring flowers along the path. At least the trees are intact, as are the rose bushes, though everything needs some judicious pruning."

"You aren't doing all the work on your own, surely?" I wondered.

She laughed. "I'm afraid I have been. I find the exercise beneficial, and the work has given me a better understanding of the plantings that are still viable. However, I recently engaged a man who will do most of the heavy labour for me. He starts next week. I hope by then the weather will be more congenial to his task."

"Has the history of the house made it difficult for you to hire staff?"

"It has taken longer to hire a gardener than I would have expected. I suspect it isn't only the house's reputation, but its proximity to the cemetery that unsettles many people."

Holmes returned to the fire and took the cup Miss Allis handed him. "Speaking of the curse," he said, as he stirred in the milk, "Watson has been fascinated by the stories you told us about the house."

"Uh, yes," I said. "It does seem very curious."

"Silly stories always seem to cling to old houses, do they not?" she said. "My friend, Emily McIntosh, grew up in a house that was alleged to have a ghost, though neither of us ever saw or heard anything untoward."

"Were you more disappointed or relieved?" I asked.

"A little of both," she admitted, laughing. "The problem with such nonsense is it seems to affect the people around. So many people are superstitious. I find it very odd."

Holmes smiled approvingly. "Do you see anything of Mr. Jessup?" he continued.

"Not very much, though he is a close neighbour. He owns Rose Cottage, directly opposite. He did come by a few times to make sure we were settling in all right, and he introduced his son, Lawrence. A pleasant enough young man, if a little . . . vacuous. Forgive me, that is unkind."

"Not at all, Miss Allis. Though I am curious as to how you formed this opinion."

"I cannot really say, Mr. Holmes. I got the impression he wasn't particularly happy to be in the house. I thought he might be one of those very superstitious young men, but I understand he had spent many happy days here as a boy. I suppose it was probably because of Felicity."

"Felicity?" I said. "Oh, was that the young lady who disappeared?"

"Yes, Felicity Bullen. She was the daughter of the previous tenant. I gather that she and Mr. Lawrence Jessup had become acquainted during one of his holidays from college."

"They were courting?" I said.

"I cannot say for certain, but I do think he was fond of her."

"Does her family still live in the area?" Holmes asked.

"They moved to Witley Road."

"And have you seen any more of Dr. Forsyth?" I asked.

She smiled. "He stopped by yesterday evening to check on Mother. While he was here, he offered to pick up anything we might need from the shops. He goes out every day on his rounds, despite the terrible weather. He's such a caring gentleman."

"Quite." Holmes stood abruptly. "May I ask you to introduce me to the staff, Miss Allis? And then, if you don't object, I should like to look around the house."

"By all means. This way."

Mrs. Allis was sitting by the window engaged in needlework when we joined her. She seemed a frail and timid lady and was effusive in her gratitude for our assistance. The maids likewise were very relieved by our presence.

By far the most imposing member of the household was the cook, a tall, robust woman who was obviously devoted to her 'misses'.

"Thank you, Miss Allis. If you don't object, I should like to explore the house."

"Please do, Mr. Holmes. Do you want me to come with you?"

"Don't disturb yourself. If you would be so good as to entertain Dr. Watson, I shall be back soon."

By the time he returned an hour-and-a-half later, he had a look on his face that promised trouble for someone.

"Miss Allis," he said, "thank you for indulging me. Well, I think we have taken enough of your time. I shall be in touch. Oh, do make sure that all the windows and doors are locked after we've gone. And please go nowhere on your own."

"But is there anything you can tell me, Mr. Holmes?"

"These are very dark waters, and our investigation is just beginning. Patience, Miss Allis. All will come right in the end. Lock the doors. Come, Watson."

As we hurried up the wet lane together, I asked, "Why the rush?"

"We have much to do, and not much time to do it in. I fear if we aren't very clever, that our young friend may be in grave danger."

"Then should we have left her?"

"It isn't for very long. We shall return soon enough, I assure you."

We puffed our way up the hill, but before we had gone too far, Holmes flagged down a cab. To my surprise, however, he didn't get in with me.

"I have a few more things to do, Watson. Don't fret. I shall do nothing of significance without you. Oh, and you might make sure your revolver and mine are at the ready."

With that, he turned away and left me on my own.

By the time I reached Baker Street, it was a little after two. I ate a lunch of mutton stew and then took a nap on the sofa, very much enjoying the peace and quiet.

Just after seven, I received a telegram:

> *Meet me at the bottom of the hill at 10 p.m. Bring the two items. SH*

For the rest of the evening, I pottered about our apartment, feeling eager to get on with things, and full of curiosity about whatever Holmes was up to. I hoped that whatever he uncovered would mean peace for our lovely client and her household.

A few minutes after nine, with a revolver in each pocket, I headed out. I would probably be early, I realised, but I was afraid to miss something of import.

I had the cab leave me at the bottom of Swain's Lane hill and waited at the corner by the cemetery. At least the night was clear and dry with a full moon. The light cast an eerie glow over the gravestones and tombs. I hoped Holmes wouldn't leave me waiting for long.

Fortunately, about five minutes later, he appeared. "Ah, there you are," I greeted him, trying not to sound too relieved.

He placed a cautionary finger on his lips. "Voices carry, Watson. We must be quiet as . . . well, not mice. As ghosts, then. We have an ugly business before us this evening. You know, I have some qualms about bringing you with me."

"Can I be of use?"

"Most certainly."

"Then I'm your man."

He gave me a brief, but heartfelt smile. "You brought my weapon?"

I handed it to him. He checked it efficiently and slipped it into his pocket.

"Let us walk up the hill a little so we're away from the street light. I know you have a dozen questions. All in good time, I assure you."

We walked a couple of hundred feet, passing more than one street lamp. At last, he stopped, looked around, and said, "This will do. Quickly, Watson!" And before I could question him, he had hoisted himself up onto the wall and over the railing into the cemetery.

"Quickly!" he hissed.

With deep foreboding and not a little exertion, I followed him.

"We'll move away from the wall, so we aren't clearly visible from the road. Anyone who does spot us will no doubt take us for spectres." He laughed softly.

"Holmes, what on earth are we doing?"

"We are walking to the back of Miss Allis's house. We may have a long wait, so I hope you dressed warmly."

"I should be all right. What did you find when you explored the house?"

He chuckled. "Very little, other than what you would expect. A pretty little house full of pretty people. Until I got to the cellar."

"The cellar? I'm surprised a house in that location could boast a cellar – assuming you mean something beyond a place to store coal."

"I do. It's an open space, with a rough floor and rough walls. It has a feeling of age. There is some of the usual clutter, of course. Old hat stands, iron basins, trunks full of gewgaws There is also a singular painting – an ancient thing by a mediocre artist. It smells of mould and has a frame quite as hideous as the painting. It's very large – at least five-feet-tall, and about three-feet-wide. At first I thought it was fixed to the wall."

"In the basement?"

He chuckled. "Exactly so. However, closer inspection revealed there was a release button beside it. I pressed it and the painting slid to the side, and behind it – " He broke off to hop over a broken tombstone. "Behind it lay half a dozen steps leading down to a tunnel. It smelled of the earth and dead things." He grinned. "At least, so it seemed at the time. I followed it."

"And it led into the cemetery."

297

"Well done. It did indeed. It was a fairly short tunnel, no more than about eight feet, crude, perhaps, but well-constructed."

"Was it new?"

"Another excellent question. You're in sparkling form tonight, my dear fellow! In fact, it was very old – more than a century, I would estimate. However, it has been used recently, and with some regularity. The inevitable cobwebs have been brushed away, the roof reinforced with new wood, and the grave where the path exits – "

"It exits in a grave?"

"Relax, Watson. It isn't occupied. You know, I wouldn't have thought you would be so squeamish about such things. You're a doctor and a former soldier. You must be well used to death."

"It isn't a matter of being squeamish. It's about respect."

Eventually, we arrived at the gravesite. I could identify it immediately by the way the stone slab had been pulled away from the empty pit.

"He's already been here," Holmes said. "Hurry, Watson!"

He dropped lithely into the hole – it was easier to think of it as that – and I, less agile and less eager, followed him.

The tunnel was dank, horrible. As Holmes had said, it smelled of death, and yet it was alive with crawling things. This was what it was like to be dead, I thought. Fortunately, just seconds later Holmes stopped and very carefully swung back the painting.

I followed him into the old cellar. Despite its lack of elegance, it felt like a palace after that wretched tunnel. I was about to say something, when Holmes put his finger on his lips and pointed upwards. That was when I saw a young man standing on the steps of the cellar.

"Put your hands up, you rascal," Holmes cried. "You are surrounded!"

The fellow turned with a start and suddenly rushed at us. I fired one shot and the villain screamed.

In an instant, the cellar seemed full of police officers. Holmes went up the stairs and knocked three times on the door.

A lock turned and the door opened.

"Do you have him, Mr. Holmes?" the sturdy cook asked.

"We do indeed, Miss Shaw. Well done!"

Eventually, after the usual confusion as the young fellow was placed in bracelets, Holmes and I, the Allis ladies and their servants, the police inspector, and two constables gathered in the drawing room.

"This is Lawrence Jessup," Holmes told the policemen.

"Trying to terrorise these ladies, you bounder?" the inspector said. "That's a serious charge."

298

"The main charge is far more serious," Holmes said. "Murder."

Now the policemen were on high alert. The women stared at Jessup in horrified silence.

"Mr. Jessup?" Miss Allis exclaimed. "But . . . *why*?"

"The truth, Mr. Jessup," Holmes said, "the whole truth."

"I meant no harm," Jessup whined. "It was just a lark!"

"Was it a lark when you tried to strangle Miss Allis in the park? Was there no harm when you tried to push her under Dr. Forsyth's carriage? And that's not to mention the murder of Felicity Bullen. The truth is the only thing that might save you from the noose!"

"I'd take that advice," the inspector said.

The young fellow paled and rubbed his neck.

"I didn't mean no harm," he said, again. "It was all Felicity's fault. She caught me pocketing a couple of pennies that had been left on the table and she said she would have nothing more to do with me."

"You had made it a habit to pilfer whatever you came across," Holmes said.

"I didn't mean anything by it. It was a joke, really. I told her I'd put everything back, but she said she could no longer trust me. I – Ah, I lost my temper."

"And you killed her," Holmes said.

"I didn't mean to! She wouldn't listen, and that made me angry. Everyone deserves a second chance, right? Anyway, I grabbed her and, well, the next thing I knew she was dead."

"It takes two to five minutes to strangle a person. That is a long time to keep your hands on her throat. You knew exactly what you were doing."

"But what has any of it got to do with me?" Miss Allis asked.

"He was worried that you would find the body," Holmes explained. "He murdered Felicity Bullen and he buried her in the garden." He turned back to Jessup. "I surmise that it was a wet or a foggy evening and you had little risk of being observed. But you aren't fond of hard labour, are you, Jessup, so you didn't bury her very deeply. You became alarmed when you saw Miss Allis working in the garden and you thought you could frighten her out of the house."

"I wasn't going to hurt her!" he whined.

"She still has bruises on her neck and her hands, you brute!" Mrs. Allis exclaimed.

I sat next to the older woman and made sure the excitement wasn't too much for her, but to my surprise, the revelations had invigorated her.

The body of Felicity Bullen was discovered the next day. The police notified her parents, and they came to thank Miss Allis for calling in

Holmes. "At least now we can give her a proper burial," Mr. Bullen said. "Lay her to rest at last."

Mr. Jessup Senior was startled to see the tunnel in the cellar. "I never even knew it was there, and I lived here must of my life. I wonder how Lawrence happened upon it."

"Small boys are, by nature, curious," Holmes said. "No doubt he found it one dreary day and kept the secret to himself. When he was older, he took pains to make it more accessible. There are boardings to keep it from caving it."

"But why was that grave empty?" I asked.

"Grave robbers, perhaps? We may never know for certain."

It wasn't until evening that I got around to asking the question that was foremost in my mind.

"Holmes, all of Highgate Cemetery lies behind the Allis's house. Why didn't Jessup bury Felicity there?"

"Come, Watson, you of all people should know how heavy a dead body is, even that of a slight woman. Getting the corpse over the wall would have been a serious challenge even to a strong and active man. Larry Jessup always prefers the easy option."

"Couldn't he have dragged her through the tunnel?"

"Perhaps, if the house were empty. But Mr. and Mrs. Bullen were almost certainly in the house, as well as several servants. The access to the cellar is via the kitchen, and that is, as you know, the busiest room in any home."

"Surely they would have heard him digging her grave, even if it was so shallow?"

"I suspect a downpour's din would have covered most of the noise. In addition, Jessup was several feet away from the house. It's not very surprising that external noises were dulled, given the peculiarities of sound in that old building."

He lit his pipe and inhaled deeply before adding, "As an architectural student, Jessup had, no doubt, observed the peculiar acoustics of the house. Words spoken in the drawing room were easily heard in the cellar as well as the attic. From my examination of the latter, I found he had been staying there for long periods at a time. He had left blankets and food stuffs there. He had been spying on the ladies ever since they moved in. I suspect the house's tragic history gave him the idea of trying to frighten the women out. When that failed to work, he resorted to deadlier measures."

"And what about the cook? She knew your plan?"

"To a point. After I explored the house and found the tunnel, I knew if Jessup returned, he'd have to make his way from the tunnel and in through the kitchen. I asked Miss Shaw to lock the cellar door. This she did and kept watch most faithfully."

"And you alerted the local constables."

"Yes. To be frank, I wasn't sure I could count on them to turn up. They seemed extremely sceptical when I told them what was going on. However, the inspector notified Lestrade, and our friend grudgingly admitted I could be relied upon." He chuckled.

The Assizes found Lawrence Jessup guilty of murder and he was sentenced to hang. His father, after initially renouncing his son, went to see him in prison and forgave him.

Miss Allis did not retain that name for long. A few months later, Dr. Forsyth proposed and she happily accepted. She, her mother, and the servants, were happy to move into the doctor's spacious home some distance from Highgate Cemetery.

Hollyhock House is again for sale.

The Sethian Messiah
by David Marcum

Chapter I

Within hours of being introduced to Sherlock Holmes in 1881, he and I – two total strangers – were sharing rooms. We met on New Year's Day for just a very few moments, long enough to agree to look at apartments that he'd identified in Baker Street. On the second morning of January, we met there and found them to be quite satisfactory. In fact, they were desirable in every way, and so moderate were the arrangements when divided between us that we entered into possession at once. I was glad to have the opportunity, since my meager wound pension would never have allowed me to afford them on my own.

I moved in with my few slight and battered possessions that very night, and Holmes began doing the same on the third – although he brought quite a bit more than I did. Soon after we'd settled in, I turned my attention back to recovering from the grievous wounds I'd received at Maiwand the previous July, and Holmes went on with his life – although at that stage, I couldn't have explained exactly what that meant.

He was often away, and I assumed that he was carrying out his further curious researches at Barts, where we'd first met. I suppose that I had some vague idea that he must be a medical student, in spite of the fact that he was getting rather old for it – he'd just turned twenty-seven that January, although I didn't yet know his actual birth date. When he began to have visitors from all strata of society, I initially believed that he might be providing them with some sort of medical treatment, using our sitting room to consult with his "patients".

Holmes was always most solicitous about my health, and he would graciously ask if I minded allowing him the use of the sitting room during those mornings when a plethora of his "clients" climbed the stairs to meet with him. I would defer and remove myself up one flight to my bedroom, or when the weather was tolerable enough I'd take a walk through the nearby streets or in Regent's Park. I learned that Holmes was generally finished with these "consultations" by about eleven a.m., and it was then safe to return to my fireside chair for the rest of the day.

But this was not what I agreed upon when we first discussed sharing a flat, and as much as I objected to rows because of my shaken nerves, I felt that I was being steadily positioned into saying something if his regular use of our joint sitting room was going to be a permanent arrangement. While I never thought that I would be there for more than a few months – I planned to return to the Army later in the year when my recovery was complete (or so I thought then) – I was paying my half-share, and that included full and free access to the sitting room, which was already more filled with Holmes's possessions than mine.

As my journal records, it was on Monday, the 28th of February, 1881, that I resolved to speak to my fellow lodger about my rising sense of injustice. I expected that it would be a civil exchange, for we had never been anything but polite with one another, and I was fully confident that my point of view would be expressed, heard, and honored.

I made a point of rising a bit early, for I had a leaning toward getting up at all sorts of ungodly hours, and knowing when Holmes's visitors started arriving, I made sure to be downstairs and fed a good fifteen minutes beforehand. I recall that I was nervous, which makes no sense at all, because just half-a-year earlier I had faced the butchering Ghazis on the worst day of my life. I suppose that even then I very much appreciated having a refuge at 221b and feared that taking my stand might muff it.

Holmes and I had finished our meals, each mostly silent, and I was preparing to speak my peace when the doorbell began clanging loudly, followed in moments by a cry from Mrs. Hudson and then scrambling thumps as someone awkwardly climbed the stairs. The door to the landing slammed open to reveal a wizened fellow of elder appearance, although later I was to learn that he'd aged prematurely due to his demanding lifestyle. With a rather wild-eyed look, he muttered, "Mr. Holmes . . . ." and then collapsed to the floor.

Although I didn't yet know it, this was Bartholomew "Bertie" Tolliver, one of Holmes's many associates in that low and gray-shadowed area of society that so many preferred to ignore. Bertie, like his forefathers before him, was a *tosher* – a "profession" whose existence I'd never even considered before beginning my medical training in London some years earlier.

For those who don't know, a word of warning: Toshers have chosen a career of sorts that places them in the filthiest of conditions and most unhealthy locations. Specifically, they venture into the city's sanitary sewers in search of lost or discarded valuables.

I first became acquainted with such men when they sought the free treatment provided by medical students when I was at the University of London, and after that when they would seek aid at Barts. As one might expect, they inevitably carried a certain . . . *aroma* about them different from that of the men who regularly worked with animals, or those who carried out the awful tasks required in the tanneries and abattoirs scattered throughout the capital. Once such a scent had been identified for us by one of my aloof professors, it was never forgotten.

Now I smelled it again as I rose from my breakfast chair and crossed the few feet to the doorway. Dropping to my knees with more than a twinge of pain, I leaned over my unexpected patient. He wasn't unconscious yet, but appearances indicated that such a condition wasn't far off.

He grasped my hand and whispered, "Food . . . ." He grasped my wrist and urgently tried to speak clearly. "I need something to stave off the shakes before it gets worse . . . ."

I understood, and further hurried examination confirmed my tentative diagnosis. This was more than simple hunger. He was one of those poor unfortunates who suffered from *diabetes mellitus*, wherein the afflicted were required to maintain very strict and careful diets, along with constant vigilance, in order to prevent a cascade of worsening symptoms, possibly resulting in death. But for now, I knew nothing of the man except that I should quickly provide him with certain items from our breakfast table.

The improvement was dramatic, and within fifteen minutes he was up and sitting in a dining chair – Holmes's, I was glad to see – as if he'd walked straight there from the door when he arrived, instead of detouring by way of a prone position upon our floor. Throughout the man's recovery, Holmes had stood to one side, watching with a gimlet eye in the same way that some of my past professors had once done when adjudicating my choice of treatment.

I questioned the man, who then provided me with his name, information about his further symptoms, and that he was already quite aware of what he needed to do to care for himself. "But I've been using myself up too freely for the last few days," he explained, "and I rather lost track of things. Won't happen again, I assure you." He was a small fellow with an unaccountable twinkle in his eye, and he spoke in a sing-song manner that would have sounded rather like a leprechaun if his accent had been Irish instead of East London. I advised that he continue to obtain medical treatment and be careful, and he agreed that he would – although I'd heard too many others promise the same thing over the years to accept such a statement on total faith.

When Bertie and I had nothing left to discuss, Holmes then spoke up, referring to me formally as "Doctor" and thanking me for jumping in so ably, and then asking – once more – if he might borrow the sitting room to speak with his visitor for a few minutes. As I wondered again if Holmes was some type of medical student, and whether he was already treating Bertie for this or some other condition, I also recalled my intent to assert my rights regarding the shared usage of our space, but decided that to do so now would appear rather petty, as my time for doing so was lost. With a nod, I swallowed the last of my now-cold coffee and retreated upstairs.

I said nothing further about the matter over the next week or so, again working to pick up my nerve, and then the matter became moot on the fourth of March, when I learned that Sherlock Holmes was a *consulting detective*, and that these visitors of his were clients in need who were seeking his unique services. I became involved that very day in the matter of the Lauriston Gardens murder, and then another case after that. More and more often in the coming months, I helped with his investigations when I could, and in ways in which I was able. Over the next few years, I saw Bertie Tolliver again on numerous occasions when he would visit us, understanding afterwards how he served as Holmes's trusted agent in that specific portion of London.

He was of particular use to us during the unreported siege of Wakeling Street, and also in the midst of the unfortunate affair of Madame Belasco's defenestration. The longer I knew him, the more he impressed me. In spite of the way he earned his bread and cheese, he was well-spoken, and more than once his comments had given me to understand that he was knowledgeable about current events, along with other learned topics. He once casually mentioned that he read a lot, and I could believe it. One curious fact about him was apparent as the years passed – I felt each and every one of those years, but Bertie seemed remain the same wizened and unchanging little fellow that I'd first met in early '81. It seemed as if the fumes of his workplace were preserving (or pickling) him somehow, and he didn't appear to noticeably age.

Bertie was perhaps of the greatest service to us just a few years before his death. It was early on the morning of Wednesday, 26 November, 1884, and Holmes and I had just returned from Knightsbridge, where a particularly grim murder had threatened to defame the carefully maintained image of Harrods store. The business had burned to the ground nearly a year before, and as the remodeling was nearly complete, a body had been discovered lodged in the forgotten framing under a stairwell. In spite of its condition, the corpse was quickly identified as Eustace Beynard, who had gone missing a decade earlier. Holmes's brilliant examination of the stitching wounds on the body identified Crane Wickham, Beynard's jealous former assistant, as the killer. The fervent thanks from the store's management were ringing in our ears as we departed the premises in the early hours

It was with these thoughts in mind that I stirred up the fire and settled into my chair, considering whether to stay where I was or make my way upstairs for a few hours of sleep. Holmes was jotting something in one of his scrapbooks, and I had just decided to wish him good-night – at six in the morning – when the doorbell rang. The perceptive reader, having seen him so thoroughly described earlier in this narrative, will rightly assume that our pre-dawn visitor was Bertie Tolliver.

I knew that Mrs. Hudson was up – her day began long before six a.m. – but I rose and went downstairs to answer the door, finding Bertie on our front step, a rather uncharacteristic grim tightness to his mouth. "Mr. Holmes in?" he asked, and I nodded and let him pass me. Then, seeing Mrs. Hudson approaching from the rear of the house, I let her know that we would apparently be staying up and would appreciate a pot of coffee. "Strong," I added.

Back upstairs, I found Holmes and Bertie standing in the center of the room, facing one another about four feet apart, with the smaller man looking up at Holmes with an alert expression. Holmes, however, was staring at something in his upturned hand, tipping it this way and that. He fiddled with it for a moment, and then began unfolding a tiny slip of paper which had apparently been attached to it. He flattened the small sheet on his palm, looked at it closely, and then offered what he'd seen to me.

I reached out with a sigh, correctly suspecting where a fellow of Bertie Tolliver's occupation would have found the object – whatever it was. And in fact it turned out to be a ring, thankfully clean – or as far as I could perceive at any rate. More curious was the tiny and stained piece of paper which had been wrapped tightly around the band.

The ring had been made for a man, apparently gold, and heavy. The object itself was plain enough, and narrow at the back side where it would rest beside one's palm. It widened on each side toward a squared front, where a stylized cloisonné black-and-white griffin was fixed in white enamel, decorated sparsely with a tiny red tongue and bloodied claws. That was curious enough in itself, but there was more. The square decoration pivoted on the connecting ring-posts, rotating to reveal a second image on the back – another white enamel space enclosing a secret emblem that would normally be kept hidden against the wearer's finger until intentionally exposed. And I had seen this wicked little sigil before.

It was the suggestion of a human figure, but drawn more like a stick figure than a man. A circle made up the head with a couple of irregular dots for eyes, and a downward slash placed a cruel and bitter-looking mouth. A few lines below sketched the shape of a body and legs. There was only one arm, holding a straight line seemingly representing a spear. Instead of the other arm, another smaller circle touched the line of the body in the semblance of a shield.

Holmes had made himself aware of countless secret societies throughout the nation, ranging from the harmless and silly to those with angry and dangerous agendas, and some with the means to create great mayhem. Through my association with his investigations, it was inevitable that I would learn more of these shadowy organizations, and the ring in my hand represented one that we had brushed against before: *The True Knights of Seth.*

The folded piece of paper was no more than an two inches square, cut sharply and neatly on two adjacent corners and ragged on the other sides – clearly it had been torn from the corner of a larger sheet, perhaps the flyleaf of a book. It had been folded many times into a tight thread, so that it would have been no wider than a sliver of wood before being wrapped around the ring's narrow band. Written in dark pencil was this curious message:

Gladstone – Thursday 10 – Return for details

As I looked at the tiny paper, Holmes was questioning Bertie Tolliver.

"Where?" he asked tersely. There was no need to query whether Bertie knew what he'd found. He'd been with us the previous February when we'd prevented a group of The True Knights from assassinating the Lord Mayor – for they were aggressive in advancing their agenda.

"Just below the Bow Street Police Station – over from the Tottenham Court trunk line."

Holmes stepped to one of his bookcases and returned with a large-scale map of that segment of the city. Pushing aside a stack of books, he unfolded it on the table and leaned down to study the arrangement of the streets.

"Once again, I'm reminded that I need to obtain a map of the capital's sewers," he said while running a finger along one of the wider thoroughfares. "The routes aren't widely known for a variety of reasons, but in my work – "

"If you don't mind, Mr. Holmes," said Bertie, pushing in beside him, "I can show you easier than you trying to puzzle it out." He put a finger down on the map. I leaned in and saw he was pointing at Bow Street, as mentioned. "The sewer here runs roughly northwest to southeast, from up here along Gower Street, and parallel to the Tottenham Court trunk which runs the same direction – but that one's set off to the west, you see. The both cross the larger Piccadilly trunk here – " He moved his finger back and forth a couple of times from west to east to west on a line north of the police station. " – and then both veer inward a bit to nearly touch one another here. Then they separate again, and the line below the Bow Street Station carries on toward the Savoy, emptying into the Victoria Embankment low-level interceptor line just west of Waterloo Bridge."

He stepped back. "As you know, we all have our areas in the sewer that we 'farm', and Bow Street is one of mine – me and a few others. I was making my rounds there this morning when I found the ring – and when I saw that symbol, I knew that you needed to see it as soon as I could get here."

Holmes nodded. "You did well, Bertie." Then he seemed to focus inward as he considered what to do next. At that moment, Mrs. Hudson arrived with the coffee, and Bertie and I quickly poured cups for each of us, and for Holmes as well, should he want it. I knew that I should drink mine as quickly as possible, as we might be leaving abruptly at any moment, and if so, Holmes would gulp his down before dashing out the door. Better that his should have a chance to cool before then.

Holmes paced slowly as he considered, staring at nothing and pinching his earlobe. I took the opportunity to retrieve the appropriate commonplace book from the shelves near his bedroom door and review what little we knew of The True Knights of Seth.

Holmes had first made note of them in mid-1881, as their actions became more public. These criminals were not to be confused with the similarly named *Knights of Seth*, an ancient religious group. As Holmes explained it to me, the original Sethians were a Gnostic sect that flourished in the Mediterranean in the early years of Christianity. They named themselves after Adam's third son, Seth, whom they believed was some sort of Messiah with secret knowledge and a special understanding of the nature of reality. It was their idea that what we perceived as the physical world was in fact an illusion, while man's spiritual side was the true reality. Their symbol was a lion's head on a serpent's body. The original Sethians had an elaborate creation myth involving events that occurred before the making of Adam and Eve, in which various spiritual powers were infused into the first humans' bodies. These beliefs then merged into what is more widely known in the book of *Genesis* concerning the Creation.

The neo-Sethian Knights of the mid-1800's were made up of wealthy young English and Germans who were more interested in an excuse for a gentleman's club of sorts than forming an actual religious movement. They simply draped the tenets of the millennia-old Sethians onto their own foolish order, which they liked to call the *Ordo Equester Sethiani*. But as is too often the case, there were a few within this group of wayward young men who felt the call to something darker.

These few believed that there is a true God and a false one, the latter being known as the *demiurge*. It was he, named by them as *Yaldabaoth*, whom they credited with actually creating the world, and in doing so replacing the true and benevolent God. They also believed that Adam's son, Seth, was the original Messiah who could enact Yaldabaoth's will in this shadowy construct we think of as the actual physical world, and that other messiahs had followed in Seth's footsteps in the ages that followed.

Holmes had first perceived that such a group was in motion after the murder of Somerset House clerk. The killer had been easily identified and caught, but he refused to provide information as to who had instigated the crime, or the reason behind it. However, a search of his possessions had turned up a ring exactly like the one now resting in my pocket. Two other murders had followed which gave every indication of being related to The True Knights of Seth, and four others had been prevented. And Holmes still had no complete idea of who the new "Seth" was, or how to identify him.

The previous February, Holmes had deciphered a coded reference to Yaldabaoth in the Agony Column, leading him to spring into action while the latest outrage was actually in progress. We had been involved in another case at the time in which Bertie Tolliver had an interest, and he was swept along with us in the mad chase across the City to save the Lord Mayor. As our growler had raced east from Baker Street, I had given Bertie a short sketch of the organization we were facing, explaining the history and the rings, and his eyes had widened at such primitive idiocy and evil going on in our modern times. It was with this awareness that he had identified the significance of the ring brought to us that morning.

And now, it was possible that we had an unexpected indication as to the True Knights' next plan – and to the identity of one of the members as well. Perhaps even the self-proclaimed modern Messiah himself . . . .

"Bow Street provides good pickings, I suppose," said Holmes suddenly, back from his reverie and with his gaze focused on Bertie.

The small man nodded. "Many are arrested with things that they don't want found on them. As soon as they can, they get them off their person and down into the sewers. Often it's money, or jewelry. The pipes downstream from the police stations are all prime, as you might suspect, and are well defended by those of us who claimed them long ago."

"Where was the ring found?" asked Holmes. "Somewhere along the pipe, or specifically at the Bow Street Police Station sewer connection?"

"At the station," was Bertie's prompt reply. "We have a basket fixed there beneath the pipe. Makes it easier to rake, and to be sure that nothing is lost. That the ring and the note came from straight above our spot – no doubt. It was lying right on top of the . . . on top of what was in the basket. It couldn't have been there for more than half-an-hour. You get a sense of how long something has been in the sewers, you understand. And when I saw it – saw what it was – I knew that you out to have it."

"Your . . . profession," pondered Holmes, "isn't well known. Whomever dropped this ring wasn't just ridding himself of it to keep it from being found on him when he was thoroughly searched at the station. The note shows that. By adding a message, it indicates that he – whomever it was that got rid of the ring – knew that it would be found in the sewers by someone who would be looking for it – someone who would know where and what it was, and what to do with it. The note instructs the finder to return for more information, so presumably another message will be sent down the pipes." He took a step forward, shortening the distance to the smaller man. "How well do you trust your fellows – the other toshers with whom you work – who regularly examine that particular area?"

Bertie frowned. "I see what you mean. They would be the ones to know where to be watching for such a message. Well, I trust some more than others. Those that I do are like family. But then, there is one . . . Willoughby. We accept him, but he isn't trusted, you see. Not yet – he's too new among us. Do you think he might be working for The True Knights – the one who was supposed to find the message?"

"Possibly. Their reach seems to be both broad and deep. If so, he hasn't received the message from the prisoner upstairs yet, because we have it – and he'll be looking for it. Was anyone with you when you recovered the ring?"

Bertie shook his head. "I made my rounds early this morning. When I found the ring, I got out as fast as I could and washed it off at the trough near Cleopatra's Needle. Then I hurried here."

"Then we have a chance to take control of the situation. Watson," he looked at me, and I thought I spied pity in his face, "put on your very oldest clothes – nothing that you need to keep." Then he stepped over to my desk, pulled a blank sheet from a pad lying there, and picked up a pencil. Leaning over, he scribbled something on a corner and then tore it off, approximating the look of the message found on the ring. Rolling it tightly, he then turned to me, his hand out. I placed the ring in his palm and he set about attaching the small slip of paper.

"I've left Gladstone's name as before, but changed the day to Sunday – four days away, instead of tomorrow – to give us time to maneuver and possibly wreck their plans. I also left instructions to deliver the ring after it's found to a house in Crutched Friars. The message barely fits." He looked at Bertie. "We need to get the ring back to the sewer as soon as possible. Is there a way in without alerting your . . . associates?"

"The easiest way is up from the Victoria Embankment by the bridge, but that's like a regular tosher highway. Instead, we can come down Goodge Street alongside the Museum. But there are only so many routes, and whoever is looking for this ring might use any of them, depending on

310

which way he decides to approach. We'll just have to be careful – and lucky."

I turned then to go upstairs and find my oldest set of clothes. This was not my first trip into the London sewers, nor even my tenth. In fact, during the years of my association with Sherlock Holmes, such journeys had been required far too often for my happiness. I had long-since learned to retain old worn-out clothing at hand for when sojourns such as this, and sometimes even worse, became unavoidable.

Downstairs, I found that Holmes had also changed into a quite disreputable outfit – his in much worse condition than mine. While Bertie warmed himself by the fire, he was drinking his coffee in one steady draw. Then he set down the cup, picked up three dark lanterns that he'd retrieved from one of the storage cabinets while I was upstairs, and led us down to the street. We walked south for just a moment before encountering an early-morning growler. "Endell Street at Short's Garden," Bertie instructed the cabbie, and we lurched into motion.

Chapter II

As we traveled, each holding to our own thoughts, I considered what I knew about the London sewer system – which wasn't very much in 1884, except for my prior visits there. I only learned about its history and construction in greater detail years later, when Holmes told me of the time in 1877 when he'd been consulted by Sir Joseph Bazalgette, the famed civil engineer. *

It was Sir Joseph who had, beginning in the 1850's, been the designer and driving force behind the construction of London's massive sewer system. By '77, he'd already completed most of his great engineering works, and was only dabbling in the occasional consultation, which was how he'd discovered an elaborate underground dene hole, far east of London. That was during those early years when my friend was residing in Montague Street and first establishing himself as a consulting detective. It was after that meeting that Holmes had bothered to learn more about the man and the sewers, and I knew that he'd remained friends with the famed civil engineer until the man's death in early 1891.

But it was back in the 1850's when Sir Joseph earned his fame, as necessitated by the terribly unhealthy conditions facing Londoners every day.

Those had been the days of The Great Stink, when the sewage for the entire massive city had emptied directly into the tidal Thames. The Pool of London had been a gigantic heaving cess-pit, toxic and festering, and the health crisis that it caused was both deadly and unceasing. Sir Joseph was appointed as Chief Engineer to the Metropolitan Board of Works and given the monumental task of fixing it.

Up to that time, the city sewers, if they existed at all, were randomly located and undersized pipes, emptying into streets or streams, which in turn filled the Thames along the length of the city. More often, raw sewage ran in the streets and ditches and was emptied from windows, making walking anywhere a hazard both above and below. As the city grew, the situation became worse, and diseases, particularly cholera, ran rampant as the local water supplies, chiefly wells whose ground water was polluted by sewage, were affected.

Growth of the city also meant that many streams and rivers were literally enclosed and covered, some lost forever as they were artificially forced underground and forgotten. Sewage choked these as well.

The famed engineer had showed amazing foresight in terms of his estimate for the future growth in the capital. After he'd completed his calculations for the size required to handle the amount of sewage being produced in the 1850's, he'd then looked at his numbers and doubled everything, stating that, "We only have the chance to do this once, and there's always the unforeseen." For me personally, that planned oversizing of the sewers meant that many of the brick passages beneath the streets of London were constructed high enough to walk through – which was the only pleasant aspect of where we were headed.

London was a stranger to me in those bygone days when I was just a boy, so I can only imagine the filth and pestilence of the place. Sir Joseph's plan was to create great underground sewers of vast diameter, oversized brick tunnels as large as the underground rivers. To these would be connected hundreds of other smaller constructed brick pipes and passages running under streets and back into the various neighborhoods and absorbed villages, all carrying the accumulated sewage downstream into larger and larger pipes like branches joining limbs, and then becoming part of a great tree trunk. Then, at the lowest elevations in the city – along the banks of the Thames – the largest of these trunk pipes, constructed underneath the Albert Embankment, the Victoria Embankment, and the Chelsea Embankment, would turn and follow the river east, out of the city and far away, keeping the sewage from directly entering the river. Many miles downstream, the sewage would then be treated, stored in reservoirs until the pollutants had been consumed and eradicated by various natural water-dwelling creatures of microscopic size. Only then, when this bacteriological treatment had occurred and the sewage water was of a more natural state similar to river water, would it then be released into the Thames to complete its journey to the sea.

The streets were still empty and dark, as our conversation with Bertie in Baker Street had lasted no longer than fifteen minutes. The cab released us in short order at the poorly lit corner on Endell Street, and our guide into the Underworld led us into Short's Garden, with Christ's Church and the workhouse on our left, and the Lying-in Hospital on our right. Our footsteps echoed off the cold black bricks rising on either side of us. Halfway down the narrow passage in the direction of Drury Lane, Bertie directed us to the left, toward a circular metal lid darkening one side of the street. Reaching into his coat and retrieving a short pry-bar (a tool of his trade), it was but a second before he had the lid raised and then lowered quietly beside the now-opened void. I smelled the unmistakable odor of our destination.

Holmes had been lighting the lanterns, handing one to each of us as he finished. Keeping the third for himself, he gestured for Bertie to lead onward. I pulled on a pair of old and thick gloves and followed the little man down into the literal bowels of London.

We had kept the lanterns darkened in the street, but after Holmes had pulled the round metal lid closed over the top of us, we each widened the apertures, illuminating our surroundings. We were in an arched brick passage, about seven feet tall, and five or six feet wide. I could only imagine the incredible effort in terms of time, manpower, and materials that had gone into the building of these vast underground passages, less than a generation earlier. At the time, the streets along the routes would have been completely removed, dug down by removing dozens of feet in depth and thousands of cubic yards of ancient soil. It was uncertain how many archeological ruins, Roman and older, had been uncovered and destroyed in passing by the workmen, as there had been little time to properly excavate and study what was revealed, as the project could not stop and would not be slowed.

Millions of bricks and tons of Portland cement had been brought into the excavations as the underground branches of the sewer line were slowly extended and connected. While this had occurred long before I arrived in London, I had seen something similar in my own adult lifetime as the Underground was being installed in much the same way – entire streets burrowed to great depths, and brick-walled tunnels formed in place before being covered over once again. I could only imagine the incredible engineering involved in designing both systems, and the problems that would have occurred when the sanitary sewer and the Underground found themselves in conflict with one another – each with a required route, slope, and depth that might be blocked by the other.

The tunnel was warmer than the street, in the way that a cave maintains a constant temperature, but that isn't to say that it was pleasant.

313

There was a fogginess to the air that held the lantern-light close to us, keeping it from extending too far in either direction. It was enough to see the nearby walls, where the cement between the bricks was somewhat swollen and crumbled, and rotten-looking. There was a dark running line on either wall about eye-high – clearly a high-water mark for those times when the rains flowed into the sewers and filled the pipes beyond their daily design capacity, accumulating more and more as they approached the river downstream, causing overflows at manholes and storm drains that even Sir Joseph's amazing plans couldn't overcome. I was relieved to recall that no rains were expected for several days, so that morning we only had to contend with the steady flow of filth beneath us, in a foot-wide channel molded into the sewer's floor. It was surprisingly clear and steady. Bertie saw me noticing it.

"It's early in the day, Doctor. Not much sewage in there yet. That's ground-water seeping into the pipes."

He saw my eyes dart to the right, where I'd sensed a movement. But it was only a rat.

"That's a good sign," explained our guide. "When they can live down here, so can we. No sour damp, you see."

I knew that he referred to the rotten-egg smell of Hydrogen Sulfide, which permeated sanitary sewers. It was detectable by the human olfactory system in the smallest amounts, mere parts per million, and deadly when present at just a bit more. As if reading my thoughts, Bertie tapped his nose. "This will keep us out of trouble. And we don't have far to go."

"Then lead on," said Holmes, surprisingly patient when considering that we weren't already in motion. "And carefully. We don't want to alert the person who will be seeking this ring, should he already be down here too."

"Willoughby," muttered Bertie.

"Possibly. You would know best."

Without responding further, Bertie set off.

It wasn't far, but I wouldn't want to repeat it, and I suppose it could have been worse. Conversation was at a minimum, but Bertie did softly call out the intersections we passed. We went back underneath Short's Gardens in the direction we'd arrived, and then turned south into a wider passage running down Endell Street. There was a slight but perceptible slope downward in the direction we were headed, enough to keep the sewage flowing steadily without pooling or ponding. The channel running along the center of the floor widened and deepened, and the fluid within became murkier, but the wide floor on either side remained relatively passable, apparently washed clean by the last rain event. Both in front and to our rear, we could occasionally hear the squeaks of the rats, but they

314

gave us wide berth, and we progressed steadily. I was always trying to sense if there was any change in the toxicity of the atmosphere, but mostly it was just a cold dampness that gave the back of one's throat a rawish feeling.

When we passed underneath manholes with their lids vented by small holes, the temperature would lower slightly, and the air seemed a bit more fresh, although that may have been my imagination. Bertie noted when we crossed the intersections of Betteron and Castle Streets, and then he laughed when the air became noticeably more unpleasant soon after. It wasn't an increase in the deadly Hydrogen Sulfide. Rather, it was a thick yeasty smell that made me want to scrape my tongue against my teeth.

"It's from the brewery just west on Long Street, at The Elms." He nodded at the flow in a floor trough joining the main channel from that direction, its contents more of a thick sludge. "Always a bit chewy. Fancy a pint, Doctor?"

He gave one of his elven laughs, but then, when he saw Holmes's pursed lips, he fell silent.

Within just a hundred yards or so, we reached a wide spot in the tunnel. It seemed as if some of the bricks were newer than what we had previously seen. "They did some work here to accommodate the Opera House," said Bertie, nodding to one side. Then he stepped to the opposite of the tunnel. "But this is what we've come for."

Holmes frowned. "I had hoped to stop and reconnoiter before we arrived," he said softly, "to make sure we aren't being watched, or to see if there were any footmarks nearby."

"I'll see," said Bertie, skipping ahead down the tunnel. He was back in a short moment. "No one down there, and no place to hide. The floor is clean – as much as it can be, at any rate. No fresh footmarks. We can do our business and be away." He stuck out a hand. "The ring, please – unless you want to place it yourself."

Holmes reached into his pocket. "You are welcome to it."

Bertie took a couple of steps to one side of the tunnel where a six-inch pipe, possibly of iron but quite tuberculated and rough-looking, jutted out of the brick-work. It had been mortared in at some point, but now there were gaps around it, and there was a small amount of clear liquid running out of the wall below the pipe and down to the floor below – more of the groundwater, I assumed, although I couldn't be certain.

A wire basket of about one cubic foot was affixed to the pipe by a thick corroded wire, so that the flow would empty there. It was a most inefficient and disgusting arrangement, but clearly one that worked, as the toshers relied it on as a labor-saving device, allowing them to retrieve all sorts of treasures that otherwise might be lost, carried away along the floor channel.

The basket was half-full, and I wrinkled my nose in disgust. Bertie placed the ring on it, message-side up, and stepped back. "Just as I found it – on top and winking in my light."

"Which means, as you said, that it was sent down the pipe not long before," added Holmes, "with the near certainty that whomever did so is still, even now, under arrest and located in one of the cells above us." He looked farther down the tunnel, as if concerned that someone might be approaching at any moment. "Time to go, Bertie. Watson and I must speak with someone upstairs."

Bertie led us thirty or forty feet onward in the downhill direction in which we'd already been heading, and then took a sharp right turn into a smaller shaft, now only about six feet in height. Leaning down to avoid brushing the ceiling, I congratulated myself upon having stayed essentially clean throughout this trip, while recalling the time in autumn 1888 when pursuit of one of the Rippers had necessitated a race beneath the streets in tunnels so small that I could barely fit by turning sideways, scraping along tighter and tighter until I feared I'd be lost and forgotten down there forever.

We exited into a wider brick chamber with the choking odor of rotting vegetation, much of which was mounded along the sides of the floor at the walls. "Covent Garden Market?" asked Holmes, and Bertie acknowledged it. He led us to a rusty ladder which he mounted carefully, climbing eight or ten feet to another of the round lids that sealed away these Stygian passages. We followed, finding ourselves in the first light of dawn and under the curious but otherwise indifferent gazes of the various vendors setting up around us. Bertie replaced the metal lid and walked us back out to Bow Street. As we stood next to the corner of the Floral Hall, Holmes gave low instructions to our short companion, confirming that there were locations within the sewer where Bertie could observe the basket beneath the police station pipe discreetly.

"Once someone finds the ring," Holmes added, "surface and let them know in the police station across the way immediately. I'll arrange to be notified."

"But what if it's one of my mates finds it who is innocent – and not Willoughby?" asked Bertie. Seeing Holmes start to answer, he added, "There are three others besides me who 'own' that spot that might check at any time, finding the ring without being guilty at all. One of them might pick it up like they would any other trinket, not knowing about messages and criminal societies.

"I know that I'm maybe suspecting Willoughby too much," he continued hurriedly, "but I have a certain feeling about him. If one of us was supposed to retrieve the ring for this Sethian fellow, it will be him, you can be certain. He hasn't been around nearly as long, and has never made himself overly trustworthy.

"Who are to ones that you do trust?" queried Holmes.

Bertie frowned. "Jacob, Harry, and Silas. Willoughby is the wrong 'un for sure.

"I honor your instincts," said Holmes. "If Willoughby is the one to retrieve the ring, let him go and follow him, but if one of the others finds it, speak to them and have them put it back. In any case, time is short. Go back to your hiding place and watch. Meanwhile, Watson and I will confer with the police."

Walking the short uphill distance a dozen or so feet above the route we'd just taken, we crossed the street and entered the station, where we were initially met with the suspicious look from the officer on duty that our shabby appearance demanded. Although we'd both been careful not to intersect with any objectionable detritus within the sewer tunnels, we'd doubtless absorbed a certain amount of the unforgettable scent within our clothing, carrying it with us like an invisible but unmistakable fog. I could see the officer's nose wrinkling as he started to speak, and then he recognized us. A bit of merry twinkle flashed in his eyes for just an instant.

"I can only imagine, sirs, where you both spent last night – " He tapped his nose knowingly. " – but I have definite ideas." He sat up a bit straighter. "Inspector Bradstreet is on duty this morning."

"Excellent, Coggins," replied Holmes, "and I'm sure you'll rejoice with us that we aren't in worse shape. Shall you announce us?"

The officer waved a hand generally toward his right. "You know the way. And may I say that I hope your day leads you along better paths than wherever you've already been."

"Amen to that," I agreed, while Holmes simply nodded and then turned toward a doorway on the left.

We made our way down a stone-flagged passage and were nearing an office when a man in a peaked cap and frogged jacket strode out, carrying an empty mug. He looked at us in surprise, and then grinned when he recognized us. "Good to see you, gentlemen. I'm must about to have some tea." He wrinkled his nose. "I expect that you could use some too."

I knew that Holmes wanted to set things in motion immediately, but I spoke quickly and accepted Bradstreet's kind offer.

"Just step into my room here," he said, "and I'll be right back."

It was no different than the many times we'd visited there before: A small, office-like space, with a huge ledger upon the table, and a telephone projecting from the wall. In a moment the big inspector had returned, carrying three mugs in his sizable hands. Placing one before each of us, he sat down at his desk with the third.

"What can I do for you, gentlemen?"

"May I see your list of prisoners currently on hand?"

Bradstreet knew of old that Holmes wouldn't be wasting his time, so he silently turned 'round the ledger in front of my friend. "The bottom six names," added the inspector.

Holmes only took a few seconds to glance along the list, and then he nodded, tapping a finger underneath one name for my attention. I leaned forward. *Brendon Hanover.* I nodded. While the other five names, all unknown to me, might be our man, their various petty crimes, along with notations of their shabby criminal history, indicated that they were not the influential man that we sought. Hanover, however, was well-known to anyone well-up on London society, and he fit with what I would have required if picking a member – perhaps even a leader – of The True Knights of Seth.

In his mid-thirties, he was the second son of a North-country textiles magnate and his American dowry wife. There was none of the idea on the part of Brendon Hanover's old father that only first sons gained the benefit of the family wealth – he would have happily made use of Brendon's innate cleverness and brutal tenaciousness had the young man gone along with the plan. But the son wanted no part of his father's operations, instead moving to London more than ten years before and then making himself over into someone completely different. He worked hard and created a successful law practice, involving himself in a number of controversial suits that steadily increased his fame. He was initially willing to take either side of a question, alternately being praised and then burned in effigy, but gradually his emphasis shifted toward an antipathy toward the establishment of his forebears. In the meantime, his hard work during the day was matched by how aggressively he pursued a social life at night – albeit with an almost palpable anger toward those with whom he associated. He went amongst the others of his age and position at dinner parties and the usual clubs, but his attitude was always truculent, as is challenging those with whom he associated, slyly reminding them that their existence was without purpose.

"And how did Mr. Hanover end up in your cells?" queried Holmes.

"The usual story – he was someplace where he didn't need to be. Specifically, a vicious brawl that erupted at the Tankerville Club after a cheating accusation. He wouldn't have been involved, but he made the mistake of being intoxicated and attacking an officer when he otherwise would have been ignored. The officer's injuries aren't life-threatening, but bad enough that Hanover won't be released anytime soon, in spite of his influence. He only became more belligerent after he arrived here – we didn't know who he was at first – and he ranted that he had somewhere he had to be this morning. Such an attitude made us decide that he needed to learn a lesson."

"It's fortunate that you did so," said Holmes. "You may have saved the Prime Minister's life."

Bradstreet removed his cap, ran a hand through his hair, and widened his eyes. "Tell me a story, Mr. Holmes."

Holmes did so. Bradstreet already knew some about The True Knights, so it didn't take much to get him caught up on that aspect. "We know that it's their ring," continued Holmes, "and that they've committed murders and tried assassination in the past. Seeing Gladstone's name written with a specific date and time – tomorrow – where he'll be on public display seems to be an indicator of planned mayhem."

"But it's no secret where the Prime Minister will be for those who want to know," countered Bradstreet. "Why take the time to leave the note on the ring, and then go to such trouble to get the message out in such a way?"

"Perhaps The True Knights have a list of several targets," I answered. Holmes nodded and I continued. "Possibly Hanover feared that he would be sequestered here for so long that he couldn't get the word out before their window closed on choosing Gladstone. And if he's seen by his lawyer, perhaps he doesn't trust the man to relay the message in the proper manner."

"But if he could make it understood to someone that he'd drop a ring into the sewer," asked Bradstreet doggedly, "couldn't he have just mouthed the word 'Gladstone' to whoever was watching him?"

"One would think," agreed Holmes, "but no doubt there were other circumstances of which we aren't yet aware. In any case, the ring *was* dropped into the sewer for someone to specifically find, and we have a chance that we wouldn't have had otherwise."

The story of the ring in the sewer a few dozen feet beneath us was of greater interest to the inspector.

"Well, I never . . ." he muttered. "I feel foolish – of course we know they get rid of things that we haven't found – our searches can never be completely thorough. Evidence – money, jewelry, what have you – it goes down the drain. But I suppose we assumed at that point it was irretrievable. Of course we know of the toshers, but if they do find anything, it's useless to us as evidence – for how can we connect it up with a specific prisoner here in the cells? To think that those fellows are straining what leaves the building right below us . . . ." He shook his head. "I'd dearly love – No, I started to say that I'd like to go down and see it for myself, but I'm not sure that I really would after all. It would be too frustrating to see the evidence appear from the pipe, and yet know we couldn't link it to the criminal who disposed of it. The lawyers would have a field day if we tried."

He shifted in his chair. "You bought us some time by shifting the day from tomorrow to Sunday – that might confuse them. But if they already have plans for a specific event tomorrow, they might not be convinced – they might not change anything. They'll likely ignore whatever confusion your new message generates and still make the effort to kill Gladstone tomorrow morning."

"Which is why I added the instruction take the ring to the house in 44 Crutched Friars – so that we can insert ourselves into whatever is happening. You may not be aware, but I know that property is currently vacant, following the recent decampment of the Wyatt brothers."

"That was not known to me, but arrangements can be made immediately to keep it under additional observation." He rose and stepped to the telephone. Soon he was speaking to officers located near Fenchurch Street Station, giving precise instructions as to how the building should be discreetly watched.

"I must also get there as soon as I can," Holmes said, rising. "I'll stop by one of my hidey-holes along the way and further alter my appearance to meet whomever shows up with the retrieved ring – Willoughby, if Bertie is right. Then I can contrive to work my way further along the chain."

He turned to me. "Find Wiggins and some of the other Irregulars. Get them into place around Crutched Friars as soon as possible to supplement the police, and then wait nearby." He glanced at Bradstreet. "You should let the boys take the lead in following whomever arrives or leaves. They will be more subtle."

Bradstreet nodded with a rueful smile. "I learned that long ago."

With that we separated. Outside, Holmes and I walked quickly south until we reached the cabs starting to congregate near the Strand. There we each went our own way without comment, he heading east and me back to Baker Street. Later, I learned that not long after we departed from the police station, Bertie Tolliver emerged once again from the Covent Garden sewers and related to Bradstreet the intelligence that Willoughby, as anticipated, had just retrieved the ring. As Bertie watched unobserved from the nearby darkness, Willoughby unfolded the revised message as soon as he picked it up, read it, and then made his way topside before hurrying east on foot. It would be close, but Holmes would be at the meeting place, in disguise, in time to intercept him.

320

Meanwhile, I rounded up a dozen lads from around Bak
gave them all instructions before we climbed into a pair of f
Like good soldiers, they understood what was required.

The streets were waking up, but our journey went qu
Friars was a narrow bow-shaped lane located in The City, severai ...
feet north of the Tower. I had the notion, based on something read long
ago, that the original Crutched Friars had been a Catholic religious order,
suppressed in the mid-1500's during Henry VIII's dissolution of the
monasteries, when he and his cronies carried out their massive theft of
properties belonging to the King's religious enemies. I had some sense that
the friars had once held a connection with St. Olave's Church, still
standing at the corner of Hart Street and Crutched Friars, and it was at that
corner where I waited after sending the Irregulars scattering in different
directions, in order to follow Willoughby in whichever direction he chose.
They needed no further instructions from me as to how they should best
carry out their business.

I was still in those same old clothes that I'd worn into the sewers, so
I felt rather inconspicuous. Still, I didn't want to draw any more attention
than necessary until I heard from Holmes. I found a place near the church
door, which was still locked tight at that early hour, and leaned against the
rather grimy stone work, as if I were someone in need of aid with nowhere
else to go. I occasionally glanced to the west toward where No. 44 was
located, pondering if it was the building located before or after a one-story
enclosed brick passage stretching over the street, connecting first floors of
the two structures on either side. It formed something of a low tunnel
across the road, and I wondered how long ago it had been constructed. I
watched idly as a dray cart barely passed underneath, the driver's body
laid over to one side, and considered how often something was knocked
against the lower side of the building by carelessness. I was still looking
that way when I heard a shuffle coming up behind me. Turning, I found a
shabby fellow, hunched in on himself as if he was hungry or sick. It was
very convincing, but I recognized Holmes none-the-less.

"Has Willoughby been here yet?" I asked softly.

He nodded. "Been and just gone. I've set the Irregulars on him. He
arrived five minutes ago. We talked for several minutes in the doorway of
No. 44. I looked past him and saw you standing here at the church. By that
point, I had another name from him – someone named Nichols. That's who
he expected to find when he got here."

"Did he accept you as legitimate?"

"I believe so. There was some initial suspicion, but I was able to speak
with enough knowledge of The True Knights that I think he was
convinced."

"And did he confirm an assassination attempt on Gladstone?"

Holmes nodded. "He did. I sent him on his way with new and erroneous instructions – to tell The True Knights to postpone tomorrow's attempt in lieu of a better opportunity on Sunday – with more information coming soon."

"All of which likely seemed credible since it went along with the reference to Sunday that he independently found in the message on the ring which brought him here."

"Which he believes came from Hanover – who may be their 'Messiah'."

"Did he tell you where is he's headed to deliver the new instructions?"

"One of the streets behind St. Paul's – where he would have gone in the first place had I not inserted this detour into his plans." He pulled his coat a bit tighter, looking every inch like one of the countless unfortunates who have nothing and fill every corner of the capital. "We'd best hurry or Willoughby and the Irregulars will leave us behind."

He walked past me and around the corner into Hart Street. We hadn't gone far before a lad of eight or nine leaned out of a dark side street, beckoning us to follow and pointing west. Soon we were trailing some distance behind Willoughby while the lads surrounded him on all sides, hurrying down side streets to get ahead of him and anticipate any changes in direction, and shifting with his path like a murmuration of starlings. I could only hope and assume that Bradstreet's forces were also somewhere behind us.

"This is more of a practice exercise than anything," said Holmes softly, "as Willoughby provided me with the address. Still, we're prepared in case he decides to bolt in a different direction."

"Or if he lied," I added. Holmes nodded with a smile.

"Any sign of the police?" I asked after a moment, looking back over my shoulder.

"No, but Bradstreet is smart enough to fall back and let the Irregulars do the work."

We walked in silence for a few moments, and then Holmes told me what else Willoughby had said.

"He was a bit puzzled when he found me there – and also suspicious. 'I don't know you,' he said. 'I expected to find Nichols.' I replied something about there being more of us than he knew, and he nodded, as if that fit his expectations. Then I asked him if he had the note from Hanover, and that settled whatever doubts he still had. He nodded and handed it to me.

322

"'And his ring?' I asked. 'Give it to me.' He provided it, but with a bit of reluctance." Holmes patted his waistcoat pocket. "Then I asked which of the locations he'd thought was his destination before being diverted to Crutched Friars, and he volunteered 'the Watling Street house'. I told him that there were other aspects of the affair which he didn't know about, and that the plans were changing. He accepted that too. 'I read the note,' he said. 'It looks like Sunday is now the day.'

"I nodded. 'You're the tosher, aren't you? We've had good reports of your service.'

"That pleased him, and I said, 'We saw the arrest at the club but lost track of what happened next. How did you know to retrieve the ring – and the message?'

"'Just luck. I happened to be near the Bow Street Station,' he answered, 'when the Maria stopped and they took Mr. Hanover out. He must have recognized me. He yelled out about being mistreated – I suppose to get my attention in case I hadn't already noticed him. "I'll take this to the Prime Minister if I have to!" he cried. Then, when he saw me looking, he managed to point to his ring, and then down to the ground. It took me a minute to work out what he was telling me. Not long after that, I went down into the sewer to wait for the ring to appear. I checked back several times through the night, and finally this morning I found where it and the message had finally come down the pipes.'"

"We were lucky," I said, "that Willoughby didn't carry out an all-night vigil by the pipe. Otherwise, Bertie never would have found the ring first, and we wouldn't have had this opportunity to derail their plans."

"Or even know about them," Holmes added. "It's almost enough to convince me that Fate occasionally takes a hand in nudging events toward a better outcome. After Willoughby told me his story, I pretended to think for a moment, and then said, 'You'd best get this message on to Watling Street,' and I gave him back the paper. 'In the meantime, I'll pass along the change of plan to some of the others.' He nodded as if that was what he'd expected to hear, and then we parted company."

"Do you have any notion as to who this 'Nichols' might be?"

"Perhaps. One of Hanover's regular confederates is Vincent Nichols. He's already been under some scrutiny for his rather heavy-handed methods at enforcing various illegalities. He comes from a good background, rather like Hanover, but he has fallen far from where he began. If it's he that's associated with The True Knights, I wouldn't be surprised in the least."

Throughout this conversation, we'd passed through Candlewick Ward, along Cannon Street, and then turned into Budge Row. We occasionally received reports from this or that Irregular who dropped back and informed us that Willoughby has proceeded without deviation toward St. Paul's, apparently completely unaware that he was being followed. It was near where Budge Row became Watling Street that little William Styers joined us, relating that our quarry had turned into a dingy brick house up ahead on the right, between Bread Street and Friday Street.

"Very good," said Holmes. "Find Inspector Bradstreet – he and his officers should be coming along behind us – and lead him and his men to surround the house." He checked his watch. "Tell him that Doctor Watson and I will enter at five after nine." As the lad ran away, Holmes added, "That gives them fifteen minutes to find their places, which should be more than sufficient." Then he took the lead, walking closer to our destination. I had no worries that we might look suspicious, as there were quite a few others on the streets by that time of morning, and our disguises were good. Still, we didn't know whom we might encounter who was also headed for the same house.

Within moments the inspector had surreptitiously joined us. As we stood just past the public house, east of Bread Street, he listened with interest to Holmes's report, and then said, "I suppose we raid the place?"

"Possibly," said Holmes. "But first, Watson and I will go in and see what we can determine, and if enough of them are present to arrest now, or whether we should give them more rope and see how they scatter, to widen the net."

Bradstreet asked the question that also occurred to me. "Is that wise, Mr. Holmes? Even if you two aren't recognized, they'll be suspicious of sudden strangers in their midst – and if we let these go, we might lose track of some of them."

Holmes brushed off his concern. "Willoughby was quick enough to accept my involvement. I believe that this group is so widespread that there are multiple cells, each with limited knowledge of the others, so that they won't know who else is involved. Speaking with confidence about the little we know should be enough to dampen their suspicions.

"But," he added, "If you hear a window break, hurry into the building with all due speed through every entrance."

Then, without any further discussion, he nodded in my direction and we continued along Watling Street.

Chapter III

One of the Irregulars was crouching near a doorway, apparently engrossed in some game of his own devising involving gravels he'd gathered from the adjacent street. He ignored us completely, but his presence at that door alerted us as to which building was our destination.

As we passed, he held up two fingers, signifying which floor. I glanced up but didn't see any lit windows. Perhaps the room in question was at the back.

Inside the narrow entryway, we were assailed by the strong odor of cooked cabbage, with something worse and old and foul underlying it – though not as foul as the sewers. I involuntarily cleared my throat and stayed with Holmes as he moved to a narrow stairway leading upward. He stepped carefully and silently, and I followed in his footsteps as well as I could, mostly managing to stay quiet. Within a moment, we were outside a closed door with a bar of light showing underneath. Through the door, I could hear the rumble of low conversation – several voices, sometimes talking over one another, but not loud enough to determine what was being said. Holmes glanced at me and I patted my coat pocket, where my service revolver rested. He nodded, and then he knocked twice, sharply, and opened the unlocked door. He boldly stepped inside, and I followed closely.

I immediately saw that we had entered very deep water.

It was a small apartment with four featureless walls. Opposite the door in which we stood was another, possibly leading to a bedroom, or perhaps simply a closet. The space was empty of any pleasantries whatsoever. There were a dozen rickety chairs of various ages and styles, and one bare table in the center. All of the chairs were circled around it, facing two men who stood there, one of them possibly Willoughby and the other Nichols. Each of the chairs facing them was occupied, and there were just as many men who were standing behind them, pressed against one another and the surrounding walls.

The man on the right had obviously been speaking when we entered. He was in his mid-thirties, tall and thin, with stylish dark hair. He was well dressed – quite incongruous for the setting in which we found him. His voice held a sneer, and he spoke in a tone that betrayed more education and advantages than most of the other men in the room had ever known. He glared at us, and his hostility seemed to be matched by the looks from the other two-dozen figures ranged around him. There was danger here, and I wondered if Holmes would have any chance to spin his tale for them before violence erupted.

Remembering Holmes's instruction to Bradstreet about how the police would be summoned when needed, I muttered with despair, "There isn't a window."

"Indeed," was Holmes's barely audible reply. Then he boldly stepped forward. "Has Willoughby told you about this morning's set-back?"

"Who are you?" growled one of the standing men, while the man who had been speaking looked Holmes up and down.

"That's him," interjected the man beside him – presumably Willoughby. "The man in Crutched Friars. He said he was going to tell the others – not that he was coming here."

"Do you refer to Hanover's arrest?" asked the other man, ignoring Willoughby. "That shouldn't have changed anything," he said. "Do you have further information as to why he's delayed the event until Sunday?"

"I do," said Holmes. "He managed to speak to me when we were both in the police van after being arrested."

The man looked at Willoughby. "Was he with Hanover when you were outside the Bow Street Station?"

Willoughby shrugged. "Might have been. I was looking at Hanover after he raised his voice to see what he wanted."

"They turned me loose early," Holmes explained, diverting the subject away from Willoughby's identification. "Hanover might have been free by now, too, if he'd kept his temper. He'll be lucky to be out by next week. But he told me to get along to Crutch's Friar and wait for Willoughby."

"Now that doesn't make any sense," said the man, the sneer now shadowing his dark features. "Willoughby was just telling us about his unexpected detour, and I can't see that it made any difference to go all the way there, just to come back here. Why would Hanover send him there to meet you, for no apparent reason except to go there, when you already knew all about it? And why would he go to the trouble of putting a message on his ring if you were with him at the station? He could have simply told you about the change of schedule. Willoughby, did you tell this man anything when you got there?"

"Not a thing. He was expecting me, and seemed like he already knew what's what."

"And then he shows up here. He likely followed you." The man moved around the table and took a step closer to us. "I'm not like the rest of these men," he said. Was there just a shade of contempt in the way he said *men*? "I've made the effort to study those who might oppose us. I expected a better disguise from someone of your reputation – *Mr. Holmes*."

There was a shuffling amongst the two-dozen True Knights who filled the room. Some might have been familiar with Holmes's name, while others simply knew that the man challenging us was becoming more hostile, and they took their cue from him.

"And you would be Nichols, I suppose," said Holmes. The man raised an eyebrow but didn't provide any confirmation. "Hanover informed us how to find you when he made his full confession last night."

The man looked at Willoughby. "Did you tell him my name?"

326

Willoughby chewed his lip. "I suppose I did."

Nichols looked back at us. "Not very clever, Mr. Holmes. Our Messiah would never confess anything."

Holmes took a step forward. There was now a low grumble from the assembled Sethians.

"Is this the lot of you, then?" He gestured toward the men. Those who had been seated were now standing. They seemed to take up more space than a moment before. Apparently The True Knights of Seth recruited from the laboring classes, as these were big men – those who labored. They could do a great deal of damage before they were stopped.

"Not entirely. These are our loyal soldiers." The sneering man looked at the crowd. Their anger was palpable. They likely didn't understand what was happening, but they knew enough to recognize enemies in their midst. "There are more than enough of them, I'm thinking – even if Dr. Watson pulls out that gun he's fondling in his coat pocket."

"And there are no more or you hiding in the other room?" asked Holmes, suddenly taking a few steps forward, into and through the midst of the crowded enemies like Daniel marching into the lions' den.

I tensed, ready to shoot the first one who made a threatening move toward my friend, but they seemed too surprised by his action to respond. Several even stepped aside, the Red Sea parting around Holmes as he passed through the taller and bulkier men. He reached the door on the opposite wall without hindrance and threw it open, revealing a darkened room beyond – but not so dark that there wasn't a window. He disappeared within and no one seemed inclined to follow, as perhaps they knew that he had nowhere beyond to go.

Immediately there was the sound of breaking glass, followed by the door to the far room slamming shut with Holmes still inside and the lock turning with an audible snick.

Taking that as my cue, I backed up through the still open door behind me, stepping into the hall and pulling the door shut. I had no way to lock it from my side, and as soon as I saw the knob start to turn, I shot into the wall beside it, only somewhat concerned whether the thick old plaster would stop the bullet, or if it would instead pass through and into one of the conspirators.

Another rattling of the doorknob brought another shot, this time aiming downward through the door. For certain that bullet passed through, and I heard a scream and knew that whomever had been at the door now had a wound in his foot or leg. I wondered how much further I would be able to discourage them, or if they had their own guns which they would begin to fire back in my direction. I only worried for seconds at most, however, before the sound of many rushing footsteps were ascending the stairs in my direction. Bradstreet was leading several dozen officers, and they swarmed past me, kicking in the door and flooding the room, their truncheons rising and falling faster than the eye could see, and the sound of strong seasoned wood hitting criminal skulls pleasantly reminding me of the break of balls on a billiard table.

Over it all, I saw the door across the room open. Holmes stepped out, eyeing with satisfaction as the Sethians fell, one by one, in very quick succession. Nichols was edging through it, his escape route before him, when Holmes grabbed him, spun him around, and dropped him with a smart right cross. Then Bradstreet was blowing his whistle, and still more constables arrived, dragging their opponents upright and then downstairs, where they would be transported back to the Bow Street cells. Holmes took Bradstreet aside and had a quick word, and then the inspector hurried out to speak with the officers in charge of the police vehicles. It was over in minutes, and in the street below, those who lived in the neighborhood watched in amazement as so many criminals were hauled away in haste. In moments, they were gone as if they it had all been a dream. Only a single growler was left for us, waiting in front of the building.

Meanwhile, Holmes also dismissed the Irregulars, who had gathered on the pavement to watch with amusement as the damaged Sethians were loaded unceremoniously into the Marias. Holmes instructed Wiggins, the head of the Irregulars, to stop by Baker Street that evening for payment. Then he and I, along with Bradstreet, were left standing on the pavement as the prisoners departed and the curious neighbors dispersed, whispering amongst themselves.

"Nichols let slip that they consider Hanover to be their 'Messiah'," Holmes explained.

"So this should mostly take care of them," commented Bradstreet.

"Possibly . . . ." said Holmes.

"But you aren't certain," added the inspector. "That's why you had me make sure that when the arrested men get to the station, no one lets Hanover know what's happened."

"That, and Nichols implied the men you just arrested were but foot soldiers. I hope that Hanover might share what else has been planned."

"He won't talk," Bradstreet pointed out.

"He will if he thinks he's been turned loose."

That statement was met with silence for a moment. Then I said, "That may be, but he might recognize you, Holmes. Nichols did, in spite of your disguise. They seem to have been warned that you would one day be on their trail."

"Exactly," replied Holmes. "Therefore, when Hanover is released, I'll follow behind him to make sure he doesn't escape the net. It will be up to

328

you, Watson, to gain his trust and find out if they have any other plans – things that only their 'Messiah' would know."

Bradstreet looked at me to see my reaction. I could only recall all the times that Holmes had commented that my forthright nature prevented me from convincingly prevaricating, or how he had withheld information from me so that I might not inadvertently reveal something before it suited his plans. Now, it seemed as if he were putting a lot of unexpected faith in my acting abilities.

"Just be yourself," he said, sensing my doubts. "The True Knights are obviously made up of men from all walks of life. The worst that can happen is that he knows each and every member, and he's never heard of you. However, I suspect that as the 'Messiah', he regularly delegates many of his affairs, including interactions with the riff-raff. And you'll have this to convince him of your legitimacy . . . ." He held up the Sethian ring.

"That's Hanover's own ring," I said. "What if he recognizes it?"

"Improvise. If he doesn't recognize it, all is well. If he does, tell him you retrieved it from your friend Willoughby. In any case, offer to take him to an emergency conference with Nichols. Head for Baker Street. When we decide to re-arrest him, it will be on home ground, and Bradstreet will have men waiting for us there."

"And what am I supposed to find out from this 'Messiah'?"

"Whatever you can. Their plans. Other members. Who else is in their sights. Timetables." He shrugged. "Or nothing at all. Do your best."

I nodded. "Why not?"

Bradstreet laughed. "Why not, indeed?"

Chapter IV

I was back at the corner of the Floral Hall, where we'd stood only hours before. Holmes had looked at my old clothing and decided that I would do. Now I simply waited for Brendon Hanover to be released. He would be accompanied to the street by Constable Giles Bates, an old acquaintance. After that it would be up to me.

Holmes was somewhere nearby, but – of course – he would only be seen when he wished to be.

I'd waited no more than five minutes, keeping back toward the building and out of the way of the hurrying pedestrians, when I saw Bates and another man exit the station. With no more than a word or two, the constable turned and went back inside. Hanover hunched his coat higher around his shoulders, looked up and down the street, and set off toward the Strand.

I crossed the street, intersecting with his path near a fire hydrant. As I approached, I made a low "*Hsstt!*" sound through my teeth, catching his attention. He stopped and tightened defensively – understandable at any time when a fast-striding stranger approaches, but more so when one has just been released from the Bow Street cells.

I maintained eye contact but raised a hand peacefully. Then, when I was within a couple of feet, I turned it so that he could see my palm, with the ring tightly on my finger, and rotated to that the sigil of The True Knights was visible to him. A curious frown settled on his face. He didn't yet relax, but I was allowed to approach.

"Nichols sent me," I said softly, allowing my voice to settle into the Scottish burr of my youth. "There are complications."

"Complications?" he asked. His voice, even in a near-whisper, was a rich baritone, and I could see that he would be a compelling and influential speaker. He wasn't as tall as I'd expected, being rather compact and athletic. His features were strong, with intelligent light-colored eyes under dark heavy brows and a high forehead, and his mouth was tight and tense. However, I could see a number of laugh lines, showing that when he was in the mood, he would appear to be charming and unthreatening.

I nodded. "Gladstone's schedule has changed. The next time we'll have a chance is Sunday."

My response was unplanned, as Holmes and I hadn't discussed what I would say. I only sensed that it must not be too outrageous – and in any case, it didn't matter what I conveyed, as Hanover would be re-arrested in the near future. I only needed to convince him to speak about any plans that might be in the offing, and with any luck reveal more about these modern Sethians.

"Your message was found in the sewer as you intended," I added. "The tosher took it to Watling Street. I'm supposed to convey you to Nichols the minute you're released."

"Where at? Watling Street, or the Lambeth house?"

"Neither. There's a fellow with more information – a clerk who works in Gladstone's office. We're supposed to speak with him at a coffee shop in Portman Mansions."

He nodded. I was thinking that perhaps this didn't seem too unexpected to him after all. Then he said, "Tell me which one."

I shook my head. "I'm supposed to bring you," I responded, my mind racing to think of a reason why that would be.

"Who are you?" he said, a new suspicious tone in his voice.

"Roylott," I said, with the first name that popped into my head. "Grimesby Roylott." I thought about elaborating – saying that I'd recently moved to London from Stoke Moran on the western border of Surrey, or

330

that I'd formerly been a doctor in India. But remembering Holmes's idea that liars often spoil their game by simply attempting to fill awkward silences, I held my tongue. Fortunately that worked. Hanover nodded. "Nichols told me that he'd been recruiting. Find us a cab."

A hansom had been moving slowly down the street, and I raised a hand to attract the driver's attention. I directed him to the coffee shop in Portman Mansions, and within minutes we were in motion, passing through several small streets and lanes until we were moving steadily north along Charing Cross Road.

"This new information," said Hanover. "Is it certain?"

"As much as can be at this point," I answered. "When Nichols got word, he called off tomorrow's sortie – the information in your message was no longer valid."

"It isn't up to Nichols to make those decisions," he said, clearly irritated.

"That's not the way I heard it," I said, suddenly seeing a way to rattle him a bit. "From what I was given to understand when it was arranged for my organization to work with you people, he's the brains, and you're the figurehead – convincing these ignorant toadies of yours that you're some kind of new Jesus."

His color darkened, and I continued. "I was at Watling Street today for the meeting. Nichols made it clear that he's doing the planning – which is probably a good thing, since otherwise we would have been trying to kill Gladstone tomorrow and he would have been two-hundred miles away."

"Nichols doesn't *plan* anything," he said tightly, his voice low and dangerous. "He doesn't *decide* anything. *I* do. It's my right – *I'm* the one with the divine gift. Who did you say you were?" he suddenly asked, his eyes refocusing sharply in my direction, new suspicion on his face.

"Grimesby Roylott. So if you're still the leader," I pressed, "then whose fault was it that the Lord Mayor is still alive? Nichols put that failure down to you. He was pretty clear about how it happened, and he promised that it won't happen again. For my people to be involved, it had better not."

By now we were well along Oxford Street, and moving surprisingly fast. It wouldn't be long before we turned north into Orchard Street.

"The Lord Mayor only escaped because of a chance accident. My plan would have worked. It *should* have worked!"

I shook my head. "I spent time in Afghanistan," I said, goading him further. "I was at Maiwand. I saw what happens when a plan is too simple – when the person making the plan is too inexperienced to account for contingencies and happenstance and the unexpected. It nearly got me

331

killed. Then Nichols said that you only think two-dimensionally – that you can't plan a campaign with the bigger picture in mind. He promised that when he's running things, it will be different." I looked him up and down, as if judging him and not liking what I saw. "That's what we signed on for."

Hanover was becoming more and more angry as I prodded him, and I was grateful that he wouldn't have been released by the police with any weapons in his possession. Still, his fists were clenched and his knuckles had turned white, and I saw the flickers of madness in his eyes. This was more than him embracing revolutionary ideas and taking on the mantle of omnipotence simply as a display to control his gullible followers – I was beginning to understand that he truly believed that he was a Messiah.

"Nichols went over your plan to kill the Prime Minister," I said. "Today in Watling Street, for all of us. And then he showed his own in comparison. Even those brutes you've recruited realized that his is far better. But I wouldn't worry any – he'll keep you around to raise funds. Can't have enough of those."

"Nichols knows *nothing*!" he hissed. "He has no *vision*!"

"I'd say that he sees exactly what needs to be done," I responded. "He told us what he has planned after the Prime Minister – one of them after another, without end. His plan – "

"*His plan?*" he shrieked, and I sensed that he was suddenly at a breaking point. "He knew nothing until I allowed him to enter into my councils – "

"Speaking of that," I interrupted. "It seems as if your organization is a bit thinner than I was led to believe. You and Nichols? Who else, besides those brutes in Watling Street?"

"Raymond Wright," he snarled. "And John Devereaux of the Foreign Office, and Colin Fraser as well. They have supported me from the beginning."

Excellent, I thought. And concerning as well. Hanover had just named a prominent banker, a Foreign Office Under-Secretary, and a cabinet secretary.

"But Nichols' plan – " I prodded.

"What does someone like him know of a *plan*? *I* was the one bold enough to suggest killing Gladstone. *I* was the one who understood how the Royal Family must be removed, and it was *me* who comprehended the way to send them to Hell where they belong! Nichols is *nothing* – Without me, he would already be dead. Without *me* – !" And then he turned, raising his hands and lunging in my direction, grabbing my coat and trying to shake me, his rage now out of control.

With a lurch the cab turned out of the traffic and stopped abruptly. The driver jumped down and then reached up, pulling apart the low front doors holding us inside. He grabbed Hanover's collar and, with a great heave, pulled the man off me, propelling him out and backwards onto the pavement, where he landed heavily and with a cry.

"I trust that you're uninjured," said Sherlock Holmes, who had been our driver.

"I didn't recognize you," I grunted, climbing out and straightening my clothes. "This was a better plan than you following along behind us."

As I spoke, several other hansoms and growlers pulled to a stop around us, and several policemen, including Inspector Bradstreet, disembarked, solely for the purpose of taking Hanover back into custody.

"Could you hear?" I asked Holmes as Bradstreet joined us.

"For the most part. Your testimony will be more effective than mine."

I shook my head. "I doubt that he will stand trial. I believe the man is teetering on the edge of insanity."

"Well, you can testify at Nichols' trial then. That was rather brilliant, by the way – nudging him with increasing evidence that his grip on The True Knights was evaporating, along with betrayal by his trusted lieutenant."

I started to sarcastically suggest that perhaps acting was in my future, but Bradstreet spoke first.

"This was all a bit too coincidental for my liking," he said. "If Hanover hadn't gotten himself arrested last night, and if your tosher hadn't found that ring, their plans might have been successful."

Holmes started to speak, but I interrupted. "Holmes spoke earlier of Fate taking a hand and nudging things in the right direction. Perhaps that's sometimes the best we can hope for."

"I would prefer something a bit more definite," commented the policeman.

Holmes nodded. "As would I. But at least we can be prepared to take advantage of opportunities when they present themselves – and find ways to be more vigilant as well. We can but try."

He looked up the street toward Mrs. Brett's coffee shop, long a favorite location. "Watson, I believe that before your improvisation with Mr. Hanover began – " He glanced toward the man, now handcuffed and raving as he was placed into one of the police vehicles. " – you directed me to the coffee shop in Portman Mansions. Shall we continue that way and have some breakfast?" He turned to Bradstreet. "Inspector, if one of your men could return the cab to its owner – he'll be waiting in Bow Street – it would be our pleasure if you would join us."

Bradstreet smiled. "That would suit me down to the ground."

It suited me as well, and soon the hot coffee was insulating us from the cold late-November morning. Yet even as we sat there, I could still smell the slightest hints of the Bow Street sewers hanging in my old garments, and I looked forward to returning home in nearby Baker Street and finding a chance of clothes.

NOTE

*   For more about Holmes's first meeting with Sir Joseph Bazalgette, see "The Civil Engineer's Discovery" in *The Collected Papers of Sherlock Holmes – Volume III* (MX Publishing 2021) or *Sherlock Holmes: Stranger Than Truth* (Belanger Books 2021)

Dead Man's Hand
by Robert Stapleton

In all the years I was acquainted with him, I never knew Mr. Sherlock Holmes to refuse assistance to any victim of a cowardly attack, even if this brought him into confrontation with the most violent and unprincipled criminals in London.

Such was the case that morning in the middle of Baker Street.

We were returning from an errand to Scotland Yard, and had just alighted from our hansom across the road from Number 221. Our attention was immediately attracted by a commotion, as two men were submitting one another to a noisy and vicious physical onslaught.

The victim lay on his back in the street, with his top-hat rolling in the gutter.

I immediately laid about the nearest thug with my sturdy Malacca, while Holmes squared up to the other attacker, ready to knock seven bells out of him.

With the tables now turned on them, the two assailants revealed their cowardly natures by turning tail, climbing into a waiting four-wheeler, and driving off in great haste, leaving their victim lying in the dust.

"That was curious, do you not you think?" asked Holmes.

"What was curious?"

"The fact that they fled so readily."

We picked up the fallen man, retrieved his top-hat, and dusted down his long black frock-coat. Then we took him inside and up to our rooms. The fellow was so dazed from his rough handling that he made no objection to being led into our sitting room and being seated before the fireplace.

As Holmes collected our decanter of brandy, our landlady appeared in the doorway, looking concerned and carrying a bowl of hot water, while I commenced a thorough examination of our man. He was tall and slim, with dark hair and trim goatee beard.

After several minutes of my careful ministrations, he looked around with urgent eyes.

"You must take it easy," I told him. "You've had a nasty blow to the head, resulting in profuse bleeding. Dramatic, but fortunately not serious. It's a good job we came along when we did."

When I had finished bandaging the man's head, Holmes offered him a glass of brandy and sat himself down on another chair facing him.

"I see you are a Frenchman," said Holmes.

The man raised his eyebrows in surprise.

"And that you have been in this country for only a short while – perhaps only a day or two. And that you are in search of something of great value."

"How can you tell so much about me?" asked the visitor. His accent showed that Holmes's initial assessment of his nationality had been correct.

"Simplicity itself, Monsieur. The cut of your clothes shows you to be from the Continent. They immediately indicate that you are a man of importance, and that you are here on business. What more pressing business could there be than a personal matter?"

"True enough."

"The fact that you sought my door suggests that you consider the matter pressing."

"Then you really are Sherlock Holmes." The man's face lit up. "I'm so relieved to have found you."

"The man who is attending to you is my friend and colleague, Dr. John Watson."

The Frenchman smiled his gratitude.

"Now," said Holmes, "you need to tell us the nature of your business here."

Our visitor looked down at his hands, and tried to concentrate. "Where shall I begin?"

"Perhaps by giving us your name."

"Naturally. I am Henri, Comte de Sancoubrey, and I am searching for something that was stolen from a relative of mine many years ago."

"Something personal?"

"Extremely so."

"Pray continue, your Grace."

"My great-grandfather – for that is how he is related to me – while serving with the army of Napoleon Bonaparte, was slain on the battlefield of Waterloo in Belgium. His horse was shot from beneath him, and he was quickly finished off by an English bayonet."

"But that was seventy years ago. Almost to the month."

"Indeed, so all I have had to go on is family gossip."

"Hardly the most trustworthy of sources," commented Holmes. "But pray continue."

"It seems that while his body lay unburied upon the battlefield, somebody removed an item of great importance from it."

We both looked on with profound curiosity. "And what was that?"

"His left hand."

336

"Interesting," said Holmes. "And do you have any idea what became of the hand?"

"That has been the abiding mystery in my family for all these years, Mr. Holmes," said the Frenchman. "The man who took the hand must have been a member of the victorious British army, serving under the Duke of Wellington."

"But why has this become such an issue now?" asked Holmes. "After so many years have passed."

"It was my own decision, Mr. Holmes. I realized that if I did nothing to resolve this issue now, then it would remain a mystery forevermore. I therefore began to use all my contacts and influences to discover what really happened to that hand."

"Just the hand?"

"That is all I am looking for."

"So what lay behind the attack made upon you out in the street just now? And why did those men flee so quickly when challenged?"

De Sancoubrey appeared embarrassed by the question. "They are cowards. My search for the missing relic of my great-grandfather has led me to encounter some particularly unsavory characters. Those men wanted to know the location of the hand, but I was quite unable to tell them."

"Mysterious," replied Holmes as he thought deeply about the matter. "Which suggests that perhaps you haven't revealed the entire matter to me. You are holding something back."

"What more do you wish to know, Mr. Holmes?"

"Only the thing that you are hiding from me."

After a tense pause, the Count leaned forward. "Will you help me, Mr. Holmes, or do I have to find somebody else who will assist me in my search for the missing hand of my relative?"

"I am inclined to refuse your request," growled Holmes, "on the grounds that you haven't furnished me with all the facts. But the mystery intrigues me. On consideration, I think that I shall accept your request for help, but be assured that, as a private consulting detective, I shall charge the appropriate rate for my services."

"Of course."

"Now, can you at least tell us how far your research has taken you?"

"I am happy to do that," said De Sancoubrey. "Since my ancestor's regiment was known to us, together with the elite cavalry unit to which he belonged, I thought I might be able to identify the regiment of foot that opposed the French attack on that part of the battlefield."

"But the man who took the hand might not have been the one who killed him."

"That is certainly possible, Mr. Holmes, but I had to follow up the only lead I possessed."

"With what result?"

"In Paris, I came across an expert on the Battle of Waterloo. He gave me the names of two men I should consult in London. One was yourself, Mr. Holmes. The other goes by the name of Aloysius Clark."

"Watson?"

"I'm already looking up the fellow," I told him from my place at our shelf of reference books. "Ah, yes, here he is. Aloysius James Clark. He is the proprietor of a small museum dedicated to the battle itself, and is an expert generally on the wars against Napoleon. His address places him at Carlington Green, Richmond."

"Have you already been to see him?"

Clark shook his head.

Holmes stood up. "Then we must pay this man a visit. But first we must at the very least warn him of our intention to visit him later this morning."

Mr. Clark was already standing at the front door of his home when we arrived. Holmes introduced each of us in turn, but our host seemed particularly impressed to have a member of the French nobility to visit him, even with his head wrapped in bandages.

"Welcome, gentlemen," Clark said. "You will have to forgive my casual attire. I'm not used to having so many visitors descend upon me in one morning."

"It is good of you to see us at such short notice, Mr. Clark," said Holmes, "but our visitor from France is anxious to pursue his investigation without delay."

Clark gave us a questioning look. "How exactly may I assist you, gentlemen?"

Count Henri explained. "I am looking into certain events which took place immediately following the Battle of Waterloo. With you being an expert on the subject, I have naturally come to consult you on the matter."

"Naturally. Then you had better come with me to my museum," said Clark, leading us down a flight of steps to the basement. "Here is my little repository of artefacts and information concerning the Battle of Waterloo, which was fought in June 1815 between the French Emperor's troops and the British Army, ably assisted by the timely arrival of Marshal Blucher's Prussians."

The museum was impressive. Maps and illustrations covered the walls of that underground room, and in the middle stood a table with a model of the battlefield laid out illustrating the turning point of the entire affair.

338

"Now," said Clark, "please tell me more."

"It is a matter of record in our family," said Count Henri, "that my great-grandfather fell on the battlefield there. But, when his body was returned to the family after the battle, they discovered that something was missing from the body. His left hand had been cut off at the wrist. *Post mortem*, I would hasten to add."

"That is a grisly tale," returned Clark, "but after all this time, wherein lies the urgency?"

"As you say, all this took place a long time ago, so that anybody who still remembers the events of those days will be of a great age now. Consequently, time is short if I am to conclude my investigations."

"And you wish me to consult my extensive collection of records. Is that your intention?"

"That is certainly my hope."

"But with what purpose?"

"I wish to identify the person who took the hand and, if possible, to retrieve that missing item from the person who stole it, so that it can be laid to rest along with the body."

"Intriguing," commented Clark. "In that case, it will be the identity of the particular British soldier involved that you are looking for."

"That is indeed my next step."

"Since I received your telegram," continued Clark, "I have undertaken a little preliminary investigation into the matter. From the brief description you gave me, I've managed to identify the British regiment that was operating on that section of the battlefield. We have no way of knowing who killed your ancestor, but further investigation has come up with an intriguing lead concerning the missing hand. With so many corpses having to be identified and removed, a large number of wooden coffins had to be constructed. One of our soldiers later put in a request for a much smaller box – with ample space for a human hand. There may of course be any number of explanations for this, and the carpenters were so busy at the time that they had no occasion to ask about details. But it remains in the records as an unexplained oddity. However, I have discovered a name mentioned in the records at the time: A fellow called Jotham Kidd."

"That could well be the man we are looking for," I suggested.

"Perhaps," said Holmes, "but we need solid facts to go on."

"That name is a solid enough fact for me, Mr. Holmes," said Count Henri. "We have little choice but to follow up on it."

"But I must caution you, gentlemen," added Clark. "These records date back seventy years. If you could ever locate Jotham Kidd, the chances are that he will have been in his own grave for many years now."

339

"And yet he may have family who are still alive," I said.

"True."

"As His Grace has pointed out, Mr. Clark," said Holmes, "we need to follow up on that information. Do you have an address for Jotham Kidd?"

Clark remained strangely silent.

"Mr. Clark," repeated Holmes, "am I correct in concluding that somebody else has been asking about this man?"

"How can you tell?"

"Deduction from what you said earlier about being busy this morning, and the fact that you are reluctant to tell me."

Clark nodded. "Two men. Foreigners. They came here much earlier this morning."

"And their names?"

"I am sworn to secrecy on that matter, Mr. Holmes."

"You say they were foreigners," said Count Henri.

"Indeed. They spoke much like yourself, Your Grace."

"Then they were Frenchmen," concluded Count Henri. "Were they brothers? And were their names perhaps Jean and Hubert Clemice?"

Clark coughed. "I see I have no need to break the promise I gave them."

"What more can you tell us?" asked Holmes.

"You have to understand, Mr. Holmes, that these two men gave me a handsome payment to obtain that address in double-quick time. And to remain silent about it afterwards."

"So you paid a visit to the War Office in Whitehall earlier today."

"Again. How can you know that, Mr. Holmes?"

"The bottoms of your trousers are showing signs of white dust – more precisely, dust associated with Portland Limestone, the kind being cut in Dorset to build and repair so many of the public buildings in London. Since such building work is currently being undertaken in Whitehall, employing precisely this kind of stone, then it is reasonable to conclude that you paid a visit to that locality recently."

"But why are you so sure I was there this morning?"

"That is simplicity itself, Mr. Clark. If this dust had been left on your clothing overnight, somebody this morning, perhaps yourself or your wife, would have employed a clothes brush to remove such an obvious sartorial disorder prior to your leaving home this morning."

"Since you already know the truth," said Clark, "then I wouldn't be betraying any confidences if I refrained from replying. But since the money was already in my hand, I was committed to helping the men. I made contact with a colleague of mine who works at the War Office, and

340

he supplied me with the address I needed. They keep all their old records with meticulous care. He and I agreed to split the money between us."

"In that case," said Holmes, "are you able to supply us with that address?"

"As a matter of fact, I have the address right here," said Clark. "And I am more than willing to let you have it, but whether it is still relevant to your investigation, or whether the man has moved on, or has died, I shall have to leave you to discover."

"And the address?"

"Goodluck Manor, in Leicestershire."

"Quite propitious," commented Count Henri.

"Then let us hope it lives up to our expectations," concluded Holmes.

The following morning, Count Henri was feeling much recovered from his head injury, and felt able to accompany Holmes and myself to Goodluck Manor in the Midland county of Leicestershire. At first sight, the building appeared to be much the same as any other country house: Solid, large, and rambling. Closer examination revealed that money had undoubtedly been expended on the building, with added rooms, details, and embellishments.

As we stood together in front of the main entrance doorway, I tugged on the bell-pull and was rewarded by a loud bell jangling somewhere deep inside.

A moment later, the sound of footsteps resulted in the door being opened, to reveal a man in his late-middle years standing on the threshold: The butler. His expression betrayed the fact that he hadn't been expecting us.

"Do you have an appointment?" he asked.

"No," said Holmes. "We are hoping to find any living relative of Mr. Jotham Kidd."

The butler's countenance returned to its normal, impassive expression.

"Please come inside," he told us, "and I shall find the mistress."

He escorted the three of us into a front reception room, where we stood waiting to discover what might transpire. The room felt cold, and the blue decorations added nothing to the uncomfortable feeling I had from being in such an austere place.

Once more the door opened, but this time a tall, elegant young woman entered. I was taken aback by her beauty, as indeed were my two companions, although Holmes would never have admitted to the fact.

"I am Adelaide Kidd," she said, casting her cold eyes round at us. "How may I help you, gentlemen?"

341

"My name is Sherlock Holmes," my friend informed her. "These gentlemen with me are my friend, Dr. John Watson, and our visitor from France – Henri Comte de Sancoubrey."

Miss Kidd looked around at each of us in turn as she pushed a lock of her dark-brown hair from her face. "Ashbourne, the butler, tells me you are here to inquire after my grandfather."

"If your he is indeed the late Jotham Kidd."

"You appear to be misinformed," said the young lady. "I can assure you that my grandfather is still very much alive – though maybe for not much longer, considering his advanced years."

"He must be over ninety years of age by now," said Holmes.

"Ninety-five, to be precise, Mr. Holmes."

"Then may we be allowed to speak with him?"

"What exactly do you wish to talk with him about?"

"Waterloo."

The young woman nodded. "After so much time? Well, I suppose you had better come along with me and meet him. Although what he might choose to tell you will be entirely up to him."

"Quite so."

With a rustle of crinoline, Miss Kidd led the three of us out into the corridor and along a passage to a doorway situated toward the rear of the building. There she knocked on the door, and entered.

We followed.

I have visited many a sick room during the course of my medical career, and not a few to see people who were nearing the end of their lives, but I have to admit this was a refreshing change. Drapes covered much of the walls, so that our voices sounded somewhat muffled. An open fireplace occupied one wall, with a pair of crossed swords mounted above it. Where these might have come from was open to speculation. A French window on one side of the room stood slightly ajar, so that the air in the room felt fresh and carried the smell of the countryside with it. The room itself was large, and filled with daylight, bearing none of the usual depressive atmosphere of a sickroom. Apart from the bed. This solid wooden structure was situated at one side of the room, and in it lay a figure propped up into a sitting position by a stack of pillows piled up him. He was an elderly man. His face looked thin, with the skin drawn tight across the skull. The hands were twisted with rheumatism, and the thin skin was the color of parchment, tarnished with age-spots, and with blue blood vessels standing out on the surface.

"You have some visitors to see you, Grandfather," said the young woman as she straightened the pillows behind the old man and laid him once more against them.

342

"Visitors? Whatever do they want?" he shot back, glaring up at us. Then he sighed. "Very well, I suppose they had better get on with it."

We gathered around the bed and introduced ourselves.

Count Henri took center stage in the questioning.

"According to my investigations," he explained, "you must be Jotham Kidd. You served as a sergeant with the British forces deployed against Napoleon Bonaparte and his French army at the Battle of Waterloo in 1815."

The old man nodded slowly. "There is no point in trying to deny the fact."

"And from that battlefield, you carried away with you a trophy."

Old Jotham Kidd fixed the Frenchman with his steely gray eyes. But said nothing in reply.

"It was the hand of an ancestor of mine," the Frenchman continued. "My great-grandfather, to be precise. You severed the hand from his dead body and took it away with you."

"There were many trophy-hunters on that field of battle, Monsieur le Comte," replied Jotham Kidd, "and some treated the remains of the dead with far less respect than I did. But be assured, I wasn't the man who killed your ancestor. I discovered him as I led my men away from that field of slaughter. He was already dead. We all considered ourselves extremely lucky to have escaped with our own lives that day."

"That isn't the issue, Mr. Kidd," said Count Henri.

"Then what exactly is the issue?"

"My great-grandfather has lain in his grave for the last seventy years with part of his body missing. After such a long time, the family and I wish to reunite the two."

"You wish me to give the missing hand to you. Is that correct?"

"Indeed."

"That sounds simple enough," opined Holmes, who until then had remained unusually quiet, "but there is something in this business that neither of you gentlemen is telling me."

Both Kidd and Count Henri turned their attention to Holmes.

"Somewhere in this business there lies a secret element," he continued.

"How do you come to that conclusion?" growled Kidd.

"Ever since I first heard the story of the missing hand, as told by His Grace here, I have had the feeling that the main point is missing. I ask myself, 'What is kept upon a hand?' Again I ask myself, 'Why would anyone wish to steal such a hand?' The answer is always the same: A ring."

Kidd stared at Holmes, as though expecting him to say more.

Which he did. "But first of all, Mr. Kidd, we need to find the box in which you placed the hand that you took from that dead man. Can you tell us where it is now?"

"No, I cannot do that."

"Why ever not?"

"A great deal of water has passed beneath the bridge since 1815. I no longer have possession of the box and its contents. The responsibility of looking after it was taken over by my son, Michael – that is, Adelaide's father."

The young woman's face took on a grim aspect as she added, "And my father went missing."

"Missing? How long ago was that?"

"It must be ten years ago now," she replied. "I was only twelve at the time that my father absented himself from our home, and he hasn't been seen since. But I remember him very clearly. He told me he was going on an adventure. At first I was excited for him, but then, when he failed to return, I fell into a deep depression from which I haven't yet fully recovered. After that, I buried myself in the life of the Manor here, and in looking after my grandfather."

We all looked to the old man in the bed. "Do you have any idea what happened to the box, Mr. Kidd?" Holmes asked him.

"None at all. But I feel certain that it didn't leave this house."

"I am sure you are right, Grandfather," said Miss Kidd. "It must be hidden within the building somewhere."

There was clearly considerably more going on in this affair than we had first imagined.

"Miss Kidd," said Holmes. "Where was your father in the habit of spending his time when he lived in this house?"

"One place in particular, as far as I remember," she replied. "The library."

"Then we must begin our search there. Lead on, Miss Kidd."

Leaving the old man, the young woman led the way to the well-stocked library. I looked around, bemused by the array of volumes. Where to begin? But Holmes had no doubts. At once, he began to search the rows of books.

Then he stopped. "All of these books are typical of a modern professionally arranged library."

"I remember that a professional librarian came in here when I was very small," said Miss Kidd. "I was fascinated watching him work."

"The books also possess numbers identifying them," continued Holmes, "so that if you want to find any particular book, you only have to visit the index in order to locate its place upon the shelves. But here the

344

tops of the books aren't on the same level, and neither is the numbering system in order. These books have been pulled out, and replaced without due care."

"But could that really have happened all those years ago, without it ever being put straight again in the meantime?" I asked.

"Since my father left, we have rarely ventured into this part of the house," said Miss Kidd, "so it is certainly conceivable."

Holmes then proceeded to pull out the offending volumes to reveal a brick wall behind them.

Someone had to take up the challenge to investigate what lay there, and it was Count Henri who volunteered. He rolled up his sleeve and plunged his right arm into the darkness behind the bookshelves. For several minutes, he used his sharp knife to scrape away at the mortar between the bricks. Eventually he pulled away first one brick, and then another, and laid them both down on the floor. The Frenchman then reached into the dark void left by the brickwork and pulled out a wooden box. It measured approximately eighteen inches in length by twelve in both height and width, and had a tightly fitting lid.

"I can hardly imagine this box has been lying here untouched for the last seventy years," said Count Henri.

"I am quite sure it hasn't," said Holmes. "Would you care to open the box so we can see what exactly lies within?"

Holding the box in one hand, Count Henri looked around at us and gave a nervous smile.

We all watched on in eager expectation as he pulled away the lid.

Inside the open box, we saw a black leather glove – and something else.

"Is that the glove that belonged to your ancestor?" Holmes asked him.

"That is hard to determine," said Count Henri. "But it certainly appears to match the one I saw in a painting of my great-grandfather that now hangs in our *château*."

Holmes nodded. "I think we need to consult the one man who is able to tell us more – Miss Kidd's grandfather."

Upon our return to the old man's bed-chamber, we once more gathered around the bed and showed him what we had discovered.

"Of course. My son must have hidden it in the library."

"You aren't surprised?" said Holmes.

"Not really. It is the sort of thing he might have done."

"A workman needs to come and repair the damage," said Holmes. "Unless, of course, you wish first to return the box to its hiding place."

"That will not be necessary," came a voice from the far side of the room.

We all turned to face the open French window. There, silhouetted against the daylight, we saw three men. Two of these were the men Holmes and I had confronted the previous day in the middle of Baker Street – the men who had attacked Count Henri, and whom we had sent packing. One of the men was wrapped in a voluminous coat, and wore a shapeless black hat on the back of his head. The second man, who remained in the background, wore a short jacket, a straw boater hat, and carried a black ebonized walking cane. The third man slipped almost unnoticed back outside.

"Jean Clemice," breathed Count Henri.

"Indeed," replied the more prominent of the two as he removed a handgun from his coat and turned it toward the man lying in the bed. "And you remember my brother, Hubert." He nodded toward the second man. "We arrived here much earlier, but we wanted to allow you to find the box before we made our presence known. We were sure that Mr. Holmes would be able to locate it for us. We were also confident that the old chatterbox, Clark, would never be able to keep his mouth shut."

"It is as I imagined," said Holmes. "That performance in the street yesterday morning was entirely for my benefit, in order to arouse my curiosity and make sure that I turned up here today."

Jean Clemice confirmed the matter by giving a sneering grin.

"I wondered when you were going to turn up again," said Count Henri. "I suppose you have come for the box."

"No," said Jean Clemice. "Merely the contents." The man looked around at the gathering. "Where is it?"

"I have it," replied Holmes, holding out the wooden box.

Jean Clemice snatched the box from his hand, and wrenched open the lid. From inside, the man took out the glove that we had seen earlier. It was a leather gauntlet of a large size which fitted the left hand. This agreed with the Count's assertion about the loss of the left hand of his ancestor on the field of battle. Around the ring finger of the glove sat a ring, made extra-large in order to fit over the gloved hand. It carried a jewel, an emerald of impressive size.

We all gazed at the ring.

"And this is what you here came for?" asked Holmes.

"No, it most certainly is not what we came for," growled Jean Clemice. He then withdrew the glove from the box, and pulled it back to reveal its contents. A mummified human hand, with skin even more diaphanous than that of Jotham Kidd himself. This grizzly object held the attention of each one of us. Jotham Kidd watched on with narrowed eyes. Miss Kidd covered her mouth in horror. And I, though no stranger to

346

seeing human remains, felt spell-bound by the sight. Even Holmes watched on with a detached fascination.

It was Jean Clemice who broke the silence. "Well, where is it?"

"Where is what?" demanded Count Henri.

"You know very well what I mean. There. The ring finger. It's bare. The ring isn't on it."

A chilling silence followed as all eyes turned to the man on the bed.

Kidd's eyes glared back at Jean Clemice. "You didn't think you were going to get your hands on it so easily, did you? Thieves! Pirates! Brigands! That's what you are. You have no right to the treasure. Any argument on that subject, if indeed there is one, is entirely between the Count and myself."

The old man turned to his granddaughter. "Adelaide, kindly bring me my pillow."

With a knowing nod, the young woman reached behind her and collected a large white pillow, which she then carried to the old man and placed into his arms.

As Miss Kidd stood back, Jean Clemice tossed the box aside, snatched hold of her, and leveled his gun at her head.

"The matter is now simplified," he growled "Tell me where the true ring is, or I shall blow her brains out."

"Take your filthy hands off my granddaughter, you monster!" croaked Jotham Kidd. "Drop your gun, or I shall kill you where you stand."

Clemice laughed as he turned both his attention and his gun away from the woman and toward the bed.

During that brief moment when the gunman was turning, Jotham Kidd lowered the pillow in his lap, to reveal a gun in his hand. It was one of the ancient military holster pistols, but of the later type, fitted with a copper powder detonation cap. Kidd immediately squeezed the trigger, and the pistol roared, sending a round ball into the middle of the gunman's chest.

Carrying an expression of intense surprise, Jean Clemice dropped to the floor like a stone.

I hurried over to him, just as his lifeblood was ebbing away onto the stone floor.

It had been a matter of self-defense on the part of Jotham Kidd, and we all recognized that.

Or most of us did.

The slain man's brother, Hubert, let out a loud cry and ran over to the body of his sibling, thrusting me to one side. Then, with eyes on fire, and a heart burning with rage, the man seized his walking-cane and withdrew from it a long and sharp sword. With this, he approached the man in the bed, as though determined on running him through.

While Hubert Clemice was struggling with his rage, Jotham Kidd looked at Count Henri, and then up to the crossed swords mounted above the fireplace. The French Count read the message in the old man's eyes and grasped hold of one of the swords. To the amazement of all, he managed to pull it away from its place on the wall with little difficulty.

With this weapon, Count Henri took his place between Clemice and the sickbed, so that the two swordsmen now faced each other.

Clemice lashed out with his steel blade. Count Henri used his blade to parry the attack, and then went himself on the offensive. Clemice stood back so that the other man's blade swung wide of its target. Both men seemed quite familiar with the art of swordsmanship, and the sharp sound of steel clashing with steel filled the room. The sword-fight progressed, with first one and then the other seizing the advantage. In time, it was Clemice who proved the better swordsman, and, as Count Henri showed signs of tiring, his attention was distracted by the door opening and the butler coming into the room. In that instant, Clemice made a move that showed him to be the more proficient and level-headed of the two. He sliced into the other man's forearm, forcing Count Henri to drop the sword, and retreat to the other side of the room.

With the quickness of a lightning bolt, Adelaide Kidd hurried over to him, and threw herself into his blood-stained arms, protecting him from any further injury. The Count had proven himself to be her hero.

Within the space of a heartbeat, Holmes picked up the dropped sword, and turned to face Hubert Clemice. Again the swords clashed. Within seconds, he had disarmed his opponent and stood with the tip of his sword pressed against the other man's throat.

Clemice visibly wilted in defeat.

"You are a better swordsman than I am, Monsieur," he admitted.

Without turning to him, Holmes called upon the newly arrived butler to send for the local constabulary.

In the meantime, the third man outside had vanished.

With the butler pointing a blunderbuss at the defeated swordsman, and Miss Kidd focusing her attention onto Count Henri's injured arm, all other eyes turned to the man in the bed.

"Jotham Kidd," growled Holmes, "I believe you owe us an explanation."

Kidd dropped his gun and looked up at him. "Very well. As you already know, I was the one who cut off the hand of the Count's great-grandfather. People were looting the bodies of other men. It was the thing that victors did after such a victory. I wouldn't have bothered otherwise, only I was attracted by the ring on the glove. So I quickly cut off the hand at the wrist. I had a suitable container constructed, an almost airtight wooden box, and I kept the gloved hand inside that box. I took the hand back home with me, as a grizzly memento of that atrocious battle. I later examined it in greater detail and discovered the other ring – the one which appeared to give the location of a hidden hoard: A treasure of great worth."

"That's right," added Count Henri. "A store of valuables had been collected by my family before the Revolution, and again during the many other conflicts into which Bonaparte led us. My family kept their heads by moving to Austria. Later, they returned and increased their wealth. But after my great-grandfather's death, they could never find the resting place of those valuables, though they searched for many years. It was clear that the key to their location had to lie in that missing ring. But others also learned about the treasure."

"The Clemice brothers."

"Just so. They pretended to be friends of the family, but they were working only for their own interests."

"But Jotham Kidd managed to locate the resting place of those riches," said Holmes.

"I kept that ring for many years," Kidd explained. "I was curious about the inscription, and managed to decipher it. It gave a map reference to a place in southern France. I can no longer remember the name of the town, but the ring led me to believe that the treasure was hidden in a vault beneath the church. My memory fails me concerning the details, but I remember that I traveled there and found the treasure. I took only a portion, and left."

"How did you gain access to the vault, Mr. Kidd?" Holmes asked him.

"I failed to mention before that I also took something else from the corpse – an official document which identified him. That document was proof enough for the priest to lend me the key to the vault and allow me to go down there. In my youth, I had received some training as a locksmith, so I was able to take a wax impression of the key. I made a replica which I placed in the box alongside the glove."

"So that if ever you decided to return, you would never again need to trouble the priest," concluded Holmes.

"Indeed," Kidd continued. "But I remember there was great danger there. That was sixty years ago now, and my memory is failing. But I know that many years after my own visit, my son, Adelaide's father, decided to go after more of the treasure. He was greedy. He studied the ring and he

349

took the key, and made his plans without consulting me. He went but never returned. If he'd told me, I could have warned him – about the danger."

"What danger?"

"With the passage of time, the details have faded from my mind. Some things I remember, Others I have forgotten. But I do remember there is real danger lurking there."

"Where?"

"In that vault."

"And the ring," Holmes demanded. "You made a point of saying the ring was studied, but the key was taken. Where is the ring now?"

Kidd turned his eyes upon his granddaughter. She reached behind her head, unhooked a fastening, and pulled her necklace from her bosom, together with the attached ring. This she removed it and held it out to Holmes, who took it and began to examine it through his magnifying glass.

"Why did you never go in search of your father, Miss Kidd?"

"My grandfather said it was too dangerous. I could never locate the reference on any map, and he refused to help me."

"Then let us take a look."

In the library, Holmes laid out a variety of maps on France. "The mystery lies in the fact that the Prime Meridian as recognized by the French passes through Paris – at least, until last year – so that it runs a couple of degrees east of the Greenwich meridian. If we use the Paris Meridian as our reference point, we can identify the place your grandfather visited: Cluce-le-Pont."

Miss Kidd nodded. "I was simply using the wrong reference longitude."

"Of course," said the old man a few minutes later. "I remember it now. But there is danger there."

"All memory of that village had been entirely lost to our family," added Count Henri.

Holmes looked around at all of us. "How do you feel about a trip to the Continent? The south of France, perhaps."

Looking down at the fallen Clemice brothers, Count Henri said, "We need to deal with these men first."

"Scotland Yard will take over custody of them," said Holmes, "so long as we each provide a statement of what has happened here today. Then we may leave for France."

The old man seemed to wither before our eyes. Soon he was asleep, dreaming of something the rest of us could only imagine.

Miss Kidd had remained close to Count Henri, and now looked up at him with adoring eyes. "I want to come with you," she declared.

"But your grandfather?"

"I know a nurse who will stay with him until we return."

"*If* indeed we return," added Count Henri. "Remember, your father never returned from his visit there."

"That is precisely why I wish to go," said Miss Kidd. "I need to find out exactly what happened to him."

"Then we must each make our preparations," concluded Holmes. "I see no reason why we need to delay our departure beyond tomorrow."

A groan arose from the bed, and Jotham Kidd awakened and sat up, his eyes staring. "The door! A deathtrap!" he declared. "Beware the door!"

But in spite of our questions, he could tell us nothing more.

For much of our journey from London, Holmes sat in a deep reverie, sometimes watching the countryside, and often enwrapped in tobacco smoke. Having taken a train from there to Dover, a ferry to Boulogne, and an express to the South of France, we finally alighted at the station nearest to our destination. A horse and carriage took us the rest of the way and dropped us off at the only hotel.

After settling into our rooms and enjoying a restorative evening meal, the four of us met to take council together in the lounge.

"The matter seems simple enough to me," said I. "We locate the vault, open the door, and retrieve the treasure."

"If only it could be that simple," replied Holmes.

"Whatever is there to stop us?" demanded Count Henri.

"It's the door, isn't it, Mr. Holmes?" said Miss Kidd. "There is something about the doorway to the vault that worries you. I recall the very last words my grandfather said while you were visiting us. 'Beware the door!'"

"Precisely so. Having studied the ring and attempted to decipher its meaning, I agree with your grandfather in sensing great danger there."

The Count stood up and stretched his long legs. "It has been a tiring day, so I intend to retire early in order to prepare for a new and demanding day tomorrow."

Miss Kidd expressed a similar opinion and departed along with the Frenchman, leaving Holmes and me to make the most of the rest of the evening.

Holmes stood up and reached for his coat. "While it's still light, I shall take a turn around the town."

"And call in at the church, no doubt," I added, following his example and joining him outside in the main street. "After all, we no longer have Kidd's key."

Cluce-le-Pont was a small community nested in a bend of a river. The town was centered on the market square surrounded by civic buildings, a cafe, a couple of shops, and the small church.

Holmes examined the graveyard, taking particular notice of the land on which the church had been built.

"It's too dark to do much here," said a voice from close behind us. We turned round to find Miss Kidd standing not far away. "I couldn't rest," she told us. "If my father really is lying here somewhere, I would like to know as soon as possible."

"But not tonight," replied Holmes. "The daylight has gone."

"I noticed a light on in the presbytery," she countered.

"Then we must disturb the reverend gentleman," concluded Holmes.

As he listened to our tale, the priest's demeanour altered from annoyance at being disturbed to intense interest. He willingly agreed to lend Holmes a lantern so that he alone could enter and wander around the church itself.

He returned not long after, looking satisfied with his investigations, but saying nothing.

Before we left, the priest promised to meet us on the following morning outside the church, and agreed to bring with him the key to the vault of the De Sancoubrey family. But he warned us that there might be a problem with the entrance, adding that he would also bring with him a couple of men whom he called the "Nephilim", or giants, to accomplish any strong-arm activity that might be required.

Before he finally turned to leave, Holmes said, "I would be obliged, Father, if you could also arrange for a crowbar to be available for my use in the morning."

"A crowbar?" came the astonished reply. "Of course."

The four of us returned to the church on the following morning, at the time determined by the parish priest.

He greeted De Sancoubrey warmly.

"It is amazing," said the Count. "All these years, nobody in the family knew about this place. But why do we need to bring these two strong men along with us?" He indicated the two burly fellows who were standing with the priest.

"You will see," replied the priest. "Come."

We followed him round to the side of the church building, where we descended a flight of stone steps down to a lower level. There, hidden among the untamed undergrowth, we came to a halt in front of a solid wooden door which was built into the structure of the building itself. It

352

was braced shut by a large stone block, shaped like a lintel, which was lying apparently unmovable upon the ground.

"Judging by the grass growing up around it, I should estimate that this block of stone has been lying here unmoved for the last ten years," said Holmes. "No less, and perhaps not much longer."

"That would be about the time that my father went missing," declared Miss Kidd, her face now distorted by the horror she imagined lying beyond the entrance. "He must have gone in there, and this stone fell down and blocked his escape."

"Horrible," said I.

"That would be a reasonable deduction to make," concluded Holmes.

"But why couldn't he simply open the door and step over the obstruction?" asked Miss Kidd.

"That we shall have to discover. But first, we have to move the stone."

The priest stood aside, and the two strong men stepped forward. "We can lift it, Father," said one of them.

"Very well," said the priest. "Do whatever you can."

The two Nephilim set about lifting the block. As the stone rose, we heard the rattle of iron chains, indicated that a counterbalance somewhere inside the walls had relaxed its strain. This, together with the efforts of the men, added to the sound of stone grinding against the stone grooves which held it in place on either side of the doorway. Eventually, the men managed to raise the block until it was level with the top of the doorway. The wood of the door was old but not decayed, and it now became clear that it was hinged so that it opened outward.

"That would explain why nobody on the inside would ever be able to open it," Holmes explained.

"How unusual," I replied.

While the two strong men continued to hold the block at head height, Holmes grasped the door-handle, turned it, and pulled the door open. Something inside the stone structure to our left clicked, and the two strong-men felt the weight of the lintel lift from their shoulders. They relaxed.

"Very interesting," declared Holmes. "As you can see, the door is already unlocked. There is no need for the key. Whoever unlocked it last never came out again."

"My father," gasped Miss Kidd.

While we looked at each other, trying to decide who should be the first to venture inside, the young woman proved the most intrepid. She took one of the two lanterns, turned up the wick, and stepped into the darkness, followed closely by Holmes, the French Count, and me. The parish priest and the two men were close behind.

"Where is the danger?" I asked.

"I'm not sure about that," said Holmes, "but whatever you do, make sure you don't close this door."

The underground vault was divided into two parts: First an outer room, and then an inner chamber secured by another heavy door.

The outer chamber contained a small number of stone coffins, each bearing the name of some member of the De Sancoubrey family. None was less than eighty years old.

"A few of my ancestors, lost in the mists of time," declared Count Henri, as Miss Kidd clung to him.

By the light of the two lanterns, and the daylight filtering in through the open doorway, we made a careful search of that chamber but found no sign of any treasure in that part of the vault.

Then we turned to the inner chamber. One of the Nephilim heaved open the inner door and stepped aside.

Adelaide Kidd swallowed hard and stepped into the darkness, followed immediately by the Count.

I went next, only to find Miss Kidd standing stock-still, struck dumb by the horror of what she saw there.

In the light of the lantern she was holding, I looked down and found a skeleton, still dressed in the clothes of an ordinary traveling Englishman. Beside the body lay a solid iron key. "Is that your father, Miss Kidd?"

She clung to Count Henri and nodded.

Indeed. Who else could it be?

It was only now that I noticed Holmes was no longer in the vault with us. Where had he gone? No doubt he was about his own business.

Keeping a respectful distance from the skeleton, we examined the rest of the inner chamber. It was smaller than the outer one, and it contained nothing apart from two wooden trunks. One of these lay open, revealing gold and silver ornaments, many decorated with precious stones – but it looked as if half the contents had been removed.

"My grandfather must have taken the rest of it back home with him," declared Miss Kidd, detaching herself from the Count.

"Then your father came out here," I reminded her, "looking for the rest of the treasure."

"And he found it," she replied, pointing to the second trunk, which Count Henri had now opened, to reveal a box full of similar precious objects.

"Your father found all of this," said the Count, "but it did him no good when he became locked inside. Even with the key."

As he was speaking, we all heard the unmistakable sound of a door slamming shut, and of a heavy weight grinding stone against stone.

354

We hurried back to the entrance, only to find that the wooden door was now closed, and was presumably blocked on the far side by the stone lintel which had once more fallen into the place it had occupied for the previous ten years. We were trapped.

Each in turn, we hammered upon the wooden door, but no answer came. I looked for a door handle, but could find none on that side of the door.

Back in the inner chamber, the young woman stood looking down at the remains of her father. "At least we shall lie here together," she said, with tears sparkling in the flickering lantern light. "Perhaps for all eternity."

"We must not give up all hope just yet," I told her. "After all, Sherlock Holmes is still out there somewhere."

"But what can he do?" asked the priest. "After all, we have the strongest men in the village in here with us, and there is nothing they can do now."

In that blackness, I tried to remember everything I had learned from the years I'd spent with Holmes. I tried to examine the situation logically as I looked around at the solid stone masonry. I was now standing at the far end of the inner chamber, fighting the temptation to give up all hope, when I heard a sound coming from the roof above me. It might have been a crowbar lifting a slab of stone. I looked upward, and watched as daylight gradually began to filter down to illuminate our Stygian darkness.

This noise attracted the others, who hurried to join me in the inner chamber. Then, as we all stood looking upward, a hole appeared in the ceiling, and Holmes's face looked down at us.

"Thank you for the loan of the crowbar, Father," came his encouraging voice. "I knew the vault had to lie directly beneath the north aisle of the church, and last night I managed to establish the most likely spot."

After widening the hole, Holmes reached down and began to help us each in turn to climb out of that pit of horrors. Count Henri himself reached down for Miss Kidd, who paused to look back into the darkness. "We shall have my father's remains removed and buried properly – back at home."

On returning to the outside entrance to the vault, we found a man lying on the ground, tied up and unable to move.

"This is the fellow who shut the door on you," explained Holmes. "He acted as coachman for the Clemice brothers back in Baker Street. He was the third man we saw at Goodluck Manor who slipped away almost unnoticed. This is the third of the Clemice brothers – Vincent Clemice. With his brothers now out of the way, he followed us all the way from London, doubtless intent upon revenge. Did you not see him on the train?"

I shook my head.

We all stared at the man on the ground. How had we failed to realize the truth?

"I was too late to prevent him from locking you all inside," continued Holmes, "and I was unable to raise the stone lintel myself."

He turned to the two Nephilim who sighed and set about the task of once more raising the lintel until it again clicked into place.

Holmes carefully examined the newly opened door. "This really is intriguing," he told us. "Look. You can see a hole in the stone jamb, which corresponds to a metal prong projecting from the wooden door on the edge farthest away from the lock. Although I have no intention of demonstrating it here and now, I believe that when the door is closed, and the projection enters the opening in the stone jamb. Whatever mechanism is holding the stone lintel in place will then release its load, preventing the door from being opened from inside."

"Fiendish," said Count Henri.

"Ingenious," said I.

"But how was my grandfather able to enter and leave without himself being caught by this trap, and entombed inside?" asked Miss Kidd.

"Now that is the really diabolic part of this whole business," replied Holmes. He turned to me. "Look carefully at the door, Watson. Do you not see it? No? Then put your hand on the projection."

"Oh yes," I exclaimed. "It pushes in when I press it. It must have a strong metal spring attached to the inside. And just below the projection, I can feel a metal plate. This seems to be hinged in some manner."

"And your conclusion?"

"You can lift the plate up so that it covers the retractable projection in the door, thus preventing it from entering the hole in the stone jamb when the door is closed."

"Quite so. And preventing it from activating whatever mechanism is hidden within the stonework. In that way, the door can be closed without allowing the stone lintel to fall down and block the entrance."

"But anyone not aware of the trigger mechanism would allow the metal plate to fall," said I, "thus trapping them inside. The building is so solid that any cries for help would not be heard."

"The church and the vault must have been constructed before the Revolution," explained Holmes.

"You are undoubtedly correct, Monsieur," the priest replied. "I knew nothing of this!"

"And at the same time, the family privately constructed this vault beneath the church."

"I suppose," said Count Henri, "we must blame my ancestors for creating such a cunning device to safeguard their riches."

"But they had to issue a warning to the family," said Holmes.

"Hence the message on the ring," concluded Miss Kidd.

"Then the secret and all records of the tomb were lost," I said, "with the only evidence lying upon the battlefield. When Count Henri revealed the existence of the lost ring, others sought access to the tomb as well."

"Now," concluded Holmes, "with the three Clemice brothers out of action, the family may safely retrieve their treasure."

Henri, Comte de Sancoubrey, removed his family treasure from the vault and showed his gratitude toward those who had helped him in his quest. He rewarded the village strong-men handsomely and made a generous donation to the church. He made sure that Adelaide Kidd could return home with a substantial gift for her grandfather, along with the body of her father, who could now be buried with due dignity in the land of his birth.

Holmes refused to accept any reward from the Count, insisting only that he meet the agreed fee, along with the expenses incurred by the two of us during our time assisting the French nobleman in his quest.

The hand, which had been removed from the nobleman's great-grandfather on the battlefield of Waterloo, was returned to the family for burial alongside the man's interred remains in his grave near the *château*. He could finally rest in peace.

It came as no surprise to me when, a couple of months after our return from France, Holmes read the announcement of the death of Jotham Kidd, aged ninety-six years, who had passed away peacefully in his bed. In the same edition, an article gave notice of the betrothal of Miss Adelaide Kidd, and Henri, Comte de Sancoubrey.

"I hope they will be very happy together," I replied.

"As do we all," added Holmes. "And I fancy that Goodluck Manor will shortly be on the market."

"Minus a mummified hand."

"Indeed."

Count Henri made me the gift of a pair of gold cuff-links, each bearing my own initials. My wife insisted that I wear them while penning this tale. A small gesture, but one I am delighted to make.

The Case of the
Wary Maid
by Gordon Linzner

"What's this, Watson?" Holmes started up as we approached our flat in Baker Street that evening. "It appears we have a visitor."

"At this time of night?" I followed his gaze.

The faint glow of a gaslit lamp coming from the first floor of 221b stood out against the thickly clouded night. We were returning from a delightful evening concert by Holmes's favorite violinist, Wilma Norman-Neruda, after a slight detour for a pint at a local pub. Given the late hour, I had expected a swift retire to our respective beds.

Now, however, Holmes was wide awake.

"It's unlikely," I agreed, "for Mrs. Hudson to admit a caller so late into our lodgings, with neither your presence nor approval. Let alone to leave him there on his own."

My right hand instinctively reached under my coat for my revolver, then stopped. Neither of us would have borne a firearm to a peaceful musical evening unless a case was involved. As far as I knew, Holmes had nothing on his current agenda.

"Him . . . or her," Holmes corrected.

I let his pedantry slide. "She certainly wouldn't tolerate such an intrusion by one of your Irregulars, considering her disdain for those urchins. The only exception I can imagine would be a visit from one of Scotland Yard's detectives in need of your abilities. Even then, it's more likely that Inspector Lestrade, or one of his colleagues, would have simply left a message."

"I'm glad to see you exercising your mind, even if you continue to miss the obvious."

"Which is?"

"Let's discover for ourselves, eh?" With that, Holmes entered the premises and immediately started up the stairs, taking them two and three at a time, his footsteps clattering against the wooden surfaces.

"Holmes!" I struggled to keep my voice low. "Our visitor will hear us coming."

"Well, after all, we are expected."

"My point exactly. It could be a trap. You've made quite a few enemies in the past half-decade, and likely more before we even met."

358

"Would an enemy be lurking with the light on?" he called back, throwing open the door to our flat.

My friend was right, as usual. There was no hostile criminal, waiting to vengefully attack Holmes in his own rooms. It was only our landlady, Mrs. Hudson, slumped awkwardly in Holmes's favorite chair. She had obviously fallen asleep, but began to stir at the sound of our arrival.

"Mr. Holmes!" she exclaimed in a low voice. "Doctor Watson!" She covered her lips with a finger as she hurriedly rose, straightening her dress and stretching her back.

"You see, Watson?" Holmes pointed out. "You had all the clues, yet did not reach the obvious conclusion: Our visitor is none other than our beloved landlady herself."

My medical instincts took over. I pushed past Holmes. Mrs. Hudson's expression reflected more than simple surprise and embarrassment.

"My apologies, Mrs. Hudson." I let my concern creep into my words. "Please stay seated. Don't stress yourself on our accounts. I don't recall seeing you this distraught – even when dealing with our Irregulars."

"Indeed," Holmes added. He, too, waved a casual hand to indicate she should settle down again, then took the seat opposite, one normally occupied by myself. I in turn leaned over the back of a chair usually reserved for Holmes's clients.

"I apologize if I have overstepped my boundaries, Mr. Holmes," she said, sitting once more. "Ordinarily I would never intrude on your private quarters in this fashion."

"Not at all. Watson and I have been acquainted with you long enough to know you wouldn't do so without good reason. Normally I would now be asking you to fetch a soothing cup of tea for my client – in this case, yourself. What is your problem?"

Mrs. Hudson shook her head. "I'm not concerned for myself, but about Mrs. Turner."

"The live-in maid you hired last week? I confess I've seen little of her so far."

"She's been helping to catch up on certain duties the previous maid, distracted by her own impending wedding, neglected. A lovely young woman – polite, hard-working, though excessively inclined to keep to herself. I fear she may be in some danger. I've indicated a willingness for her to confide in me, but she has so far ignored my hints."

"What gives you the impression she's at risk?" Holmes's tone reflected my own concern.

Our landlady shrugged. "I've encountered enough of your clients in the past five years to read the signs. After she retired to her room for the evening, I took the liberty of letting myself in here to await your return. I

359

didn't wish her to know I would be speaking to you about her. She was discomforted enough by my curiosity. She often appears so absorbed in herself that I wonder if she even knows what you do for a living."

"One moment, if you please." Holmes rose with a quick nod and strode towards his bedroom.

I leaned toward Mrs. Hudson, who appeared less tense now that she'd started unburdening herself. "He's no doubt gone to retrieve his old black pipe. It helps him concentrate." Holmes might not yet be ready to admit it, but I could tell his interest was piqued. "May I offer you a brandy?"

"I'm not much of a drinker, Doctor."

"It will help you sleep afterwards. Consider it my prescription."

"Well . . . a wee bit, then."

She accepted the glass gratefully. Then, as the evening now promised to last much longer than anticipated, I poured another for myself.

Holmes returned moments later, pipe in hand and draped in a mouse-coloured dressing gown. "Excellent, Doctor. I should have thought to offer some libation myself. None for me, thank you. What I need are details, Mrs. Hudson. If you would be so kind?"

Our landlady took another sip of brandy before replying. "As you noted, Mr. Holmes, the young woman has been in my employ less than a week. We haven't had much time to chat."

"Any little detail can be of help."

"So you have said, more than once." The landlady put down her glass and leaned forward. "Very well. Mrs. Turner lost her husband a month ago in an unfortunate accident. Something involving a stroke, I gathered. Like most young widows, she found herself desperate for money and honest employment. Despite her withdrawn attitude, she possesses a dedicated air which made her stand out among the other housemaids at the agency. In any case, keeping to herself is no less than what most employers expect of their servants. Part of her reticence, I believe, is due to a melancholy sadness, which would be expected from a new widow."

"No doubt that's what led to your hiring her in the first place. Our inevitable kindness. Go on."

"She arrived bearing few possessions: A photograph the couple on their wedding day. A long, gold-colored hatpin gifted her by Mr. Turner's mother. A few items of personal clothing. She didn't even have proper attire for the position. Fortunately, I had retained the uniforms of the previous maid, who no longer needed them. They fit her well enough, though a bit short in the sleeves."

"There may be some clue to her attitude in those belongings. When might be a good time for me to examine them? I promise I shall be discreet."

"We have no regular schedule as of yet. On those occasions when I've needed her to run a brief errand, she took with her a purse containing both that wedding photo and the hatpin. Her life had been so uncertain before I took her on, she seems worried about losing what few heirlooms she still has."

"An understandable reaction to grief," I interjected.

"Quite right," Holmes agreed. "She may also be feeling somewhat confined, spending so many hours in this new and unfamiliar environment. Might I suggest you provide her with a longer break? I can devise a few errands of my own that would keep her out in the fresh air for most of the morning. That might give her a larger sense of freedom."

"And yourself that opportunity to search her room?"

"Actually, no. As it happens, I now have business of my own to attend to tomorrow. I was thinking more in terms her mental health. You agree, don't you, Watson?"

Before I could voice my affirmation, he added, "I shall provide you in the morning with a short list of items I wish her to obtain: Notepads, fresh ink, that sort of thing. Would that suit you?"

"I put up with your indoor target practice and that group of young ruffians," Mrs. Hudson smiled. "I can accede to this request as well, if it helps her."

"Excellent! Would you like another brandy? No? Then I bid you a good night, Mrs. Hudson. I shall see you in the morning."

I escorted the landlady to our door and, once she'd started down the stairs, turned back to my friend.

"Going to bed?"

"Soon enough. I mustn't waste this tobacco." He shifted to his own chair, waved his pipe at me, and fell into a deep fit of contemplation.

I silently went upstairs to my own bedroom. One of us, at least, was determined to get a good night's sleep.

It was hardly a surprise for me to discover, on waking the following morning, that Holmes had already risen and left. Actually, I doubted he had even slept, since his bed looked undisturbed, and he was hardly the tidiest of men.

He left me a note on the dining table, situated between a half-empty cup of cold coffee and a slice of toast barely nibbled on. The content was couched as a request, but of course he assumed I would comply. He also knew I would be more than willing to do so.

In short, he wished me to visit the coroner's office to see what, if anything, I could discover regarding the late Mr. Turner's passing, and take down details of any preliminary *post mortem* report. I was to tell the

361

staff I was doing a bit of medical research in preparation for setting up my own practice, although at that time I had only the vaguest of plans to do so. He further provided half-a-dozen names of other men who had died recently under similar, non-mysterious circumstances, so as not arouse any suspicions regarding our interest in that specific tragedy.

Reading between the lines, I suspected Holmes might be expecting some more-than-superficial connections.

I was pondering my best approach when Mrs. Hudson arrived with my own fresh coffee, along with a more substantial breakfast of eggs and toast.

"How is Mrs. Turner today?" I asked.

"Oh, you should have seen her reaction when I gave her that list of errands from Mr. Holmes. Her eyes lit up at the realization she could be on her own for several hours." After a pause, she added, "I'm not sure if I should be pleased to see her express a modicum of joy, or concerned at the abrupt change in her attitude."

"Would you like me to speak with her, to see if I notice anything amiss? I'm visiting Scotland Yard later this morning, but have some time now to spare."

"I'm afraid Mrs. Turner has already left on those errands. Perhaps you can talk upon her return. Her taciturn attitude did seem to rise a bit again on her way out."

"I'm certain you've no need for concern," I assured her as I reached for my fork. "Mr. Holmes knows what he's doing."

I hoped I'd voiced that opinion with more conviction than I felt.

"What the devil have you been up to?" I growled when my friend finally returned to our rooms that evening. "Mrs. Hudson told me how distraught the maid was when she returned from her errands. So much so that she'd forgotten nearly all of the items you requested."

"I'll address your question in a moment." His tone was grimmer than usual. "Nothing on my list was essential. Had you any luck at the coroner's office?"

"I'm not sure what you expected. Mr. Turner's death was ruled natural, no question. There were some minor peculiarities in the preliminary examination, but not enough to warrant the expense of a full autopsy. I found similarities in a few of the other names you'd provided, as well."

"That isn't as much information as I'd hoped for, but more than I anticipated. I shall need full details of those peculiarities. You did make notes?"

"I'm a medical man, Holmes. I would hardly have dismissed such things out of hand."

"Excellent. In retrospect, I could have used your assistance myself this morning. Or brought along one of the Irregulars. I shall appreciate your accompanying now, however, if you can spare the time."

"Gladly. But what about Mrs. Turner? Mrs. Hudson told me that an elderly clergyman stumbled into her as she started to cross the street, and she almost fell in front of an oncoming hansom. Fortunately, that same clergyman was able to pull her to safety at the last moment. Then he mumbled an apology and took off."

Holmes nodded. "She knows, or suspects, more about her husband's fate than she is willing to share. I fear she wishes to resolve the situation on her own."

"To make matters worse," I added, "she later discovered her prized heirloom, her mother-in-law's hatpin, had disappeared That seemed more distressful to her than nearly being run over. I provided Mrs. Hudson with a small dose of laudanum from my medical kit, to calm Mrs. Turner down."

"If necessary, you may feel free to dip into my cocaine supply as well."

"I trust that will *not* be required." I rose to confront him more directly. "You know all this. The description of that clergyman sounded suspiciously like the disguise you sometimes wear. Ha! That smirk confirms my theory. I assume you changed to regular street clothes in one of your secret flats."

"Guilty as charged. I'm glad to see our relationship has been beneficial to you as well as myself." From an inner pocket, Holmes withdrew a long leather-bound item.

"Is that – ?" I exclaimed.

"Obviously," Holmes replied, unwrapping the hatpin. "Hold this up to the light. Note the numerous faint scratches in the metal, particularly along the tip. Mrs. Turner has honed her beloved heirloom to a razor-sharp keenness, far beyond what is required to keep one's hair in place. Besides, no housemaid would wear such a hatpin while on duty, let alone carry it about wherever she went."

"She was wearing it?"

"Not exactly. She gripped it tightly in her right hand. Most of the object was hidden by her dress sleeve, leaving only the tip exposed. Hardly noticeable unless, like myself, one were looking for such a thing."

"How odd. What do you plan to do with this now?"

"Why, return it, of course. Eventually. Once we have ensured she will not be tempted to attempt murder a second time. The poor woman has suffered enough."

I felt my eyes widen. "Are you telling me she murdered her husband?"

"Of course not! She had a very different target in mind. From my vantage point across the street, I clearly saw her stalking a stocky, middle-aged woman. When she suddenly quickened her pace, and I saw the glint of metal between her fingers, I knew I had to interfere. Had Mrs. Turner succeeded in her attack, in public, she would undoubtedly have been arrested, found guilty, and in all probability executed for murder. If she failed, a more likely outcome, things might turn out even worse – perhaps life in an asylum. She is safe from her own misjudgment for the time being, if sorely frustrated. Nonetheless, she will certainly seek another opportunity if we don't act immediately."

This revelation was almost too much for me to comprehend. "Did you speak to her at all?"

"There was no time. I needed to learn as much about her target as possible. Having secured the would-be weapon and assured myself that Mrs. Turner was, at least physically, safe and well, I hurried after the older woman. I would have preferred adopting a different disguise at that stage, but did not have the option. Fortunately the subject appeared unaware of either my presence or her narrow escape. Now, quickly, Watson – get ready, while I go over your notes. A third party is expecting us."

"Anyone I know?"

"I'll provide more details on the way. I have a cab waiting, and have wasted too much time already. We're about to confront one of the cruelest criminals I've ever encountered. I spent most of the afternoon gathering snippets of information, and changed my disguise twice. I'm hoping your research will fill in one or two more gaps in my knowledge."

Given the seriousness of Holmes's tone, the first thing I did was check that my revolver was loaded.

Our hansom pulled up alongside a tiny hat shop on the corner of Drury Lane at a few minutes past nine that evening. Inspector Gregson stepped forward to meet us, after signaling his two constables to stay back.

"I'm grateful to you, Inspector," Holmes called out, "for agreeing to join us for this evening's inquiry. I doubt my pugilistic skills will prove of much use tonight."

"I owe you more than one favor, Mr. Holmes, although I don't see that this visit will accomplish much." He extended a helping hand as we climbed out of our cab. "I trust your judgment but, if what you say is true, these crimes have been going on for decades, right under Scotland Yard's nose!"

"I too had no idea of these horrors, Gregson," Holmes admitted. "The clues were there, but one had to know to look for them. She's clever, this one. I've uncovered a few more details that should help us in reviewing your archives. At worst, she'll know she's being watched closely. That should save a few lives going forward."

Gregson looked at his pocket-watch. "Half-an-hour, you said?"

Holmes nodded. "If I cannot trick the woman into further revelations in that period, spending more time would wasteful. I've accumulated enough circumstantial evidence that you can at least bring her in for further questioning. As a hostile witness, if necessary."

"My men and I will enter at twenty-to-ten, then, unless we hear otherwise."

"Excellent!"

The shop looked like any ordinary millenary, save that the half-dozen hats displayed in the window appeared exceptionally dusty and unattractive. A salacious wink from Holmes directed the elderly clerk to point us toward a back door. This in turn led us down a narrow corridor lined with near-empty shelves.

A discreet knock on the door at the other end gained us access to an opulent lobby lined with chairs, couches, tables, and numerous young women in scanty disarray. Stairs on either side led to an overhead balcony that circled the room.

"Disgusting," I whispered. "These poor women – "

"Not even the worst of it," Holmes whispered back. He signaled me to be silent as one of the ladies of the night approached, dressed rather more modestly than the others.

"Good evening, gentlemen," she greeted. "Welcome to The Humble Abode. I am your hostess, Kitty. How may we serve you tonight?" Her right hand reached up to rest on Holmes's shoulder.

"I'm afraid our needs are rather specific," my friend responded curtly. "Might we have a word with Madame Amelia Blanchard herself to discuss them?"

Kitty let her hand drop. "I regret to say the Madame is otherwise engaged at present. No callers were expected. In the meantime, I can offer you a full list of our services for your perusal."

Before she could hand over the brochure, a sharp rap came from the balcony, drawing the young lady's attention, and ours as well.

A stocky, middle-aged woman stared down at us, gave a quick nod, then stepped back out of my line of sight.

Kitty stiffened as her voice took on a more businesslike tone. "It appears that Madame Blanchard is prepared to receive visitors, after all. If you gentlemen would follow me?" In a barely audible whisper, she added, "I advise you – accept no food or drink she may offer tonight."

Holmes raised a querulous eyebrow, but our hostess had already away without another word.

We were led up winding stairs to a spacious office on the first floor. There we found Madame Blanchard leaning back in her chair, hands crossed before her thick but not unattractive frame, eyeing us curiously.

"You may leave us, Kitty," she advised as her assistant approached her.

"Yes, Madame." Kitty reached for the brandy bottle on her employer's desk.

"Leave that, as well," she added. "I haven't even had a taste. You already cleared the empty bottle before you brought me this one."

"Apologies, Madame. I was . . . distracted." She cast a wary look our way as she left, which Holmes acknowledged with the briefest of nods.

I struggled to keep my own features as inscrutable as those of my friend. Madame Blanchard, however, paid me little heed.

"Mr. Holmes," she greeted. "It's an honor indeed to have a man of your stature visit my establishment."

Holmes offered a slight bow. "I'm surprised you recognized me, Madame Blanchard. I didn't think my reputation spread this far."

She gave a childish giggle that didn't quite fit her more formal decorum. "I regret to say not all of my staff are as aware as I. My clients come from all walks of life, Mr. Holmes. Many of them have reasons, directly or indirectly, to know of your accomplishments. After a relaxing session, they often become chatty. My girls, in turn, are obliged to tell me everything." She unclasped her hands and leaned forward for emphasis. "*Everything.*"

"A perfect situation for blackmail," I muttered. The woman pretended not to hear.

"I have my sources as well," Holmes countered.

"I'm sure you do." She peered at Holmes through narrowed eyes. "I should like to hear more. My assistant opened this brandy for me moments before your arrival. I was about to pour myself a glass. If you two care to join me – ?"

Holmes shook his head. "I think not."

The woman's lips tightened in anger. "You dare refuse me? I do not make such offers lightly!"

Holmes gave a sharp laugh. "You don't handle rejection well, do you, Madame Blanchard? As a certain Mr. Turner, to name but one gentlemen, recently discovered."

"Who?"

"You say you don't even know their names!" I exclaimed.

Holmes laid a firm hand on my shoulder. "Let her speak, Watson," he murmured.

"Are you implying, Mr. Holmes, that I would kill a stranger over a simple public disagreement?"

"So you do recognize the name," Holmes replied with satisfaction. "Not just one man, Madame. I've had a busy day. In only a few hours, I uncovered at least a dozen deaths over the past year of gentlemen known to have had at least some tenuous connection with this establishment. All but one of those deaths were officially declared either accidents or suicides. Most died from a variety of poisons, from arsenic to strychnine. One allegedly slashed his own throat. Another was said to have leapt – I believe he was more likely pushed – into the Thames. I shall not be surprised to eventually discover gunshots and garroting involved in similar cases, once I dig further. I'm convinced these men were murdered, likely for a variety of petty reasons."

Blanchard rose to her feet, eyes flashing. "You and your friend have outlasted your amusement value. Leave at once, or I shall have you removed."

"You might want to hold off on summoning your bouncer," Holmes replied. "Inspector Gregson of Scotland Yard is standing by outside, along with a pair of patrolmen. You don't want to escalate our friendly little chat, do you?"

Blanchard's face turned deep red beneath her rouge. She sank back into her chair, furious. "What makes you think an innocent businesswoman such as myself would have any connection to such horrid deeds?"

Holmes shrugged. "There, I fear, you may have the better of me. Nonetheless, a few of these victims, having no families to mourn them, became subjects of medical school autopsies. Some of their organs have even been preserved. Certain aspects of those autopsies appeared odd, such as strokes or heart attacks where no previous medical conditions or damaged hearts had been observed, though at the time these did little more than raise an eyebrow – unless one knows specifically what to look for."

"Even if you can prove foul play in their deaths," she replied, "how am I involved? Such flimsy evidence sounds unlikely to stand up in court."

"Not at present, no," Holmes admitted, "but it does point us in the right direction. That being so, I understand that the police would greatly appreciate your assistance with their newly reopened inquiries."

"And if I refuse?"

"They can bring you in as a hostile witness. That won't look good for you."

Her girlish laugh echoed through the room. "I've done nothing wrong. My lawyers will see that your reliance on inane coincidences and uncertain evidence leads to naught. I may even end up suing the Crown."

"Clever as you are, Madame Blanchard," Holmes responded, "now that we know where to look, I believe we will be able to form a solid case."

The woman's expression tightened at his words. "You, of all people, should know better than to confront a mother bear in her den, Mr. Holmes."

"Even if we can't bring you to justice immediately, you are now under the scrutiny of Scotland Yard. You may be a cruel, heartless woman, Madame Blanchard, but you aren't a stupid one. Otherwise you would have been caught long before now. That knowledge alone should, I trust, prevent you from doing away with any more innocents."

She laid her hands flat on the desk, as though conceding. Her tone, however, indicated the opposite.

"Be seated, gentlemen. I have something I wish to share." She opened the top right-hand drawer of her desk.

Wary of her action, I reached under my coat for my revolver.

"Really?" she said, meeting my eyes. "Do you think I have a gun in here, Doctor? That I could take you both down, with a police inspector waiting downstairs, without consequences? You, Mr. Holmes, have already acknowledged my intelligence. Impulsive, I may be. Stubborn, even. Easily annoyed, certainly." She withdrew an envelope and removed from it a small, yellowed piece of notepaper, which she then flattened and pushed in our direction.

"You've accused me of doing away with numerous complete strangers, Mr. Holmes. This is a sketch of my late mother. Crude, admittedly, but I was only six years old when I drew it. Nonetheless, I feel I captured her weary smile and haunting eyes. This is the only memory I have of her: No precious heirlooms, no beloved handkerchief, not even a faded photograph. Her murderer was never brought to justice, though most of her colleagues knew the abuser by sight, if not by name.

"The authorities abandoned me in a particularly odious orphanage – one which, I am happy to say, is now long out of business. I ran away. I was found and brought back. After my fourth escape they no longer bothered searching. I was raised by some of my mother's more sympathetic colleagues. It should come as no surprise that I would take up her trade, but with more ambition, which is why I hold my current position.

"It's true that I have little tolerance for those who abuse myself and my workers. I have seen what these women deal with, having done so myself. If, as you hint, these so-called victims had some connection with my business, I would suspect their own behaviors led to their demise."

"What you say sounds very close to a confession," Holmes responded. "While I sympathize with your misfortunes, you have taken the situation too far."

"That was hardly a confession, Mr. Holmes. Whoever killed those men, and from the variety of methods you describe I would say more than one person must be responsible, I salute them." Madame Blanchard then poured herself a glass of brandy and raised it high. "To justice, gentlemen!"

"You may yet regret that sentiment," Holmes replied. "Come, Watson. There is little more for us to do here."

We heard Madame Blanchard chuckling as we paused outside her office. I was surprised to find her assistant Kitty waiting there. I'd thought she would have more important duties to attend to.

"You overheard our conversation?" Holmes asked her.

The woman nodded, her features stoic but unable to conceal a degree of disappointment. "I've had my suspicions, as well," she whispered. "My young man Marcus was trying to free me from leave this lifestyle. He collapsed in the street last week and never recovered. I learned only yesterday that his death happened shortly after he'd visited the Madame in an effort to sort some kind of arrangement for my benefit. If I can provide you with any information that would help your own case – anonymously, of course – "

"I may be in touch," Holmes whispered back. "I assure you, I can be most discreet."

The cackling in the room behind us abruptly ceased. A heavy thud followed. Kitty's eyes widened and her face grew more animated with what I assumed, at the time, was curiosity.

I dashed back into the office to see Madame Blanchard slide off her desk onto the floor.

Holmes followed me, then paused to look back at the woman's assistant. "Inspector Gregson is waiting outside the hat shop with his men. Tell him I said he should call an ambulance, then join us up here."

The young woman nodded, heading for the stairs.

Holmes silently observed me as I bent over Blanchard. Detecting neither breath nor heartbeat, I applied the chest-pressure arm-lift method created by Henry Silvester in an effort to resuscitate her.

I had little hope of success and, indeed, eventually gave up.

"You seem uncharacteristically indifferent," I commented, looking up at him at last from my failure.

While I'd tried to revive the woman, my friend had rummaged through her desk, removing and lining up a series of bottles of various shapes and sizes from a lower drawer.

"Are you searching for some medication?" I asked. "I'm afraid it's too late for that."

"Quite the opposite, Watson." He pointed at each item in turn. "This bottle contains arsenic, and this has strychnine. I found some laudanum and a bit of prussic acid, which can be particularly nasty. I suspect the cyanide to be the likeliest source of her passing. I detected a faint bitter almond smell in the dregs of her brandy."

"That is an extraordinary collection," I remarked. "Of course, most of these items have other household uses, such as cleaning and pest control."

"Pest control!" Holmes gave a sharp laugh. "No doubt that's how she saw it. That woman murdered dozens, perhaps scores, of innocent people over a course of decades. And managed her acts so cleverly the police rarely found anything to even indicate a crime. She gets no sympathy from me. I feel a fool for not having been aware of her evil deeds sooner!"

"To be fair, neither did Scotland Yard. Nearly every murder, as you say, was planned to look like anything but."

"True enough. Even when the deaths seemed suspicious, there was no pattern, no overall technique, to indicate a single killer." Holmes sighed, not yet ready to forgive himself. "Tomorrow I'll arrange with Gregson to continue digging through the official archives. We can, I hope, at least provide comfort to some of the families."

"I'll gladly join you, if you like. After all, my assistance tonight wasn't much use."

"My dear Watson! You underestimate your value. In any case, your company is always welcome, save when the nature of my investigation requires otherwise." He drew a stiff breath. "I must ask one more favor of you."

"Anything."

"I know you have been writing up our little adventures to amuse yourself, with a possible view towards eventual publication. I ask that you add this one to that short list of tales not to be shared in our lifetimes. The less the fragile Mrs. Turner knows of our involvement in this matter, the better. She must never know who undercut her desire for personal revenge. That in turn should make it easier for her to eventually accept the same."

"As you say. Certain details are inappropriate to share with the public at large in any case."

"Good man."

"I appreciate your discretion as well," added Kitty, suddenly appearing in the open doorway to stare at her employer's corpse.

"You're very good at eavesdropping," I commented.

"I wanted to let you know that Inspector Gregson is leading his men up the stairs as we speak."

"Excellent! And, Miss Kitty, kindly assure me this is a one-time event."

"There is no question of that, Mr. Holmes."

"Good. I shall nonetheless be keeping an eye on you."

"For which I in turn shall be more than grateful."

Kitty returned to the head of the staircase to guide the officers. I looked to my friend, eyebrows raised at the implications of their exchange.

"Holmes, you don't mean – ?"

"It is obvious, is it not? Who else had access to that brandy? It's highly unlikely the Madame Blanchard would commit suicide, although I trust the police will assume the latter is the case."

"You'll let that young woman get away with murder?"

"Don't look so shocked. I firmly believe that, unlike Madame Blanchard, Kitty will refrain from further such activities, especially in view of my warning. This is hardly the first time I've condoned an illegal act to avoid a greater miscarriage of justice. Now, let us proceed homeward. Gregson will have more than enough suspects to question tonight, and I suddenly feel quite weary."

Holmes slept late the following morning, even more than usual, rising shortly before noon. Now he perched comfortably in his favorite chair – or so his posture indicated. I could not, however, miss the glint of anticipation in his eyes. He certainly couldn't have missed the same in my own as I waited by the open door of our flat.

"Mrs. Turner is coming up the stairs now," I whispered.

"Excellent!" Holmes whispered back. I took my seat as he added, in a louder tone, "Have you seen the headline in this morning's *Telegraph*? That murderous Blanchard woman's death has been tentatively ruled a suicide. I suppose she found that preferable to facing a police inquiry."

Coffee cups rattled on her tray as Mrs. Turner entered the room. She kept head bowed, though, so I could only guess at her reaction.

I forced a smile. "It appears Inspector Gregson can sometimes solve a crime on his own."

"With or without my prodding, eh?"

371

The maid cleared her throat for attention.

"Good morning, Mrs. Turner," Holmes greeted as she put down her tray. "Your timing is impeccable."

Her lips twitched, the closest thing to a smile I'd yet to see her express. "If I'm not being too presumptuous, Mr. Holmes," she said, in a low voice, "might I see that article?"

I'd never heard more than two words from the young woman before then. Initially I'd thought she was a mute. Holmes nodded, gently handing over the paper.

"By the way," he continued, "last night I encountered an elderly clergyman who has been of use to me more than once. Yesterday he found a hatpin lodged in his robe after he'd accidentally bumped into a young woman."

Mrs. Turner froze, but said nothing as she continued scan the newspaper article.

"Since the item somewhat worn, yet polished," Holmes added, "he believed it had sentimental value, and decided to leave it with me to find the woman."

"If anyone could find the owner, it would be Sherlock Holmes," I couldn't resist adding.

"I'm not that immodest, Watson, but yes. I recognized it at once from Mrs. Hudson's description. You lost this yesterday, did you not?" He reached into a nearby open desk drawer and removed the hairpin.

Mrs. Turner grasped the item, eyes wide with shock and gratitude. Which elicited a greater emotion, the hatpin's recovery or the death of her husband's killer, I couldn't tell.

"It is indeed mine, Mr. Holmes," she replied. "A wedding gift from my late mother-in-law. How can I thank you?"

"Keep it somewhere safe, and we may consider us even."

"An amazing coincidence," I offered, as Mrs. Turner started to leave.

"A fortunate one, indeed," Holmes replied, smiling.

We both knew what Holmes thought of coincidences.

The Adventure of the
Alexandrian Scroll
by David MacGregor

It was in the early days of my association with Sherlock Holmes that I began to get an inkling of how his moods would shift with the seasons. This had nothing to do with changes in the temperature or the weather itself. Rather, it reflected the kinds of clients who would appear on our doorstep asking for help. So it was that on an unseasonably warm day in late April that a steady stream of visitors had worn down Holmes's patience to a nub. In they came, one after another, men and women of all ages, and all with the same complaint – namely, they had been unfortunate enough to suffer the attentions of a pickpocket. Certainly the loss of a wallet or bracelet was no doubt dismaying, but what all of these prospective clients failed to appreciate was that Holmes's formidable talents were quite helpless in the face of this particular crime.

Even now, Holmes was at our window, gazing down at the throngs in Baker Street and shaking his head.

"Look at them, Watson. Bustling to-and-fro with no particular destination. Simply happy to be out and enjoying the sun, heedless to the fact that they are surrounded by predators."

"That's a bit of an exaggeration," I replied. "I realise that the nature of your profession has given you a somewhat dim view of humanity, but you make it sound as if we're little better than animals in the jungle."

"Worse than animals in the jungle. Far worse. Animals have only one purpose when they prey upon one another, but there is no end to the various horrors that human beings inflict upon both strangers and those they claim to love." Holmes paused and took a puff on his cherry-wood pipe, which I was quickly coming to associate with his more disputatious moods. "Ah well, it's a good thing you aren't out there, my friend. You would be relieved of your wallet within ten minutes and then be back here bleating at me for help."

"Ridiculous!" I retorted. "I'm not some callow young gentleman with his head in the clouds. And believe me, I know a pickpocket when I see one, and I would certainly notice a hand in my pocket."

"Really?" Holmes turned to me. "Prove it."

"Prove what?"

"I feel reasonably certain that I have spotted a pickpocket out in the street. Come here and see if you can spot him. Or her."

"Very well."

Standing up, I made my way to the window as Holmes moved aside and then maneuvered me for the best view along the length of Baker Street.

"You have one minute," said Holmes as he settled himself into his chair. "Describe the pickpocket in detail and I shall let you know if I concur with your judgment."

Looking down at the sea of humanity beneath me, I instantly despaired of the task at hand. The warm day had apparently brought out everyone in London, with many of the younger people wearing some striking piece of clothing with which they no doubt hoped to attract the attention of other young people. A scarlet handkerchief spilling out of a breast pocket here, a blue bonnet accentuating blonde curls there. This was easily attributable to an entirely different sort of predatory behaviour than the kind Holmes had in mind, but one just as ancient and just as primal.

"Who could it be?" asked Holmes as he gazed at the ceiling. "Man? Woman? Young? Old? A lean individual as opposed to someone of a more stout constitution, thereby making it easier to slip through the crowd? Any candidates yet, Watson?"

Leaning closer to the window, I did my best to somehow see what Holmes had seen and deduce what he had deduced, but realised that in all likelihood I would simply make a fool of myself with a guess that Holmes would quickly puncture.

"Very well," I began as I turned back to Holmes, "I'm not going to pretend that my observational skills are remotely equal to yours. However, I assure you that I am quite capable of walking the streets of London without getting my pocket picked."

"A bold claim," returned Holmes. "In fact, you were out not too long ago fetching a newspaper. Are you quite certain you returned here with your wallet intact?"

"Come now," I was familiar with Holmes's needling when he was feeling bored, but this was a bit much. "I'll thank you for giving me a bit more credit than that."

Patting the pocket that contained my wallet for emphasis, I was instantly struck with pure panic. Reaching inside it, the absence of my wallet was all too evident. In the time-honoured fashion of anyone suffering such a loss, I instantly searched my remaining pockets in the vain hope that I had somehow inadvertently placed the wallet in one of them, but my frantic search came up empty as Holmes laughed at my discomfiture.

"Missing something, Watson?"

And then, as I stared at Holmes in my distress and embarrassment, I became aware that he was holding my wallet between two fingers.

"What the devil!" I cried. In two strides I had reached Holmes and plucked it from his hand. A brief inspection of its contents revealed that nothing was missing and I thrust the wallet back into my pocket with some vigour as Holmes smiled at me.

"Holmes," I began, pointing my finger at him, "that's unworthy of you!"

"Merely making a point," he answered. "A demonstration is so much more convincing than any explanation, don't you think?"

Still trying to catch up to the unnerving series of events that had just taken place, I finally realised what had happened.

"It was when you called me to the window and positioned me to look down the street. That's when you took it!"

Holmes inclined his head slightly, "I bow to your unparalleled deductive abilities."

Clearing my throat in a fashion that I hoped adequately communicated my irritation, I picked up my newspaper with the full intention of ignoring him for the next few minutes. The headlines on the front page were the usual assortment of government fiascos and European sabre-rattling, so I opened the paper, grateful for the opportunity to eliminate Holmes and his smug expression from my view. Halfway through an article on a new railway lane being constructed in the Lakes District, I became aware of the sound of Holmes drumming his fingers on the arm of his chair. Peeking over the top of my paper, I was dismayed to see that his dark mood had returned and that his gaze was fixed on a cabinet drawer that I knew contained a certain morocco leather case filled with dubious, if entirely legal, contents. I lowered the paper.

"Here we are, Holmes – It looks like we'll be able to take a train to Grasmere later this year Won't that be nice?"

"Only if there's a murder in Grasmere," Holmes answered.

I turned another page. "And it would appear the British Museum has acquired some ancient scrolls from Egypt, courtesy of an expedition led by Lord Barwell."

"Why is it that thieving acquires a patina of respectability when it's done by the nobility?" enquired Holmes somewhat peevishly.

I hurriedly scrambled through some more pages for an entirely different topic and tried one last foray. "If the weather holds, do you fancy an outing tomorrow? It looks like England are playing Scotland at the Kennington Oval."

"Really, Watson. Rugby?" Holmes got up and strolled to the window. "Watching grown men knocking what little brains they have out of one another?"

At that, I finally concluded that anything I might say would quickly be returned to me with a good dose of cynical venom, and it was with more gratitude than usual that I heard the gentle rap of Mrs. Hudson against our door. Quickly moving to open it, I found her standing with a slight, pale man of about forty who was nervously twisting his hat in his hands. With his watery blue eyes and weak chin, he was the very picture of a man in complete and utter despair.

"A client for Mr. Holmes," announced Mrs. Hudson.

"Excellent!" I cried, with an enthusiasm that made Mrs. Hudson look at me in alarm. "Most excellent, indeed! Right this way, my good sir. Thank you, Mrs. Hudson!"

Closing the door, I ushered the gentleman further into the room, and was slightly dismayed to observe that Holmes hadn't even bothered to turn from the window.

"State your case," he announced in a bored drawl.

"My case?" The gentleman looked to me for guidance and I smiled in what I hoped was an encouraging fashion.

"Your reason for calling on Mr. Holmes. Are you being blackmailed, perhaps?" I suggested.

"Blackmailed? Oh no, sir. Nothing of the kind. It's a theft! A robbery!"

As my heart sank, Holmes turned from the window and cast a withering glare at our soon to be dismissed potential client. "Do tell. Wallet or pocket-watch?"

"Neither. It's a scroll, sir. An ancient scroll."

"Go on."

"My name is Norman Rashford, sir. I work at the British Museum in the Antiquities Department. We just received some Egyptian scrolls and I was given the job of cataloguing them, and now one of them has gone missing!"

"That's what I was just telling you about, Holmes," I interrupted, then turned to our guest. "Those would be the scrolls from Lord Barwell's expedition, yes?"

"Exactly, sir."

"Well, Mr. Rashford," began Holmes, "I am sorry indeed to hear of your loss, but a missing scroll no doubt relating to some kind of grain purchase or taxation issue doesn't particularly interest me. Beyond that, I have developed an intolerable headache. Watson will see you out."

376

With that, Holmes entered his bedroom and closed the door firmly behind him. I fully expected our visitor to meekly retreat back the way he came, but was surprised to see a spark of fire and anger in his eyes. Before I could say a word, he was at Holmes's bedroom door and banging on it insistently.

"Mr. Holmes! The scroll in question has nothing to do with grain or taxes. It's about a murder!"

Scarcely a heartbeat later, Holmes had opened the door and was peering at Mr. Rashford questioningly.

"A murder, you say?"

"Yes sir!"

"Very well. But why would I have any interest in a murder that took place in the ancient past? It isn't as if we can now bring the perpetrator to justice."

"No," returned our guest, "but you can bring the truth to light."

"Does the murder victim have a name?"

"Indeed she does, sir. Hypatia of Alexandria."

At this, Holmes's expression changed in a manner I had never before observed. Shock and excitement mingled in his features as he spun Mr. Rashford around and directed him towards a chair.

"Sit. Sit, sit, sit. What do you require to tell your tale fully, Mr. Rashford? Tea? Coffee? Something stronger, perhaps?"

"Nothing at all, sir. I can see you have heard of Hypatia."

"Of course!"

Loath though I am to confess my ignorance in any situation, I realised that any ensuing conversation between Holmes and Mr. Rashford would be meaningless to me, as I had never heard of this person. Pulling out my notebook, I expressed this as diplomatically as I could.

"If you could just fill me in?"

"Hypatia of Alexandria, Watson!" he began. "Perhaps the most remarkable woman of her age. Certainly one of the most courageous and inspiring human beings to ever walk this planet. Philosopher, astronomer, and mathematician. There are those who claim that she was the librarian of the fabled Library of Alexandria, but that great temple of learning had already been destroyed before Hypatia was born. She was a famed Neoplatonist, and students flocked to her from all over the Mediterranean. And she was a great advocate of what she termed *apatheia* – that is, consciously endeavouring to remove all emotions and affections from her thought process in an effort to see and think as clearly as possible. She was murdered in cold blood in 415 A.D., yet no one was ever charged or accused of the crime."

At this, it became abundantly clear why Holmes held such reverence for this woman, as his own attitudes towards love and emotion of any kind mirrored hers almost exactly. Mr. Rashford, pleased to have found a fellow admirer in Holmes, added, "She founded her own school, lectured in both Plato and Aristotle, and according to the Syrian philosopher Damascius, was '*exceedingly beautiful and fair of form*'."

"Indeed!" agreed Holmes. "She reputedly had many suitors, but rejected them all, prizing her own independence over any kind of security that a more domestic existence might provide."

"Or perhaps she was simply devoid of any kind of romantic inclinations," I offered.

"Unlikely," replied Holmes, "as she recommended playing or listening to music as a way to relieve lustful urges. The same remedy used by Pythagoras."

And as I cast my eye toward Holmes's violin in the corner, he continued, "She also utterly rejected Christianity, which at the time was becoming a more and more powerful political force as the Roman Empire crumbled."

"Bit of a rebel, then," I added.

"More than a bit, Watson. She enjoyed riding her personal chariot through the streets of Alexandria, no doubt earning the resentful and angry looks of men who felt that she didn't know her place. Perhaps most alarming of all, she advocated for the highest moral standards in politics, and publicly declared that politicians should act for the benefit of their fellow citizens."

"Remarkable," I muttered as I wrote all of these details down as quickly as I could manage. And to think that only moments earlier I had never heard of this woman. I looked from Holmes to Rashford. "So what happened to her? Do we know any details?"

"As a powerful and respected pagan woman," began Rashford, "the Christian leaders in Alexandria had no love for Hypatia and began a campaign of lies against her. While she herself hoped that the Neoplatonists and Christians could live together in peace, she was seen as a threat. While it was no secret that she was an unbeliever, she found herself accused of practicing magic and of being in league with evil. These efforts were led by Bishop Cyril, the Patriarch of Alexandria, who also expelled all of the Jews from the area in his attempt to create an entirely Christian city. Unfortunately for Cyril, all of his schemes to demonise and undermine Hypatia were in vain, because she was so well-known and beloved. So it came to pass that she was ultimately murdered, and as Mr. Holmes already related, her killing went unsolved. It goes down as one of the great mysteries of the ancient world and shocked the people of the

Eastern Roman Empire, who subsequently came to regard Hypatia as a martyr of philosophy."

Holmes gazed at Rashford expectantly, until it became clear that he had said his piece. Holmes turned to me. "Allow me to fill in a few small gaps that Mr. Rashford omitted, no doubt with the intention of sparing your delicate sensibilities, my dear Watson. Hypatia was not merely killed, she was *destroyed*. One fine day in March, she was waylaid by a group of Christian men as she rode in her chariot. They dragged her into a building known as the Kaisarion. This was a pagan temple that had been converted into a Christian church by Bishop Cyril. She was stripped naked and then murdered with *ostraka*. In one of those delightful details that historians battle about far into the night, the word '*ostraka*' can be defined as either 'roof tiles' or 'oyster shells'. They gouged her eyes out, then tore her body into pieces and dragged her remains outside of Alexandria where they were set on fire, thereby symbolically purifying the city of her teachings and presence."

Approximately halfway through Holmes's recitation I had ceased to write in my notebook, utterly sickened by his description of Hypatia's unfortunate end. We sat in silence for a few moments, each of us wrapped up in our own thoughts, until Holmes finally spoke.

"It's one thing to read of these events in a history book. I am afraid, however, that I am afflicted with a condition that doesn't allow me the comfort of consigning such atrocities to the dim and distant past, for I know full well that similar events still occur on a regular basis all around the world. And when I think of Hypatia's last moments, when I think of her fear and horror at what was happening to her . . . ."

Holmes trailed off with a small shake of his head, then turned to Rashford.

"This scroll. Tell me about it."

"It came along with perhaps four-dozen other scrolls," began Rashford, "all of them apparently belonging to one man who appears to have been a builder or architect in Alexandria. I began the rather painstaking task of cataloguing their contents, a process which was slower than I would have liked, owing to the fact that my proficiency in Greek lags behind my knowledge of Latin. As you surmised earlier, Mr. Holmes, the documents appeared to be related largely to the gentleman's business dealings, but just as I was about to stop work for the day and head home for dinner, my eye was caught by what was quite clearly the name '*Hypatia*'."

Holmes's glittering eyes hadn't strayed from our client for an instant. "And knowing what I know of you, Mr. Rashford, I suspect that single word served to quicken your pulse."

379

"Indeed it did, sir," replied Rashford. "But I could see that it was a long document and my colleagues were already starting to file out for the day, and so I slipped the scroll inside my coat with the intention of studying it more closely when I got home."

"And were you able to do that?" enquired Holmes.

"Yes, sir. To the consternation of my wife, I ate a rather hurried dinner and then retired to my office to examine the scroll in detail. A short time later I was perhaps halfway through the document, and it was with some surprise that I looked up to see my wife entering my office and informing me that it was two in the morning, whereas I could have sworn that only a few minutes had passed since dinner."

"I am familiar with the phenomenon," nodded Holmes. "What were you able to learn?"

"That this man, this builder, had been present at the murder of Hypatia."

"So the scroll is a confession?" I hazarded.

"Not explicitly. He stopped short of implicating himself directly in the crime, but he was most certainly part of the mob and he witnessed the events. I had reached the point in the text where he was starting to explain the forces behind the conspiracy to kill Hypatia, and had just encountered the name of Bishop Cyril himself."

"Historians have always suspected his involvement," added Holmes, "and that he ordered her assassination, but there was never any proof. Given the fact that Cyril is considered to be one of the Church Fathers and a Doctor of the Church, it would be a considerable scandal and embarrassment were it to be revealed that he orchestrated the slaughter of Hypatia. Is that what the scroll alleges?"

"It does," returned Rashford, who then faltered. "At least, I believe it does. As I said, Greek is not my strongest language, and I was reading the text quickly as my excitement grew. But what I gathered was that Cyril had called a secret meeting of his most trusted associates to arrange for Hypatia's assassination. There was still a considerable amount of the scroll left to read, but as I stated, the hour was late and I had an early appointment this morning down at the docks to monitor another shipment from Lord Barwell's expedition. I left the scroll on my desk, fully intending to pick it up and take it with me when I returned to the Museum later today, but when I arrived home . . . ."

As Rashford hesitated, tears welling up in his eyes, Holmes turned to me. "Watson, a brandy for Mr. Rashford, please."

"Of course." Moving to the sideboard and pouring a healthy snifter for our guest, I could see the poor man was almost overcome as Holmes regarded him solicitously.

"The scroll was gone," said Holmes as Rashford managed a nod. Holmes moved to the window, his grey eyes shifting back and forth in thought. "I assume you asked your wife about its whereabouts?"

Rashford nodded again as I delivered his brandy and he took a healthy gulp. "She knew nothing about it. It was my scroll and in my office. She has very little interest in my work at the Museum."

"I see," mused Holmes, "but when she entered your office in the wee hours of the morning to find you poring over the text, did you happen to relate its contents to her?"

"I believe I said a few words on the matter, yes," answered Rashford. "It was clear that I was in a state of some excitement, so I felt she deserved an explanation. But just as with Dr. Watson here, she had never heard of Hypatia, so she would hardly have any reason to take the document in my absence."

Holmes turned from the window and approached Rashford. "Then how would you account for its disappearance?"

"I don't know." Rashford drained the remainder of his brandy. "My only thought was that someone at the Museum or who was part of Lord Barwell's expedition knew of its contents. Needless to say, the translation and publication of a document attributing the murder of Hypatia to Bishop Cyril would be extremely embarrassing to not only the Roman Catholic Church, but the Church of England as well. It would be like revealing that John the Baptist had been the most noted murderer of his time. Given that, I expect that a pretty penny would be paid to keep the contents of the document secret. If the perpetrators of the crime searched my desk at the British Museum and found the scroll missing, then quite logically they would assume that I had taken it home with me. That's the only explanation I can offer."

"Then we must visit the location of this crime," declared Holmes. "I take it you have no objection, Mr. Rashford?"

"No, none. I'll escort you there myself."

"Excellent. Watson, come along. And bring your gun. We have no idea what manner of ne'er-do-wells we may encounter."

As we proceeded by cab to Upper Clapton and the home of our client, I brought out my notebook to fill in everything that I could remember of the conversation between Holmes and Rashford. In all my years of schooling I had never heard of this particularly sordid historical episode, and as I finished writing I looked across at Holmes.

"Is there anything else you think I should know about Hypatia or her death?"

"Just one minor point," answered Holmes. "If you're thinking of writing this up for your journals, you should know that Bishop Cyril is no longer referred to by that title."

"No?" I readied my pencil. "What is he known as now?"

"St. Cyril."

The remainder of our cab ride was spent in silence, with Holmes, Rashford, and I all looking out our respective windows, each wrapped in his own thoughts. Mine, I will confess, were of a particularly dismal hue as I pondered the dark history of our species, and it was with some measure of relief that I realised we were slowing to a halt. Upon descending from the cab, we approached the modest-yet-well-kept home of Mr. Rashford. Before we could enter, a dark-haired, rather handsome woman appeared in the doorway and regarded us questioningly, before turning her attention to our client.

"What's this, Norman? Shouldn't you be at the Museum?"

"Yes, of course, my dear," Rashford stammered out his response, "but the scroll I mentioned to you – I've engaged these gentlemen to aid in its recovery. Mr. Sherlock Holmes and Dr. John Watson, this is my wife, Eugenia."

As Holmes and I nodded our greeting, Mrs. Rashford cast a long and lingering look at Holmes, then stepped aside as we made our way into the house. Rashford led us straight to his office, and as we entered Holmes held up one finger.

"Please remain precisely where you are, Mr. Rashford. I need you out of the way for my investigation, but available for questions."

Bringing out my notebook, I took up a position near Rashford, who stood just inside the door. I was surprised to see that Mrs. Rashford had followed us as well, apparently interested in observing the proceedings. As she watched Holmes, she kept one hand in a pocket of her dress and appeared to be unconsciously manipulating something inside it. Holmes began by simply scanning the room, his steepled fingers up to his lips as he took in every detail visible to the naked eye. He then proceeded carefully around the perimeter, stopping at the window and lifting it up. He turned to Rashford.

"Is this window typically latched?"

"Yes sir, but I opened it yesterday to get some fresh air in. I must have neglected to latch it in my excitement of examining the scroll."

Nodding at Rashford's explanation, Holmes brought out his magnifying lens and moved to the desk, surveying it in detail. There was a pen and inkbottle, a letter opener, a photo of a small child, and some scattered papers, but very little else. After a few moments, he pulled a small paper envelope from his coat and swept something I couldn't see into it. As if reading my mind, Holmes intoned, "Some small particles of parchment from the scroll, Watson. They may be of use if we find similar particles in another location." Pocketing the envelope, Holmes's gaze swept the room until it finally landed upon our client's wife.

"Mrs. Rashford," Holmes began, "might you possibly be able to shed any light on the disappearance of the scroll your husband brought home?"

"I'm afraid I have very little interest in old, dusty documents," she answered. "If you ask me, the modern world is more than interesting enough. Why waste time wallowing in the past when the present has so many marvels to offer?"

Out of the corner of my eye, I believe I caught Rashford wincing at his wife's remarks, but what I found striking was Mrs. Rashford's bearing and demeanour as she spoke to Holmes. There was no hesitancy or hint of shyness in the presence of the detective. Instead, there was an almost challenging air as she regarded him with her striking green eyes.

"Quite," Holmes remarked as he turned back to the window, his eyes searching the street and the houses across from us. "Tell me, Mrs. Rashford, have you had any visitors today?"

"No, none." Hardly a second had passed before she caught herself. "No, actually Father Dawkins stopped by this morning. I missed Mass last Sunday due to a brief indisposition, and he kindly came by to see if I was feeling any better."

Still at the window, Holmes was almost unnaturally still, like a predator waiting for his unwary prey to stray into his path. "And did you happen to usher him into this office or show him the scroll?"

"Why should I do such a thing?"

Holmes turned to her with an enigmatic smile on his lips. "Why indeed?"

"And the scroll, Mr. Holmes? What do you imagine happened?" Mr. Rashford had remained rooted to the spot during Holmes's investigation, but now his anxiousness spilled out of him.

"I will be candid with you, sir," returned Holmes. "I believe you have seen the last of it, but we shall do what we can."

Stepping out of the house a few moments later without Rashford, Holmes inhaled deeply as he stared into the distance. "I fear we are in deep waters, Watson. Dark, fetid, almost bottomless waters." He paused, then regarded me with a sideways glance. "And yes, I agree with you. She is a most interesting woman. Particularly given the fact that she and her husband don't appear to be well-suited towards one another."

"Because of her lack of interest in his work?"

"There is that, and as we learned from her reference to Father Dawkins she is a devout Catholic, and I suspect Mr. Rashford is not."

"What makes you say that?"

"I would draw your attention to the religious iconography in his office."

"I saw nothing of the kind," I admitted.

"Because there was nothing of the kind," explained Holmes, "even as his wife was unconsciously manipulating what I feel quite sure was a rosary in her pocket. Then there is the matter of the photo of the child on the desk."

"What about it?"

"I believe we happened on a not uncommon domestic tragedy. In the spring of youth, our fancies can be unduly invigorated by almost anything, and we may be swept up in a moment that we would subsequently wish to forget, unless that moment happens to result in the appearance of a child. At that point, the expectations of society and the responsibilities of parenthood can necessitate a joining of two people who are completely unsuited towards one another, both in temperament and faith."

"I see," I nodded, bringing out my notebook. "That makes perfect sense."

"The child in the photo was quite young," continued Holmes, "and given the ages of the Rashfords and no more recent photos, I suspect that the child passed away some time ago, leaving Mr. and Mrs. Rashford to muddle aimlessly through the rest of their lives together until they tumble gratefully into their graves."

I paused to look at Holmes in shock, my pencil in midair. There was something positively inhuman in him at times, a quality that could be somewhat repellant, but no doubt aided him in his clear-eyed assessment of individuals and situations. Out of nowhere the bizarre thought came to me – Hypatia of Alexandria would be proud of him.

"By all means feel free to be appalled, Watson," remarked Holmes as he moved to examine the exterior of the window looking into Rashford's office, "for life and the actions of human beings are quite often appalling."

Crouching down, Holmes examined the ground beneath the window closely before standing back up. "Nothing. But the ground is so hard it would be difficult for any intruder to leave a trace. Now then, let's call upon the neighbours, shall we?"

Holmes walked across the street at a brisk pace and all I could do was trail in his wake with my brain still in a bit of a fog. Not thirty seconds later we were on the front step of the house just opposite the Rashfords.

"Would you like to see a front door opened in two seconds?" asked Holmes. And before I had time to reply he had rapped on the door with his cane and it had been immediately opened by an ancient, wizened woman who peered at us suspiciously.

384

"What do you want?"

"Ah, Madam! A very good day to you!" Holmes's eyes shone with friendliness as he smiled at the old crone ingratiatingly. "I am Mr. Hubert Weston and this is my partner, Mr. Oliver Crane, of Weston and Crane Architects. We have been commissioned to determine whether the spiritual needs of this neighbourhood are being adequately met by the number of churches in the area. You are a devout Catholic woman, I perceive."

"What?" The woman's eyes went wide. "How the devil do you know that?"

"The crucifix on the wall behind you suggests as much," replied Holmes. "Would you say that you and your neighbours are well served by Father Dawkins from – " Holmes turned to me. "What was the name of his church again, Oliver?"

In the time it took me to register that Holmes was addressing me by the pseudonym I had just been given, the old woman had shuffled further out on her porch to point down the street.

"St. Michael's, sir," she began, and once she started talking she seemed disinclined to stop. "Not three streets away. That's where Mrs. Rashford and I attend services. I noticed you were just over there to see her. Lovely woman. Bit of an unhappy marriage though, what with their little boy dying and all. It's a shame, really, but Father Dawkins is a wonderful priest and he's taken a special interest in Mrs. Rashford. He stops by to check on her three or four times a week."

"Excellent!" Holmes nodded his thanks. "Madam, you have been a veritable fount of information, and my colleague and I owe you our gratitude. This way, Oliver."

Once again chasing after the rapid stride of Holmes, I was struggling to understand precisely what was going on, a feeling no doubt exacerbated by the fact that I had found Holmes's instant ability to fashion new and plausible identities for both of us a little unnerving. When I finally caught up to him the best I could manage was, "What was that all about?"

"When I looked out of Mr. Rashford's office, I could see that old woman seated at her front window watching the street and instantly surmised that is where she spends the majority of her day. Who better to give us information on the comings and goings at the Rashfords?"

"Of course, yes," I managed, already a little out of breath. "And where are we going now?"

"To see the wonderful Father Dawkins," answered Holmes, as to my dismay he quickened his pace even further.

Scarcely two minutes later we were in St. Michael's Church, and with the instinct of a cat after a mouse, Holmes had unerringly made his way to

Father Dawkins' office. Crossing the threshold a good five seconds after Holmes, I entered to see Father Dawkins seated at his desk and staring up at Holmes in shock. Before him was an open Bible, to which Holmes pointed.

"I believe you will find what you are looking for in the Book of Exodus, Father Dawkins," began Holmes. "The Eighth Commandment. Thou shalt not steal."

"What?" Father Dawkins' features were twisted in alarm and fear. "What's this about?"

"It is about theft, sir," returned Holmes. "It is about entering the home of a man you barely know, taking advantage of your relationship with his wife, and making off with a document from his office. In short, sir, I must ask you for the scroll you pilfered from Mr. Norman Rashford."

In his distress, Father Dawkins rose shakily to his feet, and I could see that in other circumstances he would be a rather handsome man, with his hair greying slightly at the temples and brown eyes that were no doubt kind and gentle as he listened to the hopes and fears of his parishioners. Now, however, as he swallowed nervously, a hard defiance came over his features.

"I don't have it!" he cried.

I would be hard pressed to adequately explain my actions at that moment, but with my blood up from chasing after Holmes and now reading the guilt-ridden expression of the man before us, I found my hand reaching into my pocket. A moment later, I was holding my revolver by my side. This was not lost on Father Dawkins, who instinctively raised his hands.

"I don't have it, I tell you! It isn't here! Go ahead, search my office! Search the church! Search every square inch of the grounds if you like! It isn't here!"

Looking for some explanation to Dawkins' rising terror, Holmes glanced back at me and spied the gun in my hand. A lightning flash of approval and amusement crossed his features before he turned back to Dawkins.

"You have been extraordinarily helpful, sir. Good day. And may God forgive you."

With a serendipity that I had come to take for granted, Holmes flagged down an empty cab scarcely ten seconds after we had exited the church, and we were soon clattering down cobblestones at high speed. Looking across at Holmes, I could see that his lips were pursed together in disapproval as he shook his head.

"It won't do, Watson," he began. "I'm growing soft in my old age."

"What do you mean?" I asked as I pulled out my notebook. "Have you deduced what happened to the scroll? Where are we going?"

Observing the pencil hovering over my notebook, Holmes raised his eyebrows as he looked at me. "Very well. In recognition of your armed assistance in a moment of crisis, I shall relate the series of events as I imagine they unfolded. First, as we have established, the union of Mr. and Mrs. Rashford is not a particularly happy one. As a good Catholic woman, this is something that she would have conveyed to Father Dawkins in the confessional or in the course of receiving his condolences for her deceased son. Concerned for her mental and spiritual well-being, he took it upon himself to call upon her on a regular basis, and I don't doubt that in due course his relationship with Mrs. Rashford took on a degree of familiarity that extends beyond that typical of a priest's interactions with his flock. This morning he arrived at the house while Mrs. Rashford was alone, and with the memory of her husband's excitement regarding the scroll fresh in her mind, she no doubt showed it to Father Dawkins."

"But she denied doing that!" I objected.

"No," returned Holmes. "You must train yourself to listen more carefully, Watson. I asked if she had shown Father Dawkins into her husband's office and she replied, 'Why should I do such a thing?' She never denied it."

"Quite right," I muttered as I jotted a note and could practically hear her words in my head.

"Having shown Father Dawkins the scroll, I suspect she explained its apparent importance as best she could, based on her limited knowledge. Perhaps this alone was enough to cause him alarm, or perhaps he has some proficiency in the Greek language, but either way he rapidly determined that the contents of the scroll could not be made public knowledge."

I was writing all of this down as rapidly as I could, but paused for a moment to look at Holmes.

"Then he did steal it! He must have! Holmes, I have never seen a more guilty man in my life."

"I concur, although whether he enlisted Mrs. Rashford as his confederate or returned to the house and made off with the scroll via the open office window I really couldn't say."

"Then what of his claim that he doesn't have it?"

"He doesn't. It's at this juncture that you must bear in mind the beautifully organised, yet inherently flawed, hierarchical structure of the system within which Father Dawkins lives and breathes – that is, the Roman Catholic Church. Stealing the scroll was one thing, but taking any further action would be inappropriate for a man in his relatively low position. And so – ?"

Holmes gazed at me expectantly and I was grateful when the obvious answer came sweeping over me.

"He's passed it on!" I cried. "He's given it to someone else!"

"Precisely," answered Holmes. "Which is why I fear I'm going soft. I should have recognised that immediately instead of wasting time dashing to St. Michael's to confront Father Dawkins. Ah, but here we are!"

With a scattering of gravel, the cab came to an abrupt halt as I looked out the window at the impressive sight of a massive Georgian manor house composed of limestone and accented with manicured topiary on both sides of an oak door through which an elephant could have passed.

As we exited the cab, Holmes answered my unasked question. "Behold the residence of Henry Edward Manning, better known as His Eminence, the Archbishop of Westminster and leader of the Catholic Church in England. We're about to make a call on him."

"What if he refuses to see us?"

"He won't. A man in his position is accustomed to being deferred to and will consider himself the master of every situation. And if, perchance, there are any obstacles to a private audience with His Eminence, I would remind you that you are a gentleman with a gun in your pocket, which will take precedence over any title or pretensions he may have. This way."

Following Holmes up the path towards the house, I reflected upon the fact that a day spent in the company of Sherlock Holmes always had the potential to lead in quite unexpected directions. It wasn't so long ago that I had been reading newspaper articles aloud in an effort to distract an irritable Holmes, and now I was faced with the imminent prospect of holding a gun on the Archbishop of Westminster with the aim of encouraging him to produce a stolen Egyptian scroll.

Happily enough, I was able to keep my gun in my pocket as we were immediately admitted into the house by an elderly butler who led us down a long, dim hallway towards the inner sanctum of His Eminence. Upon entering the cavernous room and observing the Archbishop of Westminster sitting behind an enormous mahogany desk, I instantly reconsidered my assessment of the butler as being elderly. Compared to the almost fossilised creature staring at us, the butler was little more than a spry young schoolboy. As the doors closed behind us, Holmes approached the desk and I remained where I was, staring at a gaunt, hatchet-faced man whose perpetually downturned mouth spoke of a lifetime spent issuing penance to the legions of sinners who had come before him.

"Your Eminence," began Holmes, "my name is Sherlock Holmes and this is my colleague Dr. Watson. I do hope you'll forgive this intrusion, but I have come to request the return of an Egyptian scroll recently stolen from the home of my client, Mr. Norman Rashford. If you would kindly hand it over, we will be on our way."

His eyes narrowing as he looked Holmes up and down, His Eminence finally spoke, "Are you accusing me of theft, Mr. Holmes?"

"Oh no, not at all," answered Holmes. "I apologise if you mistook my meaning. I am accusing you of receiving stolen goods from Father Dawkins, which is another matter entirely."

As Holmes spoke I began to move about the room, marvelling at an atmosphere right out of the Middle Ages. It was there in the rough stonework on the walls, the enormous wrought-iron chandelier, a profusion of lit candles, and a gargantuan fireplace that was currently dark.

"Mind you," Holmes continued, "possession of stolen goods is still a crime, but one I feel certain would never be prosecuted thanks to Your Eminence's exalted position. Nevertheless, I must still ask you for the scroll."

As Holmes held out his hand, the hint of an insolent smirk passed over His Eminence's features.

"I have no such thing in my possession. Good day, sir."

Nearing the huge fireplace, I became aware that while no flame was evident, there was most definitely residual heat emanating from it.

"Holmes," I said, "this fireplace is still warm."

Holmes quickly came towards me as the Archbishop rose from his chair to observe us. As Holmes verified my observation, he turned back to His Eminence.

"Curious that you would need a fire on such a mild day," remarked Holmes.

"I find that it helps to clear the damp from the room. No crime in that, I hope?"

Kneeling near the grate, I could see Holmes's eyes flashing over every inch of the fireplace, his nostrils flaring as he took in all of the information that his senses could provide. Pulling a small paper envelope from his coat, Holmes carefully swept some almost invisible particles into it as His Eminence tottered unsteadily towards us.

"What is it you're doing there?" he asked. "You have no right to remove anything from these premises."

"I shall be happy to let the courts decide that if you will," answered Holmes as he held up two small paper envelopes. "In this envelope I have some scraps of the missing scroll that I was able to salvage from the desk of Mr. Rashford. In this other envelope I have some unburned particles from the back of your fireplace. I feel confident that microscopic and chemical analysis will be able to confirm that the contents of both of these envelopes came from the same ancient manuscript."

His Eminence stared for a long moment, then shook his head at us. "There is nothing more pathetic than a very mediocre man who thinks he has done something clever. You are venturing into realms far beyond your domain, Mr. Holmes."

"Do tell," answered Holmes as he laid a steadying hand on my arm.

"Very well. Yes, Father Dawkins did come across the document in question. Not knowing what to make of it, he very sensibly brought it directly to me and informed me of its provenance. Having specialised in Classics at Oxford as a young man, I was able to read the Greek text quite easily and determined to my satisfaction that it was nothing more and nothing less than a scurrilous attack upon the character of St. Cyril. Knowing the inclination of the press and the public to make a sensation out of nothing, it was clear to me that burning the document would save considerable scandal and consternation, which is something that the Church doesn't need."

"So you admit it!" I cried.

"Do I admit destroying a heretical document? Yes, I admit that proudly and without reservation. And if you will check your history books, I think you will find that there is a long line of distinguished and revered men of faith before me who acted similarly. I am honoured to have been given the opportunity to join their company."

"And the cold-blooded murder of Hypatia of Alexandria," began Holmes, "that isn't something that troubles you in the least?"

"Who am I to question the wisdom of St. Cyril?" answered His Eminence. "The Church was not nearly so well established in his age as it is in our own, and Hypatia was clearly an obstacle to the spread of the faith. Cyril acted as he thought best, no doubt after much prayer and with the guidance of Our Lord."

As Holmes and I stood speechless, His Eminence spread his arms and looked upward.

"It is not for us to question or understand everything that transpires in this world. For those of us in positions to guide the faithful, what we offer are answers, hope, and the certainty that there is a better life beyond this one. Our holy duty is to smooth the path to God, not to ask troublesome questions or flaunt incendiary texts in the public arena. I fully understand that you gentlemen may not agree with the means, but I can assure you that the ends are well worth it. Good day to you."

Half-an-hour later, Holmes had still not said a single word as we walked slowly back towards the heart of London. He had eschewed any form of transportation, and I had kept my peace as I knew Holmes was utterly absorbed in his own thoughts. At length, however, I ventured the only question that had been preying upon my mind.

390

"Is there nothing we can do?"

"Nothing," answered Holmes. "Only two people read the document. One of them is an underling at the British Museum with a rudimentary knowledge of Greek, and the other is the Archbishop of Westminster, who studied Classics at Oxford. Who do you think would be believed?" Holmes paused, a sombre look in his eye. "But I will tell you this, Watson. A day of reckoning is coming for the Archbishop of Westminster and his kind. We may not be alive to see it, but the truth has a way of eventually worming its way to the surface, and it is then that all of the crimes and lies of the highest of the high will reveal them for the monsters that they truly are."

Two streets further on, Holmes paused to look around us. It was in truth a beautiful day, and London was suffused in the golden glow of the setting sun as myriads of people jostled around us heading home or to more festive assignations. Holmes, I knew, was oblivious to all this.

"So we would do well to consider our day. It began with a series of petty crimes that we were helpless to do anything about, and it ended with a conspiracy to keep hidden the details of one of the most infamous murders in history, which again, we are helpless to do anything about. I ask you then, as a professional consulting detective, what is the point of my existence?"

This wouldn't do. The last thing that I wanted was Holmes returning to Baker Street in such a dark frame of mind, and so I began talking, hoping for inspiration to strike as I continued.

"It's a lovely day, Holmes. In truth, the most pleasant day of the year so far. And do you see all of these people bustling through the streets? At any moment any one of them might appear in our rooms with a case. Nothing so simple as a pocket being picked, but a false accusation, a murder that has baffled Scotland Yard, or possibly a missing child. And they come to you as a last resort, as the one man in London who can somehow see light in the darkness, who can perceive order in chaos, and who can set the world aright. That is the point of your existence. Not to be omniscient and omnipotent, but to help those who can be helped when they have been abandoned by the rest of humanity. And so, if you will permit me, I have a proposition for you."

Holmes looked at me curiously. "I'm listening."

"Dinner at Simpson's. On me. We shall sit down, we shall dine sumptuously, and we shall drink a toast to Hypatia and to a world where truth and beauty do exist, and where the pursuit of both is the highest calling of mankind."

"Watson . . . ." Holmes faltered, and I could see him endeavouring to master the emotions roiling within him. "I don't deserve you, my friend."

391

He extended his hand and I took it as we looked one another in the eye.

"Dinner at Simpson's it is," Holmes continued. "Although I have been thinking we should follow the good example of George Bernard Shaw and become vegetarians."

"Capital idea!" I agreed as we began walking again. "Let's discuss it over a jug of claret and a roast leg of lamb."

"With red currant jelly?"

"Elementary, my dear Holmes. Elementary."

The Case of the
Woman at Margate
by Terry Golledge

I was sitting alone over an early breakfast, drawn from my bed by the promise of a fine day. The summer lingered as though reluctant to give place to autumn, and I was torn between the rival attractions of Middlesex playing at Lords and a thoroughly idle day in Regents Park. My friend and colleague, Sherlock Holmes, was still abed, nursing his ill humour at the inordinate amount of political comment that monopolised the daily press,

"Confound it, Watson," he had railed. "Five governments in little more than a year is no way to conduct the business of our great country. It reduces us to the level of a Latin republic floundering from one crisis to another." He had scattered the offending papers with a petulant scowl.

"Politics! It makes small difference to the criminal classes which party is in power. Does a footpad or swindler care if we have a Conservative or Liberal administration? Does a murderer or burglar pause to reflect who leads the country? Of course not. Yet because our press is so preoccupied in influencing the minds of a fickle electorate, those parasites of society pursue their nefarious calling without the glare of publicity that is such a deterrent."

Wisely I had held my peace and waited for his peevishness to abate. Notwithstanding his discontent, the year had been a busy and productive one for Holmes. His standing had never been higher, and in the five-and-a-half years our association, I had seen his reputation flower from that of an obscure consulting detective to become the most sought-after figure in the history of criminal investigation. His services were in demand from the highest in the land as well as from the official police, yet would he be just as willing to help the poorest and most abject citizen if the case offered stimulation and challenge to his restless mind.

I reached for the last piece of toast, pausing as my ears caught the sounds of an altercation from below, Mrs. Hudson's indignant tones punctuated by those of a man. Soon the good lady's firm tread approached our door and I opened it on her knock to find her flushed and angry.

"I'm sorry, Doctor. There is a *gentleman* – " She gave the word a disparaging sound. "A gentleman who insists on speaking to Mr. Holmes and refuses to be put off." She snorted. "Barely seven of the clock, indeed!"

I gnawed at my moustache. I knew my friend had no pressing cases in hand, hence his irritability. Perhaps this was what would divert him from his present lethargy.

"Who is he, Mrs. Hudson?"

She pursed her lips and handed me an engraved card.

"'*Mr. John Ruddy*'," I read. "'*East Kent Manager, Rural and Urban Insurance Company, Margate*'." I tapped it with my thumb and spoke ruefully to our landlady.

"Well, Mrs. Hudson, if he will not go, then for the sake of peace and quiet I suggest you bring him up."

She sniffed and turned away, grumbling beneath her breath. Soon the importunate caller was shown in. He was a sallow-featured fellow, some forty years of age, thin and with lank black hair plastered damply across his narrow skull. But for his rounded shoulders he would have been as tall as Holmes, and his eyes burned feverishly as he fidgeted with the brim of the brown billy-cock hat held in nervous fingers.

Hardly was he in the room before he burst into impassioned speech.

"Mr. Holmes, you must help me or I am ruined!" he cried in a high-pitched voice. "Perhaps I am ruined anyway, but – "

"Mr. Ruddy, I am not Mr. Sherlock Holmes," I broke in. "I am Dr. Watson, Mr. Holmes's colleague and confidant. Please calm yourself and be seated while I find out if he will consent to see you."

He stared at me wildly and almost danced in his agitation. "He must hear me, Doctor! My whole career hangs by a thread!" He grasped my arm and I shook him off impatiently.

"Sit down, sir," I said with some asperity. "'Must' is not a word to be used to Sherlock Holmes. I will speak to him, but he is a busy man."

I gave our visitor a stern look, then knocked on my friend's door.

His querulous voice bade me enter.

"What the deuce is going on, Watson?" he demanded. "I could find more peace in the monkey-house at the Zoo."

"You have a client," I said, nettled by his tone. "He insists that you alone can rescue him from whatever dilemma he finds himself in. He is quite unnerved."

"At this ungodly hour? Send him away, there's a good chap. Tell him to return at a more civilized time." His eyes suddenly lit up. "No, wait. This may provide some small diversion. Ring for fresh coffee and entertain him until I am fit to appear."

Turning back into the sitting room, I found John Ruddy pacing the carpet, his sallow skin flushed with emotion as he spun round to face me.

"You are a fortunate man, Mr. Ruddy," I said, not waiting for his query. "Mr. Holmes will attend you shortly. Meanwhile I shall send for

394

fresh coffee. No doubt you left – " I looked again at his card. " – Margate well before breakfast."

"Indeed I did, Doctor. I slept but little last night and, deciding my only hope of succor lay with Mr. Holmes, I caught the milk train at the crack of dawn."

"Then some toast to stay you." I rang for Mrs. Hudson, and despite the man's protests, he attacked the food voraciously when it arrived.

It was twenty minutes before Holmes appeared, his old purple dressing gown flapping around his lean shanks. Our caller looked up, hastily swallowing a mouthful of toast, but ere he could speak Holmes held up an admonitory hand, the force of his personality imposing itself at once.

"Wait, my dear sir," he commanded. "I too have my needs." He poured coffee and picked up the card from the table where I had laid it.

He looked at it carelessly, then with great deliberation began to fill a pipe from the dottles of the previous day that were drying on the mantelpiece. Not until his head was wreathed in a halo of pungent smoke did he speak.

"Well, Mr. John Ruddy from Margate, what is the purpose of this early intrusion? Be brief but explicit and tell me why the death of Mr. Elias Burdick should cause you such unrest."

Our visitor's eyes started from his head and his hands trembled. "How – *how* – do you know that, Mr. Holmes?" he stuttered in amazement, while I struggled to contain my own astonishment as Holmes turned a sardonic eye in my direction.

"Come, sir," said my friend, "Dr. Watson and I read our newspapers, and when we see that on Monday a body was taken from the sea at Margate, and is identified by Mrs. Emily Burdick as that of her husband Elias we take note. Hard on that I receive a visit from the East Kent representative of an insurance company. Why, what could be plainer?"

Ruddy's face cleared. "Of course, Mr. Holmes, it must be obvious," he cried, and I saw the flicker of annoyance in Holmes's eyes at this casual dismissal of his powers of deduction.

"Then pray proceed," said the latter coldly. "Watson, yesterday's *Morning Post* and *Evening News*, if you will be so good. Go on, sir. My time is valuable."

His pipe gurgled as he laid back in his chair with hooded eyes while our client began to speak, Holmes's calm demeanour having a steadying effect on the man.

"As you see from my card, Mr. Holmes, I manage the East Kent region for my employers. All my working life has been spent in the insurance business, from office boy to my present position, albeit with several different companies as opportunity offered me advancement. My present post I have occupied for some three years, and the company, although small and relatively new, is both progressive and efficient."

"Yes, yes," Holmes interrupted. "Please come to the point,"

"As you say, sir. Just over three weeks ago, I had a request through the post to provide life cover for this Elias Burdick, his wife to be the beneficiary. Imagine my astonishment when the sum involved was no less than six-thousand pounds, the largest single piece of business that had come my way. Most of our policies are small affairs, what we regard as burial funds, with premiums of but a few cappers weekly, but they add up, sir, they add up. I replied at once, enclosing the appropriate forms and pointing out that I would require medical confirmation of his good health. Within forty-eight hours I had the papers back, together with a doctor's certificate of recent date and the first monthly premium of thirteen-pounds-and-ten."

As Ruddy had been speaking, I had been busy with the newspapers and found the items that Holmes had tucked away in his memory. I marked them with a pencil and gave him a brief nod.

"One moment, Mr. Ruddy," Holmes was saying. "From whence did this request emanate?"

Our client looked slightly sheepish. "From Ashford, but it was *poste restante* at the main post office in that town. Burdick explained that he was an actor with no fixed address, travelling wherever work was offered. I realise now that I should have been more cautious, but in my anxiety to secure the business, I was less so than usual."

"Indeed you were," murmured Holmes. "The certificate of health – who issued that?"

"I don't know. The signature was indecipherable, as so many are. Begging your pardon, Dr. Watson," he added hastily. "It was from rooms in Wigmore Street, though, which is a reputable address."

"Quite," said Holmes drily. "At least near enough to Wimpole and Harley Streets to inspire confidence. You have it with you?" Ruddy delved into a pocket and handed a paper to Holmes, who glanced at it and passed it to me. The signature was indeed unreadable, but something in the address disturbed me and I went to the bookshelf for the London street directory.

"By George, Holmes!" I cried. "This – " but he silenced me with a finger to his lips and I subsided into my chair.

"Pray continue, Mr. Ruddy," Holmes urged.

"On Sunday night, a pile of clothes was found on a deserted part of the beach. It was reported in the stop press of the Monday morning's paper, but it was badly smudged and I took little heed of it until in the local evening paper I read of a man's body being recovered from the rocks. Even

396

then I had no more than a feeling of sympathy for a stranger who had been foolhardy to get out of his depth and had met his fate alone and unnoticed. However, on reading further, I was shocked to find that the pile of clothes found earlier had been identified by the contents of the pockets as belonging to Elias Burdick, an actor who had that day been reported missing from his lodgings. Moreover, it was being assumed that the body was his."

"So in all probability it was your client," mused Holmes, "You had no knowledge of his presence in Margate or the reason for it?"

"No. My only contact with him had been by post, and that not for three weeks since," Ruddy took out a handkerchief and mopped his brow. "Worse was to come. Imagine my dismay when yesterday noon a policeman escorted a lady to my office. He introduced her as Mrs. Emily Burdick, who had lately been to the mortuary to identify the drowned man as her husband."

"A prompt appearance indeed," observed Holmes. "So you saw a huge claim looming up. But surely, my dear sir, that is one of the hazards of your profession, unwelcome as it might be from your point of view."

"If that was but all! Oh, Mr. Holmes, it has placed me in the most ghastly predicament. Never in my twenty years in the insurance business have I done anything dishonest or indulged in sharp practice, and even now I have behaved with perfect probity."

"Then what is your problem?" asked Holmes with some impatience.

"As I have said, this was the largest single policy I have ever been asked to issue, and in my anxiety to secure it I acted somewhat precipitately. It is a company rule that any exceptional circumstances should be referred to Head Office for approval. Nothing specific is laid down, it being left to local judgement, and I have a certain amount of discretion."

"Ah, I begin to get your drift," my colleague put in. "You conducted this matter on your own initiative and responsibility, and now you fear the wrath of your superiors."

"Exactly. My career will be finished – in ruins." The poor fellow sobbed and wrung his hands in anguish."

"But surely you hardly expected your Head Office not to perceive this large transaction? Would you not be taking commission on it?"

"Indeed, and it would have appeared in my monthly report due this very weekend. Had there been no claim, I could expect at the most a mild reprimand for excess of zeal. I was dazzled by the thought of my own cleverness, but now – "

"I appreciate your position, Mr. Ruddy, but what can I do?"

397

"I have misgivings as to the validity of the claim," replied the other fiercely. "My whole instincts and experience tell me it is wrong, yet I fear to approach the Board without firm evidence. Why, it may even be regarded as collusion on my part to defraud them. It is an immense sum."

"I see." Holmes steepled his fingers and dropped his chin onto them. For a long time he remained motionless, lost in thought. Ruddy made as if to speak, but I silenced him with a shake of the head. At last Holmes looked up, and when I saw his eyes with the old familiar light, I knew he was intrigued.

"Let me expound, Mr. Ruddy," he said. "Three weeks ago you agreed to insure the life of one Elias Burdick for the sum of six-thousand pounds, payable in the event of his death to his spouse, Emily Burdick. The business was conducted by post with no personal contact. Your client gave no fixed address, preferring to use the G.P.O. at Ashford as his postbox."

Ruddy nodded and Holmes continued. "Last Sunday, Elias Burdick is fortuitously drowned on your very doorstep, and within thirty-six hours his widow is at your office to establish her claim. It does appear that a few inquiries would not come amiss."

"Then you will help me, Mr. Holmes?" The man's eagerness was pathetic.

"I shall seek the truth, no more and no less. Tell me, did the lady offer any explanation for her late husband's presence in Margate?"

"She was very distraught, but I gathered he had come hoping for some part at a local theatre."

"She had accompanied him?" asked Holmes with a frown.

"I think not. What few words we exchanged led me to believe that she had read the newspaper accounts and had followed. The constable gave me to understand she was taking a room at the very lodgings that he had occupied. A respectable boarding-house run by a Mrs. Ellis."

"Most interesting," said Holmes, rising to his feet. "Very well, Mr. Ruddy, I shall look into the matter. "Return to Margate by the first available train and carry on as if nothing out of the ordinary had occurred. Do not under any circumstances get in touch with Mrs. Burdick or allow her to speak to you."

"But will you not come with me?" demanded Ruddy, his face falling.

"No one must know of my involvement in the matter at this stage, but rest assured that Dr. Watson and I will be on the spot later today."

"You will not approach my Head Office? That would surely bring about my downfall."

"Trust me, sir," Holmes said sternly. "Only by doing so have you any hope of retrieving your position. I shall telegraph my time of arrival. Watson, be so good as to see Mr. Ruddy to the door." When I returned it was to find Holmes on his knees, the newspapers scattered about him. He looked at me severely as I came in.

"I marked the relevant paragraphs. Have you found them?"

"I have, and also the one you chose to ignore."

"I saw nothing else of importance," I replied huffily.

"You saw but did not observe. Look, man, here." His finger stabbed at a small item tucked away on the second page of Tuesday's *Morning Post*.

"Read it, my friend."

A few lines sufficed to report that a waiter from the Stanton Hotel, Margate, one George Monk, had been missing since Sunday afternoon. All his effects remained in his room and nothing had been stolen from the hotel.

"How does that concern us?" I asked. "A coincidence, nothing more."

"I distrust coincidences, even while admitting them," Holmes said pettishly. "Two men missing on the same day from the same town with no apparent connection between them is indeed coincidence. Now, my dear fellow, you were going to tell me that the Wigmore Street address is nonexistent." I nodded and he reached out to take his book of cuttings from the shelf.

For a considerable time he leafed backwards through the pages, sometimes lingering over one page or another then moving on with a mutter of frustration. At last he gave a cry of triumph and scribbled on the back of an envelope before turning the pages more rapidly. He made one more note, then closed the book with a snap.

"The case proceeds and the sea air beckons," he cried. "Watson, the *Bradshaw!*"

By eleven o'clock, our train had left behind the sulphurous fumes of London and we were looking out on the green fields of Kent, the hops coming to fruition on the vines and the conical oast houses waiting patiently to begin their labours. Holmes had despatched three telegrams from London Bridge, announcing that one was to John Ruddy, but remaining coyly mysterious regarding the others. We had the compartment to ourselves and, defying all my efforts at conversation, my companion stared fixedly out of the window. The amber stem of his brier was clamped firmly between his teeth, only being removed to be stuffed afresh with his noxious black shag.

At last I was constrained to lower the window, and the tang of salt in the air told us we were approaching the popular seaside resort that was our objective. The train clanked to a halt, the engine giving what sounded like a sigh of relief at having completed the journey. We made our way out of the station and Holmes raised a finger to the driver of a four-wheeler who,

399

oblivious to the soft warm atmosphere, was muffled to the chin in layers of coats and comforters.

"The Stanton Hotel, cabbie, and take your time." My friend clambered in beside me and made himself as comfortable as possible on the lumpy horse-hair cushions.

"You have pondered much," I ventured to observe, nettled by his taciturnity. "Have you reached a conclusion?"

"Have you?" He turned his beaky nose towards me, "You have the same information as I, so what do you make of it?"

"Very little" I confessed. "It is plain that Mr. John Ruddy suspects or perhaps even hopes for some irregularity in the claim, and also that you support him, but on what grounds?"

"Were it only that I would be easier in my mind," he said sombrely. "No, old friend, I fear we fish in far murkier waters, but I must have more facts. Facts, Watson, are crucial."

"Is it not possible that Ruddy, with the well-known reluctance of the insurance world to disburse money, is grasping at straws? Added to which is his fear of the consequences of his unorthodox transaction?"

"That is his primary concern," agreed Holmes. "That is indisputable. A policy holder dies soon after the first premium is paid and his widow and beneficiary is on the spot almost at once to lay her claim. That is enough to disturb any responsible agent. But consider, Watson, how did Ruddy describe her?"

I thought back. "He said very little of her except that she was distraught. Surely that is natural?"

"Natural, yes, but think, man, think! We have this lady straight from seeing her husband's body on a mortuary slab making a bee-line for the honey-pot of the insurer's representative," He gave the rusty chuckle that served him for a laugh. "A neat turn of phrase, Watson. Mark it well." His face sobered. "Does that strike you as the actions of a grieving widow?"

"I suppose not, unless there was little affection between them and she was playing the part expected of her."

He bent forward and tapped me on the knee with the stem of his pipe.

"There you have it. Playing the part – but what part?"

Before I could digest this, the cab drew up before an unpretentious but pleasant hotel and we alighted to climb the three wide steps to the entrance. A young woman presided at the reception desk, and on our approach she looked up with an engaging smile.

"Good afternoon, gentlemen," she said. "You require rooms?"

"No, miss." As ever Holmes remained impervious to feminine charms and his face was stern. "I wish to see the manager at once." His tone had undergone a subtle change, no more than a slight coarsening of

400

accent, but I knew it foretold a slipping into one of those parts which he so easily assumed.

"I'll see if Mr. Hardy is free, sir," said the young lady. "Who shall I say wishes to see him?"

Holmes leaned forward confidentially and lowered his voice. "I am Inspector Lestrade of Scotland Yard, but the name is not to be bandied about. Please inform Mr. Hardy. Our business is urgent."

The young lady's eyes widened, but she hurried away without a word.

"Holmes!" I hissed in his ear. "You go too far. What if he asks for identification?"

He patted his pocket and his lips twitched mischievously. "Be easy. I am well prepared. Just back me up like a good fellow."

The young lady was back in a flash. "This way, sir," she said in an awe-struck voice.

My companion turned on the charming smile of which he was capable when it served his ends, placing a finger to his lips in a conspiratorial fashion. We found ourselves in a small office with a rotund grey-haired man rising to greet us from behind a desk.

"James Hardy, Inspector. I trust nothing is amiss?" His chubby face was creased into an ingratiating smile and a pink tongue moistened his red lips.

"Nothing to cause you worry, sir, and I'd take it kindly if you will forget that we are police officers. We are here *incognito* on an extremely delicate business in which you may assist us." The story fell easily from Holmes's lips as he fixed the manager with a penetrating look.

"Of course, gentlemen. Please be seated and tell me how I may help."

Holmes folded his long frame into a chair and brusquely signed for me to sit beside him. From his pocket he took a notebook which he studied for a while. I could see he had it open at a blank page, but his performance was impressive.

He looked up at last. "I understand, Mr. Hardy, that last Monday you reported that one of your waiters, a George Monk, was missing."

"That is correct, Insp – er – " Hardy paused uncertainly.

"Mr. Smith will serve, and my colleague is Mr. Brown." Holmes laid a finger alongside his nose, a vulgar gesture, but well in the character of Lestrade whose name he had so lightly taken. "Tell me, sir, when did this man's absence first come to your attention?"

"It was tea-time on Sunday. He had served lunch as usual, and then from two until four he was free. It was his habit, if the weather was clement, to take a stroll on the sea front each afternoon. It is but five minutes gentle walking from here."

"And on Sunday he followed his normal practice?"

401

"To the best of my knowledge," the manager replied. "Miss Hillman is positive that he went out at twenty minutes after two o'clock. She spoke to him as he passed her on the back stairs."

"Miss Hillman is the young lady at the desk? How was he dressed?"

"I questioned her and she told me he was wearing a blazer, flannels, and carrying a straw hat. Quite the young blade. But surely, Mr. Smith, all this is known to the local police from the statement I made to Sergeant Lane on Monday?"

"That's as may be, sir," said Holmes gruffly. "This is a far deeper matter that I am pursuing. Be so good as to answer my questions without wasting time." He wrote something in his notebook. "So twenty-past-two is the last known sighting of him by your staff?"

"Exactly." Hardy frowned at being thus admonished. "When he failed to appear at tea-time, I was at first most angry, assuming he had absented himself willfully, but when he did not turn up at dinner I became rather more worried." The manager picked up a pen and rolled it in the palms of his hands. "I had gone to his room at quarter-past-four, but it told me nothing. His suit was on a hanger ready to be donned, and there was no hint that he had not expected to return. Several times during the evening I looked in, but nothing had changed."

"So when he remained absent on Monday you went to the police. You have had no word from them?"

"Sergeant Lane came to interview us all – most discreetly, I may add – but I have heard nothing since."

"Was Monk a satisfactory employee?" asked Holmes.

"He would not have remained otherwise. He was my only resident waiter, all the others being local men who come in daily."

"What was his background?"

Hardy smiled faintly. "Rather unusual for a waiter. He had spent some years at sea as a steward on steamers to the East, but he had wearied of the life and, to use his own phrase, swallowed the anchor. I had one occasion to reprimand him when he first came, but he took it in good part. He wore a ring in his left ear, a common practice among seafaring men, but most improper in an hotel of this class."

"Of course," murmured Holmes. "Now, sir, first a word with Miss Hillman and then I shall want to see the man's room. Will you fetch the young lady, please?"

When the latter came in, Holmes gave her his chair and stood looking down at her. She sat with neatly folded hands, her clear grey eyes looking out from a frank open countenance that in other circumstances would have been ready for laughter.

"Now, Miss Hillman, listen carefully," Holmes began. "My name is Smith, and this other gentleman is Mr. Brown." A small wrinkle of perplexity passed across her smooth brow as my friend continued. "You will forget any other name you may have heard, Miss, for I am here on more important matters than you can conceive. No word of this visit must pass beyond these four walls. Do I make myself clear?"

She nodded gravely. "I am not a simpleton, Mr. Smith. Neither am I a chatterbox. What do you want of me?"

"I understand you were the last person at this hotel to see Mr. George Monk before he vanished. That is correct?"

"I believe so. I had been to the kitchen for a cup of tea, leaving the porter at the desk, when Mr. Monk came down the service stairs on his way out. It was precisely twenty past two when I left the kitchen."

"You spoke?"

"Briefly. He said 'Good afternoon, Miss Charlotte,' that being my name, and I replied, 'Good afternoon, George. Mind you keep out of the sun' It was a very hot day," she added. "He went out, never to return."

"You were on good terms?" asked Holmes.

"Oh, yes. He was a widely travelled man and told marvellous stories of his times when we were together in foreign parts."

"Close friends, in fact?"

Miss Hillman blushed prettily. "On friendly terms. No more than that, Mr. Smith."

"Thank you, miss, that is all. Remember, be circumspect." He waited for the door to close on her then turned to the manager. "Now, sir, the missing man's room."

We were conducted to a small room under the eaves, the door of which Hardy unlocked and threw open. When he made to enter, Holmes put out an arm to bar his way and stood surveying the cramped quarters from the threshold.

"Nothing has been removed?" he asked.

"Nothing. Sergeant Lane made a thorough search but took nothing."

Holmes sighed. "Then I doubt if there is much left for us. The trail is cold, but we may find something. Come, Brown, and do you, Mr. Hardy, remain here."

We went in and Holmes allowed his eyes to wander over the room, touching nothing. Then turned to me with a snort.

"I think we will learn more of Sergeant Lane than of George Monk," he said in a low voice. He opened the cupboard that served as a wardrobe and went through the pockets of the few clothes hanging therein, producing only a German silver pencil case and a soiled handkerchief. He dropped to his knees to examine the half-dozen pairs of boots and shoes in

403

the bottom before looking over his shoulder at the manager who hovered uncertainly in the doorway.

"Mr. Monk was not a small man, judging by his apparel, yet his feet were not large."

"Indeed not," Hardy agreed. "It was a conceit of his that a size six boot left ample room to wear two pairs of socks in the worst weather."

Holmes nodded absently and, still on his knees, let his eyes travel over the floor. Suddenly, like a rabbit darting into its burrow, he dived full length beneath the bed to came out with a small object in the palm of his hand. His eyes twinkled at me as he rose to his feet and dusted the knees of his trousers.

"So the good sergeant did leave us something," he murmured. "Tell me, Mr. Hardy, could this be the ear-ring worn by your man?" He held out his hand and the light caught a glimmer of silver. The roly-poly manager shrugged. "Possibly, but I could not take an oath on it. All I can say it is similar."

"But distinctive," said Holmes. "Come, there is no more to be had here. I need not repeat, Mr. James Hardy, I require your discretion."

"In my profession one learns discretion very early," Hardy said pompously. "My lips are sealed." He followed us to the hotel entrance and watched us descend to the street and vanish from his sight.

"Well," I asked, "what now?

"I fear we have much to do and luncheon must be a casualty to our industry. The police station is our next objective. I believe I observed it on our journey from the station."

Five minutes later we walked into the bastion of Margate's law and order and found a uniformed inspector talking to a young and intelligent looking sergeant, both looked up as we entered and the senior man turned away towards an inner sanctum.

"A moment, Inspector" Holmes said authoritatively. "A word with you, please."

"Cannot the sergeant deal with it, sir?" The inspector frowned. "I am a very busy man."

"Not too busy to speak to me, I hope." My companion took a card from his pocket to hand to the inspector, at the same time placing a finger to his lips.

The other glanced at the card then raised his eyes and spoke with alacrity. "Of course I will be pleased to speak to you, sir. Nothing will give me greater pleasure. This way, if you will. Lane, I am not to be disturbed." This last to the sergeant who nodded impassively.

No sooner had his door closed on us than he stretched out his hand.

"My dear Mr. Holmes, this is indeed an honour and a delight. Inspector Griffin, my old colleague at Sevenoaks, has spoken most warmly of you. Please sit, gentlemen, and tell me how I may assist you. My name is Purdew."

"First I must make a confession," Holmes began when we were seated. "I am guilty of posing as a police officer and of using the name of Inspector Lestrade of Scotland Yard in order to obtain information quickly."

Purdew's eyes twinkled. "I'll make a bargain with you, Mr. Holmes: If you promise to tell no one, neither shall I, Now, what brings you to Margate?"

"Two crimes which may be connected." The inspector's look invited my friend to go on, which he did. "The disappearance of George Monk from the Stanton Hotel and the alleged drowning of Elias Burdick."

"'Alleged drowning'?" Purdew looked blank. "With respect, Mr. Holmes, I see no room for doubt. The body was identified by his widow and our surgeon certified drowning as the cause of death. As for Monk, we think it probable that he has returned to his old calling of ship's steward."

"Inspector, are you aware that the Rural and Urban Insurance Company is liable for a very large sum in respect of Burdick's death?"

"I knew them to be involved, but not to what extent. A constable escorted Mrs. Burdick from the mortuary to the agent's office. I know Mr. Ruddy well."

"Mr. Ruddy is not a happy man, Mr. Purdew. He has doubts about the validity of the claim."

"As these people so often have," replied the inspector. "It is in their nature."

"I believe he has good cause in this instance," said Holmes, and went on to relate the woeful tale told us by the unhappy man.

"It seems Mr. Ruddy acted somewhat irresponsibly and is now anxious to retrieve his position." Purdew plucked at his moustache. "However, Mr. Holmes, I am at your disposal. What do you want of me?"

"What happened to the body of the drowned man?"

"Why, it is still at the mortuary pending Mrs. Burdick's instructions."

"Excellent!" Holmes clapped his hands. "May I inspect it?"

"As you wish. I should like to accompany you if I may." On receiving a nod, the inspector reached for his cap and we followed him out into the street, he pausing for a brief word to the sergeant as we passed.

"Rather young to be a sergeant, is he not?" Holmes remarked casually.

405

"A bright and ambitious young man," Purdew agreed. "Would that I could recruit more like him, but on the pittance a constable is paid, it is hard to do so." He shrugged and lengthened his stride. "The mortuary is but two streets away."

"Sergeant Lane investigated the business at the Stanton Hotel," said Holmes. "What were his views?"

"We agreed that it seemed an impulsive action on Monk's part," said the inspector thoughtfully. "However, if he suddenly made up his mind to return to sea, there was little we could do."

"And you think that is what happened?"

"In the absence of more evidence it seems likely."

"Then perhaps we shall find more evidence," Holmes replied, but refused to enlarge on his remarks.

I congratulated myself on the fact that I was following my friend's reasoning thus far, and permitted myself a little smile. So often had I been dragged along at his coat-tails and left in the dark by his incisive brain that to find myself keeping abreast of his thoughts for once afforded me no small satisfaction. He must have divined my feelings, for as we reached the doors of the gloomy building he gave me one of his thin smiles while Inspector Purdew applied himself vigorously to the bell.

The wicket-gate was opened after an interval by a shirt-sleeved man who wore a leather apron and carried an enamel mug of tea. He was of indeterminate age and had a suitably lugubrious expression on his battered features.

"Not another customer, Guv'nor?" he said complainingly.

"Not this time, Charlie. We want another look at the one brought in on Monday."

"Number seventeen." Charlie gave a jerk of the head, "This way, if you please." He led the way through the gloomy precincts and into a large cavern-like room where three or four shrouded bundles lay on slabs ranged against the wall. "There he is. Number seventeen."

At a murmured word from Holmes the inspector dismissed the attendant, leaving us looking down at the pathetic heap before us.

"Are you squeamish, Purdew?" asked Holmes, one hand on the corner of the covering sheet.

"I've seen enough in my time to be inured," said the other.

"This is your province, Watson, so I'll not ask you." He drew the sheet back to reveal a face battered beyond all recognition, at which he whistled softly.

"And this is the body identified by Mrs. Burdick as that of her husband? On what grounds, pray?"

406

"She said she would know him anywhere, but she pointed out the silver ring on his left hand. See, it is embedded in the swollen flesh." The inspector pulled the sheet down and pointed.

Holmes produced his magnifying glass and peered closely at the ring, mumbling under his breath the while. Presently he turned his attention to the rest of the piteous remains, first turning the head from side to side then touching and probing the torso as he would a joint of meat.

His eyes narrowed in satisfaction when he finally threw the sheet to the floor and stood back.

"There is no doubt as to the cause of death, Mr. Purdew?"

"Our surgeon, Dr. Stubbs, has no doubt," replied the inspector, "and he is a very competent doctor."

"Watson? Would you agree?"

"If Dr. Stubbs made a thorough examination, and I see by the incisions that he did, I would not dream of contradicting him," I said stiffly,

My friend gave and ironic smile at my defence of a professional colleague before turning back to the policeman. "The clothing recovered from the beach," he queried. "Where is it?"

"Back at the station in the property store. It will be returned to the widow after tomorrow's inquest."

"Then we must make haste. Come." Leaving the uncovered corpse as it was, he made his way out into the street, his long legs striding out as we kept pace with him as best we could. "I must see that clothing," he flung over his shoulder to the perspiring Inspector Purdew as we entered the station. "Have it brought in at once, please."

His tone was peremptory and Purdew looked at me in bewilderment, but I could only shrug and he gave the necessary orders to Sergeant Lane before leading us into his office. When the sergeant appeared laden with a linen sack, he hesitated nervously and looked uncomfortably at his superior.

"Excuse me, sir," he said in a reverential voice, "but is one of these gentlemen Mr. Sherlock Holmes"

"What the deuce is it to you, Lane?" snapped the inspector. "Do not be impertinent."

Holmes stepped forward. "I'm sorry, Mr. Purdew," he said wryly. "I forgot to tell you I asked for two telegrams to be addressed to me here. It was most discourteous of me. They have arrived, Sergeant Lane?"

"Five minutes since, sir. I thought it might be a practical joke, but I wanted to be sure. Here, sir."

He pulled them from his top pocket and Holmes snatched them from his hand, tearing them open feverishly and giving a small cry as he read the contents. "I am right, Watson, I am right." He smiled grimly and tucked the telegrams away before turning his attention to the sack of clothing.

Tipping the contents on to the floor, he crouched down to paw through them, for all the world like a rag-picker at an East End street market.

The inspector looked at me with raised eyebrows and I gave him what I hoped was a knowing smile before giving my attention to Holmes, who was wrapped in concentration.

"Jacket, trousers – nothing in the pockets – linen, socks, cap." He stood up, still talking to himself. "As I expected, no boots or shoes. Everything is here, Inspector?"

"Everything." Before more could be said, there was a knock on the door and at a sign from Purdew the sergeant answered it. He exchanged few words then brought in a constable who had what appeared to be a bundle of dirty rags under his arm.

"I think you should see this, sir," Lane said to the inspector. "Denton found these stuffed down a rabbit-hole by the big copse. Show the gentlemen, Denton."

The embarrassed constable shook out the bundle to reveal a striped blazer, once-white flannels, and various other items of men's apparel, including a pair of tennis-shoes upon which Holmes pounced avidly.

"Tell us, Denton," the inspector was saying. "How did you come to find these?"

The constable shifted his feet and looked rigidly ahead. "Sir, at one-fifty p.m. I was patrolling – "

"Yes, yes," Holmes interrupted impatiently. "You are not giving evidence in court, man. Tell us a quickly as possible."

"Do as the gentleman says, Denton," added Purdew.

"Well, sir, I'd been round the copse and was going back to make my point with Sergeant Hoskins when I saw this flapping from a rabbit-hole."

He indicated the blazer. "I dragged it out and found the rest of the stuff farther in. Sergeant Hoskins told me to bring it back here straight away."

"This is all there was?" asked Holmes keenly,

"All I could see and reach, sir."

Holmes and the inspector exchanged glances and, at a nod from the former, Purdew dismissed the constable with a brief word of commendation.

Holmes swung round sharply on Sergeant Lane, who was exhibiting signs of wanting to speak. "Come along, Lane, out with it," he urged.

408

"I am correct in thinking that these clothes belong to the missing waiter, sir?" Holmes remained silent and the sergeant continued. "If so, then should there not also be a straw hat?"

"Perhaps it is still in the burrow. A thorough search will show us."

"Organize it, Lane," said Inspector Purdew. He waited until the man had left, then turned a worried look on Holmes. "It looks as if we must look for another body. Two men drowned within hours of each other!"

"Another body, Inspector? Whose, pray?"

"Why, George Monk's, surely. Do we not agree that these are his clothes?"

"Most certainly. His name is on the laundry label inside the jacket, but I do not think a man taking an afternoon bathe would stuff a pair of pristine white flannels into a rabbit-hole, do you?"

The inspector rubbed his chin thoughtfully, then his face brightened. "Then he was not drowned. He changed into more appropriate attire before making his way to a port where he would find a ship."

"Mr. Purdew," Holmes said patiently, "we know that when Monk left the hotel he was carrying nothing, else the lady clerk would have remarked upon it to your sergeant or myself."

"Then he purchased them in town and changed in the copse?"

My friend turned to me. "What do you say to that, Watson?"

I shook my head. As much as I deplored this baiting of the inspector who had received us in such a fine spirit, I was unable to keep a note of smugness from my voice. "I think we were looking at the mortal remains of George Monk not half-an-hour since," I answered, and Holmes gave a delighted chuckle.

"Capital, Watson. You learn apace." He turned to the inspector, who had dropped into his chair wearing a thunderstruck expression.

"Are you saying, Mr. Holmes, that the body in the mortuary is not that of Elias Burdick, but that of George Monk?"

"Exactly." Holmes became apologetic. "Forgive me, Inspector. I had no intention of keeping you in the dark, but I like to verify facts before committing myself."

"Then you suspected it from the first? Why?"

Holmes seated himself opposite Purdew and began to explain. "I learned from Monk's employer that when he first came to Margate, he had cause to reprimand him for wearing an ear-ring, as is the habit of many sea-going men. Sergeant Lane was not told of this? No, but I found this under the bed in Monk's room." He produced the small silver object from his pocket.

"I think Watson will confirm its origin."

"Benares work," I said. "I saw much of it when I passed through India on my way to Afghanistan."

"We were told that Monk had extremely small feet of which he was somewhat vain," continued Holmes. "The corpse we saw had such small feet and his ear was pierced to accommodate an ear-ring." Holmes leant forward and tapped the table. "But, mark this, Inspector – the ring so deeply embedded in his finger was of Benares silver-work also."

"You make a case," said Purdew, "but how do you account for the fact that Mrs. Burdick identified the ring as her husband's?"

"Remember the face was so disfigured that it was unrecognisable. The ring was probably too tight to be removed even before the body was swollen in death, so needing to make a positive declaration, she seized on the ring." Holmes sat back complacently and eyed the inspector.

"I begin to understand," said the latter. "You believe that Burdick disposed of Monk with the intention of letting his wife claim the insurance money by identifying the body as that of her husband." His face went red with anger and jumped to his feet. "What a pair of monsters! We must take her and force her to reveal her husband's whereabouts."

"All in good time," said Holmes urbanely. "Inspector Purdew, you have been very patient with me thus far. Will you trust me farther?"

The policeman hesitated briefly before sitting down again. "What do you want of me, Mr. Holmes? I trust you implicitly."

"Then listen carefully. This is what you must do." Holmes began to speak tersely, receiving an occasional nod of understanding from the inspector. "Be sure of this, Mr. Purdew," he concluded, "I have no wish for my name to come into this matter, and any credit accruing is yours alone."

"It shall be as you say," replied the gratified inspector. "What will you do meanwhile?"

"I shall attend Mr. John Ruddy, who must surely be impatient to hear of my progress. Then we shall proceed to Mrs. Ellis's boarding establishment, where I understand the so-called widow is lodged. Remember, Inspector, be prompt, but do nothing until you have my signal, or all may be lost."

He stood up. "Mr. Ruddy's office is close?

"But five minutes' walk. Turn left out of the station. The third turning on the left is Priory Road, and his office is halfway up on the right above an empty shop. You will see his plate at the side door."

When five minutes later we came into the office to find our client impatient and anxious. He sprang up from his desk to grasp my colleague eagerly by the sleeve.

"Mr. Holmes!" he gasped. "At last! What news have you for me?"

Holmes shook himself free. "Compose yourself, sir," he said crisply. "I can guarantee your six-thousand pounds is safe. What account you will give your superiors of your actions is for you to determine, but I'm sure a little judicious wording will ease your path. At the same time, I hope this will serve as a lesson to you."

"Indeed it will, Mr. Holmes," Ruddy said fervently. "My ambitions outran my judgement, but I know better now. But what happens next?"

"We have the final act to play out – but meanwhile there is the matter of my fee."

"Ask what you will and I will gladly double it," cried Ruddy.

"That is unnecessary," replied my friend coldly. "My charges are fixed and not open to discussion. However, if you will write a cheque now you may hand it to me in exactly one hour's time when you are relieved of your troubles." He named a sum which was accepted without demur. "Now we pay a call on Mrs. Emily Burdick, to whom you present me as a financial secretary to your company." Again his impish humour showed through as it so often did when we neared the end of a case. "Mr. Gregson is a capital name for me, I think. Mr. Ruddy. Whatever you do, say nothing to alert the lady to the fact that you are anything but the sympathetic agent of the insurance company. Can you play the part?"

"Mr. Holmes, I could play Hamlet himself with what is at stake!"

"I hope so. Watson, you look put out."

"Is there no part for me in what you term 'the final act'?" I asked.

My friend laughed and laid an affectionate arm across my shoulders.

"My dear fellow, where would I be without you? Of course you have your part, but more of that later. Let us proceed."

Our objective was a neat villa a few hundred yards from the sea-front. A card in the window proclaimed vacancies, and the door was opened by a plump jolly-looking woman who smiled brightly at us.

"Good afternoon, gentlemen," she said. "You require rooms?"

"I'm afraid not, Madam," Ruddy replied in solemn tones. "You are Mrs. Ellis?" She nodded. "I am Mr. Ruddy, and I believe I am expected by Mrs. Burdick.

Her face took on an expression of sympathy. "Oh, the poor woman! How I feel for her in her grief. Come in, gentlemen, please."

We were ushered into a comfortably furnished parlour and invited to sit down. Mrs. Ellis stood in the doorway, her fingers twisting the rings she wore on both hands.

"A moment, please." Holmes took immediate charge. "I am an associate of Mr. Ruddy's. Sit for a moment and tell us about Mr. and Mrs. Burdick."

411

"There's not much to tell." She took a chair and continued to play with her rings. "Mr. Burdick came to me before lunch on Sunday asking for a room. He told me he was an actor from London hoping for a few weeks work at a local theatre before the season ended."

"Did he say which?" asked Holmes.

"No, I had very little speech with him. Within an hour of his arrival he went out, to get the lie of the town, he said, and told me he would be in for tea. That was the last I saw of him."

"He went out empty-handed?"

"He carried a Gladstone bag," She sniffed and dabbed at her nose with a wisp of handkerchief. "He had not returned by eleven o'clock, which is when I start locking up, and by midnight I thought he had fallen in with friends and was sleeping elsewhere. It happens with actors,"

"You went to bed?" Holmes encouraged her. "Go on, please."

Mrs. Ellis nodded unhappily. "I never dreamt anything was amiss. How could I? Well, Monday came and he hadn't come back, so I went to his room. I found a suit and pair of boots in the wardrobe and his razor on the wash-stand. Then I got worried and went to the police."

"Where you were told that Elias Burdick's clothes had been found on the beach," Holmes finished for her.

"Not only that," she cried dramatically. "Even whilst I was at the station, it was reported that a body had been taken from the sea and was assumed to be that of my lodger. They wanted me to look at it, but as I told them, I'd hardly seen the man and they could do without my help."

She shuddered. "What would I want with corpses I hardly knew?"

"You were well spared," agreed Holmes. "And Mrs. Burdick?"

"That was Tuesday. All of a twitter, I was, and this lady came to the door with a policeman who said she was Mrs. Burdick and she wanted her husband's old room. Not a word had she to say for herself, she was so upset, and I didn't have the heart to refuse her. I took her up, and over a cup of tea the policeman told me she'd come straight from identifying her husband at the mortuary."

Holmes pinched his long nose thoughtfully. "Tell me, Mrs. Ellis, how was the lady dressed?"

"All in black, head to toe just like a widow would be, and so heavily veiled that I marvelled she could see where she was going, Within five minutes she was down again, asking the policeman to take her to Mr. Ruddy's office." Mrs. Ellis lowered her voice. "Do you know, since she came back I've not seen hide nor hair of her. Stricken with grief, she is, and takes all her meals in her room. I just knock on her door and leaves the tray on the landing table. Number three, it is. I must say," she added, "her appetite hasn't suffered at all."

412

"Grief takes on different forms," Holmes observed sententiously, "Now, Madam, be good enough to inform the lady that Mr. Ruddy is here to do business with her. Say no more than that, you understand?" He eyed her sternly and with a nervous nod she left.

"Remember your part, Mr. Ruddy," said Holmes in a low voice. "Watson, I shall leave the door open that you may see from a suitable vantage point but not be seen. Be on your guard, old chap." He went to the window and gave a twitch of the curtain as the landlady returned,

"I'll take you up, gentlemen," she said, but Holmes shook his head,

"No, Mrs. Ellis, you will remain here. Have you any other guests in the house? No? Good, then you will lock yourself in this room and not come out until I or my other colleague tell you to." He inclined his head towards me. "It is for your own safety."

Such was the force of his personality that she nodded meekly and we heard the key turn as soon as we were in the hallway. Holmes went to the front door and quietly slipped the catch. Then we made our way silently up the narrow stairs.

We found ourselves in a poorly lit passage with several doors on either side. Number three was at the end, the door set at an angle, and at a sign from Holmes, I took up a position in the gloom where I could command a view of the room once the door was opened. Ruddy knocked on the door and a muffled voice from within bade him enter, which he did with Holmes hard on his heels.

I could see clearly into the room where a veiled figure sat in an upright chair placed with its back to the only window. As Holmes stepped over the threshold, I saw him check his stride for the merest fraction of a second, then continue.

"My dear Mrs. Burdick," said Ruddy, his voice oozing sympathy. "This is a sad occasion indeed. May I present Mr. Gregson, our head cashier?"

"Very sad," said Holmes evenly. "However, your husband's forethought and prudence must provide some small consolation." There was no reply and Holmes advanced farther into the room. "Do you not find the atmosphere somewhat close?" he went on, and not waiting for an answer, he stepped swiftly past the woman and threw the sash open to its fullest extent.

A strong breeze from the window rushed through the room and the woman turned her head in alarm. The draught took her veils and she frantically pulled them back over her face as Holmes slammed the window down. His long legs took him back to face her, his eyes blazing triumphantly.

"The game is up, Elias Burdick!" he cried. "Will you come quietly?"

413

With an unladylike oath the figure leapt from the chair, taking Holmes off balance and cannoning him into to Ruddy, who stood paralysed.

"Watson!" shouted my friend. "Seize him!"

I bounded forward and received a violent blow on the shoulder, but I grappled with the black-clad figure, realising at once that this was no woman who fought so desperately. I got in a telling punch to the ribs before a pair of sinewy hands took me round the throat and slammed me against the wall, driving the breath from my body. My assailant dived for the stairs, but hampered by the long dress was not quick enough to evade my clutching fingers which took hold of the streaming veil. It checked him for an instant then Holmes was on him and I was left gasping with the veils in my hand, together with a long black wig.

"Stout work, Watson," panted Holmes, applying a vicious arm-lock to his captive and receiving a stream of invective in return. He took a whistle from his pocket to blow a shrill blast, and within seconds Inspector Purdew pounded up the stairs with Sergeant Lane and a constable at his heels.

Not wasting time on questions, Purdew clapped a pair of handcuffs on the writhing man and left the sergeant and constable holding him in a rough grip.

"Well done, Inspector." Holmes straightened his coat. "Meet Elias Burdick, the murderer of George Monk. Also known as Luke Henry and Josiah Larkin, under which names he committed similar crimes. There are bodies buried under those names in Essex and Hampshire, but he can only hang once, unfortunately."

The prisoner continued to struggle violently until a tap from the sergeant's truncheon persuaded him of the futility of resistance, and at a signal from Purdew he was hustled downstairs to the waiting van.

"Is there anything more I should know, Mr. Holmes?" asked the inspector.

"I think not. You have a grasp of the situation that would make your London counterparts blush with shame." He thrust out his hand. "Goodbye, sir. It has been a delight to work with you."

After fulsome thanks, Inspector Purdew departed with his prisoner, leaving Ruddy to come forward to express his gratitude in more tangible form.

"I do not know how you did it, Mr. Holmes," he said wonderingly. "I can never thank you enough."

"I have my methods," smiled Holmes as he folded the slip of paper into his pocket book. "Watson, my dear fellow, are you injured? I should have inquired sooner."

414

"There is nothing wrong with me that a belated lunch will not cure," I complained. "Do you realise we have had nothing since breakfast? Also we still have Mrs. Ellis locked in her parlour."

"So we have. Good Lord, I had quite forgotten. The poor lady must be frantic."

In the event, the good lady was reasonably composed, and a few judicious words giving a bare outline of events was sufficient to soothe her ruffled feelings.

"You will read of it in the papers, and Inspector Purdew will want a statement from you," ended Holmes. "Meanwhile, speak to no one of it. Now, Watson, I believe you mentioned lunch." An hour-and-a-half later we were on our way back to London. With my notebook open, I was sketching in the affair with it still fresh in my memory, and I paused to chew my pencil when I caught my friend's eye.

"Still puzzled?" he asked with one of his impish smiles. "Why, you were with me every step of the way."

"I thought so, but I must confess I became somewhat confused towards the end." I tapped my notebook. "We knew that the body in the mortuary was that of George Monk, and it was meant to be taken for Burdick. Also it was reasonable to assume that Burdick had murdered that poor fellow in order to claim the insurance money."

"Very good, old chap. Go on."

"That is where I lose the thread," I said. "I expected to find the villain's wife there as his accomplice. Where is she?"

"There is no wife, and there never was." He pulled out his pipe and began to fill it.

"Ah, those telegrams!" I exclaimed. "You kept me in the dark."

"Not really. The telegrams were mere confirmation of similar cases I found in my commonplace book."

"Then how the deuce did you know that the supposed widow was Burdick in woman's guise?"

Holmes applied a vesta to the tobacco and surveyed me through a blue haze. He turned to look out of the window, and at first I thought he wasn't going to answer me. He sucked at his pipe and for a full minute he remained stubbornly silent. Then he turned back to me with a wry smile.

"Confound you, Watson," he said pettishly. "You have a facility for asking the most awkward questions. The whole truth of the matter is that I didn't know that until the very last minute!"

"What!" My pencil fell from my fingers to roll unheeded on to the floor. "Are you telling me – "

"Yes, Watson. Right up to the moment I stepped into that room, I fully expected to find Burdick's female accomplice."

"Then what changed your opinion?"

"You will recall that the supposed Mrs. Burdick was seated with her back to the window with her face heavily veiled and in shadow. As I went in, I saw a pair of boots peeping out from below the dress and to me they seemed somewhat over-large for a lady. There are some unfortunate women so endowed but it set me off on a new train of thought. You saw me open the window?"

"Yes, and caused a most infernal draught."

"Precisely my intention. The breeze disturbed the veils swathing the woman's head and in that fraction of a second I saw the nose."

"The nose!" I echoed. "Surely, Holmes, a nose is a nose, is it not?"

"Oh, yes." He gave me a thin smile. "You, my dear fellow, are more familiar with the whims and caprices of the fair sex, but even I am aware that no lady, whatever her other pre-occupations, would neglect to powder her nose to receive visitors, although she would remain veiled. That nose, Watson, was as shiny as new sovereign, and at that moment the whole matter became clear."

I recovered my pencil from beneath the seat and directed a quizzical look at my companion, "So you admit to a certain amount of luck at the end?"

"I admit nothing of the sort," he said testily. "It was observation and deduction that brought the business to a satisfactory conclusion, and will hang Burdick under one name or another. Now let me relax for the remainder of the journey. I fear Lestrade will be at our door this evening. He has quite lost the scent in the matter of the vanishing shop at Highgate."

"You owe the poor fellow something for the use of his name," I said drily, but he closed his eyes and uttered not another word until we came to London Bridge.

A Question of Innocence
by DJ Tyrer

I stepped out of the chill sleet and into the warmth of 221b Baker Street just as a young lady in a dark-grey travelling coat was telling Mrs. Hudson that she needed to see Sherlock Holmes immediately.

"No need to bother the boy-in-buttons," said I, removing my hat, "I shall show her up. Perhaps a pot of tea? She appears half-frozen. This way, my dear," I added, taking her arm and guiding her up the stairs.

"I'm Doctor Watson," I said by way of introduction. "And you are?"

"Miss Sally Wainwright."

"Pleased to meet you, Miss Wainwright. Rest assured, whatever your problem is, I'm sure Mr. Holmes will be able to resolve it for you."

"I pray he can," she said with a tearful urgency that frankly stung my heart.

I felt a twinge of guilt that I might have falsely raised the hopes of one who was clearly in some difficulty, but had no time to brood upon the concern as we entered the lodgings I shared with Sherlock Holmes.

My friend looked up from the fireplace where he was on his hands and knees poking at the ashes with a painting knife, some of which it appeared he was depositing in envelopes. I had no idea what he was about, but assumed he was investigating some new insight that he hoped would assist him in the solving of crimes. He was dressed in his shirt sleeves, which were rolled up, and had a smudge of dirt across his face from his vigorous poking and looked more the image of a labourer than a man of intellect and insight.

I could only imagine what our guest thought as I said, "Miss Wainwright, may I introduce you to Mr. Sherlock Holmes. This is Miss Sally Wainwright, and she has come to us with a problem – "

"Good morning," said Holmes, thrusting himself up onto his feet and extending himself to his full height, scooping up the envelopes of ashes and depositing them on the table. He clapped his hands together to rid them of some of the soot and said, "I trust you shall not be offended if I refrain from offering the usual courtesies, but I am in something of an unseemly state."

The young woman allowed herself a half-smile, despite her apparent upset, and nodded. "I quite understand."

Holmes smiled back at her and I saw he had her captivated in spite of his disheveled state.

417

"You see," said he, "I was just investigating the residue left by the burning of different types of paper and parchment and . . . Well, you didn't come here for a lecture on such an obscure subject, but, as Watson says, with a problem? How is it that we can assist you?"

She took a deep breath and gulped out, "I have been accused of murder, sir!"

"Murder?" Holmes fixed her eyes with his. "That *is* a serious problem. Please remove your coat, be seated, and compose yourself. Watson, prepare the fire. I have no further need of the ashes. I shall be but a moment, then we shall address the terrible situation in which you find yourself."

With a nod, she did as he bade, while Holmes stepped through into the next room. I got down on my knees, and began to kindle a warming blaze.

Just as Holmes returned with hands and face clean, and correctly attired in a jacket, Mrs. Hudson entered with a pot of tea and three cups.

"Thank you, kind lady," said he. "Watson will take charge of the task of pouring when it is ready."

Then, when she was gone and I'd had the chance to settle myself in my seat, Holmes steepled his fingers and said, "Please begin."

Miss Wainwright sniffed and was silent for a moment, as if rallying her thoughts. Then she spoke.

"It all began six months ago," she said. "My father was a country parson, but he had died after a long illness that had devoured his modest savings, leaving me near-destitute and homeless. What little money I had left would provide meagre lodgings for but a brief while, so that it was necessary for me to obtain some form of employment as soon as possible.

"Fortune smiled upon me, or so I imagined at the time, and an old friend of my father's recommended me for a position as a companion and lady's maid, an occupation to which the education and experience afforded to the daughter of a clergyman is well suited. I accepted without delay, of course."

She shook her head. "Perhaps it would have been better had I considered the position first, for later I learned that the family had trouble keeping staff due to the temper and ill-bearing of the master. But I gave no thought to such problems and nobody spoke of them to me.

"So it was that I found myself companion to Mrs. Mary Ashcroft in an old house in the foothills of the Pennines, not far from Bradford.

"It wasn't a bad position, Mr. Holmes, to begin with. Mrs. Ashcroft was a congenial person. Indeed, I was quite surprised upon meeting her to discover she was no older than me – younger probably. Most women who advertise for companions are older, as you know. However, it was

418

understandable why she required one, for her health was delicate and she had little energy. Of course, I wasn't entirely pleased at this, as I should have liked to walk outdoors more when the weather was good after having spent so long caring for my father, but I could hardly blame her for her infirmity and she did occasionally send me into town on errands, for which I was grateful. And though her health meant we didn't go visiting, nor did she receive many visitors, we would spend pleasant times sewing together beside the fire or with me reading to her. All in all I was satisfied, and with a nurse present to care for her needs, it was a restful position after a time of travail for me."

"But her husband was a problem," said I, and she nodded.

"Yes. Mr. Ashcroft spent most of his time in London or York, both on business and in pleasure, and showed no joy in the company of his wife, nor any compassion for her state. Every two or three weeks, he would return to the house for a day or two, during which time he would cast a critical eye about and utter the foulest language I have ever heard. Of course, I learned that my predecessors in the role of companion hadn't long tolerated him on top of the deprivations of the mistress's infirmities.

"With no alternative, I could do nothing but hold my tongue and accept the complaints and abuse that came my way, knowing that he soon would be gone again."

"Most commendable," I told her.

"Thank you, Dr. Watson. And, so it went for six months. The mistress had few visitors – as I understand it, she wasn't from the district and between her poor health and the roughness of the master's tongue, had made few acquaintances and no real friends. Indeed, the only person who visited with any regularity was the local doctor, who stopped by the house most days to check on her health and, when he wasn't too busy ministering to the afflicted, would stay for a time and read to her or play upon the *pianoforte*, or otherwise occupy her and seek to raise her spirits.

"Most of the time, it was just the two of us and the other servants, who tended not to stay long – only the housekeeper, a Mrs. Muswell, having been there for the entire period I was."

"And so," said Holmes, "we arrive at the accusation of murder." She nodded. "Of your mistress?" She nodded again.

"Yes, sir. As I have said, her husband had an awful temper. It seemed to me inconceivable that such a nice woman as her could find herself bound to one as uncouth as he, but Mrs. Muswell did tell me, one day, when the mistress had retired early to bed, something that explained it."

Now I must admit that at this point I was tempted to interrupt Miss Wainwright and demand that she get to the point of her story for, in spite of the accusation levied against her, she seemed incapable of explaining what had come to pass. But as Holmes stayed silent, I kept my temper and allowed her to continue and unravel the story in her own manner.

"They had only been married for two years – as I told you, she was a young woman – and the child that she had borne him in the first year of marriage, a treasured son and heir, had been taken by the same illness that had laid her low. From what Mrs. Muswell said, Mr. Ashcroft had never been a fine man, and his temper had worsened and he had come to lay the blame for their son's death upon his wife."

"The poor woman," I couldn't help but say.

"Indeed. It explained much, in particular the despondent moods that took her whenever he was due to return to the house and while he was present. Dark moods, if you sirs will understand me. I would take especial care to watch her at these times for I was always worried that she might do . . . something."

Holmes nodded. "We understand. Continue."

"Well, just three days ago, I took up her luncheon, only to find her collapsed on the floor of her dressing room, a bottle of medicine clasped in her hand. It was a terrible shock to me – no, not her death, though that was heart-wrenching, too – but to discover that she had chosen the path of self-destruction, for her husband was away and not due back for two weeks. I had had no reason to suspect she might try such a thing then. Indeed, the doctor had but visited just that morning and she had seemed in a fine mood to me when he left.

"He was sent for and, after examining her, declared that she had drunk the entire bottle in one go, which had killed her. Although he expressed himself shocked at her deed, he knew of her dark moods and confessed it wasn't entirely unforeseeable. With the decorum of one of good heart, he promised to obscure the cause of death to prevent any scandal attaching to either her name or mine.

"Then the master arrived home, summoned by the news of his wife's death."

"And he blamed you?" asked Holmes over steepled fingers.

"Not at first."

"Oh?"

"No. I believe he knew how his wife felt about him and could readily believe that she made such a decision. But then, he proclaimed that certain items from her jewellery box, along with money and promissory notes from his strongbox, were missing. This, he declared, showed that his wife had been murdered and, as her closest companion, it was me that he chose to blame.

"An inspector was summoned and questioned me at length, as well as the other staff, and he had his men search the house and grounds. Of course, they found nothing to connect me with any crime and I denied any involvement in murder or theft, but he made it clear that I remained his chief suspect."

"But," I interrupted, "why jump from theft to murder? Even if you had taken the jewellery and other items – and, I stress, I'm not saying I think you did – surely it would make more sense to assume you hoped to get away with the crime in the uproar surrounding your mistress's death?"

"Bravo, Watson," said Holmes. "Well observed. Yes, it is a leap. Unfortunately for Miss Wainwright, Mr. Ashcroft is a man of means and influence and, as such, his accusation carries a great deal of weight, even if it clearly lacks the merit of logic. However, fortune hasn't abandoned her entirely, for without anything to officially prove her involvement with the theft, she yet retains her liberty."

Miss Wainwright blinked away tears and said, "I worry, not for long."

"Indeed, my dear. But we have diverted you from your telling. Please, continue."

"Well, with what I would say was unseemly haste, Mr. Ashcroft had his wife buried. That was yesterday. It was a simple graveside service. It seems she had no family or friends, for only her husband, the doctor, myself, and the staff were in attendance.

"Then, this morning, I caught the train down to London and sought you out." She gulped. "The inspector had told me I wasn't to leave the district, but I just knew that if stayed that he would find some way to condemn me as a murderess, and that my only hope, even if it risked making them question my innocence further, was to find you, sir, and beg you to clear my name before the hangman can claim me."

She looked imploringly at Holmes with wide, tearful eyes. "I swear, Mr. Holmes, I neither did harm to my mistress, nor did I steal any valuables. I am an honest and God-fearing woman, sir."

Sherlock Holmes is a peculiar fellow, at times seemingly cold and without feeling, operating entirely upon logic. At others, he can be compassionate to a fault. As I watched him gaze into those desperate, fearful eyes, I was certain that, having allowed her to talk at length, he would take the case, but whether because he felt the same protectiveness for her that I did, or because his incisive brain had spotted some element that had escaped me, but which told him that she was innocent and that there was more to it all, I couldn't tell.

As I'd expected, he said, "Dry your eyes, for I shall clear your name."

I couldn't help but harrumph. "It should be easy enough to prove the woman wasn't murdered, Holmes, but can you be certain that you can prove Miss Wainwright is no thief?"

"Indeed, I believe I can." He looked at the young lady. "Now think back to the days preceding her death . . . Her husband was away, you say?" She nodded. "The staff were all present? Did any leave?"

"No, sir, they were all in the house, save for the footman who had arranged a week's holiday and was due back the day after she died."

Holmes nodded. "So nobody left, not even to go into a nearby village?"

"Not at all."

"The doctor visited?"

"Yes, as usual."

"And, did he take his bag with him when he saw her?"

"A-ha!" I cried. "You think he carried the jewellery away?"

"Perhaps," said my friend, but Miss Wainwright shook her head.

"No, he always left it in the kitchen, unless he were carrying out a full examination of her, and he didn't do that in the few days before her death. All he did was carry up his stethoscope and, that day, the medicine that she . . . ."

She trailed off and Holmes nodded.

"So," he said, "we can rule out the servants, assuming the inspector's search was adequate, and the good Doctor. Did the house receive any other visitors?"

"No."

"And you?" he asked. "Did you leave the house?"

"Me! Do you then suspect me after all?"

"I'm sure he doesn't, my dear," I interjected to calm her, "but I always find it wisest to answer my friend's questions, no matter how outlandish they might at first seem. They always have a point, even if we have yet to see it."

She straightened her skirts and said, "No."

Then she made a small noise. "Wait! It was two or three days before she died – events had put it quite out of my head – but she did ask me to take a package into town and mail it."

Holmes gave a smile then that put me in mind of a wolf that had scented its prey.

"What was the size of the package?"

She indicated the approximate size with her hands. I could see what Holmes was thinking: The parcel could easily have contained the jewellery and money.

Miss Wainwright reached the same conclusion, becoming quite pale as she did so, and said, "You think she had me post the stolen items?"

"I believe so."

"Oh! I swear, I didn't know."

422

"No, you were but an unwitting pawn in all this. Do you recall the address?"

She considered and shook her head. "No, I'm sorry." Then, she made a noise of exclamation and said, "I just remembered – I lent Mrs. Ashcroft my notepad to write the label." She retrieved it from her bag. "See, the page is torn out here, but you can make out the indentations of the letters on the next page . . . ." Her face fell. "I can just make out Essex, but that's all . . . ."

Holmes smiled and took the notepad from her, then retrieved one of the envelopes of ash from the table and sprinkled a little of its contents onto the page before rubbing them in with his thumb.

"Yes," he said, examining the words that had been revealed. "It is addressed to a '*Miss Samaria Feldspar, Care of Leigh Train Station, Essex*'."

"Well," I said, shaking my head, "that sounds like a concocted name. Feldspar, indeed."

"It may well be."

"Who was she really sending it to?" asked Miss Wainwright. "And why? And what does it have to do with her death?"

"Those are mysteries that complicate, but likely in the end, resolve this case," said Holmes. "I have one or two ideas, but this will require a little more work to unravel. Still, it is a strong lead for us to follow . . . ." Then he cocked his head and said, "By-the-by, you never named the doctor."

"Oh, his name was Landseer. Dr. Robert Landseer."

I looked at my friend. "That name sounds familiar." I tutted to myself for a moment. "Yes, I seem to recall there was some sort of scandal. He left London."

Miss Wainwright started a little. "Why, Dr. Watson, I do believe I recall him saying something about the countryside offering him anonymity once while talking to my mistress. Not that I understood him to mean for such reasons as you suggest."

Holmes laughed. "Only the distance from London offered him that, for as much as a multitude of scoundrels flee into the country each year in search of boltholes in which to hide away, the countryside offers little secrecy in comparison to the warrens that compose this city. Country folk are the most observant and prone to gossip in the land."

Then, his face grew serious again. "You're quite right, Watson – there was a scandal. I was involved with it, albeit tangentially, and have the details on file. I shall seek them out shortly. While I'm doing that, I would like you to send a telegram to – What was the name of the inspector who questioned you, my dear?"

"Inspector Wharton."

"Send a telegram to Inspector Wharton at Bradford and tell him that Miss Wainwright is here, safe and sound, and ask whether Dr. Landseer is still in the district, or if he has caught a train."

"Very good."

He returned his gaze to the young lady and told her to go join Mrs. Hudson downstairs. Handing her a *Bradshaw*, he added, "Perhaps you can locate Leigh in here. I suspect we may have to pay the place a visit." Then he smiled in an almost-paternal fashion. "I shall summon you when we have news."

Just over an hour later, the three of us found ourselves aboard a train from Fenchurch Street, headed for the village of Leigh on the north bank of the Thames Estuary.

I had returned from communicating with Inspector Wharton to inform Holmes that Dr. Landseer had indeed left Bradford by train a little earlier, only for my friend to announce our train journey to Essex.

"Surely," said I, "we ought to meet the doctor's train, if he is indeed a thief or murderer, as I take your interest in him to mean, and detain him?"

Holmes had dismissed the idea.

"We have no evidence and this is a man who can brazen his way out of such a situation. Besides, I suspect there is more to all this than there initially appears."

"Whatever do you mean?"

"You shall see soon enough, if I am right. In the meantime, we have a train to catch, if we are to arrive ahead of him and lay our trap. But here – you can read this once we're underway."

This proved to be the file to which Holmes had alluded concerning Dr. Landseer and his scandal. I read it as the train advanced its way eastwards towards the gloomy Essex marshes, then handed it to Miss Wainwright.

I found that, in essence, it served to show his guilt, for the doctor had been found to have provided the medicine used by an elderly and wealthy lady who had chosen the path of self-destruction following the death of her husband and son. Although the details had largely been kept out of the newspapers, there had been enough gossip that Dr. Landseer had been forced to abandon a rather a lucrative practice and leave London under a cloud. The role that my good friend had played in the case had been to retrieve some jewellery that had gone missing in the aftermath of the death.

Clearly, the greedy doctor had been unable to resist attempting the same crime again and, had Miss Wainwright not been accused and come to Holmes for assistance, he may well have escaped detection.

424

But if Holmes was right, it seemed that we would catch him in the act of attempting to retrieve the parcel of stolen items which Mrs. Ashcroft had doubtless been persuaded to send away by some ruse, and so prove his guilt as both thief and murderer.

The late-afternoon sun shone wanly as I watched the bleak landscape of marshland, mudflat, and snow-dappled farmland race by through the sleet-splattered window of the train. Just the sight of the dismal scene caused me to pull the collar of my coat up and huddle myself within its warmth. This was certainly country suited to villainy.

At last, we arrived at our destination and disembarked onto the platform of Leigh Station. The faint smell of ozone greeted us and told us that we were close to the sea's edge. A chill cutting breeze blew through the station, and I was relieved when Holmes directed us to the shelter of the waiting room.

The stationmaster, a large, well-rounded fellow in a fine blue uniform with brightly-polished buttons, spying us, walked over and gave us a jovial greeting, saying, "If you've come down to take the waters, you've chosen a rum day to do so. Wind's picking up and I daresay we'll be having weather later today."

I forbore from asking what he called the breeze and sleet, instead saying, "We are here on business, my good man."

"Business? Well, I trust it's indoor business. That's all I'll say on the topic."

"Actually," said Holmes at his most civil, "you may assist us with it. This young lady is expecting a parcel to have been left here in the care of the station."

"Really? And, what is your name, my dear, if I may presume to ask?"

Miss Wainwright smiled sweetly. "It is – " I held my breath, wondering if she had forgotten the unique appellation, but she finished, "Miss Samaria Feldspar," and I was able to breathe again.

The stationmaster nodded. "Ah, yes, my dear, I believe we do have a package waiting for you. I recall the name. Quite unusual."

Miss Wainwright smiled again. "If I may have it?"

"Oh, yes, of course. I'll have it for you in just a jiffy, if not sooner."

He hurried off to his office and returned with a package, which he handed to her.

Proffering a few more courtesies of thanks, as such rural station folk tend to expect, we bade him farewell and huddled close to the small fireplace that warmed the waiting room so as to conceal our purpose and had the young lady unwrap the parcel at one corner to reveal its contents. As we had expected, there were the promissory notes. There was little doubt that the money and jewellery were also inside.

425

"Well," I said, warming my hands by the fire, "there can be no doubt, can there, that Landseer is the guilty party?"

"None at all," said Holmes.

Although Miss Wainwright gave a quiet cheer at the removal of the burden of guilt from her shoulders, I was certain that my friend's tone carried a hint that there was yet more left to resolve, and I wondered just what awaited us when our prey stepped off the train.

We didn't have to wait long. There was a distant whistle and Holmes said, "Unless he tarried or was delayed, I expect the doctor to be aboard this train. We shall wait just inside the door, ready to pounce, but not evident before he steps down."

I nodded and joined him, telling Miss Wainwright, "Stay back."

"Oh, no," said Holmes, to my annoyance. "Place the young lady front and centre."

"You wish her to identify the blackguard?" I asked.

"I wish for her to see all that unfolds."

There was no time to ask him what he meant, for the train was pulling into the station with billows of steam that hung all the more thickly in the chill air, rolling out on the breeze like a thick sea fog.

A handful of figures alighted onto the platform, and I saw a man dressed in the manner that Inspector Wharton had designated – clearly Dr. Landseer. I was a little surprised to see a woman walking beside him, but I supposed it made sense if he meant to collect the package that we had intercepted.

The two figures moved through the fog of steam like ghosts towards us, then resolved out of it to reveal their faces and Miss Wainwright screamed in fright and staggered as if she might swoon.

"Mrs. Ashcroft!" she cried.

The woman, who a moment before had been smiling happily, went as pale as a sheet and an expression of horror crossed her features.

"Mrs. Ashcroft?" I responded in shock as I caught Miss Wainwright's arm and steadied her.

"Mrs. Ashcroft," said Holmes in a satisfied tone, "or Miss Samaria Feldspar, as she has also chosen to name herself."

The woman's mouth opened and closed soundlessly in a manner that, I fear, likely mimicked my own. As for the man, Landseer, he had a blank expression as if unable to work out what was occurring.

"But how?" demanded Miss Wainwright. "I saw her – she was dead – *dead*!"

Holmes shook his head. "Oh, no. I had my suspicions when you revealed that it had to be your mistress who mailed the stolen items away. That made murder seem unlikely. If she were being blackmailed, for instance, then why kill her? That she had killed herself appeared even less likely – at least not without denouncing the villain.

"Landseer here, being a medical man, had the knowledge of sleeping draughts that could fool untrained eyes – such as those of her companion and husband – and allow him to quickly certify her death, only to revive her shortly afterward."

Mrs. Ashcroft threw up her hands. "It's true. It's all true!"

"You stupid woman!" snapped the doctor, coming back to his senses. Then, to us, he said in a most-unctuous tone, "I deny everything. I may have provided her with medicine, but I had no knowledge of what she planned nor of what she did. I am as much a dupe as this poor girl here, who was wrongfully accused of murder. As you can see, Mrs. Ashcroft is alive and well, and neither Miss Wainwright nor I can be held guilty of any crime of murder or theft."

"Really? Watson, his medical bag, please."

I didn't know what Holmes had in mind, but I lunged for the case that the doctor held and, after a brief tussle, relieved him of it.

As I passed it to Holmes, the stationmaster blew his whistle and waved his flag for the train to depart. A look of pure hatred passed across Landseer's face and he seized Mrs. Ashcroft and thrust her towards the platform edge!

Without thinking, I leapt forward and took hold of her arm, pulling her back before she could fall in front of the train.

"Stop him!" I heard Holmes shout and I saw that the doctor was dashing towards the station exit. Not realising that his cry was directed elsewhere, I began to run after him, puffing and wishing I were in better condition.

As I chased after him onto a wharf, the incoming tide driven by the rising wind sending a spray of white foam up its sides, two men ran past me and towards my quarry.

They seized him and tackled him to the ground. It was then that I recognised one as Inspector Lestrade, and realised it had been to him that Holmes had directed his cry.

Pausing to catch my breath, I joined them as they hauled the criminal to his feet.

"Well done," I panted, and Lestrade acknowledged my words with a nod.

"Right. Let's get him to Mr. Holmes and see what I should charge him with."

We returned to the platform where the two women were slumped upon a bench, the one still reeling from the revelation that someone she thought dead was still alive, the other with an expression of defeat and humiliation. Holmes was calmly explaining to the agitated stationmaster that all was well and that the police had taken charge of events.

"Ah, you caught him. Well done, Lestrade. And, well done, Watson, for saving this woman from death."

I shook my head in confusion, and then looked at Landseer with narrowed eyes. "I cannot quite understand it. Were you only interested in her money?"

"Indeed he was," said Holmes, opening up the man's medical bag to reveal a syringe wrapped in a handkerchief. "When this is examined, you will find that it is a poison, likely one that causes a natural-seeming death."

"Goodness!" I exclaimed.

"No!" sobbed Mrs. Ashcroft in horror. "No, he wouldn't!"

"Oh, but he would," said Holmes in a hard voice.

"Oh!" She swooned.

"But why?" I asked as I stooped to check on her. "I mean, if he wanted her dead, why the charade? Why not just murder her then?"

"Because, unwittingly, Mrs. Ashcroft prolonged her life by seeking a cunning means to dispose of the money and jewellery with which they were to start a new life. Doubtless Dr. Landseer had intended for her to just hand them over to him, after which, as you point out, he would have allowed her to 'unwittingly' kill herself.

"But wary of his theft being detected, she chose a different course and he had to go through with what had, until then, been nothing more than a ruse."

"Faking her death, you mean?" I asked and Holmes nodded. "But," I asked him, "how did he succeed in avoiding having his artifice detected? Oh, yes, I know he was the one who pronounced her dead, but did her husband or whomever prepared her for burial not notice?"

"Given the speed with which he wished her disposed of and his greater interest in her jewels than the nature of her passing, whether due to callousness or guilt, I suspect her husband paid her no more heed in death than in life, and left Landseer to oversee her preparations."

I felt a pang of sympathy as Mrs Ashcroft sobbed loudly at his words.

"With Miss Wainwright under suspicion, I would assume the duties fell to the housekeeper, who was either quite cursory in her approach, or received an inducement from the doctor to not ask questions."

Landseer scoffed, loudly, but Holmes continued, "As the burial was conducted with a graveside service, it would not have been particularly unusual for the coffin lid to be closed – I doubt Mr Ashcroft wished to see his wife's face – and the doctor could arrange for a coffin filled with rocks or some such ballast to buried in her stead."

"It's true," sobbed Mrs Ashcroft. "I watched from a distance, and not a flicker of grief crossed my husband's face."

"You have my sympathy," said Holmes, in a surprisingly tender voice.

Then. he continued. "Clearly, Mrs Ashcroft hadn't told Landseer where the package was sent, or else he might have suborned some other woman to retrieve it for him, and she would indeed have been buried that day. But having arrived here and obtained it, she was no longer of use to him and murder would, finally, have occurred. With nothing to identify her, there would be no reason to link her with a woman already dead and buried and, as a seemingly natural death, the police would have no reason for more than a cursory investigation.

"In short, he would have got away with his crime."

I shook my head again. "Landseer, you dastard."

The man snorted and glared at me, but said nothing. Lestrade and his man hauled him off to await the London-bound train. There would be no question of his innocence in all this.

"Well, Miss Wainwright," I said after a moment, "at least you can rest assured you are no longer under suspicion of any crime."

"Oh, thank you, Mr. Holmes," she said, choking just a little as she spoke. "And, thank you, Dr. Watson. I can never express how grateful I am."

Holmes smiled. "That it has all been set aright is sufficient satisfaction for me."

And, gazing at the relief etched upon her face, I think I have to agree.

The Grosvenor Square Furniture Van
by Terry Golledge

The first day of October, and already winter signalled its approach with a chill wind that rattled the windows and sent puffs of smoke into the room from the newly-lit fire to mingle with the haze of our post-breakfast pipes. For once the table was cleared before nine o'clock, and Sherlock Holmes, my friend and fellow-occupier of the rooms at 221b Baker Street, had discarded his old blue dressing-gown to assume his outdoor clothes.

I raised a querying eyebrow as he chose a stick from the collection in the stand, receiving a negative shake of the head in response.

"No, I have no special need of your company, but of course, you are quite welcome to join me in a brisk walk to Bradley's for a pound of shag."

"In that case I shall remain here," I replied as I settled back behind the pages of *The Daily Telegraph*. "This wind promises to do my shoulder little good. Bring me half-a-pound of Arcadia Mixture if you will be so good."

The door had not closed on him before I sat up with yelp of excitement. "Holmes!" I shouted loudly, and he reappeared with a look of amused annoyance on his face.

"Really, my dear Watson, must you shout at me as though you were hailing a cab? What is so urgent?"

"This." I thrust the paper at him and stabbed a finger at it. "It sounds right up your street, or I'm a Dutchman."

He took the paper from me and ran his eye over the item I indicated. It told of the mysterious disappearance of the well-known and highly respected Sir Peter Fawkus from his home in Grosvenor Square. His butler, one Thomas Moscrop, was also missing, and the matter was made more bizarre by the fact that a large sideboard had vanished from the dining room, leaving its contents strewn on the floor.

He returned the paper with a shrug. "Nothing there for us. I see Lady Fawkus has sufficient influence for Scotland Yard in the person of our friend Gregson to show an interest. I don't doubt he will blunder his way to a solution, given time."

This time he shut the door firmly, and I was left with only the sound of his footsteps on the stairs, I went back to the paragraph and tried to fit the bare facts into some kind of logical order by using my friend's methods, I was still cogitating when Mrs. Hudson announced Inspector Gregson.

"Come in, Inspector," I said. "Holmes is out at present but should be back shortly. A glass of beer while you wait?"

"Thank you, Doctor. Most welcome." He spread himself comfortably in front of the fire. "Your very good health, Doctor Watson."

Holmes was back within ten minutes of Gregson's arrival. He divested himself of his coat and threw it on to the settee, along with his hat.

"Now, my dear Gregson," he smiled, "how may I assist you in the matter of Sir Peter Fawkus?"

The officer grinned ruefully, "Always one jump ahead, Mr. Holmes, though I'll not deny being grateful to you for that more than once. I expect you've seen what the papers have to say, and between the three of us, there's a deal of pressure from above to get the thing sorted."

"Tell me what you know," said Holmes as he filled his pipe. "Leave nothing out, however trivial you may think it to be."

"Well, sir, it's like this: On Wednesday night, Lady Fawkus returned from the theatre to find the house in darkness, the only servant in evidence being her personal maid who was dozing in her mistress's bedroom. She told Lady Fawkus that the butler, Moscrop, had told the rest of the staff that Sir Peter had given orders for them to remain in their quarters, as he was expecting important visitors. However, there was no sign of Sir Peter, nor of Moscrop. This was well past midnight, and Lady Fawkus decided that her husband had for reasons unknown left the house, taking the butler with him,"

"Surely a very casual attitude," Holmes put in. "What opinion did you form of conditions within the household?"

"I got the feeling there was something on the lady's mind. She's a handsome woman, barely thirty years of age, while her husband is all of seventy. What little I could get from the servants made me think she spends a lot of time with her own friends, while Sir Peter is at his club most evenings. Anyway, it wasn't until yesterday morning that it became clear that neither Sir Peter nor Moscrop had returned, and a footman found that a large sideboard had gone from the dining room. Lady Fawkus waited until mid-day, and when Sir Peter hadn't come home and a messenger had ascertained that he had not been to his club, she took herself straight to the Yard to demand something should be done. I've been landed with it, and quite frankly, Mr. Holmes, I don't know where to start."

Holmes gazed into the fire as if for inspiration. Then he looked up at Gregson. "What of the butler? Has he been long with Sir Peter?"

"No more than a couple of weeks. He's only there temporarily, as the regular man is in hospital recovering from an accident. Got himself knocked down by a cab in Orchard Street. Old fellow, name of Clarke – been with Sir Peter twenty years and more."

"Then," said Holmes, "I suggest you turn your attention to this fellow Moscrop. It will also be fruitful to give some thought to the matter of the sideboard and why it is missing but the contents left. That is all I can think of at the moment."

Gregson nodded gloomily, obviously disappointed that my friend had nothing more to offer. He was given some consolation by the promise that Holmes would give the matter further thought and get in touch if anything should occur to him.

Once the inspector had left, Holmes slumped into his chair with his old cherry-wood pipe clamped between his teeth, a frown of concentration furrowing his brow. He remained so even when Mrs. Hudson tapped on the door again, so I took it upon myself to ascertain her mission.

"It's a lady asking for Mr. Holmes," she whispered, casting a wary glance over my shoulder at the motionless figure.

"Who is she?" I found myself whispering also.

"Says her name is Mrs. Hebden, and her husband has gone missing. She seems a respectable body."

"Oh, for goodness sake show the lady in!" Holmes called impatiently. "Anything is better than this infernal whispering and hissing."

With a helpless grimace, the good lady turned to usher in a short dumpy middle-aged woman whose plump face was creased in lines of worry. Holmes rose to his feet, his former irritability replaced by a smile of sympathetic kindness.

"Pray forgive my ill-humour, Madam," he said gently. "I was faced with a problem that nags like an aching tooth, and any distraction can only be a relief. Be seated and I assure of you my undivided attention."

Mrs. Hebden smiled nervously and lowered her comfortable body into the chair indicated, where she sat with hands folded primly in her lap.

Meanwhile I ventured to open a window to dispel the acrid fumes of Holmes's foul pipe.

"Now, dear lady," he said soothingly, "make me privy to your problem, and I shall endeavour to advise you. A missing husband, I believe?"

"That's right, sir. I took the liberty of coming to you 'cos Harry Murcher said if anyone could help it was you. Harry's a policeman, and by way of being a friend of me and my John, lives near the Elephant."

"Ah, yes, the Lauriston Gardens affair, if my memory isn't at fault, eh, Watson? Proceed, Mrs. Hebden."

432

"Well, my husband has a small furniture van that gives us a comfortable-enough living. We'll never make a fortune, but he gets lots of jobs the big firms won't bother with, and as there's only me and the horse to keep, along of the occasional help, he can do things cheaper than most. On Wednesday, he was engaged to make a collection in the West End, and was to be told his destination when he had his load. Also, he needn't hire any labour, as that'd be supplied. He thought it a bit queer, and the lateness of the hour, too. He was to be in Grosvenor Square at exactly nine o'clock where he'd be met." At these last words my head jerked up, and Holmes leaned forward tensely.

"Grosvenor Square, you say?" he asked. "Did he tell you the address?"

"He wasn't told. Just to be there at nine, not a minute either side, and he'd be told where to go. He'd been given a goodly sum in advance, so he made no objections, and he told me to expect him when I saw him.

"Like I said, that was Wednesday, and I've heard nothing of him since. It was yesterday afternoon when I got really worried, so I spoke to Harry Murcher, and he says you might be able to help." The poor woman was about to burst into tears, and Holmes patted her gently on the shoulder.

"The good constable counselled you well, Madam, for what you tell me may have some bearing on my earlier problem. I shall not give you false hopes, for there is much that is still unclear, but leave me your address, and I promise you shall hear from me immediately I have news for you."

He led her from the room, murmuring words of comfort as he did so. No sooner had the front door closed on her than he bounded back up the stairs and into our sitting room like a whirlwind.

"Come, Watson, stir yourself! The game's afoot, and I pray we may be in time!"

He tossed my boots towards me, and I was still struggling into my ulster when he was halfway down the stairs, calling impatiently for me to make haste. By the time I reached the pavement he had secured a hansom, and seconds later we were rattling down Baker Street and crossing Oxford Street in the direction of Grosvenor Square, to be deposited at the door of the missing baronet.

"Look around you," he said, waving a hand to embrace the solid bastions of wealth and respectability. "Behind those façades exists as much hate, passion, and human frailty as you will find in Seven Dials or Whitechapel, albeit in a more genteel guise, and without the excuse of poverty and deprivation that may be advanced for the less salubrious quarters of our great city. At times I despair for the future of the human race." He turned to stride up to the front door where he applied himself to the bell-pull. The door was opened by an elderly woman, whom I judged from her attire to be the housekeeper. We were left standing in the hall while she disappeared bearing Holmes's card, but our wait was short, for she quickly returned to conduct us to a small drawing room.

A few minutes later the door opened to admit Lady Fawkus. "Mr. Sherlock Holmes," she said, tapping his card on her fingers. "I have heard much of you."

Holmes bowed. "To my credit, I hope, your Ladyship. This is Dr. Watson, my friend and confidant, whom I fear is inclined to romanticise my modest achievements. Inspector Gregson has seen fit to seek my advice in the matter of your husband's disappearance, and I deemed it best to hear the circumstances from your own lips."

Lady Fawkus nodded and invited us to sit down. "Smoke if you wish, gentlemen, and I trust you will not think too hardly of me if I indulge in a cigarette."

She was a truly beautiful woman, with large violet eyes set below the most striking crown of chestnut hair I had ever seen, while her lips were full and sensuous beneath a straight patrician nose. The only flaw in this vision was a suggestion of hardness at the corners of the mouth.

The story she told was in substance the same as we had heard from Gregson, and at its conclusion, Holmes rubbed his chin thoughtfully.

"Did Sir Peter's absence cause you immediate concern, or was it nothing out of the ordinary?"

"Well, he sometimes spent the night at his club if affairs delayed him, but he would usually contrive to apprise me if he was going to. I was more mystified by the fact that the butler wasn't to be found."

"Ah, the butler. He was a newcomer to your household, and here on a temporary engagement. How did Sir Peter come to engage him?"

"I engaged him. My husband is a very busy man, and when Clarke was injured, the arrangements were left to me."

"His references were satisfactory, of course? I assume you took them up?"

"It was unnecessary," Lady Fawkus said. "He came with a personal recommendation." She looked away as if wishing to avoid the subject.

"From whom?"

"A friend."

The name, please," Holmes insisted.

"Mr. Fulton Braddock, if that is of any importance,"

"And this Mr. Braddock is well known to you and your husband?"

"To me, Mr. Holmes." She turned her beautiful eyes on to Holmes's face. "I think you should understand that my husband and I move in our own circles. He is forty years older than I, and is occupied with affairs of national and international importance. I ensure that this establishment runs smoothly and perform the duties of hostess when it is required, but otherwise we have few acquaintances or interests in common. Do I make myself clear?"

"Quite," said Holmes austerely. "So Mr. Braddock is a friend of yours rather than your husband's, and he came to your aid when you required a temporary butler." He seemed to lose interest in the matter. "The articles from the missing sideboard were left on the dining room floor. Was anything at all taken?"

"Only Moscrop or Clarke could answer that," she said coldly. "I am not in the habit of counting the spoons daily."

"Of course not. Does Sir Peter have a valet or personal servant?"

"He had, but he was discharged a week ago for theft. My husband missed some money from his room, and Moscrop found a large sum hidden in the man's wardrobe. He denied it, naturally, but the evidence was plain enough."

"How long had he been with Sir Peter?"

"Oh, well before my marriage to him. My husband was grieved that such an old and previously honest retainer should betray his trust."

"I see," Holmes said slowly. "And except for Moscrop, the only occupants of the house would have been the servants who had been told by the butler to remain in their quarters, allegedly on orders from Sir Peter."

"Apparently so, except that Mrs. Murgatroyd, the housekeeper, had permission to visit her niece in Wandsworth and stay away overnight. The police inspector examined all the servants and learned nothing."

Holmes stood up to leave and I followed suit. "One thing more, Madam. It was past midnight when you reached home. You did not come straight back from the theatre?"

Lady Fawkus turned to the bell-rope and remained with her back to us when she answered. "No, not directly. I had supper with a friend." She turned back with a bright spot of colour burning on her cheek. "I hope I can rely on your discretion, Mr. Holmes. I wouldn't welcome the attentions of gossip-mongers, and neither would Sir Peter."

"I am always discreet," said my friend icily, "but the truth must be paramount. Good day to you. Lady Fawkus."

He was tight-lipped as we looked for a conveyance, and I was about to comment on the remarkable beauty of the lady whose presence we had just left when a growler pulled up and Gregson's head appeared at the window.

"Well met, Mr. Holmes," he cried. "I thought I might find you here, as you weren't at Baker Street. Great news! We have found the sideboard

435

missing from here – at least, I hope there isn't more than one floating about."

"Where? Tell me the circumstances, Inspector," said Holmes sharply.

"In an abandoned pantechnicon on Plumstead Common. It was seen by a patrolling constable yesterday with the horse munching away at the grass. When it was still there this morning he thought it strange, and had a look inside. The doors weren't locked, and all it contained was a large sideboard. He reported it to his station, and a sharp sergeant connected it with the description of the one we circulated as missing from here and got in touch with us."

"The van, no doubt, had the name of John Hebden painted on the side?" said Holmes eagerly.

Gregson's jaw dropped and he stared in amazement. "Lord save us, Mr. Holmes!" he gasped. "Sometimes I think you to be in league with Old Nick himself! How did you know that?"

"Are you going to Plumstead? Good. We shall accompany you and explain as we go."

On the way to London Bridge Station, Holmes told him of the visit by the worried Mrs. Hebden, at which the inspector gave a lop-sided grin.

"So our interests coincide. You think the van has a connection with what has happened to Sir Peter? Is this Hebden part of the plot?"

"You know I dislike theorising without sufficient facts to build on," my colleague said seriously, "but I fear that Hebden may turn out to be the innocent victim of some deeper conspiracy. Once we are at Plumstead, it may be that a few more pieces of the puzzle will fall into place – but let us not rush our fences."

We had the good fortune to catch a train to Plumstead almost at once, and a short walk brought us to the police station where Gregson made himself known to the sergeant at the desk.

"Where is the van now, Sergeant?" asked the inspector.

"Still on the Common, sir. I was going to have it brought in, but young Hopkins who found it reckoned it might be best to leave it where it was in case someone turned up for it. He's as keen as mustard, and quite bright, even if he has been educated." The sergeant sniffed. "He should've been off duty now, but he wanted to stay with it"

It was a weary uphill climb to the Common, but Holmes stepped out to such effect that Gregson and I were left puffing in his wake, while every so often he would stop impatiently to exhort us to greater effort. At length we came to the Common and, following the sergeant's directions, struck off to the right. Soon we came to our objective, a smartly turned-out pantechnicon with a hobbled nag cropping away at the short scrubby grass.

A uniformed constable was patrolling back and forth some yards away from the van, and on our approach stepped forward with an admonitory hand upraised.

"I'm sorry, gentlemen," he said civilly enough. "I'm afraid you aren't allowed to approach this vehicle."

"Quite right too," Holmes said approvingly. "Has anyone else shown an interest in it while you've been here?"

The young officer looked at us doubtfully. Gregson produced his warrant card, at which the constable sprang to attention and saluted smartly.

"Sorry, sir. I took you to be members of the public, and it'd not do to have them trampling all over the place."

"You've done well," Gregson commended him. "These two gentlemen are Mr. Sherlock Holmes and Dr. Watson. Answer them as you would me."

"Tell us what first aroused your curiosity," Holmes put in.

"It was yesterday evening, sir, and my beat covers this part of the Common. I saw the van and thought nothing of it, for it certainly hadn't been there an hour earlier when I came by. When I came on again late this morning it was still here, and I began to think it may have been stolen and abandoned. I decided to have a look inside, and there was this massive piece of furniture, not even covered up. Well, I recalled some talk at the station of a stolen sideboard, so I gave a boy a couple of pennies to take a note to the station asking what I should do. Sergeant Wells came to see what it was all about and reckoned Scotland Yard might be interested."

"And so we are," said Gregson warmly. "You did everything right, Constable – Hopkins, isn't it?"

"That's right, sir. Number R989, Stanley Hopkins."

"Has anyone been near the van since you stationed yourself here?" Holmes inquired.

"No one until you, the doctor, and the inspector arrived, sir,"

"Have you?"

"Once when I looked inside, and again when Sergeant Veils looked."

Holmes gave a grunt of satisfaction, then he began a slow perambulation around the vehicle, his eyes darting hither and thither as each circulation took him closer until he stopped with a hand resting on the lever to release the doors. Signalling us to remain at a distance, he clambered in to commence a systematic search of the interior. The sideboard, a substantial piece of furniture, stood at the far end, and Holmes gradually worked his way towards it, sometimes stretching up to peer at the sides and roof of the van, then dropping to his knees to crawl on the

437

floor with his lens to his eye. He was in this latter position when he gave a small cry of triumph.

"Quickly, your knife," he called over his shoulder. I climbed in and approached him gingerly, handing him the knife with the large blade already open. He inserted it in a crevice in the floor and worked it to-and-fro. Then he turned to me with a small object lying in the palm of his hand. Carrying it to the light, I saw it to be a grubby wooden button, the kind often found on the jacket of a labouring man.

Gregson looked at it and gave a sniff. "I see no help coming from that," he said dismissively, handing it to Hopkins, who studied it closely.

"If I might be so bold, sir," the constable said tentatively, "I think this could have come from a waterman's coat – what is known as a pea-jacket. See, there is a smear of tar at the edge of it."

Holmes descended from the van, taking the button to examine under his lens. He looked at Hopkins with new respect. "Go on, Constable," he urged, "What are you thinking?"

"Well, sir," the young man replied, embarrassed by the attention he was attracting, "I remember that a lot of barges tie up at nearby Erith Wharf, and there are one or two shady characters among the bargees that need watching, although most of them are decent hard-working men."

"How do you come to know that?" growled the inspector.

"I was born at Erith, sir, and my mother still lives there, running a little coffee-shop for workmen."

"We shall bear that in mind," said Holmes. "Come into the van now and tell me what you observe."

We crowded in behind him, and my nostrils were assailed by the faint but unmistakable odour of the operating theatre.

"By George, Holmes," I said, "that smells like chloroform or I've never used it!"

He forebore to answer, but began searching the interior of the sideboard with his long sensitive fingers. After a while he withdrew his hand to show us a glistening object, which on closer examination proved to be the broken portion of a cuff-link bearing the initials *P.F.* The significance of this find wasn't lost to us, but further searching revealed nothing more of value.

Outside once more, Holmes mounted to the driver's perch, the old nag turning his head to cast a disinterested eye at him before going back to his browsing. My colleague sat with a look of deep concentration, as if willing the vehicle to yield up its secrets. Suddenly he bent to retrieve a scrap of paper adhering to the footboard. He smoothed it out and studied it. Then to Gregson's offended glare, he handed it to Hopkins.

"What do you make of that, Constable?" he asked. I peered round his shoulder and saw it was part of a leaf torn from a penny notebook. Written on it in a shaky uneducated hand was part of the one word: *"Cordwainer"*. The remainder of the word was torn off.

The young man frowned, then spoke in a tone of suppressed excitement. "Why, sir, there's a public house called The Cordwainer's Arms in Erith. It sits opposite the jetty, and it's where most of the barge people gather when they aren't working."

"Capital!" said Holmes, rubbing his hands together gleefully. "The scent grows stronger." He dragged his watch out. "It approaches five o'clock. You and I must return to London, Watson. Gregson, can you arrange to have the van and nag taken care of at the police station?"

"Of course, Mr. Holmes. What have you in mind?"

"Meet us at Erith Police Station at eight o'clock. Hopkins, if you aren't averse to some extra duty, you can be there too."

Hopkins assented eagerly. Then in response to Holmes's query, he pointed out the shortest way to the railway station. We set off briskly, and soon after six o'clock, a cab set us down in Baker Street,

Holmes vanished into his room, emerging very quickly dressed in the manner of a Thames waterman, and sporting an unkempt moustache under a reddened nose. From his writing desk he took a revolver which he dropped into the capacious pocket of his reefer jacket, and taking my cue from him, I armed myself with my old service revolver, adding a stout ash-plant from the stand for good measure.

He gripped my shoulder and smiled warmly. "Good old Watson. I hope we need have no recourse to firearms, but come what may, I couldn't wish for a stouter comrade at my side. Now to Erith, for I am sure you realise that the solution to both problems lies there."

It was almost on the stroke of eight when we walked into the police station at the small riverside village in Kent where Gregson and the young Hopkins awaited us. The local man, Inspector Wray, who had been deep in talk with the Scotland Yard officer, gave a bark of laughter when introduced to my disreputable companion and shook his head in wonder.

"I must say, Mr. Holmes," he chuckled, "I would have warned my chaps to keep a very sharp eye on you, did I not know who you were. Will you be needing any assistance from us?"

"I will be grateful to have two or three of your most solid men on hand, Inspector. I trust Gregson has told you what we seek? Watson and I will make our way to this Cordwainer's Arms, and leave the official force to dispose themselves within easy hail of the tavern. Can you suggest who is the most likely candidate for our attention?"

"Sam Levett is the biggest thorn in our flesh," Wray said promptly. "A big ugly brute of a man with a temper to match. You'll not miss him with his red face, piggy eyes, and broken nose. He knows the insides of our cells well enough for his violence. Jem Milton is his lap-dog, a little weasel-faced character who's nothing on his own."

"Thank you, Inspector. That is most useful. Now, Watson and I shall see what we may stir up at the jetty."

We made our way to the waterfront and found the public house we sought directly opposite the wharf. Several moored barges bobbed gently on the river, giving the occasional creak as they rubbed sides against the wharf or each other.

Holmes whispered in my ear, then pushed his way through the entrance of the public bar, giving me a brief glimpse of a sawdust-strewn floor before the door closed on him. I entered the small private bar, which was reasonably clean and comfortable, the floor covered in brown linoleum, and with four or five chairs, their padded seats covered in American cloth.

By leaning on the counter, I could peer round the dividing partition and discern Holmes taking his first pull from a tankard of beer.

"What's it to be, mate?" The voice was that of a surly-looking man who moved along to eye me with suspicious curiosity,

"Whisky, I think, Landlord. A large one," I replied. "Quite a nip in the air tonight. Will you take something yourself?"

"Thanks, Guv. A drop of rum'll go down nicely." He brought the drinks, then leaned on the bar to eye me speculatively. "Stranger in these parts, Mister?"

"That's right," I said, improvising quickly. "I am a doctor and a bit fed up with London, so I thought I might find a nice little practice in the country. I've been scouting around this area, but without any luck."

He nodded, appearing to lose interest, then turned away at the importunate hammering of a beer-mug on the counter of the other bar.

"Come on, Charlie," a whining voice called. "Move yourself. We're all dying of thirst in 'ere."

"You mind your lip, Jem Hilton," growled the landlord. "You'll wait until I'm ready to serve you." But despite his declaration of independence, he went to obey the summons with some alacrity. I positioned myself so that by looking into the fly-spotted mirror over the bar I obtained an excellent view of the adjoining room. Holmes was leaning negligently against the beer-stained counter nursing his tankard, and next to him was the Jem Milton who had been so accurately described by Inspector Wray. He was attired in a similar manner to my colleague, and as I watched, Holmes turned to speak to him.

440

"I see you've lorst a button orf yer coat, mate," he said, his rough accent coming clearly to me.

"What's it to you?" Milton retorted belligerently.

"Would this be it?" Holmes held out his hand,

"I dunno. Where did you find it?"

Instead of answering Holmes placed the button against one on Milton's coat and nodded. "Looks like it," he said, "'Ow did you come to lose it in a furniture van?"

The weasel-faced man paled beneath his grime and shot out a hand to snatch at the button which was withdrawn too quickly for him to grasp,

"Wot's yer game, cully?" he rasped menacingly. "You lookin' fer trouble, 'cos yer in the right place to get it. So gimme the button an' sling yer 'ook."

"You are the one in trouble," said Holmes in his normal voice. "I know all about your game at Grosvenor Square on Wednesday, so why don't you come quietly and save us all a lot of bother?"

Milton gave a shout of rage as he aimed a futile blow at Holmes, at the same time yelling for the company at large to come to his aid.

"Come on, mates, 'e's a peeler!" But the words had scarcely left his mouth when a crisp upper-cut from Holmes laid him stretched out on the floor. Some of the men in the bar showed signs of joining in, and I sprang to the door where I raised my voice to summon Gregson and his party,

Not pausing for a reply, I erupted into the other bar, barging my way through the threatening mob to stand at Holmes's side. For a brief moment my sudden arrival took them by surprise, and before they could gather their wits the door again burst open for Gregson, Hopkins, and three powerfully built constables to charge in.

There was a sudden hush, and the circle around us drew back sullenly.

Holmes bent down to snap a pair of handcuffs on the recumbent Milton, whose eyes still held a glazed look. The local officers surveyed the room grimly, and the would-be assailants slunk sheepishly back to their tables. Any who attempted to leave being turned back by Hopkins who had stationed himself at the door.

"Anyone else you need, Mr. Holmes?" asked Gregson.

My colleague looked at the oldest of the local policemen. "What do you think, Constable?"

The man scanned the room before shaking his head. "I think not, sir. Most of these are straight enough. Just a touch excitable where strangers are concerned. There's no sign of Sam Levett, but our chum here could point you in the right direction." He prodded the prone figure with a not-too-gentle boot. "That's right, isn't, Jem lad?"

"Well, my man, where do we find Levett?" asked Holmes.

441

"Go to the Devil!" was the sullen reply.

Holmes shrugged. "No matter. Inspector, I think you can charge this pitiful specimen with the murders of Sir Peter Fawkus and John Hebden."

There was a howl of terror from the wretch on the floor. "You can't do that! They ain't dead! They're still – " He broke off as if suddenly realising he had said too much, his eyes on Holmes's impassive features.

"I am afraid you will have to convince us of that," said the latter in a hard voice. "Landlord, is there a quiet room where I can have a few words with this scum?"

The landlord became obsequious in his anxiety to please, the very mention of murder having reduced him to a quivering wreck.

"Of course, sir. You can have my sitting room at the back. You won't be disturbed there. I don't know nothing of what's going on, and I always try to keep – " He stopped as one of the constables stepped forward.

"Shut it, Charlie Higgins, and show the gentlemen through. We know all about you, so just watch your *P*'s and *Q*'s."

The flap of the counter was lifted, and Holmes dragged the thoroughly cowed Milton to his feet and pushed him through into a small shabby room, with Gregson and myself following, the constables remaining in the bar to ensure that nobody left to raise an alarm. The prisoner was thrust into a rickety chair while Holmes studied him coldly before starting his interrogation.

"So you would have us believe that Sir Peter and the van driver are still alive?" he asked. "How do you know that?"

The handcuffed man wetted his lips and looked up slyly. "If I peach, will you promise to go easy on me?" he whined.

Gregson thrust his face close to the other's, speaking in a dangerously soft voice. "All I promise you is an early morning walk if we don't find them alive, so if you've got anything to say, get on with it."

Milton's brief show of resistance melted away, and he raised his manacled hands as if in supplication as the rest of us stared at him.

"I'll tell yer all I know," he quavered, "They're on Sam Levett's barge just over the road, and they was both alive and kicking when I was there not an hour gorn. That's the truth, so 'elp me it is."

"Who is guarding them?" asked Holmes.

"Sam, Tom Moscrop, and the toff what paid us to take the old'un from that big 'ouse."

"Moscrop!" gasped Gregson. "Was he in it too?"

"Of course he was," said Holmes impatiently. "Come, we have no time to lose. Get one of the local men to take this rat to the lock-up, and we shall tackle those on the barge."

442

A few minutes later, having ascertained the exact location of our objective, our small party consisting of Holmes, Gregson, myself, Hopkins, and the two beefiest of the local men made its way quietly down to the waterfront. There was a slight rise and fall of the moored vessels as the tide turned, the noise made as they chafed against the wharf effectively masking any sound of our stealthy approach.

We found the barge in question, and Holmes held out a restraining arm. A small cabin perched at the stern showed a thin ray of yellow light, and my colleague pointed to it. When sure that we understood, he moved swiftly along the jetty and, abandoning any further pretence of silence, he sprang lightly on to the deck and charged the door of the cubby-hole with his shoulder.

I was on his heels, my pistol at the ready and the others crowding me from behind. The door burst open, and in the dim light of a smoky lantern I saw three figures frozen into brief immobility, while on the floor were two more bodies bound and gagged. The paralysis of the three was but momentary before they exploded into violent action, leaping at us with fists swinging wildly. Holmes struck the leading man full in the face with his clenched fist, but the man's momentum carried him on to crash into Holmes, who in turn cannoned into me so that I fell to the floor, A heavy boot swung towards me, and in a reflex action I grabbed the ankle above it to hang on desperately, bringing a heavy body down on top of me.

I wriggled out, and as I struggled to regain my feet, I heard Gregson call to someone to stop. Then came a loud splash followed by a terrible scream that was suddenly cut off. Supporting myself with a hand on the wall, I found Hopkins sitting on the man I had brought down, a big hulking brute who I took to be the notorious Sam Levett. Holmes had in his grasp a pale-faced weedy character whose teeth chattered with fear, while out on the deck I could just make out Gregson and the two local officers staring over the side into the murky water of the Thames as it sucked at the piles of the wharf.

"Quickly, Hopkins, 'cuff this pair together." It was Holmes who spoke as he came over to where I stood, concern showing on his face. "Watson, you aren't badly hurt, I trust?"

I smiled, denying any serious damage.

"Then come. Your professional skills may be needed here."

We set about releasing the two trussed men. Both were conscious, and they took deep gulps of air as I removed the filthy gags from their mouths. One was a white-haired man of advanced years. He was clad in a dress shirt and smoking-jacket, while the other man was much younger, wearing the corduroy breeches and leather gaiters favoured by cab and van drivers. They gasped for breath and flexed their cramped limbs, groaning with pain as the circulation returned. Holmes, satisfied that I was able to manage, patted me on the shoulder.

"I leave them to you, Doctor. I assume, of course, that you are Sir Peter Fawkus and Mr. John Hebden?"

A nod from each confirmed his surmise, whereupon my companion went out to the fresher air of the deck, My cursory examination told me that neither had sustained serious injury, and as soon as they were able to stand, I assisted them to rise and move out into the cool night air, where I found Gregson and Holmes gazing sombrely into the dark waters below. Of the two scoundrels who had been apprehended there was no sign, but Hopkins and another stood on the jetty, fishing with long poles by the light of a bulls-eye lantern.

Cutting short any attempts at questions or explanations, Holmes insisted on an immediate adjournment to the nearby Railway Hotel. Neither would he permit any talk until Hebden and Sir Peter, fortified with stiff brandies had removed the accumulated grime of their captivity, and were ravenously devouring a plate of sandwiches.

There was a knock on the door, which turned out to be Hopkins with the announcement that the search of the river had been unproductive.

"The tide's in full ebb now," he explained, "Anybody in there would be well on the way to Gravesend by now."

"Very well, you've done your best," Gregson replied. He was about to dismiss him when Holmes spoke mildly.

"I think Hopkins should hear the rest of the story, Inspector," he said. "After all, his contribution has been most valuable in this matter."

Gregson was plainly of the opinion that young policemen shouldn't be allowed to get above themselves, but he gave his grudging consent, and Hopkins placed himself unobtrusively in a corner of the room. With pipes and cigars drawing nicely, Holmes set the ball rolling.

"Now, gentlemen, pray let me hear your own accounts of your misfortunes so that I may compare my own conclusions. Will you begin, Sir Peter?"

The elderly baronet began to speak, hesitantly at first but with increasing fluency as his tale progressed,

"It was Wednesday evening, soon after nine o'clock, and I was settled in my study with a glass of whisky. My wife had gone out, and I was looking forward to a quiet couple of hours when the butler, Moscrop, entered to announce that two gentlemen insisted on seeing me. I wasn't best pleased, but even as I demurred, two rough characters pushed their way in and advanced towards me.

"'What is the meaning of this?' I demanded. 'Moscrop, show these persons the door.' He made no move, and to my horror I was seized violently to have a filthy rag forced into my mouth to stifle any outcry that I might make. During this outrage Moscrop stood by passively, making no move to assist me. I should add that he was a temporary – "

"Yes, yes," Holmes put in. "We know he was engaged on the recommendation of Fulton Braddock, a friend of Lady Fawkus's."

"That is so," Sir Peter said bitterly. "Have you secured the scoundrel?"

"He is dead," Gregson stated flatly. "In attempting to escape, he fell between the barge and the jetty, and was crushed to death. We haven't yet recovered his body."

A glint of satisfaction showed in Sir Peter's eyes. "Then that may save the washing of dirty linen," he said grimly. "But to continue. I was trussed up like a chicken and taken to the dining room, where a pad soaked with what I assume was chloroform was clapped over my mouth, and the next thing I knew I was in a coffin-like container being transported in some kind of vehicle. I lost consciousness again, and recovered as I was being manhandled on to that filthy barge, where I was thrown on to a pile of sacks in the hold. Shortly afterwards this gentleman," he nodded towards Hebden, "was pushed in to join me."

His face showed anger at the memory, but he took a sip of his brandy and went on. "How long we were left I have no notion, but it must have been a full day, for when the hatch again opened it was dark. To my astonishment, who should climb down was none other than Fulton Braddock. My spirits rose, thinking deliverance was at hand, but my hopes were dashed by his first words." His voice trailed away to a whisper.

"You may speak freely, sir," Holmes said earnestly. "Nothing that you say will go beyond these four walls, other than is required to serve the ends of justice, and Braddock is beyond reach of that." He looked round the room, his stern face willing Gregson and Hopkins to nod agreement.

The baronet seemed reassured by my friend's words, and after a short pause he took up his tale again, telling of how Braddock had taunted him with his wife's infidelity, before going on to describe how the old man's body would be found in some obscure reach of the Thames, when it would be assumed he had taken his own life. After a decent interval, it was Braddock's plan to marry the grieving widow, thus gaining not only a respected place in society, but a considerable fortune to boot.

During the latter part of this recital, Gregson's face had taken on a look of incredulous anger and, unable to contain himself, he now broke in on Sir Peter's narrative.

"Are you implying that your wife was party to this conspiracy?" he stuttered.

445

"Of course I am not, Inspector!" snapped the baronet angrily. "She may be a slut and an adulteress, but never a murderess!"

"I think we can trust Sir Peter's judgement in the matter," declared Holmes. "It grows late, so if you will allow me to round things off. we may save time and get back to London before midnight. I take it, Mr. Hebden, you were seen as a danger to these villains, so they intended to make away with you to ensure your silence?"

"That's about it, sir. I was uneasy about this job from the start, and must have showed it, for no sooner had we reached Erith than I was knocked on the head and found myself in the same case as this gent. They took us up top when it got dark, and I don't mind saying I thought my last hour had come. How was it you found us in the nick of time?"

Holmes told of Mrs. Hebden's appeal, and then went on: "It was too much of a coincidence that Sir Peter Fawkus and a sideboard should vanish from Grosvenor Square on the very same night that a furniture van and its owner were last heard of in that very Square. When the van was found abandoned with only the sideboard in it, the inference was certain. You both owe a lot to Mrs. Hebden's wifely concern, and to this very acute police constable whose aid was invaluable.

"Now, I am sure Mr. Hebden is keen to put his wife's mind at rest, and Sir Peter has no wish to linger at the scene of such an unpleasant experience, so if Inspector Gregson will agree to leave the formalities until tomorrow, we can doubtless secure a carriage, and any further details can be cleared up as we travel."

The hotel landlord was able to find us a not-too-dilapidated carriage complete with driver, and leaving Gregson and Hopkins to their own devices, the four of us were soon on our way. The elderly baronet, exhausted by his ordeal, fell into a fitful doze, and as we clattered through Plumstead, Holmes drew Hebden's attention to the police station where his van was held, assuring him that it would be well cared for until collected.

"One point I must reiterate, Mr. Hebden, is that you must exercise absolute discretion in the matters that have been revealed tonight."

"Trust me, sir," the man replied. "I see and hear a lot in my job that's best kept mum about." He laid a finger along his nose and winked.

Sir Peter opened his eyes and favoured him with a weary smile. "I'll not forget you, Hebden," he said. "You were a great comfort to me in our predicament, and with your permission, I will call on you as soon as I have recovered from the events of the past few days." He turned to Holmes. "After we have restored Mr. Hebden to his hearth, I have a request to make of you which I hope you will not refuse." Holmes inclined his head, and the rest of the journey passed in silence until we turned into the mews that

446

was the van-driver's home. The wheels hadn't stopped before Hebden leapt from the carriage. He was half-way across the cobbles when Mrs. Hebden rushed from a doorway to throw herself into her husband's embrace.

"We aren't needed here," chuckled Holmes, rapping on the carriage roof with his knuckles.

"Would that such a homecoming awaited me," Sir Peter said wistfully. "Will you oblige me by taking me to my club in St. James's?" He laid back, his head in shadow. "May I impose on you to go on to inform my wife of my well-being? I am in no frame of mind to face her this night, and I fear I may say things that should be left unsaid. I leave it tó your good sense as to what explanations you make, but I beg of you not to judge her too harshly."

I could see from my colleague's face that the task was distasteful to him, but he accepted the mission before lapsing into a brooding silence, his head sunk on his chest, not speaking until we turned from Pall Mail into St. James's and stopped before Sir Peter's club.

Refusing assistance, the baronet descended and leaned in to shake us by the hand. "Thank you both for all you have done. I would count it an honour if you will lunch with me on here Monday. There are matters to be discussed between us, not the least of them financial."

We watched the old man make his way up the steps of the building, and a few minutes later we reached Grosvenor Square, where the carriage was dismissed with a handsome gratuity for the driver.

"I shall not enjoy this encounter," Holmes muttered. "Don't hesitate to restrain me should my feelings betray me."

The door was opened by Lady Fawkus in person, and her hands flew to her bosom at the sight of us.

"You have no news?" she said faintly, "You haven't found my husband?"

"Sir Peter is safe," Holmes answered frigidly. "He has been saved from those who would harm him, but he elected to spend the night at his club, where we left him not ten minutes since. I think you should hear of the events that brought him near to death, but resulted in the death of his would-be murderer, Fulton Braddock."

Her beautiful face turned a ghastly pale and she clutched at the doorpost for support, her eyes widening in shock and horror at my friend's harsh tone.

"What are you saying?" she said in a strangled whisper. "You must be mad to speak so!"

"Let us enter, Madam, and I shall lay the facts before you. Then you may pronounce on my sanity."

He took a pace forward and she retreated into the hallway. I followed and kicked the door to behind me. Lady Fawkus hesitated as if to defy us. Then we were led into the same small drawing room as on our earlier visit. As she turned up the gas-light, our dishevelled appearance caused her to look askance. She faced us with a thunderous frown.

"Now, Mr. Sherlock Holmes," she demanded. "I will ask you to account for the vile and slanderous statement you made. I warn you, sir, my husband has much influence, so have a care."

"Very well, Lady Fawkus, I will be completely frank with you, and then you may take what steps you will. This afternoon you told us that on Wednesday night you had supper with a friend. Was that friend Fulton Braddock? Ah, I see it was. Have you seen him since Wednesday?"

"He called on me this morning to offer his sympathy and support, but what signifies that?"

Holmes's eyes were like chips of ice as he answered. "While you were being entertained by Braddock – no doubt to more than supper – his minions, one of whom one was your butler Moscrop, were abducting Sir Peter with a view to encompassing his death." She looked wildly from one to the other of us, then collapsed into a chair. Fearing her about to swoon, I stepped forward but was waved away.

"You have taken leave of your senses!" she cried. "Even if what you say is true, what advantage would Mr. Braddock get from my husband's death?"

"A wealthy widow is an attractive proposition to a man without honour or scruples, and he wasn't one to let a little matter of a husband stand in his way."

Lady Fawkus stood up and faced us with blazing eyes. "Mr. Braddock is a gentleman for whom I have the highest regard, and it ill-becomes you to impute such base conduct to a man who isn't here to defend his honour!"

"Honour?" sneered Holmes. "A man who would conduct a liaison with a married woman can have little of that, I declare."

For a moment I thought she would strike him. Then her body slumped as she recalled his earlier words.

"You said he is dead. Is that true?"

He nodded and she dropped back into her chair. Burying her face in her hands, she began sobbing loudly.

Holmes watched her bleakly until she regained control and looked up with reddened eyes.

"Tell me what you believe to be the truth, Mr. Holmes, but spare me your views on my personal conduct. That is between me and my conscience."

448

My companion began in a cold and detached tone as Lady Fawkus listened with a look of ever-increasing horror as the sordid tale unfolded. When all was told she sat rigidly in her chair, her lovely face ravaged by the conflicting emotions that passed over it. When she at last spoke, it was in a low humble voice.

"I cannot believe that these terrible events are a figment of your imagination, Mr. Holmes, and I presume there is evidence to substantiate it?"

"Indeed. Three scoundrels are in custody, and will be quick to confess and mitigate their own part, but Sir Peter and Mr. Hebden are alive, and will tell as much of their own story as the authorities deem necessary, so there can be no doubt of the facts."

"Oh, God!" she cried piteously. "What have I bought about? Will I ever be able to face that good man again?"

"That, Madam, is out of my hands," replied Holmes as he prepared to leave. "However, I don't think Sir Peter is a vindictive man, so there may yet be hope for you both. Good night."

We set off to walk briskly in the direction of Baker Street, Holmes now recovering his spirits. He paused under a lamp-post to light a cigarette.

"For your records, I think it will transpire that Clarke's accident, and the dismissal of the valet, were engineered to leave the gang a clear run when the time came to put Braddock's scheme into effect. Watson, is something amusing you?" he said sharply.

"I hope we don't meet a zealous policeman," I chuckled.

"Good Lord, why should that concern us?" he asked in a puzzled tone.

"Do you not realise, my dear Holmes, that apart from that outrageous moustache that was lost in the struggle, you are still attired as a Thames bargee? Hardly the type of person to be seen after midnight in this part of town."

He looked down at himself, and then joined in my merriment.

"Should that arise, old chap, we could always ask Gregson to vouch for us, and that would give great satisfaction to his sense of humour."

Still laughing immoderately, we resumed our homeward progress.

The Adventure of the
Veiled Man
by Tracy Revels

"Mrs. Spencer is the most gracious and caring lady in the world, and has treated me more like a daughter than an employee. If anything should happen to her, my heart would break. She has told me this is nothing, but I see the dark cloud that hangs over her, and I cannot wipe away the memory of that evil, repulsive man who accosted me in the orchard. It is all connected somehow. Mr. Spencer is an invalid, and so it falls on me to help my mistress, and I appeal to you."

This remarkable introduction was uttered, almost in one breath, by a slender, dark-haired girl of some eighteen years, her eyes bright and pleading, her delicate hands vigorously twisting her gloves. I was grateful for her intrusion. Holmes needed the diversion, for I had noted his longing glances towards the old morocco case, and only my loud harrumphing had prevented him from reaching for it.

"Do sit down, Miss – ?"

"Jennings. My name is Catherine Jennings."

Holmes handed her into a chair. "Your problem interests me already. You have come from the village of Huxton, near St. Albans, to consult me."

"Yes, but how – ?"

"Let us say merely that this railway return ticket, which you have dropped upon the rug, is instructive. You would not wish to lose it."

The lady's face took on a fiery blush, and she immediately lowered her gaze in embarrassment. She was clad in a beautiful mauve travelling dress, an outfit enlivened with a number of unique embellishments, little tucks, and rosettes that hinted the garment might have once belonged to a more flamboyant wearer. As lovely as it was, it hardly suited her meek and supplicant demeanor.

"Thank you, sir. I fear I am rather clumsy with everything except a needle."

"You are a seamstress?" I asked.

"Yes." The lady's glaze leapt back to Holmes. "And as such, I can offer you very little to hear my story, but I would give all that I have to bring my mistress's torment to an end."

"Do not concern yourself with payment," Holmes said. "Let us have your tale from the beginning."

"Then you should know that I am an orphan and that I was raised in a dreary Methodist institution in London. My education was only very rudimentary, but I was noted for my sewing skills. Some six months ago, I began to think seriously of what my life would be when I left the orphan's home. But on the very day I began to despair of my fate, I was called in by one of the matrons to meet with Mrs. Spencer.

"I was struck immediately by the kindness of her face. She is a short and plump lady, a bit like the Queen in a black dress and a little lace cap. She told me she was an American who had come to England with her husband, and that she was seeking an assistant who could do fancy needlework and was not averse to living a quiet life in the countryside. Her terms were most generous, and I accepted readily. The next morning, I joined her on the train.

"'Dear girl,' she said as we began our journey, 'I must be frank. There is one further condition I must impose on you, and if you find it disagreeable, then I will gladly purchase you a return ticket and compensate you for your time.'

"I wondered what it could possibly be and said as much. The lady looked down at her hands.

"'You no doubt wonder why an American couple is residing in the English countryside. Surely you have heard of the great Civil War that nearly destroyed our native land. My husband was the owner of a munition factory in Maine. He employed many girls to do this work, as most of the men had gone off to join the army.' Her voice began to quiver, and she pulled out a handkerchief to wipe away sudden tears.

"'One day in late 1864, there was a terrible accident, an explosion. Nearly twenty girls were killed. My husband was at the factory on the day that it happened. He survived the event, but he was badly burned over most of his body. There was an investigation, and while it was found that he was not at fault for the tragedy, my husband never forgave himself. His face was mutilated and scarred by the fire – and, I fear, by his shame. He wears a veil at all times. You must never ask to see his countenance. If I have your word you will make no mention of this to him, I shall be pleased to have you as my assistant for as long as you wish to stay with us.'

"I cannot express how sincere and sad her words were. I assured her that I would follow her command. She begged me also not to ask questions about their lives in America, as they wished to put this behind them forever.

"We arrived at their home. It is called Sparrow Grange, and it is a small and quaint old manor just a mile from Huxton. It is a nice farm, with some little stone cottages once used by tenants. In one of these, Mrs. Spencer has devised a workshop. She is no mere needle-worker, sir, but an artist! In her shop she creates quilts and patchwork tapestries. She equally adept with knitting needles and crochet hooks and can whip up a coverlet in a matter of days. She is also a talented dressmaker. In fact, this dress that I am now wearing was hanging on a form, and Mrs. Spencer insisted on altering it for me."

"How does she attend to her clients, if she lives in the country?" I asked.

"Almost all of her work is due on commission. At least once a week I come into the city and post packages for her and return with payments. Recently, she has entrusted me with making her deposits as well." Pride illuminated the young woman's face. "I do not know what painters and photographers receive for their services, but if they do as well as my mistress, they are quite comfortable."

"And how did you find life at Sparrow Grange?" Holmes said. "You appear to be happy in your residence."

"Oh, sir, it is wonderful. I expected to be sent to the attic, but Mrs. Spencer gave me a small suite on the first floor, only a few rooms away from her own. She insisted that I dine with her, and I may go to the kitchen at any time if I am hungry. There is a library filled with so many interesting books and magazines, and a piano and a harp – Mrs. Spencer has been giving me instruction on both. The grounds are charming, and I have made friends with all the animals. The staff is small – only a housekeeper and a farm-hand – but my sole responsibilities are to keep my room tidy and assist Mrs. Spencer in her work. I could not have asked for a better situation."

"Have you met Mr. Spencer?"

The lady's brows crinkled. "In a way. The first evening, while Mrs. Spencer was in the kitchen, he came down from his rooms to greet me. It is a startling effect, to see such a large and robust man, so perfectly dressed, but with a large hat upon his head and a heavy black veil shielding his face. Every part of his body is covered, even his hands. He gave a bow and in very few words welcomed me to his home. After that, he retired to his rooms and I did not see him again for several days. He does not dine with us, but I have caught glimpses of him riding his horse or strolling in the orchard. When he rides, his head is so wrapped up with great swaths of cloth over his mouth and nose that he looks like an Arab."

"Have you seen inside the couple's rooms?" Holmes asked.

"Oh no – they have a very large suite in the corner of the house, but Mrs. Spencer tends to it herself."

"And they never speak of their past?"

452

"Not a word. Only once did I have a hint, for Mrs. Spencer will sometimes become lost in her thoughts while sewing and begin to sing old songs. They are not familiar English songs, and one day I said to her that all her songs had colors in them, for I had heard words like 'yellow rose' and 'blue flag'. My innocent comment caused her such distress that I wish I had never spoken, for since that time she has ceased to sing."

"One last question before you tell us of the problem that has brought you to my door: Does the couple have children?"

"Not to my knowledge, though Mrs. Spencer is so kind to me, so maternal in her devotion, that I have often wondered if there might have been a child who passed away in youth. But I dare not ask her, as I have given my word not to inquire as to her past.

"And this brings me to the cloud of suffering and curious incidents which I would beg you to unravel.

"It was a little over a month ago that it all began. I had brought in the post and laid it on Mrs. Spencer's desk. My employer gave a cry of alarm upon seeing the envelope – I truly believe she must have recognized the hand in which it was written. She ripped it open, read its contents, and then thrust it into the fire. Before I could speak, she had gathered up her skirts and fled to her chamber. I did not see her again until she came down for supper.

"'I do beg your forbearance, dear,' she said to me as she settled at the table. 'I know I startled you this morning. But I just learned that an old friend from home has died, and it quite grieved me.'

"I assured her of my sympathy, but I knew, in my heart, that she was telling me a falsehood. Her cry had not been of grief, but of terror. And even more disturbing events were to occur. The next day, Mrs. Spencer gave me a bag filled with jewelry and asked me to take it to London and pawn the items. I was most nervous on the train, for I returned bearing nearly four-hundred pounds! I could not imagine why she was suddenly in need of so much cash. The following week she sent me to London again, this time with a gold watch and some old silver.

"At the end of that week, another very strange thing happened – Mrs. Spencer began to call me by a new name. She had always addressed me as 'Catherine' or 'Kate', but suddenly she started to speak to me as 'Polly'. I found this very queer, and after two days I asked her why she was doing it. She became agitated and told me that it was the name of her friend who had died, and she supposed it was very much on her mind, and that I should forgive an old woman for her errors. I resolved myself to answer to it, if it gave her comfort.

"She also changed our routine. Usually, we would work in the cottage from eight until noon, and then again from one until six, breaking only to take tea. Now, Mrs. Spencer insisted that we should walk on the grounds from one until three, casting our work aside for the benefits of the exercise. I could not deny her, for it was certainly much more delightful to amble in the garden and the lawn than to bend over a quilting frame. Mrs. Spencer surprised me with a lovely spring dress to wear while we took our 'rambles' as she called them, and insisted that I leave my hair loose beneath a large straw hat. We enjoyed walking and chatting, often arm-in arm.

"Three days ago, our walk was spoiled when I noticed a grim-faced, bearded man standing in the lane, staring at us. He was a stranger, and a most impertinent one in the way he fixed his gaze so intently on us as we gathered flowers. Mrs. Spencer didn't notice him, and I didn't wish to spoil the afternoon, so I did not draw it to her attention. Later that day, I stole out to the barn and told Jack – he is the farm-hand – about it. Jack is rather fond of me, and he promised that if the knave dared to come back on the property, he would thrash his hide and send him packing.

"And now I come to the inciting incident. Yesterday, Mrs. Spencer did not feel well. She is prone to very bad headaches and told me over breakfast there could be no work that day. She retired to her room and I amused myself with a book until luncheon. Afterward, I decided that I would go out to the orchard, as I was missing my exercise. I threw on my bonnet and was walking from the house when I noticed that the Gladstone bag which I had carried to London was now lying beneath a birdbath. I could not imagine what it was doing there, so I retrieved it and put it back in the front hallway before continuing on my quest. I was lost in a reverie, lulled by the peaceful birdsong and springtime smells, when suddenly my elbow was seized by a brute of a man who leapt out from behind a tree. He had a pointed gray beard, black stumps of teeth, and tiny, yellowed eyes. I had only the briefest impression of his clothing – a dark coat and striped pants and a slouched felt hat. He shook me so hard I could not even shriek. One great, dirty paw grabbed my face.

"'You're not her!' he growled. 'The lying wench! You aren't Dorothea! She can hang with the money – I want my girl!'

"At last, I found my strength to struggle. I jerked away so quickly that I tumbled over on the ground. To my shock, before I could gather breath to scream, the man took to his heels, scrambled over our stone fence, and ran away down the lane. By degrees I gathered myself up and calmed my nerves. Perhaps he was just some local madman, a lunatic escaped from his family's care. But the more I brooded over the thing, the more I felt that the man had been the same upstart who had glared at us in the garden. I marched to the barn and told Jack about it, then went to the house. The housekeeper had not yet seen to the bag, and so I gathered it up to place it

454

in a closet. But as I lifted it, the latch came open, and I saw that there were stacks of bank notes inside! The entirely of the money I had been entrusted with was there. It was then that I resolved to come to you, Mr. Holmes, for I see that there is some wicked persecution afoot, and my good lady is caught in it. Please, sir, you must find a way to help her."

"Allow me to put a few questions to you," Holmes said. "The man who accosted you in the orchard – was he an Englishman?"

The lady scowled. "I do not think so. His clothes didn't look English, and his voice was so gruff, but I couldn't tell you what accent he spoke with."

Holmes nodded. "Do you know when the bag was put beneath the birdbath?"

"I took my lunch with the housekeeper. While we were eating, we heard the sound of the door being opened, but I assumed perhaps it was Mr. Spencer going out. Later, of course, I learned that he had not left the house."

"Is it likely Jack would have used that door?"

"No, he always comes in through the servant's entrance."

"Permit me another inquiry: Does your master appear to be a true invalid? When you describe him as a horseman, it seems unlikely that his injuries are debilitating."

"You are correct. He seems a very hale and hearty man. I once saw him leap onto his horse when it was unsaddled and ride it across the fields with the greatest of ease."

"And finally, perhaps most crucially: Do you recall from where the letter that disturbed your mistress was postmarked?"

Miss Jennings squeezed her eyes shut, as if trying to conjure a memory. "No, but it must have been from the deceased Polly's husband, for I believe it bore an American stamp. The address was written in an ugly script – a man's hand, I am sure, and not a woman's."

"Young lady, should you no longer wish to ply a needle, you might have a future in detective work," Holmes chuckled. "Return home, have your friend Jack keep a careful watch over the place, and retrieve any bags that you find left carelessly on the yard. How did you explain your absence today?"

"I did not have to," the seamstress said. "Before I could request permission to leave, Mrs. Spencer summoned me and told me to take this item to London to pawn."

She opened her purse and held out a silver ring with a strange blue-and-green stone. Holmes made a sound of delight.

"This is wonderful, as it provides us an excellent excuse for a visit." He rose and went to his desk, removing an envelope. "In this you will find twenty pounds, which is a good bit more than a pawnbroker would offer for this specimen, I believe. Tomorrow, we will arrive at Sparrow Grange to return it to you – for, as it happens, while you were in the pawnshop the good Doctor Watson observed you, was smitten with you, learned of your residence, and redeemed your trinket for you! We must only hope that your Jack is not the jealous type. Goodbye, Miss Jennings. Look for us tomorrow, before noon."

I had a host of questions for Holmes, but as ill luck would have it, I received a summons to a patient's bedside just as Miss Jennings was departing. My case engaged me all afternoon. When I returned to Baker Street, I found a note from Holmes saying that he was investigating some developments and would not return until late that evening, but I should be ready to depart for Sparrow Grange in the morning. Left to my own devices, I struggled to divert myself with sea stories, but my imagination relentlessly dragged me back to the lonely manor house. What dark secrets were afoot? For once, I was ready to spring from my bed in the dreary hour before dawn, so anxious was I to see the resolution of this mystery.

"One might think, from reading sensational fiction, that most detective work is done by tracing footprints on darkened moors or trailing ruffians around the docks while disguised as rascally Lascars," Holmes chuckled, as we settled into our compartment. "How disappointed the public would be to learn that so much of detective work is pursued in a library."

"A library?'

"An excellent source for verification of stories, a rich vein of truth ready to be mined. A number of details in Miss Jennings's account struck me as curious, and so I resorted to that vast repository of knowledge, the British Library. I also visited several house agents, and sent off a few telegrams."

"What did you learn?" I asked as Holmes began to light a cigarette.

"I discovered that Mrs. Spencer's history is a selectively altered one. There was no Union munitions manufacturing company operated by anyone named Spencer in the state of Maine. Nor was there any record of a horrific explosion there, though such tragic accidents were sadly common – one in Pennsylvania and another in Washington, D.C. claimed the lives of dozens of young women. However – "

"Yes?"

Holmes shook out his match. "There was a small munitions plant in Kentucky that experienced a similar sad occurrence, and the operator – whose name was given as Simon Chaney – was listened among the dead, though his body was never identified."

"Which side did this factory serve?"

456

"A wise question, as Kentucky was one of the states with divided loyalties. This factory was in the southwestern corner of the state, and until its demise it provided ammunition to the Confederate rebels. Here, Mrs. Spencer's singing gives us a confirmational clue."

"Her singing?" I chuckled.

"Recall the colorful phrases Miss Jennings was taken by. The 'yellow rose' was no doubt a reference to the 'Yellow Rose of Texas', and the blue flag to the 'Bonnie Blue Flag', both of which were popular Confederate tunes that the lady would have heard in her youth. Let us therefore work on the assumption that Mrs. Spencer is, in fact, the widow of Chaney, the man who was killed in Kentucky."

"Then who is the man in the veil?"

Holmes raised an eyebrow. "Indeed, if he is not her maimed spouse, why the need to hide his appearance? No one would fault a young widow for remarrying."

"Perhaps he has some loathsome disease. Could he be a leper?"

"If so, the lady is taking an unforgiveable risk, for herself and her household. But Mr. Spencer's actions do not strike me as those of an invalid or sufferer. Recall Miss Jennings's statement about how easily he rides, as well as her description of him as a robust man."

I nodded. "What else did you learn?"

"From the house agents, I discovered that Sparrow Grange was rented three years ago. And at the time it was leased, no spouse presented himself. Instead, it was taken by a widowed American lady as a quiet home for herself and her daughter – a girl the house agent recalled as being a 'raven-haired beauty', somewhere between eighteen to twenty years of age."

"Where is this girl now?"

"Another excellent question, Watson. Where, indeed? Clearly she was the girl the offensive gentleman in the orchard was seeking."

"Were you able to learn anything about him?"

"A brief message to the local constabulary informed me that there has been something of a rash of tramps and rough sleepers in the area. However, when I made a leap of logic and sent a more specific inquiry, I was rewarded with a name and a place of residence."

"Then the case is clear to you?"

Holmes put out his cigarette, leaned back in his seat, and pulled his cloth cap over his eyes. "I can see seven possibilities. Most of them end rather unpleasantly." He yawned. "I hope you remembered to bring your Webley."

We disembarked at the village station and Holmes led the way to a decrepit, red-brick house, where a woman in an apron and a mob cap was busily sweeping the steps.

"Good morning," Holmes said, in his most pleasant and ingratiating manner. "Mrs. Carter, I presume? I would like to speak to your tenant, if he is at home."

The woman's soured face crinkled into a fierce scowl. "He's not my tenant. No sir, not since an hour ago. I've had enough of his sottish ways – staggering in drunk, singing at the top of his lungs, knocking up the whole house. And when he couldn't offer so much as a half-penny for his breakfast this morning, I sent him packing!"

"Did he say where he was going?"

"No – nor did I care to ask. He's been nothing but trouble since he came here a week ago."

"A pity. I remember him as a decent man, a traveler in linens and silks."

The woman had half-turned to go inside, but at this surprising pronouncement her face twisted into an even more repulsive grimace. "Linens and silks – ? Then he could have offered me a bolt in payment! He told me he was a reporter, and that was why he asked so many questions."

"What type of questions?"

"About the folks at Sparrow Grange. What did they do? Had they any children. What did we make of the man of the house? No one's seen him, of course, except at a distance, all swathed up in a veil. Could be a Chinaman or a Hindu for all I know. Now, sir, if you don't mind – "

"You have been most helpful," Holmes said, offering her a sovereign. "To defray some of my old friend's debt."

"It's none of my business, but you should choose your friends more wisely," the lady said. "And good heavens, that accent! Like he had a mouth full of wool."

"Come, Watson," Holmes said, picking up the pace as we crossed the street. "This development does not bode well for our gentle client. We must reach Sparrow Grange immediately."

Before I could question, Holmes had hailed a young lad driving a dog-cart, and by pressing coins into the boy's grubby hand, he secured us a rough but rapid journey from the village to the manor. I would have enjoyed the drive through the quaint countryside, where the lane was flanked with stone fences and the air was fragrant from the budding orchards, if I had not feared that I would lose my perch and be tossed head-first onto the muddy ground. It had rained the night before, and the

458

roadway was still damp. I heard Holmes give a shout and urge the boy to apply the whip to the dappled nag.

We drew up beside a neat and tidy Georgian house of yellow brick, with a slate gray roof and a lovely, graveled drive. Holmes sprang from the cart and I scampered after him.

"Watson, recall your lines. You are here to play the besotted admirer and – "

At that very moment, there came, from the room above our heads, the most blood-curdling of screams, followed instantly by a gunshot. For just a moment we were both frozen, then Holmes seized the doorknob. The portal opened instantly, and we were shocked to find Miss Jennings collapsed in the hallway, her face pale and her eyelids fluttering. I knelt beside her and was relieved to see that she bore no injury, but was only recovering from a faint.

"Hurry, please," she whispered. "That wicked man – he forced his way in. I could not stop him."

Holmes was already bolting up the stairs. I found myself caught between duties, but the brave lady urged me to follow my friend, and the timely appearance of the motherly housekeeper spared me. I placed Miss Jennings in the elder lady's care and, cocking my revolver, dashed up in Holmes's wake. There was an open doorway at the end of the hall.

"Watson," Holmes called to me, "your medical assistance will be invaluable."

I found myself inside a sizeable bedchamber. A lady – short, stout, with long gray hair loose around her face, clad only in her nightdress and a satin robe – was slumped in a chair. Holmes knelt beside her, holding a handkerchief to her throat.

"Her injury is purely superficial. His, however – "

I turned. There was a man sprawled on the floor. Half his skull was a grotesque wreckage of blood, brains, and bones. He was dark-haired and gray bearded. Hs ugly, blackened teeth were exposed in a final rictus. His coat was ragged at the cuffs and elbows, and his striped pants were nearly threadbare at the knees. In his right hand, he still clutched the long and wicked knife that had damaged the lady's throat. I noted that a sizeable revolver was just inches from the lady's slippers.

"She killed him?" I asked, even as I began to tear strips of bed linens to make a hasty bandage.

Holmes considered the weapon. "As determined as Mrs. Spencer is, and as talented as she might be with the needle, I find it unlikely that she could so skillfully wield a Colt 'Peacemaker'. No, the honor belongs to another."

It was only then that I saw the fourth presence in the room. The gentleman had been standing in the shadows, so perfectly still that he had merged with them, and now he glided forward, as silent as a ghost. He was solemnly dressed, but even in somber clothing it was obvious that he was tall, broad-shouldered, and remarkably fit. He wore a stovepipe hat, over which was draped a long and impenetrable crepe veil.

"Mr. Spencer," Holmes said. "Do you know who I am?"

The man's voice was deep and low. "I do. Last night, Miss Jennings confessed to my wife that she had spoken to you. We planned to put our problem to you when you came."

"And it seems I arrived too late," Holmes replied. "The police must be summoned, but before they intervene, let us have your story from your own lips."

Mrs. Spencer roused as I began to bandage her throat. She was confused and alarmed, but a few whispered words from her veiled husband calmed her. He easily lifted her into his arms and laid her upon the bed, drawing its curtains. Rarely have I seen such tenderness or devotion. Holmes, meanwhile, had thrown a sheet over the ghastly corpse on the floor.

Mr. Spencer turned and, with a careful movement, removed his veil.

His face was not scarred and mutilated. It was the handsome, solemn countenance of a man in his fifties, his oiled black hair bearing only a single streak of gray. His eyes were dark, his nose long, and his chin square. He studied us with a stoic expression, then folded his arms over his chest.

It was clear now why he had been willing to conceal his identity. He was an American Indian, his perfect features marked by a tattooed band across his nose, extending beneath both eyes. He began to speak, clearly choosing his words with great care.

"The man I killed was named Simon Chaney. When Elizabeth was sixteen, her widowed father sold her to that man in marriage, to pay off his debts. She loved her father and knew he would lose everything without her sacrifice. This was in 1864, when the Great War raged. Chaney owned a factory where ammunition was made. Elizabeth's father died, and then, only a month later, there was an explosion at Chaney's factory. A dozen young girls were killed. Chaney was reported as dead, but the factory burned so hot that not even his bones could be found. Elizabeth was broken-hearted – not for her husband, who was a cruel and wicked man, but for the young girls who had perished. She sold everything she possessed and resolved to leave the war behind.

"Even though she was great with Chaney's child, she found a party of missionaries and travelled with them across the plains in their wagons.

She gave birth in the Sierra Mountains, just as the snow was coming. She and the baby, Deborah, took sick and could not travel. The missionaries abandoned them, fearing that if they lingered, they would meet the same fate as the Donner Party. That was where I found her." He glanced back toward the bed. "How could I not have loved her, she who the forest and the mountain gave to me? I kept her and the little one safe all winter, hunting and providing for them in a hut that I made. She was afraid of me at first, but soon we learned words of each other's language. The missionaries had left one of their wagons behind, and in the springtime, I took Elizabeth to California, where she purchased a lonely ranch on the American River. There, we began to live as man and wife, needing no judge or preacher to tie us to each other. We raised Deborah, whom her mother fondly called Polly, as our child. Polly knew nothing of the wicked man who had sired her.

"We were happy and prosperous for three years before a trapper, who was a friend, came to us in great alarm. Chaney was not dead – he had fled the scene and hidden himself, lest he be blamed for the deaths of the girls. He lurked in Canada until after the war, then returned to find his property sold and his wife vanished. Elizabeth had written to a cousin telling her of our life in California. This woman told Chaney where Elizabeth and his daughter could be found. Chaney had come as far as Sacramento and was swearing he would have Elizabeth and his daughter back.

"Fortunately for us, he was a drunkard, and fell afoul of the law for a brawl in a tavern. He was sentenced to jail. This gave us time to sell our land and cattle. Elizabeth feared we would never be safe as long as we stayed in America. But how could we travel together as husband and wife, when I was clearly not of her race? It was Polly who gave us the answer – the little child was playing with one of her mother's old mourning veils – and we knew that we could use the story of the explosion as a way to divert attention from my strange appearance. Elizabeth chose to tell people the tragedy had occurred in Maine, to avoid any prejudice foreigners might apply to us because of the rebellion.

"And so we crossed the Pacific, spending time in Australia and then France before settling here at Sparrow Grange. Only one thing marred our happiness – a year ago, shortly after she had begun her studies at a finishing school in Switzerland, Polly died. She passed very quickly, of a tumor in her brain, and was buried in Zurich. Elizabeth's hair turned grey – she did not wish to live. But then she returned to her skill with the needle. She showed some quilts at a lady's festival in London, and soon she was surprised by the many commissions she received. There was so much work that she needed an assistant. That is how Miss Jennings came to us."

"How did Chaney find you?" Holmes asked.

"He hired an American detective, a Pinkerton agent. Chaney was a wicked man, but a resourceful one. When his letter arrived, telling Elizabeth that he was coming to expose us, we considered what to do. We were tired of running from this fiend. We though he could be sated with money, and so we began to sell every trinket we had to raise funds. But then, when he came to Huxton, he sent a message demanding to see his daughter. Elizabeth feared to tell him the truth, because she knew of his violent temper, so she sent messages to him begging him to forebear, telling him that Polly knew nothing of her father, but he was relentless. It was my thought that Miss Jennings was much the same as our lost Polly with the same black hair. We thought perhaps a glimpse of her would satisfy him, and so my wife began to call her by that name, and to take her for long walks in the garden, hoping he would spy her, be satisfied, and desist his persecution of us."

"But how did he know she was not Polly?" I asked. "If he had never seen his daughter, why would he have rebuked Miss Jennings as an imposter?"

Holmes made a soft sound, then walked over to the corpse, quickly inspecting the dead man's pockets. He rose with a small photograph in his hand.

"The Pinkerton was most thorough – written on the back is 'Dorothea Chaney.' I trust this is your stepdaughter, Mr. Spencer?"

He nodded. "It must have been made in Switzerland, just as she entered the school."

"She was clearly taller and older, and not as slender as Miss Jennings, though from a distance they might be mistaken. I assume Chaney made more threats once the deception was discovered?"

Mr. Spencer nodded solemnly. "A note arrived yesterday, while Miss Jennings was in London. It was filled with abuse and vulgar language. I sent a reply, allowing that he could finally come to our home and discuss the matter as civilized people should. We set the time for this afternoon, knowing you would have arrived and could serve as a mediator. But he came less than an hour ago, barged in, and ran to our suite. My wife was in the process of dressing. Chaney charged at her and put his knife to her throat. I shot him without hesitation." Mr. Spencer favored the corpse with a look of disgust. "If the laws of your nation require that I must hang for what I have done, I will do so gladly, because this beast will trouble my precious Elizabeth no more."

"You will find that our laws are just," Holmes said. "No man would be expected to stand aside passively and watch his wife be murdered. Let us send your farmhand for the local constable. Watson and I will bear witness to your tale."

NOTE

Some of my readers may recall the articles which appeared in our metropolitan journals under the headline "The Noble Brave of Huxton". Indeed, our courts quickly absolved Mr. Spencer of any blame, and the romance of the story was such that the village folk warmly embraced their formerly veiled resident. Mrs. Spencer's quilts were suddenly so in demand among ladies who had wept over her tale that a bevy of assistants were hired. Nothing, of course, could wipe away the pain of the loss of the beautiful Polly, but I was gratified to receive a card stating that Miss Jennings had wed the stalwart young farmhand, Jack, and that the Spencers had sponsored the nuptials and gifted the young couple with a residence, as they considered the former Miss Jennings an adoptive daughter.

One thing puzzled Holmes, until he wrote a letter to the American lady. A reply soon solved the last of the mystery.

> *Spencer was my maiden name. My husband's name, given to him in a ceremony by his Nez Perce tribe, is* Hemene Toolakasson, *or* Wolf Standing on Top.

– JHW

The Disappearance
of Dr. Markey
by Stephen Herczeg

It was in late July of 1887 that I found myself extremely occupied with quite a number of patients. Sherlock Holmes, however, found himself in quite the opposite situation. A dearth of interesting cases has plunged him into a drawn-out period of boredom, in which I caught sight of him, on many occasions, unclasping the catch of his neat Moroccan leather case containing the implements with which he partook of his horrid little habit.

Dismissing thoughts of Holmes and his addiction, I journeyed to the abode of Lady Marjorie Ingrum, a patient of mine. I had received a telegram earlier that morning that, even through the medium of the stilted printed word upon the sheet, instilled a feeling of desperation, a certain sense of urgency within me.

I was greeted by Townsend, Lady Marjorie's butler, and was quickly presented to the Lady in her sitting room. Even though she was almost twenty years my senior, her ragged appearance and drawn face made me think she was well into her seventies.

"Lady Marjorie," I exclaimed, moving across and dropping to one knee while taking her hands in mine. "Your telegram sounded frightfully urgent. What is the matter? Have you taken ill?"

A trail of tears scarred the heavy makeup she wore, lending a more sorrowful look to her appearance. A sad shake of her head. "No, Doctor, it isn't me that I've asked you here for." A glance upwards drew my stare in that direction. "It's my son."

As I helped Lady Marjorie ascend the stairs, she told me, "I haven't known what to do with him for many months now. Howard could keep the boy in train, but I've never been strong enough." I had never had the privilege of meeting Sir Howard Ingrum, as he passed well before Lady Marjorie became my patient, but his stern painted expression looked down from an assortment of vantage points around the house. "Wallace was always a willful child, and now in adulthood, is even more so. I know he's a layabout, and Lord knows I've asked him time and again, but coupled with a lazy coterie of so-called friends, he prefers an almost Bohemian existence to seeking out any form of practical application of his skills and talents."

464

Nothing that Lady Marjorie said came as any surprise to me. I met Wallace Ingrum on a few occasions, mostly as he passed by in the corridors of the house. He always presented an air of indifference or, as it seemed, intoxication, and I think we'd barely exchanged more than a few sentences. Each time he was as Lady Marjorie depicted: Regularly dishevelled, with dull eyes sporting dark shadows beneath them, and a pallid complexion as one who never ventured into the daylight.

It was even less of a surprise when I was led into the young man's bedroom to find him lying fully clothed on top of his bedclothes. The powerful smell of vomit assaulted my nostrils as soon as I entered. I reeled back slightly, before recovering and moving closer to the bed. The source of the rank odour had spilt down the other side of the bed and covered the floor.

Lady Marjorie coughed at the smell and pulled a kerchief from her sleeve. "That wasn't there when I last checked on him." Turning to her butler, she said, "Townsend, have Mary see to that, please." The butler bowed slightly and hurried off.

"How long has he been like this?" I asked, moving to the bedside, and retrieving a stethoscope from my bag.

As I placed the cup on Wallace's chest, Lady Marjorie said, "He came in late last night. A lot of banging and thumping. I could hear him all the way down the hall, and simply presumed he'd returned after an evening with those friends. It was Townsend that found him like this. I asked him to give Wallace a mid-morning call to try and get him to at least rise before midday, but this morning he was unresponsive. I was only relieved that he was simply sleeping and not . . . ."

Her voice trailed off as she suppressed a sob. Turning to catch her expression, I grew concerned for her almost as much as my patient. "Is there something more?"

Nodding, she added, "Yes. I think it's the cocaine."

"He's a user then?" I asked, turning back, and reaching for the man's wrists. There were a substantial number of puncture wounds on the underside of his left forearm, a sure sign that he shared a similar habit with my compatriot at home. Scanning the area, I noticed a small glass syringe lying in the shadow of the bed. From its position, I surmised it had dropped to the floor then rolled out of sight.

I checked the man's chest and noticed a severely accelerated heartbeat, to the point that I was surprised I couldn't hear the thumping without the aid of my instrument. I placed my hand on his forehead. He was burning up. "Can you ask Townsend to fetch some cold water and some flannel cloths? We need to get Wallace's temperature down as far as possible." When Lady Marjorie left, I set about stripping the young man

465

down to his undergarments. The room had a single window, so I drew the curtains, lifted the windowpane, and threw open the shutters. A slight breeze blew into the room. My hope was it could wash across the man's body and cool him. The only other course of action was to introduce water into his system, but with him unconscious, I could do nothing on that front until he awoke.

Thankfully, Townsend returned in a few minutes, with a young housemaid that I assumed was Mary. Averting her eyes from Wallace's half-naked form, she set about cleaning up the other side of the bed.

Retrieving the towels from Townsend and the bucket of water that he set down, I dampened and placed them on Wallace's forehead and chest. By the time Lady Marjorie joined us, it was a simple wait until Wallace regained consciousness. If he showed no signs of recovery in the next hour, I would send word to the nearest hospital and have the unfortunate man moved.

As Mary left with the dirty water, Lady Marjorie asked her to bring tea. I believe it was more to help pass the time than to alleviate any thirst. Townsend brought a pair of straight-backed chairs and a small side table and finished setting them up when Mary returned with a tray laden with a teapot, cups, and a small plate of biscuits.

After Mary and Townsend retreated to the bowels of the house, I watched Lady Marjorie for a moment and noticed her eyes barely leave her unconscious son. Taking it upon myself, I played mother and poured out the tea, establishing the need for sugar and milk as I did so.

"He will be all right, won't he?" Lady Marjorie asked.

"I'm sure he will be." Holding the plate of biscuits out to distract her attention for a moment, Lady Marjorie unconsciously picked one from the plate and bit into it.

After several minutes of silence, broken only by the sound of munching and the clink of china, Lady Marjorie seemed to calm down, possibly in anticipation of her son's recovery. "I have to confess, Doctor, that you weren't the first physician I approached to help."

Intrigued, I replied, "Really? I didn't realise you were seeing anyone else."

"Oh, I don't. It's just that I received a pamphlet from another local doctor who specialises in helping those who overindulge in the drugs."

I thought immediately of Holmes and became even more curious. "What would this physician's name be?"

"Dr. Dermid Markey. He has a practice just south of the River in Brixton."

"But he couldn't help you?"

466

"No. None of my telegrams were replied to. I stated just as much urgency and almost sent Townsend in person to seek out Dr. Markey's help, but then thought of you."

"I can only assume that Dr. Markey was simply detained elsewhere. It would seem peculiar that he didn't deem it appropriate to at least answer your telegrams."

"I was a little disappointed. From the word amongst my friends, he is very diligent, and quite against this whole epidemic of drug usage, especially amongst the younger generation. I had hoped he wouldn't just save my Wallace and help him recover, but could aid him in overcoming this compulsion to take these nefarious substances."

Thinking of my own version of Wallace sitting at home in Baker Street, I had to agree, and could only hope to find this physician and have him visit Holmes in the near future. I plied Lady Marjorie with more questions, with a view of learning more about this Dr. Markey, and to keep her mind occupied on other thoughts while we waited to see if her son recovered.

"Yes, I have heard of this Dr. Dermid Markey," said Holmes, seemingly in decent spirits following a splendid luncheon prepared by Mrs. Hudson. There were no obvious effects from any addictive substances in his system, which pleased me no end.

I had returned to Baker Street after staying with Lady Marjorie until young Wallace showed signs of recovery. Starting with a small series of groans, and a flickering of his eyes, I diagnosed that he was beginning to return to consciousness. Removal of the damp cloths brought out a series of goosebumps when the calming breeze from the windows wafted across his bare skin. His heightened temperature had indeed receded, boding well for him. Deciding there was little more I could do in any practical way, I covered him with his bedclothes and bid good day to Lady Marjorie.

"I think the worst has passed. He will need to sleep the rest of the effects off, but there is little more I can do for now. I'm happy to drop by in the early evening if you like to see how he progresses," I said.

"That would be most thoughtful," said Lady Marjorie, very effusive in her tone now that her son was on the way to full recovery. "You are a Godsend, Dr. Watson. A Godsend."

"I am a simple physician. Assisting the poorly is my duty." With that, I returned in the hope of a late luncheon before more attendances in the afternoon.

"But I neither see any need to meet with the fellow, nor how that could even be possible," said Holmes, a wry grin on his face hiding some snippet of information to which I wasn't privy.

"I simply feel that you may find some benefit from his views on the use of certain substances," I said, nodding towards the contents of Holmes's case on show in the corner. As I noticed his eyes drift in that direction, then back, the last part of his statement made itself known to my mind once more. Confused, I asked, "What did you mean by possible?"

"Ah, well," he said, moving across to a pile of newspapers and rifling through them, before turning back with the issue he sought. Placing the paper down, he opened to a page with a small article titled, "*Local Doctor Missing*".

I read and was dismayed to find that Dr. Dermid Markey had gone missing over a week before. The article stated that the last sight of him was just before attending a callout. A single witness described the hansom he hailed, but the driver was wrapped up for cold weather, a fact I felt strange given the wonderful weather of the past month. Not a word had been heard of him since.

"That explains why Lady Marjorie had no word from him then," I mumbled under my breath.

"Who?" asked Holmes.

"A patient of mine. I have just returned from helping her son overcome a cocaine overdose."

"Careless," said Holmes, matter-of-factly.

"Quite." Pointing at the article, I asked, "You didn't see fit to investigate this?"

"Not beyond a cursory examination of the facts. I have had no contact with anyone interested in instigating a formal investigation, so there has been no need."

Desperately trying to hide my annoyance at Holmes, I mumbled, "It wouldn't have anything to do with his stance on narcotics and stimulants?"

"Not at all. I will admit I don't like the man's intentions. He wishes to outlaw or bring in a higher level of Government regulation on the availability of perfectly legal drugs." Taking a deep breath to control his rising emotional state, Holmes exhaled slowly then added, "I know you wish for me to stop my usage, but it is all perfectly legal, and I only partake to maintain a level of stimulation in my mind. Besides, the product of the coca plant has proved a boon amongst your professional comrades, virtually replacing the use of ether as an anaesthetic and increasing the safety of many medical procedures."

Not wishing to look him in the eyes, I glanced down at the newsprint once more. A snatch of information buried in the middle of the short article caught my attention. "Did you pick up on this fact?"

"What would that be?"

"Dr. Markey ran for parliament in the last general election."

"Yes, I believe he ran as an independent on a strict platform of drug reform. I think the article mentions the winning Member."

Reading further, I replied, "Yes, Sir Benton McBrough, one of Gladstone's liberals, a backbencher. I haven't heard much about him."

"One can't keep abreast of all of these Parliamentarians. Why are you so interested in Dr. Markey?"

Finally glancing up into Holmes's face, I said, "He's a fellow physician, so there's a natural bond there. From what Lady Marjorie told me, he is a bit of a crusader – a do-gooder, I suppose you'd call him. That drags me closer to him as well. The fact that he is missing disturbs me, and draws me to wish to find him, or at least find out what happened to him."

"Very noble, Watson," Holmes answered, examining my expression for a time, and forming some opinion in that complex mind of his. Standing, he clapped his hands together and said, "In that case, I will seek out the whereabouts of this Dr. Markey. Consider it a favour to you, my old friend."

With that he disappeared into his rooms, leaving me slightly astonished at his change of heart.

Never one to dawdle when the scent of a case was in the air, Holmes returned within minutes, ready to depart. Where I had no idea, until he expounded that we were to start at the beginning: The rooms of Dr. Dermid Markey.

Holmes was quite effusive during our hansom journey across the Thames and into the south of London. To my ears, it was partly a relief to see a break in his sombre and distant mood, but also partly a concern that his disposition was due to something other than just the likelihood of an interesting mystery to solve.

As we turned down Kennington Road, Holmes quipped, "We don't come as a pair into this part of the city very often."

"Am I to assume that you travel here by yourself then?"

"Oh, yes," he said, a sly grin on his lips, "There is a definite undercurrent of the ways and wherefores of the criminal underbelly writhing its way through the destitute backstreets of this area. I have spent many a night wandering and slinking my way around in search of information. I'm much happier to be entering the place in the fullness of the day, though. It can be a very rough area at night." He pondered for a moment, then added in a downcast voice, "Which sadly could account as a simple solution to our little mystery."

The cab turned into a small side street and pulled up before a modest two-story yellow brick terrace. A small wooden sign hung next to the front door, the names Dr. Markey and Dr. Carlton were inscribed upon it.

"He has a partner," I said.

"It would seem," replied Holmes. "This should be a good place to start then."

The front door led straight into the surgery's waiting room. It was filled with patients, together with the sound of coughing and the gentle murmurs of discomfort. The only light came from the front window and a sole gaslight affixed above the receptionist's desk.

Holmes strode across the short distance and stood before the young woman dressed in a simple nurse's uniform. I realised the practice was small enough to warrant the duties of nurse and receptionist to be undertaken by a single person. A simple nameplate sat on the desk, informing patients that the young girl's name was Nurse Jenny Calahan.

Within a moment, the lass looked up with a slight expression of surprise, possibly at our manner of dress or stature, and said, "We don't get such fine gentlemen around here too often. How can we help you?"

"Thank you, Nurse Calahan," replied Holmes. "We'd like to speak with Dr. Carlton if that's possible?"

"Is it a medical matter?"

"No. My name is Sherlock Holmes, consulting detective, I have undertaken to investigate the matter of Dr. Markey's disappearance."

"Oh, in that case, I'll see if I can catch him for you."

Just as she finished her statement, voices echoed from a nearby doorway. "Now, Mrs. Withers, please take one each day, and stay off your feet as much as possible. The swelling should go down if you do."

"Oh, I'll try, Doctor," came the reply, "but my 'Arold's a useless fool around the 'ouse, so nuffin' will get done if'n I's just lazing around."

"Fine, but please do try."

As the old woman appeared in the doorway, followed by a young, handsome man in a doctor's coat and carrying a small card with him, an elderly man stood and shuffled across to take the old woman's arm. As they waddled towards the exit, Harold said, "Now, Diedre why's you go an' say that to the doctor?"

"Oh, don't worry 'Arold, 'e knows you well, so it comes as no surprise to 'im."

"Still," finished Harold.

I watched as they exited, then turned back towards the doctor, who eyed Holmes and myself suspiciously.

"And you gentlemen are?"

Jenny piped up, "Oh, this is Mr. Sherlock Holmes, Doctor. He's come to ask about Dr. Markey."

Carlton popped the medical card down on the desk near Jenny and reached for the top one on a small pile nearby. Reading the card he said to

470

us, "Well, I'm sorry, but my waiting room is full. Jenny here can book you in, but it may be some time."

Smiling, Holmes bowed slightly and said, "No problems there, Doctor. I can see you are busy. It is a matter of some urgency, as it's about your partner, but I'm happy to fit in with your schedule."

Regarding Holmes for several seconds, Carlton finally turned away and called out the name of the next patient. "Mr. Gareth Jones?" The call was answered by a scruffily dressed man standing. His actions were immediately met with a short coughing fit, garnering disgusted looks from others nearby. Once composed, he trundled off into the rear rooms, followed by Carlton, who gave Holmes one last look before joining him.

Seeing that there were now two seats free, Holmes stepped across and sat down. I quickly joined him, a little frustrated that we were going to have to wait, but interested in seeing how this particular medical practice operated. My observations were a little short-lived, however.

Almost as soon as he sat, Holmes garnered the interest of the old man seated to his left. He looked well into his seventies, but could have been young as sixty. His face was lined with deep wrinkles, and his weathered and sun-burnt skin looked similar to the cracked leather of an ageing couch.

"Did me ears hear right?" asked the man. "You're Sherlock Holmes?"

Looking him up and down, Holmes gave the man a quick examination, before answering. "Yes. Yes, I am."

"The detective?" Holmes nodded. "Don't you work with the Yard to bring down criminals?"

Smiling, Holmes added, "Yes, I do work with members of Scotland Yard from time to time."

"So what are ye here for? Not here for Carlton are ye? I hope not. He's been me doctor for a while now. Good man. Never had a problem with him."

"No, nothing like that. I'm here to ask Dr. Carlton a few questions."

"About any of us?" asked the man, his expression changing to a look of shock. I noticed at that point, many heads turning our way.

"Well, really I can't say. That sort of thing is private to the case at hand, and nobody can be ruled out until the evidence says they are innocent. Take you for instance. Your accent reeks of Newcastle, but you've been in London for a number of years, or you came from London initially and spent time in Newcastle." Holmes pointed to the man's hands. "You worked the mines. Your hands still have a deep-seated hint of coal dust deep in their pores. That, plus the yellow stains on your fingers, tell me you are a heavy smoker. Both could be the possible cause of why you are here."

471

The man looked flabbergasted, a common sight following one of Holmes's dissections. He coughed loudly for a few moments, bringing out a kerchief to capture the effluent.

It was then I noticed another man on the other side of the room who had been staring at Holmes quite intently stand up and head for the door.

"Mr. Smythe? You're next." said Jenny, standing and moving around her desk. "Do you not want to see the doctor now?"

"Oi'll come back later," he said, turning slightly, but keeping his eyes on Holmes. "It's a little too busy roight now." As the door banged shut, the other patients turned from staring at Smythe to staring at Holmes.

Shaking her head, Jenny turned and disappeared down the short corridor.

After she had gone, a lady sitting near to me piped up and asked Holmes, "Did you just say that nobody was innocent?"

Holding his hands up, Holmes said, "No, no, I assure you. I merely suggested that until all the evidence is gathered, one cannot rule out the guilt of any person involved. I am only establishing the facts of the case in which I'm involved, but the same concept applies."

That one statement had a galvanising effect on the conscience of the gathered group. Almost as one they stood and headed for the door. Within a couple of minutes, Holmes and I found ourselves alone in the waiting room.

I turned to Holmes and asked, "Did you plan that?"

A wry grin crossed Holmes's face, "How could I have known that the power of a guilty mind could outweigh all logic and reason?"

Before I could answer, Jenny stepped back into the waiting room. A look of shock came to her face as she spied all the empty seats. "What happened?"

"I think they had more pressing engagements," said Holmes.

"Well, you have my attention now," said Dr. Carlton, looking very aggrieved that his entire waiting room was now empty, "I have no idea how I'm going to recover the lost earnings that just walked out of here. We barely manage to make ends meet at the best of times."

"I can sympathise with you Dr. Carlton," I said. "I have a number of patients myself that can barely afford to cover the costs of any medications I prescribe before they pay for my services as well. I almost wish that the Government would step in and bolster the medical industry as a whole – to somehow make it affordable for all."

Cutting me off, Holmes added, "Yes, Watson, but you also have patients that could buy you many times over. They afford you a level of fee that, I presume, Dr. Carlton could only dream of." Turning his attention

472

to Carlton, he added, "Again, I can only apologise so many times, but our true quest here today is to ask about your missing colleague, Dr. Dermid Markey."

Carlton sat back, an expression of resignation on his face, which told me he'd been through this all before. "I've told the police everything I know, which is nothing. The last I saw of Dermid, he was heading out on a call, and he never came home. Devastating to his wife, and very damaging to the practice."

"You don't seem too affected emotionally?"

"Well, I've only known him professionally."

"For two or three years, I'd say?"

Carlton looked astonished. "How did you know that?"

"You look about twenty-four years old, give or take a year. Standard medical training should take four years. Unless you are a prodigy, you would have started in your eighteenth year. You have the look of someone from a public-school background. The clothes under your coat are neat and tailored, but starting to wear, meaning you like to appear well-dressed, but are struggling to manage of late. Could be a consequence of this practice's turnover."

The doctor merely gaped at Holmes. I took that to mean his assessment was spot on.

"You mentioned that the practice has been struggling." Carlton nodded in response. "Do you think that Dr. Markey would have taken on a loan to supplement the practice's finances?"

Carlton shook his head. "No. What I have found of Dermid was his pride and insistence on taking every burden upon his own shoulders. I would never believe he would borrow money under any circumstances. Sometimes I consider that a foolish stance, but one I had to admire. Why do you ask?"

Shrugging, Holmes answered, "Just gathering indications of any untoward attention from the more nefarious members of society. What about competitors, enemies, or any disgruntled patients?"

Again, the younger doctor slowly shook his head. "If you were to meet the man, you'd almost call him a saint. His patients all returned to him, time and again, even with another physician not far from here. I didn't know much of his private life, but he never gave me any cause to think he was hated." Stopping, he considered for a moment before continuing. "There was one incident during that d--n foolish foray into politics."

"Yes?"

"A stone was thrown through the surgery window. No note. No follow up of any kind. We didn't think much of it at the time – just youths being reckless."

"Why think of it now?"

"Because it occurred about a week before the vote. We'd never had any other incidents, but, just now, that one stuck out."

"Were there any other incidents during the campaign?"

"Just the idiotic stance taken by Dermid's opponent." He stood and moved to a small window that looked out upon the street. "McBrough stood for several hours on that street corner and handed out free samples of cocaine to any passers-by. I must admit that I watched him between patients. Couldn't believe his actions. An aged politician treating a dangerous drug as if it were sweeties."

"Intriguing. I've always taken the acts of politicians with a grain of salt. They tend to look after themselves first, then their constituents."

"Quite."

"One last question I would ask is about this final call that Dr. Markey went upon. Was it one of his addiction cases?"

A slight nod of the head was followed by a sigh and, "Yes. Damn fool. He would drop everything to go help another of these hopeless cases. They always turn out bad. The patient was either dead or so far gone that he would never recover. If it was a positive outcome, then any fee we recovered was chewed up by the costs of medicines and implements. Dermid would never ask for extra to cover them." Carlton shook his head. "I warned him it would all go wrong one day."

"How many overdoses did Dr. Markey attend – per year say?"

"Too many. One a week, sometimes two or three. Especially in this area, and down towards Brixton. The loss of time and money on such a quixotic pursuit drove me to distraction."

"And with him gone, you're feeling trapped here? Am I reading that right?"

Once again that astonished look crossed his face. "I – I – " He hung his head and shook it slightly, "I can't lie. Yes, I've been making enquiries. Looking for a place in a practice north of the river. Somewhere more salubrious." Looking up, his face took on a haggard, tired expression. "If I stay here much longer, I'll end up like my patients in the waiting room. Old before my time. One foot in the grave, the rest of my life spent just counting down the days."

As we stepped into the waiting room, I was a little pleased to see a few more patients had settled in for their wait. Holmes moved across to the nurse and asked, "Would you have the address to which Dr. Markey was last requested?"

474

Jenny said, "Oh, yes, I do." She flipped pages in a small diary and ran a finger down a column of addresses and notes. "Here. 23 Angel Road in Brixton."

"Hmm. Not a nice part of town," Holmes muttered.

"And the strangest part is, it isn't the first time we've had a call there either."

"No?"

Flipping back a few pages, Jenny pointed to another entry with the same address. I noticed the date on the page was two weeks earlier. "Dr. Markey was on another call, so Dr. Carlton went instead." Her face turned slightly dour, "He wasn't a happy chappy when he returned. He was muttering about a waste of time and something about addicts. I found out later that there was no one home, almost as if it had been a prank. I did mention that to Dr. Markey, but he dismissed it as a misunderstanding."

"Did you tell the police about this?"

"Oh, yes," she said, shrugging, "Not sure they cared or looked into it. Always too busy, the police."

"Quite so. Did you consult them when the stone was thrown through the surgery window?"

"Oh, yes. A young constable came around. Took one look, took some notes. Mumbled something about wild youths in the street, then we never heard from him again. Typical really."

Nodding, Holmes stood still for a moment, thinking on this latest information before asking, "Do you know if Mrs. Markey is in?"

"You might be in luck. She's been in a right state. I think she's looking to go off to her sister's in Windsor for a few days. I have the address if you miss her."

Nodding, Holmes said, "Thank you. I believe that the Markeys live next door, is that right?"

"Yes."

"We'll check there, but return if we need that address."

"That will be fine."

Holmes walked away, while I maintained eye contact with the lovely nurse for a moment before joining him.

"Oh Lord, have you found him?" said the distraught looking woman who opened the neighbouring door.

"No, I'm sorry we haven't," said Holmes, "I assume then that you are Mrs. Markey?"

A confused look grew on the woman's face. "Why yes. Who are you?"

"I am Sherlock Holmes, and this is my colleague, Dr. John Watson."

"Sherlock Holmes?" said Mrs. Markey, "The detective?"

"The one and the same. Your husband's disappearance was brought to my attention, and I would like to offer my services in finding him."

"I don't have any money to pay you," the woman said, accompanied by a pained expression of embarrassment.

"And like your husband, at times I do not charge. I believe that he has been offering quite a public service, and I wish to do the same."

Mrs. Markey poked her head out further, her eyes darting frantically to and fro as she scanned the street before stepping back and allowing us entrance. "Please, come in then."

We were ushered into a small sitting room near the front of the house and took the seats offered to us. It was a sparsely furnished and appointed room, a single gaslight providing a trifling amount of illumination. Looking around, I noticed a single framed photograph on the nearby mantel. From the looks of Mrs. Markey in the portrait compared to the woman sitting opposite me, the photo was several years old. It was presumptive, but I took the other two people in the picture to be Dr. Markey and probably their teenage son.

"Now we do apologise for the intrusion," said Holmes, "but I felt the need to speak with you prior to continuing my investigation."

"Thank you for even considering it, Mr. Holmes. The last week has been horrendous. I've never felt more alone. My family are all in Windsor. I'm tempted to visit, but the cost . . . ." She trailed off at that point. I made a mental note that money was high on Mrs. Markey's mind, almost akin to the loss of her husband.

"Firstly, and I'm a little loathe to ask, but is there any reason that Dr. Markey may have willingly gone missing?"

"What do you mean?"

"Again, I'm sorry to ask, but perhaps a lover?"

Affronted, Mrs. Markey sat upright, in a posture of defiance. "Certainly not. Dermid and I are firmly committed to each other." Thrusting out her left hand, I noticed a beautifully crafted engagement ring, with a less ornate but striking gold Claddagh ring. It took me a moment to realise that Markey must be of Irish heritage. "We both wear the same wedding ring, as a way of showing our connection to each other. Dermid rarely takes his off, even when seeing patients." Taking a deep breath, she forced herself to relax before adding, "Besides, he simply wouldn't have the time."

"Ah, that was my next line of questioning. The public service he has taken on, to assist those that have succumbed to addiction and overdose – I assume by your statement that this occupies much of his time."

476

"Yes. It's a double-edged sword. I can only admire his stance and his actions, but in the same breath, I find it takes him away for so many hours each week. Time he can ill-afford."

"Why is that?"

"It has affected the practice. His paying patients are made to wait while he goes off to help the next unfortunate. As it is, we're only scraping through with the surgery and the house to support."

"Therefore, I can assume that your husband took on no loans to assist with finances?"

"No. He is far too proud to rely on others. He'd rather sell off our furniture before asking for charity."

"I see. Good. I just wanted to ensure that there could be no involvement of nefarious elements looking for recompense."

"Does your son still live at home," I butted in, "or is he making his way in the world? Does he contribute or assist his father?"

With that statement, Mrs. Markey's face became a veil of sorrow. Immediately, I realised my misreading of the photograph. The boy was obviously gone from this world, hence why she had never felt so alone.

Through the onset of tears, Mrs. Markey answered, "No. Jason left us three years ago. Fell in with the wrong crowd. Took to drink and opium. He became Dermid's first overdose patient, and Dermid's first failure. It's what drives him so. He never wants another family to face the devastation that we have."

We were left in silence for a few moments while Mrs. Markey recovered herself, drawing a kerchief from her sleeve to mop the small flow of tears. Finally she looked across at the family photograph, took a deep breath, and slowly exhaled. "It's why Dermid chose to try his hand at politics." Turning she glanced first at me, then at Holmes, "He wanted to take a stand against the proliferation of drugs in the community. He has tried to spread the word through his patients and his work with addicts, but believed that he would finder a greater voice from the floor of Parliament. Sadly, that wasn't to be."

"Yes, he lost to Sir Benton McBrough, I believe," said Holmes, "a long-time Liberal. A very hard task for any man, especially one new to the cut-and-thrust of politics."

"That is true, but he did quite well, almost unseating Sir Benton in the last election. Dermid still aspires to Parliament, and holds out hope that there may be a repeat of the last two year's instability."

"He would be one of the few, other than those unseated by Gladstone's defeat. I don't generally dwell on matters of politics, but I do remember some details of the campaign. Sir Benton spent quite a large amount of effort in undermining your husband's platform."

I piped up as I recalled Dr. Carlton's comment. "Didn't Sir Benton make a bit of a fool of himself by promoting the use of cocaine, and indeed giving some away for free? I thought it very strange at the time."

A surprising smile came to Mrs. Markey's face. "Yes, the man became a little obsessed – or should I say fearful – of Dermid's commitment. I never really took much interest, but some of my friends brought that little incident to my attention. Dermid and I both found it amusing, if not a little disturbing."

"Politicians," said Holmes, a thoughtful look on his face. "Most will do anything to gain or retain power."

After bidding *adieu* to Mrs. Markey, Holmes vowed to keep in touch with any information he uncovered, and we made our way to the high street. Luckily we found a passing hansom and asked to be taken to the Brixton address. The cabbie was very hesitant at first, but a promise of a higher fee soon had us on our way.

The cab pulled up in front of a series of run-down terrace houses and, from the lack of movement within any of them, abandoned.

"Are you sure this is the right address?" I asked Holmes.

He nodded, showing me the piece of paper. "As far as we know."

"Can we at least ask the cabbie to wait? I can't believe we'll be long."

"Oh, come now, Watson – where's your sense of adventure?" Holmes vaulted from the cab and strode across to the reason for our presence.

I stepped out and paid the driver, stopping myself from asking him to stay before he drove away. Looking around, I noticed that the area was a reflection of our destination. The houses weren't quite derelict, but close to it. The street was strewn with rubbish, and there was a distinct lack of carts or wagons. The only bright spot in the street was the modest-looking church opposite. A small sign read *"St. John the Evangelist"*. The doors were shut, and the grounds quiet and vacant – not surprising for the time of the week.

Stepping up to the house in question, I found Holmes standing a few feet from the front door and examining the steps. As I watched, he pulled out his glass and leaned down, peering closely at the area.

"What have you found?" I asked.

"Something strange indeed." He stood up, replaced the glass, and pointed at the area of his concern. "Can you see?"

I examined the spot for a moment before it started to become clear. "My word," I said, dropping down for a closer look. The dust and grime on the step and stoop were quite thick, and as there was no mat on which to wipe one's feet, one could clearly see where the dirt had been disturbed

– but only from a single pair of boots that I could see. "What does it mean?"

"I can only presume that, of late, only one person has visited this door." Pointing to the few steps leading up, he added, "And that person only approached the premises and never left. Luckily for us, there hasn't been any rain for the last week or so."

"But if the person entered, then he or she must still be inside."

"Unless he or she left by a rear exit, which may be how the regular visitors gain access as well."

"Should we knock then?"

"We can, but I doubt if there is anyone inside."

The hollow sound of the knocker rang through the house, but there was no noise from within. I shrugged. "Well, I assumed you would be correct, but one must try these things."

Smiling, Holmes reached into his coat and brought out his lock picks. I glanced around to ensure we were undisturbed while he made quick work of the lock and swung the door open. I made to move inside, but Holmes placed a hand on my chest.

"Sorry, but I just want to view the scene before we enter." Intrigued, I followed Holmes's gaze and noticed that the floor within was filthy with dust and grime, much like the steps outside. However, three sets of footprints could be clearly seen in the dust. One set led to the door, with two sets leading away. "I assume you can see the sets of boot prints." I nodded and watched as Holmes stooped down once more, examining each set of prints in turn. Pointing to those leading in from outside, he said, "This pair has the look of boots worn by a city-based man, but this pair," he pointed to the other, "has a wider tread – something akin to a worker's boot."

"Strange."

"Quite," he said, entering the passageway and stepping lightly along the wall, preserving the trail of footprints as much as possible. I followed, shutting the door behind me, and keeping to his trail as closely as possible.

The line of footprints led down the long hallway and turned abruptly into a room at the end. Holmes stopped for a moment, studying the area before disappearing through the doorway.

My first view of the room brought a feeling of surprise. It was a combined kitchen and dining area, with two small windows overlooking a very overgrown rear yard. The state of the area confirmed my view that the house had been unused for some time. In the kitchen area, the small benches lay empty, devoid of cutlery, crockery, or items used for food preparation. The furniture in the dining area consisted of a small wooden table with four chairs, one of which lay upturned in the far corner. A thick layer of dust cloaked every item in the room, the floor especially.

Holmes squatted nearby, his eyeglass hovering above several impressions in the dust.

"More boot prints?"

"Yes. Two more sets in addition to those we have already seen. The scraping of heel marks and footprints through this dirt suggests that there was a scuffle of some kind." He pointed towards two parallel lines running from near the centre of the room towards the double doors that led out to the garden. "A quick summation would lead me to presume that the person entering this room was attacked, knocked unconscious – or worse – and then dragged towards the garden."

"Should we go out and check? He may still be there."

"In time. There are still many clews to uncover in this room." Then, peering closer to the floor, he cried, "Ah, yes!" Looking down, I saw him point to several dark spots on the dirty floor. "This may be blood, but I cannot tell fully in this light."

Noticing a gaslight nearby, I pulled out a small box of matches and endeavoured to light the flame, before giving up in exasperation. "There's no gas," I said, a little confused and surprised.

"That would corroborate with my assertion that this house has been unused for quite some time – at least for normal habitation, that is."

It was then I noticed a candle in a holder on the other side of the room. Deftly skirting around the periphery, I quickly lit it, shining a dull, yellow light across the scene.

"Thank you. Well done," said Holmes, snatching the candle from me and bringing it closer to the area of his attention.

Now that there was a little more light, I took the opportunity to glance around the room and noticed a glint of something metallic in the corner opposite. Pointing I asked, "What's that?" Holmes looked up as I skirted the centre of the room and retrieved the object. It was conical in shape, with circular openings at both ends. The brass had dulled slightly from age and use, but still retained enough shine to catch the light. "Intriguing," I said, "If I had to guess, I'd say this is the end of a stethoscope."

I passed the object into Holmes open palm. He quickly examined it under the glass and nodded in agreement. "I believe you're correct – different to the type you use, but common enough among your colleagues."

"Does that mean that Markey was here?"

"The idea gains credence," Holmes said.

While Holmes continued to investigate the room, my eyes kept wandering to the area outside of the rear doors. It was a singular mess and tangle of weeds and plants, though a pathway of broken cobblestones and tamped down grasses could be seen running through the brush towards the rear of the property. I almost jolted in shock when I felt rather than saw Holmes's presence at my shoulder.

"The owners of this property obviously don't entertain anyone in the rear yard," he quipped.

"I'm more worried about what they hide in there."

"Well then, let's find out, shall we?"

The first thing I saw as the door swung open was the definite line of muddied footprints leading up the garden path to the rear step. They had smudged slightly as boots walked back across them towards the rear gate once more.

"The mud only comes one way," I said.

"Yes. The owner obviously realised that his boots were filthy and cleaned them off there." Holmes pointed to a smear of dark, mud on the edge of the top step. Carefully stepping across to the dark patch, he bent down and tentatively poked his finger into the pile. I grimaced, my darkest imagination picturing where the mud came from and what it contained.

As Holmes rubbed the mud between two fingers, then raised it to his nose and sniffed. I said, "Be careful. That could be – "

"Excrement?" he asked before taking another sniff. "In fact, it is. Sheep or – " Sniffing the mud again. " – pig. There's definitely a hint of omnivore in it. Not strong enough for a carnivore. Possibly from a pig, and intriguingly still relatively fresh."

Holding back a sudden urge to gag, I said, "Where would someone find a pigsty around here?"

Wiping his fingers on his kerchief, Holmes said, "I doubt it was actually around here." He stepped to the side of the path and studied the footprints and crushed plants. After a few moments, he said, "Yes, there are actually three sets of prints. The mud-laden boots, plus two others. All came up the path in single file, then two of them moved side-by-side going back out. By the depth of the impressions in the grass, they were carrying something on their way out."

"Or someone?"

"Yes, it's starting to look likely that it was someone."

I followed Holmes as he slowly made his way down the garden path, stopping every once in a while to examine the footprints and crushed greenery. I noticed the privy set against the rear fence. It was unusable due to the build-up of weeds and grass around the door, almost hiding it from view.

The thicker weeds on both sides of the path appeared to have been completely undisturbed for weeks, if not months. Holmes confirmed this by ignoring them completely and making his way through the rear gate and into the service laneway behind. The road was a turgid mess of mud, I hoped it was mud. I knew well that the laneway was probably used mostly by the nightsoil men undertaking their nocturnal duties.

We both studied the wet trails of wagon wheels and horses' hooves, Holmes shaking his head at the state of the area. Any indications of a trap or cart behind our position had long been erased. It was then that Holmes's eyes fell on the rear door of the privy. As he carefully picked his way across to it, I gasped, "Surely you don't need to look in there?"

"Ah, but think on it. The night soil men would know by now that this house is unused, and to save themselves time and effort, would regularly skip this privy. But if you were to discard or hide something, what better place?"

As he slid the door up, I expected no less than a bucket of foul contents, but was greeted with a triumphant "A-ha!" Holmes pulled from the tiny room a brown, leather case. Even from where I stood, I could make out what it was.

Opening and peering inside, Holmes nodded and said, "A medical bag, as I'm sure you already determined. Unless there's a rush on disposing of medical professionals, I'm sure we can establish that this indeed belonged to Dr. Markey."

"The poor man. Where do you think he was taken?"

Peering down the laneway, Holmes gave a tiny shrug before adding, "To that, I have no idea as yet. I believe we need to involve the constabulary, as this case has deepened very quickly."

I was a little surprised that Holmes would look to bring in the police before having established all the facts of the case. It wasn't until we exited back into the street that it became clear.

As Holmes worked his magic and relocked the front door, I scanned the roadway for any witnesses or passers-by that might cause a ruckus, and noticed a young urchin hiding in the churchyard across the street. His attention was focused solely on us, which I thought strange, as I hadn't seen anyone on our way in, and from the looks of the boy, he knew we had entered and had been waiting all this time.

It was as Holmes turned and stepped down to the street level that the boy came out of his hiding spot and raced across towards us. I unconsciously stepped before Holmes as the boy approached.

"Mr. 'Olmes! Mr. 'Olmes!" he cried, alerting my colleague to his presence.

As Holmes stepped to one side, a smile came to his face. I realised immediately that he knew the boy.

"Jenkins, you look thoroughly flummoxed. What's the matter?"

"I'm sorry Mr. 'Olmes. One of our lads lives this way and sent word to Wiggins that you were here. He sent me in a hurry."

"Why? What can the matter be?"

"It's this 'ouse, sir. Do you know whose it is?"

"I have my theories, but obviously Wiggins was concerned about my presence, so enlighten me."

"What?" said the boy, a look of confusion on his face.

"Whose house is it?"

"Oh, yeah, it's Steelfist Wasser's."

"The criminal?" I blurted out.

"Ah, Derrick Wasser," said Holmes. "The scourge of South London,"

The little tyke nodded. "'E don't use it much, but I seen some men there last week. And a cart went off south. Big fella driving it."

A wide grin grew on Holmes's face. "The game is certainly afoot, Watson."

"Derrick Wasser," I said as the cab made its way back towards Baker Street. "I know a little about him, but mostly through reputation. Supposedly he runs a gang in South London, but the police have never been able to find evidence to actually incriminate him."

"That is true. I've kept an eye and ear open for any connection to the man, and his organisation, but until now there's been little. This could account for how self-assured he has grown."

"Yes, over-confidence leads to imprudence. I do know that the bulk of his activities are within legitimate businesses. Any mention in the tabloids have always brushed these aside as merely fronts to his other ventures."

Smiling, Holmes added, "Ah, well, I tend to read between the lines. The most important factor is that Wasser controls the importation and distribution of cocaine and opium throughout most of South London. A very large part of his business enterprises, I understand."

"That must be the motivation behind the disappearance of Dr. Markey."

"I think that's part of it, but the question I have is: Why would a man such as Wasser risk so much just to remove a minor player such as Dr. Markey?"

"If Markey's stance against these drugs were to take hold, they could severely limit Wasser's business. Would that be enough motivation?"

483

"I know only too well the legality of the drugs of which we speak. I'm more than happy for their prevalence in society to remain, while they are seen as legal. If their legal status were to change, then I would need to seriously rethink my own stance."

"To that, I would be most happy."

Slipping me a wry grin, Holmes added, "Quite, but I could only think that Wasser's business would be pushed underground, and frankly, become possibly more profitable per transaction, though much riskier."

"So?"

"I can't understand why Wasser would pursue Markey with such finality."

"Who else stands to gain from Dr. Markey's disappearance?"

"Who indeed? Who indeed? I think that I shall have to cogitate on that for a time."

Holmes slipped into silence for the rest of our journey back home. I was tied up with patient visits for the rest of the afternoon, and by the time I returned, he was nowhere to be found.

It wasn't until morning that Holmes appeared and joined me for a light breakfast. His face looked drawn from lack of sleep, but his eyes were bright with an inner eagerness. Sitting, he quickly downed two cups of coffee while I read the morning paper, seemingly composing himself before speaking.

"Watson, we must make a journey this morning. Are you free?"

"Why yes, I've nothing till later this afternoon. Where are we to go?"

"Dorking."

"What? Dorking? Why in blazes do you wish to go there?"

"We shall be visiting a piggery."

I sent notes to my afternoon patients to inform them that I wouldn't be able to attend until the morning and hailed a cab for the two of us. It soon had us at busy Waterloo Station. No sooner had we alighted than the lean form of Inspector Lestrade stepped out of the bustling crowd and greeted us.

"Ah, Inspector," said Holmes, "Glad you could join us. I thought you might send an underling in your stead."

"I'm intrigued, Mr. Holmes, plus anything that can pin an actual crime, especially one of this heinous nature, on Steelfist Wasser, is well worth following up. I'm still a little peeved at the local sergeant for not investigating that house in Brixton, but they rarely enter the area unless they have strong cause to. If this pans out, I'll be having strong words with him."

"Indeed. At this stage, I'm still a little wary of admitting success. It is a long bow that I draw, but after dwelling on the facts we know so far, and the other information I found from the voices in the street, I believe that we'll find what we're looking for."

I was still quite perplexed, but hoped that Holmes would divulge more in due time. I didn't have to wait long, as he wished for the three of us to be in solitude before speaking further.

The trip to Red Hill took all of an hour. Holmes had me purchase tickets for a compartment where we could speak undisturbed during that time. It was there that Holmes explained all he'd learned overnight.

"Inspector, this Wasser fellow: What is the word at the Yard about him?"

"He's as bent as a centuries-old willow tree," spat Lestrade, taking a breath for a moment to compose his next words, "Trouble is, we have nothing on him. Everything points to legitimate business interests, but he's got so many fingers in the wrong pies. We know it, but we can't prove anything."

"Well, hopefully, I can help you out."

"What have you got then? Why are we heading away from London?"

"One of Wasser's legitimate businesses is a pig farm on the outskirts of Dorking."

"Just another of his many."

"Yes, but he only owns the one farm. Speaking with quite a number of my contacts last night, I discovered that there have been several disappearances over the last few years. Many seem loosely associated with Wasser, in one way or another. Those facts, and the evidence of the cart, and excrement-caked boots, gives me pause to believe that this particular farm is used for very despicable purposes."

Holmes went silent at that point, leaving me to wonder further on his words. I could tell Lestrade was agitated, but I found him that way more often than not when Holmes was being cryptic.

We were met in Red Hill by a carriage with two constables aboard. Lestrade had telegraphed ahead, seeking support in case it was warranted. The bumpy ride on to Dorking was thankfully quick, and we found ourselves alighting outside of a rather run-down farmhouse and into the midst of the most God-awful smell, one that I was sure my sensibilities would take months to forget.

The farm was anything but, by my estimations. It consisted of a ramshackle house with a single large pen to one side that contained several overweight pigs. Two smaller outbuildings stood behind the pen – probably storage areas or, given the presence of the pigs, a butchery or similar.

485

Without a word, Holmes started towards the pigpen, leaving Lestrade, myself, and the two constables a little dumb-struck. A shout from the front door drew our attention.

"Oi? What the hell are you doing?" asked the husky man standing on the porch. "This is my property!" He thrust his stockinged feet into a pair of boots and shuffled off behind Holmes.

"Excuse me, sir," yelled Lestrade, stopping the man in his tracks, "Might I have a word?"

"No, you might not!" he yelled back, trailing after Holmes. "What's that blighter doing?"

"That is Mr. Sherlock Holmes, and I am Inspector Lestrade of Scotland Yard. You are?"

Stopping, the man looked Lestrade up and down before saying, "None of your business. I don't need to answer to the police, I've done nothing wrong."

"Well, if you would just let Mr. Holmes finish his inspection, we'll see if that's the case."

"What? What the hell do you mean by that?" Looking towards Holmes, the man added, "He's got no rights to be on my property or looking at my pigs."

By now all five of us were walking towards Holmes, who was entrenched in his examination of the pigpen. As we caught up with him, I grimaced in disgust, he was virtually kneeling in a pile of muck at the side of the enclosure. He had rolled his sleeve up and was pushing his hand deep into an unmentionable mess. It was then he exclaimed and pulled his hand out. "A-ha! Watson, come here – I think this will be of interest to you."

As I sidled up to him, Holmes held up several teeth. I immediately realised that they were human incisors and molars. "Good Lord."

With a grim smile on his face, Holmes pointed past Lestrade and said, "Inspector, I think we should detain that man." I turned to see the heavy-set man waddling as fast as he could away from us. Lestrade nodded and within seconds the two constables had nabbed and taken him to the wagon.

Turning to Holmes, I asked, "How?"

"It's a well-known fact that pigs can eat virtually anything, including almost every part of a human being. Flesh, organs, bone – but they struggle to digest teeth. They are also quite clean in that they will choose a specific spot in their habitat to defecate." Nodding towards the wagon, he added, "Our farmer has been helpful by pushing all the pigs excrement into one pile – probably how his boots became so caked in it."

"My word, Holmes. Good work!"

486

Without another thought, I followed the group to the cart, thinking Holmes would join us, but when I turned to find him he had disappeared. Assuming he had simply gone off to clean up or find more clues, I watched Lestrade interrogate the man as he was loaded into the back of the wagon. As the policeman plied the farmer with questions, I noticed his hands. On the little finger of his right hand, he wore a stunningly fashioned gold Claddagh ring, the twin of which I had only seen the day before.

Pointing at the ring, I almost shouted over Lestrade, "That ring – where did you get that ring?" The man's mouth dropped open in a gaping expression. "I take it from your reaction that it isn't yours. I don't wish to cast aspersions, but you don't look like the type of man to outlay so much money on jewellery."

"I . . . I found it. I liked it. So I wears it."

"Quite," I finished, placing as much cynicism on my single word as possible.

"Good observation, Watson," said Holmes at my shoulder, making me jump in surprise, "The existence of that ring, which I'm sure is the mate of Mrs. Markey's, plus what I just discovered, will certainly lead to a conviction."

"What did you find, Mr. Holmes?" asked Lestrade.

"It seems that the owner of those teeth isn't the only person to have found their final destination in the stomach of these pigs. There are multiple human teeth amongst a pile of older excrement at the rear of the property, plus in a small shed behind the house, I found clothes and other items that could only have come from elsewhere."

Turning to the farmer, Lestrade raised his voice, adding a hint of a growl to it, and said, "You're going down, my boy, but you can make things easier for yourself if you tell us who you're working for."

The look of fear on the man's face almost made me sympathetic to his plight, but as he told us everything, my anger rose.

The journey back to Red Hill was quiet. I believe it was Lestrade's way of surreptitiously sweating the farmer for information. Instead of an outright attack of questions, he let the man stew in silence until he was in the Red Hill Station, where the questioning could commence. There his reserve broke, and he wouldn't stop talking.

His name was Walter Bacon, at first an unlikely name and possibly false, until he confessed that his family had been pig farmers for generations. A chance encounter at the Spitalfields markets had seen him form a partnership with Derrick Wasser. The gangster threw money into the farm, keeping it afloat. The return agreement was for Bacon to use the pigs to eradicate the remains of anyone Wasser sent him. The pigs were the tool. Bacon eagerly, and almost proudly, told of how they could remove almost all traces of a body within a few hours. Some of the bones, especially the skull, could be troublesome, but he usually burnt those in the incinerator at the back of the property. Lestrade made a note to return for that evidence.

When asked about Markey, Bacon was nonplussed. He admitted that he never knew who the people were that the pigs devoured. He simply removed their clothes and prepared them. When he added that he used his butchering skills, learned over many years, I gagged slightly at the revolting thought of poor Dr. Markey's fate.

When pressed about the house in Brixton, Bacon admitted that he was regularly called up to London to claim the bodies and transport them away. That house was one of several that Wasser seemed to own.

By the end of the interrogation, I'd certainly had enough, and I hoped that Holmes was satisfied. Lestrade seemed to be ready to jump aboard a train and arrest Wasser, until Holmes said, "You still only have this man's word, which I'm sure won't stand up too well under courtroom scrutiny. We know how Markey was disposed of, but the reasons are still unclear. I believe our next step is to catch Wasser talking with the true villain of this piece."

An early breakfast greeted us the next day. Holmes had been resolute that we needed to be ready for a timely exit in the morning and asked Mrs. Hudson to prepare a substantial meal to set us properly for the day's adventures.

Upon arriving back at Baker Street the previous afternoon, Holmes had quickly disappeared, leaving me perplexed, but thankful as I was rather tired and looked forward to a hearty repast and a quiet night in. My colleague arrived back just prior to me making my way to bed and announced that the morrow would bring quite a few surprises.

Precisely at nine o'clock, the doorbell rang.

"Ah, that would be Lestrade," said Holmes, standing and donning his coat and hat. I followed suit and was just buttoning up when Lestrade's footsteps stopped outside our sitting room door.

As he let himself in, he looked a little weary from the previous day's journey and said, "All right, Mr. Holmes, what's this all about then? I would have had Wasser under arrest yesterday, but your words said otherwise."

"As I stated, Inspector, it is all well and good to arrest this so-called businessman, but in the case of Dr. Markey, we need the catalyst behind it all."

"As mysterious as always," said Lestrade, a wry grin on his normally dour face. "I wouldn't have it any other way."

Parked in the street outside was a covered wagon, with two bobbies sitting on the trap. "Expecting arrests then, Lestrade?" I quipped.

"Always when Mr. Holmes is on the case."

Sitting in the uncomfortable rear of the wagon, we drove through the streets for several minutes before pulling to a stop. We climbed out and looked around the area. It had the same aspect as any street in Brixton or Lambeth. "Where the devil are we?" I asked. "Back in Brixton?"

"Camberwell," Holmes said, nodding towards a building down the street. It was two storeys high, in the typical Georgian style, with a pub on the corner and what looked like residential houses behind. "That is Derrick Wasser's main office. It's where he can be found most days, and by sending telegrams to himself and one other first thing this morning, I've orchestrated a meeting between him and his client." He shrugged before adding, "Or I have wasted my money."

As Holmes spoke, a hansom drew up outside of the building. "Ah – the former it seems!"

A podgy looking man with a balding head stepped from the cab and across to the entrance. Even from our viewpoint, I could make out the insistent beating of his fist on the door. As it opened, an animated conversation began between the man and an unseen person inside.

As soon as the bald man entered, Holmes set off. Lestrade, myself, and the two constables followed in his wake. Lestrade instructed one of the uniformed policemen to remain outside, while Holmes tried the doorknob. It turned easily. The tenant was too preoccupied to lock the door as he withdrew.

As we entered the dim corridor, the sound of an argument filtered up the hallway towards us.

"By God, Wasser, what is all this twaddle? You told me it was dealt with."

"It was Sir Benton, it was."

"Then what is this?" The sound of something slamming down on a wooden desk echoed out. "Arrived this morning. Says that Markey has been found. At your pig farm."

"I received the same thing. I've no word myself, but I think someone's playing us like fools. Nobody that goes to the farm is ever found again. Mr. Bacon is very efficient."

"Well, he better be. If word about this gets out, then I won't be the only one suffering."

"Don't worry, Sir Benton. If I feel any heat, then I certainly won't be alone in Wandsworth."

"What do you mean?"

"Remember, you need me a lot more than I need you. That money you get for keeping things smooth with the law is only good while the drugs are legal. I don't care either way. If I have to go underground, then so be it. Risks are higher, but so is the profit."

"Why you – I've made things much easier for you over the years! Threatening me isn't going to end well!"

"Well, if this Dr. Markey has friends, then maybe I won't need your help much longer."

"You blackguard! I wouldn't be surprised if this was all your doing!"

"Now don't be stupid, sir. Why would I damage my operations like this? I don't know who did it, but I'd like to find them."

"Well, in that case," said Holmes, stepping through the office doorway, "here I am."

"Who the hell are you?" asked Wasser.

"Sherlock Holmes at your service." Stepping aside, he continued. "And this is Dr. Watson, along with Inspector Lestrade and Constable Conway of Scotland Yard. I think they'll be very happy to talk with you after you virtually confessed to the murder of Dr. Dermid Markey."

The looks on both their faces were priceless.

"So this Sir Benton McBrough – what was his motivation?" I asked Holmes, as we both sat down to a wonderful meal at a local pub. We thought it fitting to have a small celebration. Holmes had brought both a local gangster passing himself off as an upright businessman, and a corrupt politician to justice.

"For the last two nights, I have spent many hours scouring the backstreets of Brixton and Camberwell and Peckham, talking with many of my contacts and piecing together an interesting narrative." He took a sip from the fine brandy we had ordered before continuing. "Our fine upstanding politician, Sir Benton, was deep in with Wasser. They share interests in much of the drug trade throughout the south of London – a trade that would only continue while the drugs were legitimate.

"Sir Benton became scared by Markey's success in last year's election. The margin wasn't close, but it represented a change in the electorate's opinions of him. If Sir Benton lost his place in Parliament, his lucrative side business of supporting the drug trade within south London would be lost. Worse, if Markey's popularity grew and more politicians paid attention to his stance, then there was the possibility of a movement growing within the Government and the medical industry. Which could lead to a loss of illicit income on his part."

"Money," I sighed.

"Yes, Watson, money. There are seven deadly sins, as outlined in the theology. Whenever the other six fail to account for a motive, always rely on greed to provide the solution."

The Case of the
Irish Demonstration
by Dan Rowley

As dusk settled over London in late November 1887, I was concluding a discussion with a Harley Street medical colleague regarding a piece by Doctor Dickinson on detecting heart murmurs, found in the October issue of *The Lancet*. We both agreed that Dickinson's comments were helpful, and that he and I would keep in touch to compare our experiences. As I departed his office, I remembered that I had no more patients that day, so I decided to drop in on my friend, Sherlock Holmes. Although it was a short distance along Devonshire and Paddington Streets to Baker Street, the chill of the approaching evening and the deepening blue-grey sky persuaded me it would be preferable to take a cab. I was frankly a bit fearful that my old war wound wouldn't take kindly to a walk.

I settled into a cab and, after directing the driver, began to reflect that the year had been a significant one for Holmes. The machinations of Baron Maupertuis related to the Netherlands-Sumatra Company had so strained his health the previous spring that he was ill for some time, and we had repaired to Reigate for his recuperation. But it was another matter while rusticating there that had revived him, and not rest. That and many other fascinating cases – not least of which was one where the pips of an orange provided the solution – were what he craved. While having no interest in subjects such as literature, philosophy, and the like, his superb and utterly rational mind could hone in on subjects that assisted his detections. For example, while he could identify in an instant where in London a particular soil originated, the rest of geology was a closed book to him.

Arriving at 221b, I first dropped in to see Mrs. Hudson. "Why, Doctor, what a delight to see you! How is your wife doing?"

"Not well I fear. I suggested she stay with friends in the country to be away from this foul weather and air we've been experiencing."

"Oh, I am so sorry to hear that."

"And how is Holmes?" I tried to sound as casual as I could, because I was fairly certain that she wasn't aware that he sometimes injected himself with a diluted cocaine solution. The damnable concoction had originated with Viennese ophthalmologists trying to treat various eye ailments. They, like Holmes, underestimated the pernicious effects of the drug. His brain was a magnificent mechanism, constantly analyzing and dissecting, but the obverse of that was that he needed constant mental stimulation. When the external world failed to provide that, he turned to these injections to provide him the mental state he craved. I had warned him that the more he relied on the drug, the greater might grow his dependency. Working with him to keep him from it was a constant preoccupation of mine, as I deplored the thought that my friend and his brain might deteriorate over time. I would remain constantly vigilant.

It was with relief that I heard Mrs. Hudson's reply. "He seems fine. I think the cases do him good. Today he's been conducting those noxious chemical experiments of his. I will stand the smell as long as it makes him happy."

"He does not deserve you, Mrs. Hudson."

"Go on with you! I'm sure he will be delighted to see you. I'll prepare some tea and bring it and those shortbreads you like up in a moment."

Ascending the staircase, the smell was indeed almost overpowering. Knowing he likely wouldn't hear my knock, so absorbed would he be, I simply entered the sitting room. After a minute or two, Sherlock Holmes straightened his back and then noticed me. "Watson, what a delightful surprise! Let us sit by the fire. I'll tell Mrs. Hudson to bring us some tea."

"I have already taken care of that."

"Good old Watson! Always reliable." We sat down and I started to explain how I had come to stop by when we were interrupted by a knock on the door. Assuming it was the tea, Holmes called out, "Bring it in."

Mrs. Hudson opened the door. "Mr. Holmes, there's a young woman here to see you. She didn't tell me what it concerns. Her name is Lucy Neal."

"Well, send her up. Watson, perhaps this may be of interest. Please stay."

A young woman of about twenty years appeared in the doorway. Her clothing was plain: A simple ivory-coloured blouse, paired with a brown skirt and matching cloth belt. Reddish brown hair tied in a bun complemented blue eyes, showing a lively underlying intelligence. Her mouth, eyes, and nose were well proportioned. All in all, she was pretty and carried herself well.

She hesitated, looking at both of us. My friend said, "I am Sherlock Holmes, and this is Doctor Watson."

"Hello, Mr. Holmes. I wasn't sure about coming here."

"Please have a seat. How long have you been working in the garment industry?"

A startled look crossed her face. "But how did you know that?"

"Your fingers are red at the tips and starting to callous, which means you work with them regularly and have for some time. Similarly, your eyes have evidence of strain, likely because of poor lighting. Finally, your clothing is covered by countless fine thread scraps of different hues, which of course it would be if you are engaged in that type of work."

"It sounds so obvious when you explain it. The advertisement must be right – you are a great detective."

"What advertisement is that?"

"At night we have a labourers' reading group. Yesterday, one of the members called our attention to an advertisement in Monday's *Standard* for the upcoming *Beeton's Christmas Annual*. It said there's a story written by Dr. Watson – " She glanced my way. " – about you called *A Study in Scarlet*. It said that you're 'supremely ingenious'. The group agreed to pool our money to raise a shilling to purchase the book. And that's when I decided to come and see you about Tom."

Holmes looked askance at me, as he felt I had obscured his methods by melodrama in this, my first published effort describing one of his cases. He looked back at her. "Who is Tom? And please, start at the beginning so that I can get an accurate picture."

"Tom Carter is my . . . my young man. He moved here from Southampton several years ago, and now he works as a stevedore managing loading and unloading of ships at the London Docks. I met him through a friend, Billy Dawson. Tom and Billy are both active in the labour movement to encourage workers to organize unions. I grew up in the same building as Billy, and I met Tom when he and Billy came to our reading group to talk about unionism."

"When you say they are 'active in the labour movement' – what do you mean?"

"Tom is in the stevedore's union, and has been helping to try and organize other dock workers. Billy is a warehouseman, and so far most of the warehouses don't have unions. They attend various meetings in pubs and other places to explain the organizing movement and hand out literature. That's how Billy met Tom. He attended a meeting where Tom was speaking and decided to join the effort. Most of their time is spent in smaller groups conducting discussions to explain the benefits of being in a union, and the opportunity to have better wages, working hours, and bettering other conditions for the work being done. Tom's experience in the stevedore's union helps him to make the discussion more vivid."

"It isn't clear to me how conducting small discussion groups would lead to anything requiring you to consult with me."

"I'm coming to that. Tom and Billy were present at Bloody Sunday."

The event to which she referred was still a fresh scar in the minds of every Londoner. "Bloody Sunday" was the demonstration in Trafalgar Square on Sunday, 13 November, wherein approximately ten-thousand

494

demonstrators and over thirty-thousand spectators gathered to protest the jailing of an Irish Member of Parliament and the current administration's alleged attempts of coercion in Ireland. They were marching in all directions, and some of the demonstrators were armed with iron bars, knives, and pipes. It was a melee, and when the mounted police and soldiers intervened, there were numerous deaths.

"I take it," I said, "that Tom and Billy were there because the labour and socialist movements have taken up the Irish cause, apparently on the theory that they have a common enemy in the ruling class. Are they both members of the Socialist Democratic Federation?"

"Yes," she replied curtly. "That's why they were there. But," she hastened to add, "I disagree strongly with your characterization of it, and your assumption they are socialists. Tom and Billy simply want their rights as workers to be respected by their employers. Just as women want their right to vote recognized."

Before I could respond to her point regarding the idea of women voting, Holmes waved me off. "So I repeat, why have you come to see me?"

"The police have arrested Tom for murder and robbery. They claim he threw a brick through the window of a jewelry store on the Strand during the demonstration and stole a necklace in the window display. Then it was found that the brick struck the owner of the store and killed him."

"Yes, I recall reading about that," said Holmes. "I entered it into my index." He went to the shelves mounted on the wall near the fireplace and retrieved the relevant volume of the collection he keeps of newspaper articles and other materials to serve as his reference for crimes and similar incidents. "Here it is – I just docketed it the other day. The demonstration spilled past the jewelry store, and the brick was thrown through the store window during the confusion. As you said, the owner died from a blow from the brick, and a necklace was taken from the window display. It says here the police have an eyewitness."

Miss Neal blushed and looked down at her clenched hands, the knuckles white. Defiantly she said, "Yes. And the witness is Billy!" She looked up and said firmly, "I know that Tom would never do anything like that. He told me Saturday before the demonstration that he was attending because he wanted to peacefully show the world the wrongs being perpetrated against the Irish and the workers."

Holmes sat silently for a few minutes, her anxious gaze scrutinizing him. Finally, he said, "Miss Neal, given that the eyewitness is your young man's friend, I believe that there may be more going on than what the police believe. I'll look into your case. I'll think about it this evening and start active investigation in the morning."

"Thank you, Mr. Holmes! But . . . I don't know how I'll pay you. I'll find some way to do so."

"We can discuss that later. I'll want to talk to Billy. Where can I find him?"

"In the evenings after work he often goes to The Prospect of Whitby in Wapping, near the docks."

"Very well." He stood, as did I. "Please tell him that we'll be there tomorrow afternoon. That's all for now, Miss Neal."

She arose and looked as if she might embrace Holmes, but his look deterred her. She then took her leave, and we sat back down.

"Watson, I hope that you can join me in the morning – not too early?"

"Certainly. I'll arrange for someone to see my patients."

"Excellent. Then I'll see you then."

He returned to his chemical experiments, and I went downstairs. I put on my overcoat, went outside to again brave the cold (which had intensified now that the sun had fully set), and hailed a hansom. Sitting back, my thoughts turned to the events that had precipitated the Trafalgar Square demonstration. The agitation over giving the Irish some form of local parliament and control over some Irish matters, what people were now calling Home Rule, had started as far back as 1870. The previous year, Prime Minister Gladstone had introduced a Home Rule Bill in Parliament, but it had failed due to a split in his Liberal Party. The current year had seen an intensification of tumult over the Irish situation. In the spring, *The Times* had published letters purporting to show that the Irish leader Charles Stewart Parnell was implicated in certain crimes, including the murder in 1882 of the Chief Secretary and Permanent Under Secretary of Ireland. (Both of whom were, of course, the leaders of Her Majesty's government in Ireland, and thus symbols to the Irish of their own lack of control over their governance). Although Holmes believed the letters were forgeries, the outrage hadn't yet abated. This, in part, moved Parliament, now controlled by the Conservative Party under Lord Salisbury, to suspend trial by jury in Ireland. Then, during the Queen's Golden Jubilee the previous summer, rumors ran rampant implying that Americans who supported the Irish Republicans were plotting to blow up Westminster Abbey while the Queen and Cabinet were there.

The alliance between the Irish, the labour movement, and the socialists had intensified the protests. The socialists and workers argued that while returns on capital had increased, wages hadn't kept pace. They believed that workers should be given the franchise and that government had an obligation to own a variety of industrial concerns, on the assumption that such ownership would result in policies conducive to more employment and higher wages. In short, they felt the capitalism

496

valued profits over the well-being of workers. The working class was becoming better educated, as evidenced by Miss Neal's reading group – she herself was certainly well-spoken – and thus was more amenable to such talk. The tie to the Irish, so the argument ran, was that government actions favoring landlords in Ireland over tenants, and the absence of Irish participation in their own governance on the island, had led to the same type of economic, social, and political exploitation of the tenants as that by industrialists over their workers.

The demonstration on 13 November, so called "Bloody Sunday", was organized by the Social Democratic Foundation (an explicitly socialist association) and the Irish National League. Its purpose was to protest unemployment and low wages in England and the Government's actions in Ireland that denied political and economic rights to the Irish. The demonstration also demanded the release of William O'Brien, an Irish Member of Parliament and a confederate of Parnell. O'Brien had organized a rent strike by tenants on an estate in County Cork, resulting in a demonstration where three tenants were killed and others wounded by the local police. He was then convicted of inciting a riot under the Coercion Act passed earlier in the year.

With all this swirling through my head, and wondering about the wisdom of Holmes becoming involved with such elements, I realized that he would want to obtain further facts to help his client, if possible.

It was late the next morning when I entered the sitting room. Holmes was seated and having coffee. After pouring me some, he started to tell me what he had done the previous night after our client left, but before he got far, we heard someone coming up the stairs. "That must be Lestrade," he said. "I recognize his distinctive tread." Before there was a knock on the door, Holmes called out, "Come in, Lestrade."

The door opened and in came the familiar, wiry, ferret-like policeman. Altogether Holmes felt Lestrade was one of the best at Scotland Yard, it was damnation by faint praise, given Holmes's low opinion of the lot of them. He thought the inspector had energy, but his conventional methods lacked imagination.

"Hello, Mr. Holmes. Doctor."

"And to what do we owe this pleasure, Inspector?"

"What is the meaning of having your ragamuffins sticking their noses into this Bloody Sunday murder and robbery?"

"I assume you mean the Baker Street Irregulars." He was referring to a group of street boys that he used to run errands and collect information. He felt that they were in many ways better than the police, and only half-jokingly called them his own division of the police detectives. "I asked

Wiggins to ascertain whether there has been any attempt to sell the necklace from the jewelry store in the Strand, stolen during Sunday's demonstration. I'm unaware of any legal impediment to such an inquiry, especially given that presumably there is a reward offered by the insurance carrier. Such rewards may be claimed by private citizens – even by a humble consulting detective. Obviously one of the Yard's informants learned of my inquiries and alerted you, given that the police on their own wouldn't have discovered the Irregulars' activities in such a short period of time."

Ignoring the barb, the inspector scoffed. "After the insurance reward for the necklace, are you? Well, at least you won't be wasting your time on the murder. We have an eyewitness. It's as solid a case as I've ever seen."

"I have no doubt of that. And now, Inspector, if you have nothing further, Dr. Watson and I have work to do."

Lestrade, clearly dismissed, stood and walked to the door, saying, "Sherlock Holmes without a client and chasing after an insurance reward. How the mighty have fallen! Well, good day to you both."

After he departed, Holmes turned to me. "The man never disappoints. He makes an assumption and cannot be shaken from it. At least that saved me from prevarication with him. Now, let us go to the house for the dead where the body of the jeweler is being kept pending the inquest. I learned last night he's still at Charing Cross Hospital."

We put on our overcoats, went outside into the cold air, and hailed a cab. Holmes told the driver to take us to Trafalgar Square. When we arrived, Holmes commanded the driver to pause by Nelson's Column. I wasn't sure why we were stopping short of our destination. His expression told me he saw my puzzlement and would explain once we were out of the cab.

"I thought it would be convenient to walk from here, the heart of the demonstration, so that we can gauge the distance to the jewelry store. We'll pass it on the way to hospital." Accordingly, we walked over and exited the Square and into the western end of the Strand. Within a few hundred feet, we saw the jewelry store with a sign that read "*Throckmorton's Fine Jewelry*" and a boarded window. We paused for Holmes to scrutinize the store, street, pavement, and other surroundings. When he had satisfied himself, we continued a bit further down the Strand until coming to narrow Agar Street, which leads north a short distance to Charing Cross Hospital.

While the medical profession and some politicians had been pressing for every parish in the country to have a mortuary, progress was slow. London was no exception, and in many parishes the deceased had to be stored in graveyard structures or hospitals, these often being known as "houses for the dead". The storage could last until, in the winter, the ground was soft enough to dig a grave or, in the case of a suspected murder, the official proceedings and procedures were satisfied.

We located the morgue entrance and were greeted by a young man of rather startling appearance. He was very slight, with black hair and enormous side whiskers that overwhelmed his small face. His dark eyes were the most striking feature. They were round and wide as if in perpetual surprise. He wore a white coat and shirt with a string tie, which I suspect he affected to appear more official.

"What is your name, young man?" Holmes asked.

"George," he stammered. "Eddie George. What do you want?"

"We've just come from talking to Inspector Lestrade. We want to examine the body of the jeweler who died on 13 November. This man with me is a doctor." I was taken aback by Holmes implying we were here on official business, but it worked. At the mention of the inspector, Eddie George's eyes became even wider. He ushered us into the room where the bodies were stored.

"The one you want is on that table there."

"Thank you. If you see we aren't disturbed, I have a shilling for you."

At the mention of a reward, the man nodded and left the room.

"Come, Watson, let us take a look." And he withdrew the sheet covering the body. "Let us commence at the top. What do you see?"

I carefully scrutinized the entire head by rolling it on its side. "There is a wound on the left temple, where four bones of the skull meet. It appears that an object approximately the size of a brick struck there hard enough to fracture at least one of those bones. The deep bruising would indicate that the broken bone cut the underlying artery, leading to massive bleeding and death. Also, the wound is open, which would mean both internal and external loss of blood."

"Very good. Are there any other marks on the face or skull?"

"No, there is only the one on the temple."

With Holmes's help in moving the body, we examined the rest of it and concluded there were no other wounds or indications of violence. He stood there for several minutes with a faraway look in his eyes. From experience, I knew not to disturb his reverie. Then he turned to me.

"There's nothing else to be gained here. We shall proceed to the jewelers." On the way out, he handed Eddie George the promised shilling and admonished him not to mention our visit to anyone. Eddie nodded, wide-eyed as ever, that he understood.

We retraced our steps to the jewelry store, and Holmes once again stopped to survey it and the surroundings before entering. The front area of the shop was about twenty feet wide, and nearly as deep. A display case was in front of the window, extending from the side wall to the doorway. At the back of the room was a counter that displayed some items. Behind it was a doorway with a pulled curtain blocking our view of what lay beyond.

When we entered, a bell above the front door announced our presence. A corpulent man looked up from a ledger that he was studying on the counter. He was a few inches shorter than Holmes, with porcine eyes and small ears and nose. His greyish hair was heavily pomaded and parted in the middle.

"Hello. My name is Milvain. May I help you?"

"Yes. My name is Holmes, and this is Watson. We met with Inspector Lestrade this morning and wanted to ask you a few questions about Mr. Throckmorton's death. I assume you were his employee?"

"No, I was a junior partner in the firm. Mr. Throckmorton did all the purchasing and tended to customers out here in the store. I work in the back, keeping the books, and designing and creating the jewelry we sell. I'm now working here in front until I can find a suitable clerk."

"You said 'was' a junior partner?"

"Mr. Throckmorton's death dissolved the partnership. I don't know what his heirs will do as yet regarding our former arrangement."

"I see. I know that you've already discussed this with the police, but can you describe for us the events on the day Mr. Throckmorton died?"

"Well, we decided not to open that day because of the demonstration, seeing as how it was unlikely we would get any customers, and we're only open for a few hours on Sunday afternoons in any event. I was in the back, working on a ring that a customer had ordered. Mr. Throckmorton was out here at the counter, doing an inventory of our stock, checking it against the records.

"Suddenly there was a load crash that quite startled me. I rushed out here to find the window was broken. Mr. Throckmorton was lying on the floor with a brick next to him." He shuddered, and continued. "There was a pool of blood around his head. I tried to revive him, but to no effect. I then went outside and summoned a policeman. He came in and I told him what happened. He told me to stay behind the counter while he went for help. In a while, other police came, including an inspector. They later took a statement from me."

"So you were in the back until the incident. May I take a look back there?"

"Of course."

Holmes, Milvain, and I walked over to the doorway and pulled back the heavy curtain. Behind it was a thick door, which opened into a room

500

roughly equivalent to the public space at the front of the shop. To the left was a desk with pigeon holes for papers. At the far side of the room was a workbench with various jeweler's tools. When we entered, the door had a spring-lever that automatically swung it shut. Suddenly Holmes apologized. "I am sorry. I neglected to check something in the outer room. Watson will continue with our questions. I will be back in a moment." Then he left, and the door closed behind him.

Uncertain as to my sudden elevation to lead investigator, I asked him to show me where he normally sat. It was no surprise when he indicated the work bench. Just a moment later, Holmes returned, where he quickly examined the papers on the desk. Then he walked over to the bench and stood looking at it for a moment without speaking. Then he indicated that he'd seen enough and the three of us went back to the front of the shop, where Holmes resumed his questioning. "You said you were working on a ring. What specifically were you doing at the time the window was broken?"

"I was grinding to ensure the stone fit perfectly in the setting."

"And where did you find Mr. Throckmorton's body?"

"Over here," he said, pointing to a spot about five or six feet from the display case.

"What was the position of the body?"

"He was lying on his right side, facing the street."

To Milvain's surprise, Holmes seemed satisfied. "Thank you for your time. That's all we need for now." And then we departed, leaving the man near the counter where we'd found him.

Upon returning to the Strand, Holmes said, "Our next destination is The Prospect of Whitby to see Billy Dawson." It had been a while since I'd been to the pub, which claims to be the oldest on the waterfront. At one point it was known as the Devil's Tavern, as it was the lair for every disreputable element along the river, including thieves, pirates, smugglers, and other criminals.

"I have a suggestion," I countered. "Miss Neal said that Dawson goes there when he gets off work. It's still rather early for him to arrive, and we haven't had anything to eat since breakfast. While I know you're indifferent to food while working, my constitution is rather different. Since we are on the Strand, why not go to Simpson's?"

Holmes chuckled. "I can always count on you, Watson. Including your appetite."

We made our way past Charing Cross Station to the Savoy Building, which houses Simpson's. Passing some ardent chess players, we were seated in the dining room. After a fine lunch of roast beef, Yorkshire pudding, a bottle of claret, and post-prandial cigars, Holmes said, "Billy should be off work by now. We shall obtain a cab and go to Wapping."

There was still activity along the river as we passed the various docks. Ships came in and left as our cab made its way. I must admit my heart was stirred with pride as we saw the tangible fruits of Her Majesty's Empire. We soon pulled up in front of The Prospect of Whitby. It was a three-story building. The ground floor had two bow windows flanking the entrance door. The first and second floors each had three windows, and a sign with a picture of a schooner hung out over the street from the first floor. We entered the pub, which was rather dim. This was heightened by the dark paneling and stone floor.

Holmes's eyes adjusted more quickly than mine. "That must be Billy over there. He looked up and nodded when we entered. Miss Neal must have described us to him. You go and get us three pints, and I'll take him to a quieter table in the back."

Having procured the drinks, I proceeded to the back of the pub. Holmes had found a table near the window overlooking the Thames. Seated with him was a rather short young man in need of a shave and a proper haircut. He was wearing work clothes stained with sweat. His hands were in constant motion, and I noticed he continually glanced around the room.

"Billy, this is my associate Dr. Watson."

"I wouldn't have agreed ta see you if Lucy hadn't asked me." He took a large pull from the glass I handed him.

"Tell us how and when you met Tom."

"'Twas a year ago. I attended a meeting where they were trying ta get us ta join a union. Tom was one of the speech-makers. After, we came here for a drink."

"Were you friends?"

"Wouldn't say so."

"And you at some point introduced him to Lucy?"

"Nah, I didn't do no introducin'. We went to her reading group to talk about workers' needs, and after the talk he started chatting her up. You could see they took a shine to each other right off like."

"Fine. Tell us about the day of the demonstration."

"Well, I didn't understand why we should go hear about the bog-jumpers, but Tom said they was in the same boat. Couldn't see how, but I went. It were nothin' but a bunch of highfalutin' ponces going on and on. There was a lot of people there, and some were down that street from the Square."

"The Strand."

502

"If you say so. Anyways, I noticed Tom goin' that way, alone, so I decided to follow and get away from the ponces. Next thing I seen was Tom tossin' a brick through that window."

"Did he bring it with him?"

"Don't know. I seen other folks with stuff. We knowed the bobbies and the army would be there."

"About how far from the window was Tom?"

"How should I know?"

"The length of my height if I lay down?"

"Nah. More than that."

"Did you see him take anything from the store?"

"People moved in front of me."

"Why did you go to the police?"

"I wasn't goin' ta, but then I heard about the stolen stuff and the dead man, I decided I'd better, or I'd get in trouble."

"Thank you, Billy. On our way out, we'll pay the bartender to give you another pint."

He grunted at us. We stopped at the bar as promised to pay for another drink, and then went outside.

"Should we now speak to Tom Carson and see what his story is?" I asked.

Instead of a direct answer, Holmes replied, "Watson, you return home. I want to walk a bit to think."

I tried to protest that this neighborhood wasn't safe, but he brushed that aside and asked if I could return to Baker Street in the morning. I agreed, and he nodded and walked away.

The next morning as I took my chair in the sitting room, Holmes told me that Inspector Lestrade would arrive shortly. A bit startled, I asked if he had solved the case. He nodded, poured us some coffee, and explained that he'd sent the inspector a telegram the previous night,

Shortly, Lestrade appeared at the door. After receiving some coffee and taking a seat, he asked, "Have you learned more about the man's death?"

"More like solved it, if you please."

"What – ?"

"Allow me to explain. As is your wont, I'm afraid that you've missed the most obvious and failed to apply proper logic. Shall we begin with what you believe is the crux of your case: The throwing of the brick?"

Lestrade shrugged, which Holmes took as assent. "I'm not sure whether you took any measurements at the scene once you had Billy

503

Dawson's report. But let us examine that. Billy told us – " The inspector tried to interrupt but Holmes gave him short shrift.

"Just listen if you will. Billy Dawson told us Carson was more than my height from the window when he threw the brick. I'm a bit over six feet tall, so we will assume that Tom Carson was ten feet from the window. Inside is the display case by the window, which is approximately five feet deep. Milvain said that the body was five to six feet from the display case, further into the shop. That means Carson was at least twenty feet away when the brick was thrown.

"So the question becomes how much force the brick had after going through a window, which would slow it down, and also traveling at least twenty feet. The brick would have had to strike Mr. Throckmorton on his temple hard enough to fracture at least one of the skull bones so that it could pierce the artery, as Watson correctly confirmed. Yet consider this, Inspector: If we assume Mr. Throckmorton was looking out the window at the demonstrators and the brick hit his left temple, the natural movement of his body would have been to fall backward, and not to fall to his right, which is where the police found him, and which Mr. Milvain confirmed."

Lestrade, becoming impatient, said, "Mr. Holmes, I don't see where you are going with this . . . ."

Holmes smiled. "I'm sure not. Let us now consider further facts you have overlooked. Throckmorton had no other marks on his body, neither his hands nor face. Had he been standing facing the window when the brick came through, one would expect cuts on his face, or his hands as he tried to shield his face. The logical conclusion is that he wasn't by the window when the brick came through."

"So what are you saying happened?"

"The facts establish Throckmorton wasn't by the window. According to Milvain, Throckmorton was taking inventory behind the counter and Milvain was in the workroom. Milvain says he was at the work bench and heard when the brick came through the window. This room is separated from the shop by a heavy curtain and an even heavier door which automatically closes, and Milvain says he was operating the grinder, which I am sure you know makes a fair amount of noise. In fact, when I was there yesterday, I went back out to the outer room, closing the door and leaving Milvain and Watson in the back room. I went over by the window and called to Watson to come to me, first in a normal tone and then quite loudly. Watson didn't respond, which demonstrates he couldn't hear me."

I nodded at this, realizing we had been closer to the front room than Milvain would have been.

"What are you suggesting?" demanded Lestrade.

504

"At the time, per Milvain's statement, Throckmorton was out front, doing an inventory. But instead of Milvain being in the back as he claimed, he and Throckmorton were likely both behind the front counter when the brick came through the window – a random brick thrown as part of the riot, and not an attempt at theft. Throckmorton rushed over to see what had happened. Milvain, seizing the opportunity, came up behind him, picked up the brick, and struck him in the temple."

"But why would Milvain do that?"

"You underestimate my Irregulars, Inspector. They could uncover no attempt to fence the missing necklace."

"Well, these union rascals would lay low once they knew of Throckmorton's death."

"But the Irregulars did discover numerous fencings of individual diamonds by a man matching Milvain's description. He was stealing diamonds from Throckmorton and selling them. I believe that an examination of the books will show that Throckmorton discovered this during his inventory and confronted Milvain, with the result that I've explained. Afterward, Milvain took the necklace from the window display for multiple reasons – to cover up his own involvement, to have another opportunity for profit, and to collect the insurance proceeds."

"But the window was broken and the brick was there. So Carson still has culpability."

"Inconclusive. Dawson's account is worthless. He is the only witness you have. He claims only to have seen Carson throwing the brick, but he did not observe the aftermath. He says that he came to you to avoid trouble, but how would you have known to find him, given that no one else has come forward either before or after he did? As always, you eagerly take the path of least work."

"The brick got in through the window. How do you explain that?"

"Who knows? Perhaps Dawson threw it through the window."

"Why on earth?"

Holmes sighed. "The oldest reason, going back to Biblical times: He was jealous of Carson, who has a prestigious union position while he is a common labourer. Moreover, Carson has a relationship with Miss Neal, and possibly Dawson has always desired her for himself. After all, he stated to us yesterday that he wouldn't have seen me had she not asked him to."

Lestrade sat there contemplating the situation. "Well, Mr. Holmes, I will restart the investigation."

"I want no credit. You may have it all. Another brilliant solution by the Yard, and the vindication of an innocent man."

The inspector looked away and took his leave.

Several days later, I happened to be visiting again when Mrs. Hudson appeared at the sitting room door. Holmes looked up from a book he was perusing. "What is it?"

"Lucy is here to see you. And she has a young man with her."

"Lucy, is it? Have them come up."

Miss Neal was euphoric. She had in tow a young man neatly dressed with carefully combed red hair, clean face, and quiet demeanor. "Oh, Mr. Holmes, Doctor Watson – I can't tell you how happy I am! This is Tom, of course." The young man smiled and nodded. "The police released him yesterday. We came by to thank you."

"It was nothing. The facts were manifest once examined properly."

"And we've decided to get married!"

I stood up and said. "Congratulations! Here, let me give you an early wedding gift." I went over to my desk and retrieved a copy of the new *Christmas Annual.* "Now your reading group can use the money to buy something else."

"Doctor, how wonderful!" Eyes twinkling, and grinning impishly, she said, "Perhaps we will use the money we collected for this to purchase some literature about votes for women."

"Tom," I said with a smile and turning to the young man, "are you certain that you want to marry her?"

He blushed. "I reckon no one else can really handle her, so I'll just have to get used to it."

While we were so engaged, I hadn't noticed that Holmes had gone into his room. He returned with an envelope. "It may not be as valuable as Watson's story, but please accept this."

She looked inside the envelope and blushed. "Mr. Holmes, whatever is this?"

"The insurance reward. Had it not been for you, Tom wouldn't have been vindicated."

"But we should be paying you!"

"Nonsense. Consider it your dowry."

Despite his gruffness, I detected a warmness there that few would notice. Miss Neal started towards him as if to hug him. But remembering herself, she settled for hugging me instead.

About the Contributors

The following contributors appear in this volume:
The MX Book of New Sherlock Holmes Stories
Part XXXI – 2022 Annual (1875-1887)

Brian Belanger, PSI, is a publisher, illustrator, graphic designer, editor, and author. In 2015, he co-founded Belanger Books publishing company along with his brother, author Derrick Belanger. His illustrations have appeared in *The Essential Sherlock Holmes* and *Sherlock Holmes: A Three-Pipe Christmas*, and in children's books such as *The MacDougall Twins with Sherlock Holmes* series, *Dragonella*, and *Scones and Bones on Baker Street*. Brian has published a number of Sherlock Holmes anthologies and novels through Belanger Books, as well as new editions of August Derleth's classic Solar Pons mysteries. Brian continues to design all of the covers for Belanger Books, and since 2016 he has designed the majority of book covers for MX Publishing. In 2019, Brian received his investiture in the PSI as "Sir Ronald Duveen." More recently, he illustrated a comic book featuring the band The Moonlight Initiative, created the logo for the Arthur Conan Doyle Society and designed *The Great Game of Sherlock Holmes* card game. Find him online at:
www.belangerbooks.com and
www.redbubble.com/people/zhahadun and
zhahadun.wixsite.com/221b.

Thomas A. Burns Jr. writes *The Natalie McMasters Mysteries* from the small town of Wendell, North Carolina, where he lives with his wife and son, four cats, and a Cardigan Welsh Corgi. He was born and grew up in New Jersey, attended Xavier High School in Manhattan, earned B.S degrees in Zoology and Microbiology at Michigan State University, and a M.S. in Microbiology at North Carolina State University. As a kid, Tom started reading mysteries with The Hardy Boys, Ken Holt, and Rick Brant, then graduated to the classic stories by authors such as A. Conan Doyle, Dorothy Sayers, John Dickson Carr, Erle Stanley Gardner, and Rex Stout, to name a few. Tom has written fiction as a hobby all of his life, starting with *The Man from U.N.C.L.E.* stories in marble-backed copybooks in grade school. He built a career as technical, science, and medical writer and editor for nearly thirty years in industry and government. Now that he's a full-time novelist, he's excited to publish his own mystery series, as well as to write stories about his second most favorite detective, Sherlock Holmes. His Holmes story, "The Camberwell Poisoner", appeared in the March-June 2021 issue of *The Strand Magazine*. Tom has also written a Lovecraftian horror novel, *The Legacy of the Unborn*, under the pen name of Silas K. Henderson – a sequel to H.P. Lovecraft's masterpiece *At the Mountains of Madness*.

Sir Arthur Conan Doyle (1859-1930) *Holmes Chronicler Emeritus*. If not for him, this anthology would not exist. Author, physician, patriot, sportsman, spiritualist, husband and father, and advocate for the oppressed. He is remembered and honored for the purposes of this collection by being the man who introduced Sherlock Holmes to the world. Through fifty-six Holmes short stories, four novels, and additional Apocryphal entries, Doyle revolutionized mystery stories and also greatly influenced and improved police forensic methods and techniques for the betterment of all. *Steel True Blade Straight*.

Steve Emecz's main field is technology, in which he has been working for about twenty-five years. Steve is a regular speaker at trade shows and his tech career has taken him to more than fifty countries – so he's no stranger to planes and airports. In 2008, MX published its first Sherlock Holmes book, and MX has gone on to become the largest specialist Holmes publisher in the world with over 500 books. MX is a social enterprise and supports three main causes. The first is Happy Life, a children's rescue project in Nairobi, Kenya, where he and his wife, Sharon, spend every Christmas at the rescue centre in Kasarani. They have written two editions of a short book about the project, *The Happy Life Story*. The second is Undershaw, Sir Arthur Conan Doyle's former home, which is a school for children with learning disabilities for which Steve is a patron. Steve has been a mentor for the World Food Programme for several years, and was part of the Nobel Peace Prize winning team in 2020.

Mark A. Gagen BSI is co-founder of Wessex Press, sponsor of the popular *From Gillette to Brett* conferences, and publisher of *The Sherlock Holmes Reference Library* and many other fine Sherlockian titles. A life-long Holmes enthusiast, he is a member of *The Baker Street Irregulars* and *The Illustrious Clients of Indianapolis*. A graphic artist by profession, his work is often seen on the covers of *The Baker Street Journal* and various BSI books.

Hal Glatzer is the author of the Katy Green mystery series set in musical milieux just before World War II. He has written and produced audio/radio mystery plays, including the all-alliterative adventures of Mark Markheim, the Hollywood hawkshaw. He scripted and produced the Charlie Chan mystery *The House Without a Key* on stage; and he adapted "The Adventure of the Devil's Foot" into a stage and video play called *Sherlock Holmes and the Volcano Horror*. In 2022, after many years on the Big Island of Hawaii, he returned to live on his native island – Manhattan. See more at: *www.halglatzer.com*

Terry Golledge (according to his son Niel Golledge, who provided these stories to this collection) had a life-long love of all things Conan Doyle and in particular Sherlock Holmes. He was born in 1920 in the East End of London. He left school at fourteen, like so many back then. In 1939, he joined the army in the fight against the Germans in World War II. He left the Army in 1945 at the war's end, residing in Hastings. There he met his wife, and his life was a mish-mash of careers, including mining and bus and lorry driving. He owned a couple of book shops, selling them in the 1960's. He then worked for the Post office, (later to become British Telecom, equivalent to AT&T), ending his working life there as a training instructor for his retirement in 1980. His love of Sherlock Holmes was obviously inspired by the fact that his mother worked as a governess to Sir Arthur Conan Doyle when he lived in Windlesham, Crowborough in Sussex. She married Terry's father after leaving Sir Arthur's employment around 1918. Beginning in the mid-1980's, Terry Golledge wrote a number of Holmes stories, and they have never been previously published. A full collection of his Holmes works will be published in the near future. He passed away in 1996.

Niel Golledge was born in 1951 in Winchester, England. He retired some years ago and currently resides in Kent, UK. His last employment for over twenty years was with a large newsprint paper mill, located near his home. He is married to Trisha, a retired nurse, and they have a son and daughter who have carved out careers in mental health and physiotherapy. He is an avid football fan of West Ham and loves to play golf. He is also a keen reader – but that goes without saying.

510

John Atkinson Grimshaw (1836-1893) was born in Leeds, England. His amazing paintings, usually featuring twilight or night scenes illuminated by gas-lamps or moonlight, are easily recognizable, and are often used on the covers of books about The Great Detective to set the mood, as shadowy figures move in the distance through misty mysterious settings and over rain-slicked streets.

Arthur Hall was born in Aston, Birmingham, UK, in 1944. He discovered his interest in writing during his schooldays, along with a love of fictional adventure and suspense. His first novel, *Sole Contact*, was an espionage story about an ultra-secret government department known as "Sector Three", and was followed, to date, by three sequels. Other works include seven Sherlock Holmes novels, *The Demon of the Dusk*, *The One Hundred Percent Society*, *The Secret Assassin*, *The Phantom Killer*, *In Pursuit of the Dead*, *The Justice Master*, and *The Experience Club* as well as three collections of Holmes *Further Little-Known Cases of Sherlock* Holmes, *Tales from the Annals of Sherlock* Holmes, and *The Additional Investigations of Sherlock Holmes*. He has also written other short stories and a modern detective novel. He lives in the West Midlands, United Kingdom.

Jeffrey Hatcher is a playwright and screenwriter. His plays have been produced on Broadway, Off-Broadway, and in theaters throughout the U.S. and around the world. They include *Three Viewings*, *Scotland Road*, *The Turn of the Screw*, *Compleat Female Stage Beauty*, *Mrs. Mannerly*, *Murderers*, *Smash*, *Korczak's Children*, *The Government Inspector*, *A Picasso*, *The Alchemist*, *Key Largo*, *Dr. Jekyll and Mr. Hyde*, and his Sherlock Holmes plays *Sherlock Holmes and the Adventure of the Suicide Club*, *Sherlock Holmes and the Ice Palace Murders*, and *Holmes and Watson*. His film work includes the screenplays for *Stage Beauty*, *Casanova*, *The Duchess*, *Mr. Holmes*, and *The Good Liar*. For television, he has written episodes of *Columbo* and *The Mentalist* and the TV movie *Murder at the Cannes Film Festival*. He has received grants and awards from the NEA, TCG, Lila Wallace Fund, Rosenthal New Play Prize, Frankel Award, Charles MacArthur Fellowship Award, McKnight Foundation, Jerome Foundation, and a Barrymore Award for Best New Play. He has been twice nominated for an Edgar Award. He is a member and/or alumnus of The Playwrights Center, the Dramatists Guild, the Writers Guild, and New Dramatists.

Stephen Herczeg is an IT Geek, writer, actor, and film-maker based in Canberra Australia. He has been writing for over twenty years and has completed a couple of dodgy novels, sixteen feature-length screenplays, and numerous short stories and scripts. Stephen was very successful in 2017's International Horror Hotel screenplay competition, with his scripts *TITAN* winning the Sci-Fi category and *Dark are the Woods* placing second in the horror category. His two-volume short story collection, *The Curious Cases of Sherlock Holmes*, was published in 2021. His work has featured in *Sproutlings – A Compendium of Little Fictions* from Hunter Anthologies, the *Hells Bells* Christmas horror anthology published by the Australasian Horror Writers Association, and the *Below the Stairs*, *Trickster's Treats*, *Shades of Santa*, *Behind the Mask*, and *Beyond the Infinite* anthologies from OzHorror.Con, *The Body Horror Book*, *Anemone Enemy*, and *Petrified Punks* from Oscillate Wildly Press, and *Sherlock Holmes In the Realms of H.G. Wells* and *Sherlock Holmes: Adventures Beyond the Canon* from Belanger Books.

Roger Johnson BSI, ASH is a retired librarian, now working as a volunteer assistant at the Essex Police Museum. In his spare time, he is commissioning editor of *The Sherlock Holmes Journal*, an occasional lecturer, and a frequent contributor to *The Writings about the Writings*. His sole work of Holmesian pastiche was published in 1997 in Mike Ashley's anthology *The Mammoth Book of New Sherlock Holmes Adventures*, and he has the greatest respect for the many authors who have contributed new tales to the present mighty trilogy. Like his wife, Jean Upton, he is a member of both *The Baker Street Irregulars* and *The Adventuresses of Sherlock Holmes*.

Kelvin I. Jones is the author of six books about Sherlock Holmes and the definitive biography of Conan Doyle as a spiritualist, *Conan Doyle and The Spirits*. A member of *The Sherlock Holmes Society of London*, he has published numerous short occult and ghost stories in British anthologies over the last thirty years. His work has appeared on BBC Radio, and in 1984 he won the Mason Hall Literary Award for his poem cycle about the survivors of Hiroshima and Nagasaki, recently reprinted as "Omega". (Oakmagic Publications) A one-time teacher of creative writing at the University of East Anglia, he is also the author of four crime novels featuring his ex-met sleuth John Bottrell, who first appeared in *Stone Dead*. He has over fifty titles on Kindle, and is also the author of several novellas and short story collections featuring a Norwich based detective, DCI Ketch, an intrepid sleuth who investigates East Anglian murder cases. He also published a series of short stories about an Edwardian psychic detective, Dr. John Carter (*Carter's Occult Casebook*). Ramsey Campbell, the British horror writer, and Francis King, the renowned novelist, have both compared his supernatural stories to those of M. R. James. He has also published children's fiction, namely *Odin's Eye*, and, in collaboration with his wife Debbie, *The Dark Entry*. Since 1995, he has been the proprietor of Oakmagic Publications, publishers of British folklore and of his fiction titles. He lives in Norfolk. (See www.oakmagicpublications.co.uk)

Susan Knight's newest novel, Mrs. Hudson goes to Paris, from MX publishing, is the latest in a series which began with her collection of stories, *Mrs. Hudson Investigates* of 2019 and the novel Mrs. Hudson goes to Ireland (2020). She has contributed to several of the MX anthologies of new Sherlock Holmes short stories, and enjoys writing as Dr. Watson as much as she does Mrs. Hudson. Susan is the author of two other non-Sherlockian, story collections, as well as three novels, a book of non-fiction, and several plays, and has won several prizes for her writing. She lives in Dublin, Ireland. Her next Mrs. Hudson novel is already a gleam in her eye.

John Lawrence served for thirty-eight years on personal, committee, and leadership staffs in the U.S. House of Representatives. A visiting professor at the University of California's Washington Center since 2013, he is the author of *The Class of '74: Congress After Watergate and the Roots of Partisanship* (Johns-Hopkins, 2018) and *Arc of Power: Inside the Pelosi Speakership 2005-2010* (Kansas, 2022). His collected "history mystery" Sherlock Holmes pastiches have been published in *The Undiscovered Archives of Sherlock Holmes* (MX Publishing, 2022), in numerous volumes of *The MX Book of New Sherlock Holmes Stories*, and in Belanger Books' *After the East Wind Blows*. He blogs at DOMEocracy (johnalawrence.wordpress.com). He is a graduate of Oberlin College and has a Ph.D. in history from the University of California (Berkeley).

Gordon Linzner is founder and former editor of *Space and Time Magazine*, and author of three published novels and dozens of short stories in *F&SF*, *Twilight Zone*, *Sherlock Holmes Mystery Magazine*, and numerous other magazines and anthologies, including *Baker Street Irregulars II*, *Across the Universe*, and *Strange Lands*. He is a member of *HWA* and a lifetime member of *SFWA*.

512

David MacGregor is a playwright, screenwriter, novelist, and nonfiction writer. He is a resident artist at The Purple Rose Theatre in Michigan, where a number of his plays have been produced. His plays have been performed from New York to Tasmania, and his work has been published by Dramatic Publishing, Playscripts, Smith & Kraus, Applause, Heuer Publishing, and Theatrical Rights Worldwide (TRW). He adapted his dark comedy, *Vino Veritas*, for the silver screen, and it stars Carrie Preston (Emmy-winner for *The Good Wife*). Several of his short plays have also been adapted into films. He is the author of three Sherlock Holmes plays: *Sherlock Holmes and the Adventure of the Elusive Ear*, *Sherlock Holmes and the Adventure of the Fallen Soufflé*, and *Sherlock Holmes and the Adventure of the Ghost Machine*. He adapted all three plays into novels for Orange Pip Books, and also wrote the two-volume nonfiction *Sherlock Holmes: The Hero with a Thousand Faces* for MX Publishing. He teaches writing at Wayne State University in Detroit and is inordinately fond of cheese and terriers.

David Marcum plays *The Game* with deadly seriousness. He first discovered Sherlock Holmes in 1975 at the age of ten, and since that time, he has collected, read, and chronologicized literally thousands of traditional Holmes pastiches in the form of novels, short stories, radio and television episodes, movies and scripts, comics, fan-fiction, and unpublished manuscripts. He is the author of over ninety Sherlockian pastiches, some published in anthologies and magazines such as *The Strand*, and others collected in his own books, *The Papers of Sherlock Holmes*, *Sherlock Holmes and A Quantity of Debt*, *Sherlock Holmes – Tangled Skeins*, *Sherlock Holmes and The Eye of Heka*, and *The Complete Papers of Sherlock Holmes*. He has edited over sixty books, including several dozen traditional Sherlockian anthologies, such as the ongoing series *The MX Book of New Sherlock Holmes Stories*, which he created in 2015. This collection is now over thirty volumes, with more in preparation. He was responsible for bringing back August Derleth's Solar Pons for a new generation, first with his collection of authorized Pons stories, *The Papers of Solar Pons*, and then by editing the reissued authorized versions of the original Pons books, and then several volumes of new Pons adventures. He has done the same for the adventures of Dr. Thorndyke, and has plans for similar projects in the future. He has contributed numerous essays to various publications, and is a member of a number of Sherlockian groups and Scions. His irregular Sherlockian blog, *A Seventeen Step Program*, addresses various topics related to his favorite book friends (as his son used to call them when he was small), and can be found at *http://17stepprogram.blogspot.com/* He is a licensed Civil Engineer, living in Tennessee with his wife and son. Since the age of nineteen, he has worn a deerstalker as his regular-and-only hat. In 2013, he and his deerstalker were finally able make his first trip-of-a-lifetime Holmes Pilgrimage to England, with return Pilgrimages in 2015 and 2016, where you may have spotted him. If you ever run into him and his deerstalker out and about, feel free to say hello!

Kevin Patrick McCann has published eight collections of poems for adults, one for children (*Diary of a Shapeshifter*, Beul Aithris), a book of ghost stories (*It's Gone Dark*, The Otherside Books), *Teach Yourself Self-Publishing* (Hodder) co-written with the playwright Tom Green, and *Ov* (Beul Aithris Publications) a fantasy novel for children.

Sidney Paget (1860-1908), a few of whose illustrations are used within this anthology, was born in London, and like his two older brothers, became a famed illustrator and painter. He completed over three-hundred-and-fifty drawings for the Sherlock Holmes stories that were first published in *The Strand* magazine, defining Holmes's image forever after in the public mind.

Tracy J. Revels, a Sherlockian from the age of eleven, is a professor of history at Wofford College in Spartanburg, South Carolina. She is a member of *The Survivors of the Gloria Scott* and *The Studious Scarlets Society*, and is a past recipient of the Beacon Society Award. Almost every semester, she teaches a class that covers The Canon, either to college students or to senior citizens. She is also the author of three supernatural Sherlockian pastiches with MX (*Shadowfall, Shadowblood,* and *Shadowwraith*), and a regular contributor to her scion's newsletter. She also has some notoriety as an author of very silly skits: For proof, see "The Adventure of the Adversarial Adventuress" and "Occupy Baker Street" on YouTube. When not studying Sherlock, she can be found researching the history of her native state, and has written books on Florida in the Civil War and on the development of Florida's tourism industry.

Dan Rowley practiced law for over forty years in private practice and with a large international corporation. He is retired and lives in Erie, Pennsylvania, with his wife Judy, who puts her artistic eye to his transcription of Watson's manuscripts. He inherited his writing ability and creativity from his children, Jim and Katy, and his love of mysteries from his parents, Jim and Ruth.

Geri Schear is a novelist and short story writer. Her work has been published in literary journals in the U.S. and Ireland. Her first novel, *A Biased Judgement: The Diaries of Sherlock Holmes 1897* was released to critical acclaim in 2014. The sequel, *Sherlock Holmes and the Other Woman* was published in 2015, and *Return to Reichenbach* in 2016. She lives in Kells, Ireland.

Robert V. Stapleton was born in Leeds, England, and served as a full-time Anglican clergyman for forty years, specialising in Rural Ministry. He is now retired, and lives with his wife in North Yorkshire. This is the area of the country made famous by the writings of James Herriot, and television's *The Yorkshire Vet*, to name just a few. Amongst other things, he is a member of the local creative writing group, Thirsk Write Now (TWN), and regularly produces material for them. He has had more than fifty stories published, of various lengths and in a number of different places. He has also written a number of stories for *The MX Book of New Sherlock Holmes Stories*, and several published by Belanger Books. Several of these Sherlock Holmes pastiches have now been brought together and published in a single volume by MX Publishing, under the title of *Sherlock Holmes: A Yorkshireman in Baker Street*. Many of these stories have been set during the Edwardian period, or more broadly between the years 1880 and 1920. His interest in this period of history began at school in the 1960's when he met people who had lived during those years and heard their stories. He also found echoes of those times in literature, architecture, music, and even the coins in his pocket. The Edwardian period was a time of exploration, invention. and high adventure – rich material for thriller writers.

Tim Symonds was born in London. He grew up in the rural English counties of Somerset and Dorset, and the British Crown Dependency of Guernsey. After several years travelling widely, including farming on the slopes of Mt. Kenya in East Africa and working on the Zambezi River in Central Africa, he emigrated to Canada and the United States. He studied at the Georg-August University (Göttingen) in Germany, and the University of California, Los Angeles, graduating *cum laude* and Phi Beta Kappa. He is a Fellow of the Royal Geographical Society and a Member of The Society of Authors. His detective novels include *Sherlock Holmes And The Dead Boer At Scotney Castle, Sherlock Holmes And The Mystery Of Einstein's Daughter, Sherlock Holmes And The Case Of The Bulgarian Codex, Sherlock Holmes And The Sword Of Osman, Sherlock Holmes And The Nine-Dragon Sigil,* six Holmes and Watson short stories under the title *A Most Diabolical Plot*, and his novella *Sherlock Holmes and the Strange Death of Brigadier-General Delves*.

DJ Tyrer dwells on the northern shore of the Thames estuary, close to the world's longest pleasure pier in the decaying seaside resort of Southend-on-Sea, and is the person behind Atlantean Publishing. They studied history at the University of Wales at Aberystwyth and have worked in the fields of education and public relations. Their fiction featuring Sherlock Holmes has appeared in volumes from MX Publishing and Belanger Books, and in an issue of *Awesome Tales*, and they have a forthcoming story in *Sherlock Holmes Mystery Magazine*. DJ's non-Sherlockian mysteries have appeared in anthologies such as *Mardi Gras Mysteries* (Mystery and Horror LLC) and *The Trench Coat Chronicles* (Celestial Echo Press).

DJ Tyrer's website is at *https://djtyrer.blogspot.co.uk/*
DJ's Facebook page is at *https://www.facebook.com/DJTyrerwriter/*
The Atlantean Publishing website is at *https://atlanteanpublishing.wordpress.com/*

I.A. Watson, great-grand-nephew of Dr. John H. Watson, has been intrigued by the notorious "black sheep" of the family since childhood, and was fascinated to inherit from his grandmother a number of unedited manuscripts removed circa 1956 from a rather larger collection reposing at Lloyds Bank Ltd (which acquired Cox & Co Bank in 1923). Upon discovering the published corpus of accounts regarding the detective Sherlock Holmes from which a censorious upbringing had shielded him, he felt obliged to allow an interested public access to these additional memoranda, and is gradually undertaking the task of transcribing them for admirers of Mr. Holmes and Dr. Watson's works. In the meantime, I.A. Watson continues to pen other books, the latest of which is *The Incunabulum of Sherlock Holmes*. A full list of his seventy or so published works are available at: *http://www.chillwater.org.uk/writing/iawatsonhome.htm*

Emma West joined Undershaw in April 2021 as the Director of Education with a brief to ensure that qualifications formed the bedrock of our provision, whilst facilitating a positive balance between academia, pastoral care, and well-being. She quickly took on the role of Acting Headteacher from early summer 2021. Under her leadership, Undershaw has embraced its new name, new vision, and consequently we have seen an exponential increase in demand for places. There is a buzz in the air as we invite prospective students and families through the doors. Emma has overseen a strategic review, re-cemented relationships with Local Authorities, and positioned Undershaw at the helm of SEND education in Surrey and beyond. Undershaw has a wide appeal: Our students present to us with mild to moderate learning needs and therefore may have some very recent memories of poor experiences in their previous schools. Emma's background as a senior leader within the independent school sector has meant she is well-versed in brokering relationships between the key stakeholders, our many interdependences, local businesses, families, and staff, and all this whilst ensuring Undershaw remains relentlessly child-centric in its approach. Emma's energetic smile and boundless enthusiasm for Undershaw is inspiring.

Sean Wright makes his home in Santa Clarita, a charming city at the entrance of the high desert in Southern California. For sixteen years, features and articles under his byline appeared in *The Tidings* – now *The Angelus News*, publications of the Roman Catholic Archdiocese of Los Angeles. Continuing his education in 2007, Mr. Wright graduated from Grand Canyon University, attaining a Bachelor of Arts degree in Christian Studies with a *summa cum laude*. He then attained a Master of Arts degree, also in Christian Studies. Once active in the entertainment industry, and in an abortive attempt to revive dramatic radio in 1976 with his beloved mentor, the late Daws Butler, directing, Mr. Wright co-produced and wrote the syndicated *New Radio Adventures of Sherlock Holmes*, starring the late Edward Mulhare as the Great Detective. Mr. Wright has written for several television quiz shows and remains proud of his work for *The Quiz Kid's Challenge* and the popular TV quiz show *Jeopardy!* for which the Academy of Television Arts and Sciences honored him in 1985 with an Emmy nomination in the field of writing. Honored with membership in The Baker Street Irregulars as "The Manor House Case" after founding The Non-Canonical Calabashes, the Sherlock Holmes Society of Los Angeles in 1970, Mr. Wright has written for *The Baker Street Journal* and *Mystery Magazine*. Since 1971, he has conducted lectures on Sherlock Holmes's influence on literature and cinema for libraries, colleges, and private organizations, including MENSA. Mr. Wright's whimsical *Sherlock Holmes Cookbook* (Drake), created with John Farrell, BSI, was published in 1976, and a mystery novel, *Enter the Lion: a Posthumous Memoir of Mycroft Holmes* (Hawthorne), "edited" with Michael Hodel, BSI, followed in 1979. As director general of The Plot Thickens Mystery Company, Mr .Wright originated hosting "mystery parties" in homes, restaurants, and offices, as well as producing and directing the very first "Mystery Train" tours on Amtrak beginning in 1982.

The following contributors appear
in the companion volumes:
The MX Book of New Sherlock Holmes Stories
Part XXXII – 2022 Annual (1888-1895)
Part XXXIII – 2022 Annual (1896-1919)

Ian Ableson is an ecologist by training and a writer by choice. When not reading or writing, he can reliably be found scowling at a clipboard while ankle-deep in a marsh somewhere in Michigan. His love for the stories of Arthur Conan Doyle started when his grandfather gave him a copy of *The Original Illustrated Sherlock Holmes* when he was in high school, and he's proud to have been able to contribute to the continuation of the tales of Sherlock Holmes and Dr. Watson.

Wayne Anderson was born and raised in the beautiful Pacific Northwest, growing up in Alaska and Washington State. He discovered Sherlock Holmes around age ten and promptly devoured the Canon. When it was all gone, he tried to sate the addiction by writing his own Sherlock Holmes stories, which are mercifully lost forever. Sadly, he moved to California in his twenties and has lived there since. He has two grown sons who are both writers as well. He spends his time writing or working on the TV pilots and patents which will someday make him fabulously wealthy. When he's not doing these things, he is either reading to his young daughter from The Canon or trying to find space in his house for more bookshelves.

Hugh Ashton was born in the U.K., and moved to Japan in 1988, where he remained until 2016, living with his wife Yoshiko in the historic city of Kamakura, a little to the south of Yokohama. He and Yoshiko have now moved to Lichfield, a small cathedral city in the Midlands of the U.K., the birthplace of Samuel Johnson, and one-time home of Erasmus Darwin. In the past, he has worked in the technology and financial services industries, which have provided him with material for some of his books set in the 21st century. He currently works as a writer: Novelist, freelance editor, and copywriter, (his work for large Japanese corporations has appeared in international business journals), and journalist, as well as producing industry reports on various aspects of the financial services industry. However, his lifelong interest in Sherlock Holmes has developed into an acclaimed series of adventures featuring the world's most famous detective, written in the style of the originals. In addition to these, he has also published historical and alternate historical novels, short stories, and thrillers. Together with artist Andy Boerger, he has produced the *Sherlock Ferret* series of stories for children, featuring the world's cutest detective.

Andrew Bryant was born in Bridgend, Wales, and now lives in Burlington, Ontario. His previous publications include *Poetry Toronto*, *Prism International*, *Existere*, *On Spec*, *The Dalhousie Review*, and *The Toronto Star*. Andrew's interest in Holmes stems from watching the Basil Rathbone and Nigel Bruce films as a child, followed by collecting The Canon, and a fascinating visit to 221b Baker Street in London.

Josh Cerefice has followed the exploits of a certain pipe-smoking sleuth ever since his grandmother bought him *The Complete Sherlock Holmes* collection for his twenty-first birthday, and he has devotedly accompanied the Great Detective on his adventures ever since. When he's not reading about spectral hellhounds haunting the Devonshire moors, or the Machiavellian machinations of Professor Moriarty, you can find him putting pen to paper and challenging Holmes with new mysteries to solve in his own stories.

Mike Chinn's first-ever Sherlock Holmes fiction was a steampunk mashup of *The Valley of Fear*, entitled *Vallis Timoris* (Fringeworks 2015). Since then he has written about Holmes's archenemy in *The Mammoth Book of the Adventures of Moriarty* (Robinson 2015), appeared in three volumes of *The MX Book of New Sherlock Holmes Stories*, and faced the retired detective with cross-dimensional magic in the second volume of *Sherlock Holmes and the Occult Detectives* (Belanger Books 2020).

Craig Stephen Copland confesses that he discovered Sherlock Holmes when, sometime in the muddled early 1960's, he pinched his older brother's copy of the immortal stories and was forever afterward thoroughly hooked. He is very grateful to his high school English teachers in Toronto who inculcated in him a love of literature and writing, and even inspired him to be an English major at the University of Toronto. There he was blessed to sit at the feet of both Northrup Frye and Marshall McLuhan, and other great literary professors, who led him to believe that he was called to be a high school English teacher. It was his good fortune to come to his pecuniary senses, abandon that goal, and pursue a varied professional career that took him to over one-hundred countries and endless adventures. He considers himself to have been and to continue to be one of the luckiest men on God's good earth. A few years back he took a step in the direction of Sherlockian studies and joined the *Sherlock Holmes Society of Canada* – also known as *The Toronto Bootmakers*. In May of 2014, this esteemed group of scholars announced a contest for the writing of a new Sherlock Holmes mystery. Although he had never tried his hand at fiction before, Craig entered and was pleasantly surprised to be selected as one of the winners. Having enjoyed the experience, he decided to write more of the same, and is now on a mission to write a new Sherlock Holmes mystery that is related to and inspired by each of the sixty stories in the original Canon. He currently lives and writes in Toronto and Dubai, and looks forward to finally settling down when he turns ninety.

Martin Daley was born in Carlisle, Cumbria in 1964. He cites Doyle's Holmes and Watson as his favourite literary characters, who continue to inspire his own detective writing. His fiction and non-fiction books include a Holmes pastiche set predominantly in his home city in 1903. In the adventure, he introduced his own detective, Inspector Cornelius Armstrong, who has subsequently had some of his own cases published by MX Publishing. For more information visit *www.martindaley.co.uk*

Alan Dimes was born in North-West London and graduated from Sussex University with a BA in English Literature. He has spent most of his working life teaching English. Living in the Czech Republic since 2003, he is now semi-retired and divides his time between Prague and his country cottage. He has also written some fifty stories of horror and fantasy and thirty stories about his husband-and-wife detectives, Peter and Deirdre Creighton, set in the 1930's.

Arianna Fox is a triple-published and bestselling author, keynote speaker, actress, professional voiceover talent, award winner, and public figure whose passion is to inspire, educate, and entertain others through her work. From modern stories that connect with a teenage audience to classical-style works of literature, one of Arianna's foremost passions has always been writing. An avid Sherlockian and lover of all things Victorian, Arianna disliked reading for years until she read the first few paragraphs of *The Return of Sherlock Holmes* in a bookstore and immediately fell in love with classic literature and the intricate themes woven into its messages. As a whole, Arianna's ultimate goal is to empower others to achieve maximum success and rock their lives. Arianna can be found at *www.ariannafox.com*, Facebook: *@afoxauthor*, Twitter: *@afoxauthor*; LinkedIn: *Arianna Fox*; and Instagram: *@afoxauthor*

Mike Fox is a CEO, entrepreneur, multi award-winning filmmaker, director, producer, writer, designer, creative professional, actor, voiceover talent, and illustrator. His professional work is known across the U.S. and has received numerous accolades and awards. In addition, Mike has been named "Top Pioneer & Entrepreneur" by *K.I.S.H. Magazine*, and named "Local Business Person of the Year" by Alignable. Mike and his films and creative designs have been featured numerous times in many media channels. Mike can be found at *www.splashdw.com* and *www.crystalfoxfilms.com*; Facebook: *@splashdw*; Twitter: *@splashdw*; LinkedIn: *Mike Fox*; and Instagram: *@officialmikefox*

James Gelter is a director and playwright living in Brattleboro, VT. His produced written works for the stage include adaptations of *Frankenstein* and *A Christmas Carol*, several children's plays for the New England Youth Theatre, as well as seven outdoor plays co-written with his wife, Jessica, in their *Forest of Mystery* series. In 2018, he founded The Baker Street Readers, a group of performers that present dramatic readings of Arthur Conan Doyle's original Canon of Sherlock Holmes stories, featuring Gelter as Holmes, his longtime collaborator Tony Grobe as Dr. Watson, and a rotating list of guests. When the COVID-19 pandemic stopped their live performances, Gelter transformed the show into The Baker Street Readers Podcast. Some episodes are available for free on Apple Podcasts and Stitcher, with many more available to patrons at *patreon.com/bakerstreetreaders*.

Hal Glatzer *also has a story in Part XXXII*

Terry Golledge *also has stories in Parts XXXII and XXXIII*

Arthur Hall *also has a stories in Parts XXXII and XXXIII*

Paul Hiscock is an author of crime, fantasy, horror, and science fiction tales. His short stories have appeared in a variety of anthologies, and include a seventeenth-century whodunnit, a science fiction western, a clockpunk fairytale, and numerous Sherlock Holmes pastiches. He lives with his family in Kent (England) and spends his days taking care of his two children. He mainly does his writing in coffee shops with members of the local NaNoWriMo group, or in the middle of the night when his family has gone to sleep. Consequently, his stories tend to be fuelled by large amounts of black coffee. You can find out more about Paul's writing at *www.detectivesanddragons.uk.*

Mike Hogan's early interest in all things Victorian led to a university degree in English and research on nineteenth century literature. He taught English and creative writing at colleges in Japan, the Philippines, Libya and Thailand. He is settled now for much of the year on the island of Mersea in Essex, UK, where he writes novels, plays, and short stories, many set in Victorian London and featuring Sherlock Holmes.

In the year 1998 **Craig Janacek** took his degree of Doctor of Medicine at Vanderbilt University, and proceeded to Stanford to go through the training prescribed for pediatricians in practice. Having completed his studies there, he was duly attached to the University of California, San Francisco as Associate Professor. The author of over seventy medical monographs upon a variety of obscure lesions, his travel-worn and battered tin dispatch-box is crammed with papers, nearly all of which are records of his fictional works. To date, these have been published solely in electronic format, including two non-Holmes novels (*The Oxford Deception* and *The Anger of Achilles Peterson*), the trio of holiday adventures collected as *The Midwinter Mysteries of Sherlock Holmes*, the Holmes story collections *The First of Criminals, The Assassination of Sherlock Holmes, The Treasury of Sherlock Holmes, Light in the Darkness, The Gathering Gloom, The Travels of Sherlock Holmes,* and the Watsonian novels *The Isle of Devils* and *The Gate of Gold.* Craig Janacek is a *nom de plume.*

Naching T. Kassa is a wife, mother, and writer. She's created short stories, novellas, poems, and co-created three children. She resides in Eastern Washington State with her husband, Dan Kassa. Naching is a member of *The Horror Writers Association, Mystery Writers of America, The Sound of the Baskervilles, The ACD Society,* and *The Sherlock Holmes Society of London.* She's also an assistant and staff writer for Still Water Bay at Crystal Lake Publishing. You can find her work on Amazon. *https://www.amazon.com/Naching-T-Kassa/e/B005ZGHTI0*

Susan Knight *also has a story in Part XXXIII*

Jeffrey Lockwood spent youthful afternoons darkly enchanted by feeding grasshoppers to black widows in his New Mexican backyard, which accounts for his scientific and literary affinities. He earned a doctorate in entomology and worked as an ecologist at the University of Wyoming before metamorphosing into a Professor of Natural Sciences & Humanities in the departments of philosophy and creative writing – hence, insect-infested nonfiction and mysteries. He considers Sherlock Holmes a model of scientific prowess, integrating exquisite observational skills with incisive abductive (not deductive) reasoning.

David MacGregor *also has a story in Part XXXIII*

David Marcum *also has stories in Parts XXXII and XXXIII*

Kevin Patrick McCann *also has a poem in Part XXXII*

Will Murray has built a career on writing classic pulp characters, ranging from Tarzan of the Apes to Doc Savage. He has penned several milestone crossover novels in his acclaimed Wild Adventures series. *Skull Island* pitted Doc Savage against King Kong, which was followed by *King Kong Vs. Tarzan*. *Tarzan, Conqueror of Mars* costarred John Carter of Mars. His 2015 Doc Savage novel, *The Sinister Shadow*, revived the famous radio and pulp mystery man. Murray reunited them for *Empire of Doom*. His first Spider novel, *The Doom Legion*, revived that infamous crime buster, as well as James Christopher, AKA Operator 5, and the renowned G-8. His second *Spider, Fury in Steel*, guest-stars the FBI's Suicide Squad. Ten of his Sherlock Holmes short stories have been collected as *The Wild Adventures of Sherlock Holmes*. He is the author of the non-fiction book, *Master of Mystery: The Rise of The Shadow*. For Marvel Comics, Murray created the Unbeatable Squirrel Girl. Website: *www.adventuresinbronze.com*

Tracy J. Revels *also has stories in Parts XXXII and XXXIII.*

Roger Riccard's family history has Scottish roots, which trace his lineage back to Highland Scotland. This British Isles ancestry encouraged his interest in the writings of Sir Arthur Conan Doyle at an early age. He has authored the novels, *Sherlock Holmes & The Case of the Poisoned Lilly*, and *Sherlock Holmes & The Case of the Twain Papers*. In addition he has produced several short stories in *Sherlock Holmes Adventures for the Twelve Days of Christmas* and the series *A Sherlock Holmes Alphabet of Cases*. A new series will begin publishing in the Autumn of 2022, and his has another novel in the works. All of his books have been published by Baker Street Studios. His Bachelor of Arts Degrees in both Journalism and History from California State University, Northridge, have proven valuable to his writing historical fiction, as well as the encouragement of his wife/editor/inspiration and Sherlock Holmes fan, Rosilyn. She passed in 2021, and it is in her memory that he continues to contribute to the legacy of the "*man who never lived and will never die*".

Dan Rowley *also has stories in Part XXXIII*

Alisha Shea has resided near Saint Louis, Missouri for over thirty years. The eldest of six children, she found reading to be a genuine escape from the chaotic drudgery of life. She grew to love not only Sherlock Holmes, but the time period from which he emerged. This will be her first published work, but probably not her last. In her spare time, she indulges in creating music via piano, violin, and Native American flute. Sometimes she thinks she might even be getting good at it. She also produces a wide variety of fiber arts which are typically given away or auctioned off for various fundraisers.

Tim Symonds *also has stories in Parts XXXII and XXXIII.*

Kevin Thornton was shortlisted six times for the Crime Writers of Canada best unpublished novel. He never won – they are all still unpublished, and now he writes short stories. He lives in Canada, north enough that ringing Santa Claus is a local call and winter is a way of life. This is his twelfth short story in *The MX Book of New Sherlock Holmes Stories*. By the time you next hear from him, he hopes to have written his thirteenth.

Thomas A. (Tom) Turley has been "hooked on Holmes" since finishing *The Hound of the Baskervilles* at about the age of twelve. However, his interest in Sherlockian pastiches didn't take off until he wrote one. *Sherlock Holmes and the Adventure of the Tainted Canister* (2014) is available as an e-book and an audiobook from MX Publishing. It also appeared in *The Art of Sherlock Holmes – USA Edition 1*. In 2017, two of Tom's stories, "A Scandal in Serbia" and "A Ghost from Christmas Past" were published in Parts VI and VII of this anthology. "Ghost" was also included in *The Art of Sherlock Holmes – West*

Palm Beach Edition. Meanwhile, Tom is finishing a collection of historical pastiches entitled *Sherlock Holmes and the Crowned Heads of Europe*, to be published in 2021 The first story, "Sherlock Holmes and the Case of the Dying Emperor" (2018) is available from MX Publishing as a separate e-book. Set in the brief reign of Emperor Frederick III (1888), it inaugurates Sherlock Holmes's espionage campaign against the German Empire, which ended only in August 1914 with "His Last Bow". When completed, *Sherlock Holmes and the Crowned Heads of Europe* will also include "A Scandal in Serbia" and two additional historical tales. Although he has a Ph.D. in British history, Tom spent most of his professional career as an archivist with the State of Alabama. He and his wife Paula (an aspiring science fiction novelist) live in Montgomery, Alabama. Interested readers may contact Tom through MX Publishing or his Goodreads author's page.

Mark Wardecker is an instructional technologist at Colby College, and has contributed Sherlockian pastiches to *Sherlock Holmes Mystery Magazine* and *The MX Book of New Sherlock Holmes Stories – Part XIII*, as well as an article to *The Baker Street Journal*. He is also the editor and annotator of *The Dragnet Solar Pons et al.* (Battered Silicon Dispatch Box, 2011), and has contributed Solar Pons pastiches to *The New Adventures of Solar Pons*.

Marcia Wilson is a freelance researcher and illustrator who likes to work in a style compatible for the color blind and visually impaired. She is Canon-centric, and her first MX offering, *You Buy Bones*, uses the point-of-view of Scotland Yard to show the unique talents of Dr. Watson. This continued with the publication of *Test of the Professionals: The Adventure of the Flying Blue Pidgeon* and *The Peaceful Night Poisonings*. She can be contacted at: *gravelgirty.deviantart.com*

The MX Book of New Sherlock Holmes Stories
Edited by David Marcum
(MX Publishing, 2015-   )

"This is the finest volume of Sherlockian fiction I have ever read, and I have read, literally, thousands." – Philip K. Jones

"Beyond Impressive . . . This is a splendid venture for a great cause!
– Roger Johnson, Editor, *The Sherlock Holmes Journal,*
The Sherlock Holmes Society of London

Part I: 1881-1889
Part II: 1890-1895
Part III: 1896-1929
Part IV: 2016 Annual
Part V: Christmas Adventures
Part VI: 2017 Annual
Part VII: Eliminate the Impossible (1880-1891)
Part VIII – Eliminate the Impossible (1892-1905)
Part IX – 2018 Annual (1879-1895)
Part X – 2018 Annual (1896-1916)
Part XI – Some Untold Cases (1880-1891)
Part XII – Some Untold Cases (1894-1902)
Part XIII – 2019 Annual (1881-1890)
Part XIV – 2019 Annual (1891-1897)
Part XV – 2019 Annual (1898-1917)
Part XVI – Whatever Remains . . . Must be the Truth (1881-1890)
Part XVII – Whatever Remains . . . Must be the Truth (1891-1898)
Part XVIII – Whatever Remains . . . Must be the Truth (1898-1925)
Part XIX – 2020 Annual (1882-1890)
Part XX – 2020 Annual (1891-1897)
Part XXI – 2020 Annual (1898-1923)
Part XXII – Some More Untold Cases (1877-1887)
Part XXIII – Some More Untold Cases (1888-1894)
Part XXIV – Some More Untold Cases (1895-1903)
Part XXV – 2021 Annual (1881-1888)
Part XXVI – 2021 Annual (1889-1897)
Part XXVII – 2021 Annual (1898-1928)
Part XXVIII – More Christmas Adventures (1869-1888)
Part XXIX – More Christmas Adventures (1889-1896)
Part XXX – More Christmas Adventures (1897-1928)
In Preparation
Part XXXI (and XXXII and XXXIII???) – However Improbable . . . .

. . . and more to come!

The MX Book of New Sherlock Holmes Stories
Edited by David Marcum
(MX Publishing, 2015-   )

Part VI: *The traditional pastiche is alive and well . . . .*

Part VII: *Sherlockians eager for faithful-to-the-canon plots and characters will be delighted.*

Part VIII: *The imagination of the contributors in coming up with variations on the volume's theme is matched by their ingenious resolutions.*

Part IX: *The 18 stories . . . will satisfy fans of Conan Doyle's originals. Sherlockians will rejoice that more volumes are on the way.*

Part X: *. . . new Sherlock Holmes adventures of consistently high quality.*

Part XI: *. . . an essential volume for Sherlock Holmes fans.*

Part XII: *. . . continues to amaze with the number of high-quality pastiches.*

Part XIII: *. . . Amazingly, Marcum has found 22 superb pastiches . . . This is more catnip for fans of stories faithful to Conan Doyle's original*

Part XIV: *. . . this standout anthology of 21 short stories written in the spirit of Conan Doyle's originals.*

Part XV: *Stories pitting Sherlock Holmes against seemingly supernatural phenomena highlight Marcum's 15th anthology of superior short pastiches.*

Part XVI: *Marcum has once again done fans of Conan Doyle's originals a service.*

Part XVII: *This is yet another impressive array of new but traditional Holmes stories.*

Part XVIII: *Sherlockians will again be grateful to Marcum and MX for high-quality new Holmes tales.*

Part XIX: *Inventive plots and intriguing explorations of aspects of Dr. Watson's life and beliefs lift the 24 pastiches in Marcum's impressive 19th Sherlock Holmes anthology*

Part XX: *Marcum's reserve of high-quality new Holmes exploits seems endless.*

Part XXI: *This is another must-have for Sherlockians.*

Part XXII: *Marcum's superlative 22nd Sherlock Holmes pastiche anthology features 21 short stories that successfully emulate the spirit of Conan Doyle's originals while expanding on the canon's tantalizing references to mysteries Dr. Watson never got around to chronicling.*

Part XXIII: *Marcum's well of talented authors able to mimic the feel of The Canon seems bottomless.*

Part XXIV: *Marcum's expertise at selecting high-quality pastiches remains impressive.*

Part XXVIII: *All entries adhere to the spirit, language, and characterizations of Conan Doyle's originals, evincing the deep pool of talent Marcum has access to. Against the odds, this series remains strong, hundreds of stories in.*

The MX Book of New Sherlock Holmes Stories
Edited by David Marcum
(MX Publishing, 2015-   )

MX Publishing

MX Publishing is the world's largest specialist Sherlock Holmes publisher, with over five-hundred titles and over two-hundred authors creating the latest in Sherlock Holmes fiction and non-fiction

The catalogue includes several award winning books, and over two-hundred-and-fifty have been converted into audio.

MX Publishing also has one of the largest communities of Holmes fans on Facebook, with regular contributions from dozens of authors.

www.mxpublishing.com

@mxpublishing on Facebook, Twitter, and Instagram

CPSIA information can be obtained
at www.ICGtesting.com
Printed in the USA
LVHW100733060822
725336LV00005B/45

9 781804 240069